Lawrence Sanders

Three Complete Novels

Lawrence Sanders

THE TIMOTHY FILES	Three
TIMOTHY'S GAME	Complete
SULLIVAN'S STING	Novels

G. P. PUTNAM'S SONS   New York

G. P. Putnam's Sons
Publishers Since 1838
a member of
Penguin Putnam Inc.
375 Hudson Street
New York, NY 10014

Library of Congress Cataloging-in-Publication Data

Sanders, Lawrence,
[Novels. Selections]
Three complete novels / Lawrence Sanders.
p.   cm.
Contents: The Timothy files—Timothy's game—Sullivan's sting.
ISBN 0-399-14531-1
1. Detective and mystery stories, American.   I. Title.
PS3569.A5125A6   1999   99-21335   CIP
813'.54—dc21

Printed in the United States of America
1   3   5   7   9   10   8   6   4   2

This book is printed on acid-free paper. ∞

Book design by Patrice Sheridan

Contents

The Timothy Files

Book One
The Wall Street Dick

1

An elegant young man, plumpish but dapper, bounces down the stairs into the Union Square subway station. He is wearing a three-piece suit of pin-striped gray flannel, a fawn fedora cocked at a rakish angle. He swings an attaché case of black alligator. It is empty. Just a prop.

On the uptown express platform, he stands well back from the tracks and looks about casually. Spots the target he has been following by leading: the first at the coin booth, the first through the turnstiles. He is sure of the subject, knows the route, knows the destination. Why run the chance of being recognized as a shadow when you can go ahead?

The target leans against a pillar, starts flipping through the pages of the *New York Post*. But then the rumble of an approaching train is heard, the newspaper is closed and folded. People move closer to the edge of the platform. The elegant young man saunters up, too, and positions himself so he can get on the same car as the subject. Everyone stands patiently, waiting.

The train rounds the curve, headlight gleaming. Experienced passengers congregate in the areas where they know the doors will open when the train halts. The young man inches closer to the edge of the platform, keeping an eye on the target, ready to hold back or even jump off the train at the last minute if his quarry decides to bolt.

The train roars into the station, slowing, clattering. The dandy smiles faintly, clamps the empty attaché case under his arm.

Suddenly he is pushed from behind. A powerful thrust in the middle of his back. It propels him forward, off the edge of the platform. Hat and alligator case go flying. Arms and legs stretching, he falls directly in front of the train.

Yells, screams, the shriek of brakes. But he is hit, hurled down the track. The first car passes over him before the train can be brought to a stop. There is shouting, confusion, everyone running, peering. One old man goes down on his knees, praying, crossing himself.

The target moves back, disengages slowly from the mob. Walks up into the sunlight and takes out a cigarette. A moment later the assassin arrives.

"Beautiful," the subject says.

And they stroll off together to the nearest bar where both have martinis, very dry, straight up, with a twist of lemon.

Haldering & Co. is not as large or prestigious as Kroll Associates, Intertel, or Bishop's Service, Inc., but has a good and growing reputation as one of Wall Street's dependable "specialists in corporate intelligence." None of the firms engaged in this unique activity approve of the terms "private detective" or "private eye." But regardless of nomenclature, they are all involved in confidential investigations.

When a buyout, merger, or unfriendly takeover is in the works, inevitably the companies involved seek the advice of attorneys or investment counselors. And they more often than not turn to Wall Street's financial dicks to provide information on corporations and, more important, their owners, chairmen of the board, directors, presidents, chief executive officers, and anyone else whose probity or lack thereof might affect the deal.

Haldering & Co. has been in existence only four years, and as new boy on the block, the boss, Hiram Haldering, an ex–FBI man, does not expect to be called in on multibillion-dollar oil, steel, or chemical takeovers, friendly or otherwise. But as H.H. is fond of remarking, "You've got to walk before you can fly"—which makes little sense to anyone but him.

So Haldering & Co. contents itself, temporarily, with financial deals of modest proportions or with jobs that do not involve the activities of the better-known corporate raiders. H.H. is satisfied with assignments to investigate the principals in mergers, buyouts, and takeovers in the seven- and eight-figure range. As he likes to say, "There's enough lettuce around for all us rabbits."

The offices of Haldering & Co. are located in a dilapidated, turn-of-the-century building on John Street that is scheduled for the wrecker's ball as soon as a hotshot developer succeeds in completing a real estate parcel that will level another entire city block and fill it with a steel, concrete, and glass skyscraper that will have windows that can't be opened and high-speed elevators chronically marked Out of Service.

Haldering's offices look as if the demolition has already started. It is a floor-through of individual cubbyholes divided by painted plywood partitions. The pitted wood floor has been covered with peach-colored tiles, and the plants in the reception area are plastic.

Hiram Haldering, with a passion for chains of command and tables of organization, has divided his work force into three divisions: attorneys, accountants, and investigators. Each division is headed by a supervisor. Samantha Whatley oversees the detectives.

News of G. Edward Griffon's death at the Union Square subway station reaches the offices of Haldering & Co. at about three-thirty in the afternoon. Two New York Police Department detectives show up and inform H.H. that one of his investigators has fallen to his death under circumstances that are being investigated.

H.H. calls in Samantha Whatley, and the two offer what assistance they can. The city detectives want whatever is in the victim's employment file, and are given photocopies. Then they ask for information on the cases currently assigned to G. Edward Griffon. Hiram Haldering balks, his muttony face reddening.

"Look," he tells the detectives, "you know what we do. All our jobs are hush-hush. I mean, news of an investigation gets out, and someone could make a fortune trading on insider information. The reputation of the company would go down the drain. If we can't guarantee our clients confidentiality, we've got nothing to sell."

One of the city detectives sighs. "Do we have to get a court order?" he asks. "We've cooperated with your people in the past. Do you want to play hardball and end all that?"

Mr. Haldering is a puffy man who thinks walking upstairs to his second-floor office keeps him in splendid condition.

Running a hand over his balding pate, he looks at the NYPD detectives. "You think Griffon was scragged?" he demands.

The detective shrugs. "He fell, jumped, or was pushed. Who the hell knows? No one saw anything. No one wants to get involved. You know how these things go, but we've got to go through the drill. Now do we find out what he was working on or don't we?"

Haldering makes his decision; he can't afford to alienate the local police. "All right," he says, "as long as you abide by the SEC regulations on insider information, I'll give you photocopies of Griffon's current files. See how I cooperate? And I suppose you'll want to talk to everyone who works here. Sam, will you arrange things? I've got a meeting with a client."

Samantha Whatley nods, knowing that the "meeting with a client" is Hiram Haldering's weekly session with a doxy who services many executives in the financial community. In addition to her renown as a mattress acrobat, she is reputed to be one of the most knowledgeable and successful commodity traders on the Street, specializing in pork belly futures.

All Haldering & Co. employees on the premises are told to stand by for questioning, and the two NYPD cops get to work. Meanwhile, Samantha Whatley calls her staff into her office. Ordinarily she honchos seven investigators, but one is on sick leave and two on out-of-town assignments.

"You've all heard about Ed Griffon," she says tonelessly when the remaining four have crowded into her office. "I know how you feel. The police have notified his mother and sister. When the body is released we'll all attend the funeral. That's not a suggestion, it's an order."

They all look down at the floor, shuffling their feet. Griffon's death is an unwelcome reminder of the hazards of their profession. They are all licensed to carry handguns, but a shooter hadn't helped Ed any, had it? Recognition of their own mortality has the sound of muffled drums and the taste of bile.

"What in God's name happened, Sam?" Ernie Waters asks finally. "Do the cops know?"

"Not yet. They say he fell, jumped, or was pushed."

"He was pushed," says Timothy Cone, who has remained standing at the open office door.

Samantha looks up at him sharply. "How the hell do you know that?"

"Ed wouldn't go down in the subway unless he was tailing someone. The guy owned a Jaguar, and when he wasn't driving that, he took cabs. Take a look at his expense account chits, and you'll see."

"He could have fallen," Fred Burgess says. "Accidentally."

"No way," Cone says. "Ed didn't have accidents; he was a careful man. And he wouldn't jump. He enjoyed life too much for that. I tell you he was pushed."

"You know so much," Samantha says angrily, "tell the cops about it."

"I intend to. It may have been a crazy. Or it may have been the subject he was tailing."

"Jesus Christ, Tim," says Samantha, "I wish I could be as sure about anything as you are about everything."

"I'm sure about this," Cone says coolly. "Ed was killed. What was he working on, Sam?"

"That's why I called you all in," she says, slapping a stack of file folders on her desk. "I'm going to divide Ed's cases—one or two to each of you. Until Joe gets back from sick leave or we hire another warm body."

"My God," Sol Faber says. "Sam, we've all got more than we can handle right now."

"Tell me about it," she says bitterly. "You think I haven't been bugging H.H. for help? Maybe Ed's death will convince him we need more working eyes. But until that happens, you'll just have to forget the two-hour lunches and work harder."

"Two-hour lunches?" Cone says incredulously. "How can you spend two hours on a cheeseburger and Coke? You're spinning your wheels, Sam."

She glares at him. "If you're trying to be a pain in the ass," she says, "you're succeeding admirably."

Samantha Whatley is a tall drink of water, with the stretched body of a swimmer and the muscles of a gymnast. She is a sharp-featured woman with a lot of jaw and blue-green eyes with all the warmth of licked stones. A flattish chest and practically no ass at all. Even her long auburn hair is worn up, tightly coiled, and looks like a russet beehive.

Her background includes four years in the U.S. Army, three in the NYPD, and two working as a private investigator for a bondsman on Hester Street. She may not be feminine, but no one doubts her competence.

"All right," she says, "let's cut the shit and get back to work." She begins to hand out the folders. "Ernie, here's yours. Fred, yours. Sol, you take these. Tim, there's one left for you."

"Gee, boss," he says, "why are you so good to me?"

"Up yours," she says. "All you guys hang around until the cops have a chance to talk to you."

"Do they have copies of these files?" Sol Faber asks.

"They do," Samantha says. "And if you find anything in them that you think may have something to do with Ed's death, don't be shy about telling them. Another thing: You're all falling behind in your weekly progress reports. Will you, for Christ's sake, get on the goddamned ball? That's all. Take off."

The four investigators wander down the corridor to their own broom closet offices.

"There is one tough cookie," Ernie Waters says, sighing.

"An iron fist in an iron glove," Tim Cone says.

"The woman's a fucking barracuda," Fred Burgess says.

"I don't think so," Sol Faber says. "Just a barracuda."

They all laugh.

Timothy Cone takes Griffon's file folder to his office and slips it into a manila envelope, so tattered that he's patched the seams with Scotch tape. Then he leaves the building, figuring the NYPD detectives will catch up with him eventually; he's not about to sit around waiting.

Cone lives in a loft on the top floor of one of the few cast-iron buildings on lower Broadway, between Spring and Broome Streets. On good days he walks to and from work. It's a nice hike and gives him the chance to get some of the cigarette smoke out of his lungs and observe the changing profile of Little Old New York.

This particular evening is not all that great: a warm September mist in the air, a clotted sky, and humidity thick enough to skim his face. But he plods uptown anyway, reacting automatically to traffic signs and construction sites, and thinking about G. Edward Griffon.

Ed was no particular pal of his—but neither is anyone else. The other dicks at Haldering think him sometimes sullen, sometimes manic. Generally, they leave him alone. But Griffon really tried to be a friend. He didn't succeed, but Tim Cone appreciated the effort. Maybe Ed saw that behind Cone's love of solitude was an innate shyness.

Griffon constantly tried to get Timothy to spruce up.

"Look," he'd say, "I know you've got the money, but you live in a dump and dress like a bum. What's *with* you?"

"I don't like to go shopping," Cone would say, not admitting that department stores and salesclerks intimidated him. "Besides, I've got no interest in style or fashion."

"Tim, if I go with you, will you at least buy a decent suit?"

"No. I've got enough clothes."

In a way, Cone decides, slogging uptown, he admired G. Edward Griffon, and envied him. The guy always looked so fresh and smartly dressed. Now he is a clunk on a stainless steel table in the morgue, and some butcher in a bloody apron is carving him up to find out how he died.

"It isn't right," Timothy Cone says aloud, and passersby glance at him nervously.

The Wall Street dick is a scrawny, hawkish man who has never learned to shave close enough, so his coffin jaw always has a bluish tinge. He is tall and stooped, with a shambling gait that reminds people of a hard-scrabble farmer, although he was born in Brooklyn. His nose is a hatchet and his big ears flop.

No one has ever accused him of being handsome, but when he smiles (infrequently), his ugliness has a quirky charm. Few have heard him laugh. He moves through life, shoulders bowed, carrying a burden he cannot define. But morosity is his nature, and he is continually shocked when good things happen. He expects the end of the world at any minute.

On this day he wears a black, flapping raincoat, so ancient that the wrinkles are grayish, and the collar and cuffs greasy. Atop his spiky, ginger-colored hair is a limp black leather cap, an ebony omelet. Beneath the raincoat is a worn corduroy suit, so old that the pants no longer whistle as he walks. On his big, splayed feet are heavy yellow work shoes laced high.

When he reaches his loft building, he sees the lock on the street door has been jimmied again, the third time in as many months. He stoops swiftly, slides his Smith & Wesson .357 Magnum with a short barrel from the ankle holster and transfers it to the pocket of his raincoat.

There are commercial tenants on the first four floors, but the big freight elevator stops operating at six P.M. Cone climbs the iron stairs, gripping his handgun, carrying the manila envelope and listening to the sounds of conversation from some of the offices he passes. On the sixth floor, he pauses to catch his breath and examine the lock on his door. It looks all right to him. His place has been broken into twice. But that was months ago, and they've never come back. Why should they? He's got nothing worth stealing.

Griffon was right: It *is* a dump: one big room with cracked plaster walls. Sink, stove, and bathtub are exposed; only the toilet is hidden in a closet. Overhead are the bare pipes of a sprinkler system. There is a skylight, so filthy that it might as well be a steel shutter for all the sunshine it transmits. One of the glass panes is broken and stuffed with an old undershirt.

There is a mattress on the floor; Cone has never gotten around to buying a bedstead. A rickety desk doubles as a dining table. A few nothing chairs. A chest of drawers he found in the street and lugged home. The only decoration on the walls is a framed lithograph: *Washington Crossing the Delaware*. It was there when Cone leased the place, and he's never removed it.

When he enters, Cleo, his cat, comes up and rubs against his leg, meowing piteously.

"Shut your mouth," Timothy says. "You eat when I do." But he bends to scratch the animal behind its ears.

The cat looks like it's been in many fights and lost all of them. Cone found it one winter night in the gutter, bruised and torn, and brought it home to thaw out, lick its wounds, and gobble a slice of salami. It was originally a tom, but Cone had it neutered and declawed, and then named the castrated tom Cleo, for Cleopatra, it being the ugliest, least seductive cat he has ever seen in his life.

He inspects the contents of his obsolete waist-high refrigerator. There's a cold fried pork chop, hard as a rock; a jar of instant coffee; a chunk of cheddar covered with green mold; an unopened package of turkey pastrami. Also, four cans of Budweiser, a bottle of Gallo Hearty Burgundy, one soft tomato, and a browned head of iceberg lettuce. Not too encouraging.

But in the freezer section are two pizzas, individual size, both sausage, and a bottle of vodka with about four slugs left. That's better. He gives the old pork chop to Cleo, who grabs it and runs away under the tub where no one can take the feast away.

Cone pours himself a healthy jolt of vodka in an empty jelly jar and sits down on one of the spindly kitchen chairs to wait. He's good at that.

He's halfway through his drink when there's a knock on the door. The familiar signal: two short raps, pause, one more knock. He rises, goes over to unbolt and unlock. Samantha Whatley is standing there, wearing a belted trenchcoat.

"Hello, asshole," she says.

"Hello, shithead," he says.

Ten minutes later they're naked on his mattress, fucking their brains out.

Samantha Whatley wakes first, a little before seven A.M., rises from the mattress, relieves herself in the closet, and washes, as best she can, at the kitchen sink. She makes a grimace of distaste at the condition of the only towel she can find. It is clean enough, but fragile as Belgian lace. She puts up her hair, using rubber bands, pins, and two barrettes.

She dresses swiftly, then digs a heavy brogue into the ribs of the still-sleeping Timothy Cone.

"Get up, you monster," she says loudly. "I'm going home, but I want a cup of coffee first."

He rouses slowly, groaning, then scrubs his face with his palms. His hair sticks up like a fright wig. Cleo wanders over to sniff at his bare toes, but he kicks the cat away.

"Put the water on," he says in a growly voice, "while I shower. I smell like a goat."

"Tell me about it," she says.

She puts the kettle on to boil, searches his cupboard for two cups and saucers that match, gives up in disgust.

"You live like a gypsy," she tells him.

"I am a gypsy," he says. "And if you keep complaining, I'll put the curse on you."

"I had the curse," she says. "But not since I got spayed."

She watches him take the enameled lid off the bathtub. There is no shower, but he has a long rubber tube and spray head that attaches to the faucet. He has to hold it in one hand while he soaps with the other, standing up in the corroded tub. Water splashes onto the linoleum floor.

He has a splintery body, all sharp bones, stretched tendons, hard muscles. His fair skin is freckled across the shoulders and on his upper arms. Stomach flat, buttocks tight. He is hung like a donkey—which is okay with Samantha.

He climbs out of the tub and picks up the towel.

"This is damp," he says accusingly.

"Tough shitski," she says. "If you remembered to pick up your laundry occasionally, we'd have dry towels and clean sheets. Also, we finished the vodka last night, so you need another jug. Also, you might get some white wine; I'm getting tired of red."

"Yes, *sir*," he says, knocking off a mock salute. "And how about some champagne and caviar?"

"That'll be the day," she says. "You're the bologna-sandwich-and-beer type. I knew that the first time I saw you."

They sit at his desk and sip their steaming cups of black coffee.

"Sam," he says, "did you go over Ed Griffon's weekly progress reports for the past few months?"

"Give me credit for a little sense," she says indignantly. "Of course I went over them. The first thing I did after I heard how he died. They're strictly routine. Not a word hints of any trouble. You want to see them?"

"No," he says. "If you say they're clean, then they're clean."

She looks at him. "I get suspicious when you start acting like Mr. Nice. What do you want?"

"I may be a little late getting to the office this morning."

"So what else is new?"

"I brought that Griffon file home with me," he tells her.

"You took a file out of the office? You schmuck! If H.H. ever finds out, it means your ass. You know that, don't you?"

"Yeah, well, I'll worry about that when it happens. Anyway, I want to go over the file without the phone ringing and the cops asking questions. I'll be in later."

"Tim, you're not going to neglect your own caseload because of this, are you?"

"Yes," he says, "I am. Any objections?"

"Would it do any good if I had?" Then she covers one of his bony hands with a warm palm. "Ed's death really hit you hard, didn't it?"

He swirls what's left of his coffee around in the cup, then gulps it down. "It's just not right," he says stubbornly.

She gathers up her shoulder bag and trenchcoat, then leans to scratch Cleo's ribs. The cat purrs with delight.

"Don't forget to feed her," she says.

"It's not a her," Cone says crossly. "I keep telling you: It's a deballed he."

"He, she, it," Samantha says. "I couldn't care less."

At the door, she turns her face up to him. "Knock us a kiss," she says.

"Sentimental slush," he mutters. But he kisses her.

The moment she's gone, the door locked and bolted, he rummages around frantically for a package of cigarettes. Nothing. All gone. But he finds two long butts in the ashtray, and one more in the garbage can. He salvages them all, straightens them out, lights his first of the day. He inhales deeply, closes his eyes, and coughs, coughs, coughs.

Soothed, he fills Cleo's water bowl and gives the cat a chunk of moldy cheddar and a slice of turkey salami. That beast will eat anything. Then Cone makes himself another cup of black coffee and sits down at the desk with Ed Griffon's case file open before him.

He flips through it swiftly to see what he's got. Mostly it's a sheaf of documents Haldering & Co. call PIEs—Preliminary Intelligence Estimates. These are prepared by the company's accountants and attorneys, then handed over to the detectives for further investigation into the private lives of the individuals involved, if the facts seem to warrant it.

In addition to the PIEs, there are a few rough notes by Griffon. It gives Cone a queasy feeling to see the dead man's handwriting. Almost as bad as hearing a message left on your answering machine by someone suddenly deceased. A voice from the grave. Cone lights his second cigarette butt of the morning and starts reading the file slowly.

The case seems innocent enough. The client is Samuel Evanchat & Sons, an old and respected developer-builder of Manhattan East Side properties. The firm has the reputation of putting up elegant townhouses with a Stanford White look about them. Isaac Evanchat, the last of the clan, is now in his late sixties and has decided to retire to his Mizner-designed Palm Beach home and spend the rest of his days trying to hook a world-class sailfish.

Isaac is contemplating selling out to Clovis & Clovis, Inc., a minicon-glomerate which, if you believe New York newspapers and magazines, seems to own or manage half the real estate in midtown Manhattan. The selling price is projected at $175 million. But Evanchat, proud and cautious, wants to make sure his family business will be in good hands, and the 175 mil will be forthcoming. So he has hired Haldering & Co., asking for a complete intelligence rundown on Clovis & Clovis.

Both principals in the proposed deal are privately held companies, and it's been difficult for Haldering's attorneys and accountants to assemble an accurate balance sheet on Clovis & Clovis. But they've done what they can, using the few public records that exist, confidential sources, and talking to ex-employees, particularly the disgruntled ones. They've produced a report in which Clovis & Clovis comes up smelling like roses.

Their summary notes that the parent company, with assets of more than one billion, owns controlling interest in four other companies involved in general contracting, plumbing and electrical supplies, foundations and underpinning, and an outfit called New World Enterprises, Inc., only fourteen months old, organized, according to its corporate charter, "for purposes of building and renovating commercial and residential real estate properties."

It all seems cut-and-dried to Timothy Cone, lighting his third and final cigarette butt. Here's this big real estate corporation with four subsidiaries. Nothing sinister there. Apparently all the divisions are profitable.

Cone turns to Griffon's personal notes and reads them carefully. Mostly they're short biogs on the owners of Clovis & Clovis. That would be Stanley Clovis, forty-three, and his sister Lucinda, forty-one, each of whom owns fifty percent of the parent company. Stanley is married and has two children. Lucinda is unmarried and has no children.

Brother and sister are very active in civic affairs, Manhattan politics, and charities. They are generous donors to libraries, museums, ballet groups, and symphony orchestras. They are on the society pages frequently, and recently Clovis & Clovis hosted a big bash to celebrate the opening of a park and playground in the South Bronx that they built and gave to the City of New York.

Both Stanley and Lucinda Clovis sound like fine, upstanding citizens. With their gelt, Cone reflects sourly, they can afford to be. There seems to be little in the file that indicates further investigation into Clovis & Clovis would be justified.

But then, the last item in Ed Griffon's personal notes, there is a torn sheet of green scratch paper. On it Ed had scrawled: DUM? Cone stares at the capital letters. DUM? What the hell could that mean. Initials maybe? Department of Underwear Manufacturers? Division of Undertaker Matrons?

He closes the folder and ruminates in his stolid, methodical way. If this particular file has no connection with the death of G. Edward Griffon, then perhaps the other cases Ed was handling do—the ones that were inherited by Ernie Waters, Fred Burgess, and Sol Faber. And if those files show nothing that isn't kosher, then maybe Ed really did fall or jump to his death.

Cone doesn't believe it for a minute. The guy was wasted. Deliberately. But what the hell does DUM? mean?

Sighing, he rises, slips the Clovis & Clovis folder back into the shabby manila envelope, prepares to go to the office. He's still wearing his sleazy corduroy suit, yellow work shoes, the black leather cap. As he goes out the door, he pauses to raise an admonishing forefinger at the watching Cleo.

"Guard!" he orders the astonished cat. Then locks up and clatters down the iron stairs.

He stops first to buy two packs of Camels, then continues his amble downtown. The air has cleared, there's a sun up there, and the streets are bustling. Guys are tearing up Broadway, dancing around the steelwork on new buildings, and sidewalk vendors are heating up their franks and sauerkraut. Everyone hustling to make a buck.

When he gets to his office, he finds a NYPD dick waiting outside, sitting on a folding chair and placidly chewing on a wad of something. The detective is big and overweight. He doesn't exactly spring to his feet; he levers himself slowly upward as if he isn't sure he'll make it. The conversation goes like this:

"You Timothy Cone?"

"That's right."

"You're an investigator here?"

"Yep."

"You were told to stick around last night. How come you took off?"

"My cat was sick. The vet wasn't sure he could save her."

"That's a new one. Usually it's a wife in Intensive Care. Let's talk."

"Sure."

In Cone's minuscule office, the detective shows his ID. Neal K. Davenport. He's a ruddy-faced man with plump hands and a habit of cocking his head to one side while waiting for his questions to be answered. Cone isn't fooled by the laid-back manner. This guy, he decides, is one shrewd apple.

"You want a cigarette?" he asks.

"No, thanks. I swore off. Now I chew Juicy Fruit." He takes out a package, extracts a stick, shoves it into his mouth. He crumples the wrapper, stuffs it into his jacket pocket. "You and the deceased buddy-buddy?" he asks Cone.

"Not really."

"No, I guess not. From what I hear you're a loner."

"That's right."

"Nothing wrong with that," Davenport says, shifting his bulk in the uncomfortable chair, "if it gets results." He chews his gum steadily. "You know anything about Griffon's private life?"

"Very little. I know he lived with his mother and sister. Somewhere in the Gramercy Park area."

"Yeah. He ever talk about any girlfriends?"

"No."

"Friends? Enemies?"

"No, nothing like that. I told you, we weren't close."

"Yeah," the fat detective says, sighing. "I understand you think he was pushed."

"I think so. He'd never jump, and he was too smart to fall. Maybe it was a crazy who gave him a shove."

"Maybe." The gumshoe climbs laboriously to his feet. "He was carrying an empty attaché case. You know why he'd do that?"

"No."

"You got the file on one of his cases?"

Cone nods.

"Anything interesting in it?"

"Strictly routine."

The detective slides a personal card across the desk. "If you come up with anything," he says, "give me a call."

"I'll do that," Cone says.

"Sure you will," Davenport says with a bleak smile.

"We're both on the same side—right?"

After he's gone, Cone walks around the corridors to the section inhabited by accountants and attorneys. He stops at an office twice as large as his, with a rug on the floor and two windows. The brass sign on the desk reads: MR. SIDNEY APICELLA. Cone likes the "Mr."

Apicella is a sweet man, but the poor fellow suffers from rosacea of the proboscis. Although a nondrinker, he's got the schnoz of an alcoholic moose. The big, lumpy nose is the first thing you see when you look at him, and even the politest visitor has trouble tearing his fascinated stare away from that rosy balloon.

He looks up when Cone enters. "I haven't got time," he says.

"Sure you do, Sid," Cone says, slumping into the chair alongside Apicella's desk.

The chief accountant sighs. "I'm sorry about Ed," he says.

"Yeah, he was an okay guy. Listen, Sid, you signed that PIE on the proposed buyout of Samuel Evanchat and Sons by Clovis and Clovis."

"That's right, I did. Anything wrong with it?"

"Not that I can see, but I've got a question. Clovis and Clovis is in the business of brokering or developing properties. So why did they start a subsidiary, New World Enterprises, Inc., to do exactly the same thing?"

"I caught that and asked Stanley Clovis himself. He says the parent company handles megabuck deals: skyscrapers and luxury co-ops and industrial parks. Stuff like that. New World was organized to develop smaller parcels, like renovating old brownstones or abandoned tenements."

"Yeah," Cone says. "It makes sense." He gets up to leave, then pauses at the doorway. "One more thing, Sid: In your business does DUM mean something special?"

"Sure: 'stupid.' "

"Not D-U-M-B," Cone says patiently. "This is spelled D-U-M, all in capital letters followed by a question mark."

"You mean like in dum-di-dum-dum? Nope, it doesn't mean a thing to me."

"Me neither."

Cone's next stop is Samantha's office.

"So glad you could make it," she says, glaring at him.

He ignores the sarcasm. "Did you talk to the other guys about Griffon's cases?"

She slams a palm down on her desk top in frustration. "When the hell are you going to give me credit for having brains? Of course I talked to them. They all say they found nothing suspicious."

"Okay," he says equably. "Just asking. See you around."

He waves, goes back to his office to pick up his cap, and starts out. He takes an uptown bus, knowing it's going to be a long trip, but relishing the opportunity to look out the windows at the crazy city he loves, for reasons he cannot define. Also, the ride will give him time to think.

Cone knows very well there are cubbyhole offices on Wall Street where one honest man sits alone and shuffles billions of dollars in pension funds by telephone. There are also glitzy offices, with ankle-deep rugs and abstract and impressionist paintings on the walls, that are no better than bucket shops and will be down the tube as soon as the SEC gets wise to their shenanigans.

Despite all that, he still believes in making on-the-site inspections when working a case. Appearances may be deceiving—but not always. Sometimes you can get an accurate impression of a company's probity just by seeing where they're headquartered.

After getting off the bus at Fifty-seventh Street, Cone walks over to the main offices of Clovis & Clovis, just west of Lexington Avenue. They're in a building that seems to be all glass, sloping inward with a graceful swoop. You hit that facade in the right place, Cone figures, and the whole thing will come tumbling down, filling the street with broken glass, like a gigantic shattered windshield.

Clovis & Clovis occupies nine floors, and the reception room seems just a little smaller than Grand Central Terminal. There are plenty of people sitting and standing around, waiting, so Cone has no worries about wandering about to inspect the big blowups of color photographs, propped on easels, showing Clovis & Clovis properties.

He stands before one labeled HEADQUARTERS OF NEW WORLD ENTERPRISES, INC. It looks like a waterfront warehouse, two stories high, and appears to be the size of a football field. No address is given on the photo label, but Cone reckons that won't be hard to find.

"May I be of service, sir?" a chirpy voice says at his elbow.

He turns. A flashy blonde is giving him a beamy smile. She's wearing an office uniform of purple jacket and heliotrope skirt. Cone takes off his leather cap.

"Why, I hope so, ma'am," he says. "I've got a brownstone on West Seventy-third I want to sell, and I was hoping to talk to someone here about making a deal."

"Oh, my," she says in her girlish voice, "I do think you'd do better to write us a letter. Or go through a broker."

He nods gravely. "Very good advice, ma'am. I guess I'll do just that."

" 'Bye now," she says, and sashays away.

He stops at the receptionist's desk on the way out. It is occupied by another flashy blonde in purple and heliotrope.

"Ma'am," he says, "do you have a business card for New World Enterprises? I'd like to write them a letter."

"Certainly, sir," she chirps, handing him one. "It's in Brooklyn. That's across the river, you know."

"Yes'm," he says. "Always has been."

He takes a final look around. If the reception room is any indication, the offices of Clovis & Clovis are nothing less than sumptuous. The place is all buttery rugs, vanilla Swedish furniture, soft lighting, and wallpaper music. It could serve as a stage set for "Corporate America 1980s style." Cone wonders if the whole thing is struck at nightfall and carted off to a theatrical warehouse.

He takes the subway to Brooklyn, standing well back from the tracks while waiting for the train.

It takes him almost two hours to find the headquarters of New World Enterprises, Inc. By that time the day has soured; the sky is filled with an ocher light and the air smells of sulfur. Rain clouds are beating in from New Jersey, and Cone's corduroy suit is beginning to feel like a damp blanket.

He stands across West Street, studying New World. It really is a warehouse, set well back on a black tarmac and surrounded by a high chain fence topped with barbed wire. There's a small guard shed at the double gates. Two bulldozers and three heavy-duty trucks are neatly lined up just inside. They all look clean, polished.

There are no signs of human activity. No lights in the warehouse. It looks like it's been abandoned. Something is twisted in that scene, and Cone can't figure out what it is.

He crosses the street and strides briskly up to the gate. It's locked, but on closer examination Cone knows it would be a piece of cake to break in. He bangs on the gate and an old geezer comes limping out of the guard hut.

"Yeah?" he says.

"Anyone around?" Cone says cheerfully. "I'd like to talk to one of the officers."

"Nobody here," the guard says. "They all gone home. Come back tomorrow."

"Shit," Cone says. "Another trip. Oh, well. Say, does Vic Spagnola still work here?"

"Who?"

"Vic Spagnola. A friend of mine. He used to work night guard on the gate."

"Mister," the gaffer says, "you got your wires crossed. There's no night guard. Never has been as long as I been working, and I been here since the place opened."

"Son of a gun," Cone says. "I guess I am mixed up. Thanks for your help. I'll be back tomorrow. Better get back in your shack. Looks like rain."

"Yeah," the guard says grumpily, "that's what my hip tells me."

Cone has a long walk back to the subway through littered streets lined with grimy industrial buildings. But it's worth it; he realizes what's been bugging him about the New World premises. That tarmac in front of the warehouse looked like it had been poured yesterday. No oil stains. No tire marks. No pits or bald spots. The whole place was spotless. New and unused.

It is just beginning to sprinkle when he gets on the subway, and when he gets off at Prince Street about an hour later, the rain has stopped. Cone takes it as a good omen. He opens his second pack of Camels and does some chores.

He picks up his laundry, buys a bottle of Popov and a jug of California chablis. Then he stops at a deli and selects a frozen package of two short ribs of beef, planning to give one to Cleo. He also buys some cheese with jalapeño peppers, a can of hot chili, a kielbasa sausage—and wonders how long his stomach is going to endure these assaults before ulcering in protest.

After he and Cleo dine, they both have a nice, long nap. Cone wakes shortly before midnight. He straps on the ankle holster after checking the action of the Magnum. Dons his ratty black raincoat and leather cap. Puts a small flashlight in his pocket and adds a set of lockpicks in a suede pouch.

"Wish me luck, baby," he says to Cleo, and sets out.

He does have luck, because by the time he gets back to the New World Enterprises, Inc., headquarters in Brooklyn, there's a thick pelt of clouds masking the moonglow, and even the streetlights are dimmed by night mist. He's the only one abroad at that hour in that neighborhood, and he feels for his .357 to make certain it's there.

It takes him less than a minute to pick the lock, and then he's inside, closing the gate carefully behind him. He walks swiftly across the tarmac, still glistening from the day's rain.

He makes a complete circuit of the warehouse, not using his flashlight but peering for electronic alarms. He sees nothing.

All the windows are barred, but, shining his light inside he can see enough to make out a small office. One room with two desks, a file cabinet, a phone, and what appears to be a computer on a separate table. Then he moves slowly around the building again, peering in every window. The warehouse is huge. It looks like an airplane hangar. Steel trusses overhead but no pillars.

The place is completely empty.

"You know," Samantha Whatley says, "if you were a really wealthy man, people would call you eccentric. But you don't have all that much money, so you're just plain goofy. What if you set off an alarm or a squad car picked you up for B-and-E? Nice headlines. Great publicity for Haldering. The company would go right down the drain."

"No great loss," Timothy Cone says, shrugging.

"You're really a turd," she says. "You know that?"

It is a sparkling Saturday afternoon, and they could have been in Central Park, up at the Cloisters, or down at the South Street Seaport. But she won't be seen with him in public. She's afraid someone from the office will see them together.

That's okay with him; he plays according to her rules. So on that super afternoon they're holed up in his loft, drinking white wine and talking shop.

"Will you let me finish my story?" he asks her. "Yesterday I went back to Sid Apicella. He says New World Enterprises, Inc., was capitalized for one-three-five million when it was incorporated fourteen months ago. So far they've bought and renovated that Brooklyn warehouse, and they've got some office equipment and some dozers and trucks parked outside. How much could all that cost? A mil maybe—if that much. So what are they doing with their money?"

"What they were set up to do," Sam says. "Developing and building residential and commercial properties."

Cone shakes his head. "No record of it. Sid checked. I checked. No building permits in their name, and none applied for. So Sid called Stanley

Clovis and asked him what New World is doing. Clovis says they have several projects in the planning stage—whatever that means. I called New World in Brooklyn and pretended I was the owner of several West Side brownstones and looking for a renovator. I talked to a dese, dem and doze guy who said New World is too busy to take on any new work at this time. *Bullshit!*"

Sam is silent a moment. Then: "Pour me some more wine, Tim. Please."

She is wearing tight denim jeans and a black turtleneck sweater. Her hair is down and her long feet are bare. She's got a wide leather belt cinched tight, and it makes her waist look about the size of Cone's thigh. He thinks her stretched-out body is really neat and hopes that, later, she'll be willing to Indian-wrestle on the mattress.

"So," she says, taking a sip of her wine, "how do you figure it?"

"Let me show you something," he says. "I took the Evanchat file back to the office, but I kept something out. It was in with Ed Griffon's personal notes."

She inspects the scrap of green scratch paper. "DUM?" she says. "What the hell does that mean?"

"I didn't know, and neither did Sid Apicella. But now I can guess. DUM? is Ed's shorthand for 'dummy.' He thought New World was probably a dummy corporation, and I think so too. The goddamn thing is a front."

"For what?"

"I have no idea. But it's been in business fourteen months and hasn't done a lick of work. Those bulldozers and trucks have never moved a yard of dirt. The tarmac outside is squeaky clean. The warehouse itself is empty. But Clovis and Clovis put a hundred and thirty-five million into the business. Why? I don't know, but I think Ed Griffon found out and got wasted for being smart."

"Holy Christ, Tim, do you know what you're saying?"

"Sure I know. Clovis and Clovis are involved in some dirty scam big enough to kill for."

She shakes her head. "I can't believe it. A big outfit like that. Passing out bucks to every charity drive in town. Openings at the Met, building free parks in the Bronx. And they're killers? How can you be sure?"

"I'm sure," he says.

She sighs. "Okay, assuming you're right—what do we do next?"

"The first thing you do, Monday morning, is talk to H.H. Tell him to stall Evanchat. Tell him to convince Isaac to hold off on the deal with Clovis until we complete our investigation. Next thing you do is this: Joe is coming back from sick leave on Monday. He'll have nothing on his plate. Give him my whole caseload, except for the Evanchat–Clovis deal. Let me zero in on it."

"And get yourself murdered," she says.

"Probably," he says cheerfully.

When she arrived at his loft at noon, she brought two Rock Cornish hens and a big container of salad she had made herself. They eat at about three P.M., sitting at Cone's desk and feeding tidbits to the attentive Cleo. They even roll the cat a cherry tomato and watch the chase across the linoleum floor.

"That's one crazy animal," Cone says.

"Takes after you," Samantha says.

They're both tight, private people, and they'd rather be sautéed in oil than say, "I love you." But, grudgingly, each acknowledges an attraction, a comfort with each other. It's a no-horseshit relationship with feelings masked by cold profanity, and intimacy shielded away. Like two old soldiers cursing each other and ready to be the first to leap on the live grenade.

But they cannot deny their bodies' appetites, and when their hormones take over, they go berserk. On that lumpy mattress with clean sheets—thank God!—and Cleo watching with wise eyes.

"What are we doing?" she whispers wonderingly. "What *are* we doing?"

"You tell me," he says. "You're the boss."

They're two stick figures, all bony knobs and hard muscle. Their mating is a furious battle, not against each other so much as the emptiness and lunacy of their lives. When they strain, it is not to punish but to break out into another world. Oh, look at the meadows and the daffodils! The lawn they seek is bliss.

It's such a sweaty wrestle, not quite hysterical but frantic enough. And when they're done, staring at each other with dulled eyes, reality comes seeping back, the real world takes over again. But something remains. . . .

"Tim," she says, touching his cheek softly, "be careful."

He puts his face to her little breasts. "I always am," he says.

"Jesus," she says, "don't you ever shave?"

The first thing Timothy Cone does on Monday morning is stop by the office of Hiram Haldering's secretary. He asks for the keys to one of the two company cars.

"What do you want it for?" she says sharply.

"I'd like to take a drive in the country and see if the leaves are turning."

The old biddy sniffs. "You can't have the Impala. Mr. Haldering is using it today. You can have the Toyota, but only till noon."

He frowns, considering a long moment as if he has a choice. "Well . . . all right," he says finally, "I'll take the Toyota."

"Just make sure you have it back by twelve," she snaps, handing him the keys.

"And if I don't?" he asks. "It turns into a pumpkin?"

His next stop is at Sol Faber's office. He borrows Sol's binoculars, promising to return them in good condition. Then he walks around to the garage on Dey Street and signs out the Toyota.

It takes him more than an hour to get to the New World warehouse, but when he arrives, it looks exactly as it had before: same number of bulldozers and trucks, no human activity. Cone figures he hasn't missed a thing. He parks across West Street, scrunches down, and focuses the binoculars on the New World gates. Then he puts the glasses aside and begins reading the morning *Times*, looking up frequently to make sure nothing's going on.

About eleven-fifteen, a woman walks up to New World's gates. Cone grabs up the binocs and watches as the guard lets her in. She walks across the tarmac, unlocks the office door, and enters. Cone makes her to be five-three, 120, about thirty-eight years old, black hair, olive-skinned, poorly dressed, and carrying a brown paper bag that could contain her lunch.

About ten minutes later, a silver Chrysler LeBaron GTS pulls up at the gate, and Cone again grabs the binoculars. He can't see who's driving, but he gets a good make on the license number and repeats it aloud so he won't forget. The LeBaron crosses the tarmac and pulls up close to the office door. The driver gets out and whisks inside. Cone gets a fleeting impression of a big, husky guy—but that's all he gets.

He drives back to Manhattan and returns the Toyota's keys to Haldering's secretary.

"You're more than an hour late," she says accusingly.

He looks at her in astonishment. "You mean we're still on daylight saving time?" he says. "I could have sworn we switched back."

He gives Sol Faber his binoculars, then goes to his office, puts his feet up on the desk, and ponders his next move. He's still in the same position, smoking his fifth cigarette of the day, when Samantha Whatley appears in the doorway. She's carrying a small white envelope that she flaps at him.

"Guess what I've got," she says.

"Your draft notice?" he says sullenly. "How the hell do I know what you've got."

"What a nice mood," she says. "No wonder they call you Mr. Congeniality. This happens to be an invitation to a press conference and cocktail party being hosted by Clovis and Clovis to announce a grand plan to tear down those decaying West Side piers and create a fairy wonderland on the river: The invitation came to H.H., but he doesn't want to go. He gave it to me, and I don't want to go, So I'm giving it to you. All the Clovis bigshots will be there."

He realizes she's trying to help, but he doesn't know how to be grateful. "I'll think about it," he says.

She tosses the invitation onto his desk and stalks away, making him feel like a crumb. He doesn't touch the envelope, but searches through the mess in his top desk drawer until he finds the card of Neal K. Davenport, the NYPD detective. He calls. It rings eight times before the phone is picked up.

"Davenport."

"Yeah. This is Timothy Cone. I'm the investigator with Haldering and Company. You talked to me about the death of G. Edward Griffon."

"Oh, sure, I remember you. How're you doing?"

"Okay. Anything new on Ed's death?"

"No, nothing. These things take time; you should know that. You got something for me?"

"Not a thing. I called to ask a favor."

"Oh? What's that?"

"I got a license number I was hoping you'd trace for me. Find out who the car is registered to."

"Now why should I do that?"

"Just as a professional courtesy," Cone says, grinning at the phone.

Davenport laughs. "Kid, you've got chutzpah. Has it got anything to do with Griffon's death?"

"It might have."

Pause. "All right, give me the number; I'll see what I can do."

Cone recites the license number twice, to make certain Davenport has it right.

"I'll get back to you," the city dick says, and hangs up.

He spends the remainder of the day with Joe Washington, who has returned from sick leave and inherited Cone's caseload. Washington has a mordant sense of humor. He once said, "I am not a black, I am a person of the colored persuasion."

"Joe," Tim says, "I hope you won't take this as a personal insult, but you look a little washed-out to me."

"Still a bit puffy about the gills," Washington admits, "but I can function. I've been handed your crap."

"To ease you back into the real world. But there's nothing heavy in it."

They go through the cases: a merger, a buyout, an unfriendly takeover. They spend hours, and send out for cheeseburgers, fries, and Cokes. When they finish, Joe Washington acknowledges he can't see any great problems.

"About Ed Griffon..." he says, troubled. "Tim, what the hell happened?"

"No one knows," Cone says.

"A sweet guy," Joe says. "About a year ago I was in a bind and borrowed five bills from him. He handed it over without even asking what for. I paid it back, and he just said, 'Thanks,' and stuck it in his pocket. Like it didn't surprise him at all that I had paid him back. Tim, you working one of the cases? That's what I hear."

Cone nods.

"You think it's got something to do with Ed's death?"

"Maybe."

"You need a field hand," Washington says, "an experienced cotton picker, you know where to find me."

"I may take you up on that."

Cone goes back to his office and is opening his second pack of cigarettes of the day when his phone rings.

"Timothy Cone?"

"Yes."

"Davenport here. That license plate you gave me ..."

"Yeah?"

"I think we better talk about it. Not on the phone."

"Okay," Tim says. "Where? A bar, restaurant?"

"I don't think so," Davenport says.

"Oh-ho, it's like that, is it? Well, I live in a loft on Broadway between Spring and Broome. Wanna come up for a drink?"

"That sounds more like it. I've got your address."

"How did you get that?"

"Your personnel file at Haldering. I'll be there about six. Okay?"

"Fine."

"If I'm late," Davenport says, "don't get your balls in an uproar; I'll be along."

"I'll wait," Cone promises.

He walks home, pausing occasionally to look in store windows at things he doesn't need and doesn't want. He's got a lot of vices, he knows, but vanity isn't one of them. Maybe it should be, he thinks. A little vanity wouldn't hurt him.

He stops in front of a jewelry shop and sees a heavy necklace of chunky beads, alternating ebony and crystal, that would look great on Samantha. But he's never bought her a gift and is disturbed about starting now.

Somehow, he feels, it would upset their special relationship. Maybe change it for the worse, maybe for the better. But he's afraid to take the chance.

At home, he gives Cleo fresh water and a wing left over from Saturday's dinner with Sam. Cleo eats the whole wing: skin, meat, and bones. That cat could eat a steel anchor, Tim figures, and then belch delicately and groom its whiskers.

Davenport is only twenty minutes late. When Cone lets him in, the detective stands in the doorway and looks around.

"Be it ever so humble," he says. "Is this place available for weddings and bar mitzvahs? What's that thing under the bathtub?"

"That's Cleo, my cat."

"You're kidding. It looks like a cheetah to me."

Cone gets him seated on one of the plain wooden chairs drawn up to the battered desk.

"I have white wine, vodka, or beer," he says. "What's your pleasure?"

"Pussy," Davenport says. "But I'll have vodka on the rocks, providing you don't have to send out for the ice."

They both have heavy Popovs, sipping and talking about the weather, air pollution, the water shortage, traffic jams, and the high cost of a good corned beef sandwich.

"Enough of this idle chitchat," Davenport says finally. He's still wearing his snap-brimmed fedora because there's no place to put it that would be safe from the prowling Cleo. "Where did you get that license number?"

"Who's it registered to?" Cone counters.

They stare at each other.

Cone sees a porky guy who can chew Juicy Fruit and drink vodka at the same time. But beneath the suet, he reckons, is hard muscle. Davenport has the face of a dedicated drinker—the spider web of red capillaries and the swollen beezer. But the eyes are clear and shrewd. Cone believes he could take him, if necessary, but he doesn't want to find out.

"Look," he says to the cop, "you and I could play games forever. Why don't we level with each other? I don't mean all the way. I'm going to hold back, and you're going to hold back. We both understand that."

"Keep going," Davenport says. "You're making sense."

"Haldering isn't in the law-enforcement business," Cone continues. "We're not interested in putting anyone in the slammer. We get paid fees by clients who want other people investigated. Should I let this guy buy me out? Is he good for the dough he promises? What about this company that wants to merge? Are they legit? And what about this raider who's buying up our stock like mad? Is he a gonnif or what? We try to provide the information that lets our clients make their decision. Sometimes we give them bad news, but they go ahead anyway. You understand?"

"Sure," Davenport says, "I'm keeping up."

"What I'm trying to tell you," Cone says, "is that you and I aren't competitors. Most of the stuff I deal with is confidential. It has to be if we want to stay inside SEC regulations. But then a lot of your stuff is confidential, too. Has to be if you want to make a case."

"You're so right," Davenport says. "How about another shot from the wonderful pot? Keep your booze in the freezer, do you? I do, too."

"So," Cone says, topping off their jelly jars, "I inherited one file from the late G. Edward Griffon. It concerns a planned buyout."

Then he describes the proposed deal between Evanchat and Clovis & Clovis. He mentions nothing about Griffon's DUM note, or that New World Enterprises, Inc., might be a dummy corporation. He just says that in the course of checking out Clovis' subsidiaries, he inspected New World's Brooklyn headquarters and got suspicious.

"Why's that?" Davenport asks.

"Because the place is so clean," Cone says earnestly, avoiding the story of his break-in. "Trucks and bulldozers that have never been used. And no record of their doing any business even though they were organized fourteen months ago for a hefty one-three-five million. So, of course, I staked out the place. And eventually this big, heavy guy drives up in a silver LeBaron. I glom the license plate. And that's it."

The city dick looks at him thoughtfully. "Uh-huh," he says, "that listens. I think you're telling me the truth. Not *all* the truth, but we both agreed we're going to hold back a little. Since it's trade-off time, here's what I've got: That LeBaron you saw at New World is registered to Anthony Bonadventure. Ever hear of him?"

"No, I can't say that I have."

"He's had some publicity, off and on. None of it good. I can't say the guy is with the Families. He's not Sicilian. Not even Italian, for God's sake. Corsican, as far as we can make out. Anyway, he's been in this and that. Nothing heavy. I mean it's not prostitution, armed robbery, hijacking, or anything like that. Our Anthony is too smart. The guy's a university graduate, got an MBA. What he's into mostly is fraud, extortion, and misrepresentation with the intent to commit a felony. Like peddling fake oil leases or rigging phony tax shelters."

"Those are Federal offenses," Cone observes.

"Sure they are," Davenport agrees, "and the Feds have had him up twice, but they've never been able to pin him. I told you, the guy is smart, can afford the best legal eagles."

"So what's the interest of the NYPD? It's white-collar crime, isn't it?"

"Yeah, in a way. But some of the scams this Bonadventure has pulled, well, he could never have started them without the cooperation of the

Families. I mean, he doesn't *belong* to the mob, but when necessary, he works *with* them. Which means he pays his dues—right? Which brings our Organized Crime unit into the picture."

"What kind of scams does he do with the bentnoses?"

"Well, like for instance, he's suspected of forging green cards for aliens. Now you know he's got to be working with the locals to provide a steady stream of immigrants to make that profitable. That's how the NYPD got interested in him—his local ties. He's out of the green-card business now— the Feds got too close—and we haven't heard hide nor hair about him for almost a year. Now you come up with his license plate."

"A year?" Cone says, frowning. "New World was incorporated fourteen months ago. That's interesting."

"Yeah," Davenport says, grinning, "ain't it? I'll call you tomorrow and give you his last known address. They're running it through Records for me. Look, Cone, right now the Department has absolutely nothing we can charge Anthony Bonadventure with. But we'd love to nail that shtarker; it would really put the Feds' noses out. If you can come up with something, we'd be as happy as hogs in the mud. Why don't you take a close look at this guy? Maybe he's up to something."

"You're using me," the Wall Street dick says.

"You bet your sweet ass we're using you. But it's your job, isn't it? I mean, you're working for your client, this Evanchat, aren't you? So just do your job, and we'll provide all the cooperation we can, as long as you keep us in the picture. That's fair enough, isn't it?"

"Sure," Cone says, "that's fair."

Davenport drains off his vodka and rises to leave. "Thanks for the belt. I'll call you tomorrow with Bonadventure's home address, and I'll also try to dig up a mug shot of the guy so you can make him. By the way, he's known to pack a popgun on occasion, so watch your back. You carry?"

"Yeah," Cone says. "A short-barreled Magnum in an ankle holster."

Davenport laughs. "You been reading too many detective novels. What are you going to do in a shoot-out—pretend you're bending down to tie your shoelace?" He pauses at the door for a final look around. "I love this place," he says. "The Garden of Sleaze. It looks like my old YMCA locker room back in Topeka. Invite me again."

"Anytime you can make it," Cone says. "You're always welcome."

"Oh," the detective says, "about Griffon's death . . . We got a halfass witness who *thinks* he saw your buddy pushed. But he can't be sure, he won't swear to it, and he doesn't want to get involved."

"What else?" Cone says.

.   .   .

Davenport doesn't call the next morning, but he sends over a manila envelope, heavily sealed, with Anthony Bonadventure's last known address, a photo—taken outside, seemingly by surprise; the guy looks startled—and a copy of Bonadventure's sheet.

Timothy Cone—a cheapskate, and he knows it—carefully peels off the tape; it's a good, clean envelope; he can use it again. He puts the sheet away to read later, but he studies Bonadventure's photograph. It could be the man he saw get out of the LeBaron. Same build, same bulk.

He's a heavy guy with grossly handsome features. Plenty of brow and jaw. A massive face that's going to get jowly with age. Shadowed bedroom eyes and a full mouth: sculpted lips below a strong nose. He's really attractive in an animal kind of way, and Cone figures he does all right with the ladies.

He locks up everything and leaves the office. He takes an uptown bus, heading for the Clovis & Clovis press conference. During the trip, he wonders why Davenport has been so generous with the photo, address, copy of Bonadventure's record. Because the NYPD wants this guy real bad, Cone reckons, or Davenport's trying to establish an obligation. "I scratch your back, you scratch mine."

Timothy Cone is wearing his "good" suit. It's an old, thready Harris Tweed jacket with greasy suede patches on the elbows. The pants are unpressed gray flannel, dark enough—he hopes—to hide the spaghetti stains. When he put on White button-down shirt that morning, one of the buttons popped, so a flap of his collar swings free. His tie is a knitted black wool with several slubs where Cleo has bitten at it while dragging it across the linoleum, shaking it like a snake.

The press conference and cocktail party are being held in the mammoth reception room of Clovis & Clovis headquarters on Fifty-seventh Street. There's a uniformed security guard at the door collecting invitations.

"Thank you, sir," he says to Cone in a bored voice. "Please pass down the receiving line. Then the bar's on your left, buffet on your right."

Cone gets on the receiving line and is gratified to see several men as grungy looking as he, and supposes they're reporters. The file moves swiftly. The one man and two women shaking hands seem to be practiced. They clasp a guest's hand, give it one firm shake, and gently tug the owner along.

"Hi! I'm Stanley Clovis," the host beams, moving Cone to his right.

"Timothy Cone from Haldering and Company."

"So glad you could make it, Mr. Haldering."

"Hello. I'm Mrs. Grace Clovis."

"Timothy Cone from Haldering and Company."

"So glad you could make it, Mr. Timothy."

"Good morning! I'm Lucinda Clovis."

"Timothy Cone from Haldering and Company."

"So glad you could make it, Mr. Company."

He turns toward the bar, wondering who the hell he is. He asks the mess-jacketed bartender for a vodka rocks, and gets it with a slab of lime he didn't order and doesn't like.

He takes his drink and moves to a position where he can observe the Clovis family.

Stanley is a surprisingly small man, lean, dapper, and dark. He's wearing a raw gray silk suit with a mirror sheen. His wife, Grace, is almost a head taller: a statuesque blonde who looks like she might have been a model or showgirl. She's weaving slightly and Cone wonders if she might be bombed.

Lucinda Clovis, the sister, is as short and swarthy as her brother. She looks like a hard one, with a hatchet face and a jerky way of moving. She's flashing a spray of diamonds on the lapel of her black gabardine suit.

They make quite a trio, and Timothy Cone studies them, noting their frozen smiles, the smooth way they're greeting their guests, the public-relations performance they're putting on. They've done it a hundred times, he's sure, and wonders what happens when their public masks drop and they take off their jewelry and expensive clothes. Private masks?

But then the receiving line bunches up, and he can't get a good look at them. He wanders over to the buffet table and asks the toque-topped chef to make him a rare roast beef sandwich on those little slices of cocktail rye. He's munching on that when he notices a couple standing near the entrance, holding glasses of what appears to be white wine. They're bending toward each other in whispered conversation.

The man is Anthony Bonadventure; Cone is sure of it. That big, rugged build, heavy head, porcine features. He's wearing a pinkie ring that's got to be good for two or three carats. No doubt about it; the guy has presence. He looks assured, confident, and ready to wrestle the world.

The woman he's talking to is small, olive-skinned, poorly dressed: the one Cone saw entering the New World office.

"Hello there!" he says softly.

He finishes his tiny sandwich, licks his fingertips, and gets another vodka, without fruit. Then he positions himself where he can observe Bonadventure and his companion. They don't seem to be arguing, but they're having a very intense discussion, gesturing like mad.

The reception room has filled up, the receiving line has dribbled away. Cone, looking around, spots Mrs. Grace Clovis standing alone at the bar, working on what seems to be a beaker of scotch. He pushes his way to her side and gives her a smile.

"Lovely party," he says.

"Is it?" she says, staring at him. "Who you?"

"Mr. Haldering, Mr. Timothy, or Mr. Company. I'm not sure who I am."

"Welcome to the club," she says indifferently, taking a gulp of her drink. She looks around. "This thing sucks," she says.

He'd like to hear more, but Stanley Clovis mounts a small dais and taps a glass with a spoon. Gradually the room quiets.

"Sorry, folks," he yells, giving everyone a flash of his California caps, "you got exactly two minutes to replenish your drinks, and then we're going to close down the bar and buffet for a short presentation. And I promise you it will be short—and exciting! Then, after I make my pitch and answer questions, the bar and buffet will reopen. Okay?"

Laughter and applause. The guy handles himself well, Cone acknowledges. A real manipulator. As people crowd the bar, Tim moves away in the direction of Anthony Bonadventure and his lady. They seem to be inching closer to the exit. Cone inches right along with them.

Assistants set up easels, charts, enlarged architectural drawings on the dais. A public address system is plugged in and tested. Stanley Clovis takes his place behind the lectern. Immediately Bonadventure and the olive-skinned woman move to the door. Cone leaves his empty glass on the rug near the exit and follows.

They ride down together in the same elevator, but it's crowded and there's no conversation. If they take the LeBaron, Cone thinks, or hop a cab, I've got problems. But no, Bonadventure and the woman walk west on Fifty-seventh Street. The man moves to the outside and takes her arm. A gentleman.

Cone tails them for two blocks. The sidewalks are jammed; there's no way they're going to spot him. He moves closer, and when they go into a corner branch of the Merchants International Bank, he's right behind them. He stands at one of the glass counters and diddles with a deposit slip and a pen on a chain while he watches them.

Bonadventure stands aside, leaning negligently against a marble pillar as the woman goes up to one of the tellers' windows and pushes some papers under the brass gate. She gets a slip of paper and rejoins Bonadventure.

They leave, Cone on their heels. A cab stops in front of the bank, a woman gets out, and Bonadventure and his partner pop in and are whisked away. Cone gives up.

Back at Haldering & Co., he goes directly to the office of the chief accountant.

"You again?" Sidney Apicella says.

"Yeah, me. Sid, can you get the current bank balance of New World Enterprises? It's a subsidiary of Clovis and Clovis."

"And would you also like the mean temperature of the planet Jupiter during the month of April?"

"Cut the crap, Sid. This is important. I need to know how much New World has got in the till."

"Why do you need to know?"

"Because New World started out with a capitalization of a hundred and thirty-five million. That was fourteen months ago. Maybe they've spent a million or so on their warehouse and equipment. But they've done no jobs. There's no record of income. I'll bet my left nut that someone is looting that outfit."

Apicella sighs. "I'll see what I can do, Tim. Things like this aren't easy. But we have our contacts."

"Guys we bribe, you mean."

"Not exactly," Sid says, frowning. "We do favors for them, they do favors for us."

"You mean one hand washes the other?" Cone says. "That's an original concept. I'll be in my office. Let me know as soon as possible, will you? It really is important."

He goes back to his desk, digs out the NYPD sheet on Anthony Bonadventure, and starts reading. It's a long record, and Cone shakes his head in amazement at how many times the guy has been arrested, charged, indicted, tried, and has waltzed away whistling a merry tune.

He's still studying the transcript when Apicella comes to the door of his office, carrying a little piece of scratch paper.

"You said you'd bet your left nut that someone is looting that outfit," he says, looking down at his notes. "Well, New World Enterprises, Inc., was incorporated fourteen months ago with an initial capitalization of one hundred and thirty-five million provided by Clovis and Clovis."

"I told you all that, Sid," Cone says, sighing. "Get to the bottom line. How much is left?"

"As of yesterday," Apicella says, "their bank balance was one hundred and eighty-eight million."

"There goes my left nut."

2

He doesn't enjoy getting jerked around, and that's exactly what he thinks is happening.

"Look here," he says angrily to Samantha Whatley, "that outfit has made more than fifty million. And with no record of developing or building, which is what they were set up to do. I tell you something kinky is going down."

"Drugs?" Sam suggests.

"Nah," he says, shaking his head. "Stanley and Lucinda have to protect their reputation as public-spirited citizens and world-class partygoers. No, it's not something as heavy as drugs, but it's a scam, no doubt about it. And Clovis and Clovis must be aware of it."

They're in Samantha's gentrified apartment in the East Village. You'd think, wouldn't you—considering the woman's hard, edgy personality— that her home would be high-tech, with white walls and furniture of stainless steel and glass.

But no, her studio is one big bouquet. Lots of bright, flowered chintz, ruffles, a French doll in lace on the bed. The walls are covered with paper in a trellis and vine design, oval rag rugs scatter the polished wood floor, and there, over a fake marble mantelpiece in a place of honor, is a big, framed reproduction of Wyeth's *Christina's World*.

They've had supper—grilled knockwurst, baked beans, and cold sauerkraut with caraway seeds—and are now working on chilled bottles of Heineken dark. They're lying on one of the rag rugs, mostly because Samantha's chairs are so bloody uncomfortable. "Designed for midgets," Tim once growled, and Sam had to agree. But she likes them; they're so *pretty*.

"Did you read the paper today?" she asks him.

"Of course I read the paper. I keep up."

"Sure you do," she says. "The front page and the financial section."

"Don't forget the obituaries. I always turn to that first, looking for my name."

"You should read the society pages occasionally. Maybe you'd learn something."

She takes a folded newspaper clipping from the breast pocket of her blue denim shirt and hands it to him. He reads swiftly. It's a short account of a charity bash held at the Parker Meridien. The article lists several well-known guests.

" 'Also present,' " Cone reads aloud, " 'were the socially active Lucinda and Stanley Clovis, dressed to the nines and holding hands as usual. And where was the beauteous Mrs. Grace Clovis'?"

He looks at Sam. "What the hell does that mean?"

She shrugs. "Beats the shit out of me. I just thought you'd be interested."

"Yeah," he says, "thanks. Can I keep it?"

She nods, and he stuffs the clipping into his hip pocket.

"Getting anywhere?" she asks him.

"This guy Anthony Bonadventure..." he says. "I told you about his record. Well, I checked with our legal department, and they found out he's listed as treasurer of New World Enterprises, Inc. Now you know that anything he's connected with has got to be dirty."

"Who are the other officers of the corporation?"

"Stanley Clovis is president, Lucinda is vice-president, and in addition to Bonadventure being treasurer, there's a secretary, Constance Figlia. I just feel in my bones she's the short, dumpy broad I saw at New World and then later with Bonadventure at the press conference. They're all in it together."

"In what?"

"How the hell do I know?" he yells at her, then calms. "I'm sorry," he says contritely. "I just feel I'm getting the runaround, and I don't like it. Tomorrow I'm going to call Neal Davenport, the city dick, and ask him to run a trace on Constance Figlia. Maybe the computers can turn up something."

"And you want something from me, too, don't you?" Samantha asks.

"How can you tell?"

"You're acting so fierce."

"Fierce?" he says with his quirky smile. "I haven't been fierce since the age of eight when a kid tried to steal my best aggie. Well, yeah, Sam, I want something from you. I need wheels. Trying to requisition the company Toyota a few hours at a time just won't do. I need a car so I can run the job. I mean I've got to get around, and subways and buses and even cabs just won't do."

"H.H. won't approve."

"Sure he will. Tell him I'm on to something hot. Tell him it's going to make him King Jesus on Wall Street. Tell him anything. But also tell him it's not going to cost him a cent; he can always charge Evanchat for the expenses."

"I'll try," she says.

"That's my own dear shithead," he says, patting her cheek.

"Okay," she says, "enough shoptalk. Were you planning to spend the night?"

"I was planning," he admits. "All right with you?"

"All right," she says, "you smooth, sweet-talking son of a bitch."

"You want me to take a shower first?" he asks her. "Every time I walk into this perfumed boudoir of yours, I figure you want me to be squeaky clean."

"Fuck you," she says.

"I hope so," he says.

He gets his wheels —a little black Honda that he wouldn't select for a high-speed chase but does just fine in city traffic. What's on his mind— something he didn't mention to Samantha—is the role being played by Mrs. Grace Clovis. He figures that wobbly lady is on the sauce, or stoned, and might be willing to gabble if the time is right.

So, in the morning, he drives to the residence of Stanley Clovis. It's a triplex penthouse atop one of the Clovis & Clovis properties on Third Avenue near Eighty-fifth Street. Cone has to drive around the block three times before he finds a parking space that gives him a good view of the entrance. Then he settles down with the *Times*, a container of hot coffee, and a pumpernickel bagel.

He looks when a long blue Mercedes pulls up on the curved driveway. He watches as Stanley and Lucinda Clovis come out, both carrying attaché cases, and step into the chauffeured limousine. So Lucinda lives with her brother and sister-in-law, does she? That's interesting. Cone stays right where he is, crossing his fingers because he's a superstitious man.

His luck pays off in about a half hour. Grace Clovis comes out alone, wearing a sheath of something that sparkles and carrying a silver fox stole carelessly looped over one arm. The doorman moves out into the street to whistle up a cab, and Timothy Cone drops his newspaper and starts up the Honda. Half of the bagel is still clamped between his teeth.

Eventually a taxi stops and Mrs. Clovis climbs in, with a flash of thigh Cone can see, and appreciate, from across the street. He follows the cab downtown, almost bumper to bumper because traffic is so jammed up; there's no way Grace or the hack driver is going to spot a tail.

When they get below Forty-second Street, Cone guesses where Grace is going. Sure enough, the cab pulls up in front of a handsome converted brownstone on East Thirty-seventh Street, just off Park Avenue: the last known home address of Anthony Bonadventure.

"Well, well," Cone says aloud.

He drives by, then double-parks just long enough to watch Grace stalk across the sidewalk and enter the brownstone. Then Cone pulls away and heads for Brooklyn. Traffic is murder, but he doesn't mind; he's got a lot to think about.

He parks in front of the New World warehouse and gets out of his car. The same guard comes limping from the hut.

"Me again," Cone says cheerfully. "Is Constance Figlia in?"

"She's in," the guard says grudgingly, "but you gotta have an appointment. You got an appointment?"

"Well, no, but I'm sure she'll see me."

"No appointment, no see," the guard says. "Them's my orders."

"Okay," Cone says breezily, "I'll give her a call. If you happen to see her, will you tell her Mr. Javert was asking for her."

"Javert?"

"That's right. J-A-V-E-R-T. Thank you very much."

Cone drives back to Manhattan, satisfied with the long journey. He's a methodical man, and he's established, to his satisfaction, the presence of Constance Figlia at New World headquarters. Now he's got the cast identified; he can concentrate on the plot.

In his office, it takes three calls to locate Detective Davenport.

"Thanks for sending that stuff over," Cone says. "It's been a big help."

"Glad to hear it. Now it's your turn."

"How about this . . ." the Wall Street dick says. "Anthony Bonadventure is treasurer of New World Enterprises, Inc. In the past year or so, the company has made a profit of more than fifty million with absolutely no record of any business activity. No building, no renovation, nothing."

"Oh-ho," Davenport says, "the worms are squirming, are they?"

"I'd say so. Something is going down, but I haven't a clue—yet. Can you do something for me?"

"Depends."

"The secretary of New World is a woman named Constance Figlia. F-I-G-L-I-A. She's dark-haired, olive-skinned. I make her as five-three, one-twenty, maybe around thirty-eight years old. She dresses like she buys her clothes at a thrift shop."

"It takes one to know one," the Department man says.

"Could you see if you've got anything on her?"

Silence.

"Davenport?" Cone says. "Are you there?"

"I'm here. You think this Figlia dame is mixed up in whatever's going on?"

"Oh, yeah. Has to be."

"All right. I'll see if we've got anything on her and get back to you."

"Great. I may not be at the office. Do you have my home phone number? It's unlisted."

"I've got it," Davenport says. "I know a lot about you. Why didn't you tell me you have all those medals from the Marine Corps?"

"I hocked them," Cone says.

The detective laughs. "You're a flake, you know that?"

They hang up and then, just because he feels he's on a roll, Cone calls Clovis & Clovis and asks to speak to Miss Constance Figlia.

"Just a moment, please," the receptionist chirps, "I'll connect you with her department."

Click, click, click. Another operator comes on.

"Comptroller's office," she says.

"May I speak to Miss Figlia, please."

"I'm sorry, sir, she isn't in today. Would you care to leave a message?"

"Just tell her Mr. Javert called," Cone says. "I'll try her tomorrow."

He sits for almost an hour in his cramped office, smokes three Camels, stares at the wall, and runs scenarios through his mind like videocassettes in living color. But nothing makes sense. He just doesn't know enough.

Sighing, he pulls a yellow legal pad toward him and starts working on his weekly progress report. Progress, he thinks dourly—it is to laugh. He puts nothing in his report that Samantha Whatley doesn't already know.

He's home, he and Cleo have dined royally on pastrami sandwiches and cole slaw, and he's still running those videos through his mind and still coming up with zilch. It's past eleven o'clock when his phone rings.

"Did I wake you up?" Neal K. Davenport asks.

"No, but you woke up Cleo."

"Tough shit," the detective says. "I need sleep more than that cat. As soon as I hang up, I'm packing it in and going home for eighteen straight hours of shuteye."

"Where do you live?"

"Staten Island. You know the place?"

"No."

"There's nothing to know. About that lady of yours, Constance Figlia, we got nothing on her, she's got no record. But I talked to a pal of mine in the Organized Crime Unit, and he made her. She's a niece of Vincent Figlia. You know who he is?"

"Never heard of him."

"A lower-echelon mafioso who works out of Long Island," Davenport says, giving it the correct pronunciation: "Longuyland." "This Vincent is small-time stuff: some minor loan-sharking, bookmaking, shakedowns— things like that. But he's got connections with Brooklyn Families. And, like I say, that Constance is his niece."

"Well," Cone says, "that's something. But not much."

"Uh-huh, but here's what makes the cheese more binding: Remember my telling you that Anthony Bonadventure was mixed up in a counterfeit green-card scam? The Feds got close and broke it up, but were never able to put the thumb on Bonadventure. Well, it turns out that Vincent Figlia was one of the guys supplying the illegal aliens. Figlia and Bonadventure did business together. So your lady, the niece, Constance Figlia, probably knew Bonadventure before this New World deal, and knows he isn't a straight arrow. That's interesting—don't you think?"

"Yeah," Cone says slowly, "interesting."

"One more thing," Davenport says. "My pal at Organized Crime tells me that Constance is supposed to be a computer whiz. Good night and pleasant dreams."

They hang up. Cone starts playing more videocassettes through his mind. New ones, as senseless as the old. Finally he gets undressed, turns out the lights, and lies down on the mattress. After a while Cleo comes padding up and curls into the bend of his knees.

"What's it all about, you stupid cat?" he asks.

Cleo growls and nuzzles closer.

"Something screwy happened this afternoon," Samantha Whatley says. "Stanley Clovis himself called H.H. and asked if we have someone named Javert working for us."

"Javert?" Cone says. "Who he?"

"That's what H.H. wanted to know. Clovis said a guy named Javert has been harassing one of his execs, and he thought it might be a Haldering employee. So H.H. got huffy—you know how he can be—and said Haldering people do not, repeat *not*, harass anyone. He said there is no one named Javert working here and never has been. That seemed to satisfy Clovis, and he apologized."

Sam is in her office, heavy brogues parked atop her desk, denim skirt pulled demurely down over her knees. Cone lounges in the doorway, leaning against the jamb. As usual, he is sucking on a cigarette, tilting his head to keep the smoke out of his eyes.

"You know who Javert was, don't you?" she asks, looking at him closely.

"Nope. Never heard of the guy."

"He was the policeman in *Les Misérables*."

"*Les Misérables?*" Cone says. "Is that French for 'lousy fuck'?"

"You know," she says, "when you get that innocent look on your ugly mug, I know you've been up to something. Anyway, the reason I called you in is this: After Clovis and H.H. got over their little squabble, Clovis invited him or his representative to an open house tonight in the ballroom of the Hotel Bedlington on Madison Avenue. Stanley and Lucinda are having a cocktail party so a friend of theirs can announce his candidacy for Congress. Free booze and Swedish meatballs. From five till seven. I thought you might want to stop by."

"I might," Cone says. "The free booze doesn't interest me, but I go ape for Swedish meatballs."

"Get the hell out of here," Sam says roughly.

Cone stops at Joe Washington's office and sticks his head in.

"How you coming with my stuff?" he asks.

"Bore-*ring,*" Joe says. "Nothing but phone calls and visits to the public library."

"How would you like to go to a cocktail party tonight? From five to seven. Free booze and meatballs."

"I can live with that," Washington says. "What'll I be—the token spade?"

"Nah," Cone says. "This is a political shindig. East Side liberals. They'll be delighted to see you there. You may even get two meatballs."

"I could use them," Joe says. "According to my wife."

"I'll brief you on the way up."

"Ah-ha. So this isn't purely a social occasion?"

"Not exactly."

"Got something to do with Ed Griffon's death?"

"Maybe."

"Let's go," Joe Washington says.

In addition to being cantankerous and superstitious, Timothy Cone is also secretive. He isn't about to tell anyone anything they don't need to know. When he has it all wrapped up in a package, he'll deliver it.

So on the long, stop-and-go ride uptown, all he tells Joe is that there are probably going to be five people at the party he'd like to keep an eye on. Since he can't cover them all, Joe can take two of them: the brother-and-sister act—Stanley and Lucinda.

"I'll point them out," Cone says, "but they're the host and hostess; you won't be able to miss them. Both short, dark, expensively dressed. Charm kids."

"What am I supposed to look for?" Joe asks.

"I just want your take on them. How they act in public towards each other. If you get a chance, try to talk to both of them."

"Should I tell them I'm with Haldering?"

"Don't volunteer it, but if they ask where you're from, tell them."

The ballroom is already crowded when they get there, and jammed elevators keep bringing up new mobs. The room is filled with flags, balloons, streamers, confetti; it already looks like a victory celebration. A big banner over the dais proclaims: A NEW BEGINNING!

Cone and Washington push their way to the bar where two sweating bartenders are doing their best to quench the freeloaders' thirst.

"There," Timothy says, "over in the corner; the short couple talking to the tall guy in the seersucker suit."

"I got them," Joe says. "Now I'll get me a drink and I'll be all set."

"I'll see if I can find the others. You stay as long as you like, then take off. I'll see you in the office tomorrow and we'll compare notes."

He drifts away, sliding through the crowd. A lot of young, noisy yuppies are wearing big badges that also proclaim: A NEW BEGINNING! That slogan doesn't cut much ice with Cone. He prefers TIPPECANOE AND TYLER, TOO.

Timothy doesn't like people much, and he dislikes them most in crowds.

He moves through the happy crush with an idiot grin donned for protective coloration. But his sharp eyes are searching for a target. He spots one: Grace Clovis, standing erect in a short cocktail gown that seems to have been chiseled from one enormous rhinestone. She's not speaking, but listening to a man with three chins, two stomachs, and thighs that threaten to pop the seams of his designer jeans.

Cone watches as Grace finally staggers away, leaving the guy in the middle of a gesture with his mouth open. She moves to the bank of elevators. Cone follows. He doubts very much that she'll remember him from the press conference, but just to play it safe, he doesn't get on the Down elevator with her but waits for the next, hoping he's not going to lose her.

He doesn't. When he gets to the lobby, she's standing, looking about vaguely. She's not tottering now, but appears almost catatonic.

She wanders, with little-girl steps, into the cocktail lounge. Cone waits a few minutes, then follows. It's a dim room, almost empty. He sits at the bar, orders a vodka, and inspects the room via the back mirror. Grace is sitting by herself at a small corner table. A waiter is serving her a tall drink with a lot of fruit in it, topped with a little paper parasol.

Cone watches, and can't figure her out. She's sitting like a statue. Not smoking a cigarette, not sipping her drink, not looking around. He figures if someone touched her with a fingertip she'd topple sideways.

Finally Anthony Bonadventure comes striding into the cocktail lounge. Cone watches the action. Bonadventure looks around, walks smiling to her table. He's carrying a folded newspaper under his arm. Cone thinks it's *The Wall Street Journal*.

Anthony sits down at her table, takes one of her hands, turns it over, kisses the palm. Then he leans toward her and whispers rapidly. A waiter comes over. Anthony straightens up, gives his order. The waiter moves away. Grace gets up and walks to the lobby, carrying the folded newspaper. Bonadventure sits down again, and when his drink is served—something in a stemmed glass—sips it quietly.

Cone glances at his watch and waits for this little melodrama to be played out. In less than ten minutes, Mrs. Grace Clovis returns. No newspaper. She's practically bouncing, bopping to a tune no one else can hear. She's snapping her fingers as she walks, and kisses Bonadventure's ear before sliding onto her chair in a lithe, sexy glide.

The two chatter, heads close together again. Then they finish their drinks, Bonadventure pays the tab, and they leave together. The waiter cleans off their table and brings a small tray with their empties and crumpled cocktail napkins back to the bar. Cone reaches for the discarded paper parasol.

"May I have this?" he asks.

"Sure," the waiter says, "help yourself. Afraid it might rain tonight?"

Cone smiles dutifully. He turns the wee parasol in his fingers, opening and closing it. Made in Taiwan, probably. And here it is in Manhattan, decorating a drink in a fashionable Madison Avenue cocktail lounge.

"Go figure it," he says to the bartender.

That worthy, experienced at humoring nutty patrons, nods and says, "You're telling me."

Cone drives home, figuring Joe Washington will get back to Queens one way or another. He finds a parking space only two blocks from his loft, but he'll have to get up early to move the Honda to the other side of the street or risk it being towed away. He puts a sign inside the windshield. It came with the rented car. NO VALUABLES, DRUGS, OR RADIO. THIS CAR WIRED WITH ELECTRONIC ALARM. Lots of luck.

He isn't hungry, but Cleo is. He gives the cat a treat: a can of tuna. Topped with the tiny paper parasol. Cleo sniffs at the fish, then looks up at him, suspicious of this largesse. But starts gobbling. Half the tuna disappears. The cat strolls away, licking its chops. Then sits down to groom its whiskers.

"Not even a thank you?" Cone asks, then, suddenly famished, eats the remainder of the tuna, spooning it directly from the can. He also eats a chunk of kielbasa and a piece of moldy cheddar. He belches—which is understandable. The sudden eruption startles Cleo, who darts under the bathtub.

It is almost midnight before he calls Samantha Whatley.

"I didn't wake you up, did I?" he asks her.

"No. I'm watching the Johnny Carson show."

"Good?"

"A repeat. What do you want?"

"Not a thing. How are you?"

"I'm fine. Just the way I was this afternoon. Did you go to the party?"

"Yeah, I stopped by. Had one drink. A drag."

"Find out anything?"

He considers what he might tell her. "Lucinda Clovis, the sister, lives in the same apartment with her brother and sister-in-law. Well, in the same building, anyway."

"So?"

"Don't you think that's a little unusual?"

"Maybe," Sam says.

"What did you do tonight?" he asks. "After you got home."

"Washed my hair. Did some laundry."

"What did you eat?"

"Chicken chow mein. With fried noodles. It was pretty good. What did you have?"

"A tuna fish salad."

"You liar," she says. "You ate it right out of the can."

"Well, yes," he admits. "Cleo's leftovers. You're feeling okay?"

She sighs. "What's *with* you? Yes, for the second time, I'm feeling okay. May I go to sleep now?"

After they hang up, he wonders why he called. How are you feeling? What did you do tonight? What did you eat? A real nothing conversation—and so comforting.

He has a nagging suspicion that he's being recruited as a living, breathing, dues-paying member of the human race.

"How did you make out?" Cone asks Washington the next morning.

"Like a thief. I practically OD'd on those meatballs. Dee-licious. Then I get home, and guess what the little wifey has for dinner? Spaghetti and meatballs. Wouldn't you know?"

"Screw the meatballs. Did you get a chance to talk to Stanley and Lucinda?"

"Oh, yeah. I had a nice little chat with both of them, and I kept them in sight all the time I was there. They didn't ask me where I was from, and I didn't say."

"What's your take?"

Washington looks down at his desk and fiddles with a pencil. Then he looks up at Cone. "You think there's something kinky there, don't you?"

Timothy nods.

"I think you're right," Joe says, "but don't expect me to swear to it in a court of law. Look, I got a sister I dearly love. We meet, hug and kiss each other's cheek. Maybe I'll put my arm around her. All casual-like—you know? But Stanley and Lucinda—they're something else again. If you hadn't told me they were brother and sister, I'd have figured them for a happily married couple, or maybe lovers. I've never seen so much hand-holding, and little pats, and strokings. I really don't think they're aware of what the hell they're doing, or how it looks to other people. I spotted a few smirks and raised eyebrows, so other people probably have the same dirty, disgusting suspicions you and I have."

"Yeah," Cone says. "You got a Manhattan telephone directory?"

"Of course I've got a telephone directory. You think I'm a second-class citizen, honky?"

"Do me a favor, will you? Look up the home phone number of Stanley Clovis, then see if Lucinda has a different listing."

He waits patiently, lighting another Camel while Joe flips pages. Finally the black looks up, his face twisted into a strained grin.

"Yeah," he says, "you're right. Lucinda's number is the same as Stanley's."

"It figures," Cone says. "I know Lucinda lives in the same apartment house. I just wanted to make sure she lives in Stanley's penthouse, along with wife Grace and their two kids."

They stare at each other.

"The family that plays together stays together," Washington says.

"Maybe," Cone says. "But how are you going to nail down something like that?"

"You're not," Joe says. "Unless you're in the bedroom with a Polaroid and flash."

"Oh, I don't know," Tim says slowly. "There may be ways. Did you eyeball Stanley's haircut?"

"Oh, yeah, man. All those ringlets. Real spiffy. The Blow-dry Kid. And Lucinda has the same style. His-and-hers."

"Uh-huh," Cone says. "I think I need a haircut."

"I thought you did it yourself," Joe Washington says. "With a salad bowl and an electric shaver."

Cone grunts and goes back to his office. He spends almost a half hour with the Manhattan Consumer Yellow Pages, going through the section on Barbershops. He's happy to find a special Guide included that groups businesses according to the locations they serve. So he concentrates on the East Side, Fifty-ninth to Ninetieth streets.

He makes the same pitch to each barbershop he calls.

"Hello there! I wonder if you might help me. I met Mr. Stanley Clovis at a party the other night, and I so admired his hair styling. I'd like a do just like his, but I neglected to ask him where he goes. Is he a customer of yours?"

He strikes pay dirt on his eighth call: Venus-Adonis Hair Styling, Inc., a unisex barbershop on East Eighty-sixth Street.

"Is he a customer of yours?" Cone asks.

"Not a customer," the receptionist says coldly. "Both Stanley and Lucinda Clovis are clients of ours."

"And could I get a haircut like Stanley's?"

"Just a moment, sir. I'll have to talk to Luis. He created Mr. Clovis's styling."

Cone waits patiently. Finally the receptionist comes back on the phone.

"If you're able to get here by eleven o'clock," she says, "Luis can fit you in."

Cone suppresses an obscene reply to that. "I'll be there," he says. "Thank you, and thank Luis."

"Name, please?"

"Javert. J-A-V-E-R-T."

He leaves his black leather cap in the office and drives up to East Eighty-sixth Street. The Venus-Adonis salon is as bright and bewildering as a discotheque, with garish colors, crackled pink mirrors, and hard rock blasting from ceiling speakers.

Cone identifies himself as Javert, and the receptionist, who's wearing a black leather jumpsuit and a purple wig, looks at his spiky, ginger-colored hair in amazement.

"You *do* need help, don't you?" she says.

But she gets him into a chair and swathes him up to the chin in a Ralph Lauren sheet.

"Luis will be with you presently."

Cone waits, and waits. He's not the only client; four of the six chairs are occupied: three women and a man, all swaddled in sheets. He remembers when barbershops had copies of the *Police Gazette* available for customers. This hair-styling salon has *Elle* and *Town & Country*.

Luis shows up, looking like an anorexic basketball player. He's got to be six-eight, at least, and so thin a strong wind might blow him across to Queens, where he belongs. He's wearing white painters' overalls, with apparently nothing on underneath, and he's doused with a cologne that reminds Cone of a visit to a geisha house.

Luis claps a palm to his cheek in horror after viewing Cone's hair. "Oh, my God, my God," he groans. "Who did this to you?"

"A butcher."

"A sadistic butcher," Luis says. "There is no way, *no* way, I am going to re-create Stanley Clovis's styling with what you have. It will take at least three consultations. And meanwhile you must let the hair grow and grow to give me something to work with. The color isn't bad," he admits. "I can live with the color, but it needs brightening. And also a protein thickener and conditioner. I will start with the preliminary shaping, but you must promise to come back again in a month."

"I promise," Cone says humbly.

Luis sets to work, snipping gently, and frequently standing back to observe his handiwork through narrowed eyes.

"Stanley and Lucinda are wonderful people," Cone offers.

"Beautiful people," Luis says, clipping a bit here, a bit there. "So chic. So soigné."

Cone isn't sure what soigné means, but it sounds like a compliment. "Definitely soigné," he says. "And so devoted to each other."

Luis giggles. "Oh, you've heard those stories, too, have you? My lips are sealed."

"Everyone's heard those stories," Cone says. "With Lucinda living in the same apartment."

"Well, they do say that bro and sis are just a little *too* close, if you get my meaning. But *Que será, será* is my motto."

"Live and let live," Cone adds. "If they're happy, that's all that counts."

"You couldn't be more right, dearie," Luis says.

"It's the wife I feel sorry for."

Luis laughs. "Don't waste your sympathy. She gave him two pups, didn't she? Now she wants to spread her wings and fly. And I do mean fly, if you catch my drift."

"So I've heard," Cone says. "That magic white powder."

"You better believe it," Luis says. "Now upsadaisy and over to the sink, and we'll see what we can do with your wild mop."

Sitting on a stool, head bent into a stainless steel basin, Cone feels Luis' surprisingly strong fingers massaging shampoo in his scalp, and says, "They could be a little more discreet about it—Stanley and Lucinda."

"With their money?" Luis says. "Who needs to be discreet? It just makes their reputation a little more piquant—wouldn't you say?"

"Definitely piquant."

Luis leans close, whispering in Cone's ear. "The last time they were here together, I did her first, and when I started on him, she stood by his chair, and she was definitely groping him under the sheet. Can you believe it?"

"I can believe it," Cone says.

He has some glop rubbed in his hair. Then Luis rinses away the soap-suds and other junk, and dries Cone's hair with a big, thick towel.

"Back in the chair, ducky," he says.

When Cone is seated and sheeted again, Luis says, "I can't give you a perm; the hair is too short. But I can give you a little frizz, a little panache."

"Soigné?" Cone asks.

"Absolutely," Luis says, setting to work with blow-dryer and brush.

When, finally, Cone inspects himself in the crackled pink mirror, his heart quails. His hair looks like a Brillo pad.

"I like it," he says bravely.

"But of course," Luis says.

Cone pays everyone and tips everyone—enough money to buy Cleo a year's supply of Norwegian sardines. He wonders how he's going to get that tab approved on his expense account, but convinces himself it was solid investigative work. He wanted knowledgeable gossip, and he went to the most authoritative source.

He drives back to the office, all the Honda's windows open because he can't stand the miasma emanating from his scalp. As luck will have it, the first person he meets in the office is Samantha Whatley. She takes one look at his coiffure and collapses with laughter, leaning against the wall and holding her ribs.

In a few moments he's surrounded—four or five people—all pointing at his hair and spluttering to get out their comments: "A demented porcupine!" "Sue them, Cone, sue!" "Did you fall asleep in the chair?"

"Fuck all of you," he growls. "It happens to be soigné. With panache." Then he stalks into his office and slams the door. Runs a palm over his frizz and tells himself, "It's not *that* bad," knowing it is. He lights a cigarette and then, after a while, lights another. It takes him a moment to realize he's got two cigarettes going. He curses and stubs out both of them. Then, minutes later, rescues the long butts from the ashtray and straightens them out.

He thinks he's getting a good handle on the people involved: Stanley and Lucinda Clovis, Mrs. Grace Clovis, Constance Figlia, and Anthony Bonadventure. He's beginning to grasp the interaction there, but he's no closer to what's going down. And no closer to why, or by whom, G. Edward Griffon was pushed in front of a subway train. That, he tells himself angrily, is all that matters.

He digs out the Clovis–Evanchat file and goes over it again. He has an aching suspicion that there are questions he should be asking, and isn't. Somewhere, in all those PIEs and Griffon's reports and his own notes, is something of real import. He's convinced of it. But what?

He goes through the Preliminary Intelligence Estimates again and spots something he thinks is freaky. Clovis & Clovis do their banking at Manhattan Central, the Madison Avenue branch. But when he tailed Bonadventure and Constance Figlia from the press conference, they went into the Merchants International Bank, and seemed right at home. Of course either of them might have a personal account there.

"Oh, my God," Sidney Apicella groans, "you again? What happened to your hair?"

"Forget it," Cone says angrily. "Your PIE on Clovis–Evanchat says that Clovis banks at Manhattan Central, but no bank is listed for New World Enterprises. How come?"

Apicella sighs. "I've got it somewhere," he says. He goes to one of his many steel file cabinets, digs out a folder, flips through it rapidly. "New World banks at Merchants International. Satisfied?"

"Isn't that a little weird, Sid? The parent company banks at one place and a subsidiary banks at another."

"Nothing weird about it. When you're dealing with that much money, you like to spread the risks. It's done all the time. I mean, Clovis and Clovis is always making very heavy cash deposits and withdrawals. It makes sense to have more than one bank. Then you can shuffle funds in case of an emergency."

"Yeah," Cone says, "I can see that. Thanks, Sid. The place is Venus-Adonis Hair Styling on East Eighty-sixth. Ask for Luis."

Apicella, who wears a rug, says, "Go to hell."

Timothy spends another couple of hours on the Clovis–Evanchat file, smoking up a storm and pondering his next move. He decides he better dig into Constance Figlia, the mystery woman. He's got some good skinny on the other characters, but that Constance is a cipher.

He locks his desk and prepares to leave. When he dons his leather cap, it slides down to his ears. "Shit!" he says aloud, and sneaks out of the office.

He spends three days on the track of Constance Figlia. It's a frustrating penetration because he can't get a firm handle on that short, dumpy broad with the posture and stride of a sergeant major. But at the same time it's fascinating just because he can't pin down her time-habit pattern, and the secrets of her daily activities remain secrets.

He starts by visiting Louis Kiernan in the attorneys' section. Lou is a paralegal and custodian of Haldering & Co.'s collection of out-of-town telephone directories. Cone can't find a Vincent Figlia in Suffolk County, but finds a listing in Nassau. Lou, who lives on Long Island, tells him the address is east of Hicksville.

"Some swanky homes out that way," he observes.

"So?" Cone says. "I can do swanky. Just keep your fly zipped up—right?"

He goes back to his office and calls the Figlias' residence.

"Yeah?" A man's voice answers, sounding like a laryngitic frog.

"Could I speak to Miss Constance Figlia, please."

"Who's this?" the frog demands.

Cone decides he can keep the Javert scam going a little longer, and also get Haldering & Co. off the hook.

"My name is Javert," he says. "J-A-V-E-R-T. I'm with the Old Glory Insurance Company, and I was hoping to interest Miss Figlia in our single-premium annuity plan, with interest compounded monthly and tax-deferred until the time of withdrawal."

"Forget it. She ain't interested."

The phone is slammed down, connection broken. But Cone is satisfied; now he knows where she lives. He digs out an old, scuffed briefcase and stuffs it with outdated office memos and other junk to give it bulk. Then he sets out for Long Island, wondering how many insurance salesmen wear corduroy suits and black leather caps.

Traffic is murder, and it's almost noon before he locates Figlia's home. As Louis Kiernan said: swanky. The place looks like a Virginia horse farm, with a wide lawn and shrubs that appear to have been trimmed with manicure scissors.

There's a white picket fence around the property, with an unlocked gate leading to a flagged path to the portico. When Cone gets to the steps, carrying his bulging briefcase, the front door opens, a man steps out, closes the door behind him.

"Yeah?" he says—the frog himself.

Judging by the voice, Cone had envisioned a short, squat guy with no neck, plenty of suet, and the appearance of a thug with maybe a bent nose and a wet cigar stuck in his kisser.

But this man could be a mortician or an economist. He's tall, skinny as a rapier, wearing a black silk suit, white shirt, narrow black tie. His jacket is beautifully tailored. Cone thinks maybe he's just imagining the slight bulge under the left arm.

"Good morning!" he says brightly. "Is Miss Constance Figlia at home?"

The guy looks down with stony contempt.

"You the guy who called earlier this morning?"

Cone nods. "That's me."

"I told you she ain't home, and even if she was, she wouldn't want to talk to you. Now beat it."

Cone shrugs apologetically. "You know how it is: I get a list of insurance prospects from my supervisor, and I've got to check out each one personally and file a report. You can understand that, can't you?"

"I couldn't care less," the tall one says. "All I can understand is that you're trespassing on private property. So take a walk, sonny, while you can still walk—which might be hard to do with busted kneecaps."

"You know," Timothy says pleasantly, "it's been my experience that tough guys don't threaten. Tough guys *do* it, fast, and take advantage of surprise. I don't think you're as tough as you think."

"Want to try me?" the guy says, but something changes in his face, a shadow of doubt appears.

"What are you going to do?" Cone says. "Kill me? I honestly don't think you've got the balls for it. That hunk you're carrying under your left arm is all bluff; it's going to stay right there. And just to prove it, I'm going to turn my back to you and walk slowly down the path to my car. You want to plug me in the back, be my guest. It would be your style."

The tall man is trembling now, not just his hands but his entire body. Cone wonders if he's pushed it too far, but he can't stop now. He turns and begins to stroll toward the gate. The frog shouts something after him, two words, and not Happy Birthday.

In the Honda, Cone looks at his own hands. No shakes—which pleases him. He drives back to Manhattan, listening to the news on the radio. Something about a tropical depression north of Bermuda that might develop into a full-fledged hurricane and strike New York. Cone couldn't care less.

Back in the office, he phones out for a cheeseburger, fries, and a Coke. While munching, he calls New World headquarters. No answer. Then he tries Constance Figlia at Clovis & Clovis. She isn't in, the receptionist in the comptroller's section tells him, but is expected within an hour.

Cone spends fifty minutes finishing his lunch, smoking two cigarettes, and leaning on Sidney Apicella again.

"Tim," Apicella says, groaning. "Can't you leave me alone? I've got my own work to do, you know."

"I know, Sid. I know. But this will only take a minute. Have you got a snitch at Merchants International Bank?"

"Well..." Apicella says cautiously, "we've got a contact there who owes us one."

"Very simple request," Cone says. "Try to find out if Constance Figlia—that's F-I-G-L-I-A—has a personal account at the bank. That's all. Give me a call when you get the answer, will you? I'll be in my office."

He's lighting another Camel when his phone rings, and he grabs it up.

"Yeah?" he says.

"Tim? This is Sid. Merchants International has no customer named Constance Figlia."

So now Cone knows that Constance Figlia's visit to Merchants International was not to make a deposit or withdrawal from a personal account.

It's a fair assumption that she was depositing or withdrawing funds for New World.

He tries her at Clovis & Clovis again; she's still out. But a second call gets through, and suddenly he's talking to the lady herself.

"Miss Figlia?"

"Yes. Who is this speaking?" Her voice is husky and unexpectedly stirring.

"Miss Figlia, my name is Jeffrey B. Robbins, and I've recently been assigned to the Madison Avenue branch of the Manhattan Central Bank— with a promotion to assistant vice-president, I might add in all modesty."

"Congratulations."

"Thank you. Anyway, I've been here less than a week, and am just getting my feet wet, so to speak. One of the accounts handed to me for supervision is Clovis and Clovis."

"What happened to Fred Hartle?" Constance Figlia asks.

"Oh, onward and upward," Cone says smoothly. "He's been transferred to our trust department. Miss Figlia, the reason I'm calling is that there seems to be a discrepancy in your last deposit. Quite frankly I think it's our teller's error, but the amount involved is so large, I'd like to get it straightened out. Would it be too great an imposition to ask you to stop by in the next day or so? I'm sure we can get the whole thing resolved in a few minutes."

"A discrepancy?" she says. "How much?"

"A six-figure number," Cone says. "I suspect it's a matter of inverted digits, but I would like to get it cleared up."

"I would too," she says sharply. "Suppose I come over right now? I can be there in fifteen minutes."

"Excellent," Cone says. "I'm looking forward to meeting you personally. Clovis and Clovis are *very* valued clients. Please ask for Jeffrey B. Robbins."

"I'll be there," she says and hangs up abruptly.

"Lots of luck," Cone says softly, replacing his phone.

So now he knows Constance Figlia is handling funds for both Clovis & Clovis and its subsidiary, New World Enterprises. But whether that's significant or not Cone hasn't the slightest idea.

That's the first day. He spends the next two trying to tail the damned woman and making, he admits, a miserable job of it. She's either at Clovis & Clovis in Manhattan or at New World in Brooklyn. But she's hard to locate, seems to have no set schedule, and he still hasn't figured out how she gets from her Long Island home to the city. Train? Bus? Car? He doesn't know.

He sees her with Anthony Bonadventure several times. The two of them go to the banks together, but as far as Cone can tell, there's nothing personal to their relationship. Bonadventure treats her with respect, opening doors, assisting her down curbs, helping her get a speck out of her eye. But neither appears to have an overwhelming passion for the other.

It's business, Cone decides. Strictly business.

On the third day, something odd happens. He is lurking around the Clovis building on East Fifty-seventh Street when Constance Figlia gets out of the elevator, talking animatedly with Stanley and Lucinda. Cone dodges behind a pillar like Inspector Clouseau, peering out now and then to watch them. They're obviously waiting for someone and lo and behold, who should finally arrive but Grace Clovis with Anthony Bonadventure. Noisy greetings, hugs, and cheek kisses. Then the group, laughing and chattering, moves out onto Fifty-seventh Street. A stretch limousine is waiting, a white Cadillac, and away they go.

Cone, who has parked his Honda on Fifty-fifth Street and can't possibly get to it in time, searches about desperately for a cab. No luck. So he has to watch the white Cadillac disappear into traffic, traveling westward, and wonder where the five little elves are heading. Cocktails? A dinner? Maybe a party. Birthday? Anniversary? Or perhaps just to celebrate the frustration of Cone-Javert-Robbins.

He finds the nearest bar, on Lexington, bellies up and treats himself to a double Absolut on the rocks, figuring he can continue fiddling his expense account until Samantha Whatley lowers the boom.

He stands there, foot up on a genuine brass rail, and tries to make sense out of what he's just seen. All five exchanging hugs, kisses, giggles. A merry crew. Which probably means that whatever's coming off, they're all involved—or have guilty knowledge.

Maybe it's the vodka, maybe it's his misanthropy, but he gets some wild ideas. Perhaps the precious five are engaged in an orgy-type activity: the men stripped down to black socks and shoes, the women flaunting garter belts and mesh stockings, and all of them wearing masks—like those old blue movies.

Or they're in the counterfeiting game, with some good plates churning out quality twenties or fifties or hundreds, laundered by cash deposits at Merchants International and Manhattan Central.

Or maybe Grace Clovis isn't the only one hooked on nose candy. It's possible all five are sniffing up a storm, snickering while they soar up into the wild blue yonder. It's possible.

Anything is possible, Timothy Cone grumpily admits, and he's no closer to discovering what these people are up to than he was the day G. Edward Griffon died.

That, he decides, is what he's got to keep in mind and never forget. Ed got scratched, and it had something to do with those ha-haing, hugging, ain't-we-got-fun people. But it isn't a romp; it's the deliberate killing of a guy who tried to be a friend. And if Cone lets that slide, he doesn't want to think of what the rest of his life will be like ... remembering ...

"It's all shit," he says to the bartender, paying his tab.

"You're telling me?" the guy says, scooping up his tip. "Have a nice day."

"I'm going to make a feast for you," he tells Samantha Whatley on the phone Friday night.

"Oh, God," she says despairingly. "The last time you made a feast for me, I had the runs for two days."

"Not this time," he promises. "You'll love this feast."

He spends Saturday morning buying this and that: peeled shrimp, hot Italian sausage, mushrooms as big as yarmulkes, a small filet mignon, green pepper, scallions, a crown of garlic. And a jug of California zinfandel.

It's a blustery day. That approaching storm never did develop into a hurricane, but it's still strong enough to kick up forty-knot winds with the prediction of three to five inches of rain over the metropolitan area by nightfall. The sky already has a phlegmy look, and clouds are scudding.

He gets home with his treasures and sets to work making what he calls a "hunters' stew." It's sautéed chunks of filet and sausage, cooked up with the garlic, green pepper, mushrooms, and scallions. The shrimp will be added when he's reheating this concoction just before serving.

As he labors, helped along by a jar of zinfandel, he tosses Cleo bits of beef fat, a raw shrimp, a slice of sausage, even a nibble of garlic. That crazy cat eats everything. Afraid his creation might prove too bland, Cone adds salt, pepper, Italian seasoning, Worcestershire sauce, a dollop of wine, a dash of Tabasco and, just for fun, a couple of chopped-up jalapeños. Everything smells good.

Samantha shows up a little before five o'clock. Her trench coat is soaked, umbrella dripping. She brings a small frozen Sara Lee cheesecake for dessert.

"What a night this is going to be," she says. "Lightning to the east. Did you hear the thunder?"

"I wasn't listening," Cone says.

"No," Sam says, "you never do. Something smells good."

"Cleo likes it. When we're ready to eat, I'll pop in the shrimp for a few minutes."

"What are we having?"

"A kind of stew. I learned to make it in Nam. But with different ingredients. I won't tell you what we put in over there."

"Please don't. Will you, for God's sake, offer me a drink?"

"Sorry," he says. "Wine, beer, or vodka. And some brandy I'm saving for later."

"Wine'll be fine. Wow, listen to the thunder. You heard *that*, didn't you?"

"I heard it," he says. "Sounds like one-oh-fives. But we're in a dry, warm place with a hot meal coming up. What more can life offer?"

"Not a whole hell of a lot," she admits. "Can we eat soon? I'm famished."

They sit on the wooden kitchen chairs pulled up to Cone's desk. He serves the meal, with a baguette of French bread to be torn into chunks and used for the gravy. Cleo perches on a third chair, waiting patiently for scraps.

Samantha samples her bowl. "Jesus," she says, exhaling, mouth open, "do you think you put enough pepper in it?"

"Too much?"

"Not if you've got a flannel tongue. But I can live with it. How about a couple of ice cubes in my wine?"

All in all, the feast is a success. Even Cleo seems satisfied. Then they pile the emptied bowls into the sink and start on Sam's cheesecake.

"How was it?" Cone asks.

"It tasted just fine after my tonsils got numbed. How you coming with the Clovis-Evanchat buyout?"

"Okay," he says. "I think. Something very unkosher is in the works, so you better tell H.H. to keep stalling Isaac Evanchat."

"But you haven't pinned it down?"

"Not yet."

"How long?"

He shrugs. "Another couple of weeks maybe. Of course I could be whistling 'Dixie.' "

She looks at him thoughtfully. "You really think something stinks, don't you?"

"To high heaven."

"Want to tell me about it?"

"No," he says. "Not till I've got it wrapped up."

She accepts that. "Do it your way," she tells him. "Just don't take too long. I'm not sure Evanchat is going to stand still for the expenses you're running up."

"Screw him," Cone says, pouring them more brandy.

Samantha inspects him. He's wearing blue jeans that have been washed so often, they're a frayed pearly gray and a T-shirt that says SAVE THE WHALES.

"God," she says, "you're such a scruffy character. I can't for the life of me understand what I see in you."

"Oh, I don't know. I have my virtues."

"Yeah?" she says. "Like what?"

He stares at her. "I'm faithful," he says. "Since we've been rubbing the bacon, I haven't looked at another woman."

She takes up his hand, kisses the knuckles, then looks up at him. "Talking about sleeping together . . ."

"Yes?"

"Lock Cleo in the john, will you? The last time she kept biting my toes."

"He," Cone says. "Or it."

The storm really hits: thunder, lightning, a driving rain. They cuddle on the mattress, as if the flashy sky were a performance just for their benefit.

"Let's talk about us," Samantha says.

"Do we have to?"

"Yes," she says firmly, "we do."

"Later," he promises.

She's as bony as he, but Cone can't get enough of her long, elegant back. Her shoulder blades jut and her spine is a rope of stones, but there's a rhythm and delicacy there, all subtle curves and sly shadows.

"I want to eat you up," he tells her.

"Do," she says.

They're like two rough hawsers, braided, rasping against each other and welcoming the scratch. In no way are they gentle or tender, because they are both hard, hurt people, wanting to get out. And this is the only way they know.

So there are no proclamations of love or undying passion. Instead there is a gritty intenseness, both of them serious and hoping. Their coupling is a partnership of two bankrupts, as if all their liabilities combined might show up in black ink and make them wealthy.

"I've asked you a hundred times," she says, touching a fingertip lightly to a pink seam running along the back of his left thigh. "How did you get this scar?"

"I was born with it."

"Liar. I told you about my scars. This one was from an appendectomy, and this one I got when I was a kid. I fell against an iron railing while I was playing volleyball in the school gym. Come on, tell me: How did you get it?"

"I zigged when I should have zagged."

"My poor, wounded hero," she says, kissing the pink seam. "And all the time you were trying to make the world safe for democracy—right?"

"Something like that."

She lies back, and they both stretch out, apart but holding hands. The thunder has rumbled off, but they still hear the drumfire of hard rain, and occasionally the darkened loft is set ablaze by a distant lightning flash.

"About us . . ." she says. "How long do you think we've got?"

"Together? As long as you want. You're the boss."

"In the office maybe. Not in this dump."

"When we started," he reminds her, "we agreed: no strings and no connections."

She stirs restlessly. "Aren't you ever going to buy a bed?"

"Sure," he says. "Someday. But not while I know you."

"Why not?"

"Because you'll put ruffles on it."

They both laugh, turn to each other, embrace.

"Okay," she says, "I won't lean on you."

"You haven't," he says. "So far. And I haven't leaned on you, have I?"

"No, you haven't, you bastard. Because you just don't care."

"Oh, I care," he assures her. "In my own way."

"And what way is that?"

"I don't know. I haven't figured it out."

"Thanks a lot," she says. "That makes a girl feel very secure."

"Is that what you want—security? Forget it, babe. There ain't no such animal."

She snuggles closer to him. "All right," she says, "now I'll tell you the truth. Big confession—but you might as well know. All you are to me is a sex object. A good lay, and nothing more. I worked my evil way with you. All I want is your damp, white body—covered with freckles. I'll get tired of you eventually, I know, and trade you in for a new model."

He shakes with silent laughter. "You're as nutty as I am," he tells her. "The only thing we have in common."

"Oh, I don't know," she says, moving his hand between her legs. "Surely we have other things in common."

"Uncommon," he says, squeezing. "Damned uncommon."

"I'm ready," she says. "Has the hunters' stew given you enough strength for an encore?"

"It's the garlic," he says.

"You could have fooled me," she says. "I thought you've been gargling with Arpège."

And that's the extent of their intimate discussion of their relationship. They've done it before, never taking it too far, never digging too deeply.

Because both are afraid of what they might find, what they may admit. So it's a hard, surface thing with these two invalids, neither willing to be the first to cry, "Nurse!"

They really do get out with each other, as attuned as a duo of violinists, bowing and scraping in unison and losing themselves in mutual harmonies. Carried away and lost with closed eyes and seraphic smiles, loving life and its surprises.

"You're not going home in this shit," he says later.

"No," she agrees, "I'm not going home in this shit. Let Cleo out of the john."

And, still later, she says, "I suppose we should shower."

"I suppose," he says. "Go ahead if you want. I'm too lazy."

"Tomorrow morning," she says. "Right now I like the way I smell— all garlicky and peppery and sexy. I'll keep till morning."

So they slump at the desk, bare feet up, their nakedness minimally covered with grungy T-shirts and Jockey shorts. They sit in silence, replete, sip a little brandy, and have no desire to talk, amazed that they can be content with each other's silent presence.

Cleo chases a ball of aluminum foil across the linoleum, and they watch the cat fondly, amused by its leaps and gallops. Cleo slaps the toy here and there, whacking it, chasing it, never biting but just playing, then suddenly collapses to lie quietly, breathing heavily.

"Just like us," Samantha says. "It's a game."

"Is it?" Timothy Cone says.

Without telling Sam about it or getting permission from H.H. Cone enlists Joe Washington in the investigation of the Clovis–Evanchat deal. Joe is easy to persuade; the guy is bored with the routine cases he's handling, and he's just as anxious as Timothy to nail the person or persons responsible for the death of Griffon.

Cone doesn't tell Washington everything—just enough to hook him. He gives Joe short biogs of the characters involved.

"Crazy people," the black says, shaking his head.

"And greedy," the Wall Street dick says. "Anthony Bonadventure seems to be the only heavy, but that Constance Figlia comes from a family who play rough, so it makes sense to figure she's not in it just for laughs. The others—the Clovises—I can't figure their motive. They seem to have all the money they need—but that doesn't mean they don't want more."

Washington brings in his own beat-up Plymouth with rusted fenders, and between Joe in his clunker and Cone in his Honda, they begin to get a better idea of Constance Figlia's daily routine.

She usually takes the train at the Hicksville station. Sometimes she goes to Brooklyn and cabs over to the New World warehouse, but always gets out of the cab a few blocks away. Sometimes she rides the train into Penn Station, and takes a taxi to the Clovis & Clovis office on East Fifty-seventh, again getting out of the cab a few blocks away.

"Now why in hell is she doing that?" Joe Washington says.

"Standard operating procedure," Cone says. "Someone's taught her. If you think there's a possibility of your being tailed, you never lead the hunter directly to your home base. Walking the last few blocks away gives her a chance to look around and maybe spot a shadow. She's playing it cozy."

"She went to the bank again today," Joe reports. "Merchants International. Bonadventure was with her. That's the third time this week."

"And on Monday," Cone says, "she and Bonadventure went to the Manhattan Central branch on Madison Avenue. If they're making deposits, I'd sure as hell like to know where the loot is coming from. Listen, Joe, you stay on Constance for another couple of days. I'm going to switch over to Bonadventure and see if I can find out where that gonzo spends his idle hours."

He doesn't discover a whole hell of a lot. Anthony seems to rise late, usually has a leisurely lunch at an expensive East Side restaurant (twice with Grace Clovis), and then frequently makes his way to the Clovis & Clovis office, where he accompanies Constance Figlia to the bank.

"Goddammit it!" Cone explodes to Joe. "What's he up to?"

In the evening, Bonadventure usually meets with a bunch of pals at an uptown steak house or a downtown spaghetti joint. All the chums are heavy, florid-faced, middle-aged gents, well-dressed, with French cuffs and pinkie rings. Their gatherings look to Cone like a reunion of the Class of '65, Attica College—or maybe Leavenworth U.

One afternoon Anthony has lunch with Grace and the two of them go back to Bonadventure's brownstone. So they're shacking up. So what else is new? Cone goes back to Haldering & Co., almost convinced he's wasting his time. He finds Detective Davenport waiting for him.

"You keep lousy office hours," the city dick says, chomping on his Juicy Fruit. "I didn't snoop into anything. Besides, your desk is locked. Let's you and me have a talk."

"Why not?" Cone says, flopping into his battered swivel chair. "I wish I had something big to tell you, but I don't. Just a lot of little bits and pieces."

"Let's have them," Davenport says. "Something is better than nothing."

Cone tells him most of what he's learned, holding back a few items as bargaining chips. For instance, he doesn't tell the detective about the Anthony–Grace connection or the more than brother-sister relationship between Stanley and Lucinda.

The cop listens intently, his fingers laced over his belly.

"My, my," he says when the Wall Street dick finishes, "you've been a busy little boy, haven't you? How do you figure all those trips to the bank?"

"I don't," Timothy says miserably. "I don't know what's going on. I can understand retailers wanting to make frequent deposits if they have a heavy cash flow. What the hell, you want your money to be working for you. So naturally you deposit your cash as soon as possible. But New World isn't a retailer, and has no cash flow."

"All right," Davenport says, "now let me give you some food for thought. New World was started and capitalized by Clovis and Clovis for one-three-five million—right?"

"Right."

"Who owns the stock?"

"The four officers of the corporation: Stanley and Lucinda Clovis, Constance Figlia, and Anthony Bonadventure. They each own twenty-five percent. I got that from our resident CPA."

"Okay. And supposedly the purpose of New World is to renovate brownstones and maybe develop and build small residential and commercial properties—right?"

"Right again."

"So why do they need a hundred and thirty-five million? My God, you can fix up a brownstone for a couple of mil—at the most. And what can a small commercial parcel cost? Nowhere near what Clovis and Clovis put into New World. That outfit is overcapitalized. They were given far, far too much cash to do what they allegedly were set up to do."

Cone can feel his face reddening, and he slaps his desk wrathfully. "God*dammit*!" he shouts. "Why didn't I see that? I've been closer to this than you have, and it slid right by me."

"Take it easy," Davenport says soothingly. "Maybe you've been too close to it. Sometimes that happens. But what I said makes sense, doesn't it?"

"Of course it makes sense. I could kick myself for having missed it."

"But what does it add up to?" Davenport goes on. "New World was given too much loot by its parent company. So what? That's no crime."

Cone takes a deep breath and blows it out. "Yeah, it doesn't tell us anything. But thanks anyway. It might turn out to be something—you never know."

"All right," the detective says, "now I'm going to give you another gift. Maybe it'll convince you to open up with me."

They stare at each other a moment, two poker players not wanting to reveal their hand.

"A couple of days ago the narcs busted the biggest dealer on Wall Street," Davenport says. "You know how the kiddies down there like to snort a line of coke on their lunch hour. This guy who got busted was King Shit in the dope biz on Wall Street. They said he was actually operating in the Trinity graveyard. Anyway, the narcs grabbed his little black book of customers and credit accounts. Most listings were just initials or abbreviations. One was 'Ant. B.'"

"Bonadventure?"

"Who else? Now do you want to tell me anything?"

Cone is silent a moment, swinging back and forth in his swivel chair, considering.

"Yeah," he says finally. "I've got a trade-off for you."

"Jesus," Davenport says, "I've got to pry things out of you with a crowbar. What have you got?"

"Mrs. Grace Clovis is snorting. Bonadventure is her candyman."

"That's interesting. The Department wants that guy bad, and maybe we can nail him for dealing. What else have you got?"

Cone doesn't respond.

"Look, sonny," Davenport says patiently, unwrapping another stick of chewing gum, "I'm not one of your glory boys. I'm never going to make lieutenant or captain; I know it. All I want is to do my job and make a good bust. But you, you're all screwed up with ideas of revenge. You're the Lone Ranger gunning for the villain who knocked off your pal—right?"

"Something like that," Cone mutters. "Griffon tried to be a friend. I just can't let it slide."

"I can understand that. But don't get so involved or you'll find your brain turning to gravel. Now I've given you two choice items, so you still owe me another. Let's have it."

Cone looks at him with admiration. "You really know how to deal, don't you? All right, here's something. The gossip around town is that Stanley and Lucinda Clovis are more than brother and sister; they're making it together."

Davenport stares at him. "You believe that?"

Cone nods.

"But the guy is married."

"I know. With two kids. But the sister lives in the same apartment. And the wife is hooked on happy dust and playing bed games with Bonadventure. Go figure it."

The city detective sighs and heaves himself to his feet. "Sometimes I think I'm getting too old for this business." He starts out, then stops at the doorway and turns back. "You gave me two for two. Fair enough. Now I'm going to give you a bonus. You remember my telling you we had a halfass witness to the murder of Griffon?"

"Sure, I remember. A guy who doesn't want to get involved."

"That's right. He was hazy about everything, said he just couldn't remember. But we talked him into going under hypnosis—and guess what? While he's in a trance, he says it was a woman who pushed your friend off the subway platform. How does that grab you?"

3

In that hot and humid climate, he developed a rash in his armpits and around his scrotum, and a fungus infection of his fingers, palms, and between his toes. His fair, freckled skin was in a cruddy condition, and the docs' wonder drugs didn't help a bit. Then an old Marine gunnery sergeant told him what to do.

He was to scrub his entire body with one of those stiff-bristled brushes used on barracks floors. The soap was yellow carbolic stuff that stung like hell. After he scoured every inch of his hide and rinsed, he dried thoroughly, then rubbed on cornstarch. Crazy remedy, but it got rid of the prickly heat.

After he got home, it took two years for the fungus infection to disappear in a more temperate climate. But once a month he still gave himself the brush-yellow soap-cornstarch treatment. Samantha Whatley watched him do it once, him standing up in the tub, brushing away furiously, and shook her head in disbelief.

"Why don't you wear a hair shirt?" she suggested. "Or whip yourself with barbed wire?"

On the night after he talked to Detective Neal Davenport, Cone goes through the ceremony once again, with Cleo staring in bemused puzzlement. Scrubbing away religiously, not neglecting the places where the sun don't shine, Timothy reflects on what he's learned and what it might mean.

He ponders the possibility of a woman having pushed G. Edward Griffon to his death from the Union Square subway platform. But it's not until he's carefully dried and is rubbing cornstarch on his raw pelt, as if he's thickening himself for wonton soup, that he asks the question he should have asked weeks ago:

What was Griffon doing in Union Square?

It's obvious Ed knew New World was a dummy corporation. But Clovis headquarters are on East Fifty-seventh, and New World is in Brooklyn. So how come the guy got chilled on Fourteenth Street? What in God's name was he doing there, with his snappy three-piece suit, fedora, and empty attaché case?

Cone is still wrestling with that puzzle the next day when Sidney Apicella clumps into his office. The CPA is pulling worriedly at his swollen, roseate nose.

"Oh-ho," Timothy says, "the mountain comes to Muhammad."

"Yeah," Sid says, frowning, "something like that. Listen, Tim, you keep asking me questions about this Clovis–Evanchat deal, so I've got to figure you think there's something there that smells. Correct?"

"Correct," Cone says.

"I more or less gave the buyout a clean bill of health in my PIE, and I don't want to get my balls caught in the wringer. You can understand that, can't you?"

"Sure. Very painful."

"So I took the file home last night and spent a couple of hours going through it line by line. There's something there I didn't see before, and it bothers me."

"Yeah? Like what?"

"Well, you know that in addition to New World, Clovis and Clovis owns three other companies. They're in general contracting, plumbing and electrical supplies, and foundations and underpinning. All those three corporations are headquartered in the New York area. But one of them banks in Newark, one in Chicago, and the third in San Diego."

The two men stare at each other.

"What does that mean, Sid?" Cone asks finally.

"Beats the hell out of me," Apicella says angrily. "You can bank wherever you like. But I'd call this situation highly unusual."

"Highly unusual," Cone repeats. "You accountants do have a way with words. So what happens now?"

"Let me look into it. I'd like to find out if those three corporations have been banking out of state since they were formed or if they switched banks recently. This may take some time, Tim."

"I can understand that. Let me know as soon as you get something."

"Of course."

"I love you, Sid," Cone says solemnly.

"And I love you, too," Apicella says, "you miserable bastard. I spent two hours last night doing your work when I could have been watching *Dallas.*"

Cone stays in his cramped office, feet up on the desk, and smokes up a storm while he reviews what he knows and what he doesn't know. He's still brooding when Joe Washington slouches in and slumps into the extra chair.

"Enough already," Joe says.

Cone pushes his pack of Camels across the desk, but Washington shakes his head and lights up one of his own lowest-tar, lowest-nicotine cigarettes.

"I'll live longer with these," he says.

"Lots of luck," Cone says. "What's with the 'Enough already' crack?"

"How many times can I tail that Constance Figlia to the bank?" Washington says. "Now she's there two or three times a day."

"With Anthony Bonadventure?"

"Sometimes with, sometimes without."

"Any pattern to her bank visits?"

"Not that I can spot. Tim, am I doing any good?"

"Sure you are," Cone says. "Joe, you know where Griffon got whacked, don't you?"

Washington stares at him. "Of course I know. On the Union Square subway platform."

"Yeah. Now tell me this: What was he doing on Fourteenth Street?"

"He was investigating the Clovis–Evanchat deal at the time?"

"I think he was. The other stuff he was handling was just routine research and phone calls."

"Then I don't know what the hell he was doing in Union Square. Not eating a brown-bag lunch on a park bench, that's for sure."

Cone nods. "I think he was tailing someone. Griffon was the kind of man who'd never go below Twenty-third Street except to come into the office or do a job. I mean he was an *uptown* kind of guy."

"Right."

"So it was the job that took him to Union Square. Joe, drop Constance Figlia for the time being. I'd like you to concentrate on the Fourteenth Street area. Check all the banks around there. Try to find out about applications for new accounts in the last couple of months. Especially if Clovis and Clovis or New World Enterprises, Inc., tried to open one."

"Holy Christ," Joe Washington says, "how do I do that? A black walks in, flashes the ivories, and says, 'May I look at your new account applications, please?' They'll call the blues. You know that, Tim."

"Yeah, well, maybe you're right. But try it anyway. Show them your credentials and come on strong. If that doesn't work, here's another possibility: Go to Sid Apicella and get him to tell you the names of his contacts at all the big credit agencies. You know banks use those outfits just like department stores. Maybe you can find out if some bank in the Union Square area asked for a credit check on Clovis or New World."

Washington considers that. "It might work," he says, "but I doubt it."

"Maybe. But then, on the other hand, we could be doing something right. Do you believe in Divine Retribution?"

"Oh, hell yes," Joe Washington says. "My wife."

Timothy doesn't laugh. "Well, I think we got a kind of retribution going here. These are not nice people. They got money and reputation and social status—and all that shit. But they don't play by the rules."

"You believe in the rules, Tim?"

"Sure, I believe in the rules. If you don't, then you've got no game at all, do you? It's just a mess. I spent three years of my life with no rules, and I didn't like it. I want rules. Standards. If you can't measure up, get off the world. That's what we're dealing with: people who won't follow the rules. Fuck 'em!"

"If you say so," Washington says, looking at him queerly.

After Joe leaves, Cone wanders down the corridor to the office of Louis Kiernan. Cone lounges in the doorway, leaning against the jamb, until the paralegal looks up from the papers he's working on.

"Hi," he says.

"Lou," Cone says, "what exactly is a dummy corporation?"

Kiernan sits back and peers at the Wall Street dick over the tops of his reading glasses. "A dummy corporation? A legal entity, usually chartered by a state. But it's a fake corporation. It doesn't do any legitimate business."

"Why do people set them up?"

"A lot of reasons. To avoid personal liability. For tax purposes. Maybe even to register a name."

"But they're legal?"

"They're legal as long as the proper fees and taxes are paid, and the proper reports filed. That's all the state and federal government are interested in."

"When do they become illegal?"

"When they're caught. There are innocent dummy corporations, I suppose, but generally they're set up for fast wheeling and dealing, like hiding profits from the IRS or claiming a tax loss—stuff like that."

"But if a dummy corporation shows a profit, it has to pay taxes, doesn't it?"

"You better believe it. Unless the owners want to go to the clink."

"And anyone can set up a dummy corporation?" Cone persists.

"Anyone," Kiernan assures him. "I shouldn't tell you this, but you don't even need a lawyer. If you get the proper applications and all the other bumf, you can do it yourself. Thinking of setting up one?"

"Not today. Thanks, Lou."

. . .

The whole thing exploded so suddenly that, thinking it over later, Cone decides there was no way he could have avoided the confrontation. It's true he's a guy with a short fuse and a radioactive temper, but in this case he was goaded into it, he tells himself.

Like all experienced cops and private investigators, he knows that when you have multiple suspects, you zero in on the one with the criminal record. Christian charity has nothing to do with it; the recidivist rate does. The guy with the sheet is odds-on to be the perpetrator because that's all he knows how to do.

So Timothy sticks to Anthony Bonadventure like a leech, picking him up at his brownstone late in the morning, tailing him to lunch with Grace, following him to the banks with Constance Figlia, and then shadowing him in the evening when he meets with his coven of bentnoses who, for all Cone knows, might be plotting to kidnap the Statue of Liberty and hold her for ransom.

He's sitting in his rented Honda outside a snazzy French restaurant on East Fifty-second Street. Inside, Bonadventure and Grace Clovis are probably lunching on snails and brains and sipping a fine chablis. Cone is eating a Coney Island red-hot piled high with mustard, relish, sauerkraut, and peppers. He bought it from a sidewalk vendor, along with a can of cherry cola.

He's finished this repast and is trying to get the mess off his fingers and the stains off his lap with a paper napkin, when his two targets come out of the restaurant. Cone is double-parked across the street and watches. He sees immediately that there's trouble in paradise.

Grace is staggering, flopping around like a marionette with broken strings. Bonadventure is trying to support her, practically dragging her toward his silver Chrysler, standing in a No Parking zone. But Mrs. Clovis will have none of it. She struggles, twists away, breaks free, starts wobbling down the street. Anthony catches up with her, swings her around, and slaps her jaw, a heavy blow with all his shoulder behind it. She almost falls, but he grabs her.

Cone gets out of the car and runs across the street. When he comes up to them, they're waltzing around like a couple of drunken sumo wrestlers. By this time a dozen pedestrians have stopped to watch the action—from a distance. No one is interfering.

"May I be of help?" Cone asks pleasantly.

"Fuck off," Bonadventure snarls at him. "It's none of your goddamn business."

"But it is my business, sir. I am a paid-up member of the Society for the Prevention of Cruelty to Women, and if you attempt to strike this lady again, I shall have to restrain you."

"What?" Anthony says, astonished. "You some kind of a nut or something? This is a private matter, so butt out. She's had a little too much to drink, that's all."

Meanwhile he is holding on to Grace tightly, both arms wrapped around her. Cone sees her eyes are dulled, her head lolling on a limp neck.

"Ma'am," Timothy says in a loud voice, "would you like to get away from this man? I can drive you home."

"Yes," she says in a faint voice. "Please."

"Turn her loose," Cone orders Bonadventure. "I'll take her home."

"Who the fuck are you?" Anthony demands loudly. "Let's see your credentials."

"Certainly, sir," Cone says. He pulls up his right trouser leg, showing the ankle holster with the short-barreled Magnum. "Will that be satisfactory?"

Bonadventure looks down. His eyes widen. Slowly he loosens his grasp on Grace. Cone steps in quickly, puts an arm about the woman's waist, begins to move her gently toward the Honda.

"I'll get you, you prick," Bonadventure yells after him. "I'll find out who you are and demolish you, you no-good shit."

Cone stops and turns back. "Want to start now?" he asks. "You think you can take me? Be my guest."

The two men stare at each other, eyes locked. Then Anthony turns away.

"He's crazy!" he yells at the small mob of rubbernecks who have gathered to watch this incident. "The guy's a weirdo! Someone call the cops."

Then he runs to his LeBaron. Cone gets Grace across the street and into the Honda. She is dopey but functioning, remembers her home address, mumbles her thanks.

By the time he gets to the tower on Third Avenue near Eighty-fifth Street, she's revived enough to sit up straight, look at her face in the rearview mirror, feel cautiously along the line of her chin.

"He clipped you a good one," Cone says. "It'll probably be discolored tomorrow. You can cover the bruise with makeup."

She turns sideways on the passenger seat to stare at him. "Who *are* you?" she asks.

"Sir Galahad," he says. "Looking for the Holy Grail. Why don't you dump that miserable crud?"

"I've got no one else," she says dully. "Thanks for the lift."

She leans forward suddenly to give him a peck on the cheek, then gets out of the car and clacks across the street on her high heels. Cone watches her go, thinking that if he ever smacked Samantha on the jaw, she'd cut his balls off. But Sam isn't a victim and never will be.

He figures that little set-to with Bonadventure ends his, Cone's, effect-iveness as a shadow. With Joe Washington canvassing banks in the Union Square area, Timothy reckons his best bet is to concentrate on Constance Figlia and Stanley and Lucinda Clovis, and try to discover what those tykes are up to.

The prospect doesn't set his blood atingle. He's depressed at how *small* all these people are, despite the big money involved. They have no quality. The cash is strong, but the people are weak. The guy out at Vincent Figlia's home backed off. Anthony Bonadventure backed off. Grace Clovis said helplessly, "I've got no one else."

Stanley and Lucinda Clovis seem to be prisoners of their own selfish wants, and who the hell knows what drives Constance Figlia? Greed, probably. What disturbs Timothy Cone most is that none of these char-acters have any spine. He'd prefer staunch opponents willing to stake their lives on their sins, go down in a blaze of gunfire because no matter how rotten they might be, their pride demands they stand up for their evil.

The cheapness, the flimsiness of these people diminishes his own role. It's one thing to have the job of defusing a horrendous bomb, when the slightest, tiniest miscalculation could be your last. It's another thing to be required to quench a wee firecracker. Even if it went off, it would go "Pop."

Sometimes Cone feels like an old-fashioned whitewing, sweeping up the world's garbage and droppings. Nothing exciting, glamorous, or rewarding there. But still, it's a job that must be done—by someone. Why it should be him, and how he got to where he is now, he cannot understand.

Brought low by these mournful reflections, he still has the self-discipline to drive down to Clovis headquarters on East Fifty-seventh, hoping to get a line on Constance Figlia or Stanley and Lucinda. They may be worthless people, but he's convinced they're breaking the rules, and that's sufficient reason for this essentially puritan man to keep working.

"You didn't!" Samantha Whatley wails.

"I did," Cone says, after telling her of his run-in with Anthony Bon-adventure. "First of all, I didn't want to sit there and watch the woman get bounced around. And also, I wanted to try the guy, to see what I'm up against. I found out. He's got no moxie. All mouth."

"And if he hadn't backed down?"

"Then I probably would have."

"Oh, sure," Sam says, staring at him. "You really are an asshole—you know that? Anyway, I'm glad it went no farther than it did."

"Well," Cone says uncomfortably, "we may have a little problem there."

They're drinking dark Michelob in Samantha's chintzed and ruffled apartment after a dinner of beef stew—to which Sam added a strong dose of chili.

"All right," she says, sighing, "let's have it. What's our little problem?"

"After Bonadventure made a dash for his car, I'd bet he grabbed a pen and made a note of the Honda's license number. No trick at all to see it's a rental car, and with his bucks and contacts he can bribe the right people to find out that it's rented to Haldering and Company."

"Oh, Jesus!" Sam says despairingly.

"Not to worry," Cone reassures her. "If Clovis complains, Hiram can fuzz it over by saying the employee who was driving the car was not authorized to be in that area, and he's been reprimanded or canned. No problem."

"That's what you say," Sam says bitterly. "You're really a world-class troublemaker."

"But you love me," he says with his quirky smile.

"Yeah," she says, "like a cobra loves a mongoose. What other nasty surprises have you got for me?"

He tells her what he's learned from Davenport, and how Sid is checking the out-of-state banks used by Clovis & Clovis subsidiaries.

"And what has Joe Washington found out?" Sam asks, looking at him narrowly.

"Oh," he says, flummoxed, "you know Joe's been working with me?"

"Will you give me credit for some brains?" she yells. "Of course I know it. Don't ever get the idea that I don't know what's going on in that office, buster, because I do. But I can't keep covering your ass if you don't play straight with me. So no more secrets—okay?"

"Okay."

"Liar," she says. "Tell me something—honestly now: Why did you try that *High Noon* face off with Bonadventure? He could have pounded you to a pulp. You never would have drawn your gun on him."

"Maybe, maybe not. Listen, I just don't like people who think they own the world. Bonadventure, the Clovises—they all figure their money entitles them to shoulder everyone else out of the way. All their ego comes from *things*: bucks, new cars, expensive homes. But I tell you they're hollow people. Breathe on them hard and they blow away. Like Bonadventure. That lad will have a few scars before I get through with him, I promise you that."

She sighs. "Tim, you scare me when you talk like that."

"Look," he says earnestly, "as far as I'm concerned, those people are evil. The only way to beat them is to prove to them that they can feel pain like ordinary mortals, maybe even die if they don't straighten up and fly right."

"Who the hell are you—an avenging angel?"

"No, I'm just an ex-grunt who's eaten enough dirt to last me a lifetime. Dying isn't so bad; everyone's got to do it. And once you realize that, it gives you a big edge on those scumbags, because they think they're going to live forever."

"You really believe that, don't you?"

"You bet your sweet ass I do. And speaking of your sweet ass . . . ?"

"What if I say no?"

"I'll accept that. Are you going to?"

"Are you out of your mind? Let's go!"

She's in a wild mood, and he takes his cue from her frenzy. It's a fight to a draw: no winner, no loser, but both satisfied with their private combat, convinced it's something special that neither will ever find again with anyone else.

After, he becomes suddenly subdued and tender, kissing her ribs, stroking her hard thighs.

"Christ!" she gasps. "I swear to God you're mellowing out."

"Maybe I am," he admits. "Want me to stop?"

"Hell, no! But after all that shit you were giving me, this is a new Timothy Cone I'm seeing. Just keep it up, kiddo; I love it."

So they lie quietly, not speaking, just touching, feeling, embracing sweetly: a new kind of intimacy for them, and something both find wondrous, though neither would admit it.

He imagines what his life would be like if he spent the rest of his days with this splenetic woman. She ponders if she might dare a lifetime with this violent, crabbed man who may be a loner—but not entirely from choice.

Finally, ignited again, they come together in a different mood: all murmurings and soft twistings. They couple in a drugged tempo, slow and lazy, as if this night might last forever.

Later, drowsy and satiated, they lie entwined, peering at each other with dazed eyes. They say nothing of what has happened, not wanting the moment to slip away—as it inevitably does.

"It's late," he says. "I've got to go."

"I suppose," she says. "I've got something for you. I wasn't sure I should give it to you, but I think I will. It may help on the Clovis–Evanchat case."

"What is it?"

"I told you that you should read the society pages occasionally. You know what a house tour is? Well, every now and then a charity will arrange a tour of rich people's homes, usually on the East Side. You buy a ticket and the money goes to the charity. In the *Times* today, it listed a tour that included the Clovis triplex. Wanna go?"

"Why not? Give me a chance to see how the other half lives."

"I'll get a ticket for you."

She pulls on a flannel robe and they each have another beer while he dresses. She watches him strap the holster to his shin.

"You really need that thing?" she says.

"It's just for show. Besides, I'd feel naked without it."

"You ever use it?" she asks.

"It impressed Bonadventure," he says, not answering her question.

Their farewell is strained. Something has changed, but neither can define it nor understand. So they keep their parting short and light. A quick kiss. A hurried embrace.

He drives home through deserted streets to his empty loft. Cleo comes growling up to rub against his legs, but it doesn't help.

Wakes up with a hacking cough. Decides, for the 1,974th time, that he'll cut down on the coffin nails. Gives Cleo fresh water and the remains of a can of tomato herring. Has a cup of instant coffee and his first cigarette of the day, proud of himself for waiting so long.

Gets to work on time—a miracle. Joe Washington, waiting in his office, is amazed.

"What happened?" he asks. "Insomnia?"

"Very funny," Cone growls. "What have you got?"

"*Nada,*" Joe says. "I braced every bank within ten blocks of Union Square. They all kicked my ebony ass onto the street. Applications for new accounts are confidential, and I can't get a look at them without a court order. That's the way I thought it would go."

"Yeah," Cone says, "you're right, but it had to be done."

"So I figured to try Sid. To get the names of his contacts at the credit agencies, like you said. But he was busy. I'll hit him again, but I don't think this is going to work, Tim. We just don't have the muscle to get that kind of information."

"I guess," Cone says, then slams the top of his desk angrily. "Goddammit, I know Griffon was tailing someone involved in the Clovis–Evanchat deal because he found that Clovis's dummy corporation was up to its ass in banks."

"Someone mention banks?" Sidney Apicella asks, standing in the doorway and rubbing his big schnozzola furiously. "I'll tell you about banks!"

He seems so distraught, they look up at him in astonishment. His face is flushed, and his swollen nose is flashing like a lighthouse.

"Those three other subsidiaries of Clovis," he says. "They're all headquartered in New York, and they were all banking here up to about a year ago. Then they switched to Newark, Chicago, and San Diego."

"Oh, boy," Cone says.

"Yeah—oh, boy," Apicella says. "I'm no detective, but even I can see that a month or two after New World Enterprises was organized the other Clovis subsidiaries switched their banks. Coincidence?"

"You don't really believe that, do you, Sid?" Cone asks.

"Of course I don't believe it. Three New York corporations suddenly switching to out-of-state banks— there's something going on there that's not kosher. You going to follow up on this, Tim?"

"Sure."

"Anything I can do to help? I okayed the deal in my PIE, and I don't enjoy being played for a patsy."

"Yeah," Joe Washington says, standing up. "You can help. I'll go back to your office with you, and you can give me the names of your contacts at the credit agencies."

"What for?"

Cone answers: "We're trying to find out if Clovis or any of its subsidiaries tried to open a new account at a bank in the Union Square area."

Apicella nods gloomily. "Where Griffon was killed. Come on, Joe; I'll give you what I've got, but don't expect too much. Those guys are closemouthed. You ask them how they're feeling and they want to know why you're asking."

Alone in his office, Cone opens a fresh pack of cigarettes, forgetting his morning resolution. He blows a plume of smoke at the dingy ceiling and reflects ruefully that's what he's good at—blowing smoke. When the phone rings, he lets it shrill five times before he picks it up.

"Yeah?" he says.

"Must you say, 'Yeah'?" Samantha Whatley barks. "Can't you say, 'Timothy Cone's office' or something halfway respectable?"

"I'm not a respectable guy," he says. "You know that. What's got you in a snit? You sound ready to chew spikes."

"Get your ass in here," she commands.

"Oh-oh," he says. "Bad news?"

She doesn't answer; just slams down the phone. So he shambles along the corridor to her office. She's sitting erect behind her desk and gives him what he once called her top-sergeant stare: cold, stony, and completely without mercy.

"What's up?" he asks.

"Close the door and sit down," she orders, and he does.

"You're off the Clovis–Evanchat deal," she says.

"Oh? Why is that?"

"Because there is no deal. Isaac Evanchat got a registered letter this morning; Clovis and Clovis have decided not to go ahead with the buyout. So Evanchat called Haldering and told him to drop the investigation."

"Good," Cone says.

"Good?" Samantha cries. "Good? We lose a profitable client, and all you can say is good?"

"Bonadventure traced the Honda, like I told you he would. So he knows he's being tailed. Also, they're nervous about a guy named Javert who's been asking too many questions."

She glares at him. "You son of a bitch, that was you."

"It was me," he admits. "Don't you see what's happening? We're getting close to the jugular, and Clovis figures the best thing to do is pull out of the deal. So we stop poking into their private affairs."

"Well, they've succeeded," Sam says. "H.H. told me to drop the whole thing and reassign personnel."

"And you're going to do it?"

"Tim, for God's sake, it's my neck if I don't do as he says. So just forget it."

They stare at each other, knowing something important is happening. Not so much about the Clovis–Evanchat deal as between themselves.

"I'm not going to forget it," Cone says. "If you want to can me, then can me. I couldn't care less. But Griffon got wasted, and he was a guy who tried to be a friend. And he worked for this outfit; that counts for something. So I'm going to push it. On my own if I have to."

"Jesus," she says, groaning, "what a hard-on you are."

"Not so much," he says. "But I know what's right. I'm going to keep digging. Am I bounced?"

She takes a deep breath, blows it out. Swings back and forth in her swivel chair. Fiddles with a ballpoint pen on her desk. Rubs her forehead worriedly. Pulls at her jaw. Scratches her scalp. Finally she looks up at him.

"The Honda is leased until the end of the month," she says. "That gives you another ten days. I can cover that. And I can diddle the reports to give you some wiggle room. Can you clear it up in a week?"

"I'll try," he says. "No guarantees."

"If you blow it, we're both out on our ass."

"I know. Do I still get the ticket to the house tour?"

She takes another deep breath. "All right, idiot boy," she says, "you'll get it. I'll scam it—somehow. But I'll have to start Joe on some new assignments. You can understand that, can't you?"

"Sure."

"Okay," she says, "you've got a week. Then it's back to the salt mines for you, sonny."

"I've been there before," he says.

"I like the way you express appreciation for what I'm doing for you," she says. "Get the hell out of here. You're disgusting."

"First I'm a hard-on and now I'm disgusting. This is my lucky day."

"Out!" she says, jerking a thumb toward the door.

He goes back to his office and calls Davenport. The city detective is out, so Cone leaves a message. He works on his weekly report—a great work of fiction—for almost an hour before Davenport calls back.

"I hear Haldering is out of the picture," the NYPD man says. "The Clovis–Evanchat deal is kaput."

"My God," Cone says, "bad news travels fast. Yeah, the buyout has been canceled. But that doesn't change anything as far as I'm concerned."

"This is a goddamned crusade with you, isn't it?"

"Yes," Cone says. "I think we better meet. I've got some things for you."

"And you want something from me?"

"That's right. Why don't we stop playing games? I've only got a week to clear this."

"A hotshot like you should be able to do it in a day or two. How's about I drop by your palace around eight o'clock?"

"Sounds good to me."

"This is my week for scotch," Davenport says. "Pick up a jug, will you? I'll pay for it."

"I can afford it," Cone says. "You want soda with it?"

"Are you out of your frigging mind?" the detective says.

He buys a bottle of Chivas Regal, drives home, feeds Cleo, and eats some cold leftover lasagne. He sits at his desk and stares at that scrap of paper Ed Griffon left in his file: DUM?

"That's what I am," Cone tells Cleo. "Dumb."

Davenport arrives, wearing a clear plastic raincoat and a plastic cover on his fedora. Both are sparkling with raindrops.

"It's raining?" Timothy asks.

"No," the city detective says, "I ran under an open hydrant. Of course it's raining. Where the hell have you been for the last two hours?"

"Sitting here."

"You never look out the window?"

"What for?"

"Good answer," Davenport says. "My God. Chivas Regal! Are you trying to bribe an officer of the law? If you are, you're succeeding."

They sit at the crippled desk, feet up, and sip from jelly jars filled with
the scotch whiskey.

"I got to get home," the city dick says, unwrapping a fresh stick of
Juicy Fruit, "or the wife will kill me. So let's make it fast. Why did Clovis
cancel the deal?"

"Because they're running scared," Cone says.

Then he tells Davenport about his confrontation with Anthony Bon-
adventure. About Apicella's report on the out-of-state banks. About Joe
Washington's failure to examine applications for new bank accounts in the
Union Square area.

"That's where you come in," he says. "Griffon was down there on
something connected with the Clovis–Evanchat deal; I'm convinced of it.
But I'm getting nowhere. I want you to check the area and see if anyone
from Clovis applied for a new account the day Griffon was killed."

"What's so important about the banks?" he wants to know. "You don't
think they're being cased for holdups, do you?"

"Nah, nothing like that. These people aren't shoot-'em-up types; they
wear white collars. But whatever the con is, it's got something to do with
their banks."

"Okay," the NYPD man says equably, "I'll give it the old college try.
We're getting nowhere on the Griffon kill. Our witness can't remember
another goddamned thing."

"But he still thinks it was a woman who pushed Ed?"

"He *thinks* it was, but the guy's a flake. No way are we even going to
get an indictment on his testimony. We need more."

Cone ponders a moment. "You got a buddy at the local IRS office?"
he asks finally.

"Maybe," Davenport says cautiously. "What's on your mind?"

"I'm not sure. But I thought it might be interesting if you could get a
look at the returns of all the Clovis people involved."

"That would take a month of Sundays," the detective says. "But I can
ask my pal if any of them are under audit and for what. It's Bonadventure
we're interested in most."

"If push comes to shove," Cone says, "I think you can lean on Grace
Clovis. That lady is ready to shatter into a million pieces. I think she'll
admit Anthony is supplying her with nose candy. Then you can hit on
him, and God knows he's no Rock of Gibraltar. Maybe he'll work a deal
and sing like a birdie."

"Do you also believe in the tooth fairy?" Davenport drains his Chivas in two deep gulps and smacks his lips. "That stuff's really sippin' whiskey, but I haven't got the time. I'll check out those Union Square banks for you. What'll you do for me?"

"I'm getting into the Clovis apartment on a charity house-tour. Maybe I can come up with something."

"What are you smoking these days?" Davenport asks. "I'd like to try some of it."

"I'm going to break this thing," Cone says. "You'll see."

The detective stands and makes the sign of the cross in the air. "Bless you, my son," he says.

Two days later (both spent tailing Constance Figlia), Cone drives the Honda up to East Seventy-seventh Street, to the headquarters of the charity sponsoring the house tour. He is wearing his raggedy tweed jacket, a plaid shirt open at the neck and showing a T-shirt beneath, and his stained flannel slacks. It is, he believes, a costume suitable for visiting the homes of the rich and the famous.

The charity is located in a townhouse inhabited by what appear to be similar organizations: Society for this and Association for that. The one Cone seeks is apparently devoted to the welfare of an American Indian tribe he's never heard of, but he assumes needs all the help it can get.

The tour is assembling on the sidewalk, next to a small chartered bus. A young woman and young man, both pale, long-haired, and earnest, continually count their flock, checking off each new arrival against a clipboard list.

"Timothy Cone," he reports to the young woman. "From Haldering and Company."

"Splendid," she says brightly, ticking off his name. "You're the last. Now we can get this show on the road. Horace," she calls, "everyone present and accounted for."

"Splendid," he says, and then in a louder voice:"May I please have your attention, ladies. And gentleman," he adds, with a bob of his head in Cone's direction. "Today we're going to visit six absolutely splendid homes. We will spend approximately thirty minutes in each house. In most cases the owners will be present to conduct the visit and answer your questions. Please, I entreat you, stay together and do not wander. Remember, you are invited guests, and I know you will conduct yourselves as you would expect guests to act in your home."

They all pile into the bus: twenty-two women—mostly middle-aged

matrons with blue hair and white gloves—and Timothy Cone. He ma-
neuvers to get a seat next to Horace.

"When do we get to the Clovis apartment?" he asks.

Horace consults his clipboard. "Third on the schedule," he reports.
"Why? Is it of particular interest to you?"

"I hear it's a classy joint."

"It's splendid!" Horace enthuses. "A triplex with divinely proportioned
rooms. And wait'll you see their collections of African masks and pre-
Columbian sculpture."

"I can hardly wait," Cone says.

The first home is a nine-room apartment on East Seventy-ninth Street,
decorated in what the owner calls "New York Victorian."

"The real stuff," he says proudly. He's a stubby man, in his sixties,
chewing on an unlighted cigar.

The living room walls are covered with flocked paper in a hellish design
of mythical beasts. There are swagged velvet drapes and more gilt-framed
oil paintings of dead fish than Cone has seen outside of Manny's Restaurant
on the San Francisco wharf. There are also antimacassars, and a polished
brass gaboon on a rubber mat. The only piece of furniture Cone admires
is an armchair made of deer antlers. It looks like a sitting-down version
of the iron maiden.

The second home on the tour is a Park Avenue duplex decorated in a
style the gushy resident terms "French Provincial, with just a wee touch
of your English manor house." This one is a little more attractive, with a
lot of flowered fabrics on furniture, walls of Oriental paper, and carpeting
with a pile so deep it could swallow a hundred contact lenses.

Finally the bus pulls up in front of the Clovis building on Third and
Eighty-fifth. It takes two elevators to get the tour group up to the triplex.
Waiting to greet them are Stanley and Lucinda, both wearing silvery
jumpsuits, and if they don't exactly match, they're close enough to make
Cone think of a song-and-dance team.

The main floor of the apartment is really something. The foyer is as
large as Cone's loft, and the living room stretches away like a basketball
court. A handsome copper staircase rises to the upper floors, although
Stanley assures his awestruck visitors that there's a small private elevator
to the terrace, swimming pool, and sauna.

Brother and sister chatter on, often completing each other's sentences.
They name the Brazilian who designed the custom-made leather furniture,
the Italian who did the marble fireplace, the Frenchman who painted the
walls, and the Austrian who etched the glass for the doors.

"And who designed *le tout ensemble*?" one of the blue-haired matrons
asks. "The overall creative concept?"

"We did," Stanley and Lucinda say in unison, with such an expression of satisfaction that Cone can hardly stand it. He turns and stares at a fiendishly baroque nineteenth-century grand piano, hand-carved with painted cupids, curlicues, leaping harts, crouching hares, and a wealth of other excrescences devised by a demented woodcarver.

What interests the Wall Street dick is that on the closed lid of this monstrosity are files of standing photographs framed in silver, leather, shell, aluminum, or dark wood. Cone moves sideways behind the tour group to get a closer look. It appears to be a collection of family photos: grandparents, children, relatives, friends. And one row of Stanley and Lucinda, from the time they were toddlers to their present state of physical and spiritual perfection.

"And now," Stanley says, "before we show you the upstairs—"

"—we'd like you to see our collection of pre-Columbian art," Lucinda finishes.

"Including some really rare and amusing artifacts," Stanley says. "You won't see anything like it anywhere else."

"We hope you won't be shocked," Lucinda adds, and brother and sister giggle.

The group moves to the end of the living room, where the art collection is housed in lighted glass cases recessed into the wall. With everyone's back turned, Cone steps swiftly to the piano and scans the photographs more closely.

In the front is a four-by-five color shot of Stanley, Grace, and Lucinda Clovis, Anthony Bonadventure, and Constance Figlia. The photo is framed in blue leather. It was obviously taken on a beach somewhere. The five, wearing bathing suits, are standing in a row, arms about each other's waists, laughing at the camera.

Cone looks up to make certain he's unobserved, then swipes the framed photograph. He slides it inside his jacket, holding it clamped under his left arm. He rejoins the tour group, troops upstairs with the others to inspect the master bedroom, dominated by a "genuine Chinese opium couch."

When the visit is finished, he goes down to the street with everyone else but doesn't board the bus. Instead, he walks rapidly westward, the purloined photograph still concealed under his jacket. He doesn't take another look at it until he's back in the parked Honda on East Seventy-seventh Street.

There they all are—a grinning group, holding each other and squinting against the bright sunlight. Grace Clovis is wearing the world's tiniest bikini. Lucinda is wearing a skimpy maillot with the legs cut up to her waist. Constance Figlia is swaddled in something with a ruffled skirt. The two men are wearing conventional swimming trunks. All look healthy, happy, and maybe just a little drunk or stoned.

The photograph infuriates Cone because it refutes the scenario he had imagined, which goes like this:

Grace Clovis somehow gets evidence of her husband's incestuous relationship with his sister. In a coked-up state, Grace delivers the evidence to Anthony Bonadventure. That bandito, realizing he's onto a good thing, confronts Stanley and Lucinda and in return for his silence lures the brother and sister into some kind of a bank scam, with Constance Figlia doing the donkeywork on that computer at New World Enterprises.

That plot has a lot going for it—until Cone stares at the color photograph of five friendly people and sees how content they are with each other. And didn't he see them all drive away in a stretch limousine, laughing and chattering?

Who the hell socializes with his blackmailer? No, they're all in it together. All five are on a high, laughing up a storm as if they have the world by the nuts.

"Greed," the Wall Street dick says aloud. "It's got to be greed. Them and their African masks and private elevator and stupid piano. Screw 'em!" he adds wrathfully.

Joe Washington is a good man, thorough and conscientious. But he's not as driven as Cone. Who is? So when Joe reports he can find no pattern in Constance Figlia's bank visits, Timothy has to check it out himself.

He can be methodical when he has to be. He keeps a detailed log of Figlia's bank visits, and eventually all those hours and days spent skulking around the lobby of Clovis headquarters on East Fifty-seventh Street begin to pay off. There *is* a pattern, a rough one, but what it might signify, Cone can't yet grasp.

The woman, frequently accompanied by Anthony Bonadventure, goes to the tellers' windows at Merchants International and Manhattan Central at least once a day. On Thursdays and Fridays she makes bank visits twice or maybe three times. And on the days before a bank holiday, she's especially busy, running in and out of the two banks like some kind of a nut.

Cone is still trying to puzzle this out when, on a Wednesday afternoon, he picks up his salary check at Haldering & Co. and takes it around the corner to a branch of Workmen's Savings, where he keeps an interest-bearing checking account. He deposits his check and then draws $100 in cash. The teller punches out his number on a computer terminal to make sure he's got enough in his account, then flips out five twenties.

Cone stares at the bills and begins to get a glimmer.

"Listen," he says to the wan teller, "if I had wanted to draw against the check I just deposited, could I do it?"

The teller takes another look at the salary check Cone has just deposited. "It's local," he says, "but not our bank. Unless you can get one of our officers to okay it, better figure about five days before you can draw on it."

"Does it always take five days to clear a local check?"

"It depends."

"On what?"

"Is it a weekend? A holiday? Then it might take longer. But generally it's three to five days before a local check clears. Faster for city, state, and federal checks."

"What about checks drawn on out-of-state banks?"

"Figure ten days to two weeks before you can draw on them."

Before Cone drives home, he stops at a discount store and picks up a pocket calculator for $10.95. It's got a lot of keys he doesn't understand, but it adds, subtracts, and multiplies, and that's all he needs.

Back in the loft, he gives Cleo a dish of fresh water and some old barbecued rib bones and pulls a chair up to his desk. He gets to work with a chewed pencil stub, a pad of scratch paper stolen from his office, and his new calculator.

He works for almost an hour, interrupting his task only long enough to pop a can of cold Bud. The phone rings and rings. But he doesn't answer it. He sticks with his figuring, punching the little calculator keys carefully with his bony fingers.

When he finishes, he looks at the results with awe. He can't believe it. So he goes through his computations once again. It comes out the same way. He sits back and smiles grimly. It's a sweet scam. Simple but sweet. He can appreciate the temptation—but that's no excuse.

The next day he's back on the trail of Constance Figlia. But now that he suspects what's going down, her many bank visits don't seem so strange.

He's double-parked in the Honda across Fifty-seventh Street on Thursday afternoon after the banks have closed. He watches Bonadventure pick up Constance Figlia in the silver LeBaron. Cone makes an illegal U-turn, ignoring the horns of furious motorists, and takes off after them. He thinks he knows where they're heading, but he wants to make sure.

It's a loose tail so they won't spot the Honda. But when he gets to New World Enterprises, the silver car is parked inside the fence, next to the office. Cone drives past slowly, sees no sign of activity, and then starts back to Manhattan.

"It's computer time," he says aloud, certain he's right.

He finds two urgent messages on his desk, both asking him to call Detective Davenport immediately. He lights a cigarette and smokes awhile, staring at the ceiling. Then he picks up the phone and dials.

"Davenport."

"Yeah, this is Cone. You wanted to talk to me?"

"What are you—some kind of fucking genius or something?"

"What's that supposed to mean?" Cone asks.

"I start checking out banks in the Union Square area, telling myself I'm stupid to listen to your idiot ideas. And the second bank I hit they say, Yeah, on the day Griffon got chilled, they had an application for a new account from New World Enterprises. How do you like that?"

"I like it."

"I even saw the application," Davenport says. "Wanna guess who signed it?"

"Constance Figlia, the corporation secretary," Cone says.

"Bingo! Go to the head of the class. And also Anthony Bonadventure, the corporation treasurer. I'm going back to the bank with a mug shot of Bonadventure to see if the officer who handled the application can definitely identify him. But I don't have a photo of Constance Figlia."

"I do," Cone says.

"Oh? Where'd you get that?"

"I stole it—on that charity house-tour I told you about."

The city detective laughs. "You're a pisser, you are. Can you get it over to me so I can nail this thing down?"

"Wait a minute," Cone says. "Let me think . . ." They're both silent a moment. Then: "Can you come over here tomorrow morning? Say about ten?"

"You got something for me?" Davenport asks.

"Another of my idiot ideas. Also, you better be here when I talk to our chief CPA, Sidney Apicella. I want to get his take on what I have to tell you."

"Will it help put Bonadventure on ice?"

"For years to come," the Wall Street dick says with more assurance than he feels.

"You think he pushed Griffon?"

"No," Cone says. "I think Figlia did that. But maybe you can get Bonadventure as an accessory."

"Okay, Cone, I'll be there. You'll have the Figlia photo for me?"

"Of course. Haldering and Company is always anxious to cooperate with New York's Finest."

"Son," Davenport says, "you've got more crap than a Christmas goose."

Cone stops by Apicella's office to make sure he'll be in on Friday morning and available for a short conference. Sid grumbles but agrees to meet with Cone and Davenport at ten o'clock.

Then Timothy pauses at Samantha Whatley's office and peers in. She's watering her scrawny philodendron. She looks at him without expression.

"Who are you?" she says.

"Your humble and obedient servant, ma'am," he says.

"You're a stranger to me," she says in a low voice. "I called you last night. No answer. I guess you were out."

"I was in," he says. "I just wasn't answering the phone."

"Prick," she says. "I needed to talk."

"I needed to clear the Clovis-Evanchat thing. You gave me a lousy week—remember?"

She brightens. "You're going to do it?"

He nods.

"And get Ed Griffon's killer?"

"Sure. With a little bit o' luck. How about Saturday night? I'll tell you all about it then."

"Okay," she says. "I forgive you, your place or mine?"

"Mine," he says. "What do you feel like eating?"

She grins at him.

"You're a depraved lady," he tells her.

"Guess who taught me," she says.

They're sitting in Apicella's office. Cone is dragging on a Camel. Davenport is starting on a new stick of Juicy Fruit. Sid is stroking his swollen beezer tenderly. They look at each other.

"Well?" Sid asks. "What's this all about?"

"Tell us about kiting checks," Cone says.

The CPA stares at him. "Kiting checks? Don't tell me you've never kited a check?"

Cone stirs restlessly. "That's neither here nor there. I just want to start from the beginning. How do you kite a check?"

Apicella sighs. "Okay, I'll give you a basic course. You got, say, five hundred bucks in your checking account. But you got a mortgage payment of, say, a thousand that's due immediately. So you write a check for the thousand because you know that before your mortgage payment check clears, you're going to be able to deposit enough in your account to cover it."

"That's illegal?" Davenport says. "I've been doing it all my life."

"Who hasn't?" Apicella says wearily. "That doesn't make it any less illegal. It's against the law to write a check for funds you don't possess at the time the check is written. What you're doing is taking advantage of the float—the time it takes for a check to clear from one bank to another. Two to five days for local banks."

"Meanwhile you're using the bank's money," Cone says. "Right? I mean, you're writing a check against money that doesn't actually exist in your account."

"Correct," Sid says, nodding. "But if you cover your check in time, no one's the wiser. That's the simplest form of check kiting. There are others."

"Yeah?" Davenport says. "Like what?"

"Like overdrafting," the CPA says. "Suppose you have a lot of bucks in a checking account that pays no interest—or very little. So you draw a check on much more than you've got in the account because you've got an opportunity to make a hot, short-term investment—commercial paper, a money market fund, or maybe even a race at Belmont—that pays more than the bank. In effect what you're doing is borrowing the bank's money to make more money for yourself. If you're lucky, you earn enough to cover your overdraft plus a profit. If you're unlucky, you go to jail."

"Look," Timothy Cone says, "I got a plot I want to throw at you and see what you think. Now suppose I have a million dollars."

"That'll be the day," the NYPD man says.

"Well, just *suppose*. I got a million, and I open accounts at two different banks. In one I deposit the minimum required to keep the account active. In the other I deposit what's left of my million. Most of it. Okay so far?"

"So far," Sid says. "You haven't broken any laws."

"I don't mean to," Cone says. "These are interest-bearing, day-of-deposit-to-day-of-withdrawal checking accounts. Okay? Now, on a Thursday, I write a check for about a million against my big account, and deposit it in my little account. Both banks pay, say, six percent. So my million is making about a hundred and sixty-five dollars a day in interest. But before my check clears, I'm making that much from *both* banks. You follow? I've still got the million in my big account because the check hasn't cleared, and the little account starts paying interest the moment I make the deposit. If it takes the check five days to clear, I've made about sixteen hundred bucks in interest from *both* banks. That million dollars is working twice."

Apicella and Davenport stare at each other. But Cone doesn't wait for their comments.

"Now what I want to know is this: Is what I'm doing against the law? I mean, when I write a check for a million against the big account, the money is there. I'm not drawing against funds that don't exist. So is what I'm doing illegal?"

"It's got to be," Apicella says. "I don't know the applicable law, but what you're doing, in effect, is doubling your money. You've got a million in two different banks—the same million!—and you're drawing interest on both balances. That's got to be against the law."

"It is," Davenport says, "and you've got to consider intent. Why are you flying that million bucks back and forth? Your interest is to defraud the banks, isn't it?"

Cone suddenly smiles. "Okay, that's the way I see it. Now listen to this: Instead of switching a million dollars back and forth between two banks, I'm switching a hundred million. The interest on that, at six percent, is six million annually, or about sixteen thousand five hundred a day. If I can con both banks out of an extra five days of interest, I'm making eighty-two thousand five hundred a week. That comes to about four-and-a-quarter million a year. But what if I do it more than once a week? What if I use more than two banks where the float can be as long as ten days? That's ten days' interest on a hundred million bucks! How much am I going to take the banks for in a year?"

"Whee!" Davenport cries, throwing up his hands. "It's Looney Tunes time, folks!"

Sid rubs his nose. "Is that what Clovis and Clovis are doing?"

"That's what they're doing."

"Thank God the Evanchat deal was canceled," Sid says.

"But wouldn't the bank's computers pick up on all those big checks flying back and forth?"

"Not necessarily. Essentially, banks' computers are data-processing machines. They keep a record of deposits and withdrawals, but they're not programmed to flash a red light when a fraud like this occurs. If no bank employee takes a look at the computer printout and screams, no one's going to realize what's happening."

"Son of a bitch," Davenport says, shaking his head. "Clovis must be making zillions."

"They are," Cone says, "because they had the heavy loot to start with. That's why they set up New World Enterprises as a dummy corporation with such a big capitalization. Then, when that worked out so well, they switched their other subsidiaries' banks to Newark, Chicago, and San Diego to take advantage of the longer float. It sure beats building luxury high-rises. I'll bet the whole scam was Bonadventure's idea. It's got his prints all over it."

"I feel sick," Apicella says.

"Why?" Cone asks. "Because you don't have a piece of the action? Be happy, Sid. Haldering is out of the picture, and your ass is safe—until the next time."

Back in Cone's office, he and Davenport face each other across the desk.

"I don't want to tell you how to run your business," the Wall Street dick says, "but—"

"But you're going to," the city detective interrupts.

"Well, yeah. If I was you, the first thing I'd do is tell Merchants International and Manhattan Central to run a computer check on the deposits and withdrawals made over the past year by Clovis and Clovis and New World Enterprises. If I'm wrong, then the whole thing is dead in the water."

"And if you're right?"

"Then do the same with the out-of-state banks Clovis's subsidiaries use. It won't take them all that long to spot what's going on and you can dump the whole investigation in the DA's lap."

"Then what do I do, teacher?" Davenport says with heavy irony, unwrapping a fresh stick of chewing gum.

"Look," Cone says, still leaning forward over his desk. "As far as I'm concerned, this bank fraud is a sideshow. I want Griffon's killer."

"As if I didn't know."

"I still say Grace is the key. The woman's a balloonhead. A little pressure and she'll explode. If you get sufficient evidence on this check-kiting scheme, you should have probable cause to get into the Clovis apartment without a warrant. Maybe the lady's got some coke on the premises. Even if she doesn't, you can lean on her about her association with Bonadventure. She'll break—I swear she will—and admit he's her candyman. Then you move in on Mr. Pinkie Ring himself. That guy has got nerves of Silly Putty. Mark my words, he'll cop a plea if you tell him his cock is on the block for the murder of Ed Griffon. I guarantee he'll name Constance Figlia as the actual killer—after he makes a deal with the DA."

Davenport shakes his head. "I don't even know what I'm going to have for lunch today," he says, "and you've got all this wrapped up in a neat package with a ribbon on it."

"It'll work," Cone says. "They're all going to take a fall, one way or another. There's only one thing I want."

"Uh-huh, had to be. What?"

"I want to be there when you pick up Anthony Bonadventure. I figure if you move fast, you should be able to cuff him by tomorrow. I'll stick close to my phone. Will you let me know when you're moving in?"

"Yeah," Davenport says, rising heavily to his feet. "I owe you that."

"Wait a minute," Cone says, fishing the leather-framed photo from his top desk drawer. "Don't forget to get into the New World warehouse in Brooklyn and grab that computer. That'll give the DA all he needs for a

bank-fraud indictment. And show this photo of Constance Figlia to your
flaky witness and tell him she's under arrest. Maybe he'll be willing to
identify her."

"Maybe," the NYPD man says, inspecting the photograph. "Worth a
try. Which one is she?"

"Second from the left."

"And who's the blond broad in the bikini?"

"That's Grace Clovis."

"Oh, yeah," the city cop breathes. "I think I'll interrogate her personally."

"You're a dirty old man," Cone says.

"I was a dirty young man," Davenport says. "I haven't changed."

He doesn't leave the loft on Saturday morning, not even to run out for a
paper. He's afraid he'll miss Davenport's call and blow a chance to be in
on the kill. So he drinks black coffee, smokes cigarettes, and vapors aloud,
addressing Cleo but really talking to himself.

"I may be wrong on some of the details, kiddo," he says, "but nothing
important. Ed Griffon, a smart guy, caught on faster than I did and got
himself knocked off. Because he wasn't smart enough to watch his back.
You don't trust anyone in this world, Cleo—not even yourself. You trust
me to feed you, give you fresh water, change your litter. So you're content.
But what if some night I don't come home, and never do again? Who'll
feed you then? Ahh, you'll make out somehow, you little shit. You're a
survivor."

So the morning crawls away. Around eleven o'clock he pours himself
a brandy to stun the butterflies in his stomach. It isn't impatience so much
as anger, and he knows his furies will devour him if he can't narcotize
them with caffeine, nicotine, and alcohol—a well-balanced diet for what
ails him.

The phone rings a little before noon, and he walks toward it slowly,
too proud to send up a prayer that it'll be the call he's waiting for.

"Yeah?" he says.

"Everything's coming up roses," Davenport sings.

"The two local banks worked through the night. They figure that in
the past year, Clovis has clipped them for about fifty million. The out-
of-state banks are still figuring their losses. We grabbed the computer at
New World, and some hotshot expert in the DA's office says it's got a
complete record of everything. I mean they were *flying* those checks, and
had to use a computer to keep track of deposits, withdrawals, and interest earned."

"What about the people?" Cone demands.

"We picked up Constance Figlia this morning. Then, about an hour ago, we moved into the Clovis apartment and grabbed Stanley, Grace, and Lucinda."

"Find anything?"

"Oh, yeah. A packet of happy dust in Grace's handbag."

"Did she break?"

"Even before we could question her. She went hysterical on us, and she's in the hospital. Under treatment and under guard. I think she'll spill."

"Sure she will. What about Bonadventure?"

"After I left you yesterday we put a tail on him. Our guy says that right now he's in his brownstone. We're going to take him at twelve-thirty. Want to watch the circus?"

"Wouldn't miss it for the world," Cone says. "I'll be there."

"As an observer," Davenport warns. "Just stand back and watch. This is our job."

"Of course," Cone says.

It's a drizzly day, the sky steel, the light brass, the air tasting of a copper penny. Cone is wearing his black flapping raincoat over his corduroy suit.

He's there before Davenport arrives, leaning against a lamppost one door down from Bonadventure's brownstone. He spots the police tail: one guy in an old, dented Plymouth parked across the street. Cone waits as patiently as he can, chain-smoking. He leans down once to touch the shin holster through his pant leg. It's there.

Then two cars pull up, moving slowly, and double-park in front of the brownstone. The squad car has two blues in the front seat. The other is a smart, clean Buick with three men in mufti. Davenport gets out of the Riviera first and looks around. He spots Cone and waggles his fingers. Then he directs the others.

The squad car goes around the block. The three cops trudge up the stoop and disappear into the vestibule. Cone straightens up and moves closer.

He waits almost ten minutes, tense and agitated. Then the front door opens and a procession comes out: the three NYPD detectives and Anthony Bonadventure, hands manacled behind him. He's coatless, but wearing a beautifully tailored suit of silvery sharkskin. One of the detectives is gripping him firmly by the upper arm.

Cone has a surge of hot blood, feels his face flushing. A wild, violent thought: He could bend swiftly, slip the Magnum from the ankle holster, and plug Bonadventure. He's close enough so that he wouldn't endanger the detectives. Just take one step forward, point, and *pow!*

But Davenport is staring at Cone and sees something in his face. He steps quickly to put himself between his prisoner and the Wall Street dick. He moves to Cone and gives him a fierce, stern look. He stands there a moment, not speaking, his eyes locked with Cone's.

Then, apparently satisfied with what he sees, he turns away, and Anthony is hustled into the Buick. But as he goes, he looks back at Cone, his handsome features distorted with puzzlement and fear.

Timothy, madness passing, contents himself with giving Bonadventure the finger, twisting his hand in the air.

"Ta-ta," he calls.

He still stands in the drizzle after the police car has pulled away. Then, when his trembling has eased and he has control, he goes back to his Honda. He knows how close he came, and wonders if he's ever going to grow up.

He has shopping to do, up and down lower Broadway, and in all the funky little stores in his neighborhood. He buys a couple of barbecued chickens, some salad stuff, a package of potato skins, which he dearly loves, and a smoked chub, which Cleo dearly loves—including head, skin, bones, tail, and all.

He also buys a bottle of Korbel Natural champagne.

Samantha Whatley shows up a little after five o'clock. She brings dessert: four rum balls covered with chocolate sprinkles, sinfully rich but looking like elephant droppings.

"Well?" she demands. "What happened? Tell me this instant!"

"A drink first," he says. "My first of the day."

"Ha-ha," she says.

He mixes vodkas and water. They sit at the desk, slouched on the wooden kitchen chairs, while he tells her all about it. She listens intently, not interrupting. They're on their second drink before he finishes with an account of Anthony Bonadventure's arrest.

"I almost blew him away," Cone confesses. "Maybe I would have if Davenport hadn't stepped in."

"But why Bonadventure?" Samantha asks curiously. "You say it was Constance Figlia who pushed Griffon onto the tracks."

"Sure it was, but don't you see—Bonadventure engineered the whole thing. I'm convinced of it. I mean, here were all these people—Constance, Stanley, Grace, and Lucinda—no more larcenous than the rest of us—and then Bonadventure appears on the scene with his get-rich-quicker scam and ruined all their lives."

"You think he hooked Grace on coke?"

"I'd bet on it. And Stanley and Lucinda probably made no objection. Anthony took Grace out of the picture, and they could go on holding hands forever."

"Gross," Sam says.

"Yeah. All it took was a devil like Bonadventure to lead the way. That's why I wanted to blast him."

"I'm glad you didn't."

"I am, too—I guess. But I'll probably spend the rest of my life regretting it."

"An unarmed prisoner with his hands cuffed behind him? You'd have blown him away?"

"Hell, yes," Cone says. "You'd shoot a rattlesnake just lazing on a rock, wouldn't you?"

She looks at him a moment, then shakes her head. "Tim, you scare me. You keep forgetting you're back in civilization."

"Is that what it is—civilization? But enough of this; let's celebrate the happy ending. Isaac Evanchat escaped a fate worse than death, and Haldering and Company did its civic duty. Maybe H.H. will get a scroll or plaque or something from the city, saying what an upright citizen he is."

"He'd love that," she says, smiling.

"I'll talk to Davenport. He'll put in a good word for us. Listen, I have barbecued chicken and champagne. How does that grab you?"

"Just right," she says, "but let's eat later."

It's really raining now; they hear the drumming on the roof, but the loft is dry, warm, shadowed.

"This place is like a cave," Samantha says, undressing. "There's something primitive about it."

"Yeah," Cone says. "The plumbing."

They're naked together on the mattress and she is reaching for him when he suddenly rolls away and climbs to his feet.

"Now what?" she wails. "Where are you going?"

"Forgot something."

He goes to the kitchen cabinet and comes back with a gift-wrapped package tied with a bow. He lies down beside her again and pokes the gift at her.

"For you," he says gruffly.

She looks down at the package, then looks up at him, not believing.

"For me?" she says. "What is it?"

"Open it, for God's sake."

She strips the wrapping away with shaking hands, lifts the lid, finds a necklace of chunky beads, alternating ebony and crystal. She takes it out, eyes widening, and strokes it tenderly, then puts it around her neck. They both see the shine and glitter against her dark skin.

"It's beautiful," she says in a choked voice, and begins weeping.

"Aw, shit," the Wall Street dick says, taking her into his arms.

There is joy and shouting that night.

Book Two
The Whirligig Action

1

Late in October of that year a dramatic story from Glendale, California, titillated and bemused the entire nation. As reported in newspapers, magazines, and on network television, the facts were these:

Laura Bentley (nineteen) and Gerald McPhee (twenty-two), residents of Glendale, had met at a church barbecue and were attracted to each other. They dated for a period of ten months and then became engaged.

In addition to their youth and good looks (both blue-eyed and flaxen-haired), they had other commonalities. Both were transplanted easterners. Laura had been born and spent the first fourteen years of her life in Baltimore, Maryland. Gerald had been born and lived in Washington, D.C., for fifteen years.

In addition, both young people were fatherless, both living with their mothers. Laura's father had deserted his wife and daughter when she was nine years old. Gerald's father had died when the boy was thirteen.

During their courtship Laura and Gerald had several times discussed the possibility that both might have been adopted. It seemed all the more reasonable to them because neither resembled their mothers, and they could find no physical likeness in the photographs that had been preserved of their fathers.

Both questioned their mothers. Mrs. Bentley refused to discuss the subject with her daughter. Mrs. McPhee continually assured Gerald that he was, in fact, her natural child.

So the young people were married. Both being employed, they decided to wait a period of time until they could afford a small home before having "at least two children and maybe more."

Approximately a year after the marriage, Mrs. Bentley became seriously ill. She was diagnosed as suffering from an ovarian tumor, and surgery was scheduled. On the day before the operation, frightened and wanting to prepare for any eventuality, she confessed to her daughter that she, Laura, had been conceived by artificial insemination with sperm from an unknown donor.

Laura reported this to her husband, and they stared at each other, both suddenly aware of a dread possibility. Gerald McPhee then confronted his mother again and demanded to know the truth about his birth. Mrs. McPhee, in tears, finally admitted that Gerald, too, had been conceived by artificial insemination.

Thoroughly distraught, the young couple consulted an attorney. He immediately wrote the Washington, D.C., fertility clinic where both mothers had been impregnated. While awaiting a reply from the clinic, the lawyer sternly urged Mr. and Mrs. McPhee not to have sexual intercourse, even with contraceptive devices.

The worst fears of the young people were realized. A check of the fertility clinic's records revealed that Laura and Gerald had been conceived with live sperm from the same anonymous donor. They were half brother and sister. Their marriage was annulled.

This unusual incident was a brief sensation in the news media, but gradually faded from interest as more earthshaking stories took over the headlines.

But it was to have an unexpected and dramatic effect on several financial institutions on Wall Street.

"How could such a thing have happened?" Lester Pingle asks. He strokes his bare upper lip with a knuckle. That flap of flesh had once borne a scraggly black mustache—until the night his wife, emboldened by two brandy stingers, told him it made him look like a moth-eaten Groucho Marx. Since then the lip has been naked. "Don't you people keep records?"

Dr. Victor January tries to smile. "We at Nu-Hope certainly keep records. Computerized, I might add. We also warn patients of the possibility of incestuous relationships between offspring of the same donor. The whole subject is covered in our presentation."

"Pages thirty to thirty-four," Dr. Phoebe Trumball says.

"The chance always exists," January goes on, "but it can be minimized by the exchange of sperm, fresh or frozen, between fertility clinics in different cities, or in different countries."

Ernest Pingle stirs in his heavy club chair. He sweeps a palm over a brush of white hair, cut as short as a drill instructor's. "Tell me, Wictor," the old man starts, then asks, "You don't mind if I call you Wictor?"

"Not at all, sir," Dr. Victor January says.

"You ship this—this stuff to other countries?"

"Frozen human sperm? Yes, we airlift it in special containers. Foreign fertility clinics sometimes have requests for an American donor."

"And you buy sperm from foreigners?" Lester Pingle says, rather indignantly.

"Very infrequently," Dr. January says. "New York is a cosmopolitan city. We have an extensive file of available sperm donors of almost every nationality. If a Liberian, Korean, or Icelandic client requests impregnation by a male of her country, we can usually provide it. We had an odd one about a month ago. A woman of the Navaho Indian tribe requested she be inseminated by the sperm of a Navaho male. We were finally able to locate frozen Navaho sperm in a Phoenix, Arizona, sperm bank."

"Look," Lester Pingle says hesitantly, "suppose a woman wants a tall guy with blond hair and blue eyes. You can provide that?"

"We try to answer all our clients' requests," Dr. Trumball says. "No guarantees, of course; genetics is not *that* exact a science. But we've found that a woman who requests a blond, blue-eyed donor is perfectly satisfied if she gives birth to a dark-haired, brown-eyed baby. Motherhood conquers all."

Old Mr. Pingle shakes his head dolefully. "I can't keep up," he complains. "The world changes so fast. When I was young, boys worried about getting a girl knocked up. You wanted sex without pregnancy. The girl did, too. Now women want to be pregnant without sex."

"More and more of them every day," Phoebe Trumball says, nodding. "Including many single women who, for a variety of reasons, don't wish to be married but do want a child of their own. Our Artificial Insemination Department has never been busier."

"Understand," Dr. January says hastily, "frequently the donor is the husband, where for one reason or another the couple cannot conceive by normal sexual intercourse."

"Tell me this," Lester Pingle says. "Suppose that young couple in Glendale had never discovered they had the same donor as a father, and they had a baby. Would it be normal?"

Dr. January shrugs. "No one can say. The Egyptian Ptolemies frequently entered into incestuous marriages. But I would hardly recommend it. Too much danger of genetic damage."

"Their having a child together would be only one danger," Dr. Trumball says thoughtfully. "What about this possibility: The young married couple never discover they are half-brother and half-sister. But, for whatever reasons, the man discovers he has infertile sperm, and they decide the wife will have artificial insemination. Given the improvements in the technology of freezing human sperm, she might have been impregnated by her father. That's a very remote possibility, I admit, but it does exist."

The four stare at the walls, no one wishing to comment. Finally old Mr. Pingle looks at his son and says, "You have more questions, Lester?"

They are on the eighth floor of a Water Street office building that has all the grace and delicacy of a woolly mammoth excavated from a Siberian bog. But the conference room of Pingle Enterprises, Inc., is comfortable enough, with oak wainscotting, leather chairs, and a fireplace that appears to be veined white marble and is actually a very artful vinyl compound.

"If it's the morality of our business that bothers you," Dr. January says, "let me say this—that up to five years ago, we also provided an abortion service. But the hassle proved more than we could handle—what with the constant picketing and demonstrations. Today we are solely concerned with pro-life activities, helping people have healthy babies. There can be no legal or moral objections to that. We've included all the recent judicial decisions on our activities in the presentation."

"We've already read it," Lester Pingle says, "and we are interested. Aren't we, Father?"

"Interested," the old man says. "Not conwinced."

"As I understand it," Lester goes on, "you want to expand the Nu-Hope Fertility Clinic into a nationwide chain, either privately owned or by franchise."

"A worldwide chain," Dr. January says earnestly. "Eventually."

"And these fertility clinics would be located in shopping malls and other high-traffic areas?" Lester asks.

"For maximum exposure," Dr. Phoebe Trumball says.

"More important," Dr. January says, "we see a growing need for an organization that dominates the human fertility business. It would enable us to have a centralized computer system that could help prevent potential tragedies like that Glendale incident. Also, the various clinics could exchange fresh and frozen sperm, eggs, and embryos much more efficiently than a hundred clinics operating under individual ownership. We have given you our balance sheet. You can see how our business has boomed in the past three years."

"Our pregnancy rate is the best in the country," Dr. Trumball says. "Perhaps the best in the world. And, as head of our Research and Development Department, I can assure you that our successes with artificial insemination and in-vitro fertilization will continue to increase as we refine our techniques and improve quality control."

"Tell me, Wictor," Ernest Pingle says, "how did you come to pick our company for this project?"

Dr. January has an answer ready, so ready it might have been rehearsed. "Shelby and Hawthorne have been our financial advisers for several years. When we decided we wanted to expand, we asked them how we might locate a partner willing to make a substantial cash investment. Shelby and Hawthorne suggested we approach a venture capital company, and recommended Pingle Enterprises because of your success in raising funds for the E-Z Ortho dental chain and the Walksoft podiatric clinics."

"We have also done pizzas and tacos," the old man says wryly.

His son rises abruptly. "Thank you for coming by," he says to the two doctors. "It's a very interesting concept. But of course we'll want our attorneys to give an opinion and our accountants to go over the numbers."

"And when may we expect to hear from you?" Dr. January asks.

"Within a month," Lester Pingle promises.

His father stands up slowly and everyone shakes hands. Then Lester walks the visitors to the elevator. After they have departed, he returns to the conference room, where his father is again slumped in the club chair at the head of the table.

"I like it," Lester says.

"I don't," his father says. "Take my adwice, it's not for us."

"Why not? The numbers look good."

"It's not for us," the old man repeats stubbornly.

His son sighs. "Pop, like you said, the world is changing. We've got to keep up. What don't you like about it?"

"I don't know," Ernest Pingle says slowly. "Something isn't kosher. That Doctor Wictor—a very smart man. He talks well. The woman also is smart. They have all the answers. Even before you have the questions, they have the answers." The old man makes a soft fist and thumps his round belly. "Something here," he says. "Something in my gut tells me we should pass this one by."

"You and your gut!" his son scoffs. "Pop, if we had listened to your gut we never would have done that software deal in Massachusetts. And look how much money we made."

"Not so much," Ernest Pingle says. "I didn't understand software. I don't understand this. Frozen sperm and eggs and embryos. Feh! Frozen pizza and tacos I can understand."

"Think about it," his son urges. "Will you just do that? I really believe it's a hot proposition. Listen, I'm going to run out for some lunch. Can I bring you anything?"

"No," the old man says. "I'll have Mrs. Scherer make me a nice glass of tea and maybe I'll have one of those English biscuits. You'll be back when?"

"In an hour. At the most. And then we'll talk more about the Nu-Hope deal."

His father nods. "Something is wrong here," he says, tapping the bound presentation.

"We'll talk about it," his son says again and hurries out.

Lester Pingle, a tallish man with round shoulders and a pot that will one day rival his father's, walks quickly to the South Street Seaport. As usual, the sidewalks are crowded, and he makes better time by scuttling along the narrow streets, dodging traffic rather than trying to shove through the mob of sightseeing pedestrians.

It's a kaleidoscope, a carnival, a merry-go-round, a festival and entertainment, it's a carousel, a funfair. The costumes! The players! Everything is awhirl, and he is dizzied by the movement, colors, a shattering cacophony. Everything gigs him, and he yearns for quiet, solidity, truth—and cannot find them.

But he does find his man, browsing in a trendy shop offering maritime artifacts, including a selection of plastic scrimshaw that looks like the real thing—if you've never seen the real thing.

The man is wearing a double-breasted topcoat of herringbone tweed. It accents a barrel chest and broad shoulders: a thick, stumpy body topped with a bullethead. And atop *that*, an incongruous green felt fedora with a little clump of bright feathers in the band.

The two men stand close to the scrimshaw display and converse in low voices. The tweedy one handles a fake whalebone letter opener while Pingle fondles a darning egg.

"How did it go?"

"All right," Lester says. "Very alert, knowledgeable people. They handled themselves well."

"So you're taking them on?"

"Well—ah—not yet. It wouldn't do to make an immediate decision. It has to be vetted by our lawyers and accountants, or someone is sure to ask questions. We don't want to attract attention to this deal, do we?"

The other man turns his head slowly to stare at Pingle. His eyes are a startling blue: electric eyes. "No," he says, "we don't want to do that. But the investigation will be just routine, won't it?"

"Oh, sure. No problem. However..."

"However what?"

"The old man doesn't like it. But I'll bring him around," Pingle adds hastily.

"I'm sure you will," the man says with a mirthless smile. "That's what we're paying you for, isn't it? Mr. D. is very interested in this project. Personally interested. It wouldn't do to have it fall through."

No menace. Just a flat statement.

"I understand that," Lester says, replacing the plastic darning egg. "It won't fall through. By the way, how did you know Nu-Hope would come to us? They said we were recommended by their financial advisers, Shelby and Hawthorne."

Again that mirthless smile. "I thought you knew. We own Shelby and Hawthorne."

Pingle is too keyed up to pause for lunch. He scurries back to the office and finds his father still in the conference room, sipping his glass of tea and nibbling on a biscuit from a big English tin.

Lester doesn't even take off his hat or coat. "About this Nu-Hope deal," he says abruptly.

His father looks up at him. "You read about the Clovis scandal?" he asks.

The son stares at him in astonishment. "Of course I read about it. They were stupid. How long did they think they'd get away with it? But what has the Clovis swindle got to do with us?"

"Haldering and Company uncovered it," the old man says. "They were hired to inwestigate, and one of the Haldering detectives found out what was going on. I want to hire Haldering and Company to inwestigate Nu-Hope for us."

Suddenly hot and sweating, Lester takes off his hat and coat. "Come on, Pop," he says, "there's no need for that. We've got a lot of high-priced lawyers and accountants who can do all the investigating we need."

Ernest Pingle bares his dentures. It's intended as a smile, but looks more like a snarl. "You're outwoted," he says. "You're still a junior partner—remember? We either hire Haldering to inwestigate Nu-Hope or the whole deal is dead as far as we're concerned."

Lester has no choice. "Okay then," he says, trying to make it casual, "we'll hire Haldering. I guarantee they'll find Nu-Hope is on the up-and-up."

"You're all perspiry," his father says. "Calm down and have a biscuit. They're wery good."

On this particular afternoon, Hiram Haldering is in an expansive mood. His sausage fingers are laced across his double-breasted vest as he lounges in a high-backed leather swivel chair, beaming at two expressionless employees: Samantha Whatley and Timothy Cone.

"Pingle Enterprises, Incorporated," Haldering says happily. "They're a venture capital outfit. I met with them this morning. Checked them out first, of course. They've got a good track record. Served as general partners in a number of private and public limited partnerships. Made a mint when they took a pizza chain public. Most of their other deals have paid off. No problems with the SEC or IRS. Their reputation on the Street is as good as any risk capital company.

"Anyway," H.H. continues, "I talked to the principals: Ernest Pingle, who looks to be one year younger than God but has all his marbles, and his son, Lester, a sweaty fat guy who looks like he might enjoy a career as a flasher. Well, to make a long story short—"

"Too late for that," Cone mutters, and Samantha glares at him furiously.

"To make a long story short," Haldering repeats equably, "Pingle Enterprises has been approached by an uptown outfit called Nu-Hope Fertility Clinic."

"I know it," Sam says promptly. "They used to be into abortions, but now they only do artificial insemination and test-tube babies."

"Kee-rect," H.H. says. "Sex without joy."

His jape convulses him with laughter, and the other two smile weakly.

The boss recovers slowly. "Nu-Hope," he says, "wants to go nationwide with a chain of fertility clinics, and wants the Pingles to set up the financing. Lester, the son, is hot for the deal. The old man, Ernest, doesn't like it. He says it just doesn't smell right. He wants this Nu-Hope Fertility Clinic checked out six ways from the middle. It's a great opportunity for us. A nice fee, and a chance to get our foot in the door to the venture capital business."

"Why did they pick us, Mr. Haldering?" Whatley asks.

"Well . . ." he says, "I gather they read the news stories on the Clovis case and were impressed by our work. As they should have been; it was a neat job."

He beams at them, and they look at him with some trepidation, knowing what's coming.

"I've alerted our attorneys and accountants," Haldering goes on, "and they're checking to make sure Nu-Hope Fertility Clinic is soundly run and on the up-and-up. But we also have to run a check on the principals. That's where you two come in."

Sam and Timothy glance at each other, shifting uncomfortably in their rigid office chairs.

"Whatley," H.H. says, "I want you to work with the lawyers and accountants. Cone, the actual investigation's your baby. Hey! You'll be investigating a fertility clinic, and I say it's your baby. That's funny!"

Cone doesn't think so. "Why the hell me?" he demands. "I don't know a goddamned thing about artificial insemination."

Hiram Haldering slowly lights a cigar and blows a plume of smoke over their heads. "Learn," he says. "Buy some books and read up on it. Ernest Pingle says he's alerted the doctors at Nu-Hope, and they promise to cooperate fully with our representatives. Besides, old man Pingle insisted that the detective who broke the Clovis swindle work on this one. So you're elected. Keep me informed. We want to do a bang-up job."

Samantha and Timothy push back their chairs, wander down the corridor.

"Lots of luck," Sam says. "Do a bang-up job and keep me informed."

"Up yours," the Wall Street dick says. "What in God's name do I know about sperm banks?"

"Learn," she repeats. "Buy some books and read up on it. Who knows, maybe you'll become a donor."

"Not me," he says. "I haven't got any to spare."

He is mollified somewhat when Sam promises to relieve him of his current caseload and parcel out his files to the other Haldering investigators. Back in his cramped office, he begins to get his notes in order. Since the Clovis scam his assignments have been dull stuff, involving mostly routine phone calls and research at Dun & Bradstreet. Nothing with any pizzazz.

He is opening his second pack of Camels of the day when his phone rings, and he reaches for it absently. "Yeah?" he says.

"Mr. Timothy Cone?"

A man's voice, kind of creaky.

"That's right," Cone says. "Who you?"

"My name is Ernest Pingle. Mr. Haldering has just informed me that you have been assigned to the inwestigation of the Nu-Hope Fertility Clinic."

"I guess," Cone says, sighing. "And you're the client?"

"I am. I was wondering, Mr. Cone, if you and I could meet personally. I would appreciate it wery much."

"Sure," Cone says. "Where and when?"

"Could you make it this evening at, say, nine o'clock? At my apartment?"

"Sounds okay. Are you in the book?"

"Yes. The only Ernest Pingle listed. On Fifth Avenue. I can expect you at nine?"

"Sure, I'll be there. I don't have to dress up, do I?"

"Dress up?" the old man says, astonished. "Why should you dress up?"

"I don't visit on Fifth Avenue very often."

Pingle laughs, a nice, bubbly sound. "Don't worry about it," he says. "This will be a wery informal wisit."

"I'll be there," Cone promises.

On his way out, he stops at Samantha Whatley's office. She's pulling yellowed leaves from her mournful little philodendron. Cone stands in the doorway and watches her.

"Why don't you get rid of that thing," he says. "It's dead."

"It's not dead," she says indignantly. "Just a little peaked. All it needs is tender, loving care."

"Who doesn't?" he says. "Listen, I just got a call from Ernest Pingle. The old man. He wants to see me tonight at his place."

Sam looks at him. "What for?"

"Didn't say."

"Well, will you try to spruce up a little before you meet him?"

"Why should I? It's just an informal wisit."

"A *what?*"

"That's the way he talks. It's a wery informal wisit."

"Good night, asshole," she says in a low voice.

"Good night, shithead," he says.

On his walk uptown, Cone stops at a discount bookstore and buys three volumes on artificial insemination, test-tube birth, and human embryo transfer. Then, closer to his loft on lower Broadway, he picks up a pepperoni pizza and a cold six-pack of Bud.

The moment he's inside the door, Cleo smells the hot pizza and comes growling up to rub against his shins.

"Take it easy, monster," he tells the cat. "You'll get yours."

He cuts the pizza into six wedges and gives one to Cleo. Then he pops a beer, starts on the pizza, and begins reading the first of his three books.

It's not a thick volume, and he finds he can do a lot of skipping and skimming and still pick up the gist. Unexpectedly, he finds the subject fascinating. A paragraph that blows his mind suggests that with current techniques, it would be possible for a child to have five parents: The egg of a donor and the sperm of a donor are joined in vitro. Two parents. The resulting embryo is then implanted in a surrogate mother. The third parent. After birth, the baby is adopted by a childless couple. The fourth and fifth parents.

"And nobody got fucked," Cone marvels aloud to Cleo, who has leaped up onto the table and is licking up pizza crumbs. "What is the world coming to, you crazy cat? Who are the legal parents of the child? The lawyers are going to have a field day with that one."

He doesn't exactly spruce up for his meeting with Ernest Pingle, but he does change his shirt, discarding a faded flannel plaid number for a clean white broadcloth. He checks the short-barreled .357 Smith & Wesson Magnum in his ankle holster, then starts out, waving a hand at Cleo.

"No self-abuse," he cautions.

He takes a cab uptown, figuring H.H. is so happy with the new client that he won't scream too loudly at Cone's expense account. He arrives at Ernest Pingle's apartment house, on Fifth Avenue just north of Sixty-fourth Street, a few minutes after nine. It's a cold, sharp night, a zillion stars whirling in a cloudless sky over Central Park.

The lobby has all the charm of a crematorium, and when Cone finally gets up to Apartment 24-A, he discovers it's a gloomy cavern big enough to breed stalactites. The only thing that saves it are the floor-to-ceiling windows facing west; the view is spectacular.

Ernest Pingle, apparently the only person present, turns out to be a chubby, shortish gaffer with a big head of bristly white hair. His face may have as many lines as a Rand McNally road map, but his eyes are bright, sharp, and, Cone figures, rarely have the wool pulled over them.

"I thank you for coming on such short notice," he says, shaking hands. He takes the detective's anorak and hangs it away in a closet that looks to be as large as Cone's loft. "The truth is, it's our maid's night off, and also it's Mrs. Pingle's evening with her mah-jongg club. So I thought it would be a good opportunity to inwite you up to have a little talk."

It seems like a long, unnecessary explanation to Cone, and he wonders if this bustling little man might be a trifle nervous.

"Tell me," Pingle says, "do you take a drink?"

"Now and then," Cone says, sitting on an enormous brocade couch. "This is one of the 'now' times. It's cold out there."

"So it is, so it is. To tell you the absolute truth, I like a drop of schnapps myself. The problem is this: My wife, God bless her, has wery firm opinions about strong drink and won't allow any in the house. So, to be perfectly honest, I hide a bottle on the premises. Now, you are a detective—tell me, where do you think I conceal it?"

He stands, grinning like a plump Buddha, ready to make his startling revelation.

Cone stares at him thoughtfully. "If the cork is tight, Mr. Pingle, the best place to keep it would be in the toilet tank in your bathroom. I doubt if your wife would ever lift the lid. And you'd be helping the city's water shortage by cutting down on the volume of the tank."

"Gott im Himmel!" Ernest Pingle says, gasping. "You are exactly right. You are a wery smart man, Timothy. I may call you Timothy?"

"Of course. But I'm not so smart. The toilet tank is the first place every cop looks when he's tossing a place."

Pingle goes off, shaking his head in wonderment. He comes back a few moments later, using a hand towel to wipe a bottle of kirsch. He disappears

again and returns with two small glasses. He fills them to the rim with
the cherry brandy.

"This should warm you up," he says.

Cone looks at his glass. "This should combust me," he says. He raises
the drink. "*Prosit!*"

"*Prosit!*" his host responds, and they both take swallows. Not sips, but
gulps.

"Oh, boy," Cone says, shuddering. "Through the teeth and around the
gums; look out stomach, here she comes. Wow! That's something, that is."

"You said *Prosit*. You know German?"

"No," Cone says, "I only know *Prosit*."

Pingle smiles. "It's enough," he says. Then he sits silently, moving the
glass of brandy slowly between his blotched hands. Again, Cone gets the
impression of nervousness—or at least hesitancy.

"You wanted to talk to me about the Nu-Hope investigation, Mr. Pingle?"

"Well, in a way . . ." Pingle says in a low voice. "My son . . ." Then he
looks up from his brandy glass to stare directly at the detective. "Lester is
a good boy, and I love him wery much. He is our only child. We lost a
daughter to meningitis when she was wery young. Lester is all we have,
and we want his life to be happy. You can understand that, can't you?"

"Sure."

Pingle takes a deep breath. "You've got a closed mouth, Timothy? You
can keep it shut?"

"I don't blab," Cone says.

"Good. My son is married. I have two adorable grandchildren, God
bless them. But Lester's wife, my daughter-in-law, Sarah, she is a problem.
She suffers from shopitis. You know what shopitis is?"

"She likes to spend money?"

The old man claps a palm to his cheek. "Oy, does she like to spend
money! And I'm not talking about a dress now and then, a new lamp,
maybe a jar of caviar. I'm talking about a Rolls, a ski lodge in Vermont,
a condo on the Costa del Sol, a summer place in East Hampton, investments in Broadway shows that close the first night. That's the kind of
money I'm talking about. It is a sad situation."

"Why doesn't your son clamp down on her?"

Pingle shrugs. "He loves her, or thinks he does—which is the same
thing. Also, Lester is not the handsomest man in the world. But Sarah!
What a beauty that woman is! A lovely face and a gorgeous figure. Lester
is proud to be married to her. He will give her anything to keep her
happy. He makes a good dollar—I see to that—but he is barely keeping

his head above water. This is all confidential, you understand; I am trusting you."

Cone nods.

"So now Lester wants us to take on this Nu-Hope Fertility Clinic. He is insistent about it. I know my son, and this deal is wery important to him. Why this particular deal? Why is he perspiry over it? I don't know."

"And you want me to find out?" Cone asks.

"If you can," Ernest Pingle says humbly. "But only as part of your inwestigation into Nu-Hope. You'll find out the truth, won't you?"

"That's what I get paid for."

"Of course. I'm asking you this as a father: If you should find that my son is into something he shouldn't be in, will you tell me first? I have a lot of money, Timothy; more than I can ever spend in my lifetime. Lester will get most of it anyway, but maybe if he got some of it now, it might save him from some foolishness that would disgrace him, and me, and his mother, and the company I worked so hard to build. I don't want that."

Cone makes no reply, but finishes his brandy and rises. The old man gets the parka from the closet and stands on tiptoes to help the detective shrug into it.

"Sometimes I wonder if I know my son," Ernest Pingle says gloomily. "Sometimes I think he's a stranger."

"Thanks for the brandy," Cone says. "I really appreciated it."

"And you'll let me know if you find out anything bad about Lester? I'll take care of you."

"That won't be necessary," Cone says. "You're the client. Good night, Mr. Pingle. Better put your bottle back in the toilet tank."

He taxies back home, slumped in the corner of a ratty gypsy cab with no heater. But the radiators in the loft are hissing and thumping away like crazy, so that's a plus. The minus is that Cone is faced with the ancient axiom: "Beer, whiskey: rather risky. Whiskey, beer: have no fear." So he has a beer.

He gives Cleo a dish of fresh water and finds a slab of old lasagna in the fridge. Cleo takes it happily under the bathtub.

Cone tries to read more about human birth by syringe, birth by needle and microscope, birth in laboratory dishes. And the genesis of life kept frozen in cryogenic tanks. Who do all those rigid sperm, eggs, and embryos belong to? What parents? What families?

But his thoughts keep returning to Ernest Pingle, a nice old geezer troubled by his natural son, fearful that his heir may be acting stupidly because he's pussy-whipped by a beautiful and profligate wife.

Timothy Cone has no desire for children. No need or hope for immortality by siring a son who might beget a son, and that grandson beget, and that great grandson beget, and on and on, making the name Cone last for all time. Screw that.

"Cleo," the Wall Street dick says aloud, "when you're dead, you're fucking dead."

And he wonders if all the potential sons and daughters preserved in glass might not be better off remaining frozen forever.

The Nu-Hope Fertility Clinic occupies adjoining townhouses on East Seventy-first Street, a few doors east of Madison Avenue. The two buildings, designed by the same architect in 1928, are handsome structures of gray stone with red brick trim around bow windows on the second and third floors and mullioned windows on the top three floors.

The entrances are elegant, and the heavy front doors can be opened to the public only from within, after visitors are inspected and questioned through a grilled judas. Patients are admitted only to the west wing, where examination rooms, treatment facilities, X-ray machines, a pharmacy, and recovery rooms are located. The east wing contains executive offices, computerized record storage, and the sterile research laboratories.

Walls have been broken through between the two buildings on the third floor, but the steel door of this passageway is kept locked, and only executives and a few research staff members are provided with keys. Both structures are equipped with elevators, large enough to accommodate only one gurney at a time. Each wing has a wide staircase rising to the sixth floor.

Friday mornings are set aside for staff meetings for all Nu-Hope personnel who are not busy treating patients. These gatherings are generally held in the fourth-floor Doctors' Lounge in the west wing. It is a large, open chamber, painted a light green, looking somewhat like a factory canteen with steel tables, each set with four metal chairs. The walls are lined with machines (not coin-operated, but free) that vend everything from hot soup to plastic-wrapped wedges of apple pie.

On this particular Friday morning, the assembled staff listens to short speeches by the administrator who, as usual, urges frugality in the use of hospital supplies; by the head of data processing, who reels off the most recent statistics on new patients, sperm inseminations, and embryo transplants; and by Dr. Phoebe Trumball, who reports progress in determining the optimum time of ovulation by hormone analysis.

These mercifully brief reports concluded, Dr. Victor January stands to address his staff.

"If you can stay awake for just a few more minutes," he says, grinning at his audience, "I'd like to bring you up-to-date on the project I revealed to you a few months ago: the proposed expansion of Nu-Hope into a nationwide chain of fertility clinics. And eventually perhaps all over the world. I don't need to tell you what a marvelous opportunity this would be for all of us: an enormous increase in our caseload, our responsibilities and our income.

"I am pleased to say that the first step has been taken to make our dreams come true. We have approached Pingle Enterprises, a reputable venture capital firm, in an effort to obtain financing for our projected expansion. Their first reaction, I must tell you, was very favorable indeed. But naturally, before making a commitment, they want to know more about us.

"So I want to alert you that during the next few weeks you may see and meet several strangers wandering about the premises to size us up. These visitors will be attorneys, accountants, and private investigators from Haldering and Company, employed by Pingle Enterprises. Haldering is an organization specializing in corporate information and intelligence.

"Doctor Trumball and I will be able to handle most of their inquiries, I'm sure. But I want to make this perfectly clear: If you are questioned by any of the Haldering representatives, I want you to speak freely and answer their questions truthfully. If you have any criticism of our operation, you're completely at liberty to voice it. As far as I'm concerned, we have nothing to hide, and being absolutely honest is the best way to ensure that all our hopes become a reality. Thank you for your attention and cooperation. Now go back to work, you slaves!"

There is laughter and a spattering of applause. The lounge gradually empties out. Drs. January and Trumball, nodding and smiling at the staff, walk down to the third floor. January unlocks the steel door and they enter the east wing, going directly to his office. It is an austere, uncluttered room, with a private lavatory and small kitchen attached. He has a personal computer on his desk that can tap into the clinic's big mainframe.

They sprawl on a leather couch, look at each other.

"I think it went well," he says. "Don't you?"

"It went all right," Dr. Trumball acknowledges. "But you're taking a chance telling them they can shoot off their mouths to the Haldering people."

"What should I have told them—to clam up? That could put the quietus on the whole deal. We've got to project an open and honest image if this thing is to go through. Besides, none of these people know anything. I'm glad your crew wasn't there."

"They know enough to keep their mouths shut."

He stares at her. "Now," he says, somewhat bitterly.

"Yes," she admits. "Now."

"I hope so. How are we doing on the time, Phoebe?"

She glances at the chunky digital watch strapped tightly to her slender wrist. "It's getting close. Where are we going to meet him?"

"In Central Park. Same place. I hate this cloak-and-dagger stuff."

She shrugs. "It's got to be done," she says stonily. "He explained why we couldn't get the grant. We were such innocents when we filed. We didn't even consider the political implications. We're lucky they're doing it this way. Proves they're definitely interested."

"I guess so," January says fretfully. "Well, let's get going. It's a nice day; we'll walk over. Meet you downstairs."

The city sparkles. Light dances in spins and spirals like a giant bejeweled whirligig. The sun is a diamond, sky turquoise, pearls of tiny clouds, and all of it scintillant. The air itself seems alive and dazzling. This brilliant world promises hope and conquest.

Victor January glances at the woman striding along at his side. She too brims with purpose and resolve.

Phoebe Trumball is a tall woman, lean and hard: a greyhound look, as swift and keen. She is as slender as he, and as pale. They could be brother and sister, these two, sharing a dancer's grace. Her face is long, with wedge of chin, scimitar nose, and widely spaced dark eyes that look out at life with courage and contempt.

"One of these days I'm going to marry you," he says, and she smiles and lets her swinging hand touch his knuckles.

"Tonight?" she asks.

"No," he says. "Regretfully, no. Martha has family in from out of town. We're feeding them before the theater. Some silly musical that's been running for centuries. I've got to play the faithful hubby."

"All right," she says equably. "I'm not going to pout and stamp my foot."

"You never have," he says. "You don't even make me feel guilty."

"You?" she hoots. "Guilty? That'll be the day!"

And they both laugh.

They find their man on the same park bench where they met before, on a narrow path northwest of the zoo. There are pedestrians, joggers, babies being pushed in prams, lovers, a professional dog-walker with six hounds on tangled leashes, and one old woman trying to sell licorice strips. But the man they seek sits quietly and alone on a slatted bench, motionless and serene.

He has introduced himself as J. Roger Gibby, and that is the name on the identification he offered, along with his photograph. They checked with his directorate, of course, and were told he was a bona fide employee. But January and Trumball know that could be a cover. J. Roger Gibby could be working for one of a dozen other agencies.

He is well and strongly built, not so dapper as to be vulgar, but he shrieks with understated elegance. It is his calm, gentle manner, the doctors agree, that convinces them of his probity. That and his deep gazelle eyes that seem to have seen everything and are still ready to understand and forgive.

He does not stand when they approach, nor offer to shake hands. They sit together on his right, a little removed, and when any of the three speaks, it is with a thousand-yard stare directly ahead.

"Well . . ." Mr. Gibby says, "how did it go?"

January gives a brief précis of their presentation to Pingle Enterprises. Trumball adds that Haldering & Co. has been retained to investigate the clinic.

"Haldering?" Gibby says. His voice is velvet. "I know them. Hiram Haldering is an ex–FBI man. If there are any problems, I'm sure he'll be amenable to reason. During your discussion with the Pingles, was anything said about how the financing would be structured?"

"No," January says, "we didn't get into that."

"We would prefer a public limited partnership," Gibby says. "We can guarantee it would be totally subscribed. By our friends, of course. A private offering might prove more difficult, as would a bank line of credit. But first things first: The most important step right now is to get you approved by Pingle. I assure you the funding is there; it's just a question of getting it funneled through legitimate sources so we're completely out of the picture. Meanwhile your research is continuing?"

"As much as we can," Trumball says. "The expenses are horrendous. Do you know what a healthy rhesus monkey costs, or a mature, virile chimp?"

"I can imagine," Gibby says with a small smile, "although I haven't bought any lately."

"We may require some recombinant-DNA workups," Trumball says. "I hope you're aware of that."

"We are indeed, but genetic engineering is not your responsibility. As I told you, this project is being pursued on a number of fronts. Eventually it will all come together."

"You're very optimistic, professor," January says.

"I believe that in the world of science, if it can be done, it will be done."

"And I believe," January adds, "that a life devoted to science is a life devoted to art. Are you predicting a masterpiece?"

"That's exactly what I'm predicting," Gibby says with his sweet smile. "Other people are working toward the same goal, you know. I'm sure you realize the consequences if their masterpiece is created before ours."

They are silent then, staring out at skeleton trees sharp against a pellucid sky. All is clear, clean. It seems a washed world in late October, the final glimpse of bright before the darkness of winter.

"One other thing," J. Roger Gibby says. "Did the Pingles tell you who Haldering is sending to investigate?"

"They mentioned a man named Timothy Cone," January says. "Apparently he is not an attorney or an accountant. Just an investigator. A detective, I suppose you could call him. I promised complete cooperation."

"Timothy Cone," Gibby repeats. "A detective. Yes, by all means cooperate with him. Meanwhile I'll do a little detecting on my own. I must leave now. Please wait a few minutes before you depart. I'll be in touch through the usual channel. Nice to see you again. Be well."

He rises and moves slowly away. The two doctors turn their heads to watch him go.

"Do you trust him?" January says.

"Do we have a choice?" Phoebe Trumball asks.

"No," he says, sighing, "I guess not. But he's so damned smooth, it worries me. He acts as if every problem can be solved."

"Don't you believe that?" she demands. "If not, we never should have started this thing in the first place."

"I believe," January says hastily. "Because I believe in you."

She glances at him with an amused smile. "But you've got to go to the theater tonight with your wife."

"Yes," he says, "I do."

"Tomorrow?"

"Oh God, yes!" he cries. "Definitely tomorrow!"

Cone arrives at his office at nine-thirty—early for him—and over coffee and a bagel begins reviewing the legal PIE on Nu-Hope. Nothing in the report alerts him. Nu-Hope is legally chartered and licensed. No tax problems. No liens or lawsuits. No record of hearings before medical boards. The PIE goes into some detail on Nu-Hope's past history as an abortion clinic. It was a legal enterprise, apparently efficiently run, with no history of malpractice suits.

The changeover from abortion to fertility clinic occurred four years ago after continued harassment of patients by antiabortion groups severely interrupted business. Personal threats against January and his staff had been reported to law enforcement agencies.

Nu-Hope is totally owned by Dr. January, although he has established a very generous pension, retirement, and profit-sharing plan for his employees. In brief, the clinic appears to be a legitimate, successful enterprise, much admired in the medical community for its profits, high pregnancy rate, and the quality of its research department, headed by Dr. Phoebe Trumball.

Cone tosses the report aside and pulls his phone forward. He calls Neal Davenport, the NYPD detective he met on the Clovis swindle. It takes three calls to locate the city dick, but he finally comes on the phone.

"Timothy Cone?" he says. "The financial Sherlock and Wall Street whiz? How're you doing, buster?"

"Surviving. And you?"

"Likewise. How did you like those newspaper stories on the Clovis scam? Haldering got a nice plug—right?"

"Right," Cone says. "The old man was flying."

"And that's why you're calling—to thank me. Correct?"

"Not exactly."

Davenport laughs. "I didn't think so. What do you want?"

"I got two names for you. I thought you might run them through Records and see if either of them has a sheet."

"Now why should I do that?"

"Just for the fun of it."

"Kid, you've got chutzpah. Who are these people?"

"A couple of doctors. They run a fertility clinic on the Upper East Side."

"Fertility clinic? What the hell's that?"

"They get women pregnant."

"I used to do that," Davenport says, "but not recently. What's Haldering's interest in a fertility clinic?"

"We're checking them out for a venture capital outfit. The clinic wants to go national."

"All right," the NYPD man says, sighing. "I guess I owe you one. Give me the names and I'll see if we've got anything on them."

Cone spells out the names of Drs. Victor January and Phoebe Trumball.

"Okay," Davenport says, "I'll check and get back to you."

"Today?"

"Don't push your luck, sonny boy. This is going to cost you a couple of belts in that Garden of Delights you call home."

"Anytime," Cone says, and they hang up.

He broods a few moments, then wanders down the corridor to the office of Sidney Apicella, chief of Haldering's CPAs. As usual Sid is furiously rubbing his bugle when Cone enters.

"Leave it alone, Sid," Timothy advises. "You're just going to irritate it more."

"It irritates me," Apicella grumbles, "so why shouldn't I irritate it. If you're looking for the accounting PIE on the Nu-Hope Clinic, it's not completed yet. You'll get a copy when it is. Now leave me alone; I've got work to do."

"This isn't about Nu-Hope," Cone says. "Can you get me a financial rundown on Lester Pingle?"

Apicella looks at him with astonishment. "Since when do we investigate clients? Pingle Enterprises is in the black; we checked them out before we took them on."

"I know," Cone says patiently. "It's not the company I'm interested in; it's Lester, the junior partner. I want to know his cash assets, liabilities, and investments. You can find out."

"My God, Tim," Sid says, groaning, "that'll be a day's work—and a pain in the ass."

"Sure it is," Cone agrees cheerfully. "So is everything else around this joint. Let me know when you've got some numbers. And stop massaging your schnozz. You know, W. C. Fields had the same thing, and he used Allen's Foot Ease on it."

"No kidding?" Apicella says, interested. "You really think it'll help?"

"It couldn't hurt."

Cone goes back to his office, calls a local deli and orders a cheeseburger, fries, a dill pickle, and a cold can of Black Label Light.

On a sloppy day like this, everyone is eating in, so it's almost an hour before his lunch is delivered. Meanwhile he hacks away at the weekly progress report Samantha Whatley demands of all her detectives. That woman is a holy terror, Cone decides, and pads his expense account outrageously.

After finishing his lunch he types up the progress report on the old Remington standard that's been allotted to him. The keys haven't been cleaned in years, and all his two-finger typing comes out with the o's, p's, a's and e's filled in. Cone's finished manuscript looks like the Rosetta stone.

He takes it down to Samantha's office, hoping they'll have a chance to exchange intimate insults, but she's not in. So he flips his report onto her desk and wonders if he should go home. He's not doing any good sitting at his desk, staring at the walls. At least, back in his loft, he can read more of the books on artificial birth and discuss original sin with Cleo.

It's almost two-thirty in the afternoon, and he's preparing to make his break when the receptionist calls and tells him Detective Davenport is there and wants to see him.

"Yeah," Cone says, "send him in."

Neal K. Davenport, a big, overweight guy, shoves into Cone's office, wearing a soaked raincoat, a plastic cover on his fedora, and carrying a dripping umbrella that he props in a corner, letting it piddle on the floor.

"How come you're not out detecting?" he says. "A glorious day like this. You got anything medicinal? I think I'm coming down with something."

"Terminal thirst?" Timothy says. "I haven't got a drop, but maybe I can find something. Wait a minute."

"I'm not going anywhere," the cop says. "I just got here."

Cone goes down the corridor to Sol Faber's office. Sol isn't in, but Cone knows he keeps a pint of gin in the bottom drawer of his desk, which Cone finds, half empty. He takes it and leaves a note scrawled on Sol's desk calendar:"I lifted your jug. The Masked Marvel."

He stops at the water cooler to pull out two paper cups, then goes back to his office. Davenport has taken off his raincoat and condomed hat, and is sitting placidly in one of the uncomfortable office chairs, unwrapping a fresh stick of Juicy Fruit. He looks at the paper cups and the half-filled pint of gin.

"Bless you, my son," he says. "May your tribe increase. I never drink gin except on the third Tuesday of every month, but in this case I'll make an exception."

Cone closes the door and fills their cups. They're little triangular dunce caps—you can't set them down—so both men hold their drinks, sipping as they talk.

"Nice of you to stop by," the Wall Street dick says. "I suppose you were out for a stroll on this pleasant afternoon and just found yourself in the neighborhood."

"Uh-huh," Davenport says, drinking and chomping on his wad of chewing gum. "Something like that. You know those two names you gave me this morning? The doctors? Well, they're clean. We've got nothing on them."

"And you waded through muck and mire just to tell me that? Come on!"

"Ordinarily," the city dick says, "I wouldn't have been in any hurry to check out those names. Just something to do when I got around to it. I mean I got a full plate. You can understand that, can't you?"

"Sure. So why all the speed?"

"Funny story. Not funny ha-ha, but definitely oddball. I work out of an office with another guy, a dick too. Our desks butt up against each other. He's a nice guy, Nick Galanis, a Greek. A very sharp eye. He always smells of garlic, but that's neither here nor there. Anyway, this morning he's sitting there and he hears me on the phone repeat those two names you gave me: Doctor Victor January and Doctor Phoebe Trumball. When I hang up, he wants to know what that was all about. I tell him a guy I know wants those two people checked out— and what's it to him."

Davenport pauses to reach across the desk for the gin bottle.

"Finish it," Cone says. "The booze and your story."

"All right," the cop says, "don't mind if I do."

He empties the bottle and shakes it carefully to get the last few drops.

"Well, here's what happened: A few months ago, Nick caught a squeal from the Fulton Fish Market. You know those guys down there go to work like at two in the morning. There's a Volkswagen parked right in front of a loading dock. So the first guy to show up for work looks in and sees a Caucasian male in the driver's seat with half his head blown away. They call us, and Nick Galanis goes down to take a look.

"It turns out the clunk's name is Harold Besant. That's the name on his driver's license, and that's who the Volkswagen is registered to. There's a Charter thirty-eight Special on the seat to his right, like it's fallen from his hand. One round fired. The slug that killed Besant went into his right temple and took a lot of his brains with it when it came out. Powder burns around the entrance wound. The only prints on the gun were Besant's. So what does that tell you?"

"Suicide," Cone says.

"Sure it was suicide," Davenport says, almost angrily.

"Open and shut. But why did he pick the Fulton Fish Market? Who the hell knows? But Nick Galanis gets a hair up his ass. You know how you feel when a case is so neat and clean; you begin to wonder if you might be missing something. So Nick starts snooping, mostly on his own time. He finds out the dead guy was a research assistant at the Nu-Hope Fertility Clinic."

"Oh-ho," Cone says.

"Yeah oh-ho. That's why Nick perked up his ears when he heard me repeat those names. He had questioned Doctor January and Doctor Trumball. They claimed the guy had been depressed lately, and his fellow workers agreed he'd been in a down mood."

"Did you trace the gun?"

"Of course we traced the gun. It wasn't registered. I mean Besant had no permit. The piece was part of a shipment swiped from a Jersey warehouse. It was probably sold on the street."

"Did Besant leave a suicide note?"

"No, but that doesn't necessarily mean anything. He could have done it on the spur of the moment. Entrance wound in the right temple with powder burns. Gun found on the seat by his right hand. No prints on the

gun but his. So where does that leave Detective Nick Galanis? In no-
wheresville—right? He figures he's making a big something out of nothing. The file is closed as an apparent suicide. The ME says it was, so the
Department's home free and clear."

"You should have been an actor," Cone says. "You're leading up to your
great dramatic moment—I can feel it coming."

"Yeah," Davenport says, grinning, "something like that. This Harold
Besant's closest relative is an uncle who's in the merchant marine, and he
was on the other side of the world when Harold shuffled off this mortal
coil. About a month ago, the uncle gets back to New York and looks up
Nick Galanis, wanting to know how his nephew died. Nick tells him, and
the uncle says no way; it was im-fucking-possible. You know why?"

"I'll bite. Why?"

"Because, according to the uncle, Harold Besant was left-handed."

"Son of a bitch," Timothy Cone says.

Whatley and Cone are lounging in Sam's ruffled apartment. They've had a
fast dinner of grilled franks, baked beans, and cold sauerkraut, washed
down with bottles of Dark Heineken. While she stacks the dishes in her
little kitchen—trim as a ship's galley—Cone tells her about the books he's
been reading on artificial insemination, in vitro fertilization, and embryo
transfer.

"Keep talking," Sam says, "but pick up a dish towel. I'll wash and you
wipe."

He complies and goes on describing the laboratory technique for conception without intercourse.

"No sweat," he says, "and no grunting. No 'Was it as good for you as
it was for me?' A lot of single women are doing it. Interested?"

"No, thanks," she says, swabbing out the sink. "The patter of tiny feet
doesn't interest me. Besides, I've had all my plumbing excavated; I told
you that."

"You could always adopt."

"Who?" she asks. "You?"

He finishes the last plate, and she takes the damp towel from him and
hangs it away carefully to dry.

"And now," she says, "the surprise."

"Oh, God," he says. "You're sending me home?"

"Not yet. You know what negus is?"

"Negus? Never heard of it."

"Red wine, hot water, sugar, lemon juice, and cinnamon. I came across
the recipe in an old cookbook and stirred up a batch. Want to try it?"

"Sure," he says bravely. "Sounds like it'll go great with beans and sauerkraut."

She heats the negus in a saucepan until it begins to bubble. Then she pours it into thick mugs and adds a sprinkling of nutmeg.

"Go ahead," she commands. "Try it."

He sips cautiously. "Hey! Not bad."

"Not bad, you asshole? It's delicious."

"It's okay. A great winter drink. It warms the heartles of my cock."

"You're disgusting," she says, smiling. "I'm going to trade you in for a new model."

"Nah," he says. "You get used to an old clunker, and you never want to scrap it."

They take their mugs of hot negus into the living room and sprawl on one of the rag rugs.

"You know," Sam says, "you're the most unromantic man I've ever met. But while you were talking about those test-tube babies made in the lab, I got the feeling that you don't really approve."

"Sharp lady," he says, blowing on his drink to cool it. "To tell you the truth, I'm not sure how I feel about it. I understand that it's a boon for couples who can't have kids naturally. But something about the whole idea turns me off. It's so goddamned mechanical. Like making sausages or stamping out widgets. How do you feel about it?"

Whatley shrugs. "I guess if women want kids so bad they'll go through all that, then more power to them. It's legal, isn't it?"

"I guess so. Nu-Hope isn't breaking any laws that I know of." He pauses a moment, wondering if he should tell her about that questionable suicide of a research assistant. He decides to keep his mouth shut— about that and Ernest Pingle's fears for his son.

"You're holding out on me again, aren't you?" Sam says, looking at him closely. "You get a thousand-yard stare in your eyes, and I know something is going on in that tiny, tiny brain of yours."

"Nah," Cone says. "I'm just brooding about babies coming off a kind of assembly line. What a weird world it is."

The empty mugs are set aside.

"Bed?" she asks.

"I like it right here."

"Suits me," she says. "You don't know what a pleasure it is not to have the damned cat biting my toes."

He watches her undress, admiring the sharp-edged body, hard flanks, the twist of muscle and tendon. When she raises her arms to let down her long auburn hair, he sees the play of soft light on dark skin, warm shadows. Her body is as tight and bony as his, but the curves of hip, waist, and back are more elegant, smoothly glossed.

"At least," she says throatily, "take off your stupid work shoes."

He undresses quickly.

Their lovemaking, as usual, has a desperation about it, but never more than that night. Their coupling is a punishing duet, played furioso. They seem determined to rend walls of flesh and penetrate to a bliss that might consume them both. Perhaps their tumultuous striving springs from their talk of a brave new world with life manufactured in a sterile lab, all the ecstasy and pain of creation banished forever, along with joy and suffering, grief and laughter.

Their violence could have been a protest. Or it could have been an act of affirmation, asserting their humanness.

Whatever, it is one hell of a bang.

2

Timothy Cone figures he could call the Nu-Hope Clinic and tell them he's coming up to make a white-glove inspection. But the smart way to do it, he reckons, is to waltz in unexpectedly before they have a chance to sweep dirt under the rug or pop a skeleton into a closet.

He gets up to East Seventy-first Street about three o'clock on a dull, grimy day, a smell of snow in the air, and stands across the street a few minutes eyeballing the two townhouses. They look solid, dignified, well maintained. There are big pots of ivy outside, still green, and all the windows are sparkling.

He dodges through traffic and crosses to the east wing, rings the bell beside the heavy front door. The judas is opened almost immediately; Cone can see only the eyes and white cap of what appears to be an extremely short nurse. He holds up his identification card for inspection.

"Timothy Cone," he says. "From Haldering and Company. I'd like to see Doctor Victor January."

"Just a moment, please, sir," she chirps, and the judas is closed.

He waits patiently, stamping his feet a bit to chase the chill. It is almost three minutes before the door is swung open by a tall woman in a light-green lab coat. She holds out her hand, smiling.

"I'm Doctor Phoebe Trumball," she says. "Do come in."

Her handclasp is hard and dry.

"Doctor January is busy with a patient," she explains, "but he'll be able to join us shortly. Meanwhile, may I give you the fifty-cent tour?"

"Sure," Cone says. "I guess you were expecting me sooner or later."

"Better sooner," she says almost gaily. "Now let me put away your coat and we'll get started. I suppose you'll want to see everything. I think it best if we begin next door in the patients' wing. That's really where most of our work is done."

She takes him up to the third floor, chattering on about the architect of the townhouses and how originally they were private residences of two brothers in marine insurance. Both of them died on the *Morro Castle*.

"Which," Dr. Trumball says, "is rather ironic—don't you think?"

"Yeah," Cone says.

She reminds him a lot of Samantha. The two women have an attractive angularity and bold features. But Sam is dark, and you can read everything she feels in her eyes. Phoebe Trumball is pale and all closed in. Cone bets she's not usually so chatty. Maybe not devious, he acknowledges, but calculating.

They walk through the third-floor passageway to the west wing. Cone notes the doctor unlocking the door.

"Security," Trumball explains. "Our research labs in the east wing are sterile and off-limits to patients."

"What's in the labs?"

"You'll see them. That's where the embryos are formed. And our sperm, egg, and embryo banks. Temperature control is very important."

"Listen," Cone says, unable to resist. "I've been doing some reading about artificial insemination, and I have a question, a silly one, but it's been nagging at me. When a guy sells his sperm—well, what do you collect it in?"

Dr. Trumball laughs. "Believe it or not," she says, "we use empty baby food jars. Sterilized, of course."

They go on a whirlwind tour of the west wing, with Trumball introducing staff and answering questions before Cone asks them. She makes certain he sees it all, except the rooms where patients are being treated. He is shown offices, labs, lavatories, X-ray rooms, examination rooms, the pharmacy, recovery rooms, and the Doctors' Lounge, where they pause at one of the steel tables and have a black coffee from one of the vending machines.

"Well," Trumball says, "what do you think so far?"

"Impressive," he says honestly. "Everything clean and neat. Looks like you run a tight ship."

"We try." She looks down at her coffee cup. "Something I haven't mentioned. . . . You must realize, Mr. Cone, that most of the women and couples who come to us are under a great deal of emotional stress. They are frantic to have children. Occasionally they cause some unpleasant scenes when we are not able to help them on the first try. I just thought I'd mention it."

Cone nods. "Do you have children, doctor?"

"No," she says. "Finished your coffee? Now let me show you around the east wing. I'm sure Doctor January will be with us soon."

Back they go through that third-floor passageway. As Trumball is unlocking the door, Timothy raps on it.

"Steel," he says. "Expecting a terrorist attack?"

"Oh, no," she says, laughing, "nothing like that. Just super security."

He has the feeling that she's laughed more in the last hour than she has in the past month. This is not, he decides, a normally laughing woman. So she's nervous about passing the Haldering inspection. Which is normal. But still . . .

In the east wing, Cone peers into executive offices, the main computer room, a few open labs. One locked chamber has a thick plate glass window fronting on the corridor. He sees busy employees bending over microscopes or using stainless steel machines he can't identify. All the workers are swaddled in wrinkled green trousers and jackets, with caps that cover their hair. Some are wearing surgical masks.

"Your research lab?" he asks.

"One of them," Dr. Trumball says shortly. "We have another where you have to enter through a special air lock. I'd invite you in, but decontamination takes at least twenty minutes, including a shower. The air inside is specially filtered."

"I'll skip," Cone says.

"Don't blame you," she says. "I rarely go in there myself. It's easier to use the intercom to check on what's going on."

He finds it difficult to move away from that plate glass window. He watches the activity inside. Workers in their wrinkled green uniforms. Glittering machines. Huge tanks that steam when the lids are lifted. Computer monitors flickering. Tapes whirling around and around. A factory.

"Making babies," the Wall Street dick says.

"Trying to," Dr. Trumball says. "That's what we're here for."

"Hello, there!" Dr. Victor January carols, coming up with hand outstretched to Cone. "Sorry I'm late. A small crisis. Very small, thank God! I'm January, and you must be Timothy Cone from Haldering. Happy to meet you. Phoebe been taking care of you, has she? The grand tour?"

Cone nods, shaking the soft, slender hand. This guy, he immediately decides, is Mr. Charm himself. It comes out his pores, with a deliberate theatricality that mocks itself. "Look, I'm putting on an act. You know it and I know it. But it's fun, isn't it, and no one's getting hurt."

January herds them into his private office and closes the door. He gets them seated in directors' chairs and then flops into his own swivel chair behind the big, cluttered desk. The chair is covered with zebra skin. Very dramatic.

"All right," he says, grinning fiercely, "let's have your questions. I'm sure you've got a hundred."

"No," Cone says, "not really. I did have some, but Doctor Trumball answered them. There is just one thing I'd like to know: Where do you get your customers?"

January gives him a roguish smile. "Customers? Well, yes, you're right. We prefer to call them patients or clients—but who's fooling whom? They *are* customers. Let me get you the latest numbers."

He leans forward, punches keys on the computer terminal on his desk, peers at the screen.

"As of last week," he reports, "approximately eighty-seven percent of our patients were referrals from other doctors, clinics, and hospitals. About ten percent came in on recommendations of other patients. The rest are what we call walk-in trade. Women or couples who have read about us or have seen me on TV talk shows. Okay?"

"Sure," Cone says. "You guarantee results?"

"Of course not," Trumball says rather crossly. "How could we possibly do that? Before we accept a patient, she—or she and her husband—go through an hour-long orientation lecture. We make certain they fully understand what's involved. And then they sign a five-page legal release that spells out in exact detail what we hope to do and what they can expect. But no guarantees."

"We've been lucky," Dr. January says, rapping the wooden top of his desk. "No lawsuits—so far. We really never promise more than we can deliver. This is not an exact science, Mr. Cone. And lots of things can go wrong. Gradually we're improving our pregnancy rate, but it's still a chancy proposition. We make no secret of that, and especially not to our patients. We make certain they know the odds."

Cone reflects what a nice, amiable gathering this is, all of them sitting about a warm office on a biting November afternoon, smiling at each other. He decides to shake them up.

"A guy named Harold Besant," he says casually. "He used to work for you. Research assistant. A couple of months ago he blew his brains out down at the Fulton Fish Market."

If he expects to rock them he's out of luck. Their faces become suitably grave, their expression of sorrow suitably solemn.

"A terrible tragedy," Dr. January says.

"Dreadful," Dr. Trumball says. "The poor boy. We knew he was upset. Spells of silence. Once a horrible fit of weeping—and he couldn't, or wouldn't, give a reason for it."

"All the symptoms of depression," January says mournfully. "We tried to get him to our resident shrink, but he refused. I blame myself; I should have insisted."

"It wasn't your fault, Victor," Phoebe Trumball says.

"Did he have any close friends?" Cone asks. "Anyone on your staff?"

"No," Trumball says, "and I think that was part of his problem. We're really a family here, but he was never really a part of it. Was he, Victor?"

"No," January says. "The man was an outsider, a loner. And very talented. Too bad."

Their sadness seems genuine enough, but Cone, that cranky, misanthropic man, can't totally buy it. Maybe because January is everything Cone is not: handsome, impeccably dressed, with a magnetic appeal.

But to Cone, his gestures are too flamboyant, his smiles too wide, the waves in his blond hair too elaborate. Look for sincerity, Cone decides, and you find greasepaint.

"Are you married, Doctor January?" he asks suddenly.

"I am indeed," the man says promptly. "With two marvelous bambinos. I have their photos in my wallet—but I'll spare you that!"

Everyone laughs politely and the Wall Street dick stands up.

"Thanks for your help, folks," he says. "At the moment I can't think of anything else I need. But I may give you a call or stop by again. Okay?"

"Of course," January says, with a billowy wave of his hand. "We're anxious to get this thing approved, and we're happy to cooperate in any way we can. Our staff has been instructed to answer all your questions fully to the best of their ability. We have nothing to hide."

"Glad to hear it," Cone says, shakes hands with January and follows Phoebe Trumball down to the street floor, where he reclaims his parka. He shakes hands with her and walks out into a gloomy evening, the sky paved with slate and a mean wind gusting. He pulls his hood over his spiky hair, shoves his hands into fleece-lined pockets, and tramps over to Park Avenue.

Then he stops, reflects a moment, and retraces his steps. He takes up station across the street from the Nu-Hope Fertility Clinic. It's a few minutes after five o'clock, and he decides to give it an hour. If nothing happens by six, he'll split and go home. He pounds up and down the block to keep the circulation going.

It's almost six o'clock before January and Trumball come out. They're hatless, and Cone spots them immediately: tall, willowy blonds walking

with a jaunty grace. Timothy trudges behind them. After a while he begins
to wonder if they're heading for the South Bronx. But on Eighty-third
Street they turn eastward. And just before they come to Third Avenue,
they scurry up the steps of a nicely restored brownstone.

Cone waits a few minutes and then climbs the stairs and inspects the
names listed on the brass bell plate. Dr. P. Trumball occupies Apartment
4-B.

He wanders away. The two doctors could be having a business meeting.
It could be a cocktail party with Dr. January's wife present. It could be—

Ah, shit. Cone knows what it is.

"Big deal," he says aloud, and a bag lady mooching past him turns
sharply and snarls, "Go fuck yourself."

"Don't think I haven't tried," he yells after her.

The next morning Cone gets to work about a half hour late—which is as
close to promptitude as he can come—and finds a note on his desk to call
Lester Pingle. He lights his third cigarette of the day while he ponders
what the guy might want. He decides it will be a stern demand to hurry
up the Nu-Hope investigation.

But when Lester answers the phone, he is all sweetness and light.

"Thank you for calling back," he says. "I understand you're Haldering's
investigator on the Nu-Hope Fertility Clinic deal."

"That's right."

"I was hoping we could get together for a few minutes. There are
certain factors involved I think you should be aware of."

"Like what?"

"Well, that's what I wanted to talk to you about," Lester says, "but not
on the phone."

"Okay. You want me to come to your office?"

"No, no," Pingle says hastily. "This is, uh, confidential. You know
where Trinity Church is?"

"Sure."

"Can you meet me outside the main entrance in, say, twenty minutes?"

"I'll be there," Cone says. "How will I know you?"

"I'm wearing a black overcoat with a fur collar. And a black bowler."

"And I'll be wearing an olive-drab parka," Cone says. "No bowler."

Pingle laughs somewhat nervously and hangs up.

Timothy takes his time and ambles down Broadway to Wall Street,
pausing to look idly in shop windows. When he gets to Trinity, he sees a
tall gink in black overcoat and derby pacing back and forth in front of
the church. Cone lights a Camel before he goes up to him.

"Lester Pingle?" he says loudly.

The guy jumps like he's been goosed with an icicle, then whirls around. "Yes," he says, "yes, that's right. You're from Haldering?"

"Uh-huh. Timothy Cone. Want to see my ID?"

"No, no," Pingle says, "that won't be necessary. I just thought I'd tell you what's on my mind so you'll know what's involved."

Cone nods.

"We can just walk up and down here for a few minutes. I'd have asked you to the office, but the walls have ears."

"People keep saying that, but I've never seen a wall with ears. Although potatoes have eyes."

Pingle looks at him doubtfully, trying to decide if Cone is making a joke or is simply demented. The detective's bland expression gives him no clue.

Cone notices that although it's a nippy day, Lester's pale face is sheened with sweat.

They tramp up and down before Trinity Church as Lester launches into a spluttering monologue. Hiring Haldering was his father's idea. Lester, in his own mind, is certain that the Nu-Hope deal is clean and a potential moneymaker.

"It rates high when you consider the risk-benefit factor," he says.

The stumbling block is Ernest Pingle. Lester's father is getting on in years, and he's not keeping up so well, but without his approval, the deal is dead.

"So?" Cone says. "What do you want me to do about it?"

Well, Pingle says wiping a palm across his forehead, his father trusts Haldering because of their role in uncovering the Clovis swindle. And Lester just wanted Cone to know how hidebound his father has become, and how he seems to be prejudiced against Nu-Hope. It would be a personal favor to Lester if Cone would okay Nu-Hope as soon as possible. In that event, there would be more assignments for Haldering; Lester would see to that.

"We call them as we see them," Timothy Cone tells him.

"Of course," Pingle says, "but everyone who's looked into Nu-Hope agrees it's a sweet piece of business, so there's really no reason to stall."

"I'm not stalling," Cone says stonily. "I've just started my investigation."

Then, looking straight ahead, Lester Pingle says in a low voice: "You scratch my back, I'll scratch yours. I want this Nu-Hope deal. You okay it and there's a nice piece of change in it for you."

"Yeah?" Cone says. "How much?"

"How does five thousand sound to you?"

"Doesn't sound like much," Cone says. "This could mean millions for Pingle Enterprises."

"Ten," Pingle says desperately, still not looking at the detective. "Ten thousand. Okay?"

"No, thanks."

"Why are you so stubborn?" Lester cries.

"I work at it," Cone says and walks away.

He doesn't look back, which is a mistake. If he had, he'd have noted that Lester doesn't leave. He continues his parade back and forth in front of Trinity. In a few moments a man comes out of the church. He's wearing a herringbone tweed topcoat and a green felt fedora with a clump of bright feathers in the band.

Pingle is surprised. "You were inside the church, Martin?"

"Why not? I'm entitled. Besides, I wanted to get a look at Cone. Scruffy character, isn't he?"

Three months previously, when they first met, the barrel-chested man had introduced himself simply as Martin. Lester Pingle didn't know if it was Martin Something or Something Martin. Later, doing some investigating of his own, he learned it was Martin Gardow. He was chief of special projects for one of the country's largest conglomerates, ruled by a tyrant whom Wall Street insiders called Mr. D.

"How did it go?" Martin asks.

"It didn't," Lester Pingle says miserably. "He turned down the offer of more jobs. He turned down the ten thousand."

"You think he wants more?"

"No. I just don't think he can be bought."

"Don't tell that to Mr. D.," Gardow says with his mirthless smile. "He believes that every man has his price. But the price doesn't necessarily have to be in dollars. Our contact at Nu-Hope tells us that Cone is very smart, very inquisitive, and very persistent. We'll just have to find out what his price is."

"No violence," Pingle says, wiping the sweat from his forehead again. "I hate violence."

Martin turns to look at him. "I know you do, Lester," he says softly.

Then the two men separate, walking off in opposite directions. By that time, Cone is back at Haldering's. He goes directly to Sam's office.

"I want to tell you something," he says when she looks up. "I'll put it on paper, but I want you to know—just in case he decides to play rough."

"What the hell are you talking about?"

He tells her about Lester's proffered bribes.

"Son of a bitch," Sam says thoughtfully. "Ten thousand? Weren't you tempted?"

"Nah," he says. "My heart is pure."

"And your disposition is rancid. I better tell H.H. about this."

"No," he says quickly, "don't do that."

"Why not?"

He looks at her. "Because after striking out with me, Lester will probably try to get to Hiram himself. I want to find out just how anxious he is to seal the Nu-Hope deal."

"Jesus Christ," Sam says. "What's going on here?"

"Beats the shit out of me," he says. "I can't get a handle on the thing."

He's still brooding an hour later when his phone rings.

"Timothy Cone?"

"Yeah. Who's this?"

"Detective Nick Galanis, NYPD. I work with Neal Davenport. He says he mentioned me."

"Sure he did. What can I do for you?"

"Neal says you're investigating the Nu-Hope Clinic. Right?"

"Yeah. For a proposed expansion deal. They want to become a chain. Like fast-food joints or something."

"And he told you about Harold Besant? The alleged suicide?"

"He told me."

"Look, Cone, I had to drop that thing after the ME's report. Also, there was too much new stuff coming along. You can understand that, can't you?"

"Sure."

"But the damned thing still bugs me. I got the feeling someone's jerking us around, and I don't like it. Anyway, while you're looking into Nu-Hope, I wish you'd ask a few questions about Besant."

"I already have. The two top doctors up there tell me he was depressed."

"Yeah," Nick Galanis says, "that's what they told me, too. Did you talk to Jessie Scotto?"

"Jessie Scotto? No. Who she?"

"Works at Nu-Hope. A nurse in the west wing. She was Harold Besant's girlfriend. As a matter of fact, they were living together on the Upper West Side. I questioned her right after Besant's death, but she was shook and I got nothing from her. Maybe I'm blowing smoke, but I thought she was scared shitless and just wasn't talking. But that was like two months ago, and maybe she's calmed down by now. I'd appreciate it if you'd talk to her and see what you can get—if anything. Neal says you're a bulldog, so give it a try. That so-called suicide is still on my brain. I think about it every day."

"Well, yeah," Cone says, "I can do that. Jessie Scotto? What kind of a woman is she?"

"A little mouse," Detective Galanis says. "Don't lean on her or she'll fold. Just play the sympathetic daddy and maybe she'll talk."

"All right," Cone says. "Thanks for the tip."

"You'll let me know?"

"Of course."

It's an hour after he hangs up that Cone remembers the doctors had told him that Harold Besant had no close friends on the staff.

The black Cadillac de Ville is parked in a No Parking zone just north of Broome Street. Standing alongside is one of the biggest guys Cone has ever seen: a young hulk who looks like he's wearing football pads under his gray whip-cord jacket. As Cone goes by on his way to work, the monster steps in front of him.

"Mr. Timothy Cone?" he asks pleasantly.

Cone looks up at him. About six-feet-six, he figures, at least 280, with a neck as wide as the detective's thigh. He looks as if he's got the muscle to toss Timothy over to Lafayette Street if the mood takes him.

"Yeah, I'm Cone. Who are you?"

His question is ignored. The giant gestures toward the back of the Cadillac. "A gentleman here would like to speak to you for a few minutes."

"No, thanks," Cone says. "Mommy told me never to accept rides from strangers."

"We're not going for a ride," the young behemoth says. "Just a little talk right here. Come on, Mr. Cone, be nice."

"And if I'm not nice?"

The guy shrugs. "Then I get back in and drive away." He sounds disappointed.

But Cone believes him. He bends down to peer in the window. The man sitting back there looks innocent enough. He's elegantly dressed, with a miniature orchid pinned to the lapel of his taupe gabardine topcoat. He sees Timothy staring through the glass, gives him a sweet smile, and makes little beckoning motions with his fingers.

"Okay," Cone says.

The bodyguard, or chauffeur, or whatever the hell he is, opens the rear door and Cone slides in. He sits far back and crosses his knees so he can get to his ankle holster in a hurry if he has to.

The man turning sideways to face him has deep, soft eyes, a gentle manner. He's pushing sixty, Cone reckons, and looks like he has a massage and a manicure every day. He's wearing a cologne that makes the inside of the Cadillac smell like a cedar chest.

"Please forgive this unconventional method of meeting you, Mr. Cone," he says in a quiet voice. "I suppose I could have written you a letter or called your office for an appointment, but it didn't seem wise."

"Why not?" Cone asks.

No answer to that. "First let me introduce myself." The man slides a pigskin case from his inside jacket pocket, extracts a plastic ID card, and hands it over.

The Wall Street dick takes a quick look at it. "This doesn't mean much," he says. "I could buy a fake on the street for maybe fifty bucks."

"I don't think so," the guy says, flashing his sweet smile again. "That particular card has a microchip embedded in it."

"Well, well. Will wonders never cease?"

"No," the other man says. "They won't."

"And what's this battle monument commission? I never heard of it."

"Not many people have. It's just another federal bureaucracy."

"You promote battle monuments?"

"Among other things."

"J. Roger Gibby," Cone reads from the card. Then he looks up to stare into those dark, shadowed eyes. "That name rings a bell." He pauses a moment, then snaps his fingers. "Got it. I've been reading books on artificial insemination. They keep mentioning Professor J. Roger Gibby. That's you—correct?"

"I *was* a professor, but not any longer. Just another government employee."

"But you did a lot of work on on test-tube babies. So the reason we're having this confab is the Nu-Hope Clinic investigation. Am I right?"

"Exactly right."

"Let me make another wild guess," Cone says. "You want me to okay the Nu-Hope deal. How'm I doing?"

"Batting a thousand."

"What the hell is Uncle Sam's interest in Nu-Hope?"

"They're doing some excellent original research. The federal government is vitally interested in furthering technology in their area."

"Bullshit," Cone says roughly. "What's the research you're interested in—how to get more sperm donors to jack off into empty baby food jars?"

Gibby gives him a wry look. "You have a colorful way of speaking, Mr. Cone. I'm afraid I can't be more specific about our interest in Nu-Hope."

"Okay," Cone says. "If that's the way it is, that's the way it is. Nice talking to you."

He reaches for the door handle, but Gibby puts a light hand on his arm.

"Just a moment, Mr. Cone. Please. I've gone to a great deal of trouble to look up your record. Marine Corps. Vietnam. Your medals. You served your country well."

"Oh-oh," Cone says, "Here it comes. Hearts and flowers. Be a patriot. Do what Big Daddy in the White House wants you to do. Is that right?"

"Not quite. There are others as anxious about Nu-Hope's research as we are."

"Jesus Christ, now it's help defend America against Godless Communism. You're really pulling out all the stops."

"No," Gibby says seriously, "I'm not suggesting that at all. I'm sure the Soviets are doing research along similar lines. But that doesn't concern us at the moment. There are others interested in the same subject."

"Others? What others?"

"That, I'm afraid, is also privileged information."

Cone nods. "Glad to have met you," he says. "As for the U.S. of A., I've paid my dues. As for Nu-Hope, I'm going to keep digging. If they're clean, that's what I'll report. And if they're dirty, likewise."

He climbs out of the de Ville. The bruiser, still standing on the sidewalk, glances at him but lets him go. Cone tramps angrily southward on Broadway.

He's only an hour late for work, and gets a wrathful look from Samantha when he passes her in the corridor. But he's in no mood to endure a reaming out for his tardiness, and without even a good morning to her, heads for his office.

"Grouch!" she calls after him.

He sits at his battered desk, fishes out a cigarette, and rumbles stuff around in his brain, trying to find some logical pattern: Lester Pingle offers a bribe for an okay on the Nu-Hope deal. Cone tells him to get lost. The next morning, the U.S. Govn't, in the person of J. Roger Gibby, makes the same pitch.

Does that mean that Pingle's bribe money was going to come from the taxpayers? Or is Lester buddy-buddy with the "others" Gibby mentioned? Finally, why is everyone so goddamned interested in Nu-Hope? And why did January and Trumball lie about Harold Besant?

The whole thing reminds Cone of that nonsense riddle he loved as a child: "If it takes fourteen geese to get down off an elephant, how many Palmolive wrappers does it take to paper a boxcar?" He groans, pulls the phone toward him, and calls Jessie Scotto at the Nu-Hope Fertility Clinic.

He identifies himself, says he's coming up to the clinic to speak to several of the employees, and would like to talk to her for a few minutes.

"I'm very busy," she says in a voice so low he can hardly hear her.

He won't let her get away with that. "Doctor January told me he instructed the staff to be as cooperative as possible. Is that right?"

"Yes," she says faintly, "he told us that."

"Well, then? It won't take long."

"All right," she says. "If it's only for a few minutes."

"In the Doctors' Lounge," he suggests, "in about an hour. We'll have a coffee or something. I'm wearing an old parka, but you'll have to identify yourself."

"All right," she says again, sounding like she hears the tumbrils rolling.

At the clinic Cone flashes his ID and has no trouble getting into the west wing. He takes the elevator to the fourth floor and is happy to find the Doctors' Lounge empty. He treats himself to a free cup of black coffee and a wedge of apple pie. It comes with a plastic fork. Pie and fork taste alike.

He's on his second cup of coffee when a little nurse scurries into the lounge, looking like she's pursued by wolves. Cone rises, forces himself to smile, holds out a hand.

"Miss Scotto?" he says. "I'm Timothy Cone from Haldering. Thank you for meeting with me."

She looks like she's expecting him to slap her. But she gives him a brief, limp handclasp, then collapses into a metal chair at his table. Detective Galanis was wrong, Cone thinks: Two months haven't restored Jessie Scotto's nerves. She looks ready to shatter into a million pieces.

"Can I bring you a coffee?" he asks.

She shakes her head, so he sits down again, opposite her, and hunches over the table. He speaks quietly, trying to play the sympathetic daddy. But it's difficult; she won't look at him.

"Just a few questions," Cone says soothingly. "I know how busy you must be."

Like Galanis said: She's a little mouse. Diminutive, with frizzy hair and pale, watery eyes. She's not wearing makeup, and swims in a nurse's uniform too large for her. It's hard to believe she was living with Harold Besant. She looks like someone's maiden aunt.

"How long have you worked at Nu-Hope, Miss Scotto?"

"Six years."

"Like it?"

A nod.

"What are your duties?"

"I prep patients."

As they talk, people begin to wander into the lounge and use the vending machines. Cone notices a number of them glance curiously at Jessie and himself. He leans farther across the table, deciding he better cut this short before the place is jammed by the lunchtime crowd.

"You knew Harold Besant," he says, more of a statement than a question.

She looks up at him fearfully.

"Look, Jessie," he says, trying to keep his temper under control, "whatever you say is just between you and me. I swear to God I'll never repeat a word. You and Harold were living together."

She nods.

"Did you know he had a gun?"

"He didn't," she bursts out. "I know he didn't."

"The night he died, did he tell you where he was going?"

"No. He just said he'd be gone for an hour or so. He said he had to meet someone."

"Did he say who?"

"No."

"Do you think he was depressed, like everyone says?"

"He was—Harold was worried."

"About what?"

"His work."

"What was his work, Jessie? What did Harold do in that research laboratory?"

She looks directly into his eyes, unblinking, and Cone knows she's going to lie.

"He never discussed his work with me," she says. "I know nothing about it."

Cone sits back and regards her gravely. "There's no way I can help you if you won't let me."

She begins weeping, covering her eyes with a palm. "Just leave me alone," she says in a muffled voice. "Just go away. Please."

"All right," he says, sighing. "Haldering's phone number is in the book. If you change your mind, you can reach me there."

People look at him as he stalks out of the Doctors' Lounge, leaving Jessie Scotto alone at the table, her eyes covered, thin shoulders bowed and trembling.

He takes a cab back to John Street, furious with his failure, but not seeing how else he could have handled it. At least he learned that Harold Besant hadn't owned a gun. Or, if he had, Jessie Scotto wasn't aware of it. But if she was living with the guy, you'd think she'd know.

Back in his office, he puts in a call to Detective Nick Galanis. But Galanis has the day off, so Cone leaves a message he called and will call again tomorrow.

He leans back in his swivel chair and stares at the ceiling. He keeps seeing Jessie's pinched features and tear-filled eyes. She's such a defeated little woman, bowed by the heavy load she's carrying and too frightened to get out from under. A loser.

"Just like me," Cone says aloud.

"Who's just like you?" Sidney Apicella asks. "Typhoid Mary?"

The CPA stands in the doorway, gently rubbing his swollen beezer.

"You don't look happy, Sid," Cone says, "but then you never look happy."

"How can I be happy when you keep tossing me curve balls? Remember asking me to check Lester Pingle's financial situation?"

"Of course I remember. Well?"

"Pingle Enterprises is in good shape. A nice balance sheet. But Lester is close to being a bankrupt. The guy hasn't got two kopecks to rub together. How do you like that?"

"I like it," the Wall Street dick says.

The loft phone explodes, and he rouses from a heavy sleep. He pushes himself off the mattress and staggers over to the wall phone in his minuscule kitchen.

"H'lo?" he says sleepily.

"Jesus Christ," Davenport says, "you still snoozing? It's eight o'clock already."

"Big deal," Cone says, yawning. "What's this, a wakeup call? To get me to work on time?"

"No," the city detective says, "it's more than that. Jessie Scotto got scragged last night."

Silence.

"Cone? You there?"

"I'm here," Timothy says, slumping and wanting to upchuck. "She's really dead?"

"As a doornail. Looks like a B-and-E. Too bad you never got a chance to talk to her."

"I did," Cone says. "I talked to her yesterday morning."

"You son of a bitch!" Davenport yells at him. "Why didn't you tell us about it?"

"I tried. I left a message for Galanis. Ask him."

There's a moment's silence, then the cop comes back on. "Yeah," he says, "sorry. Nick's got your message on his desk. Anyway, the lady's dead. We just got it over the wire. Nick and I are going up there to take a look. Want to tag along and inspect the corpus delicious?"

"I don't want to," Cone says, "but I better."

"Okay. We'll pick you up outside your palace in about fifteen minutes. Don't make us wait."

"I'll be there," Cone promises.

They're in a dusty blue Plymouth, both city detectives in the front seat. Timothy scrambles into the back and is introduced to Nick Galanis, who's driving. He's a short, swarthy guy with a thick black mustache.

"This stinks," he says wrathfully. "A fake suicide and now Besant's girlfriend gets chilled. You're telling me it's a coincidence? *Bullshit!*"

"Calm down, Nick," Davenport advises. "Your ulcer will be acting up again. Cone, we picked up some black coffee. Here's yours."

He hands over a big cardboard container.

"Thanks," Timothy says gratefully. "It's plasma. When was she killed?"

"Don't know," Davenport says, gulping his coffee. "We got none of the details. Just that a Caucasian female identified as Jessie Scotto was found dead in her apartment on West Seventy-fourth. Homicide suspected. That's all they put out."

"You talked to her yesterday?" Galanis demands angrily. He's gnawing on his long mustache, reaching up with his bottom teeth.

"That's right."

"Get anything?"

"She said that Besant didn't own a gun."

"Goddammit!" Nick says furiously, banging the steering wheel with his palm. "I didn't even ask her that. I'm a fucking idiot!"

"She was still shook," Cone says. "She knew something but wasn't talking. I pushed it as far as I could, but she started crying and there were a lot of people around, so I split."

"What makes you think she knew something?" Davenport asks.

"She lied to me. She said she knew nothing about Besant's work at Nu-Hope. A woman lives with a guy and doesn't know what his job is? Maybe—but I can't buy it."

"Anything else?" Galanis wants to know.

"Yeah, she said that on the night Harold died, he told her that he was going out for an hour or so to meet someone. She claimed she didn't know who it was."

"Uh-huh," Nick says. "She told me that, too. I think the part about him going out to meet someone was the truth. But I think she knew who it was."

The brownstone on West Seventy-fourth Street, just east of Amsterdam, is roped off with sawhorses and wide Crime Scene tapes, holding back the usual crowd of rubbernecks. There are three squad cars and a meat wagon double-parked. The morgue attendants are playing gin rummy on the fender of their van. Davenport and Galanis clip their IDs to their jacket pockets.

"C'mon," Neal says to Cone. "We'll get you in. I want to make sure we're all talking about the same woman."

The blue at the door glances at the detectives' tags, then looks at Cone.

"Who's he?" he asks.

"A witness," Davenport says, and the three of them push through the door. They tramp up a stairway covered with threadbare carpeting. The place reeks of roach spray. On the third floor, another uniformed officer stands guard before a closed door.

"A witness," Davenport repeats, jerking a thumb at Cone. "Keep an eye on him; he's a dangerous character."

"Thanks a lot," Timothy says.

The two city detectives disappear inside. Cone waits in the hallway. He and the uniformed cop eye each other warily. After about three minutes, Davenport comes out.

"What did you have to eat this morning?" he asks.

"Just the black coffee you gave me."

"Try to keep it down," the city dick says. "I had my shoes shined, and I wouldn't want to get them splattered. C'mon in."

Later, Cone has a confused recollection of a squeezed one-bedroom apartment that's been thoroughly trashed: rugs torn up, pictures yanked off the walls and smashed, lamps overturned, all the shelves in the kitchen emptied onto the floor, chair and sofa cushions slashed, clothing spilled from bureau drawers.

All he remembers clearly is the body on the bed.

Davenport pulls down the bloodied sheet with his fingertips. "This the woman you talked to yesterday?"

"Yeah," Cone says, swallowing.

"What the fuck's this all about, Neal?" a plainclothesman says indignantly. "This is my squeal."

"Don't get your balls in an uproar, Harry," Davenport says. "We're not moving in on you. This one is all yours. But she was questioned yesterday on another file, and I just wanted to make sure of the ID. What made all those puncture wounds?"

"You want me to guess?" the doctor from the ME's office says, snapping shut his black case. "I'd guess a sharpened ice pick. Most of the holes look to be no more than an inch deep. Painful but not fatal."

"I saw something like that before," Nick Galanis says. "Jabs from the little blade of a jackknife. To get a guy to talk. But why did they cut off her nipples?"

"Maybe she wouldn't talk," Cone says stonily. "Then they really went to work on her."

"She was tied up and gagged when she was found," Harry says. "The legs of a pantyhose was shoved down her throat."

"I can't say definitely until the PM," the doc says, "but I think that's what killed her. Probably choked to death on her own vomit. Not a nice way to go."

"At least they spared her face," Cone says, staring at those pale, pinched features. The little mouse, trapped and destroyed.

"How do you see it, Harry?" Davenport asks.

"A junkie," the plainclothesman says promptly. "Trying to score. Maybe he heard she had money up here. When she wouldn't talk, he tortured her. Then, after she died, he tore the place apart."

"It's all yours," Davenport says, nodding. "Lots of luck."

Back on the sidewalk, the three men take deep breaths. Even the grimy city air tastes good.

"A nice way to start the day," Cone says.

"I'm hungry," Davenport says. "What say we go over to Amsterdam and get us some breakfast?"

Ten minutes later they're sitting at a table in a white-tiled dairy restaurant on West Seventy-second Street. They're all having the same thing: tomato juice with a wedge of lemon, scrambled eggs with lox and onions, french fries, toasted bagels, and more black coffee. They eat busily.

"Do you buy what Harry said about a junkie?" Cone asks.

"Harry's a good cop," Davenport says, smiling, "but when God was passing out brains, he was pretty far back in the line. I think the woman was tied and gagged, and then the place was torn apart. When the killer couldn't find what he was looking for, he went to work on her with ice pick and knife. She croaked before she talked."

"What was he looking for?" Galanis says, wiping ketchup from his mustache with a paper napkin. "She couldn't have had much cash or jewelry. Look at that apartment. You know you're not going to strike it rich in there."

"Poor Harry," Davenport says, unwrapping a stick of Juicy Fruit and sliding it into his mouth. "I got a feeling this is going to be an F and F case. File and forget."

"I know who killed her," Cone says in a low voice.

The two NYPD men look at him, blinking.

"Who?" Galanis says.

"I did," Timothy Cone says, pushing back from the table and taking out his pack of Camels. "Because I've got no more brains than Harry. I questioned the poor woman in the Doctors' Lounge. Someone saw us talking and told someone else. And that was the end of Jessie Scotto."

"What the hell are you talking about?" Davenport wants to know.

"Just blowing smoke," Cone says, lighting a cigarette.

They drive him back to John Street. But before he goes into the office, he walks around the corner to a discount bookstore on Broadway. After searching the shelves, he buys two more books on new techniques in laboratory conception. He has a vague idea of what Jessie Scotto's killer was looking for.

But it doesn't make him feel less guilty.

They're in Hiram Haldering's office.

"Now tell me," Hiram is saying, stubby fingers laced across his pot. "How are we coming along on the Nu-Hope deal? Everything hunky-dory?"

"We're coming along fine," Samantha says. "No red flags have turned up yet. Have they, Tim?"

"No," Cone says, "not yet."

H.H. stirs restlessly. "The Preliminary Intelligence Estimate from the accounting section just came in. The CPAs give the deal a go-ahead. Ditto from the legal section. So all that's missing is an okay from you people."

"I'm working it," Cone says.

The benign smile disappears. "How much more time do you need on this, Cone?"

"Hard to tell."

"Well, Pingle Enterprises is getting anxious. I got a call from Lester this morning. They want our evaluation so they can get rolling."

"Rolling on what?" Cone asks.

"On the expansion plans for the Nu-Hope Clinic," Haldering says, staring at him like he's an idiot.

"I mean how are they going to handle it?" Cone explains patiently. "Did Lester say? A limited partnership, public or private? A franchise setup or a public offering of stock?"

Haldering leans forward, frowning. "They didn't say, and I didn't ask. What the hell business is it of ours? Listen, I want you to know I'm under considerable pressure to complete this investigation."

"I'm sure Tim is giving it every priority," Samantha says. "Isn't that right?"

"Sure," Cone says. "Every priority."

Haldering looks at him suspiciously, then turns to Whatley. "I'll give you one week, Sam, and that's it."

They walk back to Samantha's office. She motions him inside but leaves the door open.

"I love the way you show respect for your employer," she says.

"What the hell was that all about?" he asks her. "He's never been so antsy."

"Well, he said Lester Pingle called him."

"Yeah, but I got the feeling someone else is leaning on him."

She stares at him a long moment. Then: "I told H.H. that no red flags had turned up on this deal, and you agreed with me. Was that the truth?"

"No," Cone says. "Red flags are flapping all over the place."

Samantha groans. "I know it's hopeless to ask what's going on—you're such a closemouthed bastard."

"All I've got are bits and pieces," he tells her. "Nothing you can take to the bank. When I've got something I can put on paper, I'll do it."

"Can you give me a glimmer, for God's sake? Do you think the Nu-Hope deal stinks?"

"To high heaven," he says.

He goes back to his office and finds, on his desk, a PIE from the accounting section.

According to Sid Apicella's gnomes, Nu-Hope is in great shape. They've got a couple of low-interest bank loans they're paying off on the button. Their cash flow is being smartly managed, and gross income shows a satisfying year-to-year increase since they converted from an abortion clinic.

But their operating expenses have also increased. Part of that is due to an enlarged staff. But a lot of it, Cone notes, is because of ballooning expenditures on research and development. The present and projected allocations for R&D seem inordinately high.

That night Cone heats up two cans of chili con carne, sparked with an extra sprinkling of chili powder. He eats that with a package of soda crackers and a cold can of Heineken. Cleo has the same thing, except for the beer. The cat sniffs at that, then wrinkles its nose and turns away.

"You're no son of mine," he tells the castrated tom.

He spends the evening reading and trying to understand the first of his two new books on artificial conception. He smokes half a pack of Camels and drinks three vodkas and water. Near two o'clock, he's dizzy with nicotine, alcohol, and all those long words in the book. What, in God's name, is ectogenesis?

He gives Cleo fresh water and promises the cat new litter in the morning. He's just beginning to undress when the phone rings.

"Yeah?" he says.

"Timothy Cone?"

"That's right. Who's this?"

"I'm the super in the building where Samantha Whitley lives."

"Whatley," Cone says. "Samantha Whatley. Is anything wrong?"

"Well, we had some excitement here. Someone tried to break into her apartment. The cops are here now."

"Jesus Christ," Cone says. "Is she all right?"

"Well, she got banged up a little. She asked me to call and see if you'd come right over."

"Sure," Cone says, thinking of Jessie Scotto. "Tell her I'll be right there."

He hangs up, rebuttons his shirt, pulls on corduroy jacket and parka. He straps on his ankle holster with the short-barreled .357 Magnum.

"Hold down the fort, kiddo," he tells Cleo, then goes clattering down the six floors of iron staircase, trying to figure his best bet at finding a taxi at that time of night.

But he doesn't have to worry about a cab. He trots about twenty feet toward Spring Street when two men come out of the shadows and close in on him.

"Suckered," Cone says aloud, knowing Sam is okay. He backs slowly away, arms half-lifted, palms turned outward.

They're not tall guys, but they've got heft. They're not wearing over-coats or topcoats or raincoats or hats. Just dark suits. They look like twin undertakers. They're both smiling, like they came to escort him to a surprise party.

"You Cone?" one of them asks.

"I gave at the office," Timothy says, hands still raised.

"You hear that, Sol?" one of them says. "He gave at the office."

"Funny," Sol says. "The guy's a comedian. Ask him if he's got any other jokes."

"Look," Cone says, "I don't know what—"

The punch comes out of nowhere, and he's not fast enough to slip it. It catches him at the corner of his mouth and splits his lip open. He tastes the blood, and Sol steps in with a short, hard jab to his gut. These guys are real bullyboys.

They swarm all over him, jack hammering with hard fists. The pile-lined parka helps, but not enough. He tries to tuck in his head and cover up, but they straighten him with stiff pokes, then bend him over with hooks to his kidneys. Professionals.

Before he knows it, he's down on the sidewalk. He vaguely remembers a lecture on unarmed combat at Quantico. "Your eyes and your nuts," the instructor had cautioned. "Always protect your eyes and your nuts." So Cone curls into fetal position on the cold pavement, arms across his face, while the two thugs give him the boot.

They don't intend to kill him, he knows that; they just want to hurt. And they do. He takes a kick to his temple that almost chills him. And finally they both jump in the air and come down hard on his ribs.

Meanwhile they haven't said a word. Just breathing heavily. Doing a job of work. When the punishment ends, he stays curled up, eyes closed. Then, suddenly, the chili comes up.

"Jesus Christ," one of them says disgustedly, as if it's all Cone's fault.

"You got the message?" Sol says to Cone. "From now on do what you're told. Be smart. Play along."

He hears them moving away. He's almost out, but hangs on to consciousness, telling himself those are the two cruds who cut off Jessie Scotto's nipples. That gives him strength to open his eyes and lift his head from the concrete.

He sees them moving away in a misty haze to a parked car. He makes it to be a four-door black Pontiac Bonneville, but can't be sure. He knows they'll have to drive by him down Broadway. He slides a hand to his ankle holster.

When they pull out with a squeal of tires, he's ready for them, forearms propped on the sidewalk, gun held in both hands. It's wavering, he knows, but at that distance he can't miss.

He shoots steadily, following the car, pumping off rounds like he's on the range. The damned car seems to absorb his shots with no effect until, thirty feet down Broadway, the Pontiac suddenly veers, climbs the sidewalk, and smashes through the plate glass window of a trendy new restaurant that serves quiche and spinach salad.

The car plunges into the darkened interior with a screech of torn metal and a crunch of splintering wood. Cone is hoping for an explosion and fire, but no such luck. Now he sees a few people on the street, running toward the crash.

Cone drags himself slowly to his feet. Stands wavering. Everything seems to be working. He goes back to his loft. It takes him almost twenty minutes to climb those six flights of iron steps, resting on every landing. Finally, he gets inside, turns on the lights, locks and bolts the door. Cleo takes one look at him and retreats under the bathtub.

"C'mon," Cone says, "I don't look that bad."

But when he strips and inspects himself in the medicine cabinet mirror, he calls to the cat, "You're right."

He knows he was conned, but he's got to make sure. So before he doctors himself, he phones Samantha. She picks up on the sixth ring.

"What?" she says sleepily.

"Cone. You okay?"

"Of course I'm okay. What time is it? Oh, my God. What are you, drunk or something, waking me up at this hour?"

"Just checking," he says. "Go back to sleep."

"You sound funny," she says. "You're not talking right."

"I think I got the flu," he says. "Maybe I won't be in tomorrow. Good night. Sweet dreams."

He takes a healthy belt of vodka and uses a little soaked in a paper towel to swab off his torn lip and assorted cuts. The adrenaline is wearing off and he's really beginning to ache.

Finally he hears the sounds of sirens and buffalo whistles, and knows that the police have come to investigate the car that crashed into the restaurant. He hopes it'll be a job for Homicide.

He finishes washing up and puts his parka in a plastic garbage bag, ready for the dry cleaners. He tries stretching, cautiously. No permanent damage that he can find. Just a bad beating. He's had that before.

He bends down slowly and collapses onto the mattress. After a while Cleo comes padding over to him, sniffs at his wounds, and whimpers.

"Yeah," Cone says drowsily. "I know."

Getting up in the morning is something else again. Every joint stiff, every bone ready to snap. He turns on the shower and stands under hot water until he begins to look like a sixfoot prune. Then steps out and inspects himself in the mirror. Beautiful. Yellow, red, black, purple, blue.

"Just call me the Rainbow Kid," he tells Cleo.

He pads naked around the loft, reflecting that it might not be the Taj Mahal, but there's always plenty of heat and hot water.

The cat gets fresh water and a chunk of kosher salami. Cone has black coffee and a Camel. Because he has no intention of going into the office, he sees no point in shaving. Especially since his face is lumpy with welts, and that split lip wouldn't take kindly to a razor. So he pulls on a grungy costume of Jockey shorts, faded jeans, and a Stanley Kowalski T-shirt.

It's about nine-thirty, and he's settling down with another black coffee and another cigarette when Davenport calls.

"Taking a day off, Sherlock?" the city dick says breezily. "I tried you at your office, but they said you're not coming in."

"Yeah, that's right. I think I've got the flu or something."

"Well, there's a lot of that going around these days. And you sure sound funny. Like you got a mouth full of marbles.

Hey, what do you think about the excitement in your neighborhood last night? On your block, as a matter of fact."

"What excitement?"

"A car plowed into a restaurant. You didn't know about it?"

"Not a thing. What happened?"

"Just what I said: A new Pontiac Bonneville drives through the plate glass window of a restaurant. You didn't hear anything?"

"What time did this happen?"

"About two-thirty in the morning."

"I was asleep. Dead to the world."

"Sure," Davenport says. "Anyway, when they dug out the car, there was a stiff in the front seat. He was ID'd as Bernie Snodgrass. How do you like that for a moniker? Bernie had a rap sheet as long as your arm, so good riddance. Guess what killed him."

"The crash?"

"Nope," the NYPD man says cheerily. "A slug in the back of the head. Fired from maybe twenty or thirty feet away. There were some other bullet holes in the car and we recovered a slug from a three-five-seven Magnum. You pack a piece like that, don't you, Cone?"

"Yeah," Timothy says. "An S-and-W."

"I thought so," Davenport says. "Interesting. We've got statements from witnesses who say they saw a second guy running away from the scene. I thought you'd like to know."

"No skin off my ass," Cone says, "but thanks for telling me. Did you ID the car?"

"Now that is interesting. It's a company car, registered to Rauthaus Industries. They're on Wall Street. Ever hear of them?"

"Yeah, they make robots and industrial computers for assembly lines. A division of International Gronier, a conglomerate that owns half the world."

"Well, Rauthalls Industries claims the Pontiac was stolen from their company garage on Cedar Street. They say they weren't even aware it was missing until we called them."

"Uh-huh," Cone says, grinning at the phone. "There's a lot of that going around these days. Listen, will you do me a favor?"

"Will it cost me?"

"Nah. Just a phone call. You know the guy Harry who's handling the Jessie Scotto kill?"

"Yeah."

"Could you find out if they picked up any prints in Scotto's apartment."

"I doubt if they did, but I'll ask him."

"Well, if they did, will you ask him to check them against Bernie Snodgrass's? You said he had a record."

Silence. Then:

"You son of a bitch, Cone!" Davenport yells at him "You're holding out on me again, aren't you?"

"Why should I do that?" Cone says mildly. "We're both working the same side of the street, aren't we?"

He hangs up softly.

He inspects the ancient, waist-high refrigerator, hoping it'll contain enough rations so he won't have to make a trip outside. But it's hopeless. There's some dried-out Havatti with dill, a chunk of moldy kielbasa, an opened tin of briefing sardines, and two cans of Heineken. That's about it. And there's that smelly parka in the garbage bag that has to be taken to the cleaners.

Groaning, he does what he has to do: Strips, cleans, assembles, and reloads his SEW Magnum, and straps it to his shin pulls on gray wool socks from L. L. Bean, and his scuffed yellow work shoes. Dons his cruddy raincoat and a sailors' knitted watch cap. Then, carrying the bagged parka, he sallies forth. Thank God the big freight elevator is working at that hour, and he doesn't have to pound down six floors.

Less than an hour later he's back in the loft with two twine-handled shopping bags. He's got a bottle of Italian brandy, a liter of vodka, a carton of Camels, a can of human-type tuna for Cleo, and some packages of frozen food: short ribs, spaghetti and meatballs, beef stew, and lasagna.

He gets everything stowed away, gives Cleo half the tuna, and changes the liner in the cat's pan. He starts to hunker down with a small vodka and resume reading one of his new books on artificial conception when there's a knock on the loft door: Samantha's signal—two short raps, pause, one more. Sighing, Cone goes to open up.

Sam starts to say, "Hello, asshole," but only gets as far as opening her mouth when she sees Timothy's face. "Oh, my God," she says. "That's what you call the flu?"

Inside, door locked, she examines him more closely. She reaches out to touch the bluish lump on his temple, but he winces away.

"Drunken brawl?" she asks.

He shrugs. "Just one of your ordinary, run-of-the-mill muggings. No big deal."

"I thought you sounded chopped last night. Why the hell didn't you tell me? I'd have come over. 1 don't suppose you have any Band-Aids or any other first aid supplies in this swamp."

"Will you stop trying to play Florence Nightingale?" he says crossly. "I'm okay. Just a little achy, that's all."

"Did you report it to the cops?"

"Of course not. You know what they'd say: 'Tough shit.'"

She stares at him, frowning. "You're not telling me the truth," she says finally.

"Shut up," he says roughly, "and have a vodka."

"At this hour?"

"Why not? It's noon somewhere in the world."

They sit at his table-desk, sipping their vodkas and water from jelly glasses. She opens her suede trench coat. She's wearing a black gabardine pants suit.

"You look okay," he tells her.

She ignores that fulsome compliment and inspects him narrowly. "Where did they hurt you?" she asks. "Besides your empty head. Ribs?"

He nods.

"Not the *cojones*, I hope!"

"No," he says, "the family jewels are safe and sound."

"What did they get?"

He shrugs again. "A couple of bucks. Maybe twenty. It really wasn't worth their time."

"When did this happen?"

"Hey," he says, "what's this—the third degree? I got mugged, lost a few dollars, and that's it. Just drop it right?"

"Christ, you're a pain in the ass."

"Did I ever deny it?"

They sit staring at each other with wary hostility.

"Thanks for coming to check up on me," he says grudgingly

"You want off the Nu-Hope case?" she asks him.

"No," he says. "By tomorrow I'll be up to speed. I'd come into the office."

She nods, finishes her vodka, rises, and belts her trench coat. She stoops to scratch Cleo, who's been rubbing against her ankles. "You never let me do anything for you," she says in a low voice.

"Well, I'm about to ask you something now. You know that dinky little pistol you own. The nickel-plated job."

"Yes."

"Where is it?"

"Top drawer of my bedside table."

"Loaded?"

"Of course."

"Do me a favor, will you? Start carrying it in your pocket or handbag. Will you do that?"

"What for?"

"Just do it," he shouts.

"I can take care of myself," she says hotly. Then she softens. "Okay, if it'll make you feel better, I'll pack it."

"Yeah," he says, coming close to slide an arm across her shoulders, "it'll make me feel better. Give us a kiss, will you? If you can find an undamaged patch."

She kisses him softly on the cheek, then holds his arms.

"Take care. I'll call you tonight to see how you're doing."

"If a woman answers," he says, "hang up."

"Up yours," she says, grinning. And then she's gone.

He goes back to his reading, and finally figures out what ectogenesis is. It makes sense to him. They already have incubators that can keep premature kids alive. It seems reasonable to believe that eventually a laboratory womb could be developed in which an embryo might live and flourish Until it reaches birth weight.

He puts the book aside and goes to his kitchen wall phone.

"Mr. Ernest Pingle," he says. "Timothy Cone of Haldering and Company calling."

"Just a moment, please."

The old man comes on almost immediately. "Hah!" he says. "And how is my favorite investigator?"

"Okay," Cone says. "And how are you, sir?"

"I wasn't listed on the obituary page this morning," Pingle says, "so I got up. You have something to tell me?"

"Not exactly, Mr. Pingle. But I've got a couple of questions. Maybe the answers would help my investigation."

"Of course. The questions?"

"Has your company ever done any business with Rauthaus Industries?"

Silence.

"Mr. Pingle? You're there?"

"Where else would I be? Why do you ask about Rauthaus?"

"Their name came up in connection with the Nu-Hope Clinic."

Pingle sighs. "Let me tell you, young man, those people at Rauthaus are nogoodniks. They are owned by International Gronier, who are double nogoodniks. And Mr. Leopold Dewers, who owns everything, is the biggest nogoodnik of them all. To answer your question, yes, we did business with Rauthaus Industries. Once. They are not nice people, Mr. Cone. We were lucky to get away with the fillings in our teeth. I am sorry to hear they are inwolved in the Nu-Hope deal."

"I'm not sure they are, Mr. Pingle. It's just one of several leads I'm working on. Their name came up."

"If they are inwolved then I know the Nu-Hope business is definitely not for us. Tell me this, Mr. Cone: Is my son Lester mixed up with Rauthaus?"

"I don't know for sure."

"I think maybe I better have a little talk with that meshuggener."

"Please don't do that," Cone says hastily. "I have absolutely no hard evidence your son has contacts with Rauthaus. Give me a little more time before you do anything."

Quiet for a moment. "I'm thinking," Ernest Pingle says, "I'm thinking. All right, I'll give you more time. I'll say nothing to Lester. But if he is mixed up with those shtarkers, it would be with a man named Martin Gardow. You have that?"

"Martin Gardow? Yes, I'll remember."

"He is a nasty piece of goods. He does all the dirty work for Mr. D. That's Leopold Dewers. Martin Gardow is presentable, well dressed, soft-spoken, but the man is a bum. That is my personal opinion, but you can tell anyone you like that I said it."

"I don't intend to tell anyone," Cone says, admiring the gaffer's feisti-ness, "but I'll keep the name in mind. Thank you for your help, Mr. Pingle."

"Don't be such a stranger. Maybe someday we'll go to lunch together and tear a herring."

"I'd like that," Cone says.

He never did think J. Roger Gibby engineered last night's assault. Nor does he believe Lester Pingle has the balls to order up a beating. But Martin Gardow has the resources and apparently the ruthlessness to apply a little physical persuasion to convince Cone to okay the Nu-Hope deal.

And that conclusion doesn't do a goddamn thing to help solve the big problem: What is going on at Nu-Hope to make the U.S. Government and International Gronier so frantic to pump money into a fertility clinic?

One of those wild, giddy November days in Manhattan . . . wind gusting, dying, gusting again . . . sun blaring, then swallowed by scummy clouds . . . spatters of rain . . . newspapers blown high . . . rumble of thunder from somewhere . . . and suddenly a blue sky . . . dust devils go bouncing . . . as men hang on to hats, women hang on to skirts, and all go bowling along, buffeted and spun.

Timothy Cone, leaning against the swirly day, fights his way down to John Street. He goes directly to the office of Sidney Apicella, who leaves off stroking his swollen nose to stare at Cone's face.

"Holy Christ," he says, "what happened to you?"

"Got caught in a revolving door. Listen, Sid, I know you've got a lot of contacts. Will you see if you can pick up any poop on a guy named Martin Gardow? He works for Rauthaus Industries."

"Why should I do that?" Apicella asks.

"Because you gave an okay on the Nu-Hope Clinic deal, and if it turns sour, you're going to look like an A-number-one schlemiel."

The CPA, who has anxiety attacks every hour on the hour, says, "You think it's going to turn sour?"

"I'm beginning to see the dark at the end of the tunnel. Check on Martin Gardow for me, Sid, and I'll say in my report how cooperative you were."

"That's extortion," Apicella cries desperately.

"Of course," Cone says. "What else?"

He goes to his office. Maybe it's because he still feels the dull throbs of the beating or maybe it's the mixed-up day, but he's in a cantankerous mood and knows it. He feels he's being jerked around, doesn't like it, and resolves to do some jerking of his own.

He calls Nu-Hope and asks to speak to Dr. January. The doctor is so full of charm that Cone can hardly stand it. He tells January he wants to come up for another meeting "to clear up a few points."

"Come right ahead," January says heartily. "We can always make time for you."

Cone hangs up, wondering why he instinctively mistrusts cheerful people.

When he gets to East Seventy-first, he stands across the street a few minutes, just scoping the clinic. He's convinced that the answers to all his questions lie behind the handsome facade of those two townhouses. But the polished windows return his stare blankly, and he's left frustrated and growly.

Phoebe Trumball is in January's office, and Cone once again thinks of how physically similar the two doctors are. He brushes aside their queries about his battered face and says, "I read about Jessie Scotto in the paper."

Immediately their faces congeal into suitable expressions of sorrow.

"A tragedy," January says. "What a city this is. A jungle."

"Just dreadful," Trumball says. "She was such a sweet girl. Quiet and shy."

"Yeah," Cone says. "Now two of your staff have died violently. I hope your other employees aren't spooked."

"Oh, no," January says. "Everyone is depressed, naturally, but things like that do happen in the city."

"Just coincidence," Trumball says. "The two deaths."

"Sure," Cone says. "But that's not what I came to talk about. I think I should visit your research labs. The ones behind the locked door. Just so I can complete my report."

"As I explained to you," Trumball says tartly, "it's a sterile lab. You would be required to strip, shower, change into a special lab uniform. It's a tedious process."

"I don't mind," Cone says.

"And then," Trumball goes on, "I'm afraid all you'd see is our research staff hunched over microscopes or taking blood samples from our experimental animals. Not very exciting."

"That's all right," Timothy persists.

"There's a legal problem involved too," January adds, frowning. "There's always a possibility of infection from our animals. We have liability insurance, of course, but it only covers our staff. I'm afraid it's just too much of a risk, Mr. Cone. For you and for us."

Cone understands that he's not going to get into that lab. "Okay," he says, "but why don't you tell me what you're working on in there?"

"Phoebe," he says to the other doctor, "that's your bailiwick. Can you give Mr. Cone a quick rundown?"

"Of course," she says crisply. "Basically, we're trying to refine optimum periods of ovulation. Especially as they relate to body temperature and hormone release. The goal is to maximize our pregnancy rate. It's a very tricky business. In the field of in vitro fertilization, we're trying to improve techniques using frozen sperm and eggs to bring the success percentage up to that of live."

"When you fertilize in vitro," Cone says, "you produce more than one embryo?"

"Frequently. Especially if fertility drugs have been used. Then we select the embryo we believe is the strongest, for implantation in the host mother."

"And what happens to the other embryos? Down the sink?"

Dr. January stirs restlessly. "Not always," he says. "Some may be frozen. I hope you're not going to accuse us of abortion."

"Abortion? I never thought of it that way—although I suppose some people might."

"Yes," January says darkly, "some people do."

"What about ectogenesis?" Cone asks. "Doing any work on that? Or cloning?"

"Oh, my," Dr. Trumball says, almost mockingly, "you have been doing your homework, haven't you?"

"I've been reading some," Cone admits.

"Well, to answer your question, no, we are doing no work on ectogenesis or cloning. Although other people are."

"No money in it," Dr. January says, turning on the charm. "Besides, it's way in the future. All we're concerned with is helping women have healthy babies."

"So that's the extent of your research in the locked lab? Ovulation timing and in vitro fertilization with frozen sperm and eggs?"

"That's it," Dr. Phoebe Trumball says.

Cone remembers the children's rhyme: "Liar, liar, pants on fire." But he doesn't recite it.

He stands and thanks them for their time. Trumball conducts him down to the street. Then she returns to January's office and slumps into one of his directors' chairs.

"He suspects something," she says somberly.

"You think so?" January says, nervously gnawing at a thumbnail. "I thought he was just fishing."

"I don't think so. He seems to know just enough to be dangerous. I think we better call Gibby. Maybe he can take care of Cone."

"You really feel that's necessary?"

"I do. And when you speak to him, tell him about Cone's face. The man has been beaten up."

"So? What has that got to do with us?"

"Just tell Gibby about it," she says patiently. "It may mean something to him."

"If you say so. You know where I'd like to be right now?"

"Yes," she says, smiling. "We could take a long lunch hour, but call Professor Gibby first," she insists. "There's too much riding on this to let Cone upset things."

"You're right," he says. "It's my whole future."

"*Our* future," she says, looking at him queerly.

"Of course," he says hastily. "*Our* future."

Back in his office, Timothy puts his feet on his desk and tries to sort out his suspicions. Nearly an hour passes before he's interrupted by the phone. When he picks it up and says, "Yeah?" all he gets is a lot of static. He holds it away from his ear and finally the line clears.

"Yeah?" he says again.

"This is J. Roger Gibby. I'm sorry we have a bad connection, but I'm calling from my car."

"Your *car?*" Timothy says, amused. "Don't you have an office?"

"I do," Gibby says. "In Washington. I'd like to talk to you, Mr. Cone."

"In your car? Where are you—on the Long Island Expressway?"

"As a matter of fact, I'm parked right outside your office. I was hoping I might prevail upon you to drop down and chat for a few minutes."

"A lot simpler than your coming up here, huh? Okay."

He takes his time pulling on his raincoat and knitted cap. He also checks his ankle holster. When he gets down to the street, the black Cadillac de Ville is not hard to spot. The young bodyguard is lounging against the front fender, examining his fingernails.

"Nice to see you again," Cone says. "How're the folks?"

The giant doesn't respond, but politely opens the back door. The car is filled with the scent of cologne. The government man is as spiffily dressed as ever, wearing a fawn wideawake and a little sprig of greenery pinned to the lapel of his topcoat.

"Parsley?" Timothy asks.

"Pine," Gibby says, smiling. "Thank you for joining me." Then he examines Cone's face. "They did a job on you, didn't they?"

"They? Who's they?"

The other man sighs. "Could we stop playing games for a moment? I just wanted to assure you that I had nothing to do with the attack."

"Why should I believe that?"

"It's simply not my style."

"Is it your style to lean on my boss, Hiram Haldering, to get quick approval of the Nu-Hope Clinic deal?"

"Yes," Gibby says calmly. "Haldering is an ex–FBI man with very strong patriotic convictions. I attempted to present his government's position. But I did not have you assaulted."

"Never thought you did," Cone says. "You're not going to tell me what this is all about, are you?"

"No. I can't."

"So why did you want to talk to me?"

Gibby gently strokes his chin, as if he had once had a Vandyke.

"Mr. Cone," he says, "I think you're a very perspicacious man."

"Perspicacious? What does that mean?"

"Keen. Shrewd. I need your advice. You've met Doctor January and Doctor Trumball how many times—twice?"

"That's right."

"I was hoping you might give me your impressions."

"Why the hell should I?" Cone asks. Then, when Gibby looks startled, he adds: "Professor, I'm in the information business. If the outfit I work for can't use it, I trade it for something I want to know. What have you got to trade?"

Gibby draws a deep breath. "All right, Mr. Cone, how's this: The Nu-Hope Fertility Clinic is engaged in original biotechnological research that *could*—and I emphasize could—have a vital effect on the security of our country. I can tell you no more than that, except to say that what we're concerned with may sound like science fiction, but it is actually in the realm of the possible. Others, individuals, are interested in that research for personal gain. Other countries are interested because they wish to remain on the cutting edge of modern science. And that, I'm afraid, is all I have to trade. Is it enough?"

Cone ponders a moment. "Okay," he says finally. "If you want my take on January and Trumball, here it is: I think he's a charm boy. A strong puff of wind would blow him away. Not only is he ambitious, he's greedy. He wants all the goodies: money, power, and maybe a Nobel Prize. Doctor Trumball is the brains of that outfit. She knows exactly where she's going. Research is her shtick, and she couldn't care less about the perks."

Gibby is silent for a moment. "Thank you, Mr. Cone. What you've said reinforces my own feelings. My fears, I should say. I think I may have a problem there."

"Welcome to the club," Timothy says. "Can I go now?"

The government man gives him one of his sweet, slow smiles. "Of course. Do watch your back, Mr. Cone. The others are not nice people."

"So I've learned." Cone starts to climb out of the car, then turns back. "By the way, Professor, here's a freebie for you: January and Trumball are rubbing the bacon."

"Yes," Gibby says, expressionless, "I am aware of that."

They stare at each other silently, hearing all the noises of the streets: the carousel city whirling to a tinkly tune.

Cone returns to his office and slumps in his swivel chair, still wearing his raincoat and knitted cap. He's brooding on the little that Gibby told him when Sid Apicella stops by.

"You coming or going?" he says.

"I don't know," Cone says, "and that's the truth."

"You asked me to find out about Martin Gardow."

"And?"

"Gardow's title is chief of special projects for Rauthaus Industries, but he's really the hatchet man for International Gronier, which owns Rauthaus. Gardow is a shark and takes orders only from Mr. D. That's Leopold Devers, who runs the whole shebang. Gardow has a nasty reputation. He broke a strike at one of Gronier's factories. Three workmen were killed and one was crippled for life. Gardow is also reputed to be head of industrial espionage for Mr. D."

"Sounds like a real charmer."

"Oh, he is. Apparently he handles Gronier's political payoffs and bribes, and is supposed to have a hefty slush fund. All Mr. D. is interested in are results. Tim, this guy is strictly bad news. What's his connection with the Nu-Hope Clinic deal?"

"Maybe he wants to make a contribution to their sperm bank," Cone says, and that's all he'll tell Apicella.

3

Cone gets back to the loft that night with a small barbecued chicken and two chilled bottles of Löwenbräu dark. He and Cleo share the chicken and he's about to get back to his reading on artificial conception when there's a sharp knock on his door. It's not Samantha's signal, and Cone approaches the door warily, standing to one side.

"Yeah?" he calls.

"Davenport. Let us in, for Christ's sake. We're not going to bust you."

Cone unlocks, unbolts, unchains the door. Neal and Nick Galanis are standing there.

"How did you get in downstairs?" Cone wants to know.

"Your outside door has been jimmied."

"Again?" Cone says, sighing. "Second time this month. Come on in."

"How do you like this joint?" Davenport asks Nick Galanis. "Luxurious—no? That monster under the bathtub is supposed to be a cat." He turns to Cone. "Aren't you going to offer us a drink?"

"What will you have? I got beer, vodka, red wine, a little brandy."

"Vodka for me. You, Nick?"

"I'll have wine," Galanis says. "I gotta get home. My daughter's birthday party. If I miss that or turn up bombed, I'm in deep shit."

They sit around the desk, the NYPD men still wearing their windbreakers and looking grim.

"Okay," Cone says, "what's the beef? You look like you're ready to roust me."

Davenport stares at him thoughtfully, unwrapping a stick of Juicy Fruit. "You're holding out on us again. Harry pulled some prints in Jessie Scotto's apartment. They belonged to Bernie Snodgrass, the punk who got killed a few doors down the block from where we're sitting. Now how did you know the prints would match?"

"I didn't *know*," Cone says. "It was just a guess."

"Listen," Galanis says. "Is there any connection to Harold Besant's death? Was Snodgrass in on that, too?"

"Look," Cone says, "you're asking me questions I can't answer. If you want me to guess, I'll try. There probably is a connection. If Besant was scragged, Snodgrass was in on it. Him and his buddy."

"His buddy?" Davenport says. "The guy witnesses saw running away from the crashed Pontiac?"

Cone nods.

"What happened?" the city dick says. "You get bushwhacked?"

"Yeah," Cone says reluctantly. "I was suckered into coming down to the street. They jumped me and did a job."

"You get a make on the other guy?" Galanis demands.

"Snodgrass called him Sol. About five-ten, maybe one-eighty. Heavy through the chest and shoulders. Wearing a dark suit. A real thug. I've got the marks to prove it."

"Could you pick him out of a lineup?" Davenport asks.

"Sure," Cone says with more conviction than he feels. "Why don't you start with Snodgrass's pals. Maybe he and that Sol did time together. You'll find him."

The two cops stare at him, expressionless, then lean forward and top their jars.

"And that's all you're going to give us?" Davenport says. "A guy named Sol?"

Cone is silent a moment, sipping his brandy and doing some fast thinking. He knows he's going to need help from these guys, and if he keeps stiffing them, they won't even return his calls.

"The way I figure it is this," he says finally. "Bernie Snodgrass and Sol were two hired hands. The kind of guys who'll take credit cards for a kill or a beating. But there's got to be a moneyman behind them—right? I have absolutely no hard evidence, but I'll give you a name: Martin Gardow. He's with an outfit called Rauthaus Industries. From what I hear, the guy's a villain, but a real handle with-care case. I mean he's got a lot of money and political clout behind him."

Davenport pulls out a notebook and ballpoint pen. "Martin what?"

"Gardow. G-A-R-D-O-W."

"And what's his company?"

"Rauthaus Industries. They're on Wall Street."

"What's his connection with Besant and Scotto?" Galanis asks.

"Beats the hell out of me," Cone says, "and that's the truth. But Gardow has a heavy interest in this Nu-Hope Fertility Clinic I'm investigating. Exactly what, I don't know. But Besant and Scotto both worked there, and my guess is that Gardow arranged both their deaths."

"Why?" Galanis says.

"Maybe Besant was going to spill the beans," Cone says, rubbing his forehead. "Maybe he had some reports or papers or something. Maybe it was just because of what he knew. After they kill him they're afraid he may have told his girlfriend, so Jessie Scotto gets whacked, too. I know I'm blowing smoke, but it does make a crazy kind of sense. Something's going on in a locked research lab at Nu-Hope, and a lot of people are interested. Interested enough to kill to keep it a secret."

"And you have no idea what it is?" Davenport asks.

"No, not yet. But I'll find out."

"Sure you will," Davenport says, finishing his drink and standing up. "And when you do, we'll be the first to know—right?"

"Absolutely," Cone says.

"When shrimp fly," Davenport says good-humoredly. "Okay, sherlock, we'll see what we can dig up on Sol and Martin Gardow. Thanks for the booze."

"Yeah," Galanis says. "Thanks." He stands and, unexpectedly, reaches to shake Cone's hand. "I knew that Besant suicide was a fake. It's been eating at me. Now we've got something to work on. Not much, but *something*. Keep in touch."

When they're gone, Timothy goes back to his books and reads about motile sperm fighting their brave way upstream to find a welcoming egg. Thinking of that, he's tempted to call Samantha Whatley, but resists. He has no desire for progeny. Still . . .

They're having an office party. Apicella's secretary is getting married, and the festivities have overflowed into the corridor. Sid has sprung for a few bottles of hard booze, mixers, colas, and platters of glutinous noshes hustled up from the local deli. The bride-to-be opens her presents with giggles and blushes.

Cone, who bought her a gross of Sheiks, stands in the hallway, nursing a plastic cup of warm vodka and listening to the sounds of joy. Samantha Whatley comes up to him, glowering.

"That was a nice, romantic gift you gave her," she says.

"What the hell," he says, "it's practical. If she doesn't want to use them, she can always fill them with water and drop them out the window. Bomb the pedestrians."

"You're nuts, you know that? Totally nuts."

"So what else is new?"

"I'll tell you what's new," she says. "Or old. The Nu-Hope Clinic case. Time's running out. H.H. gave us a week—remember?"

"Tell me about it," he says bitterly. "I'm moving on it. I really am. Things are beginning to come together."

She looks at him. "You're shitting me," she says.

"Yeah," he admits, "I am."

"Tim, why can't you tell me what you're up to? After all, I am your boss; I ought to know what the hell is going on."

"Sam, I'm spinning. It wouldn't do any good to explain what's going on. It's a fucking merry-go-round."

"If you'd tell me, maybe I could help. I do have a brain, you know."

"I know you do, but—"

Then other people crowd up to them and for almost ten minutes they're part of a laughing, chattering group. Finally the others drift away and Whatley and Cone are standing alone again.

"Another thing . . ." she says in a low voice. "You know how long it's been since we've been together?"

"Too long," he says, groaning. "Every time I sneeze, dust comes out my ears."

"Just how long do you expect me to wait?" she demands.

He gets pissed off. He can't stand to be leaned on.

"You're free, white, and twenty-one," he tells her.

She stares at him. "You really are an asshole. Who the hell but me would put up with your nasty moods?"

"Cleo," he says.

She can't help smiling, but moves away from him. He pours himself more warm vodka from Sid's bottle and carries it back to his office. That exchange with Samantha has shaken him more than she knows. She's right: What other woman would put up with his lousy disposition and cruddy habits?

But he can't waste any more time brooding about his personal happiness, or lack thereof. He's got a job to do.

He remembers a lecture on small-unit infantry tactics delivered by an old, grizzled colonel who had so much fruit salad on his chest that he listed to port. The problem posed was how to take a bald hill held by an enemy ensconced on the heights. No ravines, no natural cover, no artillery or air cover. What do you do?

"Go home," someone suggested.

"No," the colonel said, "you go up the hill and take it."

"We'd get our ass shot off," someone else said.

"Probably," the colonel said, smiling bleakly. "But what the fuck do you think they're paying you for?"

So, knowing what he is paid for, Timothy wonders how he can take that goddamn hill and keep his ass intact. He remembers what Gibby said about January and Trumball: "I think I may have a problem there."

With both doctors? Or with one? Maybe there's trouble in paradise.

He puts in a call to Victor January, but the doctor is in surgery and will get back to him as soon as possible. Cone waits patiently, sipping his drink and chain-smoking, wondering idly which will wear out first: heart, lungs, or liver.

"Hello there, Mr. Cone!" Dr. Victor January says, finally calling back. "What can we do for you today?"

"I was hoping we could have a talk."

"Of course. You want to come up here?"

"No," Cone says. "A private talk. Just you and me. I would prefer Doctor Trumball not be there."

Silence. Then, slowly: "I see. Well, I suppose that could be arranged. Any suggestions?"

"You know the Hotel Bedlington? Not too far from your place. Can you meet me there? Around three o'clock?"

"What's this about, Mr. Cone?"

"Just a meeting for our mutual benefit."

"All right," January says. "The Bedlington bar at three. I'll be there."

"If I were you," Cone says, "I wouldn't mention this to your partner or anyone else."

Again a long pause. "Very well," January says, "I won't."

After he hangs up, Cone sits back, satisfied. So far, so good. He's confident that January is going to take the bait. He returns to Sid's office, but the party is over; no more free food or vodka. So he pulls on his newly cleaned parka and goes downstairs to have a cheeseburger and fries at a fast-food joint where he stands at a chest-high counter.

Then he cabs up to the Hotel Bedlington, and is pleased to find the cocktail lounge almost deserted. Just the bartender and one guy mumbling into his martini. Cone orders a draft Heineken and takes it to a corner table where he has a good view of the glass door leading to the lobby.

January shows up a few minutes after three. He looks around, spots Cone, and comes striding toward him with one of his sugarcane smiles. "Fink," Cone says—but not aloud.

"Hi!" January says brightly. "This was a splendid idea. I'm ready for a break."

"You'll have to order from the bar," Cone tells him. "There's no waiter working."

The doctor comes back with a tall drink. "Amaretto and soda," he declares. "Delicious and refreshing."

"Uh-huh," the Wall Street dick says, realizing that with very little effort he could learn to loathe this man.

"Cheers," January says, then sips his drink and flaps his lips appreciatively. "Good, good, good! You sounded very mysterious on the phone, Mr. Cone."

"Did I?" Timothy says. "Not much mystery about it. I believe in putting my cards on the table. That's okay with you?"

"Of course. Everything up-front."

"Sure. Well, here's the way I figure it: If Haldering gives the green light, Pingle Enterprises will work the deal. They'll structure it as a public or private limited partnership, or maybe as a franchise setup, or a public stock offering. However they do it, there's going to be a lot of bucks involved, and you'll come out of it a rich man."

"Not me," January says, smiling, "the clinic."

"But you *are* the Nu-Hope Fertility Clinic, aren't you? I mean you own the whole kit and caboodle. Right now, here's how things stand: Our legal and accounting departments have given go-aheads. The final report has to come from me. I can turn thumbs up or down."

"Well, I certainly hope you'll give us your approval," the doctor says warmly. "We've done everything we can to cooperate with your investigation."

"Maybe not everything," Cone says, staring at the other man. "Like that locked research laboratory you won't let me see. I wouldn't like to insist that we bring in an independent team of scientists to see exactly what you're doing in there."

January drains his drink, rises abruptly, goes to the bar, and returns with a refill.

"Thirsty," he says. "A difficult morning in surgery. Now then, why should an independent scientific investigation be necessary?"

"It may not be," the Wall Street dick says. "Not if I file a favorable report."

They look at each other, eyeballs locked.

"How much?" January says hoarsely.

Now it's Cone's turn to make a trip to the bar for a refill. He takes his time, chats a moment with the bartender, letting the doctor sweat. Then he goes back to the table.

"How much?" January repeats.

"I figure if the deal goes through, you're going to end up a multimillionaire. It only seems right and decent that I should get a little piece of the pie. To guarantee my goodwill, you understand."

"How much?" the doctor says for the third time.

"Oh," Cone says, waving a hand, "I figure fifty thousand is a reasonable fee."

January tries to hide his shock but doesn't succeed. The hand that hoists his Amaretto and soda is trembling and some of the drink spills down his chin. He wipes it away with a cocktail napkin.

"That's ridiculous," he says, not looking at Cone.

"Is it? Doesn't seem so to me. I reckon I'm in the catbird seat. If I say go, it's go. So fifty grand doesn't seem like such a big chunk of cash."

When he planned this scenario, Cone figured this was the turning point. If January told him to go screw himself or stalked out in a snit, then Cone's house of cards would collapse with a crash that would splinter his femurs. In addition, if the doctor went to Haldering, screaming extortion, Cone would find himself out on the street. And then who would change Cleo's litter box?

But January doesn't react with anger, outrage, or even surprise. Instead, he lifts his glass a bit and replaces it on the table, several times, making a chain of interlocking damp rings.

"Fifty thousand," he says reflectively. "A lot of money."

"Not really. Not when you think of what's at stake."

January raises his eyes to look at Cone directly. "I didn't think you were that kind of a man."

"What kind is that? You're looking out for Number One, aren't you? So am I. What's so terrible about it?"

"I can't give you an answer right now."

"Of course you can't. Didn't expect you to. Just think about it awhile. Remember what I said about calling in outside MDs to investigate your research lab. And figure what you've got to gain and what you've got to lose. You can read a balance sheet as easily as you read a temperature chart. The one problem we've got is that my boss wants my report in a couple of days."

Victor January drains his drink, stands. He reaches for his wallet, but Cone holds up a palm.

"No, no," he says. "I'll take care of the tab."

January gives him a thin smile. "Thank you. I'll let you know tomorrow. About your, ah, proposition. Will that be satisfactory?"

"Sure," Cone says. "I'm as anxious to see Nu-Hope work this deal as you are."

"That I doubt," January says.

Cone watches him leave. Then he sits there, sipping the remainder of his beer. He knows the risk he's running. He's charging up that hill like a maniac, screaming and firing at anything that moves. There's just a small chance he might gain the summit, dazed, shaken, look around at the carnage and say, "Who needs the fucking hill?"

A sodden morning, with the broken skylight dripping onto the linoleum floor of the loft. Cone puts a battered saucepan under the leak, and Cleo pads over to lap at the collected rain.

"Crazy cat," Cone says grumpily.

At the office he sits at his desk, wondering if the actors in his script are going to play the roles he's assigned them. Just to kill time, he fiddles his swindle sheet, doubling all his expenses. He knows Samantha Whatley will halve them. It's a game.

His phone rings a little after ten A.M. Being a superstitious man, he crosses his fingers before he picks it up.

"Yeah?" he says.

A woman's voice, chirpy: "Mr. Timothy Cone?"

"That's right."

"Just a moment, sir. Mr. Martin Gardow calling."

Cone smiles coldly at the phone. Bingo!

"Cone?"

"Yep."

"Martin Gardow here. I think we better have a talk."

"Sure," Cone says. "Where and when?"

"Eleven o'clock at the South Street Seaport. You can make it?"

"I'll make it. How will I recognize you?"

"I'll recognize *you*," Gardow says. "There's a shop that sells nautical stuff. It's got a big tin whale over the entrance."

"I'll find it."

"Eleven o'clock," Gardow says. "Be there."

Slam!

Timothy Cone is happy. "My fondest dreams are coming true," he sings aloud to the peeling walls, and checks the short-barreled Magnum in his ankle holster.

He decides to be on time, to prove his sincerity. The drizzle has dwindled to a freezing mist. By the time he arrives at the Seaport, his parka and leather cap are pearled, and his feet feel like clumps. A fog hangs over the river, and the few tourists who have braved the lousy day look shrunken and sour.

He finds the shop that sells marine artifacts. He's hardly taken two steps inside when a thick, stumpy guy shoves in front of him. He's wearing a tweed topcoat, beaded with rain, and a green felt fedora with a sprig of feathers in the band. His face is meaty, but there's nothing soft about his eyes.

"Cone?" he says.

"That's right. You Martin Gardow?"

"Yes. The rain bother you?"

"Not so much."

"Good. Let's take a walk."

The Wall Street dick doesn't like that. Inside, he's relatively safe. Out on an almost deserted street, anything could happen. Like a long gun trained on him from a parked car. But he figures he'll get nowhere being timid with this hardnose.

They stroll along the waterfront, the river swathed with fog, tugs hooting. It's real graveyard weather, with a damp cold that eats into bones and promises death.

"Just what the fuck do you think you're doing?" Martin Gardow asks quietly.

"Trying to scorch your ass a little," Cone says. "I thought that was obvious."

"Fifty thousand?" Gardow says. "Are you really that greedy?"

"Oh-ho," Cone says, knowing now that he guessed right. "January told you, did he? Nah, I'm not greedy. But there's so much bread involved here, I thought I'd pick me up some crumbs."

"I don't think you're stupid. But you're costing me more time than you're worth. Do you realize how *small* you are? Do you know what you're up against? You're a fly, Mr. Cone. You keep making trouble, you're going to get swatted."

"Maybe," Cone admits. "You tried it once, didn't you? And now Bernie Snodgrass is pushing up daisies, and the buttons are looking for his pal Sol. Maybe they'll find him and crack him. Worried about that, Mr. Gardow?"

"I don't know what you're talking about."

"Sure you do," Cone says.

Then, infuriated by Gardow's calm confidence, the Wall Street dick suddenly plucks the little bunch of feathers from the man's hat band and tosses it over the railing into the East River.

"I hate those things," he says.

Gardow glances a moment at his bright feathers floating away on the scummy tide, then turns to stare at Cone.

"You're not long for this world," he says.

"I know. None of us are."

They're facing each other now, and Gardow's blue eyes are sparking. Timothy thinks the guy is going to get physical. He can see it in the flushed skin, bunched shoulders, the fast pump of the big chest. But gradually Gardow gets control of himself. When he speaks, his voice is as toneless as ever.

"I think it's time to lower the boom. You turned down Lester Pingle's offer of ten grand. Then suddenly you brace January for fifty. Did you learn something? I'm betting you didn't. I think you worked January to get to me. A nice move—but not too smart. All right, now you know:

I've got Lester Pingle and Victor January by the balls. So? What are you going to do about it?"

"Blow the whistle on the Nu-Hope deal," Cone says, dreading what's coming next. "What else?"

"I'll tell you what else," Gardow says. "I don't know what the relationship is between you and your boss Samantha Whatley, and I couldn't care less. All I know is that when those two bandits suckered you down to the street at two in the morning, they did it by telling you Whatley was in trouble. That's got to tell me something—right? She's *your* short hair, isn't she, Mr. Cone? And that's my leverage."

"You prick," Cone says.

"You know what happened to Jessie Scotto. Want to see Samantha Whatley with her tits cut off? Think about it. I'll give you two days. Forty-eight hours. If I haven't heard that you've okayed the Nu-Hope deal by then, we go after your friend."

"You're dead," Timothy Cone says. "As of now, you're dead."

"I don't think so," Gardow says with his mirthless smile. "As my boss says, every man has his price. I think I've discovered yours, and it isn't money. As a matter of fact, you're not going to get fifty thousand out of this deal, or even ten. You're getting Samantha Whatley. Two days, Mr. Cone. Nice to have met you."

He tips his hat with an ironic little gesture, turns, walks slowly away through the thickening mist. I could drop to one knee, Cone thinks, pull my iron, and put six between those thick shoulders.

He stands trembling, fighting down the hot anger. He doesn't doubt for a second that Gardow is capable of doing exactly what he threatens. But wasting the guy would solve nothing. His boss, the legendary Mr. D., would just come up with another Martin Gardow. And the whirligig will keep spinning.

Cone's hands are shaking so badly that it takes three matches to get his Camel lighted. And then, after two drags, the damned thing is snuffed out by moisture dripping from the beak of his black leather cap. He tosses the wet cigarette away and plods westward. He knows what he's got to do.

In the lobby of Pingle's office building Cone takes off his parka and leather cap and shakes them vigorously, spattering the marble tile with rain. The maintenance man, who's pushing a big mop back and forth to keep the floor dry, looks at him and says, "Thanks a lot."

"Listen, if it wasn't for shlubs like me, you wouldn't have a job. I mean, we muck up your floor so you can clean it. Then you've got a job—right?"

"That's one way of looking at it," the guy says.

"It's the only way," Cone assures him, and takes the elevator up to the eighth floor. "Timothy Cone," he says to the receptionist. "To see Mr. Ernest Pingle..."

"Just a moment, sir."

She mutters into a phone. Cone waits patiently. In a few minutes an elderly lady comes out, leaning on a cane. She's got a man's pocket watch pinned to the bosom of her black dress. She gives Cone a suspicious, angry stare.

"He's having his lunch," she says.

"I'll wait."

"No," she says grudgingly, "come on in."

She conducts him, hobbling on her stick, down a long corridor. Throws open a door.

"You want a glass tea?" she asks. "Coffee?"

"No," he says. "But thank you."

Ernest Pingle is propped behind an old oak desk with a glass of tea before him and an opened tin of English biscuits. There's an extra armchair in the tiny room and an old-fashioned oak filing cabinet. A bentwood coat tree. A brass wastebasket. And that's about it.

"This place is almost as small as my office," Cone says, looking around. "I thought you Wall Street types lived high off the hog."

Ernest Pingle shrugs. "I've got a telephone. What more do I need? How are you, Mr. Cone?"

"Damp, but I'm surviving," Timothy says, hanging his wet parka and cap on the coat tree. "You okay?"

"Rheumatism," the old man says. "In this weather, it acts up. Which is why I'm not standing to greet you. But I would like to shake your hand."

Cone reaches across the desk, then slumps into the armchair alongside the desk.

"Tea?" Pingle asks. "Maybe coffee?"

"No, thanks. Your secretary asked me."

"Mrs. Scherer. She's been with me almost fifty years. Would you believe?"

"Yeah, I'd believe."

"At least have a biscuit," the old man says, shoving the tin toward him. "They're wery good."

Cone inspects the contents, then selects a swirled round with a dot of chocolate in the center.

"A wise choice," Pingle says, nodding. "You've got something to tell me, Mr. Cone?"

"Something to tell you," Cone says, "and something to ask you. You've treated me square and I've got to level with you. Drop the Nu-Hope Clinic deal."

"It's not for Pingle Enterprises?"

"Or anyone else. But a lot of very strange people are interested in it. My advice is to bail out. But I've got to admit I can't give you any logical reasons. Except that I think it stinks."

"I agree," Ernest Pingle says equably. "I felt in my gut from the start that it was not for us. So I'll call Nu-Hope and cancel the deal, and I'll call Haldering and tell him to end the investigation."

"No," Cone says quickly. "Please don't do that. Give me another one or two days before you pull the plug. I think I'll have it wrapped up by then."

Pingle looks at him curiously. "One or two days? So why are you telling me now I should cancel?"

"Because I think my boss is under pressure and might give you a go-ahead without waiting for my report. Don't listen to him, Mr. Pingle. It's a sour deal."

The other man nods. "I'd offer you a bonus," he says, "but I know you wouldn't accept it."

"You're right; I wouldn't."

"See!" the old man says gleefully. "I know people. The first time I met you I said to myself, 'There's a man I can trust.' You know why I said that?"

"Because you offered me a kiss then, and I turned you down."

"No, that wasn't it. Maybe you turned me down because you were owned by someone else. But you thanked me for that little bit of schnapps I gave you. I said to myself that a man so polite can't be a thief."

"Don't be so sure," Cone says. "The most successful con men are the most courteous."

The old man shakes his big head. "Not you," he says. "I *know*. All right, I kill the Nu-Hope deal, but not for a couple of days. You'll let me know when I can move?"

"I'll let you know."

"Meanwhile, what about my son Lester? He's inwolved in this?"

"Up to his pipik."

"With that shtarker Martin Gardow?"

"Yes," Cone says. "Gardow has him on a string."

"Lester is in danger? Physical danger?"

Cone ponders a moment. "He may be," he says finally, "but the chances are small. I think it's worth the risk. I'm hoping to slice Gardow off at the knees before he can spring, and then your son will be home free. Mr.

Pingle, I hate to give advice to anyone as smart as you, but why don't you read the riot act to your son? Cut him down to size. Then bail him out of his money troubles and put him on an allowance. Tell him and the wife to straighten up and fly right. If they haven't got themselves squared away in, say, a year, then kick them out of the nest."

"Wery good adwice," Ernest Pingle says sadly. "His mother would kill me, but sometimes it's necessary to be cruel to be kind."

Cone nods, rises, struggles into his damp parka. "That's it," he says. "I saw my duty and I done it. Thanks for the cookie."

"Biscuit," the old man says, flashing his dentures. "The English call them biscuits."

"Whatever," Cone says. "It was good."

Timothy reaches across the desk to shake that unexpectedly sturdy paw.

"Are you married, Mr. Cone?" Pingle asks.

"No."

"Would you like to meet a wery nice girl?"

"No," Cone says, "thanks. I already know a nice girl."

"God bless her!" Ernest Pingle cries.

He decides not to go back to the office. He doesn't want to bump into Hiram Haldering just yet and he's afraid that if he sees Sam, he'll lose his brio and, remembering Martin Gardow's threats, insist that she take off immediately for Hong Kong, or at least go visit her parents in Idaho. Then she'll want to know why he wants her out of town and, if Cone explains, she'll be outraged and claim she is completely capable of taking care of herself.

Cone doesn't need that kind of hassle. He decides his best bet is to stay the course, do what he's doing, and eliminate the danger before telling Samantha she might be in danger. If he fails, there will be time enough for damage control.

It's impossible to get a cab, and all the buses are jammed with damp mobs that he knows will be smelling of mothballs. So he walks all the way back to his loft, cursing the wet, the gloom, and especially Martin Gardow. But not forgetting to stop at neighborhood stores to pick up a smoked chub for Cleo, a package of frozen spaghetti and meatballs for himself, and a bottle of Korbel brandy to chase the chill.

In the warm loft, he tosses the chub to Cleo and fixes his own dinner. When he's finished, he decides on a short nap. Cleo comes padding over to fit into the bend of his knees, and the two of them fall asleep.

It's almost ten P.M. when he wakes up and settles down with one of his new books on artificial conception, still seeking a clue to what's going on in that sealed research laboratory at the Nu-Hope Clinic. He sticks with it, trying to understand the techniques involved.

He's demolished a half pack of Camels and is on his second brandy when he reads a long footnote in print so small he has to play the book like a trombone, moving the page back and forth until the type comes into focus. Then he reads it again.

He looks up blinking. He thinks he's got it. It explains why the U.S. Government is interested. And why Leopold Devers, the redoubtable Mr. D. of International Gronier, would order Martin Gardow to get a lock on the research.

Timothy stares at Cleo, who is sitting primly on his desk, paws together, regarding him with cold, glittery eyes.

"Holy Christ!" Cone says to the cat.

He thinks it through carefully. If he calls Phoebe Trumball at night and demands to see her, she's going to be wary about asking him up to her place. Or even venturing out after dark to meet him at a bar. And he doesn't want to brace her in public; this has got to be a one-on-one in private.

Also, if he calls in the evening, there's always the chance January will be with her. Cone has no desire to take on the two of them together; they'll draw too much strength from each other.

So he waits until morning and calls the clinic around seven-thirty, asking when they expect Dr. Phoebe Trumball to arrive. He's told she usually checks in at nine o'clock. He thanks them, says he'll call back. But instead, he calls her home.

"Hello?" she says.

"Doctor Trumball? Good morning. This is Timothy Cone."

A short pause. "My," she says, "you *are* an early riser."

"Yeah," he says, "sometimes. Listen, something very important has come up. I was hoping you'd be willing to talk to me this morning. Not at the clinic; it can't be there."

"What is this about, Mr. Cone? If it's the Pingle deal then I think Doctor January should be present."

"No, it's about that research you're doing. I really think we should have a private talk."

"Goodness," she says with a nervous laugh, "you sound very mysterious."

"Just give me a half hour," he persists. "And then, if I'm not making sense, tell me to get lost and I'll go. Okay?"

"Well, all right," she says finally. "How soon can you be here?"

"Twenty minutes," he says happily.

There are a lot of empty cabs going uptown after dumping their fares on Wall Street, so Cone has no trouble getting a hack. He spends the trip rehearsing what he's going to say. He decides to come on hard, throw it all at her before she can get her defense organized.

She's wearing a black wool jumpsuit. Zippered and form-fitting. He's never seen her without either a lab coat or street coat before, and he's surprised at the willowy strength of her body.

She takes his parka, but offers no coffee or anything else.

"Now then, Mr. Cone," she says, all business. "What's this all about?"

He's sitting in an uncomfortable, linen-covered armchair, and he hunches forward, elbows on knees, hands clasped.

"The deal with Pingle Enterprises is dead," he says, looking directly at her. "I killed it. I told Ernest Pingle yesterday, and he agreed to pull out."

It takes a moment for that to sink in, and it really rocks her. Then she gets indignant.

"But *why*? What gives you the right to wreck our plans? Haven't we cooperated with you every step of the way? Why on earth would you turn us down?"

"Well, let me talk awhile, doctor. Most of it is guesswork, but it fits the facts I know.

"First of all, I think I've found out what you're doing in that locked research laboratory of yours. It's okay by me. If you're not doing it, someone else is or will be. But it's a long, expensive project. I figure you might have applied for a federal grant. Instead, Gibby shows up, representing a government agency that funds scientific research. Mostly on the sly. How am I doing so far?"

"I'm listening," she says stonily.

"Gibby explains that Uncle Sam is interested in your project, but there's *no* way a grant can be made. The media might get hold of it and there'd be political hell to pay. But Gibby suggests you could get the money you need for research by going to a venture capital outfit like Pingle Enterprises. It could be structured as a limited partnership or franchise, but the government would guarantee that Nu-Hope's expansion would be oversubscribed through a lot of dummy investors who would be shoveling in the taxpayers' money. That makes sense, doesn't it?"

She doesn't answer.

"I've got no objections to that scam," Cone says, figuring he's on a roll. "If that's all there was to the deal, I'd have okayed it. If the U.S. Government wants to play cute, it's no skin off my nose. But then two people got murdered, and the whole thing went sour."

She stares at him, and he believes she is genuinely bewildered.

"Two murders? What are you talking about?"

"Harold Besant and Jessie Scotto. They got dusted because your play-

mate, Doctor January, is a very ambitious, very greedy man—and you
know it. The deal suggested by Gibby wasn't good enough. If the government funded your research, it wouldn't put any bucks in January's pocket,
so he engineered another deal. A sellout I don't think you know a thing
about."

"You're lying!" she says angrily. "He wouldn't do anything like that."

"Sure he would," Cone says. "For enough money and fame. He makes
contact with a guy named Martin Gardow, who's the hit man for an outfit
called Rauthaus Industries, which, in turn, is owned by International Gronier. The top man at Gronier is Leopold Devers, known as Mr. D., who,
from what I hear, makes Attila the Hun look like a Boy Scout."

"You can't prove any of this!" she says furiously.

"The only thing I can't prove is how January and Martin Gardow got
together. Maybe your partner approached Gardow. Maybe you've got a
snitch in your lab who tipped off International Gronier to what's going
on, and Gardow was handed the assignment. However they got together,
Mr. D. and Gardow now own January, lock, stock, and test tube. That
connection I *can* prove. A couple of days ago I met with January in private,
and suggested he pay me fifty thousand to okay the deal with Pingle
Enterprises. January said he'd think it over. The very next day I get a call
from Martin Gardow, who's yelling at me for holding him up for fifty big
ones. Is that proof enough for you?"

She doesn't want to believe, but Cone can see she's beginning to. He
decides he never could have convinced her so quickly if she didn't already
have some secret doubts about January.

Cone is silent, giving her time to absorb the shock. They're sitting there,
staring at each other, when a phone in the next room rings.

"Let it go," Phoebe says dully. "It's probably the clinic wondering where
I am. Would you like some coffee? I think I better have something."

"Sure," Cone says, "that would be nice. Black, please."

While she's in the kitchen, he looks around her trim living room and
spots a couple of ashtrays, so he figures it's okay to smoke. He lights up
a Camel, inhaling gratefully. He's satisfied with the way it's going—so far.
The crunch will come when he leans on her.

She returns with a tray loaded with a Chemex of coffee, cups, saucers,
packets of Sweet 'n Low.

"There's more, isn't there?" she asks, pouring.

Cone nods. "The murders. Harold Besant's death was a setup. Someone
sat beside him in the car, put a gun to his head, and blew his brains out.
Made it look like Besant committed suicide. The killer placed the gun as
if it had fallen out of Besant's right hand, but the police learned later
Besant was left-handed."

She shudders, takes a gulp of her coffee.

"Jessie Scotto's death was an obvious homicide," he goes on. "Very brutal, very nasty. The murderer was looking for something he thought she had, or was trying to get her to talk. The cops found fingerprints belonging to a punk who worked for Martin Gardow, your playmate's pal."

"Will you stop calling him my playmate," she says furiously. "It's disgusting and I resent it."

"Okay," Cone says equably, "I won't call him that again. But there's hard evidence tying Gardow and his thugs to Jessie Scotto's murder."

"Why are you telling me all this? What do you *want?*"

"I want to hang Martin Gardow up to dry. I want to get that villain off the streets. But I need a motive. Why did Gardow kill Besant and Scotto? I think you can guess, and I was hoping you'd tell me. Harold Besant worked in your research lab. You saw him every day. I figure he knew exactly what was going on, and it bothered him. He was ready to go public. Did Besant have access to your lab records?"

"Of course."

"Is anything missing?"

"Not to my knowledge."

"Do you have a copier in the lab?"

"Yes."

"So it's possible he could have made a complete record of what's going on in there?"

"Yes, it's possible. But we trust our staff. We don't search them every night when they leave."

"Maybe you should. Was Harold Besant acting strangely in the weeks before he died?"

"Well, he was depressed. Everyone noticed it."

"Did he ever object to the work you're doing?"

"He never said anything about it to me."

"Did he talk to Doctor January shortly before he died? Did they have any private meetings?"

She finishes her coffee, and when she sets the cup down, it rattles against the saucer.

"He might have," she says cautiously. "But I wouldn't have any idea what they talked about."

"Uh-huh," Cone says, knowing she's lying. "Did Besant ever threaten to quit?"

"He seemed, ah, dissatisfied," she says vaguely.

"Doctor Trumball," Cone says, "it's possible, just possible, you may be required to testify about these matters under oath. I think you're holding out on me. I think you're remembering a lot of things. Why don't you think of yourself, your professional career, and tell—"

Just then the outside door buzzer sounds, four short, angry bursts. Phoebe is startled.

"That's Victor's ring," she says confusedly. "I'll have to let him in."

"Sure," Cone says, rising. "You do that."

January comes in fast. "Darling," he says worriedly, "is everything all—" Then he sees Cone. "Oh," January says, trying to twist his face into a smile. "I didn't know you had a guest."

"Doctor Trumball and I have been having a little discussion," Cone says.

The three stand in a tense triangle.

"A discussion?" January says. "About Nu-Hope?"

"Mostly about you," Cone says. "Your connection with Martin Gardow. How deeply you're involved in the murders of Harold Besant and Jessie Scotto. That's what we've been discussing. Stuff like that."

Suddenly, unexpectedly, Victor January falls into a martial-arts crouch. Hands clenched into fists. Arms extended. Shoulders hunched. His pale face is frozen. He shuffles toward Cone. "Hah!" he shouts.

The Wall Street dick stoops swiftly, draws his Magnum from the ankle holster, straightens, and aims casually.

"Hah yourself," he says to January. "You pull that karate shit with me and I'll pop your kneecaps. You'll spend the rest of your life wheeling around on skateboards. You want that? Or maybe I'll go for the cajones, and you'll be singing soprano in the shower. Come on, try me. At this range I can't miss."

The doctor glares at him, then melts. His arms fall to his sides. Fists open. He stands slumped. His face sags, mouth partly open. All his charm is gone. He looks spectral, leached out.

"Now behave yourself," Cone says. "I know what you're doing in that locked lab. So you can wave goodbye to the Pingle deal. To Gardow and his dirty bucks. To the Nobel Prize and TV talk shows and all that crap. Do your job, Doctor January. Help women have babies and be satisfied with that. A tycoon you ain't, and never will be."

"Oh, darling, darling!" Phoebe Trumball cries. She moves to the demolished man, embraces him. He puts his head down on her shoulder.

Cone hears sobs, but who is weeping, or if both are, he cannot tell. He slips his iron back into the holster, finds his parka and cap, and heads for the door. He knows he's gone as far as he can go with those two simples. But it was worth the try.

He turns at the door to look back. They're still hugging. Phoebe Trumball is murmuring, stroking Victor January's hair.

She's in love with the guy and won't squeal.

That's okay. Cone can understand that.

He spends the afternoon in his office, snarling at everyone who comes by, including Sam. Around one o'clock he calls down for a cheeseburger, fries, and two cans of cold Bud. Meanwhile, he's trying to devise a way to slip the blocks to Martin Gardow, that monster.

Cone knows he'll never get anywhere trying to pry testimony from Drs. January and Trumball. At the moment, those two schlumphs are probably making nice-nice and talking about how they can get out of the mess they are in with their asses unscarred.

Nor can Cone expect any assistance from J. Roger Gibby. The government man will never cooperate on any plan that might attract media attention to Uncle Sam's interest in a scientific research project that would bemuse half the nation and scarify the other half.

No, the only possibility is to use Martin Gardow's cockiness to demolish him. Timothy Cone has a few ideas on how that might be done. But he's got time working against him, Sam to protect, and his own fury to contain. One of his imagined solutions is to find Gardow, blast the fucker, and wait patiently for the blues to arrive and take him away.

He leaves the office a little after five o'clock, still seething, and is only a few feet from Broadway when a short beep from a car horn makes him look up. It's the city's dusty blue Plymouth, illegally parked, with Detectives Davenport and Galanis in the front seat. Davenport waves him over. Cone climbs into the back.

"What's up?" he says.

"My cock," Davenport says. "Watching all the young ginch stroll by." He turns sideways in the front passenger seat so he can talk to Cone. "We picked up that pal of Bernie Snodgrass. Only his name is Sal, not Sol. Salvador Guiterrez, a real sweetheart with a sheet as long as your schlong. Nice stuff, like attempted rape, assault with a deadly weapon, battery, and so forth and so on. And would you believe he's never spent a day in the slammer?"

"I believe it," Cone says. "Where is he now?"

"He walked," Nick Galanis says gloomily. "What could we hold him for?"

"Assault," Cone says. "I can ID him."

"Big deal," Galanis says. "His word against yours. And he'll come up with four witnesses who'll swear that at the time of the alleged incident, Salvador Guiterrez was in Bayonne, New Jersey, eating scungilli. It's no use, Cone. The sonofabitch knows we've got nothing on him."

"Did you run a trace on Martin Gardow?"

"Oh, yeah," Davenport says, unwrapping a fresh stick of Juicy Fruit. "He's everything you said, and more. If he was whacked, they'd narrow the list of suspects to about a thousand."

"And I'd be one of them," Cone says. "I had a meet with the guy."

Both city detectives snap their heads around to stare at him.

"About what?" Davenport demands.

"About the Nu-Hope Fertility Clinic. I told him I wanted fifty grand to okay the deal. He said I'd either okay it without the loot or he'd cut off my girlfriend's tits. Isn't that lovely?"

"Beautiful," Galanis says bitterly. "That's what happened to Jessie Scotto. You think Gardow was behind that?"

"Had to be. He bankrolled it, and Snodgrass and Guiterrez did the job. That's why Sal is hanging tough. He knows he's got money for the legal eagles."

"So?" Davenport says. "Where do we go from here?"

"I got an idea," Cone says. "A long shot, but it might just work."

"Yeah?" Galanis says hopefully. "Let's hear it."

Cone explains what he has in mind, and the two cops listen intently. When he finishes, they look at each other.

"We could set it up," Davenport says slowly. "I know a great tech. It could be done. But if it turns sour, you know what's going to happen to you, don't you?"

"Oh, yeah," Cone says, "I know. You want to fly it?"

"Why not?" Galanis says savagely. "It's got a chance."

"Okay," Davenport says.

So they talk ways and means, set up a schedule, look for loopholes and close them. When Cone gets out of the car, they all shake hands.

He walks home and feeds himself and Cleo. He gives the cat fresh water and changes the litter. He does some laundry in the kitchen sink, smokes half a pack of Camels, and drinks more Popov than he should. Meanwhile he's muttering to himself, rehearsing the part he's going to play the next day.

"Academy Award, kiddo," he tells Cleo. "I'm going to get an Oscar for this one."

He sleeps badly that night: dreams haunted with images of a war he thought he had forgotten. Once he is awakened by his own groans, to find Cleo bending over him, almost nose to nose, mewling sadly.

"Beat it," Cone says, pushing the cat away.

He tries to get back to sleep again, but it doesn't work. He finally gives up and waits for dawn, lying supine on that scruffy mattress on the floor, staring up at his broken skylight and wondering what it's all about. It's that kind of night.

He's an hour late getting to work in the morning, which is bad even for him. But he has to fight fears gnawing at him like the leeches in Nam. A terrible lassitude saps his resolve, and he beats it only by thinking of Sam and what might happen to her if he fails.

His first call is to Ernest Pingle.

"Mr. Pingle," he says, "you can pull the plug now. The Nu-Hope deal is dead."

"Wery good," the old man says. "I'll call Haldering and tell him to stop the inwestigation and send me a bill."

"It would help me," Cone says, "if you just told him you decided to withdraw from the deal without giving him any reason."

"Of course," Pingle says. "What else? Are you all right, my young friend? You sound wery tight."

"Just winding this thing up. With luck, it'll be finished today."

"Is there anything I can do to help?"

"No, thank you," Cone says gratefully. "Did you talk to your son?"

"I talked," Ernest Pingle says. "To him *and* his wife. I think maybe they'll behave."

"I think maybe they will," Timothy says, smiling at the phone. "Nice meeting you, Mr. Pingle. I hope our paths cross again."

"Why shouldn't they? I want to hear the whole story about Nu-Hope. When it's ower."

"You will," Cone promises. "I'll tell you, but you won't believe it."

"At my age I'll believe anything."

Cone's second call is to Martin Gardow. But the secretary tells him Mr. Gardow is in conference and suggests he call back in a half hour. Cone waits forty-five minutes before trying again. This time Gardow comes on the line.

"Cone?" he says. "I was expecting to hear from you."

"Yeah, I guess," Cone says, trying to make his voice as servile as he can. "I've been doing some thinking about what we discussed."

"Glad to hear it. And?"

"I don't see why we can't get together. I mean we're both reasonable men—right?"

"I hope so," Gardow says, "for your sake. So you've decided to okay the Nu-Hope deal?"

"Well, I'd like to talk to you about it first."

"What's to talk about? You know what your choices are."

"Well, sure," Cone says, "but it doesn't seem right that I come out of this empty-handed."

Martin Gardow sighs. "Another cheapski," he says. "All right, Cone, I may toss you a cookie if I'm in the mood. I'll see you at the Seaport, same place, this afternoon."

"Meeting out in the open like that gives me the willies," Cone says. "I like my back to a wall."

Unexpectedly, Gardow laughs. Not a nice laugh. "Yes," he says, "I can understand why you might feel that way. What do you suggest?"

"There's a place on Madison. The Hotel Bedlington. They got a cocktail lounge that's usually deserted in the afternoon. I thought we might meet there about three. Have a friendly drink. Our business won't take long."

There's silence, and Cone's afraid he's lost.

Then Martin Gardow says, "The Bedlington? Yes, I know it. Just let me check my appointment book."

The fink!

"All right," Gardow says after a pause, "I'll meet you at the Bedlington bar at three o'clock this afternoon. Be on time. I don't like to be kept waiting."

Cone's next call is to Davenport.

"It's on," Cone tells him. "Three this afternoon at the Bedlington."

"Okay," the cop says. "We're ready to roll. The hotel people are co-operating. We'll get there an hour ahead of time and set things up."

"Follow the script," Cone warns him. "It's my cock on the block."

"We'll do our job. Nick can't wait to get his hands on this guy."

"Like I told you," Cone says, "even if the charge doesn't stick, just busting the guy might convince Sal Guiterrez to turn canary."

"It's worth a try," Davenport acknowledges. "Stay cool."

"Yeah," Cone says. "See you later."

He gets up to the Hotel Bedlington a little before two-thirty and heads directly for the gents'. There's a sign on the door: CLOSED FOR REPAIRS. PLEASE USE THE MEN'S ROOM ON MEZZANINE. Satisfied, Cone goes into the cocktail lounge. There's one bartender, handicapping a racing sheet, one bored waiter, examining his nails, and one young couple at the bar, heads together and giggling.

The Wall Street dick takes a small table in a shadowed corner and sits with his back to the wall, where he can watch the entrance. The waiter brings him a paper napkin and a little dish of salted peanuts. Cone orders a bottle of Heineken, and when it comes, he goes to work on it as fast as he can.

The beer finished, he catches the waiter's eye and signals for an encore. When the waiter brings the second bottle, he starts to remove the empty, but Cone stops him.

"Leave it," he says. "I want to keep track."

"Whatever you say, sir," the waiter says, sighing. But Cone knows what he's doing. Those two beer bottles on his table are theatrical props.

Gardow comes striding in a few minutes after three. He looks around, spots Cone, and comes over. He's wearing his double-breasted topcoat but no hat. Cone wonders if he discarded the green fedora after the feathers drowned in the East River.

Gardow takes off his coat, folds it neatly, and places it atop Cone's parka on a nearby chair. When the waiter comes over, Gardow orders a scotch mist with a twist of lemon peel. The drink is served with a short straw, and Cone is amused to note that Gardow actually uses it.

Gardow glances at the two beer bottles. "You like the suds?" he asks. "That figures. I'll bet you go bowling, too."

"Yeah, well, sometimes," Cone says sheepishly. "Good exercise—you know?"

Gardow could have taken a chair across the table from Cone, but instead he has seated himself on the vinyl-covered banquette next to Cone. Their knees are almost touching.

Gardow takes another sip through the straw, then reaches into his jacket pocket and pulls out a small black box, no larger than a pack of cigarettes. It is inset with a switch, a round grille, two lights, and a needled dial.

"Know what this is?" Gardow says, holding it out.

Cone shakes his head.

"It's a miniaturized electronic debugger. My company makes them. In Taiwan. For instance, suppose you came in here wired with a recorder, maybe even a transmitter, to pick up our conversation. This little—"

"Wired?" Cone says, astonished. "Why would I want to do that?"

"Just suppose you did," Gardow says, staring at him. "This little beauty would tell me in a minute."

He turns the switch on with his thumb, then begins to move the little black box across Cone's shoulders and chest, around his waist, down his legs. A green light on the box is glowing. Gardow watches the dial, paying no attention to the stares of the waiter and bartender.

Finished, he flicks off the switch and slips the device back into his jacket pocket. "You're clean," he says. "But if you had been wired, I'd have known it. You've got heavy metal on your lower right leg. What is it?"

"I carry a piece in an ankle holster. I've got a permit for it."

"Sure you do," Gardow says, going back to his scotch. "You weren't thinking of plugging me, were you?"

"Come on," Cone says. "I put it on every morning like underwear. I've never fired it off the range."

"Uh-huh," Gardow says. "Tell that to Bernie Snodgrass. After you dig him up."

"Look, Mr. Gardow," Cone says, finishing his second beer, "this kind of talk is getting us nowhere. I want to discuss the Nu-Hope deal."

"So you said on the phone. And I asked you what there is to discuss."

"Wow," Cone says, "those beers . . . My back teeth are floating. Let me take a quick trip to the john and then I'll tell you what's on my mind."

"Go ahead," Martin Gardow says casually. "I'm comfortable here."

Got him!

At the entrance to the men's room in the lobby, Cone knocks three times, rapidly. Davenport opens up.

"Okay?" he asks.

"So far," Cone says, starting to take off his corduroy jacket and flannel shirt. "This is one suspicious bastard. He's got a debugger, like I figured. More than three minutes and I'm in *biiig* trouble."

"We'll make it," Nick Galanis says. "This is Marve Heimholtz, a genius. He's going to wire you. Marve, this is Cone."

"Hi," the bespectacled tech says, stripping adhesive tape off a wide roll. "I'm giving you a mike on your chest, a transmitter on your ribs, a recorder in your jacket pocket."

"Left pocket," Cone says. "He's sitting close to my right side and might feel it."

"Okay, the recorder goes in your left jacket pocket. We've also got a pickup under the bar in the cocktail lounge and another in here. We should get results from one or another. They're all miniaturized units. Japanese. Try not to cough, sneeze, or scrape things. Keep your voice loud and clear. It wouldn't hurt to lean toward him as closely as possible without spooking him."

As he's talking, the tech is wiring Timothy Cone's bare torso, carefully applying strips of tape to keep the mike, wires, and transmitter in place.

"Two minutes," Davenport says, looking at his watch. "Move it along, Marve."

"Almost done," Heimholtz says. "Put on your shirt and jacket again."

Cone buttons up, and the tech slips the recorder into his left jacket pocket. The three cops examine him.

"Looks good to me," Galanis says.

"Could you button your shirt up to the neck?" Marve says. "Just to make sure he doesn't spot the tape."

"I could," Cone says, "but the top button was open when I left him. If I close it now, he might notice. He's a real wiseguy."

"Okay," Davenport says, "leave it open." He glances at his watch again. "A bit over three minutes. Out you go. We'll listen in here. If you get anything, we'll put the arm on him when he leaves."

Cone nods, tugs down his jacket. "I'd really like to take a leak," he says, "but we haven't got the time."

"Cross your legs," Galanis says.

"What a relief that was," Cone says, sliding back onto the banquette. He notices Gardow has ordered a fresh scotch mist. Cone raises his hand, catches the waiter's attention, motions toward his empty beer bottles.

"By the way," he says to the other man, "this is my treat."

"Of course," Gardow says. "Cone, I'm going to finish this drink and take off. So if you have anything to say to me, you better spit it out now."

"Yeah, well, I wanted to talk about Nu-Hope. When I got assigned to that thing, I really didn't know how important it was."

"It's important," Martin Gardow says. "Mr. D. gives it the highest priority."

"Well, I didn't realize how much muscle was behind it. Lester Pingle tries to buy me off with ten grand, and I figure there's more there than I thought."

"Pingle handled it stupidly," Gardow says. "The man's a fool."

"Yeah, he is, you're absolutely right. Then I learn about Harold Besant and Jessie Scotto and I began to catch on to how big this thing is."

Gardow shrugs. "It had to be done. Besant was threatening to go public. Jesus, that's all we needed. So he had to be taken out."

"And you figured he had told his girlfriend?"

Gardow looks at him. "Wouldn't you?"

"I don't know. You're much smarter than I am, Mr. Gardow. I mean, you're way ahead of all of us. It's just that I saw the girl's body. Snodgrass and Guiterrez must be a couple of creeps."

"They are, but you work with what you can get. How did you find out those two slugs whacked Besant and Scotto?"

"I didn't find out; the cops did. Besant was left-handed, but the gun was dropped like it had fallen from his right hand. And they found Bernie Snodgrass's prints in Scotto's apartment."

"Shit!" Gardow says disgustedly. "How stupid can you get? Well, Snodgrass is feeding the worms, and I'll have Guiterrez taken care of. Mr. D. doesn't like loose ends."

"This Mr. D.," Cone says, "he sounds like hell on wheels."

"He's a rotten, no-good sonofabitch, but he pays a good buck for results. Well, enough of this bullshit. Have you okayed the Nu-Hope deal?"

"Not yet," the Wall Street dick says. "I guess January told you I know what's going on in that secret research lab of theirs."

"He told me. So?"

"Well, I can see how important it is."

"I told you what would happen to your girlfriend if you don't produce."

"I know, Mr. Gardow. And I know you're not just making noise. But it seems to me a little bonus would be a nice gesture on your part."

"What do you call a little bonus?"

"Well, of course I don't expect fifty grand. I just mentioned that number to January to smoke him out. But you had Lester Pingle offer me ten grand. Could you still spring for that?"

Gardow finishes the remainder of his drink and rises. "That was before I learned about Samantha Whatley. I could stiff you completely, and you'd produce just to keep her breathing. But I'm a forgiving man. The moment I hear you've okayed the deal I'll get a thousand to you—just for good-will."

"Gee, Mr. Gardow," Cone says, whining, "can't you do better than that?"

"Take it or leave it," Gardow says, pulling on his coat.

"I'll take it," Cone says hastily.

"I thought you would," the other man says. "I deal with sleazes like you all the time. You start out ten feet tall and end up on your knees. Don't call me again."

He starts toward the glass door leading to the lobby. Cone hurries after him. He wants to give Davenport and Galanis a chance to get in position.

"When will I get the cash, Mr. Gardow? I can really use it."

"You'll get it when I feel like it."

Both men go out into the lobby. The cops are waiting, IDs in their hands.

Davenport steps up. "Martin Gardow?"

"Yes. Who're you?"

"Detective Davenport, New York Police Department. This man is Detective Galanis. Here is our identification."

"What the fuck is this?" Gardow says wrathfully.

"You're under arrest," Davenport says. "Open your coat, please. We have to search you."

"Arrest," Gardow says, stunned. "For what?"

"Conspiracy to commit murder, for starters," Galanis says. "We'll probably come up with more when Salvador Guiterrez starts singing. Hey, Neal, how's about sending a cassette of this schmuck's remarks to Mr. D.? He'll get a big kick out of it—especially that part where his faithful employee calls him a rotten, no-good sonofabitch."

"I don't know what the hell you're talking about," Gardow says, his face suddenly tight and pale.

"Martin, baby . . ." the Wall Street dick calls softly.

Gardow whirls on him. Cone has unbuttoned his jacket and shirt. He displays the electronic gear taped to his bare torso.

"Surprise!" he says.

Gardow stares, shocked, then raises his eyes to glare. "I am going to have you popped," he says slowly, biting off each word.

"You think I care?" Timothy Cone says, much amused.

The whirligig is slowing down. Some of the people have been thrown off, some are still riding. But the merry-go-round is coasting now, music dying. Cone feels the tension seep out of him. It was a fast, frantic ride on the carousel, but it's good to stand on solid ground and see things in focus rather than a dizzying blur.

He figures there is no point in going back to the office. So he takes his delayed leak and lets Marve Heimholtz strip the electronic gear from his body before taking a cab down to his neighborhood. Before going up to the loft, he stops off to buy some salami and eggs, and a can of tuna for Cleo. Let the moth-eaten cat celebrate, too.

He's unlocking the loft door when his phone starts ringing.

"I'm coming!" he yells at it, and wonders, not for the first time, why people shout at a ringing phone.

"Yeah?" he says.

"What the hell are you doing home?" Sam yells. "You work here—remember?"

"I also work outside the office, and I've been busting my butt on the Nu-Hope Clinic deal."

"Forget it," she says. "Pingle Enterprises called and signed off. The case is dead."

"No kidding?" Cone says.

"You devious bastard, I'll bet you finagled it."

"Listen," Cone says, "I just picked up some salami and eggs. How's about coming by for dinner?"

"You got any salad stuff?" she asks in a low voice.

"I got a tomato. It's a little spotted."

"Beautiful," she says. "All right, I'll pick up some mixed greens at the deli. See you about six?"

He gives Cleo half of the tuna and puts fresh water in the cat's coffee can. By the time Samantha arrives, he's working on his second vodka and third Camel, and he's in a mellow mood. Not ecstatic, but satisfied every time he recalls the look on Martin Gardow's face when that yahoo realized he had been royally screwed.

"I want to know what you've been up to," Sam says angrily the moment she's inside the door.

"Calm down," he tells her. "Take off your coat, relax, have a drink."

"Don't try to sweet-talk me, buster," she says. "I always know when you've been conniving; you get that shit-eating grin."

"Christ, you're in a lovely mood," he says. "I'll tell you, I'll tell you. Just sit down and be nice."

Grumbling, she puts her package of salad stuff in the refrigerator and pours herself a jar of white wine. She sits at the table and scratches Cleo's ears.

"All right," she says, "let's have it. All of it."

He doesn't tell her *all* of it. Not about the threats to her safety. If he had mentioned that, she'd have cut him to ribbons, demanding to know what right he had to think she couldn't protect herself. She is that kind of a woman and, being that kind of a man, he can understand it.

So he tells her about J. Roger Gibby, Martin Gardow, Mr. D., Drs. January and Trumball, and the murders of Harold Besant and Jessie Scotto. Samantha listens intently, not interrupting. When he's finished and says, "That's it," she pours herself another glass of wine.

"No," she says, "that's not it. Not all of it. You still haven't told me what the McGuffin is. Why were the government and Mr. D. so interested in what Nu-Hope was doing in that research lab?"

"You won't believe it," Cone tells her.

"Try me," she says.

And, right on cue, there's a gentle rapping at the loft door.

"Now who the hell can that be?" Cone says. He slips the Magnum from his ankle holster and moves to the door, standing well to one side. "Who is it?" he shouts.

"Roger Gibby. May I come in for a moment?"

The Wall Street dick opens the door cautiously, peeks out, then pauses to slide his iron back into the holster.

"How did you get in downstairs?" he wants to know.

"I fear your outside door has been jimmied," Gibby says.

"Oh, God," Cone says. "Again? Well, come on in."

Gibby enters slowly. He's as impeccably clad as ever, wearing a trim chesterfield with a velvet collar, a black bowler, and carrying a pair of fawn gloves. There's a sprig of edelweiss pinned to his lapel.

"Where's your muscleman?" Cone asks.

"Downstairs, guarding our hubcaps." Gibby sees Samantha and removes his hat. "I beg your pardon, ma'am," he says with a small bow. "If I had known Mr. Cone had guests, I would have come at another time."

"Sam," Cone says, "this is Professor J. Roger Gibby."

"Former professor," he says with his sweet smile.

"This lady is Samantha Whatley, my boss at Haldering."

Gibby shakes her hand. "A pleasure," he says. "I envy you for having such a clever and diligent investigator on your staff."

"Oh, Cone's a pisser," Sam says, and if Gibby is shocked by her language, he doesn't reveal it.

He looks slowly about the loft. "Different," is his verdict. "And what, pray, is that animal under the bathtub?"

"Cleo," Cone says. "A sort of a cat. Take off your coat and pull up a chair. Have a drink."

"I'm only staying a minute," Gibby says, "but I would appreciate a small drink. It's been a long day."

"I've got some brandy."

"Excellent. Just a pony, if you will."

Gibby seats himself at the desk and is not at all disconcerted when Cone brings him the brandy in a jelly jar.

"Your health, ma'am," he says. "And to your continued success."

"Thank you," she says faintly.

Gibby takes a sip. "Quite nice," he says. "I presume that Mr. Cone has told you about his investigation of the Nu-Hope Fertility Clinic."

"He's told me everything except the reason everyone was so interested in them. I mean why were the U.S. Government and International Gronier involved?"

"The U.S. Government is no longer involved," Gibby says, looking at Sam steadily. "As of this afternoon we have terminated all connections with Nu-Hope. And, after the arrest of his underling, I suspect Leopold Devers of International Gronier has done the same."

"How did you find out about Gardow's arrest?" Cone asks curiously.

"Oh . . ." Gibby says vaguely, "I have contacts."

"So that's the end of it?" Cone says. "The government is dropping the whole thing?"

"Well . . ." Gibby says, "I wouldn't exactly say that, Mr. Cone. We're certainly dropping Nu-Hope. But not the project. I'm a great believer in redundancy in scientific research. It would have been foolish to have depended on one source. Actually, we have a number of teams developing the same thing. The work will continue."

"Yeah," Cone says. "That figures."

"Just to satisfy an old man, will you tell me how you got on to it?"

"I read a book," Cone says. "It was the only thing it could have been."

"Read a book," Gibby repeats, nodding. "The best way."

"Goddammit!" Samantha Whatley explodes. "Will the two of you tell me what the hell you're talking about!"

"I can understand your curiosity, ma'am," Gibby says, smiling gently, "and I see no reason why you shouldn't know. If you decide to go public—which I doubt very much you will wish to do—I can assure you there is no evidence confirming the government's interest."

"What *is* it?" Samantha cries desperately.

"It's called hybridization," Gibby says, staring thoughtfully into his jar of brandy. "An extremely complex project to explore the possibility of combining human sperm and eggs with the sperm and eggs of certain other primates, such as rhesus monkeys, chimpanzees, and others. It also involves the possibility of embryo transfer from one closely related species to another."

Sam turns her head slowly to stare at Timothy. "You were right," she says. "I don't believe it. Mate a woman with a monkey?"

"Oh, no!" J. Roger Gibby protests. "No, no, no. Actual sexual intercourse has never been suggested. We're concerned merely with laboratory techniques."

"Merely," Whatley says. "I love that merely. And you think someday you can produce a half-human/half-chimp?"

"Are you asking for my personal opinion?" Gibby says. "Yes, I think it's possible. In fact, there are reports that it's already been done by a Chinese doctor. Unfortunately, his laboratory and experiment were reportedly destroyed by terrified peasants."

"That I can understand," Samantha says.

"Look," Cone says. "Supposing the government or someone else spends a zillion dollars on this thing, finances a lot of research teams, and eventually succeeds, producing an ape-man. What I want to know is, what the hell's the *point*? Why spend so much money? Go to so much trouble?"

"Think about it, Mr. Cone. You're a smart man; just think about it. Envision any of these possibilities: an army composed of soldiers, vicious as baboons, with no imagination and hence no fear of death. Or intelligent semi-humans bred to fit into the tight, computerized cockpits of tomorrow's fighter planes. Or gifted animals able to withstand the boredom and terrors of long space flights."

"All right," Cone says grimly, "that's the government's interest. What was Mr. D.'s?"

"International Gronier is a worldwide conglomerate with factories all over the globe, a great many in third-world countries. Leopold Devers was prescient enough to realize how hybridization might revolutionize the labor force. Imagine half-animals bred to exact specifications. The missing link between robots and humans. Why, you might develop workers with abnormally long arms, prehensile toes, superior eyesight, or any other physical quality desired for efficient and low-cost production. Brilliant animals with no desire for unions or a say in management."

"Just toss them a banana," Cone says.

"Yes," Gibby says quite seriously. "That's the bottom line. Profit. Greed. That's what motivated Mr. D."

"I don't like this conversation," Sam says.

Gibby finishes his brandy, rebuttons his chesterfield, reclaims his bowler and gloves. He looks at Samantha with his kindly smile. "Religion, morality, ethics?" he says. "Is that what you're thinking about? I must tell you that science and technology have a momentum all their own. It makes no allowance for religion, morality, ethics. It's a different world. I am fond of remarking that if it can be done, it will be done. You cannot put a cap on man's creativity. It is hopeless to try by threat or edict."

"What you mean," Timothy Cone says, "is that science is your religion."

Gibby thinks about that for a moment. "Yes," he says finally, "I suppose that is what I mean: Science is my faith."

He thanks them for their hospitality, shakes hands, and flaps his gloves at Cleo, who is standing in the center of the floor, regarding him with hard, shining eyes. Then Gibby departs, and Cone locks, bolts, and chains the door behind him.

"Salami and eggs?" he asks Sam.

"Yes," she says, "that's what I need."

They speak very little that night, both burdened with secret thoughts, oppressed by nameless fears. They eat, drink, smile at Cleo's crazy antics. But it is a subdued evening, the whirligig finally stopped, music dead, lights dimmed.

It has seemed so before, and now once again that bedraggled loft becomes a cave, a refuge. Cleo is certainly not their child, but that dilapidated cat—in a manner they cannot comprehend—completes a family huddling in shelter, safe from the dark forces gathering outside.

Aloneness silences them, and it seems more a time for reflection than joy. They ponder existence and question their roles in the universe: leaves, grains of sand, dying stars. All their hopes, dreams, ambitions brought low. Evanescent things. Doomed to perish.

"What a drag," Whatley says.

"Yeah," Cone says.

They come out of it, as they inevitably must if they are to survive. They look at each other with glassy grins, tickle Cleo's ribs, stack the dishes, have another drink, embrace in a quick, clumsy dance step to no tune, fling off their clothes, have a vertical hug, flop onto the floor mattress, have a horizontal hug, nibble, yelp with laughter, stroke, the warmth and fever of living coming back now.

He stares entranced at her small, elegant breasts.

"Thank God," he says, "they're still there."

"Tim, what the hell are you talking about?"

"Just talking," he says, bending to kiss.

Book Three

A Covey of Cousins

1

Wall Street, as everyone knows, is a short, narrow, bustling thoroughfare that runs from a river to a graveyard. But it is more than a passage from deep water to deeper earth.

It is not a street at all, but a community whose backroom workers might toil in Queens, Hackensack, or Peoria. Indeed, Wall Street encompasses the world via a bewildering array of speedy electronic communication equipment: telephones, cables, satellites, facsimile reproduction, television and, faster than all of these, rumors.

Wall Street is fueled by greed and oiled by cupidity. It is a state of mind, a culture, a never-never land with all the hopeful romance of the Roseland Ballroom and the grungy despair of a Bowery flophouse. Men have soared on Wall Street—and not all of them through the nearest window because they guessed wrong.

It is a mystery, even to experienced insiders. It is a rigorous mathematical puzzle and simultaneously the most emotional and irrational of human institutions. Dealers come and go, customers come and go, but Wall Street endures, a series of nesting boxes so enormous, so artfully contrived and frustrating, that no one has ever uncovered the final secret.

Players on Wall Street, addicted to the madness, have coined a number of pithy aphorisms to serve as guides to financial adventures:

"If it sounds too good to be true, it *is* too good to be true."

"Never panic—but if you do, make sure you're the first to panic."

"Happiness can't buy money."

There are many fine buildings channeling the Street. Some house prestigious trading firms whose probity cannot be questioned. And then there are concrete barns with stalls for cash cows and others for spavined beasts not worth the feed to keep them alive, although they continue to exist until fatally stricken by Chapter Seven.

It is in one of the thriving establishments just east of Nassau Street, on a nippy Monday morning in mid-December, that the passion, the fervor of Wall Street may be glimpsed in all its crass, exciting glory. For there, on the premises of Laboris Investments, Inc., a throng of the covetous are attempting to follow the dictum of Sophie Tucker: "I've been rich and I've been poor, and believe me, rich is better."

The outer office is plain enough: plywood walls, plastic plants, and furniture that looks as if it has been rented from an outfit that supplies political campaign headquarters. The air is gummy with smoke, and the two begrimed windows look out on a shadowed airshaft that plunges to a concrete courtyard, bare and cold.

But the people coming through the door in a constant stream care nothing for the surroundings. The light of avarice is in their eyes. Many carry ads torn from newspapers, magazines, and direct-mail solicitations.

There to greet them are three personable employees of Laboris Investments, Inc. The two young men and one young woman wear large badges inscribed: ACCOUNT EXECUTIVE. And below: HI! and their names.

Each new arrival is handed a flier that, in four pages, describes the Laboris investment philosophy and technique. The thin brochure is mercifully free of the usual legal gobbledygook that fills thicker and more impressive Wall Street prospectuses. It also has the grace to state that "This is a high-risk investment, neither approved nor disapproved by the SEC, and investors should be prepared to lose the total sums invested."

But even this chilling disclaimer cannot cool the passion of the mob. They arrive with checkbooks at the ready, with money orders, even with wrinkled bills stuffed into Bloomies' shopping bags. The account executives are frantically active, answering questions, passing out applications, writing out receipts for cash received.

There is fever in the air, and all are infected. Some of those arriving are already Laboris clients come to make an additional contribution, and they happily tell strangers of a thirty-percent return on their money. "Monthly checks—regular as clockwork!" And so the contagion spreads, many angry because the account executives cannot accept their money quickly enough.

For every exultant customer who departs, two nervous hopefuls appear. There is apparently no end to the enthusiasts. The crowd importuning Laboris to take their life savings grows and grows. And all share a common affliction: the something-for-nothing syndrome for which modern medical science can offer no cure.

. . .

"Here's a crazy one," Samantha Whatley says. "Right up your old kazoo."

"How come I get all the nut cases?" Timothy Cone says grumpily. "Are you trying to tell me something?"

"Well, if you want to know, the customer asked for you, so just shut up and listen." She opens a folder and starts reading. "A private client. Mrs. Martha T. Hepplewaite. A widow. Lives in her own brownstone on East Thirty-eighth. With her only child, a daughter named Lucinda. Mrs. Hepplewaite wants us to investigate an outfit called Laboris Investments. The guy running it is Ingmar Laboris."

"Ingmar Laboris? What's that—a Swedish mouthwash?"

"Funny," Sam says without changing expression. "The legal and accounting sections already have their marching orders. You go see this Mrs. Hepplewaite and find out what the hell she wants. H.H. says she was very vague on the phone."

"How come she latched onto us?"

"Says we were recommended by Ernest Pingle, who mentioned your name. Hiram checked with Pingle, and he says the lady's got all the money in the world. Her husband was a Kansas City meat packer who dropped dead on the eighth green at St. Andrew's."

"What happened—did he miss a six-inch putt?"

Samantha shoves the file across her desk. "It's all yours. Go see the lady, and for God's sake this time keep me up to speed on what's going on."

"Don't I always?"

"Get lost," she tells him.

He takes the folder back to his office, parks his scuffed yellow work shoes on the desk, and scans the file. It doesn't tell him much more. But it does include address and phone number. So he calls.

"Hello?" A woman's voice. Cautious.

"Mrs. Martha T. Hepplewaite?"

"No, this is Lucinda Hepplewaite. May I ask who's calling, please?"
Cone tells her.

"Just a moment, please," she says, and the Wall Street dick reflects she's got a lot of "please" in her.

That's daughter Lucinda. When mother Martha comes on, she sounds like a drill instructor. No "please" at all.

"You're Timothy Cone of Haldering and Company?" she demands.

"That's correct, ma'am. I was hoping you'd have time to see me today."

"You have my address?"

"Yes."

"Five o'clock this afternoon. Precisely."

Slam!

Cone sits looking at the dead phone.

"And I love you, too," he says aloud.

He gets up to East Thirty-eighth Street ahead of time, to give himself a chance to scope the building. It snowed early that morning, a couple of inches, and it's cold enough to keep the white stuff crunching underfoot, like a beach of crusty sand. He stomps back and forth, hands in the fleece-lined pockets of his anorak.

The brownstone looks well-maintained, windows shiny and the sidewalk swept. Five stories high with bow windows and a mansard roof. Maybe seventy-five years old, he figures, and at today's prices worth a mil. At least. In the gloomy December twilight, there are lights burning in rooms on the first two floors.

The young woman who answers the door is tall, bony, and has a few too many teeth for her mouth. She's wearing an old-fashioned sweater set, a flannel skirt, and brogues almost as heavy as Cone's work shoes. A tentative smile lights her horsey face.

"Mr. Cone?"

"That's right. Miss Lucinda Hepplewaite?"

"Yes. This way, please."

He follows her down a narrow corridor and into a parlor that appears to have been untouched since World War I. Everything heavy, dark, carved, and embellished, with dried flowers under bell jars, crocheted antimacassars, needlepoint footstools, faded photographs framed in wood, an old wind-up Victrola, and whatnots and curios without end.

It's all so dated and evocative that Cone has a strong desire to cry: "Great heavens! The Boche have invaded Belgium!"

"Please take off your coat and, uh, cap," she says, "and make yourself comfortable. Mama will be with you in a moment."

She clumps away, and Cone takes off his parka and, uh, cap. But he can't see anyplace to put them. There's already *something* on every flat surface in the room, and the chairs and couches are so precisely arranged that he's afraid to desecrate them. So he stands there, holding both.

Lucinda doesn't return, but Mama comes stumping in, leaning on a cane as thick as a mizzenmast.

"I'm Mrs. Martha Hepplewaite," she declares, halfway between a bark and a snarl. "You're Timothy Cone from Haldering?"

"Yes, ma'am. Would you care to see my identification?"

"Not necessary. Ernest Pingle described you."

She makes no effort to shake hands, but plumps down in an armchair and looks up at him. He wonders if she intends to keep him standing during this interview.

"Sit down, man," she says testily.

He looks about warily and finally perches on the edge of a couch that looks deep and soft enough to swallow him.

"You're not much to look at," she says, "but I hear you know your job."

Cone remains silent, wondering whether he'll turn to stone if he stares at her long enough.

She's a massive woman, with enough wattles and dewlaps to make a bloodhound jealous. Timothy guesses a lot of good beef and bourbon went into that raddled face. Like her daughter, she's wearing two sweaters. But her broad hips are wrapped in a tweed skirt as heavy as a horse blanket. And she's also sporting a string of pearls that looks like the real thing.

"Would you like a glass of water?" she asks suddenly.

"No, thank you," he says. "But it's very kind of you to ask."

She looks at him suspiciously, but his expression is grave and attentive.

"Very well," she says gruffly. "I suppose you want to know what this is all about."

He nods.

"What do you do with your money?" she demands.

He decides it's time to clamp down. "None of your business," he says. "What do you do with yours?"

"None of your business," she replies. "But you do know something about investing, don't you?"

"A little."

"I know a lot," she says flatly. "My husband left me well-off, and I had to learn how to manage it. It wasn't easy, but I succeeded. One of the things I discovered along the way is how many crooks there are in the world."

"Yeah," Cone agrees, "you could say that."

"I *do* say it. Now my only child is engaged to be married."

"Congratulations."

"The man is a dolt," the old lady says. "But at her age and with her looks, she's lucky to get anyone."

Cone is getting pissed-off at this harridan. "I think your daughter is attractive," he states.

She ignores that. "Her fiancé is a pediatrician. Doctors are notorious for being the world's worst money managers. Because they can lance a boil, they think they can deal with options, indexes, futures, and commodities. They're the favorite targets of every con man in the country. Lucy's husband-to-be is putting a lot of money into a company called Laboris Investments. Have you heard of it?"

"Not until this morning when I was assigned the case."

"Well, it's run by a man named Ingmar Laboris."

Cone doesn't make many jokes, but when he finds one he likes, he sticks with it.

"Sounds like a Swedish mouthwash," he says.

"Don't waste your wit on me, young man," Mrs. Hepplewaite says sharply. "I warn you, I have absolutely no sense of humor. This Ingmar Laboris is promising a return of thirty percent. What would you do if someone offered you a return like that?"

"Run the other way," Cone says. "How does he claim to do it?"

"Currency trading," she says. "Switching dollars to pounds or francs or yen or pesos. Rates between various national moneys are constantly changing. I admit there are profits to be made in such trading, but it demands split-second decision-making by very experienced and knowledgeable traders. I've checked my sources on Wall Street, and no one's heard of this Ingmar Laboris. He seems to have come out of nowhere, and has no track record. Yet here he is promising a thirty-percent return. I don't like it."

"It doesn't sound kosher," Cone acknowledges. "To run a currency-trading operation you need a worldwide network: open telephone lines, computers, agents in every country—the whole bit. Has Laboris got all that?"

"How on earth would I know?" she says angrily. "What do you think I hired Haldering for? To find out. I don't want Lucy marrying a bankrupt doctor. I have no intention of bailing them out."

Cone ponders a moment. "Have you any idea how much your daughter's fiancé has invested with Laboris?"

"I don't know exactly. I'd guess it's almost a hundred thousand."

The Wall Street dick whistles softly. "A tidy sum. Can he get it out?"

"That's what infuriates me," Mrs. Hepplewaite says. "Apparently he can withdraw his money anytime he wishes, and he *has* been earning thirty percent on his investment. Of course he's delighted—the idiot!"

"Have you tried talking to him about it? Or to your daughter?"

"I've talked—to both of them. Should have saved my breath. They're convinced this get-rich-quick scheme, whatever it is, will make them wealthy. The children!"

"All right," Cone says, "you've given me enough to go on. I'll look into it."

"That's all you're going to tell me—that you'll look into it?"

"That's all I'm going to tell you," he says stonily, standing up and putting on his parka. "When I have something to report, you'll hear from Haldering. Not before."

"You're snotty," she says. "You know that?"

"Sure, I know it," he says. "And you're a mean old biddy. You know that?"

Unexpectedly she laughs. At least her spongy face creases into a grimace that might pass as a grin. She waves her cane at him menacingly.

"Stop wasting time," she says, "and go to work. That's what I'm paying you for."

He's plodding down the long corridor toward the front door when Lucinda Hepplewaite steps out of the shadows and puts a soft hand on his arm. Startled, he turns to face her.

"Please be kind," she whispers, and then she's gone.

He stands there a moment, flummoxed. Then he exits into a chilled mizzle that's put glittering halos around the streetlights. It takes him almost twenty minutes to find an empty cab, and then he gets a hackie who barely speaks English and has to be told when to turn left or right.

Cone arrives back at his loft in a foul mood, not improved when he discovers Cleo has upchucked in the middle of the linoleum floor.

"You sonofabitch!" he yells at the cat. "You been eating cockroaches again?"

He cleans up the mess, rinses his hands, pours a heavy Popov over ice. Lights a cigarette. Puts his feet up on his desk-table. Cleo comes purring over, wanting to make up.

"Miserable cat," Cone says, but he reaches down to scratch the torn ears, which the scarred and denutted tom dearly loves.

He sits there for maybe a half hour, wondering what she meant by "Please be kind." To whom? Herself, her fiancé, her mother? To everyone and everything: animal, vegetable, and mineral?

Grunting, he rouses from his reverie and opens a big can of beef stew. He heats it up in a battered saucepan. When the fat has melted and the stew is beginning to bubble, he pours out about a third of it into Cleo's feeding dish (a chipped ashtray), and eats the remainder himself, spooning it directly from the pan into his mouth. He pauses just long enough to dust some chili powder into it, then finishes. It's okay. Not a lot of meat, but okay.

He goes back to Popov and Camels for dessert. But not before he digs out the Manhattan telephone directory from the cabinet under the sink. He looks up Laboris. To his surprise, he finds three listings: Laboris Investments, Inc., on Wall Street; Laboris Importers, Inc., on Nineteenth Street at an address that would put it just west of Fifth Avenue; and Laboris Gallery of Levantine Art, on upper Madison Avenue.

Cone circles the three names with a black Magic Marker, then tears the page out of the directory. *Three* Laborises? It's such an unusual name, he figures Ingmar is either running all three outfits or there's a family connection.

He calls Samantha.

"Hello?" she says.

"Yeah," he says. "Cone."

"Call back; I'm eating dinner."

"This will only take a minute. You know everything; what does 'Levantine' mean?"

"Jesus, you're a pain in the ass," she says disgustedly. "Can't you look it up? 'The Levant' is a term used to describe all the countries around the east Mediterranean. Like Turkey, Syria, and Iran."

"Okay," he says. "Thanks."

"How did you make out with—"

"See you tomorrow," he says and hangs up.

He sits there, wondering if Laboris Investments is financing that thirty-percent return from the profits of Laboris Importers and the Laboris Gallery of Levantine Art.

"Not fucking likely," he says aloud to Cleo, who is under the bathtub, sleeping off the beef stew. The cat opens one eye to stare at him, then shuts it again.

Feeling his own eyes beginning to close, Cone finishes his last drink and last cigarette of the day. He checks the door to make certain it's locked, bolted, chained. Then he undresses, first unstrapping his ankle holster and placing the .357 short-barreled Magnum close to the mattress on the floor.

He's lying there in his skivvies, waiting for sleep, when Cleo comes padding over to curl up in the bend of his knees.

"Please be kind," he says to the cat.

He doesn't bother checking in at the office the next morning, but goes directly to Laboris Investments, Inc., on Wall Street. It's only a little after nine-thirty, but the joint is already jumping. There's a crowd swamping the three account executives and, from what Cone can see, they're all eager to plunk down cash for a ticket on the gravy train.

It's a crazy mob, hard to categorize: dowagers in ankle-length minks; starchly clad executive types carrying alligator attaché cases; cops and Sanitation guys in uniform; housewives, one with her hair in curlers; a gentleman wearing a clerical collar; a couple of punk rockers; a woman who looks like a bag lady; and two bums who look like they spent the night on the IRT subway grille.

What they all have in common, Cone decides, is a galloping case of the gimmies.

He picks up one of the skimpy prospectuses and reads it carefully. But it's weasel-worded: No promises are made, no profits mentioned. "It is hoped..." and "It is expected that..." and "Possible returns might..." And then the disclaimers: You could lose your entire investment, and there is no guarantee that past success will continue in the future. All legal, the Wall Street dick reflects mournfully, and all designed to get the chief gonnif off the hook.

The most interesting thing in the brochure is a photograph of Ingmar Laboris himself, grinning happily at the camera. He's a swarthy, plump-faced man with a heavy head of slick black hair and a brush of mustache thick enough to clean out a bird cage. Small ears flat to his skull. Full lips with a pouty look. The eyes are squinched with innocence and glint.

"May I help you, sir?" an account executive carols, suddenly appearing at his elbow.

He looks at her badge. "Maybe you can, Gwen. Any chance of my seeing Mr. Laboris?"

"Oh, I'm sorry, sir, but Mr. Laboris is out of the country at present. Expanding our operation overseas, you know."

"Uh-huh."

"Is there anything I can help you with? Do you have any questions?"

"Can I get a thirty-percent return?"

"Oh, sir, we can't guarantee any rate of return. The prospectus spells that out very clearly."

"Sure it does," Cone says genially. "But I can get my money back whenever I want it?"

"Of course, sir. We maintain a special redemption fund."

"Glad to hear it," Cone says. "You accept cash or tellers' checks?"

"Or money orders," Gwen says proudly. "And all major credit cards up to the limit of your credit rating."

"Thank you very much," Cone says. "You've been very helpful."

"Would you care to invest now, sir?"

"Not at the moment. I'd like to think about it."

Her smile flicks off, and she turns away. She's working on commission, he figures, and why should she waste time with a turd-kicker like him when there are so many other applicants with deep pockets?

He leaves Laboris Investments, not much wiser than when he arrived. The whole operation smells, but he figured that from the start. Going down in the elevator, he looks again at Ingmar's photograph and thinks: Would you buy a used Oriental rug from this man?

He stops at the office on his way uptown, just to let people know he's still alive. There are no messages and no memos on his desk, which is okay with him. Still wearing his parka and black leather cap, he wanders into Sidney Apicella's office.

"Oh-oh," Sid says, rubbing his red nose. "Bad news—I just know it."

"Nah," Cone says. "Just a question or two about the Laboris Investments case . . ."

"My God, Tim," Apicella says, "we haven't even started on that one."

"Well, could you check out our foreign contacts and see if any of them have ever heard of Ingmar Laboris? He's supposed to be a hotshot international currency dealer."

Sidney stares at him. "But you think he's a phony?"

"Yeah," the Wall Street dick says, "that's what I think."

He could take an uptown bus, but he cabs instead. He knows the client will be billed for his expenses. He figures Mrs. Martha T. Hepplewaite for a tightwad and imagines with pleasure how she's going to yelp when she gets the itemized invoice.

It's his military training; he's got to make a personal reconnaissance of the territory. So he walks up and down West Nineteenth Street, getting a feel of the neighborhood. Office buildings, lofts, small manufacturers, fabric houses, a couple of dingy bars, and a lot of importers and exporters of this and that.

Laboris Importers, Inc., is a block-wide emporium with huge plate glass show windows—and a roll-down steel shutter for nighttime protection. Dominating the window display is a six-foot brass Buddha, arms raised, belly shined. The statue stands on a dark wood base carved to resemble a rock outcrop.

Timothy Cone pushes open the door, which jangles a bell suspended overhead. He hasn't seen a gizmo like that in years. But the alarm seems to alert no one. There are maybe a half-dozen customers wandering the aisles. And in the back, behind a counter, five salesclerks are nattering and laughing. Apparently Laboris Importers doesn't believe in the hard sell.

Cone looks around, making a zigzag path through the big sales floor. He's never seen so much junk in his life. Someone has combed the world for tasteless trinkets and mass-produced art—and here it all is, displayed under fluorescent lamps in a Manhattan showroom.

Primitive African statuettes—probably made by computerized lathes in Nigeria. Imitation Navaho silver jewelry, set with stones that look like unchewed bubble gum. Moth-eaten red fezzes with limp black tassels. Glass paperweights filled with tiny Swiss chalets and a snowstorm of rice. Cigarette lighters shaped like Colt pistols. Planters' hats from Panama and puppets from India. Mexican wedding dresses and carved wooden rabbits from Guatemala. A set of Scottish bagpipes and a rack of chino pants from Taiwan. Enormous leather hippopotami from somewhere and just as large porcelain elephants from somewhere else. And tons and tons of similar stuff.

It is, Timothy Cone decides, awed, the greatest collection of schlock he's ever seen in his life.

"May I be of service, sir?" someone asks, and Cone turns slowly, hearing the hisses rather than the words.

It's a short, chubby gink, swarthy, a toothbrush mustache and teeth so white they seem to have been sandblasted. He's wearing a cologne that smells of defunct roses. And he looks like he's been dipped in Mazola.

"Just wandering around," Cone says. Then: "I hope you don't mind my asking, but does this store have any connection with Laboris Investments on Wall Street?"

The glittery teeth become more prominent. Cone figures it's a smile.

"But of course," the man says happily. "He is our cousin." He waves a hand at the other salesclerks still chattering away in the rear of the store. "We are all cousins. The Laboris family is very large. Did you invest with Ingmar?"

Cone nods. "Do you think I did the right thing?"

The guy puts a soft hand on his arm. "The wisest decision you have ever made in your life. Ingmar is a financial genius. All the cousins have invested with Ingmar."

"Glad to hear it," Timothy says. "And may I ask what your name is?"

"Sven Laboris. Amusing, no? The combination I mean. Ingmar and Sven with Laboris. I think maybe a Swede lady took one look at the Mediterranean and decided to stay."

"Yeah," Cone says, "that could happen." And then, because Sven has been so pleasant and forthcoming, he looks around for something cheap he can buy. There's a table filled with dark wooden Buddhas. They look like small versions of the big brass job in the store window.

"Those Buddhas..." he says. "What kind of wood is that?"

"Oh!" Sven says. "Very nice. Solid teak from Burma. All hand-carved, of course. Each one different."

He picks up one of the statuettes and hands it to Cone. "One solid piece of wood. Very hard. Very difficult to carve. Look at the detail."

The figure is about twelve inches high, and unexpectedly heavy. Arms are raised, plump belly protrudes, and the face has an expression of beneficent joy. It is posed in a carved rock, fists clenched, the whole posture one of jaunty pleasure.

"What are you asking for it?" Cone says.

"Oh, this must be twenty-nine ninety-five. Import duties, you know."

Cone starts to replace the Buddha on the table. "That's a little more than I wanted to spend."

"However," Sven Laboris says hastily, "because you have invested with our cousin, I can make you a special price. Twenty?"

"Okay," Cone says.

"Also," Sven says, giggling, "I must tell you about a special bonus. It is something that will delight you. If you rub the belly of a Buddha—here, let me show you how; stroke gently, like so—well then, you will have good luck for many years and all your wishes will come true."

"No kidding?" the Wall Street dick says.

He emerges from Laboris Importers, Inc., carrying the wooden Buddha swaddled in tissue paper and thrust into a brown paper bag. He figures he'll give it to Sam. If she doesn't want it, she can always give it to some relative for a Christmas present. In any case, Cone is going to put the twenty bucks plus sales tax on his swindle sheet. Let Martha Hepplewaite scream when she sees that Haldering & Co. is billing her for "One Buddha, teak, hand-carved."

He cabs on uptown, exhilarated with all the client's cash he's spending. He knows upper Madison Avenue, he doesn't have to reconnoiter the ground. A splashy neighborhood. Big bucks and big greeds. Very little schlock here. Just bring fresh money.

The Laboris Gallery of Levantine Art fits right in. It's an elegant three-story building, the entire façade covered with faded blue tiles in a vaguely Persian pattern; foliage and beasts, bearded warriors and scimitars—all contained within a severely geometrical border. Timothy Cone, who knows Manhattan real estate values, can guess what that little gem of a building cost.

There's very little of the Levantine in the interior. It's all high-tech, with white walls, track lighting, and Lucite cubes, containing works of art, set on solid ebony pedestals. Soft music is coming from somewhere: a meringue of plucked strings and flutes that is simultaneously lulling and lascivious.

"May I be of service, sir?" she says, and again he hears the hisses and not the words.

He turns to look, and curses himself inwardly for being a filthy beast, because his initial reaction is: What a *dish!* He suddenly remembers a gyrene buddy of his spotting a similar woman on the street and remarking admiringly, "All you need with *that* is a spoon and a straw."

She is young, short, chubby: a butterball. Olive complexion, killing eyes, and a smile to melt titanium. Long black hair to her buns, and such a bursting, fleshy, burning look about her that the Wall Street dick is distraught enough to remove his leather cap—more from homage than politeness.

"Miss Laboris?" he asks, scarcely believing that croak is his voice.

"Yes," she says, "I am Ingrid Laboris."

"You own this gallery?"

"Oh, no," she says, laughing gaily. "That is Erica Laboris, my cousin. You would like to see her? She has just stepped out for a moment, but she should be back shortly."

"Okay," Cone says, "I'll wait. Meanwhile I'll just look around."

"Please do," Ingrid urges. "We have so many beautiful things."

He watches her move away, knowing he could get twenty years for what he's thinking. "Down, boy," he tells himself, and resolutely makes a tour of the gallery, inspecting all those splendid antiquities locked within Lucite cubes.

There are urns, vases, plates, silver jewelry and golden bowls, lapis lazuli necklaces, clay rhytons in the shape of rams' heads, volumes of poetry, miniatures, illuminations, scraps of textiles and calligraphies, book bindings and manuscripts. There is even a crouching sphinx in faience, and two terra-cotta monkeys copulating ferociously.

No prices are posted, but he knows he can't afford a single item even if he wanted it—which he doesn't. He abjured coveting *things* years ago, when he returned from Nam. But that doesn't prevent him from recognizing museum-quality art when he sees it.

"May I be of service, sir?" she says, and once again he hears the hisses.

She has approached so quietly that he hasn't even been aware that she was in the gallery. Her fragrance should have been the tipoff: the same rose-scented cologne Sven was wearing on Nineteenth Street. Cone figures the Laboris family is importing the stuff.

"Were you looking for something special, sir?" she asks, and he realizes all the cousins have trouble with their sibilants. A lot of spit there. Maybe, he thinks, it's a genetic defect—like his own impulse to say "thoity-thoid." His old man always called it a "horspital."

"Not really," he tells her. "You're Miss Erica Laboris, the owner?"

She nods with a two-bit smile.

"I just stopped in by accident," he explains. "I was down on Wall Street at Laboris Investments, and then came uptown and was walking by and saw your name. Is there any relation?"

"Oh, yes," she says, the faint smile flickering again. "That is Ingmar, our cousin. I hope you invested."

"I did. Do you think I did the right thing?"

"Absolutely," she says firmly. "Ingmar knows all about currency trading. I've invested money with him myself."

"Glad to hear it," Cone says. "Tell me something: Where do you get all these great old things you have here?"

She starts telling him about her frequent trips to the eastern Mediterranean, how she buys from traders and private collectors, how she'll have nothing to do with grave robbers and museum thieves, how every piece in the gallery is authenticated and has an impeccable provenance.

As she's speaking, he's staring. Erica is taller than Ingrid, older, and not as bloomy. But she is a striking woman, impressive, with the oiled Laboris skin, chalk teeth, and smoldering look that could be either unspent passion or dyspepsia.

From her polished spiel and slightly aloof style, Timothy figures her for a very brainy lady. And better a friend than an enemy. He notes her fingernails: long, narrow, and lacquered a deep indigo. Want those reaching for your carotid? No, thanks.

"That's very interesting," he says when her lecture ends. "To tell you the truth, I'm out of my depth here. I'm not a collector. I know from nothing about antique art. Maybe I better stick with Laboris Importers on Nineteenth Street."

"Oh," she says with her cool, brief smile, "you've been there, have you? Sven is another cousin. He carries some nice things. Very modern. But we have many casual visitors like yourself, Mr.—"

"Cone. Timothy Cone."

"Casual visitors like yourself, Mr. Cone. But sometimes they return, captured by the beauty, the mystery, the allure. It is an introduction to a vanished world of great creativity. Perhaps you, too, will return."

"Maybe I will."

"If you would care to leave your address, I would be happy to send you an advance notice when we have a special exhibit."

"That's nice of you," Cone says. He digs the battered wallet from his hip pocket and searches. Eventually he finds a dog-eared business card stuck to a small photo of Cleo that Samantha Whatley took with her Polaroid. The cat looks depraved. Cone peels away the card and hands it to Erica Laboris.

"So glad to meet you, Mr. Cone," she says. "Do stop by again. We're always getting in new things. New *old* things. Who knows—you might find something that you *must* have. To make your life complete."

"Yeah," he says, "that could happen."

He leaves the gallery and trudges slowly south on Madison Avenue. A miserable December day. A sky that looks like beaten lead, and an icy wind that just won't quit. He stops at a corner phone booth and calls Sam.

"Wanna eat Chink tonight?" he asks. "I'll spring for it. Your place. Around seven o'clock."

"Why, Mr. Cone!" she carols. "Ah sweah you sweep a gal right off her feet."

"Stuff it," he tells her and hangs up.

. . .

They're sitting on the floor, on one of Samantha's oval rag rugs, surrounded by cardboard containers of pork lo mein, shrimp with lobster sauce, sweet-and-sour chicken, fried rice, barbecued ribs, egg rolls, wonton soup, and six bottles of cold Tsingtao beer.

"You bought enough to feed a regiment," Sam says, gnawing on a rib.

"Well, whatever we don't finish, I'll take home. Cleo can live off the leftovers for a week."

"So?" she says, slurping wonton. "How you coming with the Hepple-waite case?"

"Okay," he says, stuffing his face with an egg roll.

"That's all you're going to say—okay?"

"That's all."

"Jesus," she says disgustedly, "you're at it again. I'm your boss—remember? Is it too much to ask that you keep me informed?"

"I'm in a mulling mood," he yells at her. "You know what mulling is? It means I don't know my ass from my elbow."

"All right, all right," she shouts back. "I should have known better than to expect any cooperation from a crotchety bum like you."

"Screw you," he says.

"Fuck you," she says.

They glower at each other, then go back to the pork, chicken, and the shrimp, spooning it over the rice and gobbling the mess with soy sauce squeezed from little packets.

"You going home for Christmas?" he asks, not looking at her.

"Yes, I'm going home for Christmas. What are you going to do?"

"Who the hell knows? Make a tree for Cleo. Deck the halls with matzo balls. Get drunk. You'll be back for New Year's?"

"Sure," she says, "I'll be back."

"Good," he says. "Then I can drink champagne out of your combat boots."

She tries not to smile, still sore at him. They finish most of the food, and what's left is spooned into a plastic bag for Cleo. All the empty containers are dumped in the garbage can, and they settle down with the remaining beer.

"Why are you such a prick?" she asks him.

"Because I enjoy it. Why are you such a bitch? Hey, I've got something for you."

He rises from the floor and goes over to the cretonne armchair where he's tossed his parka. He pulls a brown paper bag from underneath and hands it to Samantha.

"What's this?" she demands. "A bomb?"

"It's for you. Open it."

"My God," she says, "don't tell me you bought me a present. For Christmas?"

"Hell, no. I'm going to put it on my expense account. It's part of the Hepplewaite case. Go ahead, look at it."

She unwraps the tissue paper, holds the carved, grinning Buddha in her hands.

"From Laboris Importers," Cone explains. "Cousins to Laboris Investments. If you don't want it, give it to your folks when you go home."

Sam inspects the statuette, turning it around and around, then looks at the little sticker on the bottom.

"Made in Burma," she reports. "You know, I like it. It's cute."

"Cute, for God's sake? Well, it's hand-carved teak. One solid piece of wood."

"I definitely like it," she says, nodding. "I'm not giving it to anyone; I'm keeping it. How much did this little gem cost?"

"Twenty bucks, plus tax. The greaseball who sold it to me claims that if you rub the belly all your wishes will come true."

"Hey," she says, "that's cool." She starts rubbing the plump belly of the Buddha.

"What are you wishing for?" Cone wants to know.

"That's between me and Izzy here."

"Izzy?"

"That's what I'm going to call him—Izzy."

"You're gone," he tells her. "You should be committed. Izzy! That happens to be a religious statue."

"What the hell do you know about religion?"

"I'm religious," he protests. "I worship."

"Yeah? Like what?"

"Let me show you."

They're out of their clothes like a shot and snuggling under the quilt on her bed.

"You son of a bitch," she says, "why can't you be nice to me."

"Come off it," he says. "Niceness you don't need. It would just turn you off."

"You're right," she says, sighing.

They've given up trying to understand the pleasure they derive from their obsessive hostility. They're able to remain lovers as long as they remain adversaries. They hide their fears with bravado and think bullying will mask their vulnerability.

Perhaps the enigma is what keeps them socked together. Mystery adds spice when the glands take over, and in their lovemaking there is always the sinful excitement of coupling with a stranger.

But that night, under the quilt, randy as all get-out, neither is concerned with self-analysis. Trading wonton breaths and soy sauce kisses, they come together as if the third week in December were the rutting season in Manhattan, and each must prove a holiday passion.

With grunts and groans, sighs, and yelps, they make great sport of demolishing each other, their bodies fevered and agile. If they could slam foreheads and lock horns, they would. For when the hormones gush, they become insensate to tenderness, love, or compassion, and know only the glory of their sweaty struggle.

What a game they play! With coarse oaths and sweet whimperings, they deflower each other for the nth time. The contest ends a draw; no winner, no loser; just two exhausted and loony combatants staring at each other with wild and wondering eyes.

Until Samantha reaches out languidly to touch the belly of the Buddha she has placed on the bedside table.

"You know," she says softly, "it really works."

Cone gets to the office a half hour late, as usual, and sits at his desk without removing his parka or cap. He lights his third cigarette of the day, coughs, and calls Neal Davenport.

"My God, Sherlock," the NYPD detective says, "I haven't heard from you in two weeks. I was afraid you were mad at me."

"Nah," Cone says, laughing, "nothing like that. Whatever happened to Martin Gardow?"

"Made bail and took a powder. We're not even looking for him. We've got Guiterrez on a homicide rap. He'll probably bargain it down, but he'll still spend a few years in the slammer where he can play pick-up-the-soap in the shower with guys bigger and tougher than he is. Is that why you called—to get caught up on my caseload?"

"Not exactly. There's something else."

"No kidding?" Davenport says. "I never would have guessed. What do you want now?"

"There's an art gallery on upper Madison, the Laboris Gallery of Levantine Art. I thought there might be someone in the Department who could give me a rundown on the place."

"What are they doing—fencing?"

"I don't know," Cone says, frowning at the phone. "I went up to talk to the lady who runs the joint, and before I know it, she's telling me how she will never have anything to do with grave robbers and museum thieves. When someone tells me how honest they are, the first thing I do is count my rings and check the fillings in my teeth."

"Yeah," the cop says, "I know what you mean. What's your interest in this art gallery?"

"The owner is a cousin of a guy who runs an outfit I'm investigating: Laboris Investments on Wall Street. They're paying out more than anyone could reasonably expect. I think there's a scam going on there, but I have no idea what it could be."

Davenport sighs. "You really come up with some dillies. I know a sergeant who works out of the Special Robberies Division. He's supposed to be a hotshot on art thefts. His name is Terry MacEver. I'll give him a call and tell him what you want. If he's interested, he'll call you back. If he doesn't, forget it."

"Fair enough," Cone says. "I'll be in the office all morning."

Then he takes off his anorak and cap, and wanders down to Apicella's office. Sidney looks up indignantly, and Cone holds up a palm.

"Don't get your balls in an uproar, Sid," he says. "I know it's too soon to hear from your foreign contacts about Laboris. I just wondered if you had anything at all on the case."

"A little," the CPA says grudgingly. "Laboris Investments has a nice bank balance. They've also got a special fund set aside for redemptions. As far as I can tell from the first look, they're solid."

"Yeah," Cone says, "and I'm Queen of the May."

"That's possible, too," Sid says.

Cone goes back to his office and lights a Camel, dreaming up loopy criminal connections between Laboris Investments, Laboris Importers, and the Laboris Gallery of Levantine Art. But none of his fantasies work; it's all smoke.

He spends almost an hour working on his swindle sheet and weekly progress report to Samantha. They're smoke, too. When his phone rings, he grabs it in a hurry, hoping.

"This is Sergeant Terry MacEver, Special Robberies Division, NYPD. I got a call from Neal Davenport. He told me what you do and gives you high marks. That's the only reason I'm calling, d'ya see."

"Yeah, well, Neal and I have helped each other out on a couple of things."

"So he says. You're interested in the Laboris Gallery?"

"Sort of."

"Got anything on them?"

"Nothing," Cone says fretfully. "But when I was up there, I was the only customer in the place. If they own that building, it must have cost a mint. And if they're renting, I don't see how they're making it."

"They're renting," MacEver tells him. "From a cousin named Leif Laboris."

"Another cousin," Cone says, sighing. "That figures. Listen, can I buy you dinner or a drink? I've got an expense account I can fiddle."

"Not dinner," the sergeant says. "I've got to get home to walk my dachshund, d'ya see, and then get uptown for an art auction. But I'll take you up on the drink."

"Good enough. Where and when?"

"You know Pete's Tavern?"

"Sure I do. East Eighteenth Street."

"Right. I'll meet you at the bar there at four o'clock. Okay?"

"Fine."

"How will I make you?"

"A little under six, about one-seventy, spiky hair, dirty parka, black leather cap. I'll be drinking vodka, and I'll have a pack of Camels on the bar in front of me."

"That should do it," MacEver says. "If I'm a little late, don't get antsy; I'll be along."

"I'll wait," Cone promises, and hangs up, feeling a lot better. If a hotshot cop who specializes in art thefts knows about the Laboris Gallery, there must be some action there.

He gets to Pete's about twenty minutes early. He sits at the bar, still wearing his parka but with his cap off, rolled, and jammed in his pocket. He puts his pack of Camels on the bar and treats himself to a Finlandia on the rocks.

He's just started his second, and it's almost four-fifteen, when someone taps his arm.

"Timothy Cone?"

"That's right."

"Terry MacEver. Sorry I'm late."

"No sweat," Cone says, and they shake hands.

The sergeant isn't dressed like a cop, even one in mufti. He's wearing an Irish field hat, an unbuttoned Burberry trenchcoat, a suede sport jacket, tattersall waistcoat, doeskin shirt with a paisley ascot at the throat. Trousers are pinkish cavalry twill. Shoes are oxblood loafers with tassels.

MacEver sees the Wall Street dick eyeballing him, and laughs. "You like the threads? No, I'm not a *fagela*. This is my working uniform, d'ya see. I spend most of my working hours at art galleries and auctions and in antique shops. If I went in dressed like your average harness bull with a gravy-stained brown suit off plain pipe racks, I'd get nowhere. Listen, I'm going to have a gin martini straight up with a twist. Then let's take a booth where we can have a little privacy."

They sit across from each other, parka and trenchcoat off and folded on the bench seats alongside them. MacEver takes a gulp of his martini and squints his eyes with pleasure.

"First today," he says. "Plasma."

He's small for a NYPD cop, but Cone notes that the shoulders under the suede jacket are hefty enough, and the guy moves well. He's got a neatly trimmed chestnut mustache and a lot of wavy chestnut hair that looks like it's been styled and blow-dried. Everything about him is so neat and well-groomed that he makes Cone feel like a slob.

"Neal Davenport says you're a screwball," MacEver says briskly, "but a valuable screwball. So when you mentioned the Laboris Gallery I figured I'd take a chance. You scratch my back and I'll scratch yours."

"What else?" Cone says.

"Look, I'm going to talk fast because I don't have too much time. Let me give you a rundown on what I do. Now, how many art galleries and antique shops do you figure there are in New York?"

"A couple of hundred?" Cone guesses.

"How does sixteen hundred grab you? And that's only in Manthattan. And there's only me and a couple of part-timers I can call in to cover them all. Don't get me wrong; most of those sixteen hundred places are on the up-and-up. But there's a lot of fencing going on, some contract burglaries, and a lot of gonnifs in the business who wouldn't blink an eye if a Bowery bum showed up with a couple of antique miniatures painted on ivory and claimed he found them in a garbage can. You follow?"

"I follow," Cone says.

"Well, these places are licensed, but we can't cover them all. Occasionally the Consumer Fraud Department gets a complaint that a 'genuine Louis XIV chair' was actually made in Grand Rapids. Generally, the complaint ends up on my desk and I have to check it out. Dull stuff. But most of my job—the fun part—involves big-money thefts of art and antiques. We get alerts from Interpol and from a special outfit that sends out regular bulletins on art work swiped from museums and private collectors."

"How much of that stuff is there?" Cone wants to know.

"Art thefts worldwide? Last year about five thousand were reported."

Cone whistles softly. "Let me get us a refill," he says. He goes to the bar, comes back with another round, slides into the booth again.

"Thanks," the sergeant says. "If I ask for a third, turn me down."

"The hell I will," Cone says. "This is *my* third. Listen, you said there were five thousand reported art thefts last year. You mean some are un-reported?"

"Sure," MacEver says cheerfully. "I'd guess at least double that number. For every one reported, the cops never hear about two others. Because the private collector who got ripped off bought his painting or silver chalice or whatever from a crook who stole it in the first place. So he can't go screaming to the cops, d'ya see. We'd want to know who he bought it from, how much he paid, does he have the proper documentation. The best part is this: The crook who lifted the work of art from the private collector is probably the same villain who sold it to him. There are sup-posed to be guys in the business who make a good living stealing and selling the same work of art over and over again."

"That's beautiful," Cone says.

"Isn't it? Can I have one of your cigarettes?"

"Sure. Help yourself."

"I'm trying to quit smoking by not buying cigarettes. Now I find myself bumming them from other people. I'm going to die a mooch with lung cancer."

MacEver lights his Camel with a gold Dunhill, inhales deeply. The smoke doesn't seem to come out mouth or nose. It just disappears. He takes another sip of his martini. "Alcohol and nicotine," he muses. "Why don't I just slit my wrists and be done with it."

"Too fast," Cone says. "We've all got to suffer first."

"Yeah," the sergeant says. "Well, let's get back to art thefts. There's something else you should know about them: They run in cycles. One year it will be French Impressionist paintings. The next year it will be pre-Columbian statuettes. Even thievery has its trends—usually following what's bringing high prices at the big auction houses. That's where the Laboris Gallery comes in."

"That I *don't* follow," Cone says.

"Well, for the past year or so, the really 'in' fashion in stolen art has been stuff from the Near East. You know what things are like over there: bombings and raids and everybody shooting at everyone else. In the pro-cess, a lot of museums and private collections have been looted. So there's plenty of Islamic and pre-Islamic art work up for grabs, and it's dollars-to-doughnuts that most of it will end up in New York."

"*Now* I follow," Cone says. "But how are they getting the stuff into the country?"

"Good question. The Customs guys do what they can, but they're as understaffed and overworked as we are. Suppose a shipment of ten thou-sand wax bananas comes in from Columbia. You think *every* banana can be checked? No way. So Customs spot-checks and finds only wax bananas. But five hundred could be filled with pure cocaine. Who's to tell? Now, to get back to art thefts from the Near East, you think a pirate is going to airmail his loot directly from Beirut to New York? Fat chance! That valuable work of art is going to be transshipped and travel halfway around the world before it gets into this country, maybe from Mexico or Canada. We had a case about six months ago: a sword with a silver hilt set with diamonds and rubies. A real beauty. It was swiped in Lebanon, went to Turkey, to India, to Korea, to Taiwan, to Venezuela, to Cuba, to Miami, and eventually ended up in Manhattan as part of a shipment of office furniture. And the guy who engineered all this lives in Switzerland. How do you like that?"

"Did you nab him?" Cone asks.

"Couldn't touch him. But we recovered the sword. We're holding it until the rightful owner can be determined—which will probably never happen. Anyway, right now the art scene in New York is being flooded with booty from Iran, Lebanon, Iraq, and Turkey."

"Where do you start on something like that?"

"Since I'm such a cynical bastard, with the apparently legitimate art galleries and dealers who handle Islamic stuff. Some of them sell to the public, some only to private collectors. I've got a list of about fifteen possibles. The Laboris Gallery is one of them."

"Oh-ho," Cone says.

"Yeah, oh-ho. But I've checked them out and they seem to be clean. You don't think so?"

Cone takes a swig of his vodka. "Don't know. All I can say is that they're occupying a prime piece of Manhattan real estate and aren't exactly thronged with customers. And the owner, a deep lady named Erica Laboris, made a point of telling me how honest she is. I'm itchy about that place."

Terry MacEver sighs and finishes his martini. "See what you can come up with," he says. "Anything, and I do mean *any*thing, will be gratefully appreciated." He fishes in his inside jacket pocket, pulls out a pigskin wallet, extracts a card, and hands it across the table to Cone. "There's my number. If I'm not in, you can leave a message and I'll get back to you. Right now this whole business of smuggled Near East art is driving me right up the wall. Listen, I've got to run. Thanks for the refreshment."

They shake hands, and then Sergeant MacEver is gone. Cone carries the empty glasses and his parka over to the bar and orders another Finlandia. His third or fourth? He can't remember—and who the hell cares?

He sips his fresh drink slowly, smoking another Camel and reviewing all the stuff MacEver told him. Good background, he decides, but what has it got to do with Laboris Investments on Wall Street? Is Ingmar paying that thirty percent from the proceeds of smuggled Levantine art? Ridiculous. Who ever heard of a thief needing financing and going public? It would be like the Mafia selling shares.

Because MacEver was so ready to meet with him, Cone figures the sergeant is holding out. He knows something, or suspects something, about the Laboris Gallery he's not mentioning. That's okay; Cone said nothing to him about Laboris Importers on Nineteenth Street.

He looks into his empty glass of vodka and reflects that everyone wants the glory of the collar. It's understandable; it comes with the territory. But cops—locals, state, Feds, or whatever—have to think about their records and their careers. All Cone has to think about is his own satisfaction.

"Another, sir?" the bartender asks.

"Splendid idea," the Wall Street dick says, wondering if he'll get home alive.

It's a honey of a hangover. Nausea, dry heaves, headache, tremors, a parched throat, a cold sweat, gummy eyes, cramping of the bowels, self-disgust—the whole bit. Cleo looks at him sorrowfully.

"Don't *you* start," he tells the cat.

He drinks a quart of cold water, two cups of black coffee, pops four aspirin, takes a hot shower, starts a cigarette, and puts it out. He inhales twelve deep breaths, striding up and down the loft, tries to drink a cold beer and puts it back in the fridge. He belches, frequently, and Cleo retreats under the bathtub.

He's getting it together, pulling on his white wool socks with trembling hands, when his phone rings.

"The boss," he says to Cleo.

"Where the hell *are* you?" Samantha Whatley demands angrily.

"On my way," he says. "I overslept."

"Horseshit," she says. "I can smell your breath over the phone. Come to my office as soon as you get in. I've got something to show you."

"I've seen it," he says.

"Very funny. Just *be* here."

He walks to work as usual, figuring the fresh air will perk him up. But it isn't fresh; it's thick and smells of snow and sewer gas. He plods along, all scrunched up in his parka, heavy work shoes slapping the pavement, and wonders why he smokes too much, drinks too much, and generally plays the fool. He can solve other people's mysteries, but he can't solve his own.

"Screw it," he says aloud, and passersby glance at him nervously.

He lumps into Samantha's office, still wearing his cruddy cap and parka. She stares at him.

"Jesus!" she says. "You didn't shave, did you? Afraid you'd slit your throat? You look like the wrath of God."

"I *am* the wrath of God."

"Did you remember to feed Cleo?"

"Yes, I remembered to feed Cleo. Is that what you wanted to see me about?"

"Sit down," she says, "before you fall over."

He slumps gratefully into the armchair alongside her desk.

She looks at him a long, sad moment. "You're killing yourself," she says.

"Tell me about it," he says bitterly. "Come on, lectures I don't need. What's up?"

"You know that Buddha you gave me? I broke it."

He straightens in his chair. "You *broke* it? How? With a sledgehammer? That was one solid piece of teak."

"The hell it was," Sam says. "I didn't exactly break it, but take a look at this."

She reaches into the well of her desk, pulls out a Macy's shopping bag, and plucks out the Buddha.

"Looks okay to me," he says.

"Yeah?"

With a hard twist of her wrists, she separates the Buddha into two parts, base and figure. She displays the sections.

"Son of a bitch," Cone says wonderingly. "The momser who sold it to me swore it was one solid piece of wood."

"That's not all," Samantha says. "It unscrews the wrong way—clockwise. And then there's this . . ."

She holds up the butt of the separated Buddha. There's a hole drilled into the figure, about an inch in diameter and three inches deep.

"What the hell," Cone says. "Now why did they do that? To lessen the weight for shipment? Nah, that doesn't make sense. Listen, how did you find out it comes apart?"

"This morning I reached to shut off my Snooz-alarm and knocked him onto the floor. When I picked him up, I noticed the base was loose. I couldn't figure out how the two parts were connected until I tried twisting it the wrong way."

"It's interesting," Cone says. "Let me take it."

"I want it back," Samantha says sternly. "It's Izzy, and I love him."

"Cut the shit," Cone says roughly. "Give me the goddamned thing. I'll let you know what I find out."

"In a pig's ass," Whatley says, but she lets him take the Buddha dumped into the Macy's shopping bag.

He goes back to his office, takes off his cap and parka, and lets them fall to the floor, because some office bandit stole his coat tree. Then he sits down to examine the Buddha. He screws the two parts together tightly, turning them counterclockwise. When they're snug, he leans forward to examine the joint. You'd never notice if you weren't looking for it. Nice workmanship. The little label MADE IN BURMA is still stuck to the base.

He puts the Buddha under his desk and shambles down the corridor to the legal department. He's passing Apicella's office when the CPA calls, "Hey, Tim, got a minute?"

Cone pauses.

"Listen," Apicella says. "I got cables from three of my overseas contacts. None of them ever heard of this Ingmar Laboris. If he's trading in foreign currencies, he's got to be doing it through fronts. I don't like it."

"I don't either," Cone says. "Take my advice, Sid, and hold off on your PIE until I can get more skinny on this guy."

"Keep me informed," Apicella says anxiously.

"Oh, sure," Cone says, and continues on to Louis Kiernan's office.

"Hey," Cone says, "we got like an atlas or an encyclopedia around this joint?"

The young paralegal peers at him over his reading glasses. "No big encyclopedia," he says. "I've been trying to get a set of the Britannica, but Mr. Haldering won't okay the cost. But he did spring for a one-volume job. It's that thick book in the white cover on the top shelf."

Cone takes down the heavy volume and flips through it. He reads the paragraph on Burma. Chief products: teak, rubies, sapphires, and jade. He closes the book, replaces it on the shelf, starts out of the office.

"Find what you were looking for?" Kiernan asks.

"Who the hell knows?" Cone says.

Back in his own office, he separates the Buddha again and peers at the hole drilled into the base of the figure. It's a nice, smooth job. He can't see the residue of anything. He sniffs at it, but all he can smell is oiled wood. He puts the figurine aside, digs out his wallet, and calls Terry MacEver.

The sergeant is on another phone, so Cone leaves a message and waits patiently. Meanwhile he turns the Buddha over and over in his hands, shaking it once or twice. Nothing rattles. But closer inspection does reveal a lot number burned lightly into the bottom of the base—30818-K. Whatever that means.

True to his word, MacEver calls back.

"You got something for me?"

"More questions," the Wall Street dick says. "Yesterday, when you were talking about smuggled Levantine art, I didn't ask what the stuff was. Paintings? Sculpture?"

"A lot of things," MacEver says. "Miniatures. Manuscripts. Figurines. Illuminations. Weapons. Could be almost anything."

"Listen," Cone says, "could any of that fit in a container about an inch across and three inches long?"

"Very little of it. Maybe coins, a gold chain, a rolled-up page from a book. But we're talking about drinking cups and statuettes and old weapons."

"Yeah," Cone says. "Thanks for your time. I'll keep in touch."

"You do that," MacEver says.

After he hangs up, Cone realizes he is ravenous, having drunk his dinner the night before. He pulls on parka and cap, takes the Buddha along in the shopping bag, and leaves the office. He heads for a sloppy Irish pub on Broadway where he stuffs himself with Dublin broil, hashed browns, overcooked string beans, a lousy salad, four slices of soda bread, and two bottles of Harp.

Feeling a lot better, his violent eructations reduced to gentle burps, he takes a cab up to West Nineteenth Street to pay another visit to Laboris Importers.

The huge brass Buddha is still in the show window, a king-sized version of the teak job Cone is carrying in his shopping bag. While staring in the window, he spots something he hadn't noticed before: a small sign propped on a bamboo easel. LABORIS IMPORTERS, INC. THE DIFFERENT AND THE BEAUTIFUL FROM ALL OVER THE WORLD. STORES IN NEW YORK, BOSTON, BALTIMORE, WASHINGTON, ATLANTA, MIAMI, NEW ORLEANS, DETROIT, CHICAGO, ST. LOUIS, DENVER, LOS ANGELES, SAN FRANCISCO.

Cone is impressed. He hadn't realized this House of Schlock was a nationwide chain. He has a sudden vision of an army of grinning teak Buddhas, arms raised in triumph, taking over the country.

The store has plenty of customers prowling the aisles. Cone goes directly to the table where his Buddha had been displayed. It's laden with a phalanx of little stuffed rabbits from Taiwan. When you wind them up, they twirl and bang tiny cymbals affixed to their paws.

He marches to the sales counter at the back. There's a flock of clerks twittering away to each other. They all look like Laborises: swarthy skin, flashing eyes, teeth like sugar cubes. He can even smell that rose-scented cologne.

He holds up a hand, and a little lady comes scampering over.

"May I be of service, sir?" she asks with the familiar hiss.

"I'll bet you're a Laboris," he says.

"Oh, yes," she says, giggling. "I am Karen Laboris. We have met?"

"No, but I know some of your cousins." He fishes into his shopping bag, hauls out the Buddha. "Listen, I bought this a few days ago."

"And it's damaged? Your money will be cheerfully refunded, sir. No trouble at all."

"No, no," he says hastily. "Nothing like that. It's just that I like it so much—and my wife does, too—that we'd like to buy another one. But I can't seem to find any on display."

"Ahh," she says, "that was a very popular item. Handcarved. One solid piece of teak. So enchanting, don't you think? I am afraid we are out of stock."

"Oh, no," he says. "I promised I'd get one for my mother-in-law, who is in a nursing home, wasting away. Don't you have a single one left?"

She frowns. "Let me look in the stockroom, sir. It's possible there may be one on a back shelf."

"Thank you," he says. "I'd appreciate that."

While she's gone, he takes a look around. There's a lot of new stuff that wasn't displayed on his first visit: suits of armor from Spain, Korean chests with brass hardware, enormous marionettes from India, leather hassocks from Turkey, quilts from Iowa, Portuguese wine flasks, and cuckoo clocks from Switzerland.

Cone is examining a Brazilian armoire when Karen Laboris comes trotting up to him, carrying a teak Buddha.

"I found one!" she announces happily. "The last in the store. You are in luck."

"Hey, that's great," he says, taking a quick look at the Buddha she's holding. It appears to be a double of the one in his shopping bag.

"That will be thirty-five dollars," she says. "Plus tax."

He doesn't quibble about the price. While she's making out the sales slip, he says, "I suppose your stores all over the country carry this."

"Oh, yes, sir," she says. "Everyone loves it. We've sold hundreds. If you rub the belly, it will—"

"I know," he says. "And I've been told it really works."

"It does," she says, giggling again. "Sir, Laboris Importers is going into the mail-order business. We plan to bring out a catalog of our most enchanting items twice a year. If you would care to leave your name and address, we will be happy to add you to our mailing list."

"That would be enchanting," he says, and gives her his name and home address. "That's a lovely perfume you're wearing," he adds.

"You like it?" she says archly. "It's made exclusively for us. It is called Nuit de Fou. I think that means Night of Craziness. Or something like that."

"Yeah," Cone says. "It figures."

He cabs back to the office, toting the two Buddhas in the Macy's shopping bag. He resists the temptation to inspect his new purchase until he's safely seated behind his desk. It appears almost identical to the first. A few variations here and there—but no more than you might expect from handcarved works.

He picks up the latest acquisition, grips it firmly, and tries to unscrew the base. Nothing. He applies more force. Still nothing. He looks more closely, his nose squashed against the Buddha's belly. No hairline joint. The new statuette really is one solid piece of teak.

"Son of a bitch."

Cone sits back in his creaking swivel chair and glares at the two figures. Four arms upraised, two shiny bellies, two plump faces with beneficent grins. Cone grabs the latest purchase, turns it over, inspects the base. There's the label MADE IN BURMA. But the lot number reads 30818-M. So? The two Buddhas were imported in different lots, maybe different shipments.

He puts them close together on his desk, lifted arms almost touching, and he sits there, brooding. The more he stares at those plump, smiling faces, the more they remind him of something.

It doesn't take him long to make the connection. That stupid prospectus he picked up at Laboris Investments with the photo of Ingmar on the cover. Shave off the bushy mustache and he would look exactly like the grinning Buddhas.

2

"Well, man," Mrs. Hepplewaite says. "What do you have to report?"

"Nothing," Timothy Cone says.

"Nothing?" she repeats angrily, thumping her heavy cane on the floor. "Then what am I paying you for?"

"You want me off the case? Call my boss and ask for a replacement. If you want to fire Haldering and Company, then fire them. It's your decision."

She glares at him. "You're as snotty as ever," she says.

"It's my nature," he tells her. "Look, if it'll make you feel any better, I think Ingmar Laboris is running a scam. But I've got absolutely no hard evidence. As of now, the guy is delivering, and apparently no one has lost any money."

"Did you check his background?"

"Yeah. No one's ever heard of him, in this country or overseas. He came out of nowhere."

"I told you so," she says triumphantly.

"So what? He could be trading currencies through agents or front companies. It's done all the time. And he's got a solid bank account with a special fund for redemptions."

"The man is a thief," she insists.

Cone stands and fastens the toggles on his parka. "Is that why you brought me up here? You could have told me on the phone. Now you're going to be billed for my transportation. By cab. Think of that."

She stares at him fixedly. "I don't like you much," she says.

"Welcome to the club," he says, stalking out.

"I expect immediate results!" she yells after him.

He can think of several choice rejoinders, but he doesn't voice them. He's halfway down the block, heading toward Madison Avenue, when he hears the sound of running feet. He turns and sees Lucinda Hepplewaite flying toward him, a big green loden cape floating out behind her.

"Hi," he says.

"Mr. Cone," she says breathlessly, "have you found out anything?"

"Nothing definite."

"Mama thinks Francis is a dolt," she says with an anxious, toothy smile. "But he's not."

"Francis? Your fiancé?"

She nods. "He's trying very hard to prove to Mama that he can take care of me. She doesn't think he's right for me. She doesn't think *any* man is right for me. Because she doesn't want to let me go. She wants a companion in her old age."

"I get the picture," Cone says.

"Please, Mr. Cone, if you hear anything bad about Laboris Investments, will you tell me first, before you tell Mama?"

He doesn't answer. "Is your fiancé still getting checks from Laboris?"

"Oh, yes."

"Thirty percent or more?"

"Well, the last check he received was a little under twenty percent. But that's still good, isn't it?"

"Uh-huh."

"And you'll tell me if you find anything wrong?"

"I'll see what I can do," Cone says, and watches her go running back to the brownstone, the cape billowing behind her.

He continues on to Madison Avenue and takes an uptown bus. He doesn't know why he's decided to stake out the Laboris Gallery of Levantine Art for a few hours. Maybe, he admits, because he hasn't anything better to do.

He walks by the place and looks through the window. Lights are on, the gallery is open, but it looks empty. No customers, no Ingrid or Erica Laboris. Cone crosses Madison and starts tramping up and down the other side of the street, his eyes on the gallery entrance.

It's a cruel, naked December day with a wind that flays and a lowery, sunless sky that presses down. Cone lights a cigarette, stuffs his hands into the pockets of his anorak, and plods back and forth, figuring he'll give it till noon. Then maybe he'll grab a Coney Island red-hot, with all the trimmings, from a street vendor, have a wild cherry cola, and then head back to the office.

He's been patrolling for almost a half hour when he sees two mink-clad matrons enter the gallery. They're inside for maybe fifteen minutes and then come out and go on their way. They weren't carrying any packages when they entered, and none when they exit. Zero plus zero equals zero.

During the next hour the gallery has two more visitors: a big, heavy man in a tweed coat, and a spindly woman wearing a knapsack over her down jacket. Neither stays long, and Cone figures maybe they just went into the gallery to look around and warm up.

It's about 11:45 when he spots another visitor. A shortish man wearing a beret and a three-quarter-length coat of black fur pops inside so quickly that Cone can't get a good look. But he has an itchy feeling that he's seen the gink before. So he takes up station almost directly across Madison and keeps watching the gallery, though sometimes it's difficult because the Christmas traffic is murder.

He stands there, stamping his feet and smoking his third Camel. Eventually, almost a half hour later, the gallery door opens. The beret starts to exit, then ducks back inside for a moment. Finally he comes out, closes the door, moves to the curb. He starts waving a hand for a taxi. Cone takes a long look and makes him. It's Sven from Laboris Importers on Nineteenth Street.

"Hello, there," the Wall Street dick says softly.

It takes Sven almost five minutes to get a cab. Cone watches him go, then trudges eastward to Lexington or Third, looking for his Coney Island red-hot. He tries not to make too much of Sven's visit to the Gallery. They're all cousins, aren't they? The family that plays together, stays together. Whatever the hell that means.

Except that when Sven entered the gallery, Cone could swear he wasn't carrying anything. But when he came out, he was lugging a bulging briefcase.

It's almost two o'clock before Cone gets back to the Haldering office. There's a memo from the receptionist centered on his bare desk: Please call Terry MacEver. So, his stomach still grumbling from that hot dog with sauerkraut, onions, piccalilli, and mustard, the Wall Street dick calls the sergeant.

"Listen," MacEver says, "I've been thinking about your interest in the Laboris Gallery, d'ya see, and I did something I should have done before: I ran the owner, Erica Laboris, through Records."

"And she's got a sheet?" Cone says hopefully.

"Nope, she's clean. But Neal Davenport told me you were interested in Laboris Investments on Wall Street. What's the name of the boss?"

"Ingmar Laboris."

"Shit," MacEver says. "Close but no cigar. Nothing on Ingmar. But the computer did cough up the name of Sven Laboris. Does that mean anything to you?"

Cone is silent a moment. "Yeah," he says finally, "Sven works at a place called Laboris Importers on West Nineteenth. I think maybe he's the boss."

"Is that so?" the sergeant says, his voice suddenly cold. "You didn't mention Laboris Importers before. Not holding out on me, are you?"

"I wouldn't do that," Cone says righteously. "You're interested in smuggled art. Laboris Importers is a junk shop. Besides, they're listed in the telephone book; it's no secret. Nah, I wasn't holding out on you. I just didn't think it was important."

"Look," MacEver says, "if you and I are going to work together, just tell me what you know and let me be the judge of whether it's important or not. Okay?"

"Of course. Absolutely. So Sven Laboris has a sheet?"

"Not much of one. About six months ago the blues busted an after-hours joint on East Eighty-third Street. A penthouse yet! They shook down all the customers, which was probably a stupid thing to do because their warrant only covered the owners. Anyway, when they frisked Sven Laboris, they found a glassine bag of shit in his jacket pocket."

"No kidding. Was he held?"

"Maybe for a couple of hours. But he had no needle tracks, no previous criminal record, and there was no evidence that he was dealing in what the government laughingly calls a 'controlled substance.' So he walked. Happens all the time. But here's the kicker: When the lab analyzed the heroin he was carrying, they said it was the purest they had ever seen. That stuff could have been cut six ways from the middle and still zonked fifty junkies. Shoot it uncut and it's instant DOA. Sven Laboris claimed someone must have slipped the skag into his jacket pocket after the blues broke in."

"Oh, sure," Cone says. "And that's it?"

"That's it," the sergeant says. "I don't know if it means anything, but I'm giving it to you. Now what have you got for me?"

Long pause.

"Come on, come on," MacEver says impatiently. "There are no freebies in this business—you know that. What have you got?"

Cone decides he better play along; so he tells MacEver how he staked out the Laboris Gallery that morning and saw Sven Laboris enter empty-handed and emerge about a half hour later carrying a briefcase.

"What has that got to do with your guy on Wall Street?" asks MacEver.

"Beats the hell out of me," Cone admits. "I can't see Ingmar financing drug or art smuggling with investors' funds and then paying off thirty percent. Banditos don't go looking for public money. They've got other ways to raise cash. Mostly from their profits on the last deal."

"I know what you mean," the sergeant says. "Well, you keep plugging, and I'll keep plugging, and maybe between us we can make a score. I won't hold out on you, but you don't hold out on me. Understood?"

"Oh, sure," Cone says, hanging up. And if you believe that, there's a swell bridge to Brooklyn you may be interested in buying.

He lights a cigarette and ambles down to Joe Washington's cubicle. It's identical to his own, except that Joe has a coat tree and a coffee maker he locks up in his desk every night.

"Hey, it's the Cone-head," Washington says, looking up. "How's it going, old buddy?"

"Getting by. And you?"

"Surviving. What're you doing for the holiday?"

"Celebrating Christ's birth."

"Yeah?" Joe says, looking at him closely. "Wanna come out to my house for Christmas dinner? Roast turkey, mashed potatoes with gravy, cranberry sauce—real honky soul food."

"Nah," Cone says. "You'll want to be alone with your family. But thanks anyway. Listen, I need some poop. Didn't you work a drug case about two years ago?"

"Closer to three," Washington says, leaning back in his swivel chair and laughing. "What a giggle that was! The client was a brokerage house on the Street. They suspected one of their account executives was dealing, so they called us in. Dealing? That idiot was trying to become the IBM of dope. He had even started a mail-order business. If we hadn't scuttled him, he'd have been selling futures in heroin and cocaine. The guy was blitzed out of his gourd."

"You worked with the City on this?"

"Oh, sure. An undercover narc named Petey Alvarez. A wonderful guy.

I still see him for drinks occasionally. What's your interest, Tim? You got a drug case?"

"I don't know what the fuck I've got," Cone says fretfully. "But there may be a heroin angle. The stuff usually comes over in kilo bags—correct?"

"Yeah. Two-point-two pounds."

"Where does it come in?"

"Boston, New York, Baltimore, Miami, the Texas coast, Los Angeles, San Francisco, Seattle. Here, there and everywhere."

"And how does it come in?"

"Hidden away in everything from office furniture to VCRs. There's a million ways to get the shit into the country. Every time the Feds close off one pipeline, ten new ones open up."

Cone is silent, thinking that over.

"Mostly from where?" he asks finally.

"Oh, hell," Joe Washington says. "A hundred places. If the climate is right, you can grow opium almost anywhere. The guy I helped nab was getting his supply from Turkey and Iran after it was processed in Marseilles and Sicily."

Cone perks up. "Turkey and Iran? The Middle East?"

"Yeah, but that was three years ago. Turkey and Iran claim they've put the opium growers out of business. Fat chance! Look, if you're a piss-poor farmer, you know you can make more money squeezing a poppy than growing rutabagas. So I'd guess there's stuff still coming from the Middle East. And of course there's always Cambodia, Vietnam, or Laos."

"And Burma?" Cone asks.

"Burma? Sure, Burma."

"Listen, Joe, could you call this Petey Alvarez and pick his brains a little?"

"I guess I could," Washington says slowly. "What do you want to know?"

"Well, you keep talking about how things were three years ago. Ask him about how things are now. Is there a lot of heroin on the street in New York? Or is it all cocaine? And does he have any idea where it's coming from and how it's getting in?"

Joe looks at him. "He could probably tell me all that, Tim, but what's in it for him?"

"Maybe a nice bust, maybe nothing. Will he go along with you on that basis?"

"I'll try," Washington says, sighing.

Cone goes back to his office and finds two file folders Samantha Whatley has dropped on his desk. Two new cases.

"Goddammit!" he shouts.

He sits down in his swivel chair and flips through the files. They look dull: Check out a proposed merger of two outfits that sell water pumps, and investigate a franchiser who's selling a chance to get rich by raising worms in your basement. The Wall Street dick already knows the answer to that one.

He tosses the folders aside, lights a Camel, leans back to review the day's happenings. He's got a possible drug-smuggling caper. He's got a possible art-theft scam. But what—if anything—is the connection with Laboris Investments on Wall Street?

Maybe, he thinks morosely, Ingmar is the Mr. Nice Guy of the family and strictly legit.

"And I also believe in the Tooth Fairy," Cone says aloud.

He gets up early the next morning, shaves, and even takes a shower. Cleo looks at him in amazement.

"What are you staring at?" he asks the cat. "It's Christmastime, isn't it?"

Sitting in his skivvies, he has two cups of black coffee, each with a cigarette. Then he sips a small shot of Italian brandy because he feels in a festive mood. He lets Cleo lick the rim of his empty glass.

"Stick with me, kiddo," Cone says, "and you'll be wearing diamonds."

He puts on what he calls his "good suit": a frowsy tweed jacket with suede patches on the elbows, flannel slacks (not too stained), a plaid shirt open at the neck to reveal a clean but somewhat grayish T-shirt. He straps the Magnum to his ankle and is ready for a fight or a frolic.

When he gets outside, he finds it has snowed during the night; there's almost an inch of powder on the sidewalks. But it's melting rapidly, and the air is razory, the sky washed. As usual, he hikes down Broadway to the Haldering office on John Street. Before he goes up, he stops at the deli for a container of black coffee and a buttered bialy.

At his desk, working on his breakfast, he calls Laboris Investments, Inc. If he can get through to Ingmar, he's decided to zap the guy with honesty. Not too much, of course, but enough to get him interested and willing to talk.

"Has Mr. Laboris returned from overseas?" he asks the perky receptionist who answers the phone.

"May I ask who's calling, sir?"

"My name is Timothy Cone, and I'm with Haldering and Company on John Street. I'd like to speak to Mr. Laboris if he's available."

"Just a moment, please," she chirps—from which Cone figures Ingmar is on the premises.

He munches on his bialy a couple of minutes before she comes back on the line.

"Thank you for waiting," she says. "Could you tell me what this is in reference to?"

He's got his scenario plotted. "Haldering and Company represents a private client who would like to make a substantial deposit with Laboris Investments. We have been asked to investigate. I was hoping for the opportunity to have a personal interview with Mr. Laboris."

"Just a moment, please, sir," she repeats, and she's gone again. He has finished his breakfast and lighted his third cigarette of the day before she comes back on again. "Mr. Laboris is tied up at present," she says. "But if you'd care to leave your number, he'll get back to you as soon as possible."

"That'll be fine," Cone says, and gives her the Haldering number.

"Thank you, sir," she says.

He sighs, hangs up, and doesn't do anything but smoke and count the walls for the next twenty minutes. He hopes Ingmar has taken the bait and is checking out Haldering & Co. When his phone rings, he picks it up, determined to be humble.

"Timothy Cone," he says instead of his usual "Yeah?"

"This is Ingmar Laboris speaking."

"Thank you for calling back, Mr. Laboris. I realize what a busy man you are, but I was hoping you might be able to give me a few moments to discuss an investment one of our clients wishes to make."

"So I understand," Ingmar says. The voice is plummy, with the churchy resonance of a monsignor or a proctologist. No hisses for Ingmar. "I must tell you I do not ordinarily meet with individual investors or their representatives. My time is almost totally devoted to managing our currency portfolio."

"I appreciate that, Mr. Laboris, but perhaps you'd be willing to make an exception in this case. The investment our client is planning is of such a size that we feel a personal interview is necessary."

"What amount are we speaking about?"

"A quarter of a million," Cone says, hoping that won't be too small to turn Ingmar off or too large to make him suspicious.

"I see," the other man says thoughtfully. "Well, let me take a look at my appointment calendar."

Got him! Cone exults, recognizing the ploy.

"If you can be here at ten-thirty this morning," Laboris says, "I will be able to fit you in. But I must tell you it can only be for a limited time. I am flying to Zurich at noon."

"I appreciate your help," Cone says. "I'll be in your office at ten-thirty on the dot."

It's only after he hangs up the phone that he says, "Fink!"

He gets to Laboris Investments ten minutes early, intending to scout the territory. The outer office is crowded with plungers, but nothing like the mob scene he had witnessed on his previous visit. Speculators are still signing up and plunking down their bucks, but Cone wonders if the bloom is off the rose.

He wanders about, picks up one of those skimpy brochures and reads it again, once more noting the caveat: "Past performance is no guarantee of future results." And then there's the photo of Ingmar: plump, glossy, with that gleeful look of the Buddha statuettes.

And when Cone is ushered into the inner office, the man himself, standing behind an enormous mahogany desk, looks even more like a mustachioed Buddha, for he has a smooth, round belly that bulges his vest. His skin has the Laboris margarine sheen, and his handclasp is slippery.

"Mr. Cone," he says in that orotund voice. "Delighted to make your acquaintance."

"Likewise," the Wall Street dick says. "I certainly do appreciate your making time for me in your busy schedule."

Laboris waves that away, and with the same gesture indicates the leather armchair facing his desk. But he doesn't, Cone notes, offer to relieve him of his anorak. Since the office is overheated, that's probably Ingmar's tactic to make his visitor's stay as short as possible.

"Would you be offended if I smoked a cigar?" Laboris asks. "I fear I am addicted."

"Go right ahead," Cone says. "As long as I can light up a spike. I'm hooked, too."

"Of course," Ingmar says, moving a heavy ashtray halfway between them. It's a solid chunk of smoky quartz, faceted like a diamond but with a shallow depression to hold ashes. "A Nepali prince gave me that. It's amusing—no?"

"Yeah," Cone says. "Amusing."

He watches solemnly as Laboris goes through the slow ceremony of lighting his cigar.

"Now then, Mr. Cone," he says, "how may I be of service?"

"I don't know if you're familiar with Haldering and Company, sir, but we do financial investigations for corporate and individual clients. You can check us out if you like."

"I already have," Laboris says with a soft smile. "You're not one of the biggest firms in that business, but you have a good reputation."

"Well, we try. Anyway, we have a client who wants to put a quarter-million in your operation and is paying us to take a look-see. No reflection on you, of course; it's just prudent investing."

"I understand. And naturally you cannot reveal the name of this client."

"Naturally."

Ingmar regards the lengthening ash on his cigar with pleasure. "I must tell you," he says, "each time I smoke I play a game to see how long an ash I can produce before it falls off. To prove the steadiness of my hand."

"It looks steady enough to me," Cone says, realizing that there is no way this guy is going to be surprised, shaken, or angered.

"Foreign-exchange trading is a minute-by-minute thing, isn't it?" Cone asks. "How do you keep up?"

"Through open telephone lines to my chief agents overseas. We avoid computers and telecommunications equipment, but I must tell you, I am in constant touch with market changes, no matter how frequent or how small. The exchange rate between, say, British pounds and Israeli shekels may suddenly vary by a tenth of one percent. Doesn't sound like much, does it? But when you're dealing in hundreds of millions, as I am, there's money to be made on that tenth."

"Or lost."

"That," Ingmar Laboris says, "I try very hard not to do."

"You mentioned your overseas agents. We've checked with currency traders in several European cities, Mr. Laboris, and none of them has ever heard of you."

The ash falls from Ingmar's cigar onto the polished desktop. He makes no effort to scoop it up or brush it away, but looks at it sorrowfully. "What a shame," he says. "I had hoped to grow it longer. About my not being known to foreign-exchange traders overseas, I must tell you that I am delighted to hear it. You see, Mr. Cone, I deal daily in vast sums. If I did it in my own name, my trades would be sufficient to quirk the market. Even a rumor of my interest might destroy a potentially profitable deal. So I am happy to remain anonymous. I employ almost a hundred agents all over the world who trade for me and who are wise enough, I trust, not to mention the name of Laboris Investments. I must tell you that money trading is a very ancient and arcane art."

"Yeah," the Wall Street dick says. "Jesus drove them from the temple, didn't he?"

Laboris tries to smile. "I believe the biblical reference is to money *changers*. Somewhat different from modern currency traders."

Cone could have argued that but decides he's pushed it far enough. "Mr. Laboris, I haven't seen anything that looks like an annual report. You issue them, don't you?"

Ingmar sets his cigar carefully aside in the quartz ashtray.

"I certainly intend to. I must tell you that Laboris Investments has been in existence for less than a year so, as of this date, no annual report has been issued. However, I have organized a special staff for that purpose, and we anticipate having a complete report available by the middle of March."

He glances at his gold Rolex, and Cone knows he's not going to prod this guy into making any mistakes or unexpected disclosures. Sitting back, manicured fingers laced across his vested belly, Laboris looks bland, oiled, and satisfied. The slick black hair is without a wayward strand, and the full lips are rosy enough to be rouged. He's wearing a suit of smooth gray flannel. He also sports a gold pinkie ring with a rock just slightly smaller than the Kohinoor.

"A couple of final questions," Cone says. "What is the minimum investment you accept?"

"Five thousand. But additional funds may be deposited in existing accounts in thousand-dollar increments."

"And what is your current rate of return?"

Ingmar pauses a moment, then sighs heavily. "Unfortunately, at present it is only a little over ten percent—due mainly to the unexpected rise in value of the Japanese yen."

"Uh-huh," Cone says. "The yen'll do you in every time."

"However, I have every confidence that we will improve on net profits in the next few weeks. I am especially interested in the relationship between German marks and Swiss francs. It's a very volatile situation, and I think there's a small fortune to be made."

"Yeah," Cone says, "if you start with a large fortune."

Both men laugh heartily, each as falsely as the other, and Cone rises to leave. Ingmar comes up close to give him that slick handshake again. Cone gets a whiff of the familiar Laboris scent: desiccated roses.

"I certainly hope I have addressed all your questions adequately, Mr. Cone."

"You've impressed me," the Wall Street dick says.

"And you'll recommend Laboris Investments to your client?"

"I'll certainly make a recommendation. You'll probably be hearing from us shortly. Thank you for your time, Mr. Laboris."

He can't wait to get into the hard, clean December sunlight. The stench of con is overpowering, and it takes the long walk back to John Street to rid himself of that odor of glib thievery. What *is* the sonofabitch up to?

Back in his office, the answer still eludes him. He doodles a rough equilateral triangle on a scratchpad. At the apexes he writes the names of three cousins: Sven Laboris, Erica Laboris, Ingmar Laboris. Sven gets the notation: "Possible dope smuggling." Erica gets "Possible art theft" after her name. And Ingmar gets a big, fat question mark. It's a triangle, Cone is convinced, but he can't see the connection between cheap gimcracks, expensive Levantine antiques, and Laboris Investments, Inc., of Wall Street.

"Screw it," he says aloud, and calls down to the deli for a hot corned beef on rye, with cole slaw, a half-dill pickle, and two cold cans of Michelob Light.

That afternoon, Joe Washington comes slouching into Cone's office and finds Timothy drowsing, chin down on his chest. Joe grins and calls softly, "Hey, Tim, got a minute?"

Cone opens his eyes. "I got a lot of minutes—all empty. Pull up a chair."

"You feeling okay?"

"If I felt any better I'd be unconscious. What's doing, Joe?"

Washington pulls a small notebook from his jacket pocket and starts flipping pages. "I talked to Petey Alvarez, that narc pal of mine."

Cone straightens in his swivel chair. "That's great. Come up with anything?"

"More than you want to know," Joe says, reading his notes. "The opium poppies are squeezed in Bhutan, Bangladesh, Laos, Thailand, Vietnam, Cambodia, Burma, Turkey, Iran, Pakistan, Afghanistan, and points north, east, south, and west. The raw stuff used to be sent to Marseilles and Sicily for processing, but most of those labs have been busted. The latest thing is to set up plants close to the source of supply. Cut out the middleman. So the shit is coming in from all over the Middle and Far East."

"That's nice," Cone says.

"Yeah. Some of it is quality, some of it probably has sand, sugar, or talcum powder mixed in. To answer your specific questions, the price on the street right now has gone up. You get less in your nickel and dime bags. But there's plenty available. If you've got the gelt, you get your melt."

"And that's it?"

"Just about," Joe says, closing his notebook. "One more thing: Petey says in the last six months or so, some really high-quality smack has been coming in. Which means a small amount goes a long way after it's been cut. And that's all I got. Any help, Tim?"

"Who the hell knows?" Cone says. "But thanks anyway."

After Washington leaves, Cone opens the bottom drawer of his desk and stares down at the two Buddha statuettes. It takes him a moment to identify his first purchase, the one with the removable base. He separates the two sections and peers into the neat hole drilled up into the figure.

That hollow could never contain a kilo. It might, he estimates, hold six ounces of a white powder packed tightly. Six ounces. Not much. He pulls a scratchpad toward him and does some quick figuring.

Say Laboris Importers brought in a thousand hollowed Buddhas for distribution all over the country. Six ounces of heroin per Buddha. Six thousand ounces. About 375 pounds. Or about 139 kilos. If the stuff is pure, maybe they could get $30,000 per kilo. More than four million for the lot. Nice. And then, because the cousins are all business, they sell the emptied Buddhas in their schlock shops.

And the solid Buddha, the one that doesn't separate? Maybe that's one of the dummies put up front in the shipment in case Customs wants to take a look.

And, Cone realizes, they would use more than the Buddha statuettes. The stuff could be hidden in leather hassocks from Turkey, porcelain elephants from Korea, huge marionettes from India. Those things are big enough to contain a whole kilo of shit.

And also, Cone thinks, big enough to conceal Levantine art, like urns, bowls, rhytons, manuscripts, weapons—anything. What a sweet setup. You deal in crazy cuckoo clocks and end up with a zillion bucks from smuggled dope and stolen art work. Beautiful.

But all smoke, he acknowledges. He hasn't got a smidgen of hard evidence to prove what he guesses is going down.

He puts the two teak Buddhas away and slams the desk drawer. He's no sooner done that than Samantha Whatley comes storming into his office.

"Where's Izzy?" she demands. "I want him back—now!"

"What's the rush?" Cone says mildly. "You'll get him back eventually."

Sam leans down and lowers her voice so no one will overhear. "Listen, bubblehead," she says, "you don't give me so many gifts that I'm going to give up Izzy without a fight. You give me something and then you take it back. What kind of bullshit is that? And if that isn't enough, you cheap bastard, you're not even paying for it; it's on your swindle sheet, for God's sake. Come on, let's have it."

Sighing, Cone opens the lower desk drawer, fumbles inside, pulls out the solid Buddha, and shoves it at her.

"Here," he says, "take the goddamned thing."

Samantha takes a close look at the statuette and then, without even trying to untwist the base, glares at Cone wrathfully. "What are you trying to pull? This isn't Izzy."

He groans. "How do you know?"

"Because my Izzy has a cute little dimple in his chin. This one doesn't."

"A cute little dimple? Jesus Christ!" He hauls the other Buddha from the desk drawer and hands it to her. "Go ahead, unscrew the base. The first one is a solid piece of wood."

Sam inspects the two statuettes carefully, then looks at Cone, perplexed. "What the hell's going on, Tim?"

"Damned if I know."

"Oh, you know," she says angrily. "You're just not telling me."

"Nothing to tell."

"What a hardass you are. Well, I don't care, I'm taking Izzy with me."

"Okay, but keep it safe; I may have to borrow it again one of these days."

"Lots of luck," Samantha says, sweeping out of his office, the Buddha cradled in her arms.

Cone opens a fresh pack of Camels, lights his umpteenth cigarette of the day. He sits smoking slowly, staring at the solid teak statuette on his desk. Its arms are stretched high in a banzai gesture, plump face creased in a happy grin. Finally, he pulls the phone close and calls Sergeant MacEver.

"What's happening?" MacEver wants to know.

"Nothing's happening; that's why I'm calling. I've got a wild idea I want to try on you."

"About the Laboris Art Gallery?"

"Yeah. Would you be willing to try a sting?"

"How do we do that?"

"Well, you told me you get reports from Interpol and other places on stolen works of art. Right?"

"That's correct."

"Suppose you pick out one of the items and we send someone to the Laboris Gallery to ask if Erica can find them a similar item. If she refuses to bite, she's clean. If she says she'll see what she can do and then actually delivers, we've got her. What do you think?"

Silence.

"Sergeant?" Cone says. "You there?"

"I'm here," MacEver says finally. "It's not a *bad* idea, but it needs a lot of work. Most art galleries get photos and descriptions of stolen objects, so you can't just waltz in, describe a piece of loot, and say you want to buy it. That would alert any art dealer, especially if they don't know you from Adam."

"Yeah, I can see that. So you think a sting is out?"

"I didn't say that. But it would have to be rigged very carefully."

"Have you ever met Erica Laboris?" Cone asks. "Would she recognize you?"

"No, I've never met her, and I doubt if she'd make me."

"Okay, how about this: I go up to the gallery and tell Erica I've got a wealthy brother-in-law who's a nut on collecting antique daggers or pis-spots or whatever. You select the item from your list of stolen stuff. I say the guy is coming to New York from Topeka on a business trip and he'd like to stop by and see if she's got anything to add to his collection. You follow? We suck her in slowly."

"And I play the brother-in-law?"

"Sure," Cone says heartily. "I mean, you know the business, don't you? This is one shrewd lady, and she'd know in a minute if you're a genuine expert or just a plant."

"It just might work," the sergeant says slowly, "but I may have some trouble convincing my boss. At any rate I'll give it the old college try. I'll get back to you as soon as possible."

Cone hangs up, satisfied that he's started one wheel turning. Figuring he's given Hiram Haldering enough sweat for one day, he pulls on his parka and cap, shoves the solid Buddha in Samantha's shopping bag, and, carrying that, heads for home.

As he leaves the building, he spots a tall, scrawny guy wearing a ratty trench coat and a black slouch hat, like a foreign correspondent from the 1930s. He's leaning against a mailbox, mumbling to himself and shifting his weight slowly from foot to foot.

Just one of your Manhattan weirdos, Cone figures, and turns north on Broadway. Two blocks later, he stops for the sign to change from DON'T WALK to WALK, and sees the nut case in the trench coat standing at his elbow, still mumbling.

Having learned to live defensively in New York, Cone slows to let the mumbler get ahead of him. But no dice; the trench coat begins to saunter, too, staying about fifteen feet behind the Wall Street dick. Cone stops to look in a shop window with a tasteful display of plastic Christmas trees and Styrofoam ornaments. The weirdo stops and stares around vaguely.

If he's shadowing, Cone figures he's got to be the most inept tail since General Hood lost track of General Sherman at the Battle of Atlanta. The mumbler sticks at Cone's heels for three more blocks. Then the investigator decides to dump him. Cone darts out into oncoming traffic on Chambers Street, sprinting, pausing, pirouetting like a ballet dancer. He makes it to the other side, bones intact, ignoring the screams of infuriated drivers. He looks back. The trench coat is still hesitating on the curb, waiting for the light to change.

He walks home at a faster pace, proud of his performance. He stops at a local deli, picks up barbecued pork ribs, a container of potato salad, and a cold six-pack of Heineken. When he comes out of the store, the mumbler is across the street, inspecting the heavens.

"Shit!" Timothy says aloud, startling a young couple who are walking by, holding hands.

Up in the loft, door locked, bolted, and chained, he sets out his evening meal. Cleo sits patiently on the floor at his side, waiting for discarded bones.

Cone works his way through two pounds of ribs, a half pound of potato salad, and two cans of beer. Then he goes to the front window and pulls the torn shade aside. The tall, scrawny guy is standing in the doorway of a closed Japanese sushi joint across Broadway. Even at a distance, Cone can see him slowly weaving from side to side. Got to be stoned out of his gourd, Cone decides.

"Ah, the hell with it," he tells Cleo. "I shall return carrying my shield or on it."

That doesn't impress the cat at all.

He pulls on his cap and anorak. Then he transfers the .357 Magnum from ankle holster to the parka's right-hand pocket, goes downstairs, and crosses to the other side of Broadway.

"Mr. Laboris, I presume," he says, walking up to the tail.

"Beat it, bum," the guy says. He doesn't look like a Laboris: too tall, too pale, too thin. He's got a saber of a nose, his teeth are tarnished clunks, the eyes are black aggies.

"What are you on?" Cone asks. "I'll make one guess: smack—right? Really good stuff?"

"Get lost," the man says hoarsely. "I'm waiting for someone."

"You're waiting for death," Cone says. "It could be me if you keep tramping up my heels. Who hired you?"

The guy straightens up from his slouch. He takes a deep breath. "You asked for it," he says.

"Oh-ho," the Wall Street dick says. "We seem to have a little altercation brewing here. Okay, put up your dukes."

Cone raises balled fists, begins dancing about the other man, tossing short punches at the air, stubbing his nose with a thumb.

"Come on," he says. "Lay on, Macduff, and damned be him who first cries, 'Hold, enough!' "

"My name ain't Macduff."

Cone reaches out to slap the man's face lightly. "No?" Slap. "What is it?" Slap. "What is it?" Slap.

"You stop that!" a woman says. "Stop beating that man!"

Cone turns to see a middle-aged couple: mink coat and British short-warm. The man is trying to tug the woman away.

"I'm not beating him," Cone says. "I just want to punish him. He raped my cat."

"He what?!"

"You heard me," Cone says. "Bestiality. Disgusting."

"Come along, Cynthia," the man says.

"I'm going to call the police," the woman says defiantly.

"Yeah," Cone says, "you do that. Tell them I've cornered the mad cat-rapist who's been terrorizing lower Manhattan."

"You prick," the mumbler says when the couple scurries away. "You're a rotten, no-good prick."

"Who hired you?" Cone asks, slapping the guy's face again, harder this time.

Cone thought he was stoned, out on his feet, but the gink moves fast. His hand comes out of his trench coat pocket, there's a snick and a click, and six inches of raw knife blade gleam dully. And he knows how to use it, not gripped like a dagger, hand raised to strike a blow, but knuckles down, ready for a smooth stab or slash.

"Come ahead," Cone says, knowing he hasn't got time to start fumbling for his iron. "Make your play. Do what you're getting paid to do."

The guy lurches, but he's clumsy, hasn't got the moves. Cone feints, then goes in under the steel. He gets a solid wrist lock, twists, then turns the whole arm. He raises his own knee and brings the other man's arm down hard. There's a satisfying *crack!* The knife clatters to the sidewalk.

"You hurt me," the man says wonderingly, looking down at his dangling arm. "I think it's busted."

"I think so, too," Cone says. "I'll bet it hurts."

Then, when the guy's eyes glaze over and he begins to fall, the Wall Street dick catches him under the arms and eases him down. He'd like to search him, but Cynthia in the mink coat might have made good on her threat to call the cops. So Cone recrosses Broadway and climbs the six floors to the loft.

He mixes a muscular vodka and water and paces up and down the loft, drinking, waiting for his adrenaline level to get back to normal, and trying to figure who sicced the mumbler on him, and for what reason. It just doesn't make sense. Why hire a spaced-out junkie to scrag someone? And Laboris Importers already knew his home address—if the hophead was paid to track him to his wallow.

He gives up trying to puzzle it out. He freshens his drink (with vodka, not water), and sits again at the rickety table. He takes the solid Buddha from the Macy's shopping bag and sets it on the floor. Cleo comes padding over to investigate.

The denutted tom stares at the statuette, sniffs it all over, then begins rubbing his flanks against the smooth teak belly.

"Keep rubbing, kiddo," Timothy Cone says, "and make a wish. Maybe you'll get your balls back."

The next morning, he's on his second cup of black coffee and second cigarette when the wall phone rings in the kitchen. It makes a loud, shrill jangle and sends Cleo scuttling under the bathtub.

"Yeah?" Cone says.

"Neal Davenport," the NYPD detective says. "Don't you ever go to work on time?"

"Nah. But I make up for getting in late; I leave early. What's up?"

"Not me, that's for sure," Davenport says. "Had your first laugh of the day?"

"I could use a mild chuckle."

"Late last night the blues in your precinct picked up a clunk in the doorway of a sushi bar right across the street from where you live. That's a laugh, isn't it?"

"A corpse?"

"Deader than Paddy's pig."

"How'd he go?"

"Knife. The preliminary report says he was stabbed three times in the gut, and then a final cut tickled his heart, and that was it. He's been ID'd as Sidney Leonidas. That name mean anything to you?"

"Yeah," Cone says. "Leonidas was the king of Sparta in the fourth century B.C."

"I don't think it was him," Davenport says. "This one was a junkie. He was covered with ulcerated needle tracks. The docs figure that even if someone hadn't offed him, he'd have OD'd from shooting shit, probably sooner than later."

"Very interesting. But why are you telling me all this?"

"Because every time something happens on your block, I get antsy about you. You do crazy things and then leave it to us to pick up the garbage."

"Yeah, but I deliver, don't I? Maybe not right away, but eventually."

"Well...maybe," the city dick says grudgingly. "How's the Laboris thing coming along?"

"Slowly. Nothing to report."

"And if there was, you wouldn't talk, you tight-mouthed bastard. Look, Cone, if you've got anything that'll help us on this homicide, spit it out."

"I don't know a damned thing about it."

"The guy had a busted right wing. You know anything about that?"

"Not a thing."

"Shit!" the city bull says disgustedly. "You and your goddamned secrets. One of these days you're going to realize that you've got to go along to get along."

"Did you find the knife?" Cone asks.

"What?"

"The knife that killed this Sidney Leonidas. Did you find it?"

"That's just when I mean," Davenport says indignantly. "You want to pick my brains, but you won't open up to me. All right, I'll toss you a crumb: No, we did not find the murder weapon. Now just remember you owe me one."

"Thanks," Cone says. "I'll be in touch." And he hangs up.

He peers out his front window and, across Broadway, sees NYPD sawhorses around the sushi bar. There's one uniformed cop on duty, talking to a few of the rubbernecks. Otherwise no activity. Cone pulls on cap and parka, checks his ankle holster, and sets out to trudge down to John Street.

Meteorologists have been predicting a white Christmas, and it sure smells like one. It's cold enough for a wet snow, and the air is thick, clotted, and beads on Cone's leather cap. He plods along steadily, reacting automatically to traffic lights and pedestrian flow, but oblivious to the cityscape. He's pondering the murder of Sidney Leonidas.

He knows from experience that nine times out of ten the solution to any problem is the most obvious one. In the case of the mumbler's death, the evident explanation is that some villain came along, maybe a junkie himself, saw a guy passed out in a dark doorway, and decided to pick him clean. But Leonidas roused and put up a fight. The knife was there, handy on the sidewalk, so the mugger grabbed it up and made the muggee's quietus with a bare bodkin.

It listens—but could Leonidas put up a fight with a busted right arm? Cone doesn't think so. A little old lady on crutches could have lifted the guy's wallet and shoes; he was in no condition to offer resistance. He was *out* when Cone left him.

So the obvious doesn't have all the answers. The next best guess is that Sidney Leonidas was done in deliberately, with malice aforethought. Someone wanted him gone.

The Wall Street dick doesn't enjoy that idea. Because the logical perpetrator might well be a guy who hired the mumbler to waste Cone and followed him to make sure the job was done properly. Then, when he witnessed the confrontation between the two and saw his assassin chopped down and laid to rest in the doorway, the boss decided he better get rid of his junked-up thug in case he had told or might tell Cone or the cops who he was working for.

That scenario holds together, but it makes Timothy look like a pointy-head. It means that while the mumbler was following him to his loft from the office, there was a second shadow behind both of them, keeping an eye on the action and ready to take over if things got hairy. And Cone had never been aware of a second tail.

He doesn't like it. There are a lot of desperadoes in New York, and the knave who hired Sidney Leonidas will probably not quit after one failure. He'll come on again. And again. That realization makes for an itch between the shoulder blades and a tendency to flinch at any loud street noise.

Now I know how the President feels, Cone thinks—but that's no comfort.

Sergeant MacEver is waiting in the reception room of Haldering & Co. He's dressed dapperly and carrying an attaché case of black alligator. Cone leads the way to his office.

"Beautiful," the sergeant says, looking around. "This place should be condemned."

"It has been," Cone tells him. "We're just waiting for the wrecker's ball. I think they're going to build a skyscraper or a parking lot or something. Take a chair."

MacEver sits down, still wearing his natty fur-collared chesterfield and a trooper's cap of black mink.

"About that sting on the Laboris Gallery," he says. "I think maybe we can finagle it."

"Good," Cone says. "Best news I've had today."

"But I don't have an absolute go-ahead. You know how the Department works; no one wants to stick his neck out, in case it ends up a complete disaster. But I did get tentative approval to put the play in action. Here's how I plot it: We follow your original scenario. You make the first approach. I'm your rich brother-in-law, in New York on a business trip. I'm a nut collector of antique swords, and I'm especially interested in getting hold of some old blades from the Near East. You with me so far?"

"I'm following."

"Okay," the sergeant says. He leans down to open his attaché case, pulls out an eight-by-ten black-and-white photo and hands it to Cone. "That's what we're looking for."

Cone inspects the grainy photograph. "Looks like a hunk of junk to me."

"Does it? Well, they're maybe seventy or eighty of them in the world that have been definitely identified and dated. This particular blade is

Assyrian and was hand-forged around the sixth century B.C. They were still making iron swords then, but using bronze for the hilts. Anyway, this one was stolen from a Beirut museum about six months ago."

"What's it worth?" Cone asks.

"Hard to say. Who would want a rusty piece of old iron except a museum or a collector? It's worth whatever you can get for it. I'm just telling you all this stuff as background, d'ya see. When you make your pitch to Erica Laboris, all you know is that you've got a wealthy relative who's ape for antique swords from the Middle East."

"I dig. I make the intro and then you show up and take it from there."

"Right," MacEver says approvingly. "We'll play this very cozily and see what the lady suggests. When can you start the ball rolling?"

"Today," Cone says. "Maybe this morning. You want me to use your real name?"

"No," the sergeant says. "Too risky. I've got some business cards from an insurance outfit in Dallas that I've helped out on a few things. They'll cover for me. Here, take it and leave it with the mark."

He hands a card to Cone. It reads: J. Ransom Bailey, Agent, Fugelmann Insurance Co., Inc., Dallas, Texas.

"If Erica Laboris checks with them," MacEver says, "they'll swear I'm one of their most successful salesmen."

"J. Ransom Bailey," Cone says, pocketing the card. "Very elegant. And what are you doing in New York?"

"Attending a convention of insurance agents at the Hilton: guys who have topped fifty million in sales for the past year. It's legit; the convention is starting tomorrow, and Bailey is registered at the Hilton."

"You make a great diddler," Cone says admiringly. "Looks to me like you've covered your tracks just fine."

"Not the first time I've done this," Terry MacEver says. He snaps shut his attaché case and rises. "Give me a call after you've seen Erica Laboris and tell me how it went. Don't press too hard and don't, for God's sake, mention that stolen Assyrian sword I showed you."

"I'm not an amateur bamboozler myself," Cone says. "I'll act the rube. I'll do everything but say, 'Aw, shucks.' Don't worry; if the lady can be had, she will be had."

"Tell her I'll only be in New York till Christmas Eve, and then I'm flying back to Dallas. Just to put a little heat on her, d'ya see. When I talk to her, I'll turn the burner up a bit higher. If she's dealing stolen art, she'll want to close the deal as soon as possible."

"I'll call you as soon as I've made contact," Cone promises.

After MacEver leaves, he lights a Camel and reviews the planned sting. He can't see any glaring loopholes. If Erica Laboris is foursquare, then the whole scam is dead. But if she takes the bait, then they should be able to hang her by the heels. It all depends on the intensity of the lady's greed.

Which has, of course, apparently nothing to do with Laboris Investments, Inc., of Wall Street. This case, which started as a simple investigation of an investment firm, has now flushed a covey of cousins, and Cone is up to his pipik in possible heroin smuggling and possible art theft.

What it calls for, he decides, is juggling, sleight of hand, and a dark vision of the human race which may or may not be one of God's jokes.

He gets up to the Laboris Gallery a little before noon, and walks by once, scoping the place. As far as he can see, no customers—which pleases him.

When he goes marching in, doffing his cap, Ingrid Laboris, the cream puff, comes dollying up, giggling like a maniac.

"I knew you would return," she says. "I just *knew* it!"

"Did you?" Timothy Cone says, beaming. "That's more than I did. How'ya doing? Busy?"

"Not so much," Ingrid says, pouting prettily. "Not so many people shop for Levantine antiques for Christmas presents. You are interested in something?"

"Yeah. Your cousin Erica. Is she around?"

"Oh, yes. In the back office. I shall tell her you are here."

She sashays away. He watches her go, cursing his unbridled lust.

But then Erica comes stalking, cooling him down. She's wearing a black leather sheath that looks like a tube, tight enough to squeeze her out both ends. But there's no come-on about her; she's aloof, sure.

"Ah," she says. "Mr. Cone of Haldering and Company."

"You remembered," he says. "That's nice."

"But of course," she says with her distant smile. "How may I be of service?"

The hisses sound like a whistling teakettle.

"Listen," Cone says, "I've got a brother-in-law, J. Ransom Bailey, a rich-type insurance agent. He's in from Dallas for a convention at the Hilton. Randy is a nut on swords, and when I told him I had visited your gallery, he wanted me to ask if you had anything he could add to his collection."

"Oh?" Erica Laboris says. "What exactly is he looking for?"

Cone shrugs apologetically. "I know from nothing about swords. The one time I saw his collection in Dallas, it just looked like an assortment of junk to me. A lot of rusted iron and tarnished bronze."

"Iron and bronze? Then he's interested in antiques?"

"Oh, yeah—he's hooked. I mean he hasn't got any modern sabers or things like that; his stuff is *old*. Here's his business card."

He hands it over and Erica examines it closely.

"Fugelmann Insurance," she says, reading. "I have heard of them."

"It's supposed to be a big outfit. I guess Randy is one of their star performers. At least the Hilton convention is for hotshot insurance agents. Do you have any antique swords he might be interested in?"

Erica puts a fingertip to pursed lips and ponders a moment, frowning. "Nothing at the moment," she says. "But if you could wait a few minutes, I'll call two other dealers who handle antique weapons. We sometimes exchange requests for rare or unusual items."

"Sure," Cone says, "go ahead and make your calls. I'll just wander around and look at all your pretty things."

She's gone for almost five minutes which, Cone figures, is time enough for her to call the Hilton in New York and Fugelmann Insurance in Dallas to make certain that J. Ransom Bailey exists. When she returns, her frosty smile has thawed a bit.

"Your brother-in-law may be in luck," she says. "One of the dealers I spoke to has a very old iron blade in good condition. I'll be happy to borrow it and show it to Mr. Bailey if he'd care to stop by."

"Hey, that's great," Cone says. "He's flying back to Dallas on Christmas Eve, so he hasn't got much time. Can I tell him to call you and set up an appointment?"

"Of course. I will be delighted to meet with Mr. Bailey."

"Good enough," Cone says. "He'll be in seminars most of the day, but I'll get hold of him later this afternoon and have him give you a call. Thanks for your trouble."

"No trouble at all," she says, putting her indigo talons lightly on his arm. "That's what we're here for."

Cone walks over to Fifth Avenue to get a cab heading downtown. He reckons the meeting with Erica went okay. No evidence that she's dealing in loot, but she didn't turn him down cold either. Now it's up to Terry MacEver.

When he gets back to the office, he calls the sergeant to report.

"I told her you'd call for an appointment later this afternoon. She's going to show you an iron sword she says she's borrowing from another dealer. Is that kosher?"

"Oh, sure," the sergeant says. "Art dealers are always borrowing from each other or taking stuff on consignment. Then they split the profit. Nothing illegal about it. Did she act suspicious?"

"Hard to tell what that lady is thinking, she's so buttoned up. Let me know what happens, will you?"

"Sure I will. You got a home phone number?"

"Yeah. It's unlisted, so don't write it on any men's room walls."

He gives MacEver his telephone number and hangs up. He lights a cigarette, calls down to the deli for lunch, and starts hacking away at his expense account and weekly progress report. There are a few early Christmas parties starting in the offices, but no one invites Cone.

He plods home through the mottled dusk, using every trick in the book to make certain he isn't being tailed, and wondering if hired killers knock off work for Christmas. Why not? They've probably got family celebrations, trees to decorate, gifts to buy.

Gifts to buy? Holy Christ! Tomorrow is Christmas Eve, and he hasn't bought anything for Samantha, or for Cleo, either. The cat is easy; a big hunk of garlic salami will do the trick. But that won't satisfy Sam. Cone tells himself he can always pick up some drugstore perfume—or maybe a gag gift like five pounds of horehound candy. Whatley would get a laugh out of that.

When he gets to his building, he finds the street door has been jimmied again. It's getting to be a weekly occurrence. He climbs six floors to the loft and finds his door open a few inches. He stoops swiftly, draws his Magnum from the ankle holster.

He kicks the door wide open and goes in fast, crouching. He looks around quickly. Nothing. He turns back to check the locks and doorjamb. No nicks or scars. A nice professional job.

Cleo is cowering under the bathtub.

"You're a lousy attack cat," Cone says sourly. "Couldn't you have fought to the death to preserve the sanctity of our home?"

He wanders around a moment and soon discovers what's missing: the solid teak Buddha statuette. He stands in the middle of the loft and sniffs. No doubt about it: The warm air of the loft smells of faded roses. Nuit de Fou. The exclusive scent of the Laboris cousins.

Christmas Eve turns out to be a cheerless day, with a clayey sky and a wild wind that won't quit; it blows warm, then cold, dies, and revives. There are a few dusty snow flurries, but nothing to carol about.

The Wall Street dick spends the morning futzing around the office, hoping for a call from Terry MacEver. But the sergeant doesn't phone, and Cone doesn't want to bug him. Office parties are beginning to swing and, unable to endure all the jollity and high spirits, Timothy takes off and taxis uptown to buy Samantha a Christmas gift.

That task accomplished, he decides to kill time walking uptown to Central Park. It is not a pleasant hike; Fifth Avenue is scattered with last-minute shoppers scurrying to get home, and holiday decorations already look tired and worn. When he finally cabs back to his neighborhood, he stops at his local deli to pick up some beer and Cleo's garlic salami. Then to the liquor store for supplies to see him through the holiday blues. He washes up, changes his shirt, and starts out for Samantha's apartment, carrying a bottle of Asti Spumanti.

Sam is leaving for her parents' home on an early-morning flight, and she's busily packing when he arrives.

"Where the hell were you today?" she demands. "We had a great party going at the office, and everyone wanted to know where you'd disappeared to."

"I was working," he says.

"In a pig's ass. You were probably sleeping in your loft. Listen, I want to get rid of all the leftovers in the fridge, so that's what we're going to have. Then you take off and let me finish packing and get some sleep. Okay?"

"Sure," he says equably. "Why not?"

She pulls out bits and pieces of this and that: a bowl of cold lamb stew, baked beans, a piece of flounder, some cole slaw, foil containers of creamed spinach, noodles, and green beans, a hunk of cheddar, two potato pancakes, a dish of curried rice, cherry tomatoes, a few dried-up gherkins, slices of head cheese, heels of pumpernickel. Both being blessed with efficient digestive tracts, they devour everything and polish off the bottle of sparkling wine.

"Hey," Cone says, "that teak Buddha in two parts—you've still got it?"

"Izzy? Of course I've got him."

"I need it for a while."

"What for?"

"Evidence."

She stares at him. "Son, you've got more crap than a Christmas goose. What evidence?"

"Just an idea."

"Tell me."

"Not yet. It's too crazy."

"That figures," she says. "All your ideas are crazy."

"Not so," he protests. "I happen to have a very logical brain."

"You haven't got a brain," she tells him. "You've got tapioca in your skull."

"Oh-ho," he says. "Now that you've worked your evil way with me and enjoyed my damp, white body, it's insult time."

"Go to hell," she says, "and let's open our presents."

She's bought Cleo a red net Christmas stocking packed with a catnip-stuffed mouse, three plastic balls, a package of munchies, a can of poached

salmon, and a plastic-framed picture of Garfield. She gives Cone a cashmere muffler in a Black Watch tartan.

"Nice scarf," he says, examining it. "Thanks."

"Muffler, not scarf, idiot," she says. "And you better wear it."

"Oh, I will," he says, "I really will."

Cone gives her a $100 gift certificate from Altman's.

"That's the most romantic gift I've ever gotten," she tells him.

"Yeah, well, I didn't know your measurements, so I figured you could
buy something for yourself."

She puts a palm against his cheek and looks into his eyes. "You're really
a mutt—you know that? Mutt, mutt, mutt!"

"I suppose," he says, sighing.

They slow down and drink some of Sam's vodka. No sex tonight; they
both know it and accept it with only a small twinge. They talk about her
plans to return to New York for New Year's Eve and what they might
do.

"Stay in," he says. "New Year's Eve is amateur night. We'll spend it
at the loft. I'll buy balloons, a small package of confetti, and two funny
hats."

"I can hardly wait," Samantha says. "I may call you during the week.
Just to make sure you're not shacked up with some tootsie."

"Not me," he says. "Cleo maybe, but not a tootsie."

"Have a happy Christmas, Tim," she says. "Now drag your ass out of
here. I've got to finish packing and get some sleep."

"Let me have the Buddha."

"Jesus," she says, "you never give up, do you? Will I get it back?"

"Sure you will."

"The original Izzy?"

"Absolutely."

"You better be telling the truth," Sam says, "or you'll be singing soprano
for the rest of your life."

She puts his cashmere muffler, Cleo's Christmas stocking, and the two-
part Buddha statuette in a brown paper sack and taps his cheek. "On your
way, buster," she says.

"Yeah," Cone says. "Have a good time. Don't talk to any sailors."

She comes up close. "Take care of yourself, asshole."

"You too, shithead."

They embrace lightly, exchange a small kiss and a sad smile. Then he
leaves.

He cabs back to the loft and gives Cleo the gift-packed stocking. The
cat isn't interested in any of the toys but goes whacko over the empty net
stocking and starts wrestling it across the linoleum.

Cone pours himself a brawny brandy.

"She's gone," he tells Cleo. "Merry Christmas, kiddo."

He sits at his desk, wraps his new muffler around his neck and sips his drink, feeling bereft.

3

Christmas turns out to be a broody day for Timothy Cone, with not much Ho-ho-ho about it. He grumps about the loft all morning, drinking black coffee, demolishing cigarettes, and growling as he gives Cleo fresh water and changes the cat's litter.

He goes out about noon to buy a paper and plods a half dozen blocks before he finds a newsstand that's open. The sky is low and looks like wrinkled parchment. There's still snow in the air, and the wind is cold and sharp enough to make his teeth ache. He returns thankfully to the warm loft and decides to drink and sleep the day away.

There's no one, family or friends, he has any desire to call and wish a Merry Christmas. But then his phone starts ringing. Joe Washington wants to extend season's greetings. So does an uncle in Brooklyn who's full of hearty cheer and asks to borrow a hundred bucks. Then a gyrene buddy who served with Cone in Vietnam calls to exchange ribald insults.

Then, later in the afternoon, Terry MacEver phones.

"Merry the hell Christmas," he says. "I should have called yesterday, but I had a Christmas Eve party to go to and got taken by the sauce, d'ya see."

"Yeah," Cone says, "that happens."

"Well, I went up to see Erica Laboris. Like you said, there is one smart lady. She starts asking me questions about my collection of antique swords—pumping me. I had boned up on the subject, so I think I convinced her I was a compulsive collector and knew what I was talking about. Then she brings out the blade she claims she borrowed from another dealer. It was a piece of shit and I told her so. It looked like it had been hammered from old sardine cans. That thing couldn't cut braunschweiger. She was just testing me, d'ya see. I told her I was looking for something better. She pretended to think awhile and then said a European agent she dealt with had mentioned a choice item that was available. She described it: an Assyrian relic of the sixth century B.C. It sounded exactly like that stolen sword I showed you in the photograph. She said it was museum quality. Sure it was, if it was lifted from a Beirut museum. She said the

European agent wanted twenty K for it, but she thought he might be willing to come down a bit. I told her it sounded interesting, and twenty thousand didn't scare me if it was the real thing. But of course I'd have to see it first. She said she could have it flown over and would be able to show it to me in a couple of days."

"Do you believe all that?" Cone asks.

"Hell, no! I think she's got the sword in the country right now and scammed the story of the European agent to give herself an out if the deal turns sour. Very suspicious, our Erica. Anyway, she's going to give me a call when the blade arrives, and I promised to fly up to New York to take a look."

"How is she going to phone you?"

"She'll call Fugelmann Insurance in Dallas, and if I'm not in—which obviously I won't be—she'll leave a message and I'll call her back. I've got all that set up with my contact there. I don't want to start celebrating, but so far it looks good. I swear she's peddling that stolen Assyrian iron."

"I'll bet my *cojones* on it," Cone says. "She's playing it cozy, but visions of sugarplums are dancing in her head. She thinks she's found an A-number-one sucker. Play it out, Sergeant; I think you're going to score."

"I'm hoping," MacEver says. "How do you figure she got the sword into the U.S.?"

"Inside a leather hassock from Turkey," Cone says. "Or a porcelain elephant from Korea. But that's another story. Keep me up to speed, will you?"

He hangs up, convinced they're going to bust the Laboris Gallery. That leaves Laboris Importers and Laboris Investments, Inc. And how to land Sven and Ingmar snares his thoughts for the remainder of that Christmas day, which now seems suddenly merrier and more hopeful.

On the morning after Christmas, Cone gets to work late. He breakfasts at his desk (black coffee and a Mae West) while he flips *The Wall Street Journal* and the Business Day section of the *Times*. All the economic pundits predict interest rates will continue to fall, and Cone wonders how long Ingmar Laboris is going to be able to pay that high rate of return. Even junk bonds are down to twelve percent.

It's almost noon when he leaves the office and grabs a taxi up to West Nineteenth Street. Laboris Importers is crowded, which is what he figured. All those people are returning Christmas presents. The flock of cousins is busy behind the sales counter in the rear of the store, and Cone is free to wander around and take a look at the latest in imported monstrosities.

No teak Buddhas in sight, but there is a table of curious statuettes arranged in precise ranks like a company of Marines on parade. They are all about eight inches tall, and identical; no hand-carving here. They look to be a resin and sawdust compound, colored black and produced from a mold.

There is a small placard set on a bamboo easel:

THE HINDU GODDESS KALI, WIFE OF SHIVA. SHE IS KNOWN AS THE BLACK ONE, OFTEN DESTRUCTIVE. KALI IS DEPICTED IN INDIAN ART AS WEARING A NECKLACE OF SKULLS, AND SOMETIMES SNAKES. SHE IS THE GODDESS OF DEATH AND FREQUENTLY WIELDS A SWORD TO CUT THE THREAD OF LIFE. KALI MEANS "TIME," TO REMIND US OF OUR SHORT LIFE SPAN.

"Right on," Cone says softly.

Glancing around to make certain he is unobserved, he picks up one of the statuettes. Kali is standing on a low base, her hefty bosom pressing thin drapery. About her neck is a string of skulls. In one hand she holds a sword, scissors in the other. Charming lady.

Cone twists the base in a clockwise direction. Nothing. Then he tries a conventional twist to the left. Again nothing. The doodad is solid, a single casting. He replaces it on the table and tries another, with the same result. He looks around again to make certain no one is noticing his strange behavior, then continues trying other statuettes.

He hits pay dirt on the sixth; the base unscrews when turned to the left. He puts that Kali aside and goes on with his search. He finds another with a screw-on base. He takes the two to the sales clerk and waits patiently for almost fifteen minutes before he can pay for his purchases. They are swaddled in tissue paper and slid into a plastic bag. Printed on the outside of the bag is: LABORIS IMPORTERS, HOUSE OF WONDERS.

He cabs back to Haldering & Co., goes directly to his office, and shuts the door. Still wearing parka and cap, he sits at his desk, unwraps one of the Kali statuettes, and carefully unscrews the base. Drilled upward into the goddess is a hole about an inch in diameter and three inches deep. Cone peers inside, turning the figure this way and that to catch the light. He sees a slight coating of white powder.

Bingo! Maybe.

The second Kali yields the same results. Cautiously, Cone licks a finger and swabs it into the recess. It comes away with some white powder adhering. He sniffs at his finger. Nothing—except nicotine. Then he takes a small lick. The powder tastes bitter. He wonders what the hell he's doing; he has no idea what high-grade smack tastes like. It could be talcum powder for all he knows.

He sits there a long time, staring at the two disassembled Kalis on his desk. Goddess of death and destruction? Could be. He pulls the phone close and calls Neal K. Davenport. But the city bull is out, can't be reached. So Cone leaves a call-back message.

Suddenly he realizes he's famished. He phones down for a sausage hero, a kosher dill, and two cans of beer. He's finished all that and is wiping his lips and belching mightily when Davenport calls back.

"Hey, Sherlock," he says. "What're you selling today—cancer?"

"Listen," Cone says, "how about having a drink with me up at my loft?"

"The Garden of a Thousand Delights?" the NYPD man says. "Why this sudden attack of hospitality? You must want something."

"You know a guy in the Department named Petey Alvarez? He works out of Narcotics."

"Petey Alvarez? No, the name doesn't ring a bell. I know some narcs, but no Alvarez."

"I was hoping you could get hold of him, and the two of you could drop by. This Alvarez doesn't know me from Buster Keaton, but maybe you could talk him into coming along."

"Now why should I do that? What's in it for me?"

"It might help solve that homicide on my street. That Sidney Leonidas who got scragged. You want to break that, don't you?"

"Not especially," Davenport says. "The guy was a doper. Who cares? His kill comes pretty far down on my anxiety list."

"Come on," the Wall Street dick says. "It would look good on your record to clear that file, wouldn't it?"

"Has this got something to do with your Laboris job?"

"Well, yeah, it might have."

Davenport sighs. "What a pisser you are. Okay, I'll try to get hold of this Petey Alvarez and see if I can con him into visiting your mansion. By the way, I'm drinking bourbon this week."

"You'll get it," Cone promises.

It's almost two hours before the city dick calls back. He's located Petey Alvarez and talked the narc into showing up at Cone's loft. The meet is set for six o'clock. And Alvarez drinks rum and 7-Up.

"Holy Christ!" Timothy Cone says.

But on his hike back to the loft that night, making certain he's not being tailed, he stops at local stores to pick up a jug of Jim Beam, one of Puerto Rican rum, and a six-pack of 7-Up. He feeds Cleo, checks his ice cube trays, and places the plastic bag with the two Kali statuettes under the table. Then adds Izzy, the two-part Buddha he borrowed from Sam.

Petey Alvarez turns out to be a short, whippy guy with a walrus mustache and hair long enough in back to support a brass barrette. He's wearing a braided Greek captain's cap and a black trench coat gray with grime. His dirty Reebok running shoes have broken and knotted laces, and a small gold ring hangs from his left earlobe.

He looks around the loft in amazement.

"Sonnenbitch," he says. "I live better than this in the barrio. Wassamatta, you busted?"

"Nah," Cone says. "I got some money."

"But you got no fucking taste," Alvarez says. "Bathtubs like that we throw out on the street."

"It's an antique," the Wall Street dick explains.

"Yeah," Neal Davenport says, "and so are you. Do we stand here passing the time with idle chitchat or do we have something to drive the chill?"

Cone gets them seated on kitchen chairs and brings them drinks. He leaves the bottles of bourbon and rum on the table so they can help themselves. He pours a jelly jar of vodka for himself.

"L'chaim," Petey Alvarez says, raising his glass.

They drink to that, and then sit looking at each other.

"So this is it?" Davenport finally says. "A nice quiet drinking party? This is what you dragged us up here for?"

"It's a long story," Cone says.

"I got time," Alvarez says. "My woman expects me when she sees me."

Cone starts by telling them about the client, Martha Hepplewaite, who wants Laboris Investments investigated because she's suspicious of their high rate of return.

"That's Ingmar Laboris," he says. "I still don't know where he fits into this action, but I'll bet he's a nogoodnik."

Then he tells them about Laboris Importers on West Nineteenth Street and the foreign schlock they sell. Cousin Sven Laboris, he reminds them, was picked up in a raid on an after-hours joint and was found to be carrying a bag of high-grade heroin.

"Now look at this," Cone says, and pulls the two-part Buddha from beneath the table. He unscrews the base and shows them the recess drilled up into the statuette. "That's how I think they're bringing junk into the country, packed inside things like this."

Alvarez jerks a thumb at Cone. "Is this guy for real?" he asks.

Davenport laughs. "The jury is still out on that one. But he hasn't fucked me up—not yet he hasn't."

"Look," the narc says, "how much shit could you jam in that little bitty hole? It wouldn't be worth the trouble."

"Sure it would," Cone says, "if you're bringing in hundreds or thousands of these doodads. Now we're talking about kilos. And Laboris Importers has stores all over the country—a perfect distribution setup."

The two cops look at each other. Then Davenport shrugs.

"Thin stuff," he says. "All smoke."

"Well, yeah," Cone admits, "if this Buddha was all I have. But today I dropped by Laboris Importers and got these."

He drags out the two statuettes of Kali and unscrews the bases. He hands a figurine to each of the other men.

"Notice?" he says. "Same-size drilled hole. But these have some white powder in them."

They examine the Kalis, peer into the recess. Then, just as Cone did, the narc licks a forefinger and probes the hole.

"It could be flour," Cone says.

Petey Alvarez licks his finger. "Flour, my ass," he says. "High-octane horse. I be a sonnenbitch."

They all sit, staring at each other. Then they reach forward to fill their glasses.

"It's not only these statues," Cone tells them. "Laboris Importers brings in stuff from all over the world. Big clocks and porcelain elephants and hassocks and crap like that. They could be sneaking in kilo bags for all we know."

"Beautiful," Alvarez says. "I love it. But the Customs guys check shipments."

"Sure they do," Cone agrees. "But like everyone else, they're overworked and understaffed. So they spot-check. Not *all* the statuettes are going to carry junk. Just the ones with a special lot number burned into the base. The ones up on top will be legit."

The narc looks at Neal K. Davenport. "You think I should take a ride with this nut?"

"What have you got to lose? If it doesn't pan out, no harm done. If Cone's right, you got yourself a nice bust and maybe a commendation."

"Yeah," Alvarez says. "Look. Let me take one of these statues to the lab and get a test on the powder."

"Be my guest," says Cone.

"Then, while they're testing, I'll find out where this Laboris Importers has its warehouse. If they have stores all over the country, they've got to have a warehouse. Makes sense?"

"It does to me," Davenport says. "Their stock is probably trucked to the warehouse from the docks or airports after it clears Customs."

"That listens," Cone says. "Maybe they got their own trucks. I don't figure they're mailing the stuff to other cities by parcel post."

"Yeah," the narcotics man says, sniffing at the hole drilled into the Kali figurine. "If this is as pure as I think it is, it could zonk half the junkies in the Bronx out of their gourds." He looks up at Cone. "You work with Joe Washington—right?"

Cone nods.

"I was wondering why he called to pick my brains," Alvarez says. "That's cool. One hand washes the other, and you're coming through."

"Enough of this bullshit," Neal Davenport says, pouring himself more Jim Beam and unwrapping a fresh stick of Juicy Fruit. "What do I get for bringing you two lovers together? Cone, you said something about the Leonidas homicide."

"Look," Cone says, "the guy was tailing me, and I braced him the night he was chilled. But I didn't do it. I could tell he was stoned out of his skull."

"But you broke his arm?"

"Well, yeah, but I had to; he pulled a shiv on me. When I left him, he was blotto in that doorway, and his knife was on the sidewalk."

"Uh-huh," Davenport says. "And who do you guess put him away?"

"The guy who hired him. Probably one of the Laboris cousins. Listen, this family is a fucking corporation. Like an idiot I gave Laboris Importers my home address, to get their mail-order catalog. And Ingmar at Laboris Investments has my office address. I think maybe they compared notes, got spooked at the idea that I was getting nosy and might have bought one of the hollow Buddhas. They wanted to take me out of the picture."

"What's Laboris Investments got to do with all this?" Davenport asks.

"Beats the shit out of me," Cone admits.

The NYPD detective stares at him a long time. "You're holding out on me again," he says. "You and your goddamned secrets. There's something you're not spilling. I know it when your eyes go blank."

"Hey," Cone says, "one thing at a time. If you can bust Laboris Importers for drug dealing and lean on some of the cousins, one of them is going to break and cop a plea—right? Then you'll find out who slid the blade into Sidney Leonidas. And you'll get brownie points for clearing a homicide."

Davenport sighs, turns to Alvarez. "Why do I let this fruitcake con me like this?" he says. "Every time he calls, I know it's trouble and more work."

"I don't know," the narc says. "He's beginning to get to me. And you gotta admit the price of his drinks is right."

The two cops drain their glasses and stand.

"I'll be in touch," Petey Alvarez says, shaking Cone's hand. "Thanks for the wallops."

"Where's the cat?" Davenport asks.

"Under the bathtub. Sleeping."

"That's what I should be doing," the city dick says. "See you around."

After they're gone, Cone puts the bottles under the sink and rinses out their jelly jars. He figures he's started some action, and maybe it'll pay off.

He stalks about the loft, pondering, and Cleo slithers out from under the bathtub, yawning and stretching. Then the cat starts padding after Cone, turning when he turns, sticking close to his heels, mewing steadily.

"You hungry again?" Cone says. "I've got some nice ham hocks for us. Just be patient."

He figures Petey Alvarez for a cowboy—just the kind of gritty guy needed to put the arm on Sven Laboris. Cone knew hot dogs like Petey in 'Nam: real outlaws who pushed and pushed until they earned medals or body bags.

Cone is happy he didn't blab about Sergeant Terry MacEver and the sting planned for the Laboris Gallery of Levantine Art. Davenport and Alvarez have no need to know. And Cone likes to keep his hole card facedown until the call.

"Okay, kiddo," he says to Cleo, "let's have the ham hocks. One for you, three for me."

He lumps into the office the next morning, an hour late. He's carrying his breakfast in a brown paper bag: container of black coffee, buttered bagel.

"You're late," the receptionist says sternly.

"Morning sickness," Cone explains. "I'm pregnant."

"Well, you got a call. Two calls. From Mr. Ingmar Laboris. He wants you to call him as soon as you get in."

He goes back to his office, drinks coffee, eats bagel, smokes third Camel of the day. *Then* he calls Ingmar Laboris. He guesses what that oily knave wants—and he guesses right.

"Hello there, Mr. Cone!" Laboris says heartily. "And how are we this morning?"

"We're fine," Cone says. "We have a slight twinge of the liver, but we think that'll pass."

"Excellent, excellent!" Ingmar carols, obviously not listening. "The reason I called, Mr. Cone, was to ask if your client had made up his or her mind to place that investment you mentioned."

"The quarter-mil?" Cone says. "I've made a recommendation, and I expect the client will come to a decision shortly. Probably in the next day or so."

"And how do you read the client's mood? Do you feel the investment will be made?"

"I'm not allowed to comment on that," Cone says virtuously. "But I think you're in for a surprise."

"Splendid!" Ingmar Laboris, obviously a terminal optimist, says happily. "I must tell you I am deeply appreciative of your efforts on behalf of Laboris Investments. Incidentally, you might wish to consider taking a flier yourself. In all confidence, I can assure you that our future looks very bright indeed, and while I can make no promises, of course, I anticipate a very rapid increase to a thirty-percent return."

"I'll certainly consider it seriously," the Wall Street dick says.

After he hangs up, he sits staring at the phone. Ingmar's call is worrisome. It sounds to Cone like the man is getting itchy. Maybe that mob of new investors has dwindled to nothing, or maybe Ingmar is planning a final big score before he closes up shop and walks off into the sunset.

Cone drags himself down to the office of Sidney Apicella. The CPA looks up from an enormous ledger, then sits back and begins massaging his swollen beak.

"You haven't bugged me for days," he says. "What's wrong—you sore at me?"

"One easy question, Sid," Cone says. "Remember when you checked the bank accounts of Laboris Investments for me? You said they had a special redemption fund set aside to pay off investors who wanted their money back."

"That's right; I remember."

"Do you recall how much was in the fund?"

Apicella rubs his beezer vigorously. "I think it was about a million five when I checked."

"Could you find out what it is now?"

"Oh, Christ," Sid says. "That's Ollie March at Merchants Interworld. He's done so many favors for me lately, I hate to hit him again."

"Come on," Cone urges, "it'll only take one short phone call. You can send him a bottle of booze. I'll finagle it on my expense account."

"Well . . . okay," Apicella says grudgingly. He flips through his Rolodex, finds the number, and dials.

"Mr. Ollie March, please . . . Hello, Ollie. Sid Apicella here. How are the hemorrhoids? . . . Uh-huh . . . Jesus, that's a shame . . . Ollie, I hate to bother you again—I know how busy you are—but this is important. Remember my asking you about the position of Laboris Investments? . . . That's right; Wall Street. Well, what I need right now is the current status of their redemption fund. Could you take a look? . . . Sure, I'll hang on."

He covers the phone with a palm and looks up. "The poor guy is really suffering," he says. "He has to sit on an inner tube."

"Tough," Cone says.

Apicella goes back to the phone. "Yeah, I'm here, Ollie . . . Uh-huh . . .

I've got it. Thanks very much; I owe you more than one. I hope the new treatment helps . . . Right . . . I'll be talking to you."

He hangs up and swings around in his swivel chair to face Cone. "Laboris's redemption fund is down to a little below three hundred thousand."

The two men stare at each other.

"From a million and a half about ten days ago," Cone says. "Sounds like someone's pulled the plug."

"I'd say so," Apicella agrees. "Does the client have any money in Laboris Investments?"

"Not the client. The husband-to-be of the client's daughter."

"Better tell him to get it out," the CPA advises. "The sooner the better."

"Yeah," Cone says, "that's what I figure. Thanks, Sid."

"Don't forget that bottle for Ollie," Apicella calls after him.

Cone goes back to his office and calls the Hepplewaite brownstone. He's in luck; Lucinda answers the phone.

"Miss Hepplewaite, this is Timothy Cone at Haldering and Company."

"Oh, yes, Mr. Cone. Do you want to talk to my mother?"

"No, I want to talk to you. In private. Can we meet somewhere?"

Silence. Then: "Is it about you-know-what?" she asks in a whisper.

"Yes," Cone says, "it's about you-know-what. Can you get out of the house for a few minutes?"

Long pause. Then faintly: "Maybe for a few minutes."

"That's all it'll take. How about meeting me on the corner of Thirty-eighth and Madison in half an hour? If you're late, don't worry—I'll wait."

"All right," she says in her wispy voice, "I'll meet you there."

He gets up to Madison and Thirty-eighth Street about five minutes early. It's a snappy day with a sturdy westering wind and a brilliant sky. Cone stomps up and down, hands in pockets to keep his parka from flapping. He's not wearing Samantha Whatley's Christmas gift. Cleo is probably sleeping on the muffler right now.

Lucinda Hepplewaite comes flying down the block, loden cape billowing out behind her. Her long face is wrenched. She grips Cone's arm.

"I hope you have good news for me," she says breathlessly.

"I got lousy news for you. That boyfriend of yours—what's his name?"

"He's not my boyfriend; he's my fiancé. And his name is Francis."

"Yeah," Cone says. "Well, you tell Francis to get his money out of Laboris Investments as fast as he can."

"Oh, my God," she says, then grimaces. She's all teeth. "Is it that bad?"

"Bad enough."

"Are you sure?"

"No, I'm not sure," he says angrily. "But you asked me to tell you first if I found out anything, so I'm telling you: Laboris is going down the tube."

They walk up and down: ten paces, turn, ten paces, turn. Lucinda has a stride as long as his. She's huddling inside her loose cape. Once or twice she shivers. Cone figures it's the cold; he doesn't think she's nervous or fearful.

"What should we do?" she asks finally.

"No use writing a letter or phoning," he says. "That'll get you nowhere. This Francis of yours—can he come on hard? I mean can he yell, threaten, really lay on the muscle?"

"Oh, no," she says. "Francis is the dearest, sweetest man who ever lived. He's very quiet and mild. I've never heard him raise his voice in anger."

"Oh, boy," Cone says. "You're sunk."

Pace, turn, pace in silence. Then he stops. She stops. He turns to face her.

"Unless . . ." he says, "unless you can do it."

"Do what?"

"Collect Francis, and the two of you get down to Laboris Investments as fast as you can. Demand the return of Francis's hundred thousand. They'll try to stall, tell you to write them a letter, and all that. But you scream and shout and insist on a check immediately. There will probably be potential investors in the outer office, so if you create enough of a scene, they'll probably give you your money to get rid of you. Can you do that?"

"I'll do it," she says decisively, "if I have to."

"You have to," he tells her. "And the moment you get the check, take a taxi to Francis's bank and deposit it. Even then there's no guarantee; Laboris may stop payment the moment you leave. But it's the only chance you've got. If it doesn't work, you'll be listening to your mother say, 'I told you so,' for the rest of your life."

"I'll go right now," she says determinedly. "I won't even tell mother where I'm going."

"Atta girl," he says. "Remember to come on strong. Yell and stamp your foot and even squeeze out a few tears if you have to. Just don't leave Laboris without your boyfriend's money."

"My fiancé," she says.

"Whatever. Where's his office?"

"Sixth Avenue and Fifty-seventh Street."

"I'll get you a cab. Pick up Francis and go straight to Wall Street. Let me know what happens."

He puts her in a taxi, raises a hand in farewell and benediction. Then he stops another empty cab and rides down to John Street.

The first thing he does is phone Laboris Investments. Ingmar is out, which is another lucky break; Cone figures he's on a roll. He leaves a message with Ingmar's secretary: Please tell Mr. Laboris that Timothy Cone of Haldering & Co. called, and the investment they discussed that morning has been approved by the client. The funds will be in Mr. Laboris' hands within two days.

Cone hangs up, satisfied that he's done all he can to protect the client's interest. Or rather, the client's daughter's interest. The two are not necessarily identical.

He reckons that when Ingmar hears he's getting a quarter of a million in a couple of days, he'll be more inclined to sign a 100-G check for Lucinda Hepplewaite's fiancé.

It takes a con man to con a con man.

Later in the afternoon, Lucinda Hepplewaite calls him, all excited. She did just as he instructed, created a rambunctious scene at the Wall Street offices of Laboris Investments, and eventually her fiancé was issued a check for a hundred thousand.

"Just now. We got to Francis's bank a few minutes before it closed."

"Good for you," Cone says. "Now if Laboris doesn't stop payment, you're home free. Lots of luck."

He starts on his progress report, opening a fresh pack of Camels— second of the day. By four o'clock he's ready to call it quits and wander home. As a matter of fact, he's halfway out the door of his office when his phone rings again, and he returns to his desk.

"Yeah?" he says.

"Petey Alvarez, you crazy sonnenbitch," the narc says, laughing. "That stuff in the statue's asshole tested out as high-grade smack. We got a make on Laboris Importers' warehouse. It's over on Eleventh Avenue. We haven't got enough guys for a twenty-four stake, but we're covering the place from midnight till eight. Listen, you wanna have some fun?"

"Sure," Cone says. "I like fun."

"I'm taking the watch from midnight to four. How about coming along and keeping me company?"

"Okay. Should I bring what's left of the rum and Seven-Up?"

"I was hoping you'd say that," Petey says happily. "Yeah, bring it. We can have a few and chew the fat while we're planted there. How's about I pick you up at your loft around eleven-thirty. All right by you?"

"I'll be waiting," Cone says.

He goes home, feeds Cleo, changes the cat's water, and has a belt of vodka before he lies down, fully clothed, on the floor mattress. He figures if he's going to be awake from midnight to four, he better get a start on his shut-eye.

He rouses a little after ten-thirty, fixes himself a salami sandwich with a dry slice of greenish Swiss cheese. He wolfs that down with another vodka, wondering how long his gut can take the punishment. He puts the rum and 7-Up in a shopping bag, then adds his own jug of Popov and a couple of empty jelly jars. He also adds a plastic bag of ice cubes. Timothy Cone knows how to live.

He waits outside on the sidewalk for almost ten minutes before Alvarez drives up. He's behind the wheel of a clunker so old and battered that Cone isn't sure what it is: a '74 Dodge, he thinks, or maybe a '73 Chrysler.

"Don't let the looks fool you," Alvarez says. "Plenty of horses under the hood. This baby can move when it has to."

"And nothing falls off?" Cone asks.

"What's to fall? The lights and bumpers are stuck on with picture wire and masking tape. Don't worry, sonny boy; it'll hold together."

They head north, and Alvarez fills Cone in on what he's learned, which isn't much. The heroin in the Kali statuette tested out as almost pure, probably from Thailand. The Laboris Importers' warehouse is owned by a company named Sirobal, Ltd.

"Sirobal," Cone says. " 'Laboris' spelled backwards."

"You got it," Petey says. "The schmucks!"

He tells Cone the Customs guys have no rap sheet on Laboris, but they do a big business by ship and air. The warehouse is busy during the day, but at night there's only one watchman. The building has an alarm system, but it's self-contained, not wired to a security agency or local precinct.

"Oh, they're bringing the stuff in," Petey says. "No doubt about it. If we can't get evidence of them dealing, we'll have to tell the Feds to clamp down with dog searches and all that shit. But I wouldn't like that; I want to engineer this bust myself."

"Why not," Cone says. "You're entitled."

They park in the shadows on Fifty-third Street, where they have a good view of the Laboris warehouse. It's a squat, ugly building with stained brickwork and blacked-out windows above the ground floor. But there are interior lights on the street level, and they can see figures moving about inside.

"Hey-hey," Petey Alvarez says, "what's this? The place is supposed to close at six o'clock when the night watchman comes on. Maybe they're having an office party."

"Yeah," Cone says. "Maybe."

They settle down, and Cone mixes a rum and 7-Up for Petey, and pours himself a jelly jar of vodka on the rocks. They drink slowly, and for almost two hours the narc regales the Wall Street dick with stories about the wild ways dope is brought into the country.

In sealed condoms swallowed by couriers. In small metal containers shoved up the rectum or pushed into the vaginas of female mules. In tubes of toothpaste and jars of cosmetics. In kids' teddy bears and cripples' hollow crutches. Under toupees and inside sanitary napkins.

"How about this one," Alvarez says. "They dissolve coke or heroin in a tub of water. Then they dunk a woman's fur coat in it. Let the fur dry. She waltzes through Customs carrying the fur coat over her arm. Once she's in, they soak the fur coat again and extract the dope from the water. Isn't that beautiful? The bastards are always one step ahead of us."

But as he's talking, Cone notes, the narc rarely takes his eyes from the Laboris Importers' warehouse.

"I don't get it," Alvarez says fretfully. "The place is supposed to be closed with just a night watchman on duty. But I make out two guys moving back and forth. You see them?"

"At least two," Cone says. "Maybe three. One's a hulk. The others are small and skinny."

"Yeah," Petey says. "So what the fuck's going on at this hour?"

It's almost two A.M. when a long, silver-gray Cadillac limousine glides to a stop in front of the warehouse.

"Oh-oh," the narc says. "We got some action. Scrunch down a little. Just in case."

They watch as two men get out of the Cadillac and look around before walking up to the dimly lighted doorway of the warehouse.

"Sonnenbitch," Alvarez says softly, "I make those guys. The short one in the black leather coat is Simon Juliano, a hotshot drug dealer in East Harlem. He's a real kink. Digs little Chinese girls—and I mean *little*. The monster in the plaid mackinaw is his muscle, Ollie Jefferson. He's got feta between his ears, but he's fast."

The two men look around again, then ring the bell. In a moment the warehouse door opens and they disappear inside.

The narcotics cop drums on the steering wheel with heavy fingers. "Something's going down," he says. "It's a buy; I swear it's a buy."

They straighten, stare at the lighted ground floor of the warehouse. But there's no movement, nothing to see.

"Listen," Petey says to Cone, "you loaded?"

"Yeah. A short-barreled Magnum in a shinplaster."

"Good enough. Well, those two shtarkers weren't carrying anything when they went in, were they?"

"I didn't see anything."

"So if they come out with a suitcase or bag or whatever, I'll *know* it's a buy. I'd like to bust their asses. You game?"

"Sure," Cone says. "Why not."

"Okay," Petey says, "here's how we work it. . . . If they come out with a package, we let them get in their yacht and drive away. We follow them. Because I don't want to spook Sven Laboris—not yet I don't. Then, when they're a few blocks away, we cut them off and see what they picked up at the warehouse."

"It's legal?" Cone asks.

"Hell, yes. I've got probable cause. Both those pricks have drug sheets."

"No," Cone says, "I mean my being in on the bust. I'm a civilian. I'm ready, willing, and able, but won't it put your ass on the line in the Department?"

"Fuck it," Alvarez says roughly. "I'll scam my way out of it. I've done it before."

"Then let's do it," Cone says.

He slides his .357 out of the ankle holster and holds it on his lap. Petey Alvarez pulls a cannon from a shoulder holster and places it on the seat beside him. It's the biggest handgun Cone has ever seen.

"What do you use that for?" he asks. "Elephants?"

"It'll crack an engine block," Petey says proudly. "Once I knocked off a guy standing behind a half-inch steel door. Jesus, was he surprised."

They wait in silence. It's almost fifteen minutes before the warehouse door opens again. Several men can be seen shaking hands. Then Juliano and Jefferson start back to their limousine, looking about carefully. The muscle is carrying a small suitcase.

"That's it," Alvarez says. "They made a buy. Let's get this show on the road."

The Cadillac pulls away. In a moment, the narc starts up his clunker and follows the big car. They go south for a couple of blocks, then the limousine makes an illegal U-turn and heads north. Alvarez follows, keeping a block back. The avenue is deserted; only the two cars are moving.

"They're going to get antsy in a minute," Alvarez says. "They'll spot us on their tail and speed up. I think we better move in. You set?"

"I'll never be setter," Cone says.

The old car leaps forward. The narc wasn't lying about the power under the hood. In moments they're alongside the Cadillac, and then ahead. Petey wrenches the wheel sharply to the right.

"Whee!" he screams.

Screech of brakes. Squeal of skidding tires. Thud of crumpling metal. The limousine is forced up onto the sidewalk. It crunches to a stop, the front end digging into the tin shutters of an abandoned store.

The narc is out of the car, howitzer in his fist. Cone is close behind, Magnum gripped tightly. They rush the big car. Alvarez jerks open the door on the driver's side.

"You're dead!" he yells. "Out, out, you fuckers!"

But it's not that easy. Juliano, driving and apparently stunned, sits slumped with his head bent forward, pressed against the steering wheel. But Ollie Jefferson piles out the other side, fumbling at his hip. Cone circles behind the Cadillac and aims, crouched, with a two-hand grip on his shooter.

"Don't do it," he says, not recognizing his own voice.

But, as Alvarez said, the muscle has no brains. He pulls a revolver from a hip holster. Cone pumps off two. The first misses. The second shatters Jefferson's left kneecap, spins him around, dumps him. Cone moves in fast, kicks the revolver away. He stands over the fallen man, Magnum still gripped in both hands.

"This fink is out," Alvarez calls. "How's yours?"

"No problem," Cone says.

"Beautiful!" Petey says. "I love it!" He digs into the limousine, hauls out the suitcase, snaps it open. "Three kilos," he reports gleefully. "Everything's coming up roses. Keep an eye on these two cocksuckers, will you, while I call for backup."

The Wall Street dick stands motionless, gun still aimed, while the narc goes back to use his radio. Then Alvarez returns to his side and looks down at the fallen Ollie Jefferson, now writhing in pain, clutching his shattered knee.

"Suffer, you scumbag," Petey says. Then he claps Timothy Cone on the shoulder. "I love you, baby," he says. "You did real good. But look, I think you better take off. It'll make things a lot easier for me if you're gone when the brass arrive."

"Sure," the Wall Street dick says. Then: "Thank you for an enjoyable evening."

"You nutty sonnenbitch!" Alvarez cries, embracing him. "You like action—no? Me, too. Shoot 'em up! Bang-bang!"

"Keep in touch," Cone says.

He walks over to Ninth Avenue and after waiting ten minutes gets a cab heading downtown. He's still wired, on a high, waiting for his adrenaline to drain away. He tries to breathe deeply and slowly. But he's still surging inside, half-sick, half-drunk with sorrow and pride.

He left his vodka jug in Petey's car, but he's got some California brandy in the loft. He has a beefy slug to calm the jits while he recalls what happened that night: what Petey said, what he said, what Alvarez did and what he did.

He lets Cleo lick a brandy-dipped finger, and the cat's purr and lazy movements help him thaw and remember his philosophy.

"Just don't give a damn," he advises Cleo. "That's the secret."

He's still awake, lying in his skivvies on the mattress, and it's almost four A.M. when his phone jangles. Oh-oh, he thinks, Petey's in trouble.

"Yeah?" he says.

"You bastard!" Samantha Whatley wails. "Where the hell have you been? I've been calling all night."

"I worked late at the office," he says, happy to hear her voice.

"Bull*shit!*" she says. "You never worked late at the office in your life. You've been out tomcatting around."

"Nah," he says, "I wouldn't do that. Where are you—back in town?"

"Coming back tomorrow," she says. "But it'll be late in the afternoon so I won't show up at the office. How are things going?"

"Okay."

"That's all—just okay? How you doing on the Laboris thing?"

"All right," he says. "Coming along."

She sighs. "What a chatterbox you are. Come over to my place tomorrow night?"

"Sure," he says. "How's about a big pizza and a jug of red ink?"

"Sounds great. I haven't had a decent pizza since I left. See you tomorrow. Good night, asshole."

"Good night, shithead," he says, and hangs up.

"Sam is coming home," he tells Cleo, and goes back to the mattress, content.

"Sergeant Terry MacEver to see Mr. Timothy Cone," the receptionist says primly.

"Yeah," Cone says, "send him in."

He hangs up the phone, stands, brushes croissant crumbs off his corduroy jacket. He drains the dregs of his black coffee, crumples the container, and tosses it at his wastebasket. Misses, and leaves the garbage on the floor.

MacEver, a dandy, enters wearing a black bowler with a curved brim. He looks at the littered office with some distaste and declines Cone's offer to take his hat and coat.

"Just stopped by for a minute," he explains. "Good news: I think Erica Laboris has taken the bait."

"Hey," Cone says, "I like that."

"She called Fugelmann Insurance in Dallas, and they got back to me. So I phoned the lady, pretending I was deep in the heart of Texas. She says she's got an iron sword that she thinks would make a splendid addition to the collection of J. Ransom Bailey. Then she proceeds to describe, almost exactly, the blade that was stolen from the Beirut museum. It's hand-forged, Assyrian, and dates from around the sixth century B.C. I'm betting she's already got the loot in her hot little paws."

"Sounds good," Cone says. "When are you going to see her?"

"Tomorrow," the sergeant says. "I didn't want to be too anxious, d'ya see. So I told her I'd fly up from Dallas and meet her in the gallery in the afternoon to inspect the merchandise. You want to be there?"

"Hell, yes," Cone says. "If it's the genuine article, you're going to cuff her?"

"What else?" MacEver says. "I'll arrange for some backup in case we have a hassle. I'll give you a call tomorrow morning and we'll synchronize our watches. I'm really high on this thing, Cone; I think we're going to score."

The sergeant leaves, and Cone lights a cigarette, feeling perky. Alvarez made a nice bust last night that will probably lead to the indictment of Sven Laboris. And now Terry MacEver has a good shot at putting Erica Laboris in the slammer. The Laboris cousins are being decimated.

But . . . but . . . Cone begins to wonder if he might be engineering a monumental balls-up. The arrest of one Laboris cousin will surely spook the rest of the clan. Groaning, he gets on the horn and tries to locate Petey Alvarez. No luck; the narc is not available, and no one knows where he is. Beginning to sweat, Cone calls Davenport and almost sobs with relief when the detective answers.

"Hey, Sherlock," the cop says breezily, "I hear Petey Alvarez had himself quite a time last night."

"Did he?" Cone says.

"You weren't along for the ride, were you?"

"Not me," Cone says. "I went to bed early last night. Slept like a baby."

"I know what that means," Davenport says. "You woke up crying every two hours."

"Listen, I've been trying to locate Alvarez. Do you know where he is?"

"Not at the moment. He's busy organizing the Shoot-out at the O.K. Corral. We're going to raid the Laboris warehouse tonight and really tear the place apart. I'm going to grab every Laboris cousin in sight and lean on them. Maybe I really can clear that Sidney Leonidas homicide."

Cone takes a deep breath. "You can't do that," he says.

Silence. Then: "Why can't I do that?"

"Not you," Cone says. "The raid on the warehouse—it can't go down tonight."

"No?" Davenport says coldly. "Why not?"

"There's something I didn't tell you."

"I knew it, I knew it!" the city bull screams at him. "Oh, you tight-mouthed idiot! I knew you were holding out on me. All right, all right, what is it?"

Cone tells him about the sting he and MacEver have planned for the Laboris Gallery. And how they're going to pull the plug on Erica Laboris the following afternoon. If the Laboris Importers' warehouse is raided that night, and a covey of cousins picked up, it'll send Erica running.

"You can see that, can't you?" Cone says. "She'll close up shop and get out of town. You know she will."

"And you couldn't have told me all this before?" Davenport demands.

"Look," Cone says, "it was MacEver's deal, and I didn't want to queer it. I'm just as tight-lipped when you and I work together."

"Yeah?" the NYPD man says. "Well . . . maybe. But now we got a world-class fuckup on our hands."

"Not necessarily," Cone says. "Get hold of Alvarez, explain the situation, and get him to postpone the warehouse raid until tomorrow afternoon. Then call Terry MacEver and fix it so the warehouse and the art gallery are hit at the same time. That way none of the birds will fly away."

"Mmm," Davenport says thoughtfully. "It might work."

"Sure it'll work," Cone says. "You manage the whole thing. You'll direct two important busts and probably close the Leonidas file. You'll make lieutenant out of this."

"You really know the way to a man's heart, don't you?" Neal Davenport says. "You lunatic! Where were you when God passed out brains—at the end of the line? I'll give you a call if I can straighten out this mess."

He hangs up.

Cone is satisfied that he's done all he can. From now on it's up to the Department to run the show. He's convinced they'll find enough evidence in the warehouse to justify the raid. And if Sergeant MacEver is right about the antique sword being offered by Erica Laboris, that cousin will take a fall, too.

That leaves only Ingmar Laboris.

When he goes out for lunch, he's still thinking about Ingmar and what that pascudnyak might be up to. He wanders about lower Manhattan, head bowed, shoving his way through the lunchtime throng. He buys a gyro and a cherry cola from a sidewalk vendor and continues his hike, eating and drinking as he walks.

He figures that if the coordinated busts of the Laboris warehouse and art gallery go down as planned, Ingmar might decide to make a fast exit. But Cone doesn't think so. The guy has bank accounts he'll want to clean out first. And he'll need to make cash transfers to someplace that doesn't

have an extradition treaty with the U.S., and where government officials
are not insulted by the offer of a small pourboire.

He drags himself back to Haldering, wondering how he's going to
spend the afternoon while waiting for Davenport to phone and report a
go or no-go. But his first call, after taking off parka and cap, is from
Hiram Haldering himself.

"Cone," he says in his chief executive officer voice, "I want to see you
in my office right now. Immediately. Is that clear?"

"Shit!" the Wall Street dick says—but only after he's hung up the
phone.

H.H. is sunk in the high-backed swivel chair behind his desk. His
muttony face is flushed with either anger or a three-martini lunch. Plump
fingers are clamped across his vested belly. His balding pate gleams dully
in winter light leaking through corner windows.

Alongside his desk, Mrs. Martha T. Hepplewaite sits grimly in an armchair. She's leaning forward like a figurehead, propping herself on the
heavy cane. Her raddled features are as purplish as Haldering's, and all
the wattles and dewlaps are quivering with fury.

They glare at Cone.

"Hi, folks," he says, and since no one asks him to sit down, he slouches
limply and wonders if he'll be offered a final cigarette and blindfold before
the execution.

"Cone," the boss says—a high-pitched bark—"how long have you been
on the Laboris Investments case?"

"Oh . . . I don't know. Two weeks or so, I guess."

"And what, exactly, have you discovered?"

"Nothing much. Little bits of this and that."

"But you have no evidence that Laboris is a fraud?"

"Nope," Cone says. "No hard evidence."

"Then why," Mrs. Hepplewaite says, almost strangling on her wrath,
"why did you see fit to advise my daughter to tell her fiancé to withdraw
his investment?"

"Oh, she told you that, did she?" Cone says. "It was a judgment call.
I think Ingmar Laboris is a crook. Right now I can't prove it. But I thought
it best to tell your daughter about how I felt. She and her fiancé decided
to bail out."

The harridan bangs her cane on the floor—two loud thumps. "Why
didn't you tell me first?" she demands. "I am the client. I am paying the
bills. You went behind my back."

The Wall Street dick doesn't like being hollered at.

"I'll tell you why I didn't go to you first," he says. "I called you a mean
biddy, and you are—in spades. If I had told you I think Laboris Invest-

ments is probably a fraud, you might not have passed the news along to your daughter."

"Cone," Hiram Haldering says, shocked, "you're talking to a valued client."

"Big deal," Cone says. "She's a conniving old lady who wants to keep her daughter unmarried and at home, slaving as a cook, secretary, housekeeper, servant, scullion, and all-around Cinderella. She's vindictive enough so that, if I said I think Ingmar Laboris is a gonnif, she might not tell Lucinda. She might keep her mouth shut and let the investment of her daughter's fiancé go down the drain. Then maybe they couldn't get married. Then maybe she could keep Lucinda cleaning up slops and winding clocks in their mausoleum for the rest of her life. Then maybe she could keep repeating, 'I told you so,' at least once a day until she died."

Mrs. Hepplewaite collapses back into her chair. The hand holding the cane begins to tremble. "You're a dreadful man," she says in a hoarse whisper. "Dreadful."

"Sure I am," Cone says cheerfully. "And you don't do so bad in that department yourself. My advice to you, ma'am—unsolicited, and you can tell me to go to hell if it'll make you feel better—my advice to you is to make peace with your daughter, give her your blessings, and wish her the best. That lady has more gumption than you give her credit for. She's going to marry her Francis, and maybe they'll have a kid or two. You told me he was a pediatrician, didn't you? Then he should know how it's done. If you turn her out, you'll never get to see your grandchildren. Is that what you want?"

She stares at him with widening eyes, and he thinks he sees the beginning of tears, but can't be sure.

"Snotty," she says in a low voice. "The snottiest man I've ever met."

"Dreadful and snotty all in one afternoon," he says. "My my, this is my lucky day. If all goes well, your daughter's fiancé has recovered his original investment plus a nice profit. Lucinda will be married. Doesn't that bring the roses to your cheeks?"

She growls, tapping her cane angrily on the floor. The three are silent a moment. Then Hiram Haldering, unwilling to grant his employee a complete triumph, clears his throat.

"About these expense accounts you've submitted on your investigation," he says sternly. "Two teak Buddhas and two statuettes of the goddess Kali. What is that all about?"

"Yes," Mrs. Hepplewaite says, raising her head and regaining her confidence. "And all those bills for cab fares. Do you *live* in a taxi, you disgusting man?"

"All legitimate expenses," Cone says blithely. "You're also going to pay for a bottle of cognac for a banker who helped me out. I knew you were a shrew, Mrs. Hepplewaite, but I never figured you for a cheapski. Pay the tab and think of the joy you'll feel when your first grandchild pees in your lap."

And he stalks out, wondering if he'll have a job in the morning and not much caring.

He gets back to his office feeling pretty good. He laid it on the line to H.H. and the client, and kept his dignity reasonably intact. He lights a Camel and sits chain-smoking for almost an hour, reviewing what might be going down the next day, but unable to drag his mind away from the part Ingmar Laboris could be playing in this mishmash. A puzzlement...

When his phone rings, he stares at it for a moment, wondering whether he really wants to talk to anyone and maybe get leaned on again. Finally, sighing, he picks it up.

"Yeah?" he says.

"Davenport," the city detective says. "All right, I've cleaned up your mess. Everything's coordinated. We're hitting the art gallery and warehouse at eleven-thirty tomorrow morning."

"So early?" Cone says.

"It's New Year's Eve, you schmuck," the NYPD man says. "You want us to wait until late in the afternoon when everyone's gone home?"

"Oh, yeah, I didn't think about that."

"There's a lot you didn't think about, Sherlock. MacEver says you're going with him."

"That's right. We're supposed to be brothers-in-law."

"God forbid," Davenport says. "Better he should have Godzilla for a relative. Anyway, he says to meet him fifteen minutes early across the street from the art gallery. Think you can remember that?"

"I'll remember," Cone says. "You're sore at me, aren't you?"

"Goddamn right I'm sore. I've had to spend all day on this Laboris thing. And it's not the only turnip on my plate, you know. But I had to push everything else aside while I got it organized."

"No one could have done it but you."

Davenport has to laugh. "What a bullshit artist you are!" he says. "Nah, I'm not sore at you. But next time be a little more up-front with me, will you?"

"Sure I will," Cone says. "Absolutely."

"Yeah," the city dick says, "I should live so long." And he hangs up.

Cone walks home through the violet twilight, still playing games occasionally to make sure he's not being tailed. He stops at a liquor store to pick up two bottles of Chianti Classico, figuring he'll buy the pizza on his way to Sam's place so it'll still be warm when he arrives.

Back in the loft, he feeds Cleo—some leftover breaded chicken nuggets he finds in the fridge. The omnivorous cat cleans up the plate, then sets to work grooming its whiskers. Cone strips and takes his ritual brush treatment under a hot shower, lacerating his skin with stiff bristles and rubbing on cornstarch after he's dried off.

He calls Samantha. She's home and waiting for him. So he dresses, checks his armament, and leaves the loft, not forgetting to take the wine. He feels excited and scary, like he's heading for the first date with a new woman. Nice feeling. Being young again.

It seems like a long time since they've been together, and seeing each other now is a little tight, stiff, confused. It takes them awhile to adjust— about two minutes. Then they slide into their comfortable roles, sit on the floor to chomp pizza and drink wine. Sam tells him everything that happened during her visit home, and he nods, smiling, stuffing his mouth, and realizing, as if for the first time, how complete she is.

She's wearing her long auburn hair up and pinned, and her sharp-featured face is devoid of makeup, washed and gleaming. Lots of jaw there, and steady blue-green eyes. Much woman, he thinks, and can see that stretched body under the jeans and turtleneck. He doesn't even want to imagine how empty his life would be without her. But, of course, he doesn't tell her that.

They demolish the pizza, clean up the mess, and open the second bottle of wine. They look at each other, and with no invitation from either, accepted or rejected, begin undressing lazily, still chattering about Samantha's trip and Cleo's new habit of sleeping under the kitchen sink.

It's only when their naked bodies are pressed does their gossip falter.

"Ah, Jesus," Sam says, sighing. "I thought of this a lot. Did you?"

"Yeah," Cone says.

"Do you know what I want to do right now?" she asks.

"What?"

She whispers in his ear.

"Well . . ." he says, "if you insist. If I don't enjoy it, I'll fake it."

"You louse!" she says, and sets to work.

They're possessed by demons that night, trying to make up for time lost. Their hard bodies are jangled with need, and sensation is not the answer. Neither knows what is, but they rend each other in a frantic effort to find relief. Not physical, for that is a mosquito bite compared to the hunger that gnaws at them.

Both prideful, they will not let go, unwilling to acknowledge that victory might lie in surrender. So they play their skin games, unable to yield to the heart's want, and settling for the satisfaction of greedy glands. Their lives are half-wins; they know it but cannot make the sacrifice total triumph demands. They show their naked bodies to each other, but will not present themselves flayed.

When their horizontal aerobics are concluded, they lie awhile, insensate and numb. Then Samantha stirs groggily to fetch the remainder of the chianti and their glasses. The wine, sipped slowly, revives them, and they look at each other with sappy smiles as if they had climbed Everest and returned intact.

And it is while they are in that loopy mood that Timothy Cone makes his Great Discovery.

"Where's Izzy?" Samantha demands. "You still have it, don't you?"

"Oh, sure. In the loft. I'd have brought it over tonight, but I had too much to carry. You can pick it up tomorrow night. You're coming over, aren't you?"

"Of course," she says. "It's New Year's Eve, isn't it? What are we eating?"

"I thought I'd pick up a roasted chicken and some odds and ends. And I suppose we'll have to drink champagne."

"What else? And do me a favor, will you: Change the sheets on that lumpy mattress of yours."

"Sure," he says equably. "I'll pick up my laundry tomorrow."

"Oh, boy," she says, "fresh laundry. A great way to start the New Year. Tim, why are you looking at me like that? Your face is all twisty."

"Laundry," he says wonderingly. "Jesus Christ, what a fucking moron I am!"

"So what else is new?" Samantha Whatley says.

He figures there's no point in going into the office at all on New Year's Eve. There will be a party. Guys will be nuzzling their secretaries, the secretaries will be goosing their bosses, and everyone will be drinking some lousy punch spiked with rotgut and decorated with slices of kiwi. Worst of all will be the forced jollity that Cone cannot endure.

So he spends the morning doing chores. Changes Cleo's litter. Goes out and picks up those bundles of laundry. Goes out again and returns with two bottles of Korbel champagne and puts them in the refrigerator. Goes out again to buy the largest roasted chicken he can find, some frozen yams in syrup, and salad stuff. Also a frozen apple pie and a package of sliced cheddar.

On one of his trips back to the loft, the phone shrills just as he's about to go out again. It's Samantha at the office.

"Why aren't you here?" she demands.

"I'm working," he says. "On the Laboris case."

"Bullshit," she says. "Are you going to show up at all today?"

"No."

"Well, you're going to miss one hell of an office party."

"Darn it," he says.

"Another thing," she says, "why didn't you tell me you had a hassle with H.H. about your expense account?"

"Oh, that," he says. "I left it on your desk, figuring you'd clean it up when you got back. But I guess he picked it up. Besides, it wasn't exactly a hassle. I explained every item."

"Oh, sure," she says. "He's still boiling."

"See you tonight," he says, and hangs up.

By 10:45 he's finished all his donkeywork. He tosses Cleo the tip of a chicken wing to gnaw on, checks his ankle holster, and heads uptown.

He finds Terry MacEver standing across Madison Avenue from the Laboris Gallery and about a block north. The sergeant, wearing his black bowler, has two plainclothesmen with him, a couple of Neanderthals who look like they dine on haunches of mammoth every night.

MacEver greets Cone with a grin. "Things almost got screwed up, didn't they?" he says.

"Almost doesn't count," the Wall Street dick says. "Everything's copacetic now."

"It is indeed," the sergeant agrees. "Here's the deal: My appointment with Erica Laboris is for eleven-thirty. You go in with me. That won't spook her. After all, I'm supposed to be your brother-in-law. When I get in the gallery, I take off my lid. Then she shows us the sword. Meanwhile, these two men have moved to the sidewalk in front of the gallery and are scoping the action through the window. If the sword is the real thing, I put my hat back on, and they come into the gallery like Gangbusters— just in case we have any problems with Erica. If the blade offered is junk, I keep my hat off and we leave the gallery with no harm done. How does that sound?"

"Simple and neat," Cone says. "It'll go like silk."

"Let us pray," MacEver says, glancing at his watch. "Okay, it's time. You guys," he tells the plainclothesmen, "don't stand in front of the window and gawk, but station yourselves where you can watch what's going on inside without being spotted."

"I gotta take a leak," one of them says.

"Tough," the sergeant says. "Clench your teeth."

MacEver and Cone cross Madison and walk south to the art gallery. They enter. MacEver removes his derby. Ingrid Laboris, the cream puff, comes swaying forward.

"Good morning, sirs," she says with the Laboris hiss. "How may I be of service?"

"J. Ransom Bailey to see Miss Erica Laboris," the sergeant says.

"Of course," Ingrid says. "I shall tell her you have arrived. And how are you today, Mr. Cone?"

"Surviving," he says. "Happy New Year."

"Likewise," she says. "Just a moment, sirs. Erica will be with you shortly."

They wait stolidly. Cone turns casually, as if to inspect a crusty old pot on display, and glances out the front window. He can't spot the two plain-clothesmen. He doesn't know if that's good or bad.

It's almost three minutes before Erica Laboris comes stalking out of a back room. She's really a put-together woman, Cone thinks admiringly, with her hair elaborately coiffed and lacquered. She's wearing a black silk dress that hints. Her fingernails are painted a jade green.

"Good morning, gentlemen," she says with her mirthless smile. "So nice to see you again."

She's carrying a long box of rough wood with a hinged lid. Cone notes that her clamping hands are white at the knuckles, and her long talons dig into the wood.

"Over here, please," she says, leading the way to the receptionist's desk. "I think you will be enchanted with this, Mr. Bailey. Authentic, very old, very unusual."

Opens the long box. Lifts out a bundle of tissue paper. Unwraps it carefully. Withdraws an ancient sword. Holds it out to them.

To Cone, it looks like a piece of rusted iron that's been reclaimed from a junkyard. But Terry MacEver, bending low to inspect it, is impressed.

"Beautiful," he breathes. "A real museum piece."

"It is indeed," Erica Laboris says with her chilly smile. "You wish to add it to your collection?"

She puts the blade down on the tissue paper. The sergeant replaces his bowler atop his head. He reaches slowly inside his coat and withdraws his ID wallet. He flips it open and displays it to Erica.

"Sergeant Terry MacEver of the New York Police Department," he says. "You are under arrest for receiving and possessing stolen property. I shall now read you your rights."

She stares at him. Then turns her head to stare at the two Neanderthals piling through the front door of the gallery. Then she stares at Timothy Cone.

"You prick," she says.

"Yeah," Cone says, "I know."

. . .

It takes him almost twenty minutes to stop an empty cab, and by the time he gets over to the Laboris warehouse on Eleventh Avenue, there's not much to see. There are several empty cop cars parked outside, and a couple of blues wandering about, but otherwise things are quiet.

Cone marches up to the uniformed officer stationed at the warehouse door.

"Detective Neal Davenport around?" he asks. "I'm Timothy Cone. I'm supposed to meet him."

"Yeah?" the cop says. "I'll see. You wait here."

He goes inside, and the Wall Street dick waits, lighting a Camel and pacing up and down the driveway. A couple of plainclothesmen come out, their IDs clipped to their lapels. They take camera equipment from one of the cars and go back into the warehouse.

Cone has almost finished his second cigarette before Davenport appears. He looks a little bedraggled, but happy.

"Hey-hey," he says, "sherlock himself. How did things go at the art gallery?"

"MacEver cuffed Erica Laboris," Cone reports. "She was peddling a sword stolen from a Beirut museum. After she's booked, the sergeant is going back to the gallery to toss it. He figures he'll find more goodies. How are things going here?"

"Bingo," the city bull says. "So far we've found eight kilos of horse, a sweet arsenal of handguns and some small amounts of coke and pot."

"Much cash?" Cone asks.

"A few bucks. What's your interest in cash?"

"Something has come up I think you should know about."

"Oh, Jesus!" Davenport says despairingly. "Have you been holding out on me again?"

"I swear I haven't," Cone vows, holding up a palm. "I only got a line on it last night, by accident. It's about Laboris Investments and where Ingmar fits into this whole schmear."

"Yeah?" the NYPD man says. "Let's hear it."

Cone talks rapidly for almost five minutes, as the two men walk up and down. Davenport listens intently, not interrupting. When the Wall Street dick finishes, the NYPD man looks at him narrowly and then slowly peels the wrapper from a fresh stick of Juicy Fruit.

"Could be," he says, frowning.

"Got to be," Cone says. "The entire Laboris clan are natural-born villains, and this puts Ingmar right in the middle of the picture."

"But you've got no evidence?"

"No. Nothing."

"So? What do you want from me?"

"Move in on Ingmar this afternoon. Take him for questioning."

"Whoa!" Davenport protests. "On what grounds? This is one for the DA. Or the SEC."

"Can't you bring the DA in on it?"

"Hey, come on! It's New Year's Eve. Everyone will be partying. And tomorrow is New Year's Day. Maybe the next day."

"Too late," Cone says desperately. "Ingmar will hear about the art gallery and warehouse by tonight. If we wait until the day after tomorrow, he'll be long gone. Listen, are you leaning on any of the cousins in the warehouse?"

"Yeah," the Department man says, "the shipping manager, a nerd named Edvard Laboris. We read him his rights and he started crying. I think he's ready to crack."

"Why don't you brace him and see if he'll talk about what I just told you. If he does, then you'll have enough to get the DA's okay to take Ingmar."

Davenport stares at him a long time. "Well, you gave us this package, so I can't complain. All right, I'll see if Edvard will break. You wait here."

He goes back into the warehouse. Cone tramps up and down, smoking furiously. A few minutes later, Petey Alvarez comes bounding out of the warehouse, rushes over to Cone, embraces him.

"You crazy sonnenbitch!" he yells. "I love you, baby. Now we're up to ten kilos. What a score! Listen, you want to hear something nutty? This Laboris outfit brings in its own brand of perfume, cologne, and after-shave lotion."

"I know," Cone says. "Nuit de Fou."

"Right. Well, half those cologne bottles are filled with high-grade shit. How do you like that? Isn't that beautiful? Look, I gotta go. We're still searching. Going for the world's record. Thanks, bubbalah. I owe you one."

He runs back into the warehouse. Cone lights another cigarette and resumes his pacing. It's a raw, biting day, but he can feel the sweat dripping from his armpits. He wants Ingmar. It's important to him, but for reasons he doesn't completely understand.

It's almost twenty minutes before Davenport comes out again, accompanied by two uniformed officers. The detective is pulling on a pair of gloves.

"Okay," he says, "I got enough out of Edvard to make me think you guessed right. I also got a good lead on the Leonidas homicide. I've called the DA's office. There's an assistant prosecutor I've done a few favors for. I spelled it out for him. He grumbled about leaving his office party, but agreed to meet us at Laboris Investments in an hour. That'll give us time to pick up some burgers. I'm starved."

The man from the DA's office is a tall, skinny gink wearing black horn-rimmed glasses. Davenport doesn't bother with introductions, and Cone figures the city detective doesn't want the assistant prosecutor to know that he's working with a lousy civilian.

The outer office of Laboris Investments is empty except for a blond receptionist filing her nails. The five men descend on her, the two uniformed officers moving close to the desk. She isn't interested.

"Could we see Mr. Ingmar Laboris, please," Davenport asks.

"Who shall I say is calling?"

The NYPD man looks at the two uniformed cops, then back at the blond. "The Salvation Army," he says. "On second thought, don't bother announcing us. Go back to your nails, honey; we'll surprise him."

Cone leads the way to the inner office and opens the door. Ingmar Laboris is leaning back in his swivel chair, Gucci loafers parked atop his huge mahogany desk. He's sucking on a Louisville Slugger cigar and leafing through *Penthouse*. He looks up when the five men come crowding in, but doesn't change his expression. A ballsy guy, Cone decides.

"Ah, gentlemen," he says, "what can I do for you?"

"Ingmar Laboris?" Davenport asks.

"That is correct."

The detective and the man from the DA's office proffer their IDs. Laboris glances at them.

"So?" he says.

"We'd like you to come down to the office and answer a few questions," the prosecutor says.

"Now why should I do that?"

"Because it's more comfortable than the precinct house," Davenport says.

Ingmar takes a long drag from his cigar. Then he sets it carefully aside in the smoky quartz ashtray. He sits back again, and regards the detective gravely.

"I must tell you," Laboris says in his sonorous voice, "I would find it very inconvenient to accompany you gentlemen. At the moment, I am waiting for a very important overseas call."

"I'm afraid it'll have to wait," the DA's man says. "Let's not play games, Mr. Laboris. Do yourself a favor and don't make trouble for us."

Ingmar reflects a moment. "May I call my attorney?" he asks.

"If you feel it's necessary," the prosecutor says.

Laboris reaches for his phone, punches out a number. "Ingmar Laboris calling," he says. "May I speak to Mr. Bjorn Laboris, please." He looks up at the men standing in front of his desk. "My cousin," he explains.

"What else?" Cone says.

Ingmar speaks rapidly into the phone in a low voice, concealing his lips with a palm. Then he hangs up.

"Very well," he says briskly. "Bjorn will meet us at the district attorney's office. I presume this concerns Laboris Investments?"

"That," Davenport says, "and other things. Can we go now?"

Ingmar rises, takes a cashmere overcoat and gray homburg from a small closet. He carries the coat over his arm, but dons the homburg, adjusting it to a rakish tilt.

"You stay here," Davenport says to one of the uniformed officers. "No one in. Not a scrap of paper removed. Got that? I'll make sure you get a relief in a couple of hours."

"Oh, sure," the cop says bitterly. "On New Year's Eve?"

On the way out the door, Ingmar Laboris pauses before Cone. "I never did get that investment from your client," he says with a wan smile.

"The check is in the mail," Cone says.

Samantha Whatley comes directly to the loft from the office. She swears she's not swacked, but Cone can tell she's got a nice mellow buzz on. That's okay; he's feeling no pain himself. After he returned from Wall Street, he had a couple of stalwart vodkas while preparing the evening's festivities.

"The yams are thawed and baking," he tells her. "The chicken is warming up on the stove. The salad is made. We'll eat in about an hour. All right?"

"Fine with me."

"Meanwhile, why don't we crack a cold bottle of bubbles, just to get in the mood."

"Splendid idea," Sam says. "You missed a great office party, though I could have done without the Diet Pepsi in the punch. By the way, H.H. told me that Mrs. Hepplewaite paid her bill in full, your expenses included. And her daughter's fiancé got all his money back."

"That's nice," Cone says.

"How the hell did you manage that?" she asks, sipping her champagne.

"I didn't; you did."

"Me? What the hell are you talking about?"

"It's a long story."

"We've got all night," she says. "Come on, buster—*give*."

"Well, it started when you discovered Izzy came apart."

"I didn't discover it; it was an accident."

"Whatever. Anyway, that's what broke the whole thing."

He tells her about his purchase of the Kali statuettes, the traces of heroin found inside, and how Petey Alvarez, the narcotics cop, took over from there.

"They raided the Laboris Importers' warehouse this morning," he says, "and found kilos of the stuff. Petey should get a commendation at least. And all because you knocked Izzy off your bedside table."

"Crazy," Sam says, shaking her head. "Can we eat now? I'm famished."

While they're tearing the chicken apart—tossing scraps to a delighted Cleo—Cone tells her about Sergeant Terry MacEver and the sting operation.

"Another Laboris cousin," he says. "She was hawking stolen art smuggled in by the importing company. It probably traveled halfway around the world before it got to Manhattan. Anyway, Erica's in the clink."

"You *have* been a busy little boy," Sam says. "You want that last piece of yam?"

"No, you take it. Empty bottle? I'll open the other."

"I'll get smashed," Sam warns.

"That's okay; you're amongst friends."

"So keep talking," she says. "What's all this got to do with Mrs. Hepplewaite and Laboris Investments?"

Cone has already decided to tell her nothing about his run-in with Sidney Leonidas and the junkie's subsequent murder. Nor of the shootout on the night he and Petey Alvarez took the drug dealers. If he did, she'd just scream at him. Investigators for Haldering & Co. weren't supposed to get involved in such vulgar activities.

"Laboris Investments," Cone repeats. "I couldn't see the connection with drug dealing and art smuggling. I felt in my gonads that Ingmar was an A number-one wiseguy, but I couldn't figure his angle. He was paying a hefty return on investments, but that guy's no foreign-exchange dealer. He doesn't know a rand from a rupee. So it had to be something else—right?"

By this time the roasted chicken is destroyed, and Cleo is working on the carcass. The yams are gone, and so is most of the salad. They're deep into the second bottle of bubbly, and decide to save the apple pie and cheddar for a late-night snack. Or morning.

They're still at the desk, feet up on the littered newspaper tablecloth. They sip their champagne very, very slowly, eyes a mite glazed, movements slow and precise to prove their sobriety.

"What was I yakking about?" Cone asks.

"Laboris Investments. What Ingmar was up to."

"Oh, yeah. Well, here's where you come in again. You broke it."

"Now how the hell did I do that?" Samantha says.

"Last night you said you wanted me to put fresh sheets on the mattress and to be sure to pick up my laundry."

She stares at him a long moment before she gets it. "Laundry!" she yells. "Laboris Investments was laundering the cash from the dope dealing and art smuggling. Feeding it into their investment funds."

"Right," Cone says approvingly. "That's exactly what Ingmar was doing."

"But he was paying thirty percent. I can't see any villain cutting his profits like that."

"Ever hear of the Ponzi swindle?" he asks her.

"Vaguely," Samantha says. "It works like those pyramid clubs, doesn't it? You get a list of ten people, send five bucks to the name on top, add yours to the bottom, and send the chain letter to ten friends. When your name hits the top of the list, you're supposed to get a million dollars. Right?"

"Right. If you get in on the start, you might make a little. If you're down on the list, you're just out five bucks. The Ponzi scam, which was dreamed up by Charles Ponzi in the 1920s, works something like that. You promise investors a big return on their money. Ingmar Laboris started out paying thirty percent. But he was using the money coming in from new investors. He wasn't doing any foreign-exchange trading. He wasn't putting the money to work in *anything*. He was just paying off that thirty percent from funds coming in from fresh suckers. And pocketing the rest. The swindle will work if the pool of new investors is limitless. But of course it never is. As soon as the new money stops coming in, the whole con collapses. That's what was happening to Laboris Investments. Lucinda Hepplewaite's boyfriend got his shekels out just in time."

Samantha frowns. "You mean this Ponzi scheme was a cover?"

"Sure it was," Cone says. "For the laundering operation. All of Ingmar's cousins were putting in dirty money and then taking out clean cash. Ingmar knew it couldn't last, but the Laboris clan did okay while it was running. I reckon they planned to close up shop in the next month or so. Then Ingmar would retire to the French Riviera and spend his remaining years indulging in Havana cigars and nymphets."

"Where is he now?"

"In durance vile, I hope. The DA picked him up this afternoon."

"On your anonymous tip, no doubt," Sam says.

"Something like that."

"Tim," she says, staring at him, "how did you figure it all out?"

"I've got a criminal mind."

"I really think you have."

"Sure I do. Every cop in the world has a criminal mind. How else are we going to keep up with the bad guys?"

It's getting on as they finish the second bottle of Korbel, talking lazily of this and that. Samantha looks down at the clean sheets tucked around the mattress on the floor.

"You ready?" she asks.

"Not yet," Cone says. "Let's wait until after midnight. There's something about the first shtup of the new year."

"You're the most romantic man I've ever met," she says, kicking his shin.

But they're lying together on the clean sheets, fooling around, when they hear sirens, bells, firecrackers, and the crash of breaking glass. Samantha sits up and unpins her glorious hair. She touches Cone's face.

"Happy New Year, Tim," she says softly.

"Yeah," he says, "the same to you."

Timothy's Game

"Sex is dead. Money is the sex of our time."

—Sally Steiner

Book One
Run, Sally, Run!

1

Jake Steiner, a crude and growly man, slams down his fork. "What *is* this shit?" he demands.

"It's fettucini primavera, Pa," Sally says. "Martha made the pasta herself, and all the spring vegetables are fresh. Try it; you'll like it."

"I won't try it, and I won't like it. Whatever happened to a nice brisket and a boiled potato?"

"You know what the doctor told you about that," his daughter says, then jerks a thumb at his tumbler of whiskey and water. "And about *that*."

"Screw the doctor," Jake says wrathfully. "There are more old drunks than old doctors."

He gets up from the table, stalks over to the marble-topped sideboard, takes a cigar from a humidor. He bites off the cigar tip and spits it into a crystal ashtray.

"I'll pick up something to eat later," he says. "I gotta go out."

"Yeah," Sally says. "To Ozone Park. It's payoff night. Those fucking bandits."

"Watch your mouth," he says sharply. "Act like a lady, talk nice."

She finishes her fettucini, watching as he scrapes a kitchen match across the marble slab and lights his cigar.

"I gotta import these matches from Florida," he tells her. "You can't buy scratch-anywhere matches around here. Would you believe it?" He puffs importantly, twirling the cigar in his heavy lips. "What are you doing tonight?"

"I'm going up and sit with Ma awhile. Give Martha a chance to have some dinner and clean up."

"And then?"

"I thought I'd drive into New York and take in a movie. There's a new Woody Allen."

"Bullshit," her father says. "You're going to see that fairy brother of yours. Well, don't give him my love."

"Believe me," Sally says, "he can live without it."

They glare at each other, then Jake pushes back the sliding glass door and stamps out onto the tiled terrace to smoke his cigar, taking his whiskey glass with him.

Sally goes up to her mother's bedroom on the second floor. Martha is feeding the invalid. Rebecca Steiner's hands and lower legs are so crippled with rheumatoid arthritis that she cannot walk, cannot hold a spoon.

"How was dinner, Ma?" Sally asks.

"Delicious," Becky says, smiling brightly. "And I'll bet your father wouldn't take even a little taste."

"You'd win your bet. Martha, why don't you go down and have your dinner. I'll sit with ma for a while."

The old black woman nods. "There's a nice piece of strawberry cheesecake, Miz Steiner," she says to the woman in the wheelchair. "Just the way you like it."

Sally leans over her mother. "How about the cheesecake?" she asks.

"Well, maybe just a bite. I hate to disappoint Martha, she works so hard."

"Ho-ho," Sally says. "If I know you, you'll finish the whole slice. Come on now, open wide."

She feeds the cheesecake to Rebecca, then holds the mug of coffee close so her mother can sip through a straw.

"You're going out tonight?" Becky asks. "It's Saturday. You got maybe a date?"

"Nah, Ma. I'm driving over to New York to see Eddie."

"That's nice. You'll give him my love?"

"Of course. Don't I always?"

"Listen, Sally, in New York you'll be careful?"

"I'm always careful. I can take care of myself, Ma, you know that."

They watch the evening news on television, and then sit gossiping about an aunt who is on her third husband and has recently taken up with a beach boy in Hawaii.

Rebecca Steiner is shocked, but Sally says, "Let her have her fun; she can afford it."

Martha comes back up, carrying her knitting, and she and Mrs. Steiner settle down for a night of television. Then, at eleven o'clock, Rebecca will be put to bed, and Martha will retire to her own bedroom to read the Bible.

"Dad still downstairs?" Sally asks her.

"Oh, yeah," Martha says. "Stomping up and down and cursing."

"Sure. What else."

She goes downstairs to find her father pulling on his leather trench coat. He has a fresh, unlighted cigar clamped between his teeth.

"How is she?" he asks.

"Why don't you go up occasionally and take a look?" Sally says angrily.

"I can't take it," her father says, groaning. "I see her like that, and I remember . . ."

"Yeah, well, she's the same, no change."

He nods and tugs down a floppy tweed cap. "It's chilling off out there, Sal. Wear a coat."

"I will, pa."

"You want a lift?"

"No, I'll take my car."

"You got your pistol?"

"In the glove compartment."

"You get in trouble, don't be afraid to use it."

"I'll use it. Pa, watch your back with those ginzos."

"Listen, when I can't handle momsers like that, I'll be ready for Mount Zion."

Suddenly, unexpectedly, he comes close to touch her cheek with his fingertips.

"It's a great life if you don't weaken," he says, looking into her eyes.

"I'm surviving," Sally Steiner says.

"Yeah," he says. "See you tomorrow, kiddo. Don't take any wooden nickels."

She watches from the window until he drives away in his black Cadillac Eldorado. Then she struggles into a long sweater coat that cost a week's salary at one of those Italian boutiques on Madison Avenue. She backs her silver Mazda RX-7 out of the three-car garage. She checks the glove compartment to make certain the loaded pistol is there, then heads for Manhattan.

Jake Steiner drives from Smithtown into Ozone Park. He parks in front of a narrow brick building, windows painted black. There is a small sign over the doorway: THE MIAMI FISHING AND SOCIAL CLUB.

Jake gets out of his Cadillac, knowing the hubcaps are safe. There is no thievery on this street. And no muggings, no littering, no graffiti. Maybe the cops drive through once a week, but the locals take care of everything.

There are a few geezers in the front room, playing cards and drinking red wine. They don't look up when the door opens. But the mastodon behind the bar eyeballs Steiner and pours a waterglass of whiskey, splash of water, no ice. Jake pulls out a fat roll of bills, peels off a twenty, hands it over.

"For your favorite charity," he says.

"Yeah," the bartender says, and moves his head toward the back room.

Steiner carries his whiskey through a doorway curtained with strings of glass beads, most of them chipped or broken. There is one round wooden table back there, surrounded with six chairs that look ready to collapse at the first shout. The tabletop has a big brownish stain in the center. It could be a wine spill or it could be a blood spill; Jake doesn't know and doesn't wonder.

Two men are sitting there: Vic Angelo and his underboss and driver, Mario Corsini. They've got a bottle of Chivas Regal between them, and their four-ounce shotglasses are full. Only Vic gets to his feet when Steiner enters. He spreads his arms wide.

"Jew bastard," he says, grinning.

"Wop sonofabitch," Jake says.

They embrace, turning their heads carefully aside so they won't mash their cigars. They look alike: short, porky through chest and shoulders, with big bellies, fleshy faces, manicures, and pinkie rings.

"Hiya, Mario," Jake says.

Corsini nods.

"How's the family?" Angelo asks, pulling out a chair for Jake.

"Couldn't be better. Yours?"

"Likewise, thank God. So here we are again. A month gone by. Can you believe it?"

"Yeah," Steiner says, taking a gulp of his drink, "I can believe it."

He tugs a white envelope from the inside pocket of his jacket and slides it across the table to Angelo.

"My tax return," he says.

Vic smiles and pushes the envelope to Corsini. "I don't even have to count it," he says. "I trust you. How long we been good friends, Jake?"

"Too long," Steiner says, and Mario Corsini stirs restlessly.

"Yeah, well, we got a little business to discuss here," Angelo says, sipping his scotch delicately. "Like they say, good news and bad news. I'll give you the bad first. We're upping your dues two biggies a month."

Steiner slams a meaty fist down on the table. It rocks; their drinks slop over.

"Two more a month?" he says. "What kind of shit is this?"

"Take it easy," Vic Angelo says soothingly. "Everyone in Manhattan and Brooklyn is getting hit for another grand."

"But I get hit for two? That's because I'm such a good friend of yours—right?"

"Don't be such a fucking firecracker," Vic says. He turns to his under-boss. "He's a firecracker, ain't he, Mario?"

"Yeah," Corsini says. He's a saber of a man, with a complexion more yellowish than olive.

"You didn't give me a chance to tell you the good news," Angelo says to Steiner. "We're giving you a new territory. South of where your dump is now. Along Eleventh Avenue to Twenty-third Street."

"Yeah?" Jake says suspiciously. "What happened to Pitzak?"

"He retired," Vic says.

"Where to? Forest Lawn?"

"I don't like jokes like that," Corsini says. "It's not respectful."

"What the fuck do I care what you like or don't like," Steiner says. He swallows whiskey. "So the bottom line is that my tariff goes up two G's, and I get Eleventh Avenue down to Twenty-third Street. Right?"

"And all the garbage you can eat," Corsini says.

"Listen, sonny boy," Jake says. "One man's trash is another man's trea-sure. You're drinking Chivas Regal. That's where it comes from—my garbage."

"Hey hey," Angelo says. "Let's talk like gentlemen. So you start on Monday, Jake. You can handle the business?"

"Maybe I'll need a new truck or two. Let me see how much there is."

"You need more trucks," Vic says, "don't buy new ones. We can give you a good deal on Pitzak's fleet."

"Oh-ho," Steiner says. "It's like that, is it?"

"That's the way it is," Corsini says. "You take over Pitzak's district, you take over his trucks. From us."

"I love you wise guys," Jake says. "You got more angles than worms."

"If you're shorting," Angelo says gently, "we can always make you a loan to buy the trucks. Low vigorish."

"Thanks for nothing," Steiner says bitterly. "I wouldn't touch your loans with my schlong. I'll manage."

"One more thing," Vic says. "We want you to take on a new man. He's been over from the old country six months now. Strictly legit. He's got his papers and all that shit. A good loader for you. A nice young boy. He'll work hard, and he's strong."

"Yeah?" Jake says. "He speaka da English?"

"As good as you and me," Angelo assures him.

"What about the union?"

"It's fixed," Vic says. "No problem."

"If I'm taking over Pitzak's organization," Steiner says, "what do I need a new man for?"

"Because he's my cousin," Mario Corsini says.

They drain their drinks, and Jake rises.

"It's been a lovely evening," he says. "I've enjoyed every minute of it."

He nods at them and marches out, leaving his empty whiskey glass and chewed cigar butt on the table.

"I don't trust that scuzz," Mario says, filling their shot glasses with scotch. "He's got no respect."

"He's got his problems," Vic says. "A crippled wife. A fag son. And his daughter—who the hell knows what she is. What a house he's going home to."

"Only he ain't going home," Corsini says. "He's going to Brooklyn. He keeps a bimbo on Park Slope. He bought a coop for her."

Angelo stares at him. "No shit?" he says. "How did you find that out?"

"I like to know who we're dealing with. You never know when it might come in handy."

"A young twist?"

"Oh, sure. And a looker. He makes it with her three or four times a week. Sometimes in the afternoon, sometimes at night."

"The old fart," Vic Angelo says admiringly. "I never would have guessed. I wonder if his wife knows."

"I'll bet that smartass daughter of his knows," Corsini says. "I can't figure her. You never know what she's thinking."

Manhattan comes across the bridge, the harsh and cluttered city where civility is a foreign language and the brittle natives speak in screams. Sally Steiner loves it; it is her turf. All the rough and raucous people she buffets—hostility is a way of life. Speak softly and you are dead.

She dropped out of Barnard after two years. Those women—she had nothing in common with them; they had never been wounded. They were all Bendel and Bermuda. What did they know about their grimy, ruttish city and the desperate, charged life about them? They floated as Sally strode—and counted herself fortunate.

Her brother lives in Hell's Kitchen on a mean and ramshackle street awaiting the wrecker's ball. Eddie works on the top floor of a five-story walk-up. The original red brick façade is now festooned with whiskers of peeling gray paint, and the stone stoop is cracked and sprouting.

His apartment is spacious enough, but ill proportioned, and furnished with cast-offs and gutter salvage. But the ceilings are high; there is a skylight. Room enough for easel, taboret, paints, palettes, brushes. And white walls for his unsold paintings: a crash of color.

He has his mother's beauty and his father's body: a swan's head atop a pit bull. When he embraces Sally, she smells turps and a whiff of garlic on his scraggly blond mustache.

"Spaghetti again?" she asks. "A'la olio?"

"Again," he says with his quirky smile.

"I can't complain; we had fettucini. Ma sends her love. Pa doesn't send his."

Eddie nods. "How is the old man?"

"Terrible. Smoking and drinking up a storm. I don't know why he's paying that fancy Park Avenue doc. He never does what he's told."

"He's still got the girl in Brooklyn?"

"Oh, sure. I can't blame him for that. Can you?"

"Yes," Eddie Steiner says, "I can blame him."

They sit side by side on a dilapidated couch, one broken leg propped on a telephone directory. Eddie pours them glasses of a harsh chianti.

"How you doing, kiddo?" Sally asks him.

"I'm doing okay," he says. "A gallery down in the East Village wants to give me a show."

"Hey! That's great!"

He shakes his head. "Not yet. I'm not ready. I'm still working."

Sally looks around at the paintings on the walls, the half-blank canvas on the easel.

"Your stuff is getting brighter, isn't it?"

"Oh, you noticed that, did you? Yeah," he says, laughing, "I'm coming out of my blue mood. And I'm getting away from the abstract bullshit. More representational. How do you like that head over there? The little one on top."

"Jesus," Sally says, "who the hell is *she*?"

"A bag lady. I dragged her up here to pose. I did some fast pencil sketches, gave her a couple of bucks, and then did the oil. I like it."

"I do, too, Eddie."

"Then take it; it's yours."

"Nah, I couldn't do that. Sell it. Prove to Pa you're a genius."

"Who the hell cares what he thinks. I talked to Ma a couple of days ago. She sounded as cheerful as ever."

"Yeah, she never complains. Where's Paul?"

"Bartending at a joint on Eighth Avenue. It's just a part-time thing, but it brings in some loot. Including that wine you're drinking."

"Paul's a sweetheart," Sally says.

Her brother smiles. "I think so, too," he says. "Hey, listen, there's something I've been wanting to ask you."

"Ask away."

"I want to do a painting of you. A nude. Will you pose for me?"

"A nude? What the hell for? You've seen me in a bathing suit. You know the kind of body I've got. My God, Eddie, I'm a dumpster."

"You've got a very strong body," he tells her. "Good musculature. Great legs."

"And no tits."

"I'm not doing a centerfold. I see you sitting on a heavy stool, bending forward. Very determined, very aggressive. Against a thick red swirly background laid on with a palette knife. And you looming out. What do you say?"

"Let me think about it—okay? You've never seen me naked before."

"Sure I have," he says cheerfully. "You were five and I was seven. You were taking a shower, and I peeked through the keyhole."

"You louse!" she cries, punching his arm. "Well, I've added a few pounds since then."

"And a few brains," he says, leaning forward to kiss her cheek. "So *good* to see you, sweetie. But you seem down. Problems?"

"Well, you know, with Ma and Pa. And you."

"Me?" he says, amused. "I'm no problem."

"And me," she goes on. "I'm a problem. I'm not doing what I want to be doing."

"Which is? Making money?"

"Sure," she says, challenging him. "That's what it's all about, isn't it?"

"I guess," he says, sighing. "The bottom line."

"You better believe it, buster. I see these guys raking in the bucks. . . . Like those banditos Pa went to pay off tonight. I've got more brains than they've got, but they're living off our sweat. What kind of crap is that?"

"Life is unfair," he says, smiling and pouring them more wine.

"If you let it be unfair. Not me. I'm going to be out there grabbing like all the rest—if I ever get the chance."

He looks at his paintings hanging on the walls. "There's more than just greed, Sally."

"Says who? What? Tell me what."

"Satisfaction with your work. Love. Joy. Sex."

"Sex?" she says. "Sex is dead. Money is the sex of our time."

He doesn't reply. They sit silently, comfortable with each other.

"You're a meatball," she says finally.

"I know," he says. "But a contented meatball. Are you contented, Sal?"

"Contented?" she says. "When you're contented, you're dead. Once you stop climbing, you slide right back down into the grave."

"Oh, wow," he says. "That's heavy."

She drains her wine, rises, digs into her shoulder bag. She comes up with bills, smacks them into his palm.

"Here's a couple of hundred," she says. "Go buy yourself some paint and spaghetti. And a haircut."

"Sally, I can't—"

"Screw it," she says roughly. "It's not my dough. I'll take it out of petty cash at the office. Pa will never know the difference."

"You're sure?"

"I'm sure."

Before she leaves, he embraces her again.

"You'll think about posing for me?"

"I will. I really will."

"I love you, Sal."

"And I love you. Stay well and say hello to Paul for me. I'll be in touch."

She gets back to Smithtown a little before midnight. Goes up to her mother's bedroom and opens the door cautiously. The night-light is on, and Becky is snoring grandly. Sally goes back downstairs to the office-den. The books for the accountant and tax attorney and IRS are kept in the office safe of Steiner Waste Control on Eleventh Avenue in Manhattan. The *real* books are kept here, in a small safe disguised as a cocktail table.

She spends a half-hour crunching numbers, using a pocket calculator that has no memory. Profits are up over the corresponding week of the previous year. But not enough. The tax paid to the bentnoses for the right to collect garbage is a constant drain. Go sue city hall.

Next she flips through the current issue of *Barron's* to see how their equities are doing. A small uptick. Jake lets his daughter do all the investing. "I can't be bothered with that shit." He doesn't know an option from a future, but he can read the bottom line. Every month. Then it's a grudging "Not bad" or a furious "You trying to bankrupt me?"

Sally pushes the papers away on the big, leather-topped desk scarred with burns from her father's cigars. She sits brooding, biting at the hard skin around her thumbnail.

They're doing okay—but nothing sensational. Most people would consider the Steiners rich, but they're not *rich* rich—which is all that counts. It's not for lack of trying; the want is there. But what Sally calls the Big Chance just hasn't come along. She can buy a thousand shares of this and a thousand shares of that, and maybe make a few bucks. Terrific.

But she's also bought some dogs and, on paper, the Steiner portfolio is earning about ten percent annually. Hurrah. She'd be doing better if she socked all their cash away in tax-exempts. But where's the fun there? She doesn't go to the racetracks or to Vegas; stocks are her wheel of fortune. She knows that playing the market is a crapshoot, but once tried, never denied.

Later, naked in bed, hands locked behind her head, she tries to concentrate on the Big Chance and how it might be finagled. But all she can think about is Eddie asking her to pose in the nude.

That's the nicest thing that's happened to her in years.

Judy Bering, the receptionist-secretary, opens the door of Sally's office and sticks her head in.

"There's a guy out here," she says. "Claims he was hired and told to report for work this morning."

"Yeah," Sally says, "Pa told me he'd show up. What's his name?"

"Anthony Ricci."

"Sure," Sally says. "What else? What's he like?"

Judy rolls her eyes heavenward. "A Popsicle," she says.

Ricci comes in, an Adonis, carrying his cap and wearing a smile that lights up the dingy office.

"Good morning, miss," he says. "I am Anthony Ricci, and I am to work here as a loader."

"Yeah," Sally says, "so I heard. My name is Sally Steiner. I'm the boss's daughter. Sit down. Have a cigarette if you like. You got all your papers?"

"Oh, sure. Right here."

He digs into his jacket pocket, slides the documents across Sally's desk. She flips through them quickly.

"Everything looks okay," she says. "You been over here six months?"

"Maybe seven," he says. "I never want to go back."

"You speak good English."

"I thank you. I study hard."

"Good for you," Sally says. "You know what a loader does? He lifts heavy cans of garbage and dumps them into the back of a truck. You can handle that?"

Again that high-intensity smile. Ricci lifts his arms, flexes his biceps. "I can handle," he says.

"Uh-huh," Sally says. "We've had three hernias in the past year. They call you Tony, I suppose."

"That's right. Tony."

"Well, Tony, the boss isn't in right now. He's out inspecting a new territory we just took over. He should be back soon, but meanwhile I'll show you around. Come along with me."

As they're going out the door, he flashes those brilliant choppers again and asks, "You married?"

"What's it to you?" Sally says sharply.

She shows him around the dump: sheds, unloading docks, compactors, maintenance garage, shower and locker room. She leaves him with old gimpy Ed Fogleman who got a leg caught in a mulcher but won't quit. Jake Steiner keeps him on as a kind of plant caretaker, and is happy to have him.

Sally goes back to her office, draws her third cup of black coffee of the day from the big perk in Judy Bering's cubbyhole, and gets back to her paperwork.

She is vice president and truck dispatcher at Steiner Waste Control. She directs, controls, hires, fires, praises, berates, curses, and occasionally comforts a crew of tough men, drivers and loaders, who make a living from their strength and their sweat. They work hard (Sally sees to that), and they live hard.

But Sally does more than schedule garbage trucks. She's the office manager. She leans over the shoulder of the bookkeeper. She solicits and reviews bids on new equipment. She negotiates contracts with old and new customers. She deals with the union and approves all the city, state, and federal bumf required, including environmental reports.

Big job. Stress. Tension. Dealing with a lot of hardnoses. But she thrives on it. Because she's a woman making her way in this coarse men's world of the bribed and the bribers, the petty crooks, the thugs on the take, and the smiling lads with their knives hidden up their sleeves. Sally Steiner loves it because it's alive, with a gross vitality that keeps her alert and steaming.

At about 12:30, she runs across Eleventh Avenue and has a pastrami and Swiss on a seeded roll, with iced tea, at the Stardust Diner. She and Mabel, the waitress, exchange ribald comments about the crazy Greek chef who recently flipped a hamburger so high that it stuck to the tin ceiling.

She returns to the Steiner dump. A loaded truck is coming in, driven by Terry Mulloy, a redheaded, red-faced harp. Sitting beside him is his loader, a black named Leroy Hamilton who's big enough to play noseguard for the Rams. Both these guys are beer hounds, and on a hot day you want to stand well upwind from them.

"Hey, Sally baby," Terry calls, waving. "How'ya doing?"

"Surviving," she says, walking up to the truck. "How you two putzes doing?"

"Great," Leroy says. "We're getting a better class of crap today. You know that restaurant on Thirty-eighth? I picked out enough steak scraps to feed my Doberman for a week."

"Bull*shit!*" Sally says. "You two morons are going to have a barbecue tonight."

They laugh. "Hey, baby," Terry says, "when are you and me going to make it? A night on the town. Maybe a show. A great dinner. All you can eat."

"No, thanks," Sally says. "I got no use for shorthorns."

She flips a hand and starts away. "Don't knock it until you've tried it," Terry Mulloy yells after her.

She goes back to her office, smiling. That guy will never give up. But it's okay; she can handle him. And she enjoys the rude challenge.

She works on the next week's schedule, assigning drivers and loaders to the Steiner fleet of trucks. For a couple of years now she's been trying to convince her father to computerize the whole operation. But Jake continues to resist. It's not that they can't afford it; he just doesn't want to turn control over to machines; he's got to see those scraps of paper with numbers scrawled on them.

Late in the afternoon he comes lumping into Sally's office, collapses in the armchair alongside her desk.

"Jesus, Jake," she says, "you smell like a distillery. You been hitting the sauce hard today."

"A lot of people I had to see." He takes off his hat. His balding head is covered with sweat. It's been a warm April day; he looks wiped out.

"You want something?" she asks anxiously. "Coffee? A cold Coke?"

"Nah," he says, "I'm okay. Just let me rest a minute."

"You look like the wrath of God."

"Yeah, well, I've been on the go since this morning. What's been going on around here?"

"Nothing much. The new guy showed up. His name's Tony Ricci."

"That figures," Jake says. "He's Mario Corsini's cousin. Did I tell you that?"

"Yeah, pa, you told me."

"What kind of a guy?"

"A good-looking boy. Fresh—but that's okay."

"Wait'll he puts in a week lifting hundred-pound cans of dreck, he won't be so fresh. You can handle him?"

"Oh, sure, pa. No problem. So tell me, how does the new territory look?"

"Not so bad," Jake says. He takes out his handkerchief, wipes his face. He straightens up in the chair. "Pitzak had some good wheels. Three

Loadmaster compactor trucks only a few years old. The rest of the stuff
is shit, but still rolling. Their dispatcher is a lush; he doesn't know his ass
from his elbow; you'll have to take over."

"Okay, pa, I can do that. What about the customers?"

"Mostly industrial, thank God. Some restaurants, some diners, two
apartment houses. But most of the stuff is clean. Like scrap wood, steel
shavings, and so forth. There's one paint factory and one chemical outfit
that might give us some trouble. We'll have to dump in Jersey. And three
or four printers. But that's only paper, so that's no problem there. We can
bale and sell."

"What kind of printers?"

"One does magazines, a couple do catalogs and brochures, and one does
printing for Wall Street outfits. Annual reports, documents, prospectuses,
stuff like that." ·

"Yeah?" Sally Steiner says. "That's interesting."

2

Late in May, Timothy Cone comes off a case that's a real doozy. Cone's an
investigator for Haldering & Co., an outfit on John Street that provides
"financial intelligence" for corporate and individual clients.

Early in May, a venture capital partnership hired Haldering to look into
something called Ozam Biotechnology, Inc. Ozam had been advertising in
the business media with big headlines: NEW ISSUE! Shares of Ozam available at ten bucks.

The legal and accounting departments of Haldering & Co. couldn't find
any record of Ozam anywhere. It apparently had no bank accounts, wasn't
chartered by the State of New York, nor was it registered with the Securities and Exchange Commission.

So Timothy Cone went to work. He soon found there were two other
eyes doing the same thing: a guy from the SEC and a woman from the
Manhattan District Attorney's office.

The three finally discover that Ozam just doesn't exist. It is an out-and-
out stock swindle dreamed up by a con man named Porfirio Le Blanc.
How much loot he took in on those fraudulent ads they never do determine, but it must have been hefty because when Porfirio flies the coop, he
flies first-class to Bolivia.

No one is interested in trying to extradite the rascal; just getting him out of the country is enough. So the Immigration and Naturalization Service is told to put Señor Le Blanc on the "watch list," and Timothy Cone returns to his cubbyhole office to write out his report.

When he tosses it onto the desk of Samantha Whatley, who bosses the five Haldering & Co. investigators, he slumps in the doorway while she reads it.

"You're a lousy speller," she tells him. Then she shakes her head in disbelief. "Can you believe this? A guy takes out ads in newspapers, and people send him money. *Fan*-tastic."

"It's happened before," Cone says, shrugging. "Years ago there was an ex-carny pitchman working the Midwest. He bought ads in small-town newspapers. All the ad said was: 'Last chance to send in your dollar,' with a P.O. Box number in Chicago. He was doing okay until the postal guys caught up with him."

"Barnum was right," Sam says. "Well, here's a new one for you."

She holds out a file folder, and Cone shuffles forward to take it.

"What is it?" he asks. "Some guy selling the Brooklyn Bridge?"

"No," Sam says, "this is heavy stuff. The client is Pistol and Burns. You know them?"

"The investment bankers? Sure, I know them. Very old. Very conservative. What's their problem?"

"They think they may have a leak in their Mergers and Acquisitions Department."

"Oh-ho. Another inside trading scam?"

"Could be," Samantha says. "Tim, this is a new client with mucho dinero. Will you, for God's sake, try to dress neatly and talk like a gentleman."

"Don't I always?"

She stares at him. "Out!" she says.

Back in his office, he opens a fresh pack of Camels (second of the day) and lights up. He parks his scuffed yellow work shoes atop the scarred desk, and starts flipping through the Pistol & Burns file.

It's a sad story of unbridled greed—and a not uncommon one. About a year ago, P&B is engineering a buyout between a big food-products conglomerate and a smaller outfit that's making a nice buck with a nationwide chain of stores that sell cookies, all kinds, made on the premises, guaranteed fresh every morning. The takeover is a marriage made in heaven. Or, as they say on Wall Street, the synergism is there.

As usual, the ladies and gents in the Mergers and Acquisitions Department of Pistol & Burns work in conditions of secrecy that would do credit to the CIA—so word of the impending deal won't leak out prematurely. But it does. The computers of the Securities and Exchange Commission pick up evidence of heavy trading in the cookie company in the weeks prior to the signing of the buyout documents and the public announcement. The cookie stock goes up almost ten points.

So the SEC launches an investigation to try to discover the insider leak. It turns out that a yuppie-type in the Mortgage Insurance Department of Pistol & Burns, who has nothing to do with mergers and acquisitions and is supposed to know zilch about them, is a drinking buddy of another yuppie in the M&A section. Not only that, but they're both doing coke and shagging the same twitch who supplies the nose candy and also dances naked at a joint on East Thirty-eighth Street called Aristotle's Dream.

The whole thing is a mess. The two Pistol & Burns' yuppies confess their sins and admit they made almost a quarter-mil dealing in shares and options of the cookie corporation in the month prior to the takeover. What's worse, they were paid for their insider information by arbitrageurs and attorneys who work for other investment bankers.

This clique of insiders, all with MBAs or law degrees, make a nice buck until the SEC lowers the boom, and everyone has to cough up their profits, pay fines, and is banned from the securities business for three years. The two original Pistol & Burns insiders also get a year in the slammer, which means they'll be out in four or five months. There is no record of what happens to the skin dancer at Aristotle's Dream.

The entire scandal is a painful embarrassment for Pistol & Burns. It is one of the few remaining investment-banker partnerships on the Street. The original partners, Leonard K. Pistol and G. Watson Burns, have long since gone to the great trading pit in the sky, but the present partners try to preserve the stern probity and high principles and ideals of the two founders. Their oil portraits glower down on the executive dining room, spoiling a lot of appetites.

But Pistol & Burns muddles through, cooperating fully with investigators and prosecutors from the SEC and district attorney's office. P&B also appoints one of the senior partners, Mr. G. Fergus Twiggs, to be Chief of Internal Security. He institutes a series of reforms to make certain such an insider coup will never again tarnish the reputation of such a venerable and respected institution.

(Which somewhat amuses students of the history of our nation's financial community. They happen to know that Leonard K. Pistol kept a teenage mistress, and G. Watson Burns drank a quart of brandy every day, without fail, and once had to be dissuaded from making a cash offer to buy the U.S. Government.)

Timothy Cone, reading all this with enjoyment, pauses long enough to light another cigarette and call down to the local deli for a cheeseburger, an order of French fries, a kosher dill, and two cold Heinekens. He munches on his lunch as he continues reading the preliminary report provided by the client.

After enduring the shame of what comes to be known on Wall Street as The Great Cookie Caper, and after tightening up their internal security precautions, Pistol & Burns now finds itself facing another disgrace involving insider trading.

They're in the last stages of finagling a leveraged buyout of a corporation that makes clothes for kiddies, including diapers with the label of a hotshot lingerie designer and little striped overalls just like gandy dancers once wore. The buyers are a group of the company's top executives, and the transaction includes an issue of junk bonds.

Everything is kept strictly hush-hush, and the number of people with a need to know is kept to a minimum. But during the last two weeks, the volume of trading in Wee Tot Fashions, Inc., usually minuscule, has quadrupled, with the stock up five bucks. An investigator from the SEC is already haunting the paneled corridors of Pistol & Burns, trying to discover who is leaking word of the upcoming deal.

"This state of affairs cannot be allowed to continue," Mr. G. Fergus Twiggs concludes firmly.

So Timothy Cone calls the phone number on the letterhead of the client's report.

"Pistol and Burns." A woman's voice: brisk and efficient.

"Could I speak to Mr. Twiggs?"

"May I ask who is calling?"

"Sure," Cone says cheerfully.

Long pause.

"Who is calling, please," she says faintly.

"Timothy Cone. I'm an investigator with Haldering and Company."

After a wait of almost a minute, he's put through. Twiggs has a deep, rumbling voice. Cone thinks it sounds rum-soaked, aged in oak casks, but maybe that's the way all old investment bankers talk. Cone wouldn't know; he doesn't play croquet.

Their conversation is brief. G. Fergus Twiggs agrees to meet at ten the following morning to discuss "this disastrous and lamentable situation."

"Uh-huh," Cone says. "Okay, I'll be at your office at ten tomorrow morning. Who's the SEC investigator?"

"His name is Jeremy Bigelow. Do you know him?"

"Yeah," Cone says, "I know Jerry. I worked a case with him earlier this month. Good man."

"Seems rather young to me," Twiggs says, and then sighs. "But at my age, everyone seems rather young to me."

Cone smiles. The guy sounds almost human.

. . .

It's a close and grainy evening; when he walks home from John Street to his loft on lower Broadway, he can taste the air on his tongue. It isn't nice. He stops at local stores to buy a large jar of spaghetti with meat sauce, a jug of Gallo Hearty Burgundy, and a link of kielbasa for Cleo, his neutered tomcat, who eats everything, including cockroaches, fish heads, chicken bones—and thrives.

Cone notes mournfully that the outer door of his cast-iron commercial building has once again been jimmied—an almost weekly occurrence. Since it is now later than 6:00 P.M., the ancient birdcage elevator is shut down for the night, so he climbs the six flights of iron staircase to his apartment.

Cleo is waiting for him, and gives him the ankle-rub treatment, crying piteously, until he hands over the sausage. Then the cat takes its treasure under the old claw-footed bathtub and gnaws contentedly while the Wall Street dick mixes himself a vodka and water. He works on that as he heats up the spaghetti in a battered saucepan and sets his desk that doubles as a dining table. The china and cutlery are bits and pieces of this and that. The wineglasses are empty jars of Smucker's orange marmalade.

Samantha Whatley shows up a little after seven o'clock. She's picked up container of mixed greens at a salad bar, and also has two strawberry tarts for dessert and a small chunk of halvah for Cleo.

An hour later, they've got their feet up on the littered table and are drinking noggins of cheap Italian brandy with black coffee. They decide to save the tarts, but Cleo gets the halvah, mewling with delight.

"Good dinner," Cone says.

"Not very," Sam says. "Do you have to buy canned spaghetti?"

"It wasn't canned," he tells her. "It came in a jar."

"Whatever. Is it so difficult to buy a package of pasta, boil it up, and add your own sauce?"

"Oh-ho," he says, beginning to steam, "now I'm supposed to be a gourmet cook, am I? Bullshit! Either eat what the kitchen provides or bring your own. And now that we got that settled, you staying the night?"

"Half the night," she says. "Maybe till midnight or so."

"Okay," he says equably. "I'll put you in a cab."

"My hero," she says. "You talk to Pistol and Burns?"

"Yep. I'm seeing G. Fergus Twiggs tomorrow morning at ten. I'll be in late."

"So what else is new?" She looks at the mattress on the linoleum floor of the loft. It's been spread with clean sheets. "I feel horny," she says.

"So what else is new?" he says.

Timothy Cone is a scrawny, hawkish man who's never learned to shave close enough. Samantha Whatley is a tall drink of water with the lean body of a fashion model and the muscles of a woman at home on a balance beam. He is taller, but stooped, with a shambling gait. She is sharp-featured: coffin jaw and blue-green eyes. His spiky hair is gingery; her long auburn hair is usually worn up, tightly coiled. His nose is a hatchet, and his big ears flop. Her back is hard and elegant. His skin is pale, freckled. She is dark, with a ropy body that holds secret curves and warm shadows. He is all splinters, with the look of a worn farmer: pulled tendons, used muscles.

They have nothing in common except. . . .

Naked on the floor mattress they have another skirmish. Not combat so much as guerrilla warfare with no winners and no losers. They will not surrender, either of them, but assault each other with whimpers and yelps, awaiting the end of the world. They think capitulation shameful, and their passion is fed by their pride.

They recognize something of this. Their relationship is sexual chess that must inevitably end in a draw. Still, the sweat and grunts are pleasure enough for two closed-in people who would rather slit their wrists than admit their vulnerability.

Shortly after midnight, he conducts her downstairs and stops an empty cab.

"Take care," she says lightly.

"Yeah," Cone says. "You, too."

Then he goes back up to his desolate loft, eats both strawberry tarts, drinks a jar of vodka, and wonders what the hell it's all about.

The offices of Pistol & Burns, Investment Bankers, on Wall Street, look like a genteel but slightly frowsty gentlemen's club. The paneled walls display antique hunting prints in brass frames. The carpeting seems ankle-deep. Employees tiptoe rather than walk, and speak in hushed whispers. Even the ring of telephones is muted to a polite buzz. The atmosphere bespeaks old wealth, and Timothy Cone is impressed—not for the first time—by the comfortable serenity that avarice can create.

He is kept waiting only ten minutes, which he endures stoically, and then is ushered into the private office of G. Fergus Twiggs, P&B's Chief of Internal Security. This chamber, as large as Cone's loft, is more of the same. But on the floor is an enormous, worn Persian prayer rug, and on the beige walls are oak-framed watercolors of sailing yachts, most with spinnakers set.

G. Fergus Twiggs is a veritable toby jug of a man: short, squat, plump, with a smile and manner so beneficent that the Wall Street dick can see him with a pewter tankard of ale in one fist and a clay pipe in the other.

He is clad in a three-piece, dove-gray flannel suit of such surpassing softness that it could have been woven from the webs of white, Anglo-Saxon, Protestant spiders. But the pale blue eyes are not soft, nor do they twinkle. They are the unblinking basilisk eyes of an investment banker.

"Thank you for coming by," Twiggs says genially, shaking hands. He gets Cone seated in a leather chair alongside his mastodonic desk. "I needn't tell you how upsetting this entire matter has become; the whole house is disturbed."

"Look, Mr. Twiggs," Cone says, "there's not much I can do about the Wee Tot Fashions deal. The cat is out of the bag on that one. You'll just have to take your lumps."

"I realize that. The problem is how to prevent it from happening again."

"You can't," Timothy says. "Unless you figure a way to repeal human greed—and I doubt if you can do that. Listen, how do you define insider trading?"

"Define it?" Twiggs says, looking at him curiously. "Why, it's the illegal use of confidential information about planned or impending financial activities for the purpose of making a personal profit."

"Yeah, well, that sounds very neat, but it's not that simple. Insider trading has never been exactly defined, even by the Supreme Court. Let me give you a for-instance. Suppose one of your guys is working every night on a megabuck deal. His wife is furious because he's continually late for dinner. So, to explain his long hours, he tells her he's slaving on this big buyout of the ABC Corporation by the XYZ Corporation. His wife mentions it to her hairdresser. He mentions it to another customer. She tells her husband. The husband mentions it to his car dealer, and the dealer runs out and buys ABC Corporation stock and winds up making a bundle. Now who's guilty there? The original investment banker didn't profit from his inside knowledge; he just had a big mouth. And the guy who did profit, the car dealer, was just betting on a stock tip. He didn't have any inside knowledge. How do you stop that kind of thing?"

"Yes," Twiggs says slowly, "I see what you mean."

"Also," Cone goes on, "the leak on the Wee Tot Fashions deal may not have been in your house at all. The arbitrageurs have a zillion ways of sniffing out a deal in the making while it's still in the talking stage. They pick up one little hint, hear one little rumor, that XYZ is going to make an offer for ABC, and they go to work. They try to track the whereabouts of the chairman, president, and CEO of both corporations. They'll even check the takeoffs, flight plans, and landings of corporate jets. They'll bribe secretaries, porters, pilots, chauffeurs, office cleaning ladies, security guards—anyone who can possibly add to their poop on who is meeting whom and what's going on. There's a lot of money to be made on advance knowledge of deals in the works, and the arbs want some of it. But I wouldn't call that insider trading—would you? It's just shrewd investigative work by guys who want a piece of the action."

"I suppose you're right," the little man says, rubbing his forehead wearily. "Very depressing. That men would go to such lengths to make a profit. It wasn't like that in the old days."

"Maybe, maybe not," Cone says. "In the old days there was only a handful of people who knew about a deal in the making—just the principals and a few lawyers—so it was relatively easy to spot the gonnif if someone leaked or made an illegal profit on his own. But now, in any big-money deal, there are hundreds of people with inside knowledge: corporate officers and their staffs, the investment bankers and their staffs, attorneys and their staffs, accountants and their staffs. Then you've got secretaries, telephone operators, and messengers. Any one of them could spill or make a dirty buck."

"Ah, me," Twiggs says, sighing. "So you believe it's impossible to stop insider trading?"

"Sure it is," Cone says cheerily. "As long as people's itch for a dollar overrides their ethics or morals or whatever the hell you want to call them."

"I should think that heavier penalties might be effective."

"Yeah?" Cone says. "Ever hear of the 'hangup gimmick'?"

"The hangup gimmick? What on earth is that?"

"An arbitrageur hears a rumor that ABC Corporation may be bought out by the XYZ Corporation. The arb has a drinking buddy with the legal firm that handles ABC. He calls his lawyer buddy and says, 'I hear XYZ has made an offer for ABC. If the rumor is true, don't say a word. I'll stay on the phone. But if you're silent and then hang up after ten seconds, I'll know which way to jump, and you'll get your share.' So the ten seconds pass in silence, the lawyer hangs up, and the arb rushes to buy ABC stock. Who do you prosecute? The attorney, the insider, hasn't leaked a word, and can swear to it in a court of law. How do you prosecute him? There are a hundred scams like that. So when you talk about heavier punishment for insider trading, you've got to realize how tough it is to get a conviction."

G. Fergus Twiggs gives him a quirky smile. "Are you trying to talk yourself out of a job, Mr. Cone?"

"Nah. I just want you to understand the problems involved. And I'd like to know what you expect Haldering and Company to do about them."

The investment banker takes a handsome pipe from his top desk drawer. He looks down at it, fondles it, then strokes the bowl slowly between his fleshy nose and cheek, inspecting it as skin oil brings out the grain of the brier.

"Being Chief of Internal Security at Pistol and Burns," he says ruefully, "is not a task I sought or relish. I have had no experience in this rather distasteful field. I suppose I was selected for the job because, though it may be difficult for you to believe, I am the youngest of the senior partners. In any event, what I'd like you to do is spend as much time in our offices as you feel is necessary and review all the security precautions I have instituted. Be as critical as you like. Make any suggestions you wish that will make insider trading at Pistol and Burns, if not impossible, then at least more difficult."

"Yeah," Cone says, "I can do that. As long as you understand I can't make the place airtight. No one can. I'll tackle your setup like I was an employee, out to make a dishonest buck from trading on inside secrets. That should be easy; I've got a criminal mind."

Mr. Twiggs smiles again and rises. "I think you're exactly the man for the job," he says. "When do you plan to start?"

"How about tomorrow? Could you spread the word to guards and secretaries and such that I'll be wandering around the place and have no intention of boosting women's purses or swiping a typewriter?"

"Certainly. Is there anything else you need?"

"I don't think so, thanks. I'd start today, but first I want to compare notes with Jeremy Bigelow, the SEC investigator. Maybe he's got some ideas on how the Wee Tot Fashions deal was leaked."

He walks back to John Street. It's a warm, springy day, but the wind is boisterous, and Cone isn't sweating in his ratty olive drab parka and black leather cap. He shambles up Broadway, thinking of the interview and wondering if Twiggs himself might not be making a quick, illicit buck on Pistol & Burns' deals. The guy looks like Santa Claus, but maybe his bag is stuffed with illegal greenbacks.

The Wall Street dick ponders how much gelt it would take for him, Cone, to turn sour. Half a mil? A mil? Five mil? But that kind of thinking is strictly wet dreams; no one is going to offer him that much loot to go rancid. Besides, what's the point of being rich? Right now he's got a job, a place to sleep, a rotten cat, and enough pocket money to buy beer and ham hocks. He even has Samantha—sort of. What more could a growing boy want?

.   .   .

Back in his cubbyhole office, he takes off cap and anorak and lets them drop to the floor because some office thief has snaffled his coat tree. He lights his fourth or fifth cigarette of the day and sits down behind his scarred desk. He calls Jeremy Bigelow at the Securities and Exchange Commission.

"Jerry?"

"Speaking. Who's this?"

"Timothy Cone at Haldering and Company."

"Hey, old buddy! I was thinking of giving you a call. I hear you guys got the Pistol and Burns account."

"Bad news travels fast. Listen, Jerry, you looked into a possible leak on the Wee Tot Fashions deal, didn't you?"

"That's right." Bigelow's voice turns cautious. "I've been working it. You got something for me?"

"Not a jot or tittle, or tot or jittle, whichever the hell it is. Anyway, it adds up to zilch. But I'd like to buy you lunch and pick your brains."

"Lunch? Today?"

"Sure."

"Why not," the SEC investigator says. "Where?"

"I feel like eating street food. Okay by you?"

Bigelow sighs. "The last of the big-time spenders," he says. "All right, I'll eat street. I'll even come over to your place. Meet you outside at, say, twelve-thirty. How does that sound?"

"Just right. There's a new stand near Trinity that's selling hot roti goat. How does that grab you?"

"Instant ulcers—but I'll give it a go. See you."

They meet outside the Haldering & Co. office and start ambling down Broadway. The day has thickened, with clotted clouds blocking out the sun. There's a smell of rain in the air, but it hasn't stopped the lunch-hour throngs from flocking to the street for their falafel fix.

Manhattan is the biggest outdoor buffet in the world. Especially in the financial district, the umbrella carts, vans, trucks, and knockdown booths are all over the place. Foul weather or fair, the street vendors are out hustling and probably dreaming of the day they can build their taco stand into The Four Seasons or maybe sell franchises.

What do you feel like eating? Not falafel? Not hot roti goat? Not tacos? Then how about fried chicken with jalapeño sauce, seeded rolls with cold cuts, sausage heroes, gyros, foot-long franks, turkey hamburgers, pizza, soups hot and cold, Acapulco salads, shish kebab, Philadelphia steak sandwiches, burritos, shrimp parmesan, tortillas, Ben & Jerry's ice cream, chocolate-covered Oreos, coffee, tea, milk, colas, cakes, pies, pastries, nuts, fresh fruit? Sound okay? And you never have to leave a tip!

Cone and Jeremy Bigelow begin their peripatetic luncheon. The first stop is for barley and mushroom soup. They throw away the plastic spoons and drink the rich sludge directly from the foam containers. They try the hot roti goat. Not bad. Then they stop at a Chinese booth for slivers of bamboo stuck through chunks of barbecued pork and kiwi slices. Then cans of cola and ice cream bars covered with a quarter-inch of dark Belgian chocolate.

They eat as they stroll, as everyone else is doing. Meanwhile, between sips and bites, they talk shop.

"What's your take on that Twiggs?" Cone asks.

"I think he's straight," Bigelow says. "A gentleman of the old school. But not too swift when it comes to street smarts. He wanted to hook up everyone at Pistol and Burns to a lie detector. I had to explain to him how easy it is to beat the machine."

"Yeah," Cone says. "Like urinalysis for drugs. There's a couple of ways you can beat that even with an observer there watching you pee in a plastic cup."

"Please," the SEC man says, "not while I'm eating."

"So how do you figure the Wee Tot Fashions leak? The arbitrageurs?"

"I think so, and that's what I'm going to put in my report. I don't believe anyone at Pistol and Burns was on the take. It was just rumor and good detective work by the arbs. Those guys can put two and two together and come up with twenty-two. We checked all the trading in Wee Tot in the last few weeks. Not the odd lots, of course. Just the big trades, like ten thousand shares and up. Most were handled by brokerage houses the arbs use. I looked for personal connections with Pistol and Burns staff, and came up with zip. There was one big trade, ten thousand shares, by an amateur. A woman named Sally Steiner. But she works for a garbage collection outfit on Eleventh Avenue. She couldn't have any access to inside information. She plays the market for fun and games, and just made a lucky pick. Other than that, there's nothing to justify our pushing this thing any farther. What's your interest in this, Tim? What does Twiggs expect Haldering and Company to do?"

"He just wants me to double-check his security precautions."

"That sounds easy enough," Jeremy Bigelow says. "Most of these investment banking houses are as holey as Swiss cheese. You could stroll in and walk out with their checkbooks, and no one would notice, especially if you were dressed like a Harvard MBA."

The SEC investigator is a self-assured guy with such strength of character that he can eat one salted peanut. When Cone first met him, Bigelow came on strong, like working for the Securities and Exchange Commission was akin to holding high office in the Papacy. The Wall Street dick had to swat him down a few times, but then Jerry relaxed, and they were able to work together without too much hassle.

He's a beanpole of a gink who equates height with superiority—but that's okay; superior shrimps cause more trouble. Cone admires him because he can drink gin martinis. Cone loves gin martinis but can't handle them, and leaves them strictly alone—especially since an incident several years ago when he ended up in Hoboken, New Jersey, in bed with a lady midget.

"I got to get back to the treadmill," Bigelow says. "Thanks for the lunch. I'll probably be popping Tums all afternoon, but it tasted good. Let's eat street again—my treat next time."

"Sure," Cone says. "Listen, that woman you mentioned who made the big trade in Wee Tot Fashions ... What was her name?"

"Sally Steiner. Why the interest?"

"Did you talk to her?"

"Of course," Bigelow says, offended. "That's what they're paying me coolie wages for. She's a tough bimbo who practically runs that waste disposal business I told you about. Her father owns it. She claims she bought Wee Tot stock because she wants to get out of garbage and open a store that sells kids' clothes. She figured the annual reports of Wee Tot would help her learn the business. It makes sense."

"Sure it does," Timothy Cone says. "Nice seeing you again, Jerry. Give my best to the wife."

Bigelow looks at him. "How do you know I'm married?" he asks. "I never told you that."

"Beats me," Cone says, shrugging. "I just assumed. You've got that married look. Also, you've got a pinched band of skin around your third finger, left hand, where I figure you wear a ring but maybe take it off during the day in case you meet something interesting."

Bigelow laughs. "You goddamn sherlock," he says. "You've got me dead to rights. I better watch myself with you; you're dangerous."

"Nah," Cone says, "not me. I'm just a snoop. Thanks, Jerry."

"For what?"

"All the info you gave me—like Sally Steiner and so forth. I owe you one."

"Look," the SEC man says, "if you find out anything more about the Wee Tot Fashions leak, you'll let me know?"

"Absolutely," the Wall Street dick vows. "I'm no glory hound."

They shake hands, and Cone watches the other man move away, towering over everyone else on the street. Then he trudges back to Haldering & Co. He stops on the way to buy a knish. He's still hungry.

3

May is a rackety month for Sally Steiner. She is living in a jungle and giving as good or better than the blows and bites she endures.

"Listen, Jake," she says to her father, "I'm going to take a few hours off this afternoon to go see some customers."

"Yeah?" he says, looking up from his tipsheet. "Who?"

"The new people we got from Pitzak."

"I already seen them."

She sighs. "You *saw* them, pa. But so what? I'm the one they call with their kvetches. I want to know who I'm dealing with."

"So do what you want to do," he says. He puts aside his chewed cigar and picks up his whiskey and water. "You're going to do it anyway, no matter what I say. So why ask?"

"I didn't ask," she says, as prickly as he. "I'm telling you."

But there is only one customer she wants to visit: Bechtold Printing, downtown on Tenth Avenue. She's planned this interview and dressed for it. Black gabardine suit. High-necked blouse. No jewelry. Opaque panty-hose. Clunky shoes. With a leather portfolio under her arm. The earnest executive.

"Mr. Frederick Bechtold, please," she says to the lumpy blond recep-tionist, handing over her business card. "From Steiner Waste Control."

The klutz takes a look at the card. "He's in the press room," she says. "I'll see."

It's almost five minutes before the owner comes out, a chunky slob of a man. He's wearing a cap of folded newsprint and an ink-smeared apron that doesn't hide a belly so round that it looks like he's swallowed a spit-toon.

"Zo," he says, peering at her card. "Sally Steiner. You are related to Steiner Waste Control?"

"Daughter," she says brightly. "I just stopped by to see if you're satisfied with our service, Mr. Bechtold. Any complaints? Any way we can im-prove?"

He looks at her in amazement. "Eight years with Pitzak," he says, "and he never came around. No, lady, no complaints. You pick up twice a week, right on schedule. My contract with Pitzak is still good?"

"Absolutely," Sally says. "We'll honor the prices. Nice place you got here, Mr. Bechtold. I've heard about your reputation for top-quality financial printing."

"Zo?" he says, with a smile that isn't much. "I do the *best*. The *best!* You'd like to see my pressroom?"

"Very much."

It's a cavern, with noise and clatter bouncing off cinder-block walls. There's one enormous rotary, quiet now, and four smaller presses clanking along and piling up printed sheets. Sally is surprised at the small workforce—no more than a half-dozen men, all wearing ink-smeared aprons and newsprint caps. Two guys are typing away at word processors. One man is operating a cutter, another a binder. A young black is stacking and packing completed work in cardboard cartons.

"This is my pride," Frederick Bechtold says, placing his hand gently on the big rotary. "West German. High-speed. The very *best*. Six colors in one run. And I use high-gloss inks from Sweden. Expensive, but the people I deal with want only the best."

"You have some big Wall Street accounts, Mr. Bechtold?"

"Absolutely," he affirms. "For them, everything must be just zo."

"Annual reports?" Sally suggests.

"For the color, yes. And in black-and-white, we do brochures, documents, instruction booklets, proxy statements—everything. They know they can depend on Bechtold Printing. They give me a deadline, and I meet it. I have never been late. Never!"

Sally shakes her head in wonderment. "A marvelous operation," she says. "Nice to have met you, Mr. Bechtold. You ever have any complaints about our service, you just give me a call and I'll take care of it."

She goes back to the office and gets to work. First, she finds gimpy Ed Fogleman, who runs the dump.

"Ed," Sally says, "we got a new customer: Bechtold Printing, on Tenth Avenue. It's a clean job; practically all their shit is paper. We'll pick up twice a week. Is there any place we can store the barrels for a day or so before we bale?"

He peers at her, puzzled. "Why do you want to do that, Sal?"

She's prepared for questions. "Because I got a look at their operation, and they use everything from coated stock to blotting paper. Up to now we've been baling everything from good rag to newsprint in the same bundle. I figure maybe we could make an extra buck if we separate the good from the lousy and sell different qualities of scrap paper at different prices."

"Yeah," the old man says slowly, "that makes sense. But who's going to spend the time separating all the stuff? Sounds to me like a full-time job—and there goes your profit."

"That's why I want to hold out the Bechtold barrels," Sally says patiently. "To see if it would be worth our while. Where can I put them temporarily?"

Fogleman chews his scraggly mustache. "Maybe in the storeroom," he says finally. "I can make space. It's against fire regulations 'cause we got inflammables in there, but if it's only for a day or so, who's to know?"

"Thanks, Ed," Sally says gratefully. "I'll get the barrels out as soon as I can."

She goes back to her office and looks out the window every time a truck rolls into the dump. She goes running when she spots Terry Mulloy and Leroy Hamilton in their big Loadmaster compactor.

"Hey, you paskudniks," she yells, and they stop. Terry leans out the window.

"Sally baby," he says, grinning. "You've finally decided you can't resist my green Irish joint."

"Up yours, moron," she says. "Listen, I'm revising schedules and pulling you two bums off that chemical plant on Twenty-fourth Street and giving you Bechtold Printing on Tenth Avenue."

"God bless the woman who birthed you," Leroy Hamilton says. "That chemical place smells something fierce. Gets in your hair, your clothes; you can almost taste that stink."

"Yeah," Sally says, "well, now you've got Bechtold. A nice clean job. Practically all paper. Pickups on Tuesday and Thursday. When you get the stuff, keep it in separate barrels and leave them in the storeroom. Ed Fogleman will show you where."

"What the hell for?" Mulloy asks.

"You know what curiosity did to the cat, don't you?"

"I don't know from cats," he says. "All I know is pussy."

She gives him the finger and stalks away, followed by their whistles.

On Thursday night, she complains to her father and Judy Bering about having to work late on a couple of workmen's compensation cases. It's almost seven o'clock before they leave, and she sees Ed Fogleman drag himself home. Then the dump is almost deserted; only the night watchman is in his hut at the locked gate, flipping through his dog-eared copies of *Penthouse*.

She goes out to the storeroom, puts on the light, starts digging through the barrels of scrap paper from Bechtold. It's almost all six-color coated stock. Someone is running a slick annual report, and the discarded sheets are preliminary press proofs with colors out of register and black type too heavy or too faint.

That's not what she's looking for. She spends more time with black-on-white proof sheets: documents, proxy statements, prospectuses. Nothing of any interest. She gives up and drives home. The next morning she tells Fogleman to empty the barrels and bale everything.

She goes through the same routine on the following Tuesday evening with similar results. She's beginning to think her wild idea, her Big Chance, is a dud. But on the next Thursday night she finds some interesting proof sheets on Pistol & Burns letterheads. She scans them hastily. They look like a plan for a leveraged buyout of Wee Tot Fashions, Inc. She gathers up all the pages she can find that mention Wee Tot, crams them in her leather portfolio, and drives home to Smithtown, singing along with Linda Ronstadt on her stereo deck.

She stops up to visit with her mother for a while. Then when Becky and Martha settle down for an evening of TV, Sally rushes downstairs to the den. She's too excited to eat, but pours herself a Perrier before she goes over the Pistol & Burns documents scavenged from Bechtold's scrap. She reads them three times because some of the type is blurred, and she has to use a magnifying glass to make out certain words and phrases.

Then she does swift computations on her pocket calculator. The next morning she calls her stockbroker and sells some of the dogs in the Steiner portfolio, taking a tax loss. But she accumulates enough funds to buy 10,000 shares of Wee Tot Fashions at a total cost of about $48,000, including commission. Have a hunch, bet a bunch.

A week later, after following the market anxiously, she sells out her Wee Tot stake for about $112,000, and is so elated and unbelieving that she doesn't know whether to weep or laugh.

And a week after that, she's having a coffee with Judy Bering in the outer office when a tall, thin guy, nicely dressed, walks in and smiles at the two women.

"I'm looking for Sally Steiner," he says.

"That's me," Sally says. "Who are you?"

He hands her a card. "Jeremy Bigelow," he says. "Securities and Exchange Commission."

She's sitting naked on a three-legged kitchen stool, hunching forward.

"I think I'm getting splinters in my ass," she says.

"Shut up," Eddie says, "and try to hold that pose. Don't relax. Make yourself tight and hard."

She *is* tight and hard. Her body has a rude grace, heavy through shoulders and hips. Not much waist. The thighs are pillars tapering to unexpectedly slender ankles. A muscled woman. Her skin is satin.

"When's Paul coming back?" she asks.

Her brother sighs. "I told you. He'll ring before he comes up. Don't get so antsy."

He continues sketching, using a soft carpenter's pencil on a pad of grainy paper. He works swiftly, limning her body with quick slashes, flipping pages, trying to catch her solidity, the aggressiveness of her flesh. He was right: She does loom.

After a while she forgets that she's exhibiting herself in front of her brother and thinks about why she's there. Because she wants something from him—or rather from his consenting adult, Paul Ramsey.

That visit from the SEC investigator spooked her. The guy wanted to know how come she had sprung for 10,000 shares of Wee Tot Fashions, Inc. Had she heard something? Did someone tell her something? Did she know anyone at Wee Tot? At Pistol & Burns? Why, suddenly, did she buy such a big block of that particular equity?

Without pause, she scammed the guy silly. She was proud of that. She wanted to get out of garbage hauling, she told him, and open a store that sold kids' clothes. She bought Wee Tot to get their annual reports so she could learn more about the business. Besides, she owned a dozen other stocks. She was in the market for kicks.

He departed, apparently satisfied, and Sally went back to her own office. She was sweating. What if Jeremy Bigelow subpoenas Steiner's customer list and discovers they're collecting trash from Bechtold, who does confidential printing for Pistol & Burns? What if he comes poking around, asking questions of Ed Fogleman, Terry Mulloy, Leroy Hamilton, and learns she's been putting aside barrels of Bechtold waste? Curtains!

She decides she handled her Big Chance stupidly. Too many people involved, too many potential witnesses. And she purchased the stock in her own name. Idiotic! And she bought 10K shares. That would be a trip wire to alert anyone investigating the possibility of insider trading.

Eddie's phone rings. Three times. Then stops.

"That's Paul," he says. "He'll be up in about ten minutes. You can get dressed now. I got some good stuff. But I'll need a couple more sessions."

"Sure," she says. "Anytime."

To her surprise, she finds she's no longer self-conscious, and when Eddie helps her hook up her bra in back, she thinks it's a nice, brotherly thing for him to do. By the time Paul Ramsey shows up, Sally is dressed and sipping a glass of their lousy chianti.

Paul is a tall blond with a sweet smile and more teeth than he really needs. He's got a laid-back manner, and Eddie says that when the world blows up, Paul is going to be the one who murmurs, "Oh, yeah? Cool."

Sally has already decided what she wants to do. She's going to continue picking through Bechtold Printing trash. But if she finds another lead on a takeover, merger, or buyout, she can't invest in her own name, or in the name of anyone else connected with Steiner Waste Control. Too risky. And the stock purchase has got to be less than 10,000 shares.

"Paul," she says, "I got a proposition for you."

"Sorry," he says with his seraphic grin, "my evenings are occupied."

She tells him what she wants. She'll give him the name of a stockbroker. He's to open an account by purchasing shares of AT&T. She'll give him the money. After that, he'll buy and sell on her instructions.

"I'll pay all the losses," she says. "You get five percent of the profits. How about it?"

The two men look at each other.

"Go for it, Paul," Eddie Steiner advises. "My little sister is a financial genius."

"Okay," Paul Ramsey says, shrugging. "Why not?"

Sally has come prepared. She hands over a manila envelope with $2,500 in cash and the name and phone number of her stockbroker.

"Stick with me, kid," she tells Paul, kissing his cheek, "and you'll be wearing diamonds."

"I prefer emeralds," he says.

She goes back to the office, pondering her next move. She's walking from her parking slot when she meets Anthony Ricci. The kid is wearing tight jeans and a Stanley Kowalski T-shirt, and he looks beautiful.

"Hey, Tony," Sally says. "How's it going? You like the job?"

"No," he says with his hundred-watt smile, "but the money is good."

"All money is good," she tells him. "The loading—you can handle it?"

"Sure," he says. "I've done worse. Maybe someday I'll be a driver—no?"

"Why not? We have a lot of turnover. Hang in there, kiddo."

She goes into her office, parks her feet on her desk, and tries to figure how to paw through the Bechtold garbage without endangering Steiner Waste Control. She decides she can't do it by herself. She's got to use fronts, some bubbleheads who won't have a glimmer of what she's doing. She looks out the window and sees Terry Mulloy and Leroy Hamilton wheeling onto the tarmac to dump their load.

"Oh, yeah," Sally breathes.

The next morning, at breakfast, Jake Steiner says to his daughter, "You better take your car. I'll be gone all afternoon. I got things to do."

"Sure, pa," she says. "I'll drive in."

They don't look at each other. She knows about his "things to do." He's going to shtup his twist in Brooklyn.

He drives to the dump in his Cadillac and she follows in her Mazda. By the time she arrives at the office, Jake is on his second cigar and third black coffee. He's also nibbling on a tot of schnapps from a bottle he keeps in his desk.

"You're killing yourself, pa," Sally says.

"Tell me about it," he says, not looking up from his *Times*.

She keeps glancing out her window, watching for the big Loadmaster crewed by Mulloy and Hamilton. Finally, a little after noon, she sees it coming in. She knows the guys are going to take their lunch break. She grabs her shoulder bag and goes running out. She has to wait until they wash up in the locker room.

"Hey, you bums," she says. "Want a free lunch?"

"Whee!" Leroy says. "Christmas in May. What's the occasion, Sally baby?"

"She wants to make nice-nice," Terry says. "I told you she'd come around eventually."

"This is strictly business, you schmuck," Sally says. "Come on, let's go over to the Stardust."

She picks out a table in a back corner of the diner. They give Mabel their order: three cheeseburgers, home fries, cole slaw, and beer.

"Can either of you guys get hold of a pickup or a van?" she asks them.

They look at each other.

"What for?" Mulloy says.

"It's a special job. I need a pickup every Tuesday and Thursday. I want you to load it with the barrels of Bechtold Printing scrap, drive out to my house in Smithtown, and leave the barrels in the garage. The next Tuesday or Thursday when you bring the new barrels out, you pick up the old ones and bring them back here to the dump for baling. Got that?"

"What's this all about?" Terry asks.

"It's about an extra hundred a week for each of you. In cash. Off the books."

They think about that awhile, chomping their cheeseburgers.

"I got a cousin with an old, beat-up Chevy van," Hamilton says slowly. "I could maybe borrow it on Tuesdays and Thursdays. Probably get it for five bucks a shot and gas."

"I'll pay," Sally says promptly. "However you want to work it. Just get those Bechtold barrels out to Smithtown twice a week. I'll rig your Tuesday and Thursday schedules so you'll have plenty of time to make the round trip. Maybe one of you better stick in town on the big truck, and the other guy makes the drive out to the Island in the van."

"But we get a hundred each?" Mulloy says.

"That's right. Per week. Cash. Off the books."

"No trouble with the buttons?" Hamilton says.

"What trouble?" Sally says. "Anyone asks questions, you know from nothing; you're just following the orders of the boss."

"Sounds good to me," Mulloy says, glancing at Hamilton.

"I'll play along," Hamilton says.

She goes back to the office, sets to work rearranging pickup schedules. She lightens up on Mulloy and Hamilton's Tuesday and Thursday assignments so one or both of them will be able to work in the round trip to Smithtown. It's about three o'clock, and Jake is long gone in his Cadillac, when Judy Bering comes into her office.

"There's a woman on the phone," she says. "She's crying. Sounds hysterical. Something about your father."

"Jesus," Sally says, knowing this can't be good. "All right, put her on my line."

She listens awhile to the wails, the sobs, the incoherent babbling. Finally she figures out what has happened.

"What's your name?" she says sharply, interrupting the woman's desperate howls.

"What? What?"

"Your name. What's your name?"

"Dotty. My name is Dotty."

"Dotty what?"

"Uh, Dotty Rosher."

"All right now, Dotty, listen to me. Lock your door and get dressed. Go into the living room and just sit there. Don't do a goddamn thing. Don't call anyone or talk to anyone. I'm coming to help you. To *help* you, Dotty. I'll be there as soon as I can. Now give me your address and phone number."

She makes quick notes, hangs up, then has the presence of mind to go to the office safe. They keep the petty cash in there, but it's hardly "petty"—almost five thousand in small bills in case the local cops come around, or the fire inspectors, plumbing inspectors, electrical inspectors, sanitation inspectors. The petty cash is not for bribes, exactly. Just goodwill.

Sally grabs up a handful of twenties and fifties, stuffs them in her shoulder bag. She stalks out, grim-faced.

"I listened in, Sal," Judy Bering says, beginning to weep. "I'm sorry."

"Yeah," Sally Steiner says.

She drives her Mazda like a maniac, but crosstown traffic is murder, and it's almost an hour and a half before she gets over to Park Slope.

Dotty Rosher turns out to be a little thing, a piece of fluff. A strong west wind would blow her away. She's got wide blue eyes, a mop of frizzy blond curls, Cupid's-bow lips, and a pair of lungs that make Sally look like a boy. She's fully dressed—for all the good that does.

"Where is he?" Sally demands.

"I got your phone number from his business card. It was in his wallet, but I swear I didn't—"

"Where is he?" Sally screams at her.

"In the bedroom. He just, you know, just went out. I thought he had fainted or something, but then I couldn't—"

"Shut your yap," Sally says savagely.

She goes into the bedroom. The body of her father, naked, is lying on rumpled pink sheets. His mouth is open, eyes staring. He is dead, dead, dead. She looks down at the pale, flaccid flesh and varicose veins with distaste. His shrunken penis is lost in a nest of wiry gray hair.

"You son of a bitch," Sally says bitterly, then bends to kiss his clammy cheek.

She goes back into the living room and tells Dotty Rosher what must be done.

"I can't. I just can't."

"You do it," Sally says stonily, "or I walk out of here right now and leave you with a naked corpse. You can explain it to the cops. Is that what you want?"

So, together, they dress the remains of Jake Steiner, wrestling with his heavy body while they struggle to get him into undershirt and shorts, knitted sport shirt, trousers, jacket, socks and shoes. They remember to lace up the shoes, close his fly. Then they drag him off the bed into the living room, tugging him by the armpits, his heels scuffing the shag rug. They get the body seated in an armchair, head flopped forward, arms dangling.

Dotty Rosher looks ready to pass out. Her mouth is working, and she's beginning to claw at her throat.

"You better get a drink of something," Sally advises.

"I think I'll have a Grasshopper," Dotty says faintly. "They're really delicious. Would you like one?"

"No, thanks. Go have your Grasshopper."

Sally fetches her father's half-full tumbler of cognac from the bedroom and sets it on the end table alongside his armchair. Then she tips it over so the brandy spills on the table and drips down onto the rug. She inspects the scene, then knocks the tipped glass to the floor. Now it looks authentic: man with history of heart trouble stricken with an attack while drinking.

Dotty comes back with her Grasshopper, looking a little perkier. Sally outlines the scenario for her, speaking slowly and distinctly.

"My father owned this apartment, but you rented it from him. Got that? He and I came up to collect next month's rent. *He and I* came here together. That's very important. Can you remember that? We were sitting in the living room talking, and you offered us drinks. I didn't want anything, but Jake had a glass of brandy. He took a couple of swallows and suddenly collapsed. We tried to revive him but nothing helped. Got all that?"

Dotty nods.

"Just keep your mouth shut," Sally says, "and let me do the talking. Okay? You behave and there'll be a nice piece of change in it for you. Capeesh?"

"What?"

"Do you understand what I'm telling you?"

"Oh, sure."

So Sally calls 911 and explains that her father has died unexpectedly, and since he had a history of heart trouble, she thinks it was a sudden attack.

While they're waiting for the paramedics and cops, she makes three more calls. The first is to Judy Bering.

"He's gone," Sally says. "I may not be in for a couple of days. I'm depending on you to keep the wheels turning."

"Sally, I'm sorry, so sorry."

"I know, kiddo, and thanks. Listen, if anyone comes around asking questions, just tell them you know from nothing and refer them to me. Okay?"

"Of course, Sal. I can keep my mouth shut."

"That's the way to do it. I'll let you know when the service is scheduled in case you and any of the guys want to come."

"I'll take up a collection. For flowers."

"Yeah, that would be nice."

Her second call is to Jake's personal physician. She explains that her father dropped dead after drinking half a glass of brandy.

"I'm not surprised," the doctor says. "I warned him, but he wouldn't listen. I'm sorry, Sally."

"Yeah, thanks. I guess they'll take the body to the Medical Examiner, won't they?"

"That's the customary procedure if no physician was present at the time of death."

"Do you know anyone there? I mean, I'd like to get the body released as soon as possible."

"I understand. I'll do everything I can."

"Thanks, doc. I knew I could count on you."

Finally she calls Eddie, tells him the true story of their father's death, and what she's doing to cover it up. Her brother starts weeping, a soft, keening sound.

"I loved him," he says. "I really did."

"I know, baby."

"Jesus," Eddie says, "this will be the end of ma."

"Nah," Sally says. "Becky is stronger than you think. Eddie, can you come out to Smithtown? I want you there when I tell her. Take a cab if you have to. You've got enough money?"

"I can manage. I'll be there as soon as possible."

"Bring Paul if you like. You can stay there for a few days. Until the funeral. Plenty of room for both of you."

"Yeah, maybe we'll do that. Sal, are you all right?"

"I'm surviving."

"My God," he says, "I couldn't have done what you did. I wouldn't have the balls for it."

"Sure you would," she says.

The paramedics and cops show up. Jake Steiner is pronounced definitely dead. Statements are taken from both Sally Steiner and Dotty Rosher. While a uniformed cop is scribbling in his notebook, the plainclothesman in charge, a big, beefy guy, wanders about the apartment, hands in his pockets. He seems to be whistling noiselessly.

The body is finally removed on a gurney, covered with a rubber sheet. The plainclothesman crooks a finger at Sally, and the two go into the kitchen. The cop fishes in his pocket and comes up with a little plastic bag. Inside is a chewed cigar butt.

"You forgot this," he says, staring at Sally. "It was in the ashtray on the table next to the bed."

She dips into her shoulder bag, picks out two fifty-dollar bills.

"For your favorite charity," she says.

"Thank you," he says, taking the money and handing her the plastic bag. "My sincere condolences on your loss."

She's in the funeral home, holding herself together while a parade of old guys come up and tell her what a mensch her father was. They were Jake's gin rummy and pinochle pals, and all Sally can say is, "Thank you very much."

Then the uniformed doorman tells her there's a man downstairs who'd like to talk to her. His name is Mario Corsini.

"Jesus X," Sally says. "All right, I'll be down in a minute."

She looks around. Everything seems under control. Eddie is holding up well, and they hired a special van with a lift so Becky in her wheelchair could be transported to the funeral home and eventually to the cemetery. Paul is there. Martha is there. And a crowd of relatives, friends, and neighbors. More people than Sally expected. Dotty Rosher isn't there. *Got tsu danken*!

The hearse is parked at the curb, followed by a long line of black limousines. The chauffeurs have congregated, and are smoking up a storm and laughing. The single Cadillac limousine parked across the street is a stretch job, silver-gray.

"Mr. Angelo would like to talk to you," Corsini says.

"Now?" Sally says indignantly. "Can't it wait?"

"Just a couple of minutes," he says. "We didn't want to come inside."

"I'd have kicked your ass out," she says, and means it.

She crosses the street and climbs into the back, alongside Vic Angelo. Corsini sits up front behind the wheel, but turns sideways so he can keep an eye on Sally and listen to what's going on.

"My sincere condolences on your loss," Angelo says.

"Thanks."

"Your father was an old friend."

"Uh-huh."

"But now we got a business problem. The garbage dump. Who inherits?"

"My mother, my brother, me."

"And who's going to run it?"

"Who do you think?" Sally says angrily. "Me. I've practically been running the joint for the past ten years."

"It's no business for a woman," Angelo says, shaking his head regretfully. "Too rough. We'll make you a nice offer."

"Screw your offer," Sally says wrathfully. "I'm hanging on to the dump. You'll still get your tax. Jake is dead, but the business belongs to my family and that's where it's going to stay."

Mario Corsini grins. Or at least he shows a mouthful of big, yellowed teeth. "I don't think so," he says.

Sally stares at the two bandidos. If she had her pistol she would have popped both of them, right there. She knows exactly what they can do to Steiner Waste Control: trouble with the union, trouble with city inspectors, maybe firebombs in the trucks if they want to play hard. There's no way she can fight that. She could run to the DA and scream about the monthly payoffs—but where's the proof?

"All right," she says, "you want to take over, you can do it. But you'll be throwing away a fortune."

"What's that supposed to mean?" Angelo says.

"You guys ever play the stock market?" Sally asks.

4

"I'm going to gird a loin," Timothy Cone says.

"You're going to *what?*" Samantha Whatley demands.

"Haven't you ever girded your loins? It's something like hoisting yourself with your own petard."

"Oh, shut up," she says crossly, "and get to work."

"That's what I'm trying to tell you," he explains patiently. "I'll be out of the office the rest of the week. I'm supposed to investigate internal security at Pistol and Burns, and make suggestions for improvements."

"Then *do* it!"

He slouches out of her office and ambles down Broadway to Wall Street. It's a sultry day, and he's happy he left his raincoat at home. He's wearing his black leather cap and his old corduroy suit.

G. Fergus Twiggs must have spread the word because, after identifying himself, the Wall Street dick has no problems getting into Pistol & Burns. He's allowed to roam the hushed corridors, examine offices, poke into closets, and check the fire escape doors to see if they can be opened from the outside.

Cone doesn't leave the offices during the lunch hour because he wants to see if any high-powered executives come reeling back, their eyes glazed with a three-martini lunch. He strikes out on that; all the P&B employees seem sober, industrious, and dull.

"Look," he says to Mr. Twiggs at the end of the first day, "I'll put everything in a final report, but there are things you should do immediately, so I think I better pass them along to you personally every day."

"It's that bad, is it?" the cherubic senior partner says.

"It's not a disaster," Cone says, "but you've got to learn to operate defensively. I don't mean you've got to make this place into a fortress, but you should take some more precautions. Or one of these days some outlaws are going to stroll in here and waltz out with the family jewels."

"What kind of precautions?"

"Well, for starters, you've got one security guard on the front door. I'm sure he's a fine old gentleman, but he is old and he is fat. It would take him a while to suck in his gut before he could get that big revolver out of his dogleg holster. Get a younger guy on the door. Get another two or three to wander around. They can be nicely dressed, but armed and maybe wearing badges."

"What else?" Twiggs says, making notes.

"All your typewriters and business machines should be bolted to the desks. You can even get attachments with burglar alarms, if you want to go that far. But you've got a zillion dollars' worth of portable machinery in here that could be carted off with no trouble at all. Bolt it down."

"Good idea," the senior partner says. "Anything else?"

"Yeah, those paper shredders you're using to destroy confidential documents. . . . They're antiques. Shredded documents can be pasted together again. The Iranians taught us that when they re-created CIA secret memos from strips of paper lifted from the shredders in our embassy. You need new models that turn paper into confetti."

"Excellent suggestion. More?"

"Not today," Cone says. "I'll be back tomorrow and take a closer look. I'll stop by at the end of the day and give you my report."

"I think you're doing a fine job."

"It's all practical stuff. It's not going to stop insider leaks, but it may help. Like keeping a cleaning woman who's on the take from delivering the contents of your wastebaskets to some wise guys."

At the end of the second day, he says to Twiggs, "This one is going to cost you bucks. You've got your Mergers and Acquisitions people scattered all over the place. An office here, an office there. That's an invitation to leaks. You've got to consolidate that whole department. They can still have their individual offices, but all of them have to be in the same area. And that area has to be behind a locked door that can only be opened by authorized personnel with a computer-coded card."

"It's beginning to sound more and more like a fortress," Twiggs says with a wan smile.

Cone shrugs. "You want to cut down on the possibility of leaks? This is one way to do it."

On his final day at Pistol & Burns, he says to the senior partner, "This one is going to cost you *big* bucks. Your M-and-A people are writing too many office memos, too many suggestions, projections, analyses of upcoming deals—and all on paper."

"We've got to communicate," Twiggs protests.

"Not on paper you don't. Computerize the whole operation. If anyone has something to say on a possible takeover, buyout, or merger, he puts it

on the computer. Anyone else who's involved can call it up on his moni-
tor—but only if he knows the code word. You understand? Nothing typed
on paper. And everything in the computer coded so that it can only be
retrieved by personnel who have a need to know, and have the key word
or number allowing them access. Also, the computer can keep a list of
who requests access to the record."

G. Fergus Twiggs shakes his head dolefully. "What's the world coming
to?" he asks.

"Beats the hell out of me," Timothy Cone says.

He plods back to Haldering & Co. to pick up his salary check. He
figures he's done a decent job for Pistol & Burns. If they want to follow
his suggestions, fine. If not, it's no skin off his ass.

But something is gnawing at him. Something he heard or saw that flicks
on a red light. Maybe it was something Bigelow said, or Twiggs. Maybe
it was something he observed at Pistol & Burns. He shakes his head violently, but can't dislodge whatever it is. It nags him, a fragment of peanut
caught in his teeth.

When he gets back to his office, there's a message on his desk: Call
Jeremy Bigelow. So, without taking off his cap, Cone phones the SEC
investigator.

"Hiya, old buddy," Jerry says breezily. "How did you make out at Pistol
and Burns?"

"Like you said, it's as holey as Swiss cheese. I gave them some ways to
close the holes."

"But no evidence of an insider leak?"

"I didn't find any."

"That's a relief. I wrote in my report it was the arbs who caused the
run-up of the stock. I guess I was right."

"Uh-huh," Cone says.

"So much for the good news. Now comes the bad. We got another
squeal on insider trading."

"Oh, Jesus," the Wall Street dick says. "Don't tell me it's a Pistol and
Burns' deal."

"No, this one is at Snellig Firsten Holbrook. You know the outfit?"

"The junk bond specialists?"

"That's right. They're supposed to have the best security on the Street,
but they're handling a leveraged buyout and someone is onto it. The stock
of the takee is going up, up, up. Listen, could you and I meet on Monday?
Maybe we can figure out what's going on."

"Maybe," Cone says, striving mightily to recall what he cannot remember.

·   ·   ·

He wakes the next morning, hoping the night's sleep has brought to mind what he's been trying to recollect; sleep does that sometimes. But all he can remember is the entire pepperoni pizza he ate the night before.

He goes over to Samantha's place on Saturday night. She won't be seen with him in public, fearing someone from Haldering will spot them and office gossip will start. That's okay with Cone; he's willing to play by her rules.

She serves a dinner of baked chicken, Spanish rice, and a salad. They also have a bottle of chilled Orvieto, which puts them in a mellow mood. They have a nice, pleasant evening of fun and games, and Cone is home by 1:00 A.M. He gives Cleo fresh water and some of the chicken skin and bones he doggie-bagged from Sam's dinner.

Sunday is just as relaxed. He futzes around the loft, smokes two packs of Camels, drinks about a pint of vodka, with water, and digs his way through *Barron's* and the business section of the *New York Times*. In the evening he has a one-pound can of beef stew with a heel of French bread he finds in the refrigerator, so hard that he has to soak it in the stew to render it edible. Cleo gets the remainder of the chicken scraps.

On Monday he's late for work, as usual. Jeremy Bigelow shows up at ten o'clock, carrying a fat briefcase. Cone calls down to the local deli for two black coffees and two toasted bagels with a schmear. They wait for their breakfast to arrive before they get down to business.

"Look," Cone says, "it would help if you could tell me how the SEC works on insider trading scams. Then maybe I'll know what you're talking about."

"It's a two-level operation," Jerry says, gnawing on his bagel. "We get a lead and start gathering facts. That's where I come in. If we can't find any evidence of hanky-panky, the investigation is usually dropped. If things look sour, the staff goes to the Commission and gets an order for a formal inquiry. That's when we get power of subpoena."

"Yeah, but what gets you moving? Where do the leads come from?"

"Computers mostly. We couldn't live without them. You know how many companies are listed on all the stock exchanges in the country?"

"No idea."

"Neither do I—exactly. But I'd guess about twelve thousand. How could you check all those every day by hand? Im-fucking-possible. So the computers are programmed to pick up unusual activity. Say a stock has been trading an average of fifty thousand shares a day for months and months. Suddenly the trading volume goes up to maybe a million shares a day. The computer flashes a red light, bells go off, and an American flag pops from the top of the machine and starts waving madly back and forth."

"And that's when you move in?"

"Sure," Bigelow says. "We want to know who's trading. Most of the time it's entirely innocent. A rumor got floated on Wall Street, and a lot of amateur arbitrageurs are hopping on what they hope will be a band-wagon—and probably won't."

"So your computers do it all?"

"Hell, no. Just the first line of defense. We also get tips from brokerage houses. *Their* computers pick up unusual trading activity. They report to us because they don't want to get their balls caught in the wringer. Also, we get anonymous tips from divorced wives and husbands who want the boom lowered on their former mates. And sometimes we get squeals from honest executives who know or suspect the guy in the next office is buying or selling illegally on the basis of the next quarterly earnings report."

"You check out the executives first?"

"Of course. If they're officers of the company, they've got to declare buys and sells. If they don't, they're in the soup."

"Look," the Wall Street dick says, "I know you haven't got the time or staff to check out every piddling little trade. I mean you're not going to investigate Joe E. Clunk of Hanging Dog, North Carolina, who bought ten shares of this or that. So what do you look for?"

"Generally I look for trades of ten thousand shares or more. But if a corporation officer is involved, he's as guilty if he trades a hundred shares as he would be if he traded a hundred thousand on the basis of inside knowledge."

"But he could get his relatives and friends to trade for him."

"Of course," Jerry says, grinning. "Happens all the time. That's when we've got to play detective, track down relationships, and tell them all they've committed a no-no."

"And what do they get for that?"

"Usually they have to surrender their profits, pay a fine, and are put on probation. A few go to the clink."

"For how long?"

"I think the longest sentence for insider trading has been four years."

"Which means the guy is out in eighteen months."

"Probably," Bigelow says, shrugging. "But that's not my problem. I'm supposed to make the case. What the judge decides is something else again."

Cone lights up a cigarette, after offering the pack to the other man. But Jerry declines.

"I stopped smoking four years ago," he says virtuously. "You know what those things are doing to your lungs and heart?"

"Please," Cone says, holding up a hand. "I've heard all the lectures and none of them take. Let me enjoy my vices. Now what's this Snellig Firsten Holbrook deal you mentioned on the phone?"

"Like I said, it's a leveraged buyout. An old outfit named Trimbley and Diggs, up in Massachusetts. They make brooms, brushes, wooden clothespins, and stuff like that. But they also own some choice shorefront real estate. They went public about twenty years ago and have been paying a small dividend—but never missing a quarter. It's a small outfit, Tim, General Motors it ain't. If their daily trading volume hits, say, ten thousand shares, it's a big day. Now the top executive officers want to buy them out, take the company private again, and develop their beachfront properties. Snellig Firsten Holbrook is handling the deal. But suddenly the daily volume is way up—almost a hundred thousand shares last Friday. Nobody can figure how the buyout leaked. Someone is gobbling up shares, and we want to know who."

"The arbs?" Cone asks.

Bigelow shakes his head. "I doubt it. Not enough loot in it for them."

"Yeah," Cone says, "I can understand that. But what's all this got to do with me? I work for Haldering, and we don't have Snellig Firsten Holbrook as a client, or Trimbley and Diggs either. So why am I supposed to get involved?"

"One," Jeremy says, holding up a thumb, "as a personal favor to me. Two," he says, pointing a forefinger, "because it's a puzzle, and I've got you made as a guy who likes puzzles. And three," he adds, extending his middle finger, "who the hell do you think recommended you to Pistol and Burns?"

"Jesus," Cone says, "you're really calling in your chits, aren't you?"

"Just take a look at it, will you? I brought you computer printouts of trading and a record of the stock since the leveraged buyout got started."

"What's it selling for now?"

"About eight dollars a share. A week ago it was four."

"All right," the Wall Street dick says, sighing. "Leave your bumf and I'll take a look. No guarantees."

"Thanks, Tim," Bigelow says gratefully. "In return, the SEC can be very cooperative with Haldering and Company if the occasion ever arises."

"Who the hell cares?" Cone says roughly. "When are you going to buy me a street lunch like you promised?"

"You give me a lead on this, I'll take you to The Four Seasons for dinner."

"Yeah? They got ham hocks?"

.   .   .

He would never lie to Samantha Whatley on a personal matter. But he will lie to her *officially*, as his boss at Haldering & Co. That he can do with nary a qualm.

He lounges in the doorway of her office. "Listen," he says seriously, "I've got to go back to Pistol and Burns and finish up that job."

"Yeah?" she says. "I thought you were all done with them."

"I need a couple of more days. Clean up some odds and ends. Then I want to talk to Twiggs about the final report."

She looks at him suspiciously. "So what you're telling me is that you'll be out of the office again this week."

"Just until Wednesday or so. I'll have it wrapped up by then."

"You better," she says. "I've got three new files waiting for you."

"Gee, thanks, boss," he says. "That makes me feel warm all over."

Jeremy Bigelow has left his battered briefcase stuffed with all the skinny on the Trimbley & Diggs buyout.

"You can borrow the briefcase," he tells Cone. "But I want it back eventually."

"What for?" Cone asks. "Sentimental attachment? It's a piece of junk. You should pay me for taking it off your hands."

So he plods up Broadway in a warm drizzle, lugging the case and feeling no guilt at having conned Sam. The world isn't going to come to an end just because he finagled a couple of days off. Besides, it is a good cause: cooperation with an agency of the U.S. Government.

Back in his loft, he pops a tall can of Bud. Then he opens Bigelow's briefcase and dumps the contents onto his wooden table. He sets the empty case on the floor, and Cleo immediately jumps in and curls up contentedly.

"Leave your fleas in there," Cone tells the cat.

He reads all the papers and reads them again. Then he sits back and considers the case. It's pretty much as Bigelow described it. The first printed documents are dated about three weeks previously and deal with Snellig Firsten Holbrook's suggested plan for the proposed buyout of Trimbley & Diggs, Inc.

Subsequent printed documents amend and refine the plan. Then there's a letter assuring the principals involved that the required funds can be raised through the sale of high-risk bonds, and Snellig Firsten Holbrook has "every confidence" the bond issue will be oversubscribed.

All that is routine stuff, and Cone can't see anything freaky going on. What interests him more are the computer records of trading activity in Trimbley & Diggs. The volume began to climb about ten days ago, and the stock, listed on the Nasdaq National Market, rose in value steadily from about $4 a share to its current price of slightly over $8. Nice. The buyers are probably rubbing their sweaty palms with glee and wondering whether to hold on or sell and take the money and run.

Cone leans down to address Cleo, who is snoozing in the briefcase. "Sometimes the bulls make money," he says, "and sometimes the bears make money. It's the pigs who always get stuck."

But who are these lucky investors who doubled their stake in about ten days? Cone goes over the computerized trading records again, and what he finds amuses him. He can't spot any trades of 10,000 shares or more, but there are plenty for 9,000 shares. Timothy figures that's because a lot of wise guys have heard that the SEC is interested in trades of 10K shares and over. If they buy or sell 9,000 shares, they think they're home free. Cone is surprised Jeremy Bigelow didn't spot that, and he wonders just how swift the guy is.

The big buyers of Trimbley & Diggs' stock are from all over the country, but seem to be concentrated in New York, Atlantic City, Miami, New Orleans, and Las Vegas. Also, most of the buyers' names end in vowels. That gets Cone's juices flowing because all those cities are big mob towns—which may mean something or absolutely nothing.

Since no one is going to finance his travels to investigate out-of-state buyers, he concentrates on the names of New York investors. One that catches his eye is a man named Paul Ramsey, who lives on Forty-seventh Street at an address that would place his residence west of Tenth Avenue.

That sets off alarm bells because, after Cone returned from Nam, he lived for two years in a five-story walk-up on Forty-eighth east of Tenth, and he knows what a slummy neighborhood that is. It's in the middle of Hell's Kitchen, with rundown tenements, sad mom-and-pop bodegas, dusty beer joints, and boarded-up buildings awaiting demolition.

Unless the whole area has been gentrified since Cone lived there, it's hard to believe one of the residents is a stock market plunger. Not many ghetto dwellers deal in gold coins either.

He goes through the computer printouts for the fourth time, checking Paul Ramsey's trades. It looks to Cone like the guy now owns 27,000 shares of Trimbley & Diggs, Inc., bought at an average of six bucks a share. If he sells out today, he'll walk away with a profit of about $54,000. Not bad for someone who lives on streets where a mugger would be happy with a take of $10—enough for a vial of crack.

Cone pulls on his leather cap and takes his grungy raincoat in case the drizzle has thickened. Just before he leaves the loft, he checks the short-barreled S&W .357 in his ankle holster. Reassured, he ventures out to visit his old neighborhood.

"Guard!" he admonishes a startled Cleo before he leaves.

Down on the street, he finds the drizzle hasn't just thickened, it's as if someone has turned a tap on over Manhattan. And there's not a cab in sight. Cursing his luck, Cone bows his head against the rain and humps his way to the nearest subway station. He tries to figure the best way to get to Forty-seventh Street and Tenth Avenue, and finally realizes there is no "best" way. No matter what his route, he's going to get soaked.

But almost a half-hour later, when he exits at Fiftieth Street and Eighth Avenue, the downpour has ended. The city remains a sauna, and Cone reflects morosely that all he needs is someone to beat him with birch branches. He carries his raincoat and splashes through puddles and running gutters down to Forty-seventh Street and westward to Tenth Avenue.

Ramsey's building looks the way Cone imagined it: peeling paint, torn shades, cracked windows. It is dreary and dying, and no way would you figure it as the residence of a Wall Street plunger.

There's a spindly-legged little girl on the sidewalk. She's about nine, and she's skipping rope to the repeated chant:

Hubba, hubba, hubba,
You better use a rubbeh,
Or your ma will be a bubbeh.

A freckled, red-haired boy is sitting on the sagging stoop, watching her. He looks to Cone to be about eleven, going on forty-six.

"You live here?" Cone asks him.

The kid stares at him coldly. "What's it to you?"

"I'm looking for Paul Ramsey. You know him?"

"I don't know nothing, I don't."

"He's supposed to live in this building."

"I'm not saying, I'm not."

"But you heard the name?"

"I told you I don't know, I told you."

Cone sighs. "Who are you—Joey Echo? All right, I'll see for myself." He starts up the stoop. The kid stands up.

"Hey," he says, "you want to know about this guy, you want to know? Cost you a buck."

Cone digs out his wallet, fishes out a dollar, hands it over.

"I don't know nothing, I don't," the kid yells and darts away.

Outraged, Timothy watches the juvenile con man race down the street. Then he laughs at how easily he's been scammed. He figures that kid will end up President or doing ten-to-twenty in Attica.

He goes into the cramped vestibule that smells of urine and boiled cabbage. There's a bellplate but no names are listed in the slots. But there are names on the mailboxes. Two are listed for Apartment 5-A.

One is Paul Ramsey.
The other is Edward Steiner.

He gets a cab going downtown on Ninth Avenue. The hackie wants to talk baseball, but Cone isn't having any; he's got too much to brood about.

There's this woman, Sally Steiner, who goes for 10,000 shares in Wee Tot Fashions, Inc., in an insider trading scheme at Pistol & Burns. And there's this man, Paul Ramsey, who buys 27,000 shares of Trimbley & Diggs, Inc., in what is apparently another insider scam at Snellig Firsten Holbrook. And this Ramsey lives in an apartment with a guy named Edward Steiner.

Maybe the two Steiners aren't related, don't even know each other. Coincidences do happen—but don't bet on it. The Wall Street dick wonders how far he should push what he's already calling the "Steiner Connection."

He's back in the loft, pacing back and forth, when a light bulb flashes over his head, just like a character in a cartoon strip. And suddenly he remembers what he's been trying to recall these past few days, something he heard that struck a tinny note. It comes to him now.

Jeremy Bigelow said that when he interviewed Sally Steiner in the course of his investigation of the Wee Tot Fashions deal, she claimed she bought her 10,000 shares because she wanted to get Wee Tot's reports. She was planning to quit the garbage business. She hoped to learn more about the manufacture, distribution, and sale of children's clothing.

Now, as Cone well knows, people sometimes do buy stock to get a company's reports and possibly learn about the business. And sometimes they buy stock just so they can attend the annual meeting of stockholders and may get a free box lunch. But those objectives can be achieved by purchasing one share, ten, or maybe a hundred. But buying 10,000 shares just to get quarterly reports? Ridiculous!

Cone curses his own stupidity; he should have caught it from the start. It's obvious to him now that Sally Steiner bought her stake because she knew something or had heard something about the takeover of Wee Tot Fashions, and was out to make a quick buck.

He goes to the wall telephone in his greasy little kitchenette and calls Neal K. Davenport, a detective with the New York Police Department. He's worked with Davenport on a few things, and the city bull owes him.

"Hey, sherlock," the NYPD man says cheerily. "How'ya doing? I haven't heard from you in weeks. You've found another patsy in the Department?"

"Nah," Cone says, "nothing like that. I just haven't been working anything you'd be interested in."

"Glad to hear it. Every time you get me involved, I end up sweating my tush. So why are you calling now?"

"It's about the commercial garbage-collection business."

"Oh?" Davenport says. "Thinking of changing jobs, are you? I'd say you're eminently qualified. You want a letter of recommendation?"

"Cut the bullshit," Cone says, "and just tell me if I'm right. Private garbage collection, waste disposal, and cartage in Manhattan is pretty much controlled by the Families—correct?"

"So I've heard," the NYPD man says. "They're supposed to have the whole fucking city divided up into districts and neighborhoods. If you want to pick up shit, you've got to pay dues to the bentnoses. There was an investigation years ago, but nothing came of it. The DA's witness disappeared and hasn't been heard from since. So what else is new?"

"Thanks," Cone says. "Nice talking to you."

"Hey, wait a minute," Davenport says. "You got something on the mob's connection?"

"Not a thing," Cone assures him. "If I come across anything, you'll be the first to know."

"I won't hold my breath," the city cop says.

Cone hangs up and stares at Cleo thoughtfully.

"Something stinks," he tells the cat. "And it ain't garbage, kiddo."

5

Sally Stalls Vic Angelo and Mario Corsini for two weeks. It's a gamble; if she can't come up with a winner, then she loses Steiner Waste Control and access to inside secrets in trash collected from Bechtold Printing. And that'll be the end of her Big Chance.

She conned the two villains in Angelo's car outside the funeral home where Jake lay in his coffin.

"Look," she says to them, "I got a boyfriend on Wall Street. He's a lawyer in the Mergers and Acquisitions Department of a big investment banker. I won't tell you which one. Anyway, he gets in on the ground floor on mergers, takeovers, and buyouts. There's a lot of money to be made if you get advance notice of these deals. I've been making a mint. You guys let me keep Steiner Waste Control, and I'll feed you the same inside information I get from my boyfriend."

The two men stare at her, then turn to look at each other.

"I don't like it," Angelo says. "Insider trading is a federal rap. Who needs it?"

"Wait a minute, Vic," Corsini says. "The insider here is this girlie's boyfriend. If he wants to shoot off his mouth, it's his problem. The people he tells can claim they bought on a stock tip."

"Right!" Sally says enthusiastically. "I tell you it's foolproof. I've played four deals and haven't lost a cent."

Corsini gives her a two-bit smile. "And you invest for the boyfriend and then kick back to him. Have I got it straight, girlie?"

"Of course," she says. "Whaddya think? And don't call me girlie."

"I still don't like it," Angelo says, slowly peeling away the band from one of his fat Havanas. "Trouble with the Feds I don't want."

"Wouldn't hurt to take one little flier, Vic," Corsini says.

That's when the shtarkers agree to give her two weeks to come up with a winning tip. If she can do that, they'll talk a deal. If she fails, they'll buy Steiner Waste Control—on their terms. Sally goes along with that; she's got no choice.

By this time she's got Terry Mulloy and Leroy Hamilton organized. Trash from Bechtold Printing is being delivered to her Smithtown garage, and the stuff she's already pawed through is taken away and brought back to the Eleventh Avenue dump.

By the ninth day she's getting panicky. She's broken three fingernails grubbing through the Bechtold scrap, and all she's found is worthless first proofs of prospectuses and mass mailings to stockholders. But then, on a Thursday night, she hits paydirt.

There are crumpled pages with the letterhead of Snellig Firsten Holbrook. They outline a suggested plan for a leveraged buyout of an outfit called Trimbley & Diggs, Inc. Financing will include junk bonds and a hefty cash payment by company executives who are going to take T&D private as soon as they get control. The purpose, as far as Sally can make out, is to sell off or develop valuable shorefront real estate.

She looks up Trimbley & Diggs in that day's *Wall Street Journal* and finally finds the stock listed in Nasdaq. It's selling for four dollars a share. The next day she calls Paul Ramsey, tells him to buy 9,000 shares of T&D; she'll get the cash to him as soon as possible. Then she calls Mario Corsini at the number he gave her. He isn't in, but she leaves a message, and he calls back in fifteen minutes. Sally tells him she's ready for a meet.

He says they don't want to be seen with her in public, and that's okay with Sally. She suggests they come out late that night to her Smithtown home, say at midnight when her mother and housekeeper will be asleep, and they can talk without being interrupted or overheard.

Corsini doesn't like it. He implies her place may be bugged. He can't take the chance.

"Oh, for God's sake," Sally says disgustedly. "Why would I want to do a stupid thing like that? I'm in this thing deeper than you are. Look, if it'll make you feel any better, you drive out there, park in the driveway, and I'll come out and sit in the car. Your Cadillac's not bugged, is it?"

Corsini mutters darkly that he doesn't think so, but these days who the hell knows? Finally he agrees that they'll drive out that night and try to arrive at midnight. Sally gives him the address and directions on how to find her home.

She gets home early, fills a plate with the shrimp salad Martha has prepared, and takes it upstairs to have dinner with her mother. She and Becky watch the evening news on TV while they're eating, and then Sally goes downstairs while Martha gets her mother ready for bed. She works on her records and books in the den. Steiner Waste Control, with the addition of Pitzak's territory, is making a bundle. Jake would have been happy.

By eleven o'clock the house is silent. Sally sits quietly, plotting how she's going to get the cash to Paul Ramsey and how much, if anything, she should give to Dotty Rosher. That bubblehead has written a letter to Sally, claiming she's broke, and after all she did for Jake, she figures she should have something for her time and trouble. And silence.

Sally decides to turn Dotty's letter over to the Steiners' attorney, Ivan Belzig. He's a toughie and will know exactly how to handle an attempted shakedown like that.

At fifteen minutes before midnight, she's standing in the dimly lighted living room, peering out a window at the graveled driveway. It's almost ten minutes after twelve when the silver gray limousine comes purring up and coasts to a stop. The headlights are doused.

Sally snaps on the porch light and steps out the door. But before she can get down the steps, she sees Vic Angelo and Mario Corsini get out of the Cadillac and start toward the house, looking about them.

"You decided to come inside?" Sally asks as they approach.

"Yeah," Angelo says. "I figure you're straight. You'd be a fool not to be."

She leads the way into the den and offers them a drink, but they decline.

"We won't be here that long," Angelo says.

Both men light up cigars, Vic one of his thick Havanas and Mario a short, twisted stogie that looks like a hunk of black rope. The air grows fetid, and Sally switches the air conditioner to exhaust. She comes back to sit behind the desk. She looks at Vic Angelo, suddenly shocked at how much he reminds her of Jake.

"So?" she says briskly. "Have you decided? You want in? If you do, I've got a hot tip for you."

"Nah," Angelo says. "The stock market ain't for us. I talked to my lawyer about it. He says the risk of our being racked up on an insider trading charge is zip. But if we *do* get involved, then maybe the Feds start looking into our other activities—and that we can do without. So we're turning down your proposition."

She stares at the two men, feeling as if she's been kicked in the cruller. They return her stare with all the expression of Easter Island statues.

"So," Angelo goes on, "we take over Steiner Waste Control. My lawyer is drawing up the papers now. We'll pay you a nice price."

"A nice price!" Sally explodes. "My father started that business with one lousy, secondhand pickup truck. He worked his ass off to build it up, doing the driving and loading himself. And after I joined him, I worked just as hard. How can you put a 'fair price' on that? Goddamn it, that dump belongs to the Steiner family."

"Not anymore it doesn't," Angelo says coldly. "Look, private garbage collecting and cartage is a rough, dirty business. It's no place for a woman."

"Screw that!" Sally says wrathfully. "I can handle it."

"You don't need it, do you?" Mario Corsini says, speaking for the first time. "I mean, you got this boyfriend on Wall Street and you're cleaning up on inside tips. You've been making a mint. That's what you told us—right?"

"Well, yeah, sure," Sally says, beginning to feel desperate. "But the money to play the market comes from the business."

"That's your problem," Vic Angelo says, rising. "You're a smart lady; you'll find a way to work it. The papers for the sale of Steiner Waste Control will be ready in a couple of weeks. We've got to find someone to take over, but that's our problem. Thanks for inviting us to your home. Nice place."

Then they're gone. She watches the limousine pull slowly away. She digs her nails into her palms, determined not to cry. She turns off the porch light, locks and bolts the front door. Then she goes back into the den, slumps in her swivel chair, and in a low voice calls those two snakes every filthy name she can think of.

It's almost ten minutes before she begins to weep.

By Monday morning she's got her act together again. But her brain is churning like one of the compactors at the dump as she tries to find an out. All she knows is that no way, *no* way, are those skunks going to get control of her family's business.

She drives into the city, and before going to the office, stops at the bank that handles the company's accounts. She withdraws $36,000, telling the bank officer she's made a deal on a new truck, but the seller wants cash. She gets the money in hundred-dollar bills, neatly packed in a manila envelope. It's small enough to fit into her capacious shoulder bag, next to her loaded pistol.

When she gets to the dump, Judy Bering jerks a thumb at Sally's private office. "You got a visitor," she says in a low voice. "He wouldn't wait out here. Wouldn't give me his name. A mean bastard. He scares me. You want I should call the cops?"

"Not yet," Sally says. "If I need help, I'll yell."

She walks into her office with a hand in her shoulder bag, gripping the gun. Mario Corsini is seated in the armchair alongside her desk. Sally stops short, glares at him.

"Don't tell me," she says. "You came to count the paper clips. Afraid I'll steal something before you take over?"

"Nah," he says with a bleak smile. "Close the door and sit down. You and me gotta have a private talk."

"We did," Sally says. "On Friday night. Remember? So what more have we got to talk about?"

But she does as he says: closes the door and sits down behind her desk. She examines him in silence.

He really is a repellent man, with a pitted, ocherous complexion and eyes like wet coal. His shiny black hair is parted in the middle and plastered to his long skull like a gigolo or tango dancer of the 1920s. He's wearing morticians' clothes: black suit, white shirt, black tie, black socks, black shoes. No color. No jewelry. He looks like a deep shadow.

"I gotta tell you," he says. "I think Vic is making a big mistake."

"Don't tell me," Sally says bitterly, "tell him."

"I did," he says. "My point is this: We can take over this place anytime we want—but what's the hurry? Why not give you a chance to deliver the stock tips you promised? If you come through, maybe we could make more loot on the market than we can by taking over. If you can't deliver, then we grab the business. I told him all that but he wouldn't listen."

"And Vic's the boss," Sally says.

"That's right," Corsini says. "Vic's the boss. So I go along even when I don't agree. But there's more than one way to skin a cat. We got a lot of things going on, and there are ways I can stall our moving in on you."

"Yeah? What ways?"

"Just believe me when I tell you I can do it," Corsini says evasively. "But it means you'll have to play along with me. With *me*, not with Vic and me. You understand? He knows nothing about this. If he knew I was

talking to you alone, he'd cut off my balls. I told him I was coming here
to see how my cousin, Tony Ricci, was being treated."

"Well, he's doing okay. The kid's a hard worker—and ambitious."

"Yeah, I know. I had breakfast with him about an hour ago. He's all
right; he does what I tell him. Anyway, what I want to toss at you is this:
On Friday night you said you had a hot tip for us. Vic turned you down.
I want you to give me the name of that stock. I'll invest my own money.
Not Vic's money or our company's money, but *mine*, my personal funds.
Now if your tip pans out, and I make a nice buck, then I go to Vic and
say, 'Hey, that Sally Steiner wasn't shitting us; she really can deliver. Why
don't we let her keep the dump as long as she keeps feeding us inside info
on stocks.' What do you think of that?"

"I think it sucks," Sally says. "There are two things wrong. First of all,
you could do exactly like you tell me, and Vic would still say screw it,
we're taking over the business."

"Yeah," Corsini says, nodding, "that could happen. He's a stubborn guy
who likes things his own way."

"Second of all," Sally says, "how do I know you're not scamming me?
Maybe you just want to make a quick dollar on my tip and you couldn't
care less if or when I lose the dump."

He looks at her admiringly. "You got more between your ears than
pasta fagioli," he says. "And sure, you're exactly right; I could be conning
you. But you're forgetting one thing: You got no choice. Without me,
you're going to lose the business for sure. Play along with me and at least
you got a chance."

"I got other choices," she says hotly.

"Yeah?" he says with a death's-head grin. "Like what? Like running
to the DA and ratting on us? You'd be cold in a week, and so would your
mother and brother. Is that what you want?"

They sit a few moments in silence, eyes locked. They hear the sounds
of the dump: trucks rumbling in and out, gears grinding, shouts and laughter. And beyond, the noises of the harsh, raucous city: sirens, whistles, the
roar of traffic, and under all a thrumming as if the metropolis had a
diapason of its own, coming up from underground vaults and vibrating
the tallest towers.

Sally Steiner pulls a pad of scratch paper toward her and scribbles on
the top sheet.

"The stock is Trimbley and Diggs," she says. "Nasdaq Market. Right
now it's selling for about four bucks a share. And don't, for God's sake,
buy more than nine thousand shares at a clip or the SEC might get interested."

Mario Corsini takes the slip of paper. "Nice doing business with you," he says politely.

He starts out the door. "Hey," she calls, and he turns back. "Thanks for not calling me girlie."

He inclines his head gravely as if her gratitude is merited.

She sits for about five minutes after he's gone, thinking about their conversation and wondering if she's doing the smart thing. But then she realizes the bastard was right: She really has no choice. As for his threat of what might happen to her, Becky, and Eddie if she goes to the cops, she has no doubt whatsoever that he and his thugs are capable of doing exactly what he said.

She pulls the phone toward her and calls Eddie.

"Hey, bro," she says. "How'ya doing?"

"Hanging in there," he says. "How are you, Sal?"

"Couldn't be better," she says brightly. "Paul around?"

"Won't be back till noon. He's auditioning for a commercial for a strawberry-flavored laxative."

"Beautiful," Sally says. "Could I pop over for a while? I've got some cash to leave for him. Our first step on the way to fame and fortune."

"Sure," he says. "Come ahead. Got time to pose?"

"Maybe an hour or so. Okay?"

She walks down to Eddie's apartment, stopping on the way to buy him a decent burgundy. It's a sprightly day, summer around the corner, and the blue sky, sharp sun, and kissing breeze make her feel like she owns the world. Life is a tease; that she knows. All souls dissolve; but meanwhile it can be a hoot if you keep running and never look back.

She poses nude for Eddie for almost an hour, sitting on that stupid stool and trying to make her body as tense, muscular, and aggressive as he commands. Finally he slaps his sketch pad shut.

"That's it," he says. "I've got all the studies I need. Now I'll start blocking out the canvas. This is going to be a good one, Sal; I just know it."

"Make me pretty," she says. "And about six inches taller and twenty pounds thinner."

"You're perfect the way you are."

"Marry me," she says. "And also pour me a wine while I get dressed."

They're sitting on the couch, drinking her burgundy, talking about their mother and whether or not they should try another doctor, when Paul Ramsey comes ambling in. He gives them a beamy smile.

"I didn't get the job," he reports. "They decided I wasn't the strawberry laxative type."

"Thank God," Eddie says. "I don't think I could stand seeing you in a commercial, coming out of a bathroom and grinning like a maniac."

"Paul," Sally says, taking the manila envelope out of her shoulder bag, "here's thirty-six thousand in hundred-dollar bills."

"Hey," he says, "that's cool."

"You opened a brokerage account?"

"Oh, sure. No sweat."

"Well, dump this lettuce in your personal checking account. Draw on it to buy nine thousand shares of Trimbley and Diggs. Your broker will find it on the Nasdaq exchange. I wrote it all out for you. Buy the stock today, as soon as possible. You've got five days to get a check to the broker."

"Does this make me a tycoon?" Paul Ramsey asks.

"A junior tycoon," Sally tells him. "But we're just getting started."

She sits in the one comfortable armchair in the apartment. Eddie and Paul sit close on the rickety couch. The three kid along for a while, chattering about this and that. But then Sally falls silent and listens while the two men, holding hands now, chivy one another as they plan what they're going to have for dinner and whose turn it is to do the cooking.

She can see the intimacy between them, a warm bond that may be fondness, may be affection, may be love. Whatever, each completes the other. They are easy together, and no strains show. There is a privacy there, and Sally finds it disturbing. For that kind of sharing is a foreign language to her and yet leaves her feeling cheated and bereft.

The stock of Trimbley & Diggs, Inc., is going up, up, up, and Sally is ecstatic. When it hits seven dollars, she has Paul Ramsey buy another 9,000 shares.

She also notes the trading volume of T&D is increasing as the value of the stock rises. She figures there's either an inside leak at Snellig Firsten Holbrook or the arbitrageurs have ferreted out the takeover and are looking to make a bundle. So is Sally. And so, apparently, is Mario Corsini. He calls her at home, late at night, a week after their talk in her office.

"Good tip," he says, his raspy voice revealing neither joy nor enthusiasm. "You buying more?"

"Thinking about it."

"How high do you think it'll go?"

"Who knows?" she says. "Ten. Twelve maybe."

"Twelve?" he says cautiously. "If it hits twelve; you think I should bail out?"

"Hey," she says, "I'm not your financial adviser. I gave you a good tip.

What you do with it is your business. And what about *my* business? What's going to happen to Steiner Waste Control?"

"I'm working on it," he says. "Listen, one of the reasons I called: Tony Ricci will be late for work tomorrow. There's a family funeral, and I want him to be there. He'll show up around noon. Okay?"

"I guess it'll have to be," Sally says. "It'll screw up my truck schedules, but I'll work it out."

"You do that," Corsini says. "And if you get any more tips, let me know."

He hangs up abruptly, leaving Sally staring angrily at her dead phone. It infuriates her that she's enabling that gonnif to make even one lousy buck. It's she who's breaking her nails digging through garbage from Bechtold Printing. All Corsini has to do is call his broker.

She drives to work early the next morning, checks in at the office, then crosses Eleventh Avenue to the Stardust Diner. Terry Mulloy and Leroy Hamilton are seated at the back table. Both men are working on plates of three eggs over with a ham steak, a mountain of home fries, a stack of toast with butter and jelly, and coffee with cream and sugar. Sally joins them.

"You're both going to have coronaries," she says, and tells Mabel to bring her a plain bagel and a cup of black coffee.

It's payoff day, and she slips each man an envelope under the table.

"I thank you kindly," Hamilton says, pocketing his hundred. "And the best part is my wife don't know a thing about it."

"How long is this going to last?" Mulloy wants to know.

"Till I tell you to stop," Sally says. "What's the matter—getting all worn out, poor baby? I can always find two other imbeciles to handle Bechtold Printing."

"Nah," Leroy says, "no call to do that. We like the job, don't we, Terry?"

"Well, yeah," the redheaded harp says. "The money's good, but I'd like to know what's going down. I don't want to get my ass busted for a hundred a week."

"You worry too much," Sally says. "You know those three monkeys: See No Evil, Hear No Evil, Speak No Evil. That's the way you monkeys should be."

At about the same time, a silver gray Cadillac limousine pulls into a No Parking space in front of the marquee of the Hotel Bedlington on upper Madison Avenue.

"What're we stopping here for?" Angelo asks.

"Vic," Mario Corsini says, "we got plenty of time to get downtown for the meet. I figured we'd grab some breakfast. You like it here. The French toast—remember?"

"Oh, yeah," Angelo says. "Good idea."

They get out of the car. The uniformed doorman comes forward, and Corsini slips him a sawbuck. "Take care of it," he says. "You have any trouble, we'll be in the dining room."

"No trouble, sir," the doorman says. "No trouble at all."

The cavernous dining room is almost deserted; just one wimp by himself and two old ladies together, sipping tea and nibbling on dry rye toast. The two men take a corner table so their backs are against the wall. Vic Angelo orders a large glass of freshly squeezed orange juice, French toast with plenty of butter and syrup, and decaf coffee. Mario Corsini has warm blueberry muffins and regular coffee, black.

"Nice quiet place," Angelo says, looking around.

"Yeah," Corsini says. "You could plan a revolution in here and no one would be the wiser. Also, it gives me a chance to speak my piece."

"Oh, Jesus," Angelo says, groaning. "Not that Steiner thing again. Lay off, Mario. We been over that twice, and what I said still goes."

"I gotta tell you, Vic, I called and leaned on her. She gave me that stock tip she told us about. I played it—on my own, Vic, on my own—and it's almost doubled in a week."

Angelo stares at him, face rigid. "That wasn't very smart, Mario. I told you I want no part of Wall Street. We're going to take over the Steiner dump and that's it."

"Vic, will you listen just for a minute," Corsini says, leaning over the table. "She wasn't conning us; she really does have an inside pipeline. Maybe I'll triple my stake. Jesus, we can make more with her than we can from garbage and linen supply. And the—"

But then their breakfasts are served, and neither man speaks until the waiter moves away.

"And the best part," Corsini continues earnestly, "is that we don't have to kick anything upstairs. Let's face it, Vic, we're hired hands. Messenger boys—right? Sure, we collect plenty, but how much sticks to our fingers after we pay our dues and grease the lousy politicians, the cops, the union guys, and everyone else and their uncles? This thing with Sally Steiner is a nice clean deal. What we make is what we keep. No dues, no payoffs."

"You're talking shit," Angelo says, smothering his French toast with butter and syrup and beginning to wolf it down. He talks with his mouth full. "How long do you think it would take Fat Lonny to find out what's going on? He's no dope. Then he'll want to know why we didn't cut him in, and our ass is in a sling. Just forget about it, will ya, and let me finish my breakfast in peace. No more stock deals with Sally Steiner. As soon as the papers are ready, we're moving in on her. And that's final."

"If you say so, Vic. You're the boss."

They finish their food in silence, then light up cigars from Mario's gold Dunhill. When they get up to leave, Corsini stays behind a moment to inspect the check. He leaves enough cash on the table to cover it, with a generous tip.

They exit from the hotel together. Their Cadillac is still parked in front of the marquee.

Corsini slaps his jacket pocket. "Shit," he says, "I must have left my lighter on the table. I'll be right back."

He reenters the hotel. Vic Angelo gets into the front seat on the passenger side. He has closed the door when a young man comes out from between parked cars behind the limousine. He's wearing a black raincoat with the collar turned up and a black slouch hat with the brim pulled down.

He walks swiftly to the Cadillac. He pulls an automatic pistol from the pocket of his raincoat. He sticks his arm through the open window and fires four rapid shots into the startled face of Vic Angelo.

Then he walks quickly to a car double-parked north of the hotel. He gets in. The car pulls away.

The doorman, hearing the shots, comes running from the lobby. Mario Corsini comes running from the hotel. Pedestrians come running from all directions. They peer into the front seat of the limousine where Vic Angelo lies sprawled in a fountain of blood, still spouting. His face and half his head are blown away.

"Oh, my God," the doorman cries.

"I saw who done it," someone shouts. "It was a guy in a black raincoat."

"Call the police," someone yells.

"There's never a cop around when you need one," says Mario Corsini.

Sally Steiner wasn't born yesterday; after watching TV reports and reading newspaper accounts of the assassination at the Hotel Bedlington, she makes a shrewd guess at what actually went on and who's responsible. It's no skin off her teeth. Let the bastards kill each other; she couldn't care less.

The only thing that concerns her is how the death of Angelo is going to affect the future of Steiner Waste Control. She doesn't have to wait long to find out. Three days after the murder, she gets a call at the office from Mario Corsini.

"I'm driving out to your place tonight," he states. "About twelve. You'll be there?"

"Sure," she says. "Sorry about Angelo."

"Yeah," Corsini says. "He was an okay guy."

The prospect of being alone with that mobster at midnight is not a prospect that fills her with glee. She puts her loaded pistol in the top drawer of the desk. She doesn't think he'll try any rough stuff, but still. . . .

It's a balmy night, and she's strolling around the front lawn when the silver gray Cadillac pulls into the driveway a little after twelve. Sally goes back to the lighted porch and waits for Corsini to come up.

"Still got the same car," she observes.

"Yeah," he says. "I had to have the front seats re-covered."

In the den, she offers him a drink, and this time he accepts. She hasn't any Chivas Regal, but he takes a snifter of Rémy Martin. That was Jake's favorite, and no one has touched the bottle since he died.

"I'm taking over from Vic," Corsini announces. "It's been cleared. I don't want you coming to Ozone Park, so from now on you'll make your monthly payments to Tony Ricci, and he'll deliver. I'm bringing him along slowly. He'll be my driver one of these days."

"My monthly payments?" Sally says. "Does that mean I keep the dump?"

"For the time being," he says coldly. "Just keep running it the way you have, and we'll see. You got another stock for me?"

"No. Not yet."

He takes a sip of his cognac. "You better be extra nice to that boyfriend of yours," he advises. "Figure it this way: As long as you keep coming up with inside tips that pay off, that's how long you'll own Steiner Waste Control. You can understand that, can't you?"

"Yeah, sure; it isn't all that complicated."

"Well, now you know where you stand. I like everything open and aboveboard."

"Uh-huh," Sally says.

He sits back in the armchair, beginning to relax. He crosses his knees, inhales the aroma from his glass of brandy.

"Now about that Trimbley and Diggs stock," he says, watching to catch her reaction. "Right now I'm holding about a hundred thousand shares."

"What!"

"You heard me. A hundred thousand. But don't get your balls in an uproar. I only bought nine thousand in my own name. The other buys were made by friends of mine around the country. They'll get a cut of the profits. And none of them bought more than nine thousand shares each, so there's nothing to worry about."

"I hope you're right," Sally says nervously, biting at her thumbnail. "Jesus, you must have well over half a million tied up in that stock."

"About," he says carelessly. "I had to borrow to get up the kale. And the people I borrowed from wouldn't like it if I stiffed them. So I'm going to start taking some profits."

"Oh, my God!" Sally says despairingly. "Don't tell me you're going to dump a hundred thousand shares all at once? It'll kill the market."

"Whaddya think—I'm a klutz? Of course I'm not going to dump it all. I'm selling off little by little. It won't hurt the stock price. But I want to see some money. Enough to pay off the sharks. How much you in for?"

"As much as I can afford," Sally says. Then she figures she better prove her confidence in T&D. "I had eighteen thousand shares," she tells him, "and bought another nine this morning. Through a friend."

"That's smart," he says, nodding. "You really think it'll go to twelve bucks a share?"

"Now I think it may go to fifteen. It's a leveraged takeover, and from what my boyfriend tells me, it's going through."

He finishes his drink, sets the crystal snifter carefully on the desk. He stands up to go.

"Just remember what I told you," he says. "Your family keeps the business as long as you keep coming up with cash cows. That's fair enough, isn't it?"

"Oh, sure," Sally says, "that's really fair."

At the front door, he pauses and turns to her. He reaches out to stroke her cheek, but she jerks angrily away, and he gives her a mirthless smile.

"You're some woman," he says. "You've got guts. I'd teach you how to be nice, but I don't want to ruin what you've got going with your Wall Street guy. That's where our loot's coming from, isn't it?"

She doesn't answer. Just glares at him. She watches until he gets in the Caddy and drives away. She goes back into the den and stares at his empty brandy glass. Enraged, she backhands it off the desk, hoping it will shatter into a hundred pieces. But it bounces harmlessly on the shag rug, and she leaves it there.

She sits stiffly in the swivel chair, thinking of what happened. After a while she cools, and the fact that he came on to her seems small potatoes compared to the fact that the stupid prick has sunk over a half-mil on a stock tip. Suddenly she strikes her forehead with a palm and groans.

Feverishly she digs out the most recent issue of Standard & Poor's Stock Guide. She looks up Trimbley & Diggs, Inc., and follows the numbers across to the column headed Capitalization. As she feared, T&D is very thinly capitalized. There is no preferred stock and only about 800,000 shares of common stock outstanding.

Then she begins laughing. It's possible that there's an insider leak at Snellig Firsten Holbrook, and it's possible that arbitrageurs have learned of the leveraged takeover and are buying T&D for a quick profit. But it now seems obvious that the run-up of the stock's price is mostly due to Sally buying 27,000 shares and Mario Corsini buying almost 100,000 shares.

Unknowingly, the two of them have been manipulating the goddamn stock! She can't stop laughing, but eventually sobers long enough to realize that their manipulation can work both ways. If Corsini is liquidating his holdings, she better do the same. Take the money and run—before the whole thing blows away like a house of cards in a sudden belch.

So she unloads her first purchase of 9,000 shares the next morning, making a profit of about $36,000. She gives Paul Ramsey his five percent, and he looks at the cash in bemusement.

"Cool," he says.

"I told you my sister is a financial genius," Eddie tells him. "She's a lousy cook, but she knows money."

So everything's coming up roses, and looking even better on Tuesday night when Sally, digging through the latest delivery of Bechtold Printing trash, finds smeared proofs on the letterhead of Pistol & Burns. There's a merger in the works between two food processing companies, one small, one big and cash-rich.

Sally smiles grimly. That should keep Corsini happy until she can figure a way to get that murdering punk out of her life—permanently.

6

Timothy Cone looks up the telephone number of Edward Steiner, West forty-seventh Street, in the Manhattan directory and calls from the loft.

"Mr. Steiner?"

"Yes. Who's this?"

"Our name is Silas Farthingale. We are the director of client data for the Carlton Insurance Company. A Miss Sally Steiner has applied for a single-premium annuity policy with Carlton. It pays a death benefit, of course, and Miss Steiner has listed you as one of her beneficiaries, giving us your name and address. Unfortunately, she neglected to fill out the space in which the relationship should be stated. We have attempted to contact Miss Steiner, but she seems to be out. We wonder if you'd be willing to state your relationship to Miss Steiner so her application can be processed as expeditiously as possible."

"Sure," Eddie says, laughing. "I'm her brother."

"We thank you very much, Mr. Steiner."

So now Cone knows that much. The two, brother and sister, could be in it together, but he's inclined to think the woman is the mover and shaker in these stock deals. After all, she's the one who bought 10,000 shares of Wee Tot Fashions in her own name. Then Jeremy Bigelow shows up and asks questions. So now Sally is using a front: Paul Ramsey, her brother's roommate. And she's buying Trimbley & Diggs in 9,000-share lots, figuring that will keep the SEC off her tail.

And those other 9,000-share buys in cities all over the country? Maybe those buyers are friends of Sally Steiner, too. But that's so neat a solution that Cone is inclined to doubt it.

But none of his theorizing sheds any light on the Steiner woman's pipeline into Wall Street. She must have an informant down there—unless . . .

She runs a garbage collection outfit, doesn't she? So maybe she's picking up trash from Pistol & Burns, Snellig Firsten Holbrook, and God knows how many other investment bankers and stockbrokers. And maybe she's flipping through that rubbish to glean her inside information. It's possible. Cone remembers warning G. Fergus Twiggs about safeguarding the contents of Pistol & Burns' wastebaskets by purchasing more efficient shredders.

He digs out the Manhattan Yellow Pages and, in the section headed Rubbish & Garbage Removal, finds the address and phone number he wants. He calls.

"Steiner Waste Control."

"My name is Herschel Dingby. I'm opening a restaurant in the Wall Street area in a month or so, and I'd like to talk to someone at your company to arrange for daily garbage collection."

"We don't service any customers below Fourteenth Street."

Bang! goes the phone. And *bang!* goes Timothy's theory of how Sally Steiner is getting her inside poop. He sighs and makes one more call.

"Pistol and Burns. May I help you?"

"Could I speak to Mr. G. Fergus Twiggs, please. Timothy Cone of Haldering and Company calling."

"Just a moment, please, sir."

It's more than a moment, but Cone waits patiently. Eventually the senior partner comes on the line, and they exchange brief pleasantries. Then the Wall Street dick gets down to business.

"Are you a betting man, Mr. Twiggs?"

Short pause, then: "I wouldn't be in this business if I wasn't. What do you want me to bet on?"

"Me," Cone says. "Look, I know that technically Haldering's job is finished at your shop. I submit a final report, you pay us off, and that's it. Only I don't want it to end right now. I'd like you to call Hiram Haldering and tell him you want to keep us on the payroll for another couple of weeks."

"And why should I do that, Mr. Cone?"

"Because I think I'm onto something that may—with heavy emphasis on the *may*—uncover that Wee Tot Fashions leak from your office. And other insider leaks from other investment houses. No guarantees, but I think it's worth the bet that I'll come up with something. If not, then just write me off as another con artist."

"No, Mr. Cone, I'd never do that." There is a long silence, then he says, "All right, I'll place a wager on you. I'll call Mr. Haldering immediately and tell him we require your services for another two weeks."

"Thanks," Timothy says. "But I better warn you: I plan to rent a car. I'll need it to do the job. You'll get stuck for the expenses on that."

G. Fergus Twiggs laughs. "Why not?" he says. "In for a penny, in for a pound."

That night Cone picks up a big box of baked lasagna, a container of cucumber salad, and a jug of burgundy. He cabs over to Samantha's apartment in the East Village. She pops the lasagna in the oven to warm it while he pours tumblers of wine. As usual, they plop down and eat on one of the oval rag rugs in her artsy-craftsy apartment.

"You'll never guess what happened," she says. "This afternoon that guy Twiggs called H.H. He wants you to keep on the Pistol and Burns case for another two weeks."

"No kidding?" Cone says, eating busily. "I wonder what he's got in mind."

Sam looks at him suspiciously. "When you get that look on your puss," she says, "I begin to worry. You didn't have anything to do with Twiggs' call, did you?"

"Me? Come on! How could I convince a guy like that to spend more money on something I thought was signed, sealed, and delivered? I figured to complete the final report and that would be that."

"Uh-huh," she says, still staring at him. "Well, now I'll have to parcel out those three new cases to the other guys, and they'll scream bloody murder. Tim, is there something you're not telling me?"

He holds up a palm. "I swear there's not. Have I ever lied to you?"

"Oh, Jesus," she says, sighing. "Now I *am* worried. You tight-mouthed bastard! I should have known better than to ask you."

They finish their dinner and clean up the debris. Then they sit on the rug again, sipping fresh glasses of burgundy.

"Want to stay the night?" she asks him.

"Of course I want to stay. I'll split early in the morning, before you're awake."

"What a life we lead," she says. "Fast action and quick goodbyes."

"Hey," he said, "don't get started on that. We agreed—remember? Either of us can blow the whistle any time, with no explanations, no excuses, no apologies."

She looks at him coldly. "I'd like to blow your whistle," she says, and they both crack up.

She wants to watch some stupid TV documentary about the Richest Man in the World. So Cone undresses and slips naked into bed, after removing her French dolls and chenille bedspread covered with little pink balls of fluff.

She keeps the volume down, and after a while he dozes, not really sleeping but floating drowsily between clean, crisp sheets, wondering if this really is, as he believes, the best time of his life.

He is dimly conscious of Sam clicking off the TV set and checking the chain and bolt on the outside door. He hears her moving about, going into the bathroom and coming out, undressing.

Then she slides into bed alongside him.

"Sleeping?" she whispers.

"Yes," he says.

"Liar. Want to wait till morning?"

"No."

She molds herself to his back, spoon-fashion, then reaches around to hold him. He can feel the fever of her body, and it's so nice having her close that he doesn't want to move.

"*Do* something," she urges.

"Whistle 'Dixie'?" he suggests. "Sing an aria? Crack my knuckles?"

She punches his ribs. "I'll crack more than that, buster."

Then he is no longer drowsy, and they attack each other with moaning kisses and caresses as hard as blows. Their bodies join in a curve as convoluted as a Möbius strip. Within moments they are engaged in hostile assaults, as if each is guilty of the other's need—for which there is no forgiveness.

They rampage across the bed, back and forth, and if there had been a chandelier overhead, they would have swung from that, two nutty acrobats socking together in midair. Curses are muffled, oaths gritted, and when they finally come to a sweated juncture, each believes it a selfish victory and is beamy and content.

. . .

Cone rents a Dodge Shadow because the name appeals to him. He intends using it to shadow and, if things get hairy, to dodge. It's a black two-door compact and has all the performance he'll need for city driving.

He gets the feel of it on a jaunt uptown. He drives by Steiner Waste Control on Eleventh Avenue and is surprised by the size of the dump—almost a city block wide. It's late afternoon, and the place seems relatively quiet with only a single truck unloading at a shed and another on the tarmac awaiting its turn.

He returns to the loft and phones Neal K. Davenport.

"Now what?" the NYPD detective demands. "I'm trying to eat a sausage hero, so make it fast."

"That's your lunch? At this time of day?"

"You think we get a regular lunch hour like you nine-to-five types? Fat chance! What's on your mind, Sherlock?"

"You know anyone in the Organized Crime Bureau?"

"I might. Why are you asking? You got something for them?"

"Nah," Cone says. "Just a couple of questions."

"What the hell is this—a one-way street? When are you going to start coming up with some answers for us? What a hardnose you are! Okay, I'll play your little game. The guy I know in the Organized Crime outfit is Joe D'Amato. He looks and dresses like a college professor, but he's got more street smarts than you and I will ever have. I'll give him a call and tell him you're the worst brain-picker in the city. If he wants to talk to you, that's his problem."

"Thanks," Cone says. "That's one I owe you."

"One!" the city bull says, outraged. "What're you doing—counting on your thumbs? Use all your appendages and it comes to twenty-one. Do you read me, sonny boy?"

Cone hangs up softly. He finds the computer printouts Jeremy Bigelow gave him, and makes a list of all the out-of-town buyers who purchased 9,000 shares of Trimbley & Diggs, Inc. There are ten of them, and Cone jots down their names and the cities where they bought the T&D stock.

Cleo has started to mewl sadly, so he changes the cat's litter, puts out fresh water, and then inspects the contents of his scarred, waist-high refrigerator to see what kind of a banquet man and beast can share. He finds three eggs, a hunk of salami, and a piece of greenish cheese sparked with jalapeño pepper flakes.

He cuts the salami into cubes, fries them up with the eggs, and sets out the cheese to provide his cholesterol overdose of the day. There's also a blackened banana for dessert. But everything tastes good to him, and Cleo has no objections except perhaps to the pepper cheese, which makes the tom sneeze.

The phone doesn't ring until almost nine o'clock and, being a superstitious man, Cone goes to answer it with his fingers crossed.

"Yeah?" he says.

"Is this Timothy Cone?"

"That's right. Who's this?"

"Sergeant Joseph D'Amato. Neal Davenport said you wanted me to contact you."

"Yeah. Thanks."

"I should tell you this call is being taped. In the business I'm in, that's SOP. Okay with you?"

"Sure. All I got is a list of names and where they live. I was hoping you might be able to give me some skinny on them."

"Who are they?"

Cone sees no reason to hold back, especially if he wants a favor from this guy. "All of them bought big blocks of the same stock in the last two or three weeks. I think it may be an inside trading scam."

"Hey, wait a minute," D'Amato says. "That's a federal rap. No interest to us."

"It might," Cone says. "I think these guys are getting their tips from a woman who operates a private garbage removal service on the West Side of Manhattan. I got a feeling these guys are all wrongos, and they're in your files."

Silence a moment, then: "All right, let's have the names. Try to speak slowly and distinctly. My tape recorder is an antique. And spell out all the last names."

Cone does as he's told.

"That's it," he says when he's finished.

"A couple of the names ring a bell," the sergeant says. "And you're right: They are not nice people. I'll run them through the computer and see what turns up. I'll get back to you."

"Thanks."

"Neal tells me you're a secretive sonofabitch. If you're holding back, now's the time to tell me. I don't like doing a private eye's work unless there's something in it for me."

"I understand that, and I'm not holding back. I've given you all I've got."

"All right," D'Amato says. "But you cross me just once, and you've had it, pal. You capeesh?"

"I capeesh," Cone says.

That night, around eleven o'clock, he drives uptown again. He parks two blocks away from Steiner Waste Control and walks back. The dump is surrounded by a heavy chain-link fence, and the truck-filled tarmac is lighted by two floods. There's also a night watchman's shed inside the locked gate, and the guy himself is outside, looking up at the star-spangled sky. He's a chunky bruiser, and he's not carrying a kielbasa in that belt holster.

Cone knows at once that there's no way he's going to break into the Steiner office and waltz out with their customer list. That leaves only one alternative, and he groans aloud when he thinks of the stultifying labor that will entail.

But he won't let go; he's done his share of donkeywork before and lived through it. So on Thursday morning, early, he's parked across Eleventh Avenue from Steiner Waste Control. He's come prepared with two deli sandwiches (bologna on rye with mustard, roast beef on white with mayo) and four cans of Miller beer in a plastic bag filled with ice cubes.

The garbage dump comes to life. Cone watches as the gate is unlocked and thrown open. Employees arrive, trucks are revved up, the gas pump is busy, and a short, stocky woman comes out of the office to yell something Cone can't hear at an old guy who comes limping from one of the corrugated steel sheds.

There are six huge Loadmaster compactor trucks, all painted yellow. Timothy thanks God and his good-luck angels when he sees that not only do the garbage trucks bear the legend Steiner Waste Control, but each has a big number painted on the side, 1 to 6. At least Cone won't be following the same truck for a week.

Because that's his plan; he can't think of a better way to find out who Sally Steiner is dealing with. He doesn't think she's got a Wall Street informant, so she must be getting her inside info from one of her customers. It's a long shot, but the only one Cone has.

Truck No. 4 pulls out first, and Cone starts up the Dodge Shadow and goes right after it. For the next seven hours he eats the truck's exhaust, going where it goes, stopping when it stops, returning to the dump when Truck No. 4 returns to drop a load.

Meanwhile he's making scrawled notes on the back of a brown envelope that originally contained a nasty letter from the IRS warning him that he owed Uncle Sam an additional $17.96. He logs the schedule of Truck No. 4: names and addresses of places it services: restaurants, apartment houses, diners, industrial buildings, taverns.

By the end of the day, sandwiches and beers consumed, Cone is bored and cranky, wondering if he's got the fire to keep this up for a week. What bugs him is the fear that each numbered truck may have a different schedule of rubbish pickups every day. If that's true, it'll take a month of Sundays to list all of Sally Steiner's customers.

But on Friday morning, he's there again, parked and waiting. Now there are big flatbeds pulling through the Steiner gate to load up with strapped bales of paper, and open-bed trucks being filled with cubes of compacted garbage to be taken, Cone presumes, to landfills on Long Island or New Jersey. And smaller trucks loading up with tons of swill for what eventual purpose Cone doesn't even want to imagine.

On Friday he follows Truck No. 2. On Monday he shadows Truck No. 5. And on Tuesday he takes off after Truck No. 3, beginning to think he's just spinning his wheels. But then, early Tuesday afternoon, something happens that makes it seem likely he hasn't been diddling himself.

Cone has already noted that the big Steiner trucks are operated by a crew of two, driver and loader. On Tuesday, Truck No. 3 is being driven by a redheaded guy with the map of Ireland spread all over his face. The loader is a broad-shouldered black who looks like he could nudge a locked door off its hinges with no trouble at all.

Everything in their Tuesday routine is normal and dull until about 1:00, when Truck No. 3 slows and turns into an alleyway alongside a one-story cinderblock building on lower Tenth Avenue. Cone parks across the street and opens his second pack of Camels of the day. From where he sits, he has a good view of the action.

The loader climbs down from the cab. But instead of hefting the cylindrical barrels of trash that have been put out for pickup, he exits the alley and starts walking up Tenth Avenue. Cone straightens up, interested enough to forget to light his cigarette.

In a couple of minutes, a battered Chevy van pulls into the alley and stops right behind the Steiner truck. The loader gets out of the Chevy, opens the back doors, and begins to lift the barrels into the van. "What the hell?" Cone says aloud, and then realizes he's now got two cigarettes going at once. He licks thumb and forefinger and pinches one out, saving it carefully in the ashtray. The van, loaded with four barrels, backs out of the alley and starts north on Tenth Avenue. Cone takes a quick look at the cinderblock building. It's got a brass plate next to the front door, but it's so small he can't read it from across the street. The yellow truck hasn't moved, so Cone gets rolling and follows the van.

What a journey that turns out to be! Up Tenth Avenue to Fifty-fourth Street. East on Fifty-fourth to Eighth Avenue. North on Eighth and onto Broadway. Up Broadway to Seventy-second Street. East on Seventy-second to Central Park West. North on CPW to Eighty-sixth Street. A right turn and they're going through the Park at Traverse 3. Cone is happy he's got a full tank of gas.

He's keeping a tight tail on the van, but city traffic is heavy and it's doubtful if the loader will spot him, even if he's looking for a shadow. Cone doesn't think that likely; the guy is driving steadily at legal speeds and making no effort to jink.

On the East Side, they turn up First Avenue and continue north, almost to 125th Street. Now Cone guesses where they're heading: the Triborough Bridge. He wonders if this guy is making a hegira to Long Island to dump his four barrels in some deserted landfill. But that doesn't make sense; by rights, the contents of those barrels should have been taken back to the Steiner dump for disposal.

On they go, picking up speed now as traffic thins. They stop briefly to pay their tolls, then head across the span. Cone accelerates to pull the Dodge Shadow alongside the van. He glances sideways. The loader looks like he's enjoying life. He's smoking a plump cigar and slapping the steering wheel in time to radio music Cone can't hear.

They get onto the Long Island Expressway, moving at a lively clip. They turn off onto the Northern State Parkway, turn again onto the Sunken Meadow State Parkway. The van is slowing now, and Cone has time to look around. Pretty country. Plenty of trees. Some impressive homes with white picket fences.

Down Main Street in Smithtown and into an area where the homes are even bigger, set on wide lawns with white graveled driveways leading to the house and two- or three-car garages.

The Chevy van turns into one of those driveways. Cone continues down the road a piece, pulls onto the verge and parks. He hops out, lights a cigarette, and saunters back. He stands in the semi-concealment of a small copse of pines and watches the loader lug the four barrels, one at a time, into a neat white garage with a shingled roof.

The four cardboard barrels inside, the man starts bringing them out again and sliding them into the van—or so it seems; the barrels are identical in appearance. Timothy is flummoxed until he realizes what's going on. The guy has delivered four new barrels; he's picking up four old barrels that were already stored in the garage.

Cone sees the Steiner loader climb behind the wheel of the van. Away he goes. Cone will make book on exactly where he's heading: back to the city to make contact with Truck No. 3, dump the trash in the big yellow Loadmaster, and then return the empty barrels to the alleyway alongside that building on Tenth Avenue.

Cone stays where he is, eyeballing the garage and home. Nice place. The house is two stories high with a lot of windows. Weathered brick halfway up and white clapboard the rest of the way. A tiled terrace at one side with French doors from the house. All set on what looks to be a one-acre plot, at least, with a manicured lawn and a few pieces of Victorian cast-iron furniture scattered about.

He figures he'll meander up and see if there's a name on the mailbox. If someone braces him, he'll tell them he's the Avon Lady. But he doesn't have to use any subterfuge. He's no sooner started up the bricked walk to the front door when he spots a sign on a short post driven into the lawn. It reads: THE STEINERS.

"Ho-ho-ho," Cone says aloud. He goes back to his car, turns around, and heads for the city. He drives as fast as the cabs on the parkways and expressway, hoping to get back to Tenth Avenue before that business closes for the day. Traffic is heavy, but nothing like what's coming *from* the city; that's bumper-to-bumper.

He's back in Manhattan by four o'clock, but it takes him almost forty-five minutes to work his way over to the West Side. He finally parks on Ninth Avenue, with his watch nudging 5:00 P.M. He practically runs back to the one-story cinder-block building. The brass plate next to the front door reads: BECHTOLD PRINTING. Just that and nothing more.

The front door is still open, but when he pushes his way in, a blowsy blonde in the front office is putting on her hat. It looks like a velvet chamberpot.

"We're closed for the day," she tells Cone.

"Nah," he says, giving her what he fancies is a charming smile. "The front door is open. I just want to get some letterheads, bills, and business cards printed up."

"We don't do that kind of work," she says tartly.

"You don't?" he says. "Well, what kind of work do you do?"

"Financial printing," she says.

"Thank you very much," the Wall Street dick says, tipping his leather cap. "Sorry to bother you."

Back in the Dodge Shadow, he realizes he hasn't eaten all day. So he wolfs down his two deli sandwiches (salami and egg salad) and gulps two beers. All the ice cubes in his plastic sack have melted, and the beer is barely cool. But at least it's wet.

Then he drives back to his loft, whistling a merry tune.

He wakes Wednesday morning, mouth tasting like a wet wool sock and stomach ready to do a Krakatoa. He resolves never again to drink Italian brandy with kosher hot dogs, baked beans, and sauerkraut. Even Cleo, who shared the same meal, looks a mite peaked.

He trudges down to the office. It's an unexpectedly sharp day, with a keen, whistling wind. Breathing that etheric air is like having a decongestant inhaler plugged up each nostril. But by the time he hits John Street, he's feeling a lot better and figures he'll live to play the violin again.

"Thanks for stopping by," Samantha Whatley says bitterly. "So glad you could make it. And it isn't even payday."

"Hey," he says, "you know I've been busy with Pistol and Burns. Practically living with G. Fergus Twiggs."

"Practically living with him, huh? That's why you've got three messages on your desk to phone him as soon as possible."

"Oh," Cone says. "Well, something must have come up. I'll give him a call."

"That's more than you do for me," she says in a low voice. "You bastard!"

"I've really been busy," he says lamely, and flees to his own cubbyhole office before she starts bitching about his missing progress reports.

There are the three messages from Twiggs, and one from Joseph D'Amato. Cone calls the sergeant first.

"Christ, you're a hard man to get hold of," the NYPD detective says. "I called you at home a couple of times, then figured I'd try your office. Listen, you and I have got to have a talk."

"Sure. How about noon here in the office? We can have a sandwich and schmooze as long as you like."

"Suits me," D'Amato says. "I'll be there."

"You got something for me?" Cone asks hopefully.

"See you at noon," the sergeant says and hangs up.

Cone then calls G. Fergus Twiggs. Getting through to the senior partner of Pistol & Burns is akin to requesting an audience with the Q. of E., but the Wall Street dick waits patiently, and eventually Twiggs comes on the line. His normally cheery voice sounds dejected.

"I'm afraid we have another one," he reports.

"An insider leak?"

"Yes. On a deal that's barely gotten under way. I just don't understand it. Very depressing."

"I can be in your office in half an hour. I won't take much of your time, but I think it'll make you happier."

"Then by all means come ahead."

Timothy is in the office of P&B in twenty minutes, and moments later is closeted with the Chief of Internal Security. The plump little man is sagging. All he can manage is a tinselly smile.

"It's a merger," he tells Cone. "Two food processing companies. I prefer not to mention the names."

"Sure. That's okay."

"Anyway, it's still in the early stages. Surely no more than fifty people know about it. But there's already increased trading in the stock of the smaller company. The share price is up two dollars since Monday."

"Uh-huh," Cone says. "I suppose documents have been prepared."

"Of course. Preliminary proposals. Suggestions for stock swaps between the two companies. Analyses of the problems of merging the two management groups."

"And the documents have been printed up and distributed to those fifty people?"

"Naturally. They're all involved and have to be kept informed of what's going on."

"Who's your printer?"

"Bechtold Printing on Tenth Avenue. We've been using them for years. Absolutely trustworthy. Every Christmas Frederick Bechtold sends me a smoked ham."

"Do you know anyone at Snellig Firsten Holbrook?" Cone asks suddenly.

Twiggs looks at him, puzzled. "Yes, I know Greg Vandiver, a risk arbitrage attorney. He crews for me in the Saturday yacht races at our club."

"Will you call him right now, please, and ask him the name of the printer used by Snellig Firsten Holbrook. They got caught, too."

Twiggs makes the call and asks the question. Then he hangs up and stares grimly at Cone.

"Bechtold Printing on Tenth Avenue," he reports.

"Sure," Cone says. "And I'll bet a dozen other investment bankers and brokerage houses print at Bechtold."

"You mean Frederick Bechtold, that fine, upstanding man who sends me smoked hams, is leaking all his customers' secrets?"

"Nah, he's clean. But he's throwing out some valuable garbage."

Then Cone explains what's going on: How first press proofs are invariably discarded and more proofs are pulled until the density of the ink is correct, colors are in register, copy is properly centered on the page.

"All those fouled-up proofs are wadded up and thrown out. And along comes a private carter who picks up the barrels of trash and empties them into a truck. In this case, it's a garbage collector called Steiner Waste Control, on Eleventh Avenue. The boss is Sally Steiner, and she's a stock market maven. She knows what kind of work Bechtold is doing, and whenever a pickup is made at the printer, she has the barrels taken to her home in Smithtown. Then she paws through all those discarded press proofs looking for goodies. And finds them."

Twiggs' face reddens, he seems to swell, and for a moment Cone fears the senior partner is going to have cardiac arrest, or at least bust his braces. But suddenly Twiggs starts laughing, his face all squinched up, tears starting from his eyes. He pounds the desk with his fist.

"The garbage collector!" he says, spluttering. "Oh, God, that's good! That's beautiful! I'll dine off that story for years to come! And I believe every word of it."

"You can," Cone says, nodding. "A few years ago a financial printer was reading the stuff delivered to him by his Wall Street customers and buying and selling stocks on the basis of the documents he was given to print. He did great, and the SEC charged him with inside trading. I think it was the first insider case to end up in the Supreme Court. They found the guy Not Guilty, but they never did define exactly what constitutes inside trading. The garbage angle is just a new variation on an old scam."

"And what do we do now?"

"Nothing you can do about the merger that's in the works. The cat is out of the bag on that one. But for the future, you've got some choices. You can get yourself a new printer, with no guarantee that the same thing won't happen again. Or stick with Bechtold, but every time you give him something to print, send over a couple of guys who can make sure all preliminary proofs are destroyed. Or—and I like this one best—equip your Mergers and Acquisitions Department with the new desktop printers. You won't get six-color work or jazzy bindings, but you'll be able to reproduce most of the documents you need right here in your own shop, including graphs, charts, and tables. It's all done by computers, and the finished documents can be counted and coded so none of them go astray. The machines aren't cheap, but they'll save you a mint on commercial printing costs. And your security will be umpteen times better than if you send your secrets to an outside printer."

"I'll look into it immediately," Twiggs says. "It makes sense. You're going to report this garbage collector to the SEC?"

"As soon as possible."

"And what's going to happen to—what's her name?"

"Sally Steiner. Well, I figure her for a smart, nervy lady. She probably thinks that if she's caught, she'll walk away from all this with a smile on her lips and a song in her heart. If she's the stand-up gonnif I think she is, she'll fight any attempt by the SEC to charge her or make her cough up her profits. What, actually, did she do? Dig through some barrels of rubbish, that's all. She's home free. That's what she thinks, and I hate to admit it, but she may be right."

"I wonder," says G. Fergus Twiggs thoughtfully, "if she'd consider employment with an investment banker."

Cone smiles and rises to leave. "You could do a lot worse," he says.

"Nice meeting you, Mr. Twiggs. You put in that electronic printing system. It'll help."

The senior partner shakes his hand fervently. "I appreciate everything you've done, Mr. Cone. It's a pleasure dealing with someone who enjoys his work."

"Do I?" Timothy Cone says. "Yeah, I guess I do."

Neal Davenport is right: Sergeant Joseph D'Amato looks and dresses like a college professor. He's a tall, gawky guy with a Mount Rushmore face and big, spatulate hands. His tweed jacket has suede patches on the elbows, and his cordovan kilties are polished to a mirror gloss. He's smoking a long, thin cigarillo, so Cone thankfully lights up his ninth cigarette of the day.

He calls the local deli for cheeseburgers, fries, a couple of dills, and four cold cans of Bud. They talk and eat at the same time, occasionally waving a pickle slice or French fry in the air to make a point.

"Those names you gave me," D'Amato says. "All illegals. Members of the same Family."

"New York?" Cone asks.

"Yeah, but not the Big Five. These schmoes belong to a second-rate gang, bossed by a slimy toad whose monicker is Alonzo Departeur. He's not even an Italian, I'm happy to say, let alone Sicilian. He's known as Fat Lonny, and if you ever see him, you'll know why. The guy is obscenely obese."

"This Family of his—what're they into?"

D'Amato gestures with a pickle. "Think of them as hyenas, waiting around for scraps after the big Families make the kill. They couldn't operate without permission of the heavies. And, of course, they pay through the nose for the go-ahead."

"How do you know all this?" Cone asks curiously.

"Snitches," the sergeant says promptly. "We have informants in every New York Family. We catch a guy pulling something foul, and we give him a choice: Either he does ten years in the slammer or he turns and becomes our property. You'd be surprised at how many of those scuzzes are willing to work for us, singing their rotten little hearts out. We've even got some of them wired."

"Whatever happened to the code of silence?"

"Omertà? Forget it. Maybe ten years ago, but today it's every pirate for himself. Organized crime is becoming disorganized crime. Anyway, the names you gave me are all associated with the Departeur mob, headquartered in New York but with people all over the country. They do routine collections for the Big Five and are allowed to run some drug deals, loan-sharking, extortion, and a few other things like restaurants, nightclubs, and after-hour joints."

"Any connection with garbage collection?"

"Oh, yeah. And linen supply, liquor wholesaling, and some minor ri-poffs of concrete companies, construction unions, plumbing contractors, and electrical equipment suppliers."

"Anything on Wall Street?"

"Not to my knowledge. The Big Five keep a lock on that. The reason I'm telling you all this is that one of the biggies in the Departeur Family was, until recently, a hood named Vic Angelo. You probably read of how he was scratched outside the Hotel Bedlington not too long ago. His job was taken over by his underboss, Mario Corsini. And Corsini was one of the names on your list—so that accounts for our interest."

"You think this Corsini arranged for Vic Angelo being chilled?"

"Definitely. It's common talk on the street, but we can't get enough real evidence to justify busting Corsini, let alone indicting him. But we keep hoping."

"Is this Corsini into extortion of private carters and garbage collectors?"

"Sure he is. Why do you ask?"

So, for the second time that morning, Cone describes the activities of Sally Steiner, and how she's been able to come up with those profitable stock tips.

"That's lovely," D'Amato says when Cone finishes. "I'd guess that she's passing her inside information along to Corsini. For what reason I don't know. Maybe she's got the hots for the guy. Some women think mobsters are king shits."

"Maybe," Cone says, "or maybe he's leaning on her, and those stock tips are what she has to pay to stay in business."

"Could be," the sergeant says. He blots his mouth delicately with a paper napkin, sits back, and lights another of his long cigarillos. "On the list you gave me, Mario Corsini's address was given as Atlantic City. Actually he lives in Queens but probably bought his stock through an Atlantic City broker. No law against that. Maybe the broker's a pal of his, or maybe one of the Departeur Family. Something bothering you?"

"I don't know," Cone says fretfully. "We've been blowing a lot of smoke, but there are damned few hard facts. It's all 'suppose' and 'maybe' and 'perhaps.' I don't think *every* private garbage and rubbish collector in New York is paying dues to the mob. I mean, we have no hard evidence that Mario Corsini or any other Mafia type is ripping off Steiner Waste Control. How can we prove a connection?"

Sergeant D'Amato gives Cone a soft smile. "About seven or eight months ago, Corsini brought a cousin over from the Old Country. It's legal; the kid has all his papers. His name is Anthony Ricci. Anyway, in that list you gave me, there were two heavy stock buyers in Atlantic City. One was Mario Corsini. The other was Anthony Ricci."

"So?" Cone says. "What does that prove?"

"Anthony Ricci works for Steiner Waste Control."

"Let me buy you another cheeseburger," Timothy Cone says.

7

"There you are," Eddie Steiner says, gesturing. "In all your primitive glory."

Sally stares at the completed oil painting propped on an easel. "Jesus!" she bursts out. "You made me look like a tough bimbo."

"You *are* a tough bimbo," her brother says. "But forget your vanity for a minute; what do you think of it as a painting?"

"It's good, Eddie," she says grudgingly.

"Good? The goddamned thing is magnificent. It's just one hell of a portrait. The best I've ever done. Ever will do. But then I'll never find a model like you again."

She moves closer to inspect the canvas.

"Careful," he warns. "Don't touch. It's still wet; I just finished it last night."

"I'm going to have to lose some weight," Sally says. "Look at those hips. And that ass. My God!"

"You're just a strong, solid woman, sis. Don't knock it."

"What are you going to do with it?"

"I told you about that gallery in the East Village that wants to give me a show. I finally agreed. I'll bet this thing will be the first to sell."

"I hope you're not going to call it *My Sister* or anything like that."

"Nah," he says, laughing. "I'm calling it *Manhattan*."

Good title, she thinks. In the nude body of a thrusting woman, he's caught the crude, exciting world she lives in. The colors are so raw they shriek, and sharp edges and jagged composition reflect the demonic rhythm of the city.

"Yeah," she says, "I think you got something there. If no one wants it, I'll buy it."

"And cut it up?" he teases.

"Never. When I'm old and gray, I'll look at it and remember," she says, smiling. "Well, look, here's a package for Paul. Cash and a note telling him what stocks to buy. Okay?"

"Sure. I'll give it to him. He likes the idea of being the Boy Wonder of Wall Street. Listen, Sal, you're not going to get into any trouble on this, are you?"

"Trouble? What trouble? I'm giving stock tips to a good friend, that's all. Nothing illegal about that."

"I hope not," Eddie says. "I'd hate to visit you up the river on the last Thursday of every month, bringing you some of Martha's strudel."

"Not a chance," she says confidently. "No one's going to lay a glove on me."

She walks back to the office, thinking of her portrait. It lights up that entire dingy apartment. The more she recalls it, the better she likes it. It's Manhattan, all right, but it's also Sally Steiner, shoving belligerently from the canvas.

"That's me," she says aloud. "A tough bimbo."

It's almost noon when she gets back to Steiner Waste Control. There are four big yellow trucks on the tarmac, waiting to unload. Most of the guys have gone across to the Stardust Diner for lunch, but Anthony Ricci is waiting in the outer office. She knows what he wants.

"Why don't you go to lunch," she says to Judy Bering. "I'll hold down the fort until you get back."

"I may be a little late, Sal. I want to get over to Bloomie's. They're having a sale on pantyhose."

"Take your time. Tony, come into my office."

The kid really is a beauty, no doubt about it, and she wonders what Eddie could do with him—and then decides she's never going to bring them together and find out. Paul Ramsey would kill her.

Ricci has a helmet of crisp, black curls, bedroom eyes, and a mouth artfully designed for kissing. That chiseled face might be vacuous except that, occasionally, the soft eyes smolder, the jaw sets, lips are pressed. And there, revealed, are temper, menace, an undisciplined wildness when the furious blood takes over.

He's got a muscled body and moves with the spring of a young animal. He's been working all morning, but he doesn't smell of garbage; he smells of male sweat with a musky undertone from the cologne he keeps in his locker and uses every time his truck returns to the dump.

"How's it going, Tony?" Sally asks him. "Like the job?"

"It's okay," the kid says. "For a while. I'm not about to spend the rest of my life lifting barrels of shit."

"You're not?" she says, putting him on. "And what have you got in mind—an executive job where you can wear monogrammed shirts and Armani suits?"

"Yeah," he says seriously, "I think I would like a desk job."

"With a secretary? A blue-eyed blonde with big knockers?"

He gives her the hundred-watt grin. "Maybe. But not necessary."

"No, I don't imagine you have much trouble in that department. You got someone special, Tony?"

He shrugs. "I have many friends, but no one special, no. Mario, he'd like me to marry a woman he has picked out for me, but I don't think so. Her father is respected and wealthy, but she looks like a—like a— what is it that farmers put in their fields to frighten birds away?"

"A scarecrow?"

"Yeah," Ricci says, laughing, "she looks like a scarecrow. Not for me."

"What kind of a woman are you looking for?"

He leans toward her slightly, his dark, burning eyes locked with hers. "An older woman," he says in a low voice. "I am tired of young girls who talk only of clothes and rock stars and want to go to the most expensive restaurants and clubs. Yeah, I'm interested in older women."

"Because they're grateful?" Sally suggests.

He considers that. "It's true," he says finally, and she decides he may be an Adonis, but he's got no fucking brains. "Also," he continues, "older women are settled and know about life. They are smart about money, and they work hard."

"Uh-huh," Sally says. "Sounds to me like you've got it all figured out. An executive desk job—with or without a secretary—and an older woman you can tell your troubles to. And what would you give her? You'd be faithful, I suppose."

He doesn't realize she's kidding him, but sits back with a secret smile. "She would not care about that," he says. "Where I come from, a man provides a home, food on the table, and takes care of his children. What he does outside the home is his business. The wife understands."

"Well, I wish you luck," Sally says. "I hope you find a rich older woman like that."

"I intend to," he says solemnly, staring at her with such intensity that she begins to get antsy.

"Well," she says, "let's get down to business." She slides a sealed white envelope from the top drawer of her desk and hands it to him. "You know what's in that, Tony?"

He nods soberly. "More than I make in a month for lifting gar-bage."

"You better believe it," Sally says. "So don't lose it or take off for Las Vegas. A receipt isn't necessary."

Her sarcasm floats right over those crisp, black curls. "A receipt?" he says, puzzled. "Mario didn't say anything about a receipt."

She wonders if this boy has all his marbles. "Forget it," she says. "Just a joke. Nice talking to you, Tony."

"Maybe some night we could have dinner," he says, more of a statement than a question. "I know a restaurant down on Mulberry Street. Not expensive, but the food is *delizioso*. Would you like to have dinner with me?"

She realizes that if Terry Mulloy had made the same proposal, she'd have told him to stuff it. "Sure," she says to Anthony Ricci. "Why not?"

After he's gone, she questions why she didn't cut him off at the knees. Not, she decides, because he's so beautiful and dumb. But he's Mario Corsini's cousin, and she has a presentiment that he might, someday, be of use to her. She has never forgotten that on the morning Vic Angelo was murdered, Ricci didn't get to work until noon.

She calls Mario, leaves a message, and he calls back in twenty minutes.

"I delivered the mail to Tony," she tells him.

"Okay," he says. "You got anything else for me?"

"Yeah," she says, and gives him the name of the smaller food processing company involved in the merger being engineered by Pistol & Burns.

"A good one?" Corsini asks.

"I'm in it," Sally says. "You suit yourself."

"It better be good," he says. "You know what's riding on it."

"You scare the pants off me," she says scornfully.

"I'd like to," he says, and she hangs up.

Timothy Cone and Jeremy Bigelow are "eating street" again. They're sauntering down through the financial district toward the Battery, stopping at carts and vans to pick up calzoni, chicken wings in soy sauce, raw carrots, chocolate chip cookies, gelato, and much, much more.

"I never want to work a case with you again," the SEC investigator says. "Every time we eat like this, I gain five pounds and my wife tells me she can't sleep because my stomach keeps rumbling all night."

"I got a cast-iron gut," Cone brags. "But nothing compared to my cat. That monster can chew nails and spit tacks."

"Lucky for him. How did you make out with those Trimbley and Diggs trading records I gave you?"

"I made out like a thief," Timothy says. "I found the leak."

Jeremy stops on the sidewalk, turns, stares at him. "You're kidding," he says.

"Scout's honor," Cone says, and for the third time he describes how Sally Steiner is digging through trash from Bechtold Printing and finding smeared proofs of confidential financial documents.

He tells Bigelow nothing about the Mario Corsini connection.

Twiggs had succumbed to hysterical guffaws after hearing the story, and Joe D'Amato had been amused, but the SEC man is infuriated.

"Son of a bitch," he says angrily. "I should have caught those nine-thousand-share trades. How did you break it?"

"A lot of luck."

"You told Pistol and Burns?"

"Oh, sure. Twiggs called me this morning. They've canned Bechtold and are switching to another commercial printer until they can put in a desktop printing system. Listen, Jerry, you better tell Snellig Firsten Holbrook."

"Yeah," the other man says worriedly. "I'll do that. You think the printer was in on it?"

"Nah," Cone says, "I think he's clean. He's just careless with his garbage, that's all."

"My God," Bigelow says, trying to wipe drips of gelato from his lapel, "do you realize what this means? We'll have to get hold of Bechtold's customer list—get a subpoena if we have to—and alert all his Wall Street customers about what's going on."

That's exactly what Cone wanted him to say. This guy is brainy, but not the hardest man in the world to manipulate.

"Yeah," he says sympathetically, "a lot of work. Maybe an easier way to handle it would be for you to pay a visit to Frederick Bechtold. Come on strong. Tell him what's been going down, and if he doesn't get rid of Steiner Waste Control and put in an incinerator or pulverizer, you're going to report him to every Wall Street customer he's got. He'll believe you because he'll already have the bad news from Pistol and Burns."

"It could be handled that way," Jeremy says thoughtfully. "A lot less work. No subpoenas, charges, and court trials."

"Sure," Cone agrees. "And why should an innocent printer suffer just because Sally Steiner has larceny in her heart."

They stop at an umbrella stand for a final giant chocolate chip cookie. They munch on those, holding paper napkins under their chins as they walk.

"Sally Steiner," Bigelow repeats. "What are we going to do about her?"

"What can you do?" Cone asks. "Let's face it: Your chances of making a legit charge against her for inside trading are zilch. She's a shrewd lady, and I'm betting she'll fight you every inch of the way. Maybe you can force her to cough up her profits—but I doubt it. Meanwhile the SEC will be getting a lot of lousy publicity. Everyone will be on Steiner's side and getting a big laugh out of how clever she was to beat the stock market."

"Yeah, you're right. If this was a megamillion deal, I'd push for a formal inquiry by the Commission. But how much could she have made? Half a million?"

"Probably less than that," Cone says, not mentioning how much Corsini and his pals might have cleared. "But the important thing is that you're closing her down. The moment you brace Bechtold, you know he's going to get rid of Steiner. She'll be losing a good customer and getting cut off from her source of inside scoop."

"It makes sense," Jeremy says, nodding. "I'll just keep the whole thing on the investigative level and file a report saying the leak's been plugged."

"And take all the credit," Cone advises. "I don't want any glory. My job was with Pistol and Burns, and they're happy. The rest belongs to you."

"Thanks, Tim," Bigelow says gratefully. "Listen, you don't mind if I split, do you? I want to get uptown and start the ball rolling."

"Go ahead," the Wall Street dick says. "Tell the printer it was all Sally Steiner's fault."

He watches the SEC man hurry away, tossing the remnants of his cookie into a litter basket. Cone finishes his, then turns and meanders uptown to Haldering & Co.

He's satisfied that he's put the first part of his plot into place. If he can stage-manage the second part, his scheme will have a chance. Except, he admits, everything depends on the reaction of Sally Steiner. All Cone can do is put the pressure on and hope she'll cave. She might not, but he's got to try it. It's his civic duty, he tells himself virtuously. And besides, the whole thing is a hoot.

Back in his office, he calls Joe D'Amato. Sorry, he's told, the sergeant is out and can't be reached. Cone leaves a message and begins to get skittery. A lot depends on timing, and if he can't get hold of D'Amato and persuade him to play along, the whole scam will collapse.

He chain-smokes two cigarettes and makes a half-assed attempt to compose his long-delayed progress reports. They should be submitted weekly to Samantha Whatley, but at the rate he's going, they've become monthly progress reports.

His phone doesn't ring until after four o'clock. By that time his throat is raw from smoking, and his "Yeah?" comes out like a croak.

"Joe D'Amato," the sergeant says. "Something wrong with your voice?"

"Too many coffin nails. Thanks for calling back. I need a favor."

"Yeah? And what might that be?"

"You got a phone number for Mario Corsini? I'd like to call him."

"What for? Wanna have lunch with him?"

"Nah, nothing like that." Then Cone explains what he has in mind. "It's risky," he acknowledges, "but I think it's got a chance, don't you?"

"Damned little," D'Amato says. "You're playing with fire, you know that?"

"Sure, but what have I got to lose? I figure if I go ahead with it, she'll think seriously about turning."

"Umm. Maybe."

"You want to make the call to Corsini yourself?"

"Hell, no. Self-preservation are the first, second, and third laws in this business, and I've got to cover my ass. I'm even going to erase the tape of this call."

"Does that mean you're going to give me Corsini's phone number?"

"I haven't got it. But I've got the number of a social club in Ozone Park where he hangs. Maybe they'll get a message to him to call you back. That's the best I can do."

"Good enough," Cone says. "Let's have it."

That evening, on the way home, he stops to buy some baked ham hocks, which he and Cleo dearly love, and a container of potato salad. But back in the loft, he postpones laying out the evening's feast until he calls that Ozone Park social club.

A man answers. "Yeah?" he says in a voice that sounds like someone has kicked his Adam's apple.

"I'd like to speak to Mr. Mario Corsini," Cone says politely.

"Who?"

"Mario Corsini."

"Never heard of him."

"Sure you have," Cone says.

"I'm telling you, mister, there's no one here by that name, and I never heard the name before."

"Well, look, if a man named Mario Corsini happens to stop by, will you ask him to call this number. It's really very important. Tell him it's about Sally Steiner. Got that? Sally Steiner."

He gives his phone number, repeating it twice, and hangs up. Then he and Cleo go to work on the ham hocks and potato salad. Cleo takes a hunk of gristle under the bathtub for a late-night snack, and Cone mixes himself a vodka and water to cut the grease.

He doesn't read, listen to the radio, or watch TV. He just slouches at his desk, feet up, planning what he's going to say if Corsini calls.

The phone rings a little after eight o'clock, and he moves quickly to the kitchenette.

"Hello, asshole," Samantha Whatley says. "What're you doing?"

"Will you get off the line," he says. "I'm expecting an important call."

Silence. Then: "And what's this—chopped liver? Fuck you, buster!"

"Listen," he says desperately, "I'll call you when—"

But she hangs up, and he goes grumbling back to the vodka bottle. "Who needs her?" he shouts at a startled Cleo, then answers his own question. "I do," he says.

It's almost 9:30 when the phone rings again, and by that time Cone is feeling no pain and is ready to take on the entire Cosa Nostra and its Ladies' Auxiliary.

"Who's this?" a voice shouts.

"Am I speaking to Mr. Mario Corsini?"

"You tell me who you are or I hang up."

"Mr. Corsini, my name is Smedley Tonker, and I am an investigator with the Securities and Exchange Commission."

"So?"

"Forgive me for calling at this late hour," Cone goes on, wondering how many years he can get for impersonating a federal officer, "but we're working overtime investigating recent stock trading in Trimbley and Diggs, Incorporated. In the course of our investigation, careful examination of computer records shows that you and your associates took a very considerable long position in that stock."

"I don't know what the hell you're talking about."

"I'm sure you do, Mr. Corsini. Our records show a purchase of nine thousand shares by you personally through a broker in Atlantic City."

"I tell you it's all horseshit to me; I don't know nothing about it. And you said this call was about Sally Steiner. I never heard of the broad."

"You haven't? That's odd since your cousin, Anthony Ricci, works for Steiner Waste Control. Come on, Mr. Corsini, let's stop playing games. Our investigation shows you and your friends made your stock purchases on the basis of inside tips from Sally Steiner. Do you know how she got her information, Mr. Corsini?"

So, for the fourth time, Cone relates the tale of how trash from Bechtold Printing was delivered to Sally's Smithtown home, and how she rummaged through the garbage to find confidential financial documents.

"Are you claiming you knew nothing about Ms. Steiner's illegal activities, Mr. Corsini?"

"Talk to my lawyers, you putz!" the other man screams and hangs up.

Smiling happily, Cone goes back to his unfinished drink, polishes it off, and then returns to the phone to call Samantha Whatley.

It takes almost twenty minutes of sweet talk to soothe Sam into a growlingly genial mood. But finally they're calling each other "asshole" and "shithead" and planning a Saturday night dinner in the loft. Cone promises to supply pounds of barbecued ribs, a basket of extra-thick potato chips (garlic flavored), and some dill pickles as a green vegetable.

"I'll bring the dessert," Sam volunteers.

"Okay."

"What would you like?"

"You," he says.

Sally Steiner thinks of it later as Black Friday. It starts bad and gets progressively worse. On the drive into the city, some fucking cowboy cuts her off on the Long Island Expressway, and she almost rolls the Mazda onto the verge.

Then, when she gets to the office, she discovers the air conditioner has conked out, and it's a bloody hot day. There's a letter from the bank informing her that a check she deposited, from the guy who buys their baled paper, has been returned because of insufficient funds. There's also a crusty letter from the IRS telling her that Steiner Waste Control owes an additional $29,871.46 on the previous year's return, and they better come up with the funds—or else.

She's on the phone to the IRS for a long time, and when she finally hangs up, sweating, Judy Bering comes in to tell her that Frederick Bechtold has called three times.

"He sounds like he's got steam coming out his ears," Judy reports. "He kept shouting in German. All I could catch was *verdammt, verdammt, verdammt*. It sounded like he wants to feed you into one of his high-speed presses."

"All right," Sally says, sighing, "I'll give him a call."

Bechtold immediately starts spluttering, roaring, and cursing her in German. She knows enough of the language to recognize some of the words he's using, and they're not nice.

"Now wait a minute," she says, getting pissed off.

"Zo!" he shouts. "I should wait a minute, should I? You, you *Dirne*, you will wait five years in jail. In prison you will wait."

"What the hell are you talking about?" she demands.

"Oh, yes, oh, yes," he says furiously. "My best customer you have cost me. And who knows how many more? Maybe all. Because you go through my trash, and you read my first proofs, and then you buy stocks, you *Schlampe!* You are fired, you understand that? And you will hear from my lawyers. For my loss of business, you will pay plenty, you bet."

Sally has been listening to this tirade while standing behind her desk. Now, knees suddenly trembling, she collapses into her swivel chair.

"Who told you all that?" she asks weakly.

"Who? I tell you who. A man from the United States Government, that's who. They know what you have been doing. Oh, yes, they know everything. And you will pay for what you have done. Thirty-six years I have been in this business, and my work is the best. The best! And you, you slut, you have destroyed—"

She hangs up softly and sits slumped forward, forehead resting on the heels of her hands. She tries to make sense of what's happened, but her brain's awhirl. Thoughts come, go, jostle, scream for attention, dissolve, return.

The government man he mentioned must have been that creep from the SEC. How did he find out? And if he knows about Sally's stock trading, then maybe Paul Ramsey is in danger. What can they do to him? What can they do to her? Goddamn it, she'll fight them! She had no inside knowledge of those deals—exactly. But will they charge her anyway? Make her return the profits and fine her? A prison term? Ridiculous! It was no big deal. How the hell did they find out?

Suddenly frightened—not at possible punishment, but at possible loss of her investments—she phones Paul Ramsey. Thank God he's in, and she tells him to call his broker immediately and sell everything at the market price. Just unload totally.

"That's cool," he says.

"You'll do it, Paul? Right away?"

"Sure," he said, and his placidity helps calm her.

She closes the door to her office, and then calls Ivan Belzig, her attorney, and tells him everything. After he stops laughing, he gets indignant.

"And you couldn't pass the tips along to me?" he says. "What am I—an enemy?"

"Cut the shit, Ivan," Sally says. "Tell me, what can the SEC do to me?"

"I'll have to research it," he says cautiously, "but if you want a top-of-the-head opinion, they can't do a thing to you. You had no personal contact with any of the insiders who knew about those deals. All you did was use typical American chutzpah. They might want you to return your profits, but we'll fight that. Listen, they've closed down your operation, haven't they? That should be enough. If you hear from them, don't tell them a thing, not a thing—you understand? Just tell them to contact me; I'll handle it. And don't worry, honey; you'll come out of this smelling like roses."

"Thanks, Ivan," Sally says gratefully, feeling a lot better.

But when she hangs up the phone, she sees Mario Corsini standing in the doorway of her office.

"Thanks for knocking," she says angrily.

He comes close to the desk, leans forward on whitened knuckles. He stares at her with dead eyes from under the brim of a black fedora.

"Cunt!" he says venomously.

"I can explain," she starts. "I can—"

"You can explain shit!" he says, voice cold and hard. "A boyfriend on Wall Street, huh? And all the time you're digging through garbage. I should have known; that's your style, you no-good bitch. Now I got the SEC on my ass, and who knows what—"

"Listen," she interrupts desperately, "I just talked to my lawyer, and he says—"

"Fuck your lawyer," Corsini says, "and fuck you. The SEC works hand in glove with the Federal District Attorney, and he works with the FBI and God knows who else. So now I got the whole fucking government asking questions, like where did I get the money and do I know those guys who invested in other cities, and maybe the IRS is auditing my returns. All because of you, you lousy twat. Vic Angelo warned me this could happen. I should have listened to him. I swear to Christ I could off you right now for what you did to me."

"Hey," Sally says, "take it easy. You're imagining a lot of things that might not happen. Maybe you'll have to give back your profits and pay a fine. That's no big deal for a hotshot like you."

"No big deal, huh? And I should tell the sharks that? You got shit for brains? Oh, I'll work my way out of this, but I'm going to have to grease a lot of people. It's going to cost me, and guess who's going to pay?"

She doesn't answer.

Corsini looks around the office, goes to the window to peer out at the busy tarmac. "Nice place you got here," he says. "Good business, real estate, trucks. Plenty of assets. The papers are ready, and I've got a front lined up to make you a nice offer."

"I'll bet," Sally says stiffly. "But the business isn't for sale."

"Sure it is," Corsini says, taking out one of his twisted black cigars. He lights it and tosses the spent match onto Sally's desk. "This place is how I'm going to get my money back."

"But you haven't *lost* any money!" she yells at him. "You've *made* money on the tips I gave you. So why are you coming on so hard?"

He leans across the desk and blows cigar smoke in her face. "Because you tricked me," he says, his face twisted. "You played me for a sucker, you fucking whore. Now's my turn. You want to go on living, you sell the business; it's that simple."

She learned a long time ago that if you show weakness in the world she inhabits, you're finished. Jake taught her that. "Give 'em an inch, and they'll take a mile," he told her. "You gotta stand up to the hardcases.

They push, you push back. Otherwise you're flat on your tuchas, and they're walking all over you."

"Listen you cocksucker," she says stonily, "you and your lousy front aren't coming anywhere near this place. The business belongs to my family, and that's where it's going to stay. I'm not signing any papers. Stick them up your ass and smoke them, you crap-faced motherfucker."

The hand holding the cigar starts to tremble, and he presses it against the side of the desk to steady it. She wonders how close he is to popping her then and there and doesn't care.

"Oh, you'll sell," he says in an unexpectedly soft voice. "Maybe you got the balls to fight me, but does your crippled mother or faggot brother? I'd start with them. I'd leave you for last, because before I was through, you'd be down on your knees, begging to sell."

"Screw you," Sally says with more bravado than she feels.

"There is one way you can keep the dump," Mario Corsini says thoughtfully, still staring at her. "You put out for me and maybe we can work a deal."

"Christ Almighty!" she cries. "Is that the only way you can get a woman?"

"I can get a lot of women," he says, snapping his fingers. "Like that. But I want you. I want to break you. Really put you over the hurdles." Then he starts describing exactly what he wants to do to her.

She jerks to her feet. "You prick!" she screams. "Get the hell out of my office."

"*Your* office?" he says, looking at her with a stretched grin. "Not for long."

8

It's still Friday, and Sally Steiner wonders if this frigging day will ever end. If just one more schmuck starts swearing at her and calling her names, she's going to take out her pistol and *Bam!*—right in his family jewels.

Judy Bering goes out for lunch, and Sally calls over to the Stardust Diner for a tunafish on wheat and an iced tea. But when the sandwich arrives, it tastes like wallpaper paste, and after one bite she dumps the whole thing in her wastebasket. The tea is cold and wet, but that's about all.

Her stomach is still bubbling after that go-around with Mario Corsini. She rummages through her father's desk, still in the office, and finds his bottle of schnapps in the bottom drawer. It hasn't been touched since Jake died. She pours a dollop into her iced tea, but the mixture is so awful that she can't swallow more than a sip.

So she gets a plastic cup from the stack alongside the coffee percolator in the outer office and fills it with ice cubes fished out of her tea. Then she pours in the schnapps, a pear brandy strong enough to take the kink out of her hair. After the first swallow, which almost makes her gag, it begins to slide down a lot easier, killing off those butterflies in her gut.

She's pouring another when she looks up to see a tall, gangly man standing in the doorway. He's wearing a ratty corduroy suit and a black leather cap. He looks like a nut, and that's all Sally needs on this Black Friday: another brouhaha with an airhead.

"I'll take one of those," he says, jerking his chin at the schnapps bottle. His smile is quirky, but Sally decides he's not going to be a problem.

"Who the hell are you?" she demands, putting the bottle away.

"Sally Steiner?"

"That's right. And if you're selling, I'm not buying. So take a walk."

"I just wanted to talk to you for a few minutes."

"About what?"

"About Paul Ramsey."

"Oh, Jesus," she says, "are you from the SEC?"

"Nah," the gink says. "Do I dress like a guy from the SEC? My name is Timothy Cone, and I'm with Haldering and Company on John Street. We do financial investigations, mostly for corporate clients on Wall Street."

"Beat it, will you?" Sally says wearily. "I've already been investigated up and down, inside out, and both ways from the middle."

"I know," Cone says. "I'm the one who did it. Our client I was Pistol and Burns. Wee Tot Fashions—remember that stock? And I was also in on the Trimbley and Diggs takeover leak."

She stares at him. "You're the bastard who blew the whistle on me?"

"I'm the bastard," he says cheerfully.

She sighs. "You make my day complete. All right," she says, taking out the bottle of pear brandy again, "get yourself a cup out there and we'll drink to my destruction."

"It's not that bad," he says. "Just listen to me for a minute."

He comes back with a plastic cup, sits in the armchair alongside her desk, and takes off his cap.

"How did you do it?" she asks, pouring him a stiff wallop of schnapps.

"Find out you were going through Bechtold's trash? I followed your trucks."

Her eyes widen. "You're kidding."

"No, that's how I did it. You were on the computer printouts of trading in Wee Tot Fashions. Then, on the records of Trimbley and Diggs, there was Paul Ramsey. I went up to see him, but came away when I found out he was living with your brother. So that led me back to you."

"How did you find out Eddie was my brother?"

"I called and told him he was a beneficiary on an insurance policy you had bought, and asked him what the relationship was. He told me you were his sister. Pardon me for saying it, but he's not too swift in the street-smarts department."

"Tell me something I don't know. For instance, tell me how many days you followed my trucks."

"Four."

"You were lucky."

"I know. I tailed the van with Bechtold's scrap out to your garage in Smithtown. After that it was a breeze."

Sally takes a deep swallow of her drink. Now it's going down as smooth as silk. "You're a real buttinsky, aren't you?" she says.

"That's right," he agrees, and his smile is unexpectedly charming. "That's what they pay me for. So I got Pistol and Burns to dump Bechtold, and I turned you in to the SEC. Sore?"

"Sore? Why should I be sore? You just ruined my life, that's all."

"Nah," Timothy says, leaning forward to pour himself another shot, "it's not that bad. Nothing is going to happen to Paul Ramsey. I just mentioned his name so you'd talk to me. And I doubt if the SEC will move in on you. They may want you to return your profits, but if you've got a good lawyer, you can fight that. Look, they've closed you down, haven't they? That's the important thing as far as they're concerned."

"So that's why you're here? To cheer me up?"

"Not exactly," Cone says, looking at her directly. "I wanted to talk to you about Corsini."

"Who?"

"Mario Corsini."

"Never heard of him," she says.

"Sure you have," Timothy says. "His cousin works for you. Anthony Ricci."

"My, you've been a busy little boy," she says, but her smile is glassy.

"It's all guesswork," he admits. "But I figure that Steiner Waste Control, like a lot of private carters in the city, pays off the mob to stay in business. I think Corsini is your collector. You gave him stock tips. What I don't know is whether you did that voluntarily or if he was leaning on you."

She stands suddenly, begins to pace back and forth behind her desk, arms crossed, holding her elbows. "You really are a meddler, aren't you?"

"That's right. So which was it? You gave him the tips out of the kindness of your heart or because he came on heavy?"

"None of your business," she says.

"It *is* my business," he insists. "I think Corsini is giving you a hard time, and you gave him the tips to keep him off your back."

She turns on him suddenly. "All right!" she cries. "I gave him the tips. What difference does it make why I did it? It's all over now, isn't it?"

"No, it's not all over," Cone continues doggedly. "By this time he and his pals have heard from the SEC, and Corsini knows where your tips were coming from. And he knows the SEC has closed you down. No more inside stock tips. So if he was squeezing you before, he'll squeeze you all the harder now. If he hasn't already."

She flops into her swivel chair, drains her drink, peers into the empty cup. "All right," she says, "but you didn't come here just to tell me the story of my life and brag how smart you are. You want something. What is it?"

He looks at her admiringly. "You've got the brains of the family," he says. "I want you to turn and blow the whistle on Corsini. Go to the cops and tell them about the shakedowns."

"And get my ass shot off," she says with a sour grin.

"No," Cone says, shaking his head. "The cops will give you and your family protection. Corsini and his bullyboys won't dare try anything. No way! They're shrewd enough to know that any rough stuff would raise a stink strong enough to convict them without a trial."

"You don't know them," Sally says. "They may be smart, but when someone crosses them or plays them for saps, they stop thinking. Then it's just their stupid pride, machismo, and hot blood. Then all they know is revenge."

"Bullshit!" Cone says. "Maybe ten years ago, but the new breed are weasels. They'll rat on their mothers to keep out of the clink. Listen, these guys aren't like they were in *The Untouchables*. It just takes one person like you to stand up to them. Then maybe a lot of other people in your business will say enough's enough, and help the cops put the shtarkers away."

"And if I don't?"

"You want to go on the way you've been going? Paying a lot to bent-noses just to make a living? What makes you think you'd still have a business?"

"What's that supposed to mean?"

"I told you that the SEC probably won't bring criminal charges. But what if the SEC and the Federal DA decide you're not being cooperative?

You know what they can do if they want to? Just give the story to the newspapers and TV. It'll be the talk of Wall Street for at least eight hours. Long enough for a lot of people to decide to bring civil cases against you. Maybe even class-action suits. They'll say you manipulated the stocks—and there's something to that. Suppose a guy sold short in Trimbley and Diggs. He lost his stake because you drove the stock up on the basis of what he'll claim was inside information. The people trying to take over Trimbley and Diggs will probably have to pay a higher price because of what you did. Ditto the ones who bought Wee Tot Fashions. They can all sue if they want to. I'm not saying they'll collect, but your legal fees to fight those suits could bleed you dry."

"Oh-ho," Sally says. "First the carrot and now the stick."

"I'm just telling you what your situation is," Cone says. "You may be home free as far as the SEC is concerned, but you're not out of the woods yet. Those civil suits could demolish you. But if you become the Joan of Arc of the garbage business, I think the cops and the Manhattan DA will pass the word, and those civil cases will be quietly dropped. No one wants to sue the city's star witness who's performing a noble civic duty. Think it over. If you decide to play along, give me a call. Haldering and Company on John Street. I know a couple of New York's Finest. Like all cops they're hard-ons, but these guys you can trust. Say the word, and I'll set up a meet."

Sally makes no reply.

The Wall Street dick rises, pulls on his cap. "Thanks for the belts," he says. "Take my advice and go to the cops. Do yourself a favor."

After he's gone, she sits behind her desk a long time, swinging slowly back and forth in her swivel chair. What Cone said makes a lot of sense—to him. But, smart as he is, he doesn't know everything. He's got half the equation. Sally has the whole thing, all the pluses and minuses. And, at the moment, not a glimmer of how to solve it.

She rises, wanders over to the window. Truck No. 2 has just pulled up at the shed to unload. Anthony Ricci swings down from the cab. Sally stares at him a moment, then hurries out of the office.

"Tony!" she yells, and when he looks up, she beckons. He walks toward her smiling and wiping his face and neck with a red bandanna.

"It's a hot mother," he says as he comes up to her.

"Yeah," Sally says, "a killer. Listen, what about that dinner you were going to buy me?"

He looks at her, startled. "You wanna go? Hey, that's great! How about tomorrow night?"

"Suits me."

"The joint is Brolio's on Mulberry just below Grand Street."

"I know a girl who got screwed on Delancey Street and thought it was Grand. All right, I'll meet you at Brolio's tomorrow night. What time?"

"About eight. Is that okay?"

"I'll be there," Sally says.

She sleeps late on Saturday morning. It's almost ten o'clock before she rises and pads naked to the window to peer out. Everything is swaddled in pearly fog, and Sally can't even see the garage. The house is silent, and the stillness is everywhere: no traffic noises, no bird calls, no distant thrum of airliners. She feels isolated, wrapped in cotton batting, and yearns for a shout or a whistle.

She pulls on jeans and a T-shirt and goes downstairs barefoot to the kitchen. She has a glass of V-8, an English muffin with orange marmalade, a cup of black coffee. She may be awake, but her brain isn't; she's moving senseless through a muffled world, unable to concentrate; the fog is in her.

She picks up the Times from the stoop, but can't read it. She pours herself another coffee, but can't taste it. She stubs, her toe, but can't feel the pain.

"Zombie," she says aloud.

It angers her, this dazed feeling of being out of control, and it frightens her. She goes back upstairs to her bedroom and takes a shower as cold as she can endure. She stands under the water for almost twenty minutes, letting the needle spray bounce off her skull, face, shoulders, back, breasts, stomach, thatch, thighs—and start all her corpuscles dancing.

Gradually consciousness returns, confidence is reborn, resolve swells. She dresses again, goes down to the den, sits at her desk. She pulls a pen and scratch pad close and starts doodling, making scribbles: arrows, flowerpots, a radiant sun, stick figures running. She ponders what to do, how to do it, when.

Timothy Cone offered one option: go to the cops and spill the beans. That way she'd be able to hang on to Steiner Waste Control. Maybe she could get her mother and brother out of the city to reduce the danger to them. She has a queasy faith in her ability to protect herself.

A second option is to play along with Mario Corsini, put out for that devil until she can figure a way to fix his wagon for good. She actually considers letting that slob have his way, but then realizes it's impossible; the first time he tried, she'd vomit all over him; she knows it.

What it comes down to is that both options represent surrender, and that she cannot tolerate. She considers herself capable of coping with a raw, turbulent world. It's a matter of pride. If she gives up now, then her life is make-believe, and she is pretending to be someone she is not.

What would her father have done? Jake would never run to the cops for help; she is certain of that. Nor would he sacrifice his personal dignity to Mario Corsini or anyone like him. Making payoffs to the mob was distasteful to Jake, but just another business expense. If they had demanded something more, something that would diminish Jake as a mensch, Sally knows what her father's reaction would have been: He would have died fighting.

It's an ego thing, Sally decides, and there's no use denying it. She has bragged (to herself) that she is a woman with the brains and will to succeed in the violent, dog-eat-dog world of savage, scrambling men. If she is defeated now, her self-esteem shattered, she doesn't want to imagine what her future will be like. No future. None at all.

She draws the number 1 on her pad and strikes it out. Sketches the number 2 and crosses that out also. Then makes a big 3, and stares at it. A third option that did not suddenly occur to her, but has been growing in her mind like some kind of malignant tumor ever since she learned that her Big Chance was down the drain.

Option 3 is scary, no doubt about it, and she wonders if she has the balls for it. She thinks she might be able to bring it off, but the risks are horrendous. Failure would mean the loss of the business and, possibly, the loss of Sally Steiner.

It's a gamble, the biggest gamble she's ever made in her life. But she underlines the number 3 on her scratch pad with heavy strokes, and decides to go for broke. Jake would approve; she's certain of that. She starts plotting the details.

Later that day she calls Eddie. Paul Ramsey isn't there, but her brother assures her that Paul unloaded all the stocks and asked the broker to send him a check.

"Good enough," Sally says. "And you haven't had any unexpected visitors—like a guy from the SEC?"

"No one's showed up," Eddie says. "What's going on, Sal?"

"Nothing to worry about. When's your show at the gallery?"

"In about a month. Cocktail party at the opening. You'll come, won't you?"

"Wouldn't miss it for the world. I'll even tell everyone I posed for your masterpiece. Eddie . . ."

"Yeah, Sal?"

"I love you, baby."

He laughs. "What brought that on?"

"I just want to make sure you know."

"I know," her brother says, his voice soft. "And I love you, dear, and want the best for you."

She hangs up before she starts bawling. She goes upstairs to her mother's bedroom where Becky and Martha are playing backgammon, with the housekeeper shaking the dice cup for both of them. Sally sits with them awhile, watching the game and making them laugh with her ribald comments.

Martha goes downstairs to start dinner, and Sally pulls up a hassock alongside her mother's wheelchair.

"I won't be home for dinner, ma," she says. "I'm driving into the city. I got a date."

"A date?" Becky says, then smiles happily. "That's wonderful! But listen, you deserve, you work so hard. A nice boy?"

"Very nice. And very, very handsome." Then, knowing what her mother's reaction will be: "A regular John Garfield."

"Mazel tov!" Becky cries, and adds dreamily, "John Garfield. How I loved that man. So tell me, how did you meet?"

"Through business."

"He's got money?"

"Plenty."

"And what's his name?"

"Anthony. He's Italian."

"That's all right, too," her mother says. "I know some very nice Italian people. So where are you going?"

"To an Italian restaurant," Sally says, laughing. "Where else?"

"You'll be home early?"

"I don't think so. But I'll tell you about it in the morning."

"He lives in the city?"

"Yeah, ma."

"So you'll be driving home alone?"

Sally nods.

"Be careful. Drive with your windows up and the doors locked. You promise?"

"I promise."

Sally rises, then bends over her mother, embraces her, kisses her velvety cheeks. "I love you, ma."

Tears come to Becky's eyes. "I love you, too. I am so lucky, having a daughter like you. Every day I thank God."

"Yeah," Sally says huskily, "we're both lucky. Eat all your dinner and have a nice evening."

"You, too," her mother cries gaily. "Enjoy! Enjoy!"

Sally goes to her bedroom to get ready. Another shower, warm this time, with scented soap. She decides to wear her high-necked black sheath, figuring all the floozies Anthony Ricci has been dating probably dress like tarts with their tits spilling out. So she wears her conservative black with a pearl choker. And, examining herself in a full-length mirror, wonders sourly if she looks like the older wealthy woman that Ricci seeks.

It's a long drive into the city and down to Mulberry Street. But the trip goes swiftly as she runs scenarios through her mind, trying to decide the best way to spin this simpleton. It's been a long time since she's come on to a guy, and she hopes it's like riding a bicycle: You never forget how.

She gets down to Little Italy in plenty of time, but has to cruise around for a while, looking for a parking space. She finally finds an empty slot two blocks away. She slips the loaded pistol into her purse, locks the car, and walks back to Brolio's. It looks like a scuzzy joint to her, but you never know.

Tony is already there, thank God, waiting for her at a tiny, two-stool bar to the left of the entrance.

"Hey!" he says, coming forward to take both hands in his. "You made it! Have any trouble finding the place?"

"Not at all," Sally says, looking around. And then, with feigned surprise: "Tony, I like it. Very pretty."

"Nothing fancy," he says, shrugging. "But the food's great, and you can't beat the prices."

Sally sees a typical third-rate New York trattoria. Small, only nine tables, and all occupied except one. Crude murals of Vesuvius, the Colosseum, Venetian canals painted on wrinkled walls. Plastic plants in plastic pots. Checkered tablecloths. Dripping candles stuck in raffia-bound Chianti bottles. Paper napkins. And hanging in the air, a miasma of garlic strong enough to scare off a hundred vampires.

Tony snaps his fingers, and a waiter swathed in a filthy apron comes hustling to usher them to the empty table and remove the Reserved card.

"A little wine first?" he suggests.

"Tony, you order," Sally says. "You know what's good."

"A glass of Soave to start," Ricci says rapidly to the waiter. "Then the cold antipasto, lobster diavolo, linguine, and maybe a salad of arugula and radicchio. With a bottle of that Chianti Classico I had the other night. The Monte Vertine."

"Very good," the waiter says, nodding approvingly.

"Sound good to you?" Tony asks Sally.

"Sounds yummy. You eat like this every night?"

He gives her his sizzling smile, eyes half-lidded. "This is an occasion. Dinner with the boss."

"Let's forget about that," she says, touching his hand, "and just enjoy."

The food is unexpectedly good. Maybe a little harsh, a little too garlicky, but Sally exclaims with delight over every course, the wine, the crusty bread, the prompt and efficient service.

"You know how to live," she tells Tony.

"Everyone knows how to live," he says. "All you need is money."

"That's so true," Sally says. "It's what makes the world go 'round, isn't it?"

She gets him talking about himself, his family, his boyhood in Salerno, a motor scooter he owned, a job he had making plaster statues of saints. She bends close to listen to his nonstop monologue over the loud talk and shouted laughter of the other diners, all the deafening sounds bouncing off the low tin ceiling. But, by leaning forward, she gets a whiff of his cologne mixed with the garlic, and she sits back.

She has one glass of the red wine and lets him finish the bottle. He drinks and eats enthusiastically with, she is bemused to note, a corner of the paper napkin tucked into his collar and the remainder spread over his chest, hiding a tie of hellish design.

He insists on tortoni and espresso, and then amaretti with ponies of Strega. Sally takes one sip of the liqueur and then pushes the glass toward Tony.

"You finish," she says.

"Sure," he says, and downs it in one gulp.

It's after ten o'clock when they rise to leave. He pays the bill with cash, Sally sees—no plastic for him—and leaves a lordly tip. They come out into a black, close night, the sky clotted with clouds and a warm, soft mist drifting. They stand for a moment in the doorway.

"Hey," he says, "I didn't tell you how great you look. That's the way a woman should dress. Very *elegante*."

"Thank you," she says, smiling.

"I mean, a woman doesn't have to show everything she's got in public. Am I right?"

"Absolutely," Sally says, taking his arm. "Where are you parked, Tony?"

"Well, uh, my car's in the garage right now. Transmission trouble. I cabbed down."

She knows he's lying; the poor shlumpf doesn't own wheels.

"Then we'll take mine," she says brightly. "It's only two blocks away; we won't get wet."

They skip, laughing, through the mizzle until Sally tugs him to a halt alongside her silver Mazda RX-7. "Here we are," she says.

He looks at the car with astonishment. "This is yours?"

"All mine. You like?"

"Fantastico," he breathes, and walks around the car admiring the lines.

"C'mon, get in," Sally says. "You can drive."

They slide into the bucket seats. Tony caresses the wheel with his palms, staring at the dash. "Radio, air conditioner, cassette deck," he says. "Even a compass. You got everything."

"All the comforts of home," she says lightly. "I also own a Cadillac, but this baby is more fun to drive."

"I wish—" he starts, then suddenly stops.

They sit in dimness, windows opened a few inches to let in moist night air. The windshield is beaded with mist, and illumination from streetlights is broken into watery patterns, as irregular as pieces from a jigsaw puzzle.

"If you had your druthers, Tony," she says quietly, "what kind of a car would you like?"

"A Jaguar," he says promptly. "The XJ-SC Cabriolet. You know the car?"

"I've seen it. A beauty. You have expensive tastes."

"Yes," he says sadly, "I do. Maybe someday . . ."

"Maybe sooner than you think," she says. "Do you mind if we sit here a few minutes? There's something I want to talk to you about."

"Sure," he says. "The night's young."

In spite of all her rehearsals and imagined scenarios, she finds it difficult to state or even hint at what she wants. But Tony is no great brain, she tells herself, so she figures her best bet is to come on as blunt and obvious as possible. Then she can gauge his reaction and play him from there.

"That cousin of yours," she says. "Mario. What do you think of him?"

Ricci shrugs. "He's okay, I guess. Sometimes he thinks he's my father. He knows what he wants."

"Yeah," Sally says with a short laugh. "He wants me."

Tony turns to peer at her in the gloom. "What do you mean? What are you saying?"

"The guy is driving me crazy. He's after me every day. He won't let up. I don't know what to do about it."

"He is after you? I don't understand. You pay your dues promptly."

"Do I have to spell it out for you, Tony? That cousin of yours is trying to get me into bed. He's told me a hundred times what he wants to do to me."

"No!"

"Oh, yes. You didn't know?"

"I swear I didn't."

"I thought he might have said something about it. I know how men talk."

"Mario is not like that. He is very—how do you say it?—very near-mouthed."

"Closemouthed."

"Yes, closemouthed. He tells me nothing. Just Tony, do this; Tony, do that. He keeps his secrets."

"Well, I'm one of them. No way am I going to spread my legs for that guy. He disgusts me. But I don't know how to make him leave me alone. I'm not going to ask you to talk to him about it."

"Holy Mother, no! I couldn't do that."

"Of course you couldn't. Because then he'd know I had talked to you about it. He'd get jealous because you're young and handsome, and he'd think you and I have something going."

"Yes," he says, "that's true."

"Tony," she says, putting a hand on his thigh, "what am I going to do?"

"You told him you don't want, uh, what he wants?"

"I told him a hundred times, but he won't take no for an answer. He just keeps after me. Calls me almost every day. Sends me letters. Dirty letters—you know?"

Tony nods. "He is acting like a fool. If a woman says no to me, I say goodbye. There is always another."

"You think I haven't told him that? But it hasn't done any good. I've got to get him out of my life, but I don't know how."

No response from Tony.

"Sometimes," Sally says, deciding this is the moment, "sometimes I wish the same thing would happen to him that happened to Vic Angelo."

"What? What are you saying?"

"You heard me. I just want him gone, and I'm at the point now where I don't care how it's done. I hate the guy, and I hate what he's doing to my life."

They sit in silence then, and Sally gives him time to absorb what she's said. If he belts her, she's sunk. If he gets out of the car and stalks away, she's sunk. If he tells Mario of their conversation, she's sunk. That's a lot of sinking, and her only life preserver is Tony's ambition and greed.

"I'd pay," she says in an aching voice, and she doesn't have to fake the desperation. "I'd pay a nice buck to have it done. Cash. I'd even help plan it. Make it look like an accident."

He doesn't answer, and her hand tightens on his thigh. She moves closer.

"And maybe a good job for the guy who does it," she goes on. "An inside job. No more straining your kischkas lifting pails of garbage in all kinds of weather. You saw that extra desk in my office? That was my father's. I've been handling everything since he died. But the business is getting too big. I need another executive. Someone I can trust. Someone who's done me a big favor by putting Corsini down."

She looks closely into his face and sees something new: stoniness. His eyes are hard and shiny as wet coal.

"No," he says flatly, "I cannot do it. Anyone else, but not Mario. He is my cousin. You understand? He is *family*."

Sally slumps. "Then I'm dead," she says dully.

"No, you are not dead," Anthony Ricci says. "There is a way out for you."

"Yeah?" she says in a low voice. "Like what?"

"Marry me."

She looks at him. "Are you nuts?"

"Listen to me," he says, taking her hand, holding it tightly. "You marry me and Mario will never bother you again. I swear by my mother. And you get to keep the business. Sure, you will still pay dues, but no one will hassle you—because you will be my wife."

"And what's in it for you?"

"First, I marry a smart, beautiful, older woman. It will help me stay in this country. Also I get a good inside job, a desk, maybe a secretary."

"And a piece of the business?"

He gives her his megawatt smile. "Maybe a little piece."

"And what about the sex department?"

"What about it? Am I so ugly?"

"No," she says. "Ugly you ain't."

"So? What do you say?"

"Let me think about it," Sally Steiner says, and doesn't object when he kisses her.

Timothy Cone has covered his table with several thicknesses of old newspaper, and they need it; the barbecued ribs, potato chips, and pickles make for a messy meal. Cleo prowls around, waiting for scraps.

"My live-in garbage disposal," Cone says.

"Cut the small talk," Samantha Whatley says, "and get on with your story. I want to know how it comes out."

As they eat, he describes for the fifth and, he hopes, final time how Sally Steiner was trading stocks on inside information gleaned from the printer's trash. He tells Sam about the mob's control of the private carting business and how Sally was giving tips to Mario Corsini.

"For what reason I don't know, exactly," Timothy admits. "But I think he was leaning on her; that's my guess."

Then he recounts how he went up to see Steiner and did a little leaning of his own, trying to turn her so she'll go to the cops and end extortion by the skels.

By the time he's finished his narrative, they've demolished ribs, chips, and pickles. Sam has provided chocolate éclairs for dessert, but they put those in the fridge and settle down with their beers, feet parked up on the littered table.

"My, oh my," Sam says, "you really have been a busybody, haven't you? But you know what burns my ass?"

"A flame this high?" he asks, holding his hand a yard off the floor.

"Shithead," she says. "When you found the insider leak for Pistol and Burns, your job was finished. Keerect? That's what they hired Haldering for, and you delivered. It should have ended right there. But no, you had to push it and get involved with the Mafia shaking down garbage collectors, and trying to get this Sally Steiner to blow the whistle. Why did you do that, Tim?"

He looks at her. "I don't know," he says. "It just seemed the thing to do."

"Bullshit!" Sam says. "You know what I think your problem is? I think you see yourself as nemesis. Death to all evildoers!"

"Nah, not me. I just saw a chance for the good guys to make a score, so I played out my hand. Listen, the cops helped me plenty. If I can fiddle a good bust for them, then they're happy and willing to keep cooperating. I wasn't acting out of anything but pure selfishness."

"Uh-huh," Samantha says. "Get me an éclair, you Masked Avenger."

"Up yours," he says.

They sip their beers, nibble their chocolate éclairs, and agree it's a loathsome combination—but tasty. Their conversation becomes desultory, with Cone doing most of the talking, and Sam replying with monosyllables or grunts.

"Hey," he says finally, "what's with you? Got the fantods or something?"

"Just thinking."

"About what?"

"That Sally Steiner. I feel sorry for her."

He snorts.

"What's that supposed to be?" Sam asks. "A laugh?"

"If it is, it's on me. I went up to see that put-together lady to find out if she was ready to talk to the cops."

"And?"

"She told me to get lost. She's marrying Tony Ricci, Corsini's cousin."

"You're kidding."

He holds up a palm. "Scout's honor. She snookered me. I thought I had her in a bind, but she wiggled out of it. By marrying Ricci she gets to keep the business. And she gets Corsini off her back. Maybe she'll have to give her husband a piece of the action, but I'll bet that garbage dump is going to stay in the Steiner family for another generation. She's a real survivor."

"Is she pretty?" Sam asks.

"She's okay."

An hour later, they're lolling naked on the floor mattress. Popped cans of beer have been placed within easy reach, and Cleo, protesting mightily, has been locked in the loo.

Samantha, sitting up, begins unpinning her magnificent hair. Timothy watches with pleasure the play of light and shadow on her raised arms, stalwart shoulders, the small, hard breasts. Suddenly she stops and stares at him.

"Listen," she says, "you made it sound like Sally Steiner is marrying that Tony Ricci just so she can keep the business in the family. Did it ever occur to you that she might love the guy?"

Cone shrugs. "Could be. There are all kinds of love."

"Yeah," Sam says, reaching for him. "Here's mine."

Book Two
A Case of the Shorts

1

John J. Dempster, Chairman and Chief Executive Officer of Dempster-Torrey, Inc., comes charging out of his office bathroom, a dynamo in overdrive. Gray brush-cut hair is wet from a shower; he scrubs his scalp furiously with a towel. He's wearing only boxer shorts imprinted with monetary insignia: dollar, pound, deutsche mark, yen.

Mrs. Esther Giesecke, his executive secretary, follows him to the dressing room, picking up his damp towel. She stands in the doorway as he dresses swiftly.

"All right," he says, "what have we got?"

"Tommy called from La Guardia. The Lear is fueled and ready to go. He wants to know when you'll be leaving."

"The idiot!" Dempster snaps. "We'll be leaving when I get there. What else?"

"Hiram Haldering called to confirm your appointment on Monday afternoon at three."

Another woman appears at the secretary's side. She is Eve Bookerman, Chief Operating Officer of Dempster-Torrey.

"You sure you want to go to Haldering's office, J. J.?" she asks. "Why not have him come over here?"

"No," he says brusquely. "I want to get a look at his operation. Twiggs at Pistol and Burns says it's a raggedy-assed outfit, but apparently they get results. Eve, I'll want you to come with me. And Ted Brodsky, too. Tell him about it. Anything else?"

"Your case is packed," his secretary tells him. "The takeover papers are in there, with a photocopy of your letter of intent. And a preliminary draft of your speech to the Chicago analysts."

"That's it?"

"That's it," she tells him.

"Eve, you got anything?"

"*Time* magazine wants to do a profile. They'll assign someone to follow you around for a day. Twenty-four hours in the life of a magnate—that kind of thing."

"A cover?" he asks sharply.

"They didn't say, and I didn't ask."

"Tell them no cover, no story. Did you send flowers to Ed Schanke's funeral?"

"I took care of it, J. J."

"Good. That union should be easier to deal with now. He was a sonofabitch. Well, I guess that's it. If I think of anything else, I'll call from the car or plane. You know where to phone me in Chicago and St. Louis. I'll be back in town Sunday night, so you can reach me at home then if anything comes up."

He inspects himself in a full-length mirror. He's wearing a black suit of raw silk, white shirt, regimental striped tie. His black kilties are polished to a high gloss. His only jewelry is a gold wedding band.

"Okay, Esther," he commands, "check me out."

"Wallet?" she says. "Keys? Handkerchief? Sunglasses? Reading glasses? Credit cards? Pen? Cigarettes? Lighter? Pillbox?"

As she enumerates all these items, he taps trouser and jacket pockets. "Got everything," he reports. "Esther, take my case out to Tim. I'll be along in a minute."

They move into his outer office, a baronial chamber paneled with bleached pine. It is dominated by an enormous desk-table: a solid slab of polished teak supported on chrome sawhorses.

Mrs. Giesecke carries his attaché case into the corridor, closing the door behind her. Dempster puts his back against it and beckons. Eve Booker-man comes into his arms: a long, fervid embrace, lips mashed, tongues seeking.

She pulls away, gasping. "You'll call me tonight, Jack?" she asks.

"Don't I always? That ear of yours still giving you trouble?"

"It's better. The drops are helping."

"Good. I better get moving."

"Jack, you be careful."

"I'm always careful," he says. "See you on Monday."

Tim, his bodyguard, is waiting at the executive elevator. The two men ride down forty-two floors to Wall Street.

"Nice day, Mr. Dempster," Tim says cheerily. "Good flying weather."

"Too bloody hot. But we'll be going from one air-conditioned cocoon to another."

A gray Lincoln limousine is at the curb. Bernie is behind the wheel. He hops out to open the back door, and Dempster slides in. Tim walks around to the traffic side to get in next to his boss.

A black Kawasaki motorcycle is idling about twenty feet to the rear of the limo. It starts up, moves forward so slowly that the man in the saddle drags his steel-toed boot on the pavement. Both driver and the man on the pillion are wearing blue nylon jackets, jeans, massive crash helmets with tinted visors that extend to their chins.

The bike pulls up alongside the Lincoln and stops. The rear rider unzips his jacket. He pulls out an Uzi submachine gun, stock folded down. Firing the weapon with one hand, he sprays the three men in the limousine, shooting through the opened door and the closed windows.

The chauffeur and bodyguard die first, their bodies riddled, jerking as the 9mm slugs cut them open. The muzzle is turned to Dempster. He throws up both hands in angry protest, but the bullets slice through. He is slammed back on the seat, then toppled onto the floor.

The assassin coolly empties the thirty-two-round magazine, then slips the gun back into his jacket. The Kawasaki accelerates, roars away, weaving through traffic. In a moment it is gone.

And so is John J. Dempster.

News headline: MASSACRE ON WALL STREET!

Post headline: WALL STREET BLOODBATH!

Times two-column head: Executive and Two Aides Slain by Motorcyclists in Financial District.

Photographs were gory, but facts were few. Knowledgeable witnesses identified the bike as a black Kawasaki Ltd. 650, and the weapon as a 9mm Uzi submachine gun with folding stock. Descriptions of the killers were meager: two young male Caucasians, medium height, medium build, wearing blue jackets, jeans, visored helmets, boots.

Shortly after the murders, three New York newspapers received phone calls from an organization calling itself "Liberty Tomorrow," and claiming responsibility for the killings. More attacks against "corporate America" were promised, and the callers warned that assassinations of business executives would continue until the "people sit in the seats of the mighty."

The New York Police Department, the FBI, CIA, Interpol, and anti-terrorist organizations of foreign governments reported they had no information on a revolutionary group called Liberty Tomorrow, but all cautioned that such anarchic cells formed frequently, were usually short-lived, and sometimes consisted of no more than a half-dozen members.

The police investigation concentrated on finding the Kawasaki and checking all the threatening letters that John J. Dempster, like many business executives, received over the years. Detectives also sought to determine who was aware of Dempster's schedule, knew of his projected flight to Chicago, and was able to direct the killers to the right place at the right time, enabling them to commit their crime quickly and escape with ease.

John J. Dempster was buried on Friday, but even before his funeral (attended by a Deputy Under-Secretary of Commerce), the Board of Directors of Dempster-Torrey, Inc., met in emergency session and appointed a subcommittee to search for and recommend a possible successor to Dempster. Meanwhile the responsibility for keeping the conglomerate functioning was assigned to Chief Operating Officer Eve Bookerman.

On the day of the murders, the common stock of Dempster-Torrey, Inc., was listed on the New York Stock Exchange at $155.250 per share. By the following Monday, it was trading at $119.625.

And on Monday afternoon, at precisely three o'clock, Eve Bookerman is ushered into the private office of Hiram Haldering on John Street.

"My dear lady," he says, taking both her hands in his and twisting his meaty face into a suitable expression of grief, "may I express my extreme sorrow at your loss and my horror at this tragedy."

"Yes," she says, looking at their scabrous surroundings with some astonishment, "thank you. May I sit down?"

"Of course, of course," H.H. says hastily. He drops her hands and pulls an armchair closer to the side of his desk. "After what you've been through in the past few days, I would have been happy to postpone this meeting or at least come to your office."

"No," she says decisively. "Mr. Dempster wanted to come here, and I'm carrying out his wishes as best I can. Our Chief of Security, Theodore Brodsky, was supposed to come along, but he's tied up with the New York police and the FBI."

"I understand completely. And tell me, has there been any progress at all?"

"They don't tell me anything," she says fretfully. "Only that the investigation is continuing. Infuriating!"

Haldering nods his fat head benignly. "I can understand that, having worked for the FBI for many years. They're making progress; I'm sure they are. But nothing will be released until all the facts are nailed down, and either the perpetrators have been taken into custody or suspects identified. I hope, dear lady, that you and other Dempster-Torrey executives are taking extra precautions for your personal safety."

"The police insisted on it," she says, not happily. "My bodyguard is sitting in your outer office right now. Ridiculous! I can take care of myself."

"I'm sure Mr. Dempster thought the same thing," he says. And then, fearing that comment didn't show the proper respect for the departed, he clasps his pudgy hands and leans across the desk. "Well!" he says with a treacly smile. "I'm sure you didn't come here to discuss the murder of Mr. Dempster. Now what can I do for you, ma'am?"

"You're familiar with Dempster-Torrey?"

"Of course. Who isn't? One of the largest conglomerates in the country, I believe."

"Eighth largest," she says, lifting her chin. "Two years ago we ranked number twelve. If J. J. had lived, we would have been the largest within five years. Fantastic! Dempster-Torrey owns twenty-seven subsidiaries with a total of eighty-three divisions. We're into everything from peanut butter to sheet metal. We produce golf carts, paper napkins, scuba-diving gear, ventilation ducts, potato chips, ponchos for the U.S. Government, pasta, hair dryers, forklift trucks, and more. That chair you're sitting on was made by a Dempster-Torrey subsidiary. One of our industrial divisions made the tile on this floor. You name it and the chances are good that it is produced by Dempster-Torrey."

H.H. shakes his head in wonderment, although he knows the chair he's sitting on was purchased secondhand, and the floor tile was part of a job lot—and cruddy stuff it is, too.

"For the past six months or so," Eve Bookerman goes on, "our factories, warehouses, and distribution centers all over the country have been hit by a series of attacks. Deliberate! Fires, vandalism, unexpected strikes, and consumer lawsuits. There have been eighteen separate incidents. Mr. Dempster did not think that was coincidence, nor do I. He was convinced there is a plot by some person or some group directed against Dempster-Torrey. He had no idea what the reason for such hostility might be, nor do I, nor does anyone else in our organization. Mystery!"

"Surely Mr. Dempster must have made enemies during his career."

"Of course he did. How could a man do what he did without making enemies? But I can't believe any of them would take revenge by setting a fire in a little flag and banner factory we own, a fire that killed two innocent workers. Despicable!"

"You said that Mr. Dempster considered the possibility of a plot by some group. Liberty Tomorrow, for instance—the terrorists who called the newspapers after the murders?"

"It was the first time I ever heard the name. That's one of the most frustrating things about the attacks against Dempster-Torrey. There were no telephone calls, no threatening letters. No one claimed responsibility."

"And I presume each of these incidents was investigated?"

"Of course. By local police and by our own security people. No arrests, not even a theory on who is responsible. Maddening!"

"Tell me, dear lady, have you told all this to the officers investigating Mr. Dempster's death?"

"I told them," she says grimly. "I don't believe they think there is any connection between the attacks on our factories and J.J.'s murder."

"But you think there is?"

"I don't know what to think. Nightmare!"

Hiram Haldering, nodding, begins swinging slowly back and forth in his swivel chair. He's getting to look more like a dumpling every day. The double chin is going for a triple. The waistcoat is ready to pop its pearl buttons. And what he fancies is an executive stride comes perilously close to a waddle. He is not totally bald, not quite, but his pate glistens, the color of a peeled apple.

He stops swinging to lean on his desk once again, suety palms clasped.

"I should tell you at once, ma'am," he says, "that Haldering and Company cannot investigate the murder of Mr. Dempster. We have neither the resources nor the personnel. We consider ourselves specialists in corporate intelligence. Buyouts, takeovers, mergers—things of that sort. We provide confidential information on individuals and companies, for a fee. But we are not equipped to conduct homicide investigations."

"I didn't think you were," Eve Bookerman says sharply. "J.J. made an appointment with you on the recommendation of Mr. G. Fergus Twiggs of Pistol and Burns, our investment bankers. The express purpose was to get to to the bottom of this series of assaults against our property and our people. We've gotten nowhere in trying to solve them or stop them. Mr. Twiggs suggested you might be able to help."

"Very kind of Twiggs," Haldering says, preening. "It is true that in several cases we have had remarkable success where others have failed."

"Then you'll be willing to take on the job? You can write your own ticket."

"With the understanding that our investigation will deal only with the industrial sabotage and not the assassination of Mr. Dempster."

"I'll accept that," she says crisply. "When will you be able to start?"

"Immediately!" he cries, picking up on her monosyllabicity.

"Excellent! In the hope that we might come to an agreement, I've brought along copies of a file that will give you an idea of what we've been up against. Along with a list of personnel involved, addresses and phone numbers—all of which may be of help."

"I admire your foresight," he says with an unctuous smile.

"Oh," she says, snapping her fingers, "one more thing: Mr. Twiggs urgently recommends that we request the problem be handled by one of your investigators—Timothy Cone. Is that his name?"

"Timothy Cone," Hiram Haldering repeats, smile fading. "Yes, we do employ an investigator by that name. But unfortunately, Mr. Cone is busy with several other cases at the moment. However, we have a number of other investigators who are fully qualified to—"

She interrupts him. "No Cone, no deal," she says.

He shifts uncomfortably in his chair. "As you wish," he says. "Perhaps I should warn you that Timothy Cone is—"

"Mr. Twiggs described him," she says impatiently. "I know what to expect. If he can do the job, it doesn't matter." She rises, holds out her hand. "Nice doing business with you, Mr. Haldering. I'm depending on your shop to make sense out of this whole awful affair. Monstrous!"

He starts to thank her for her trust and confidence, but she is out the door, leaving behind a taped accordion file bulging with documents. H.H. picks up his phone and punches the intraoffice extension of Samantha Whatley.

"Sam?" he says. "Come into my office, please. At once. And if Cone isn't sleeping or beering it up, drag his scruffy ass in here."

Cone lumps up Broadway, that humongous accordion file clamped under his right arm. It's heavy enough so that he lists to starboard, and occasionally has to pause and get a fresh grip.

"Don't you dare take that file out of the office," Sam had warned.

"Sure, boss," he replied. "I'm not about to carry that blivet home with me."

"What's a blivet?"

"Eight pounds of shit in a four-pound bag."

"You're disgusting!" she yelled at him.

"Yeah," he said, "I know."

So now he's plodding home to his loft, lugging the blivet and wondering what he and Cleo might have for dinner. He decides hot Italian sausage might be nice, fried up with canned potatoes. Maybe a charlotte russe for dessert. That sounds like a well-balanced meal.

He stops at local shops for the makings, not forgetting a cold six-pack and a jug of pepper-flavored vodka—something he's been wanting to try for a long time. Thus laden, he trudges up the six flights of iron steps to his loft.

The meal turns out to be okay, but that pepper vodka is sparkly enough to make Cone's scalp sweat. He's afraid to light a cigarette, figuring a single belch might ignite and, like a flame thrower, incinerate the joint.

He switches to cold beer to soothe his scorched palate and settles at his desk, feet up, to dig through the contents of that Dempster-Torrey file.

The first thing he finds is three pages stapled together that list names, addresses, and phone numbers of people connected with John J. Dempster and his corporation. Included, Cone sees, are the names of his widow, three young sons, his brother, his parents, his deceased bodyguard and chauffeur, and the top rank of Dempster-Torrey execs, the Board of Directors, attorneys, and bankers.

Also on the list, Cone notes with some bemusement, are the names of Dempster's tailor, masseur, physician, dentist, physical fitness instructor, servants, golf pro, pilot, and proctologist.

"Some people know how to live," Cone calls to Cleo. But the tom, sleeping off the Italian sausages under the bathtub, pays no heed.

He starts flipping swiftly through the documents on the attacks that have bedeviled Dempster-Torrey, Inc., for the past six months. There are eighteen reports, all signed by Theodore Brodsky, Chief of Security. They include arson, sabotage, vandalism, product tampering, and similar crimes, all apparently designed to erode the profits and tarnish the public image of Dempster-Torrey. Cone can understand why John J. thought there was a plot against him and his conglomerate; the guy wasn't just being paranoid.

He pops another beer and starts reading the reports again, slower this time, wondering if there's a pattern or link everyone else had missed. He's halfway through and hasn't found a damned thing when his wall phone shrills. He carries his beer into the cramped kitchenette.

"Yeah?" he says.

"You putz!" screams Neal K. Davenport. "Just what the fuck do you think you're doing?"

"Hey, wait a minute," Cone says. "What's this—"

"The Dempster kill!" the NYPD detective shouts at him. "Why are you sticking your nose into that?"

"Come on," Cone says, "don't get your balls in an uproar. Who told you Haldering is involved in it?"

"Eve Bookerman, that's who. She's been running the outfit since Dempster got chilled. She told us that she hired Haldering."

"Then she must have told you that all we're doing is investigating industrial sabotage in their plants. Look, Neal, we don't do windows and we don't do homicides. That job is all yours; Hiram Haldering made it plain to Bookerman. You know about the accidents they've been having?"

"Yeah," the city bull says grudgingly, "they told us."

"You think there's a connection with Dempster's murder?"

"We can't see it."

"So where's the conflict? The Department is after the guys on the motorcycle. We're after the people who are trashing Dempster-Torrey's property. Listen, what's your interest in this? Are you handling the file?"

"Shit, no! I caught the original squeal. I got there right after the blues. But it's too big to leave to little old me. They think I'm only good for busting pickpockets and flashers."

"Tough titty," Cone says. "So who's in charge?"

"Some wet-brained lieutenant who's got a rabbi in the Department with a lot of clout. The guy's a real cowboy. He's riding off madly in all directions. Well, I can't really blame him. This is an important one, and he wants to cover his ass. The first case of terrorism in the Wall Street district."

"The hell it was," Cone says. "A few years ago Fraunces Tavern was bombed by revolutionaries, and long before that a guy drove a horse-drawn cart down Wall Street and set off a bunch of bombs in the wagon. They called them anarchists in those days. Anyway, the explosion blew the hell out of the horses. You can still see the scars on some of the buildings if you look for them."

"Jesus," Davenport says, "you're a veritable gold mine of useless information. Well, regardless of past history, this is still a big case, and everyone wants a piece of it. Not only the Department, but the Manhattan DA, the Federal DA, the FBI, New York State, and the CIA. It's as fucked up as a Chinese fire drill."

"The CIA? What's their interest?"

"They're investigating those wackos, the Liberty Tomorrow gang, to see if it's a terrorist organization with pals overseas, like in Germany, France, or the Middle East."

"Lots of luck," Timothy says. "So everyone is walking up everyone else's heels and fighting for interviews on the TV talk shows. Where do you fit into this mishmash?"

"Christ!" the city cop says. "You know what they've got me doing? A couple of witnesses swear the driver of the motorcycle was wearing a steel-toed boot. So I'm supposed to check out every joint in the city that puts steel tips on shoes and boots. That's like looking for a needle in a keg of nails."

"Yeah," Cone says, "I know what you mean."

"If we could handle it as a simple dusting," Davenport goes on, "an ordinary, run-of-the-mill homicide, things would be a lot easier. But all the people involved are real nobs—or think they are. I mean Dempster-Torrey is a powerhouse in local politics. Charitable contributions, campaign donations, and all that shit. So the heat is on. I get pushed every hour on the hour, and when I heard you were joining the pack, I blew my cork. Sorry I yelled at you."

"That's okay," Cone says. "I can understand how you feel. But believe me, Haldering and Company has no interest in getting involved in Dempster's death. All I'm supposed to do is find out who's torching their factories."

"And you don't think it has anything to do with the murder?"

"Hey, I've just started on this thing. I was reading the file when you called. But you said yourself that you can't see a connection."

"That's right. But that's today. Maybe tomorrow you'll trip over something. You'll let me know?"

"Hell, yes. I'm no glory hound; you know that. If I find anything that sets off bells, you'll be the first to know. You can have the headlines."

"I don't know why I trust you," Davenport says. "You're such a flake."

"Yeah, well, I haven't ever bollixed you up, have I?"

"Not lately you haven't," the NYPD man says, considerably mollified. "Okay, go back to your boozing; you sound half in the bag already. Every time I think of a wild card like you rampaging around in something like this, my ulcer starts acting up. Keep in touch, will you?"

"Depend on it," Timothy says.

He goes back to his desk, back to reading the Dempster-Torrey reports, back to pepper vodka—which now seems mild, light, dry, sparkling, and guaranteed to dull the senses and make life seem interesting and even meaningful.

Finished with the documents, he tosses them aside, parks his feet on the desk, dunks a charlotte russe in the vodka, and ruminates.

As far as finding a link between the eighteen crimes—zero, zip, and zilch. But the lack of a pattern might have significance. It's unlikely one guy is racing around the country setting fires, dumping rice in gas tanks, blowing up warehouses, and slipping cyanide into sealed bottles of diet pills made by Dempster-Torrey's drug subsidiary.

Those sophisticated techniques were devised by someone with a lot of criminal know-how. That makes Cone think it's a gang, bossed by a villain who knows exactly what he's doing and what he wants to accomplish. But what does he want to accomplish? Revenge?

That would point the finger at a fired or disgruntled employee. Or maybe the former owner of some small and profitable company that John J. Dempster gobbled up on his march to power. God knows Dempster must have made enough enemies to last him a lifetime—which didn't, after all, last very long at all.

The Wall Street dick pours another small vodka, swearing to himself it will be a nightcap and knowing it won't because his mind is churning, and he'll be able to sleep only with high-proof oblivion.

He's halfway through that snort when his peppered brain spits out an idea that's so elegant he feels like shouting. It's a neat solution: an organization controlled, or hired, by a tough, determined, brainy guy who knows exactly what he wants and how to get it. Cone walks around his brilliant inspiration, and the more he inspects it from all angles, questions it, analyzes it, the stronger it seems.

And the motive? That's the best part!

"I do believe . . ." he says aloud, and Cleo comes slinking out from under the bathtub to yawn and stretch.

Later, lying in his skivvies on the floor mattress, lights out, his last conscious thoughts are of Neal K. Davenport, and how rancorous the detective must feel at being relegated to a minor role in a big case he thinks of as his own.

Cleo pads up to curl into the bend of his knees.

"He wants praise, kiddo," Cone says, reaching down to scratch the cat's torn ears. "Or maybe justification. He wants recognition that he's doing important work in this screwed-up world. Do you want praise, justification, and recognition, Cleo? The hell you do. I don't either. We've got a roof over our heads and all the hot sausage we can eat. What more do we need?"

Cleo growls agreement.

2

The secretary is a middle-aged woman, with a glazed ceramic complexion and wiry gray hair up in a tight bun. She gazes at the world through hard eyes. He figures it would take a helluva lot to surprise her—and nothing would shock her.

"Timothy Cone from Haldering and Company," he says. "To see Miss Bookerman. My appointment's for ten-thirty."

She glances down at a watch pinned to her bodice. She doesn't have to tell him he's late; her look is accusation enough.

"I'll tell her you're here, Mr. Cone. Please be seated."

But he remains standing, eyeballing the place. Nothing lavish, but everything crisp, airy, and looking as if it was waxed five minutes ago. The carpet has the Dempster-Torrey corporate insignia woven into it. A nice touch. Reminds Cone of the linoleum in his loft. That bears *his* insignia: cracked, worn, with the brown backing showing through in patches.

"Ms. Bookerman will see you now," the secretary says, replacing her phone. "Through that door and down the hall to your left."

"Right," he says.

"No," she says, "left."

He looks at her and sees a glint of amusement in her steady eyes.

"How about tonight?" he whispers. "Same time, same place. I'll bring the herring."

That cracks her up. "I'll be there," she promises.

He had called that morning from the loft. Eve Bookerman could see him at 10:30. Precisely. For a half-hour. Precisely. Cone said that was fine, and he'd also like to talk to Theodore Brodsky, Chief of Security. Bookerman said she'd arrange it. Her voice was low, throaty, stirring. Cone liked that voice.

He figured that if he had a 10:30 appointment, there was no point in going into the office first. So he spent an hour drinking black coffee, smoking Camels, and finishing the last charlotte russe. He was a mite hung over, but nothing serious. Just that his stomach was queasy, and he was afraid of what might happen if he yawned.

So he plodded all the way down the Wall Street. A hot July day, steamy, with a milky skim over a mild blue sky. By the time he arrived at the Dempster-Torrey Building, he was pooped; the air conditioning was plasma.

Now, scuffing down the inside corridor to his left, he passes a succession of doors with chaste brass name plates: JOHN J. DEMPSTER, SIMON TRALE, THEODORE BRODSKY and, finally, EVE BOOKERMAN. He wonders if, having taken over the murdered man's duties, even temporarily, she has moved into the CEO's office. But when he raps on the gleaming pine door, he hears a shouted "Come in!" and enters slowly, leather cap in hand.

She stands and comes forward to greet him. He is startled. From her voice and determined manner on the phone, he had expected a tigress; he sees a tabby. A short woman, almost chubby, with a great mass of frizzy strawberry-blond curls. She's trying to smile, but it doesn't work.

"Glad to meet you," she says. "Mr. Twiggs has told me so much about you."

"Yeah?" he says. "That's nice."

She's wearing a seersucker suit with a frilly blouse, a wide ribbon bow-tied at the neck. She looks clunky, but she moves well and there's strength in her handshake. Her eyes are great, Cone decides: big, dark, luminous. And she's got impressive lungs. Even with the blouse and suit he can see that.

She gets him seated in an armchair, not alongside her desk but facing her. Then she slides into an enormous, high-backed leather swivel chair. It swallows her, makes her look like a cub.

"Do you smoke?" she asks.

"Thanks," he says gratefully, reaching into his jacket pocket for his pack.

"Please don't," she says sharply. "I can't stand cigarette smoke. Atrocious!"

"Okay," he says equably, "I can live with that."

She sits on the edge of her chair, leans forward, elbows on the desk, hands clasped: a position of prayer. Her fingers Cone notes, are unexpectedly long and slender.

"Did you read the material I left with Mr. Haldering?" she demands.

"Yep."

"I hope you realize those reports are confidential. I wouldn't care to have them leaked to the media."

"I don't blab," he tells her.

"And do you have any questions?"

"A lot of them," he says. "Here's one for starters: What's the difference between a Chief Executive Officer—that was Dempster—and a Chief Operating Officer—that's you?"

"It varies from company to company," she says. "At Dempster-Torrey, J.J. made the big decisions and I made the small ones. He got the ulcers and I got the headaches."

"He had ulcers?"

"Of course not. It was just a figure of speech. What I'm trying to say is that he set policy and I carried it out. Expedited things. Found the people he needed and liaised with bankers, attorneys, accountants."

Cone stares at her. "Made his dreams come true?" he suggests.

"Yes," she says with that forced smile, "something like that. But the dreams were his."

"You've been with Dempster-Torrey—how long?"

"Almost eight years."

"Started out as Chief Operating Officer?"

"God, no! I was an MBA fresh out of Harvard. I started in the Planning Section, practically a gofer. I didn't get to be Operating Officer until three years ago."

"And then you worked closely with Mr. Dempster?"

"Yes."

"He made a lot of enemies?"

"Not a lot, but some, certainly. Any man in his position would."

"Any hot-blooded enemies? The type that'll say, 'I'll get you, you dirty dog. No matter how long it takes, I'll ruin you'?"

"None like that I know of. You think it's an old enemy who's engineering all our trouble?"

"I don't think much of anything," Cone says. "I'm just getting started. Trying to collect stuff. Maybe it would help if you could tell me what kind of a man he was."

"Very strong," she says promptly. "He couldn't stand to be denied anything he wanted for the company. Couldn't endure defeat. A very forceful personality. Goal oriented. An overachiever. He knew what he wanted and went after it."

"For himself? Or for Dempster-Torrey?"

"Mr. Cone, he was Dempster-Torrey. You cannot separate the man from the company he built. They were one. It wasn't just an ego trip. He wanted to make us an international conglomerate, bigger than IBM, General Motors, or the Vatican. And if he had lived, he would have done it. Absolutely!"

"Doesn't sound like the easiest guy in the world to work for."

She slumps back in her big swivel chair, begins curling a strand of hair around a slim forefinger. Those dark eyes glimmer, and Cone wonders if she's trying not to cry. For the first time he sees a wad of cotton batting stuck in her right ear.

"Got a bad ear?" he asks, trying to get her mind off Dempster's death.

She shakes her head impatiently. "A mild infection," she says. "I think I picked it up in the pool at the health club I go to. It's getting better.

Look, Mr. Cone, I've tried to describe J. J.'s business personality. Yes, in his business dealings he was hard, demanding, occasionally even ruthless. He believed that was the way he had to be to build Dempster-Torrey. But away from the office, when he could temporarily forget about takeovers and mergers, he was the kindest, sweetest man who ever lived. He was tender, sympathetic, understanding. That's the John J. Dempster you never read about in *The Wall Street Journal* or *Fortune*. The press was just interested in the tycoon. But the man himself was more than just a money- and power-grubber; he was a mensch. You know what a mensch is, Mr. Cone?"

"I know."

"Well, J. J. was a mensch. In his personal life, a man of honor and integrity. I'm trying to be as cooperative as I can. I'm sure that as you get deeper into this thing and talk to more people, you'll hear a lot of bad things about Mr. Dempster. I just want to make sure you understand how I felt about him. I thought he was a marvelous man. Marvelous!"

"Uh-huh," Cone says. "I appreciate that. And how are things going since he died?"

"Lousy," she says with a short, bitter laugh. "It's disaster time, folks. You saw what happened to our stock?"

"I saw."

"All the way down. Because Wall Street knew J. J. was Dempster-Torrey. And with him gone, what's going to happen? The market hates uncertainty more than anything else, so the heavy investors and big institutions are dumping shares. Can't say I blame them, but it hurts."

"Sure," Cone says, "it would. But you've still got the factories, the farms, the warehouses, the railroad, the airline, the work force, the management organization. The assets are still there."

"But he's dead," she says darkly. "He was our biggest asset. And the Street knows it."

She peers at a man's digital watch strapped to her wrist.

"Your time's up," she announces. "I've got Ted Brodsky standing by. You want me to bring him in here?"

"No," Cone says. "I'll go to his office."

"Whatever you want," she says, shrugging. "I know you're going to be talking to a lot of people. Just don't believe everything you hear."

"I never do," he assures her. "Thanks for your time. I may be back with more questions."

"Of course. Whenever you like. Just call first. I'm up to my eyeballs until the Board elects another CEO. But I want to help you any way I can."

"Sure," the Wall Street dick says.

. . .

Theodore Brodsky's office is small, cramped, and jumbled with file folders, reports, and manuals. There's a national map framed on the wall, studded with pushpins. An American flag on a wooden staff is held erect in a cast-iron base. The room reeks of cigar smoke.

The Chief of Security clears off a two-cushion leather couch, and that's where they sit, half-turned to face each other.

"She wouldn't let you smoke, would she?" Brodsky says with a knowing grin.

"Eve Bookerman? Nah, but that's okay; she's entitled."

"Go ahead, light up. That's why I chain-smoke stogies—to keep her out of here. She can't stand the stink. Says it gets in her hair."

Cone lights a Camel, watching as the other man puts a kitchen match to what's left of a half-smoked and chomped cigar.

"I gotta tell you right out," Brodsky says, "I wasn't in favor of Dempster bringing in outside people to investigate what's been happening at our plants. It's a reflection on me. Right?"

Cone shrugs. "Sometimes it helps to get a fresh angle."

"I don't need any fresh angle. When Dempster said he was going to Haldering, I raised holy hell—for all the good it did me. That guy got an idea in his head, you couldn't blast it out with nitro. Anyway, I checked you out with Neal Davenport, and he says you're okay, so I guess we can get along."

"Oh? You and Neal are friends?"

"Haven't seen much of him lately, but him and me go back a long way. Did a tour together in the Two-one Precinct. Then I took early retirement and got this job. Listen, I don't figure you're out to cut my balls off. I mean, you've got a job to do; I can understand that."

"Uh-huh," Cone says. "And I'm not out to make the evening news on TV."

"Sure," Brodsky says. "And if you fall into anything, you'll let me know first—am I right?"

"Absolutely," says Timothy, an old hand at skillful lying.

"Then we can work together," Brodsky says, sitting back and chewing on his cigar. "Like they say, one hand washes the other."

"That's what they say. Suits me fine."

"As I get it, you're just assigned to the industrial accidents—am I right? No interest in the homicide?"

"Nope. I'll leave that to the uniforms."

"Yeah, that's the best thing to do."

Mention of Dempster's murder makes him scowl. He leans forward to drop his cigar in a smeared glass ashtray that already contains three dead butts. Then he rises, begins to pace around the room, jacket open, hands in his pants pockets. He's got a gut, and his belt is buckled low, under the bulge.

If you had called Central Casting, Cone thinks, and said you wanted a middle-aged flatfoot, they'd have sent Theodore Brodsky, and he'd have gotten the part. A big-headed guy with heavy shoulders and that pillowy pot. A trundling gait and a truculent way of thrusting out his face. It's a boozer's face, puffy and florid, with a nose like a fat knuckle.

"My name is shit around here as it is," Brodsky says morosely. "After all, I'm supposed to be Chief of Security, and my A-number-one job was to protect the boss—am I right? Look, I did what he let me do. I'm the one who talked him into hiring a bodyguard. Tim was an ex-Green Beret, and he'd never dog it. Ditto the chauffeur, Bernie. He used to be a deputy sheriff out in Kansas or someplace. Both those guys were carrying and would have drawn their pieces if they had a chance. But what can you do against a couple of nuts with an Uzi?"

"Not much," Cone says. "And you can't stop a guy with a long gun on a roof across the street. It was just bad luck, so don't worry it."

"I gotta worry it," Brodsky says angrily. "It may mean my ass. I know that Bookerman dame would like me out."

"How come Dempster's limousine didn't have bulletproof glass?"

"You think I didn't think of that? I been after him for months to spring for a custom BMW. It goes for about three hundred Gs, and it's got bulletproof glass, armored body steel and gas tank, remote control ignition, bomb detectors—the whole schmear. He finally agreed, and that car's on order. But it'll take a couple of months to get it. Too late. But the new CEO can use it."

"Who's that going to be—Eve Bookerman?"

"Bite your tongue," Brodsky cries. "If she gets the job, I'm long gone. That lady and me just don't see eye-to-eye."

"What's the problem?"

"Chemistry," the other man says, and Cone lets it go at that.

"Look, Brodsky," he says, "when we first started talking, you said you didn't need any fresh angles on the sabotage. Does that mean you've got an idea of who's behind it?"

"That's exactly what it means."

"There was nothing in your reports even hinting at who's been pulling this stuff and what their motive is."

"Because I didn't have any proof," the Chief of Security says grimly. "But I'm getting it, I'm getting it." He pauses to consider a moment. Then: "I guess there's no reason why I shouldn't tell you. It's the labor unions."

Timothy stares at him.

"Yep," Brodsky says, nodding, "that's who it is. The unions that Dempster-Torrey deals with have got together and are causing all the trouble as bargaining chips to get better terms when their contracts come up for renewal."

"I gotta level with you," Cone says. "I think that idea sucks."

Brodsky flares up. "What are you," he demands, "a wisenheimer? What the fuck do you know about it?"

Cone stands, walks over to the framed map on the wall. He jerks a thumb at it. "All those pins show the location of Dempster-Torrey facilities in this country—correct? There's gotta be over a hundred of them."

"Hundred and fifty-nine."

"So how many local and national unions does Dempster-Torrey deal with? Ten? Twenty? Probably more like fifty, at least. And you're trying to tell me all those unions have joined in some grand conspiracy to damage the company they work for so they'll get better terms on their next contract? Bull*shit!* It just doesn't listen. First of all, you'd never get that many unions to agree on *anything.* Second of all, I'd guess that their contracts come up for renewal at different times. Maybe some next month, some in three years. And finally, what the hell's the point in burning down the place where you work? Manufacturing jobs are too hard to come by these days. No union in its right mind is going to trash a factory where its members earn a living. It's not labor that's causing all the trouble."

"Then who the hell is it?" Brodsky yells.

Cone spreads his hands. "Hey, give me a break. This is my first day on the job. I can't pull a rabbit out of a hat."

"I still think it's the unions," Brodsky says stubbornly. "Who else could it be? Some of those labor guys are out-and-out Commies. Maybe they're doing it for political reasons."

"To destroy American capitalism? I don't know what kind of cigars you smoke, but you better change your brand. You're way off in the wild blue yonder."

"Yeah? Well, you go your way, and I'll go mine. I'm still going to work the union angle."

Cone shrugs. Then, figuring he's gone as far as he can, he collects his cap and starts for the door. But he pauses.

"It might help," he says, "if you could tell me what kind of a man this John J. Dempster was."

Brodsky finds a fresh cigar in the mess on his desk. He bites off the tip, spits it into the overflowing ashtray. He moves the cigar around in his mouth to juice it up.

"They say you should only speak good of the dead," he says, "but in his case I'll make an exception. The guy was a dyed-in-the-wool bastard.

A real ball-breaker. When Wall Street heard someone had offed him, the list of suspects was narrowed to ten thousand. He didn't let anyone get in his way, and if you tried, he squashed you. He was just a mean bugger. And he didn't have to be; he had all the money in the world—am I right?"

"You ever have any run-ins with him?"

"Plenty. And so did practically everyone else who works here. His Bible was the riot act. Used to read it all the time."

"Yeah," Cone says, "I know what you mean."

He starts out again, but Brodsky calls, "Hey, Cone," and he turns back.

"I bet what I told you about Dempster doesn't jibe with what Eve Bookerman told you."

"You're right; it doesn't."

Brodsky holds up a hand, middle finger tightly crossed over forefinger. "Dempster and Bookerman," he says with a lickerish grin. "That's Dempster on top."

"Thanks," Timothy Cone says.

He figures plodding back to John Street in that heat will totally wipe him out. So he cabs uptown, but before he goes to the office he stops at the local deli and buys a cream cheese and lox on bagel, with a thick slice of Bermuda onion atop the smoked salmon. He also gets a kosher dill and two cans of cold Bud.

Sitting at his desk; scoffing his lunch while still wearing his leather cap, he reflects that there is no way he can separate an investigation of the industrial sabotage at Dempster-Torrey plants from an inquiry into the assassination of John J.

Despite what Hiram Haldering said, and regardless of what he himself told Neal Davenport, Bookerman, and Brodsky, Cone suspects the sabotage and homicide are connected. Also, there's a practical matter involved. To limit his detecting to the sabotage, he'd have to travel to eighteen different localities and try to pick up cold trails on cases that had been thoroughly investigated when fresh by local cops and Brodsky's security people, with no results.

All Cone's got to work with is the murdered man's family and friends, his acquaintances, employees, and business associates. Cone pulls out that list of personae that Eve Bookerman provided, from his inside jacket pocket. He looks up the address and phone number of the widow, Teresa Dempster, and dials.

It rings seven times at the other end before it's picked up.

"The Dempster residence." A woman's voice. Chirpy.

"Could I speak to Mrs. Teresa Dempster, please."

"Just a moment."

Long wait. Then:

"This is David Dempster. To whom am I speaking?"

"John J. Dempster was your brother?"

"He was."

"Well, this is Timothy Cone. I'm with Haldering and Company. We're investigating a series of industrial accidents at Dempster-Torrey plants, and I was hoping to talk to Mrs. Dempster for a few minutes. And you're on my list, too."

"Eve Bookerman informed us you'd probably be calling. I must tell you in all honesty, Mr. Cone, that neither Teresa nor I know the slightest thing about Dempster-Torrey operations. But naturally we'll be happy to cooperate in any way we can."

He shouldn't have said "in all honesty." Every time Cone hears that, he gets itchy. Also, Dempster has the plummy voice of a priest who's been unfrocked for waving his dork out a vestry window. Cone wonders what the guy does for a living. His business address on the list is David Dempster Associates, Inc., on Cedar Street.

"Can I see Mrs. Dempster?" he asks.

"As long as you're not a reporter or policeman," the other man says. "I rather think she's had her fill of those."

"I could be up there in a half-hour."

"Come ahead then; I'll tell her to expect you. I'm afraid I'll be gone by the time you arrive, but you'll be able to reach me at my office whenever you wish to see me. You have the address and phone number?"

"Yeah, I've got them. I'll probably get to you tomorrow if that's okay with you."

"Of course. And, Mr. Cone, please make your meeting with Teresa as brief as possible. She's been through a great deal in the past week. She's bearing up well, but we don't want her unduly disturbed, do we?"

"I won't disturb her," Cone promises. "Just a few questions. Won't take long."

But before he starts out, he stops at the office of Sidney Apicella, chief of Haldering's CPAs. As usual, Sid is massaging his nose. The poor guy suffers from rosacea of the beezer. It's big, magenta, and swollen, and he can't leave it alone.

He looks up as Cone enters. "Whatever you want," he says, "I can't do it. I'm too busy."

"Come on, Sid; this'll only take one phone call."

"The last time you told me that it took four days' work."

"One phone call, I swear. I'd do it myself, but you've got the contacts.

There's this guy named David Dempster. He's the brother of that pooh-bah who got blasted on Wall Street last week. Anyway, this brother has a business, David Dumpster Associates, on Cedar Street. All I want to know is what kind of a business it is, assets, liabilities, cash flow, and all that financial shit."

Apicella groans. "And you think I can get that with one phone call? You're demented!"

"Give it the old college try, Sid. I'll make sure you get special mention in my final report."

"Thanks for nothing," the CPA says. "When are you going to buy yourself a new suit?"

"What's wrong with this one? Sleaze is *in* this year—didn't you know?"

Figuring an outfit as big as Dempster-Torrey isn't going to quibble about expenses, he takes a taxi up to the Dempster residence on East Sixty-fourth between Third and Lex. The place is practically a mansion and, scoping it from across the street, Cone figures it was probably originally two five-story brownstones. But now, with an expensive face-lift, it's red brick with wide plate glass windows.

The old stoops have been removed, and entrance is via a street-level doorway protected with a wrought-iron gate. There's a uniformed police-man leaning against the gate, eyeballing all the young ginch passing by.

Cone crosses over and gives the cop what he thinks is an innocent smile. It doesn't work. The blue takes a long look at his black leather cap, cruddy corduroy suit, and yellow work shoes, and says, "Beat it, bum."

"Hey," Cone says, hurt, "watch your language. I'm Timothy Cone from Haldering and Company. I've got an appointment with Mrs. Dempster."

"Yeah? Let's see your ID."

Cone digs out his Haldering & Co. card with his picture attached. Sa-mantha Whatley claims that photo should be on a post office wall with the warning: This man wanted for molesting children.

The officer takes the card, steps inside, and calls on the intercom. Then he opens the gate, returns the ID to Cone, and unlocks the heavy oak door.

"Sorry about that," he says.

"No sweat," Cone says. "You guys on twenty-four hours?"

"Yeah," the cop says. "About as exciting as watching paint dry."

There's a young, uniformed maid waiting for him in the foyer, and he follows her up a wide marble staircase to the second floor. Cone tries to keep his eyes on the stairs, with scant success. Down a carpeted hallway to the rear of the townhouse he gets a quick impression of high ceilings, light, airy rooms, plenty of bright graphics, polished wood, and green plants everywhere.

He is ushered into a greenhouse extending from the back of the building. Wide panes of glass are set in a verdigrised copper framework. The whole faces south and east, and sunlight floods in through glass walls and domed roof. A system of bamboo shades has been designed to mute the bright light, but air conditioning keeps the place comfortable.

The greenhouse is crowded with rough wooden tables, bags of potting soil, fertilizer, crushed shell, sand, and gardening tools. On the waist-high tables, in neat rows, is arranged an impressive assortment of bonsai, each dwarf tree in a splendidly proportioned pot of brown, cream, or dark blue glaze. Other pots are decorated, and a few are set on lacquered wood pedestals.

The woman who comes forward, brass watering can in her hands, is tall, reedy, and wearing a long, flowing dress that billows as she moves. The gown is voluminous, made of some thin, diaphanous stuff the color of vanilla ice cream. But no paler than the woman herself.

"Mrs. Teresa Dempster?" Cone asks.

She nods vaguely, looking around at her plants. "And you're Mr. Timothy?"

"Cone," he says. "Timothy Cone."

"Of course," she says.

"Thank you for seeing me. I hate to intrude in your time of trial."

At last she looks at him directly. " 'Time of trial,' " she repeats. "What a nice, old-fashioned expression. Are you an old-fashioned man, Mr. Timothy?"

He gives up on the name. "I guess I am," he says uncomfortably. "About some things. Beautiful plants you have here, Mrs. Dempster."

"Trees," she corrects him. "All my babies. But such old babies. This one, for instance, is said to be forty-five years old. It's a Japanese red maple. Do you like it?"

"Yeah," he says. "Real pretty."

She puts down the watering can, picks up the little red maple and thrusts it at him. "Then take it," she says. "It's yours."

He moves a startled step backward. "Oh, I couldn't do that," he protests. "It's probably valuable."

"No, no," she says. "If you promise to love it, I want you to have it."

Getting a glimmer of what he's up against here, he, says earnestly, "Look, Mrs. Dempster, I appreciate your offer. It's very kind of you. But where I live, there's no sunlight at all. And I've got a nasty cat who'd demolish that thing in two seconds flat. It really wouldn't be fair to the tree for me to take it."

She looks so hurt that he's afraid she might start weeping.

"Tell you what," he says. "Why don't I accept the gift in the spirit in which it's given. But you keep it for me and take care of it. But it'll be my tree."

She gives him a smile as simple and charming as a child's. "I think that's a wonderful idea!" she says. "I'll tell everyone it's Mr. Timothy's tree, and you can visit it whenever you like. Do you want to name it?"

"Name it?"

"Of course. Most of my trees have names. This juniper is Ralph. That Norfolk pine is Matilda. Would you like your Japanese red maple to have a name?"

"How about Irving?" he suggests, willing to play her game—if game it is.

"How lovely," she says with such evident enjoyment that he stares at her, wary and perplexed.

Everything about her is long: face, limbs, hands, feet. She looks like a tree herself, but not a bonsai. More like a fullgrown willow, soft and drooping. There is an ineffable languor, she seems to float, her gestures are flutters. The big azure eyes are more innocent than any eyes have a right to be, and the unbound hair streaming down her back is flaxen and wispy.

Something ethereal there, something unworldly, and Cone has a vision of her galloping through the heather and caroling, "Heathcliff! Heathcliff!" He shakes his head to clear his mind of such nonsense and, to see if she is completely bonkers asks:

"And what are the names of your boys?"

She looks up into the air as if striving to recall. "Edward," she says. "He's the oldest. And then there's Robert, and then Duane."

"They live here with you?"

"Usually they're away at school. But this summer they're all on a bicycle tour through Europe. They're having tons of fun."

"Did they come back for their father's funeral?"

"No," she says, "they didn't. By the time we got in touch with them, it was too late. Besides, there was no point in their returning, was there?"

Cone has his own idea about that, but doesn't voice it. "Your husband's death must have been a tremendous shock to you, Mrs. Dempster."

"Oh, Jack didn't die," she says, almost gaily. "He just passed over. Nobody and nothing ever dies, Mr. Timothy. Just assumes another form. But everything is immortal: you, me, these trees, the world about us."

Oh, God, he thinks despairingly, she's one of *those*. And he resolves so wind up this interview as speedily as possible, figuring it a total loss. But suddenly Teresa Dempster becomes talkative. He thinks at first she's swaying as she speaks, but then realizes she's standing in the blast of an air-conditioning vent set into the interior brick wall, and the draft is moving her insubstantial gown.

"David, my brother-in-law, was such a help," she says. "He just took care of everything. I know people wanted to be kind, but why did they have to cut down all those flowers? Jack was buried near Schroon Lake. We have a summer home up there, you know, and a family plot in the dearest, sweetest cemetery you ever did see. Mom and daddy are there, and now Jack, and there's a place for me."

The idea seems to enchant her, and she pauses to smile fondly.

"Of course," she goes on, "he's not really there; just the envelope he temporarily inhabited. Because he came to me last night. Yes, he did. 'Terry,' he said. He always called me that. 'Terry, I'm very happy here. I've crossed over, and it's beautiful. I'm waiting for you, Terry.' That's what he said to me last night."

The Wall Street dick can't take much more of this.

"Mrs. Dempster," he says sternly, "did your husband ever mention any enemies he had? Anyone who had threatened him or sworn revenge for one reason or another?"

"So many people have asked me that," she says, and seems genuinely puzzled. "Of course Jack didn't have any enemies. How could he—he was such a *good* man. I've been so fortunate, Mr. Timothy. He was certainly the best husband in the whole wide world. He was away so much— traveling, you know—doing whatever it was he did, but I could, understand that; men are so busy. But when he returned, he always brought me a gift. Always! Sometimes it was just a funny little thing like a hand puppet. But he never forgot to bring me something. Never!"

"My sympathy on your loss," Cone mumbles. Then, louder: "Thank you for your time, Mrs. Dempster. I appreciate it."

"You're going away now?" she says, sounding disappointed.

"Yeah, I've got to. Another appointment."

"I suppose I should have offered you a drink or something."

"That's okay. You gave me a tree. Irving."

"And you'll come visit him, Mr. Timothy?"

"I certainly will," he says, and then tries one last time. "The name is Cone. Timothy Cone."

"Oh," she says. "Well, it's not important, is it?"

"Not important at all," he assures her.

He's hoping the lissome maid is lurking around to show him out, but there's no one in sight. He makes his way along the hallway, down the staircase, and out into the hot afternoon sunlight. The same uniformed officer is still on duty at the gate. Cone pauses to light a cigarette.

"You ever talk to Mrs. Dempster?" he asks.

"No," the cop says, "I never have."

"You're lucky," Cone tells him.

"Maybe it was her husband's death that made her flip out," Samantha Whatley suggests. "Maybe she was a perfectly normal woman, but then that awful, bloody murder pushed her over the edge."

"I don't think so," Cone says. "I'm guessing she's been that way all her life. She's not a wetbrain, you understand, but her gears have slipped a little; they don't quite mesh. Not bad enough to have her committed, but the lady is balmy, no doubt about it."

They're sprawled on an oval rag rug in Sam's tiny apartment in the East Village. She's prepared a mess of chicken wings cooked in an Italian sauce with onions and small potatoes thrown in. The big cast-iron pot rests on a trivet between them, and they fill their plates with a ladle. There is also a salad of Bibb lettuce and cherry tomatoes.

"Good grub," Cone says, sucking the meat from a wing. "Maybe a little more pepper and garlic next time."

"Now you're a cordon-bleu? If you stopped smoking, you'd be able to taste food the way it's supposed to taste. So you got nothing from the widow?"

"Nah, nothing important. Except that I'm immortal. That makes me feel swell. Maybe I'll do better with David Dempster, the brother. I called him and set up a meet for tomorrow. I'm also seeing Simon Trale, the Chief Financial Officer of Dempster-Torrey."

"What do you expect to get from him?"

"Nothing, really. I'm just fishing."

She looks at him suspiciously. "When you get that dopey look on your puss I know there's something going on in that tiny, tiny brain of yours. What are you up to, buster?"

"Me?" he says innocently. "I'm not up to anything, boss. Except maybe illicit sex. But I better tell you: I don't think you can separate the industrial sabotage from the murder. I think they're connected. Scratching the Chairman and CEO was just the ultimate act of sabotage. To damage Dempster-Torrey."

"Why? What for?"

"Beats the hell out of me. What's for dessert?"

"Tapioca pudding."

"I'll pass," he says. "You eat the fish eyes and I'll take my portion home to Cleo. That cat'll eat anything."

"Thanks for the compliment. Coffee?"

"Sure," he says. "And I brought a bottle of Spanish brandy. How about a noggin of that?"

"I'm game," she says. "And later do you intend to work your evil way with me?"

"It had occurred to me," he admits.

They watch *n*th return of *The Honeymooners* on TV while still lounging on the floor, sipping their brandies. It's a nice, lazy evening, but when the show is over, Timothy stirs restlessly.

"What's with you?" Sam demands.

"I don't know," he says fretfully. "I think I'm mellowing out. Look at us: curled up on a rug, watching TV and inhaling brandy. It's all so domestic and comfy I can't stand it."

"The trouble with you is—" she starts, then stops.

"Go ahead," he says, "finish it. What's the trouble with me?"

"You can't endure being happy," she tells him. "You don't know how to handle joy. The moment you start feeling good, you pull back and ask, 'What's the catch?' You just can't believe that occasionally—not always, but now and then—it's perfectly normal to be content."

"Yeah, well, you may be right. I know I don't go around grinning. So I admit I get a little antsy when things seem to be okay, but only because I haven't had the experience. Being happy is like a foreign language. I can't understand it, so naturally I get itchy and think someone is setting me up for a fall."

"You think I'm playing you for a patsy?"

"Oh, Christ, no. I'm talking about God."

"Since when have you been religious?"

"I believe in God," he protests. "He looks a lot like my drill instructor at Parris Island. A mean sonofabitch who kept kicking our ass and telling us it was for our own good. Like my pa walloping me with his belt and telling me it hurt him more than it did me. God always has a catch. Maybe not right away, but sooner or later. You pay for your pleasure in this world, kiddo."

"I'm willing," Samantha says. "Fly now, pay later."

Ten minutes later they're in bed together.

Both would be shocked if someone had suggested anything admirable in their allegiance to each other. Not only their sexual fidelity but their constancy for more years than most of their acquaintances have been married. Each is a half-filled glass, needing the other for topping off. Alone, each is half empty.

But no such dreary soul-searching for them; all they know, or want to know, is sweat and rut: a gorgeous game of shouted oaths and wailing cries. And in slick slide and fevered grasp they are oblivious to all else. Not even aware that the TV screen has gone blank after the closing rendition of "The Star-Spangled Banner."

3

A midsummer heat wave has Manhattan by the throat. The air is humid, so supersaturated that one drinks rather than breathes it. Clothing clings, feet swell, hair uncurls, and even paper money feels greasy, as if all those engraved presidents are sweating.

Cone shuffles slowly down to Cedar Street, carrying his cap and jacket. He tries to keep to the shady side of streets, but there's no escape. It is the kind of day, as Sydney Smith said, that makes you want to take off your skin and walk around in your bones.

David Dempster Associates, Inc., is located in a building of stainless steel and tinted glass. The lobby is blessedly chilled by air conditioning turned down so low that sides of beef might be hung on the walls without fear of spoilage. Cone just stands there for almost five minutes until his blood stops bubbling. Then he consults the lobby directory and takes a high-speed elevator to the twenty-seventh floor, donning his jacket en route.

The anteroom is small: desk, typewriter on a stand, file cabinet, wastebasket, and a plump, hennaed secretary reading a copy of *Elle*. She looks up as Cone enters and gives him a saucy smile. "Hot enough for you?" she asks.

"It's not the heat," he says solemnly, "it's the humidity." And having completed the New York catechism, he gets down to business. "Timothy Cone from Haldering and Company to see Mr. Dempster. I have an appointment."

"Sure," she says blithely. "I'll tell him you're here."

She pops through an inner door and is out again in a moment. "This way, please, Mr. Cone. Would you like to leave your cap out here?"

"Nah," he says. "Someone might steal it."

"I doubt that," she says. "Very much."

David Dempster's office is large, but only in comparison to the reception room. Actually, it's a modest chamber, skimpily furnished: executive-type desk with leatherbound accessories and two telephones, swivel chair and two armchairs, steel file cabinet and small bookcase. And that's about it.

The only wall decoration is a large color photograph of a golden retriever, with an award and blue ribbon affixed to the frame.

The man standing smiling behind the desk is tall and stalwart. He's wearing a vested glen plaid tropical worsted, and the suit is snug across shoulders and chest. Cone figures that if he doesn't pump iron, he does something equally disgusting—like exercise regularly. His handshake is a bonecrusher, as if he's ready to arm wrestle right then and there.

But he's affable enough: gets his visitor seated in one of the armchairs, holds a gold Dunhill to light Cone's Camel and his own Benson & Hedges (filtered). He asks, with a boomy laugh, if it's hot enough for Cone, and the Wall Street dick gives the proper reply. They're like lodge brothers exchanging the secret code.

They settle back, sucking greedily on their cigarettes and regarding each other with cautious ease.

"Teresa informed me you were up to see her," Dempster says. "She was quite embarrassed that she continued to address you as Mr. Timothy."

"That's okay. She said it wasn't important, and it's not."

"What did you think of her?" the other man asks suddenly. "Tell me, what was your initial impression?"

Cone shrugs. "She's different."

Dempster smiles; more fangs than teeth. "Teresa is her own woman. Many people, meeting her for the first time, are put off by her manner. But I assure you, she is not as simpleminded as she might appear. When it is necessary, she can be quite practical and quick-witted. She has handled the tragedy of Jack's death remarkably well."

"He didn't die," Cone can't resist saying, "he passed over."

Dempster becomes serious. "Yes, well, that's what she believes—sincerely believes. And it does no harm to anyone, does it?"

"Not a bit. I asked if her husband had any enemies, and she said no. Now I'll ask you the same thing."

"So have all the police and reporters," Dempster says ruefully. "You must realize, Mr. Cone, that my sister-in-law was not totally aware of her husband's business activities. Or even what Jack did for a living. Not that he ever attempted to conceal anything from her, but she simply wasn't all that interested. She had her sons, her homes, her bonsai, and she was content. As for your question to me: Did Jack have any enemies? Of course he did. He was a ruthless and, at times I fear, a brutal CEO. He built an enormous conglomerate from a small machine shop in Quincy, Massachusetts. You don't do that without making enemies along the way. But no one, to my knowledge, hated him enough to murder him. That is what I have told the police, and it is the truth as I know it."

"Mr. Dempster, I'm not involved in the homicide investigation. I'm

supposed to be looking into all the industrial accidents Dempster-Torrey
has had lately. You know about those?"

"Vaguely. Jack mentioned them one night at dinner."

"Any idea of who might be pulling that stuff?"

"Discharged or disgruntled employees would be my guess."

Then they are silent. Cone lights another cigarette, but this time David
Dempster takes a handsome silver-banded brier from his desk drawer and
fills it from a silken pouch. He tamps the tobacco down slowly with a
blunt forefinger. Then he lights the pipe carefully, using a wax match
from a tiny box. He sits back, puffing contentedly.

Lord of the manor, Cone thinks. With a picture of his favorite hound
on the wall.

Dempster has a big face, long and craggy. Big nose, big teeth, and
biggest of all, a mustache trimmed in a guardsman's style. It spreads
squarely from cheek to cheek, brown with reddish glints. And he has a
thick head of hair in the same hues, so bountiful that it makes Cone's
spiky crew cut look like a cactus. Dempster's only small feature are his
eyes; they're dark aggies.

"What kind of a man was your brother?" Cone asks.

"You know, you're the first investigator who's asked me that. Odd, isn't
it? You'd think that would be the first thing the police would want to
know. Well, Jack was an enormously driven man. With tremendous energy. And enough ambition for ten. Not for money or power, you understand. He had enough of both to last him two lifetimes. But Jack was a
builder. He wanted Dempster-Torrey to become the biggest, richest international business entity in the world. He was intensely competitive. I think
business was really a game to him. He played squash, golf, poker, and was
a devil at three-cushion billiards. And he always played to win. He couldn't
endure losing."

"Did he ever cut any corners to make sure he won?"

Dempster laughs, flashing the fangs again. "Of course he did! But he
rarely got caught. And when he did, he would admit it, grin, and people
would forgive him. Because he had so much charm. He was the most
charming man I've ever known. And I'm not saying that just because he
was my brother."

"And his opponents in business deals—did they forgive him when he
cut corners?"

"That I doubt. I told you he made enemies. But of course I can't speak
firsthand. I never had any business dealings with Jack. We went our separate ways."

"What kind of business are you in, Mr. Dempster?"

"You didn't know?" the other man says, surprised. "Corporate public relations. Not a great number of clients because I prefer to keep this a one-man operation. I am not an empire builder the way Jack was. None of my clients are what you might call giants of industry, but they stick with me and pay their bills promptly. That's all I ask."

"What sort of things do you do?" Cone asks. "Turn out press releases? Plant photos and bios of clients? Sit in on planning sessions for new products?"

"Ah," Dempster says, relighting his pipe, "I see you know the business. Yes, I do all that, but I suppose my most important function is keeping my clients' names *out* of the newspapers after they've pulled some exceptionally stupid stunt or gotten fouled up in their personal lives."

"Yeah," Cone says, "there's a lot of that going around these days. How well did you and your brother get along?"

Dempster sets his pipe down carefully. "We weren't as close as we might have been, I suppose. We had such a small family. Our parents are dead, and our few aunts, uncles, and cousins are all out in South Dakota. We should have been closer. And now Jack is gone. I'd say our relationship was cordial but cool. We didn't socialize much. An occasional dinner when he could make it; he was an extremely busy man. And I'd spend a weekend up at their summer place now and then."

"You ever do any public relations for Dempster-Torrey?"

"No, and I never made a pitch for that account. I didn't want anyone accusing Jack of nepotism. And besides, Dempster-Torrey has a very effective in-house PR department. So it was better all around if I stayed away from my brother's business."

"Uh-huh," Cone says. "Well, you promised to cooperate, and you have. Thanks for your time."

"If there's anything else I can do to help, don't hesitate to give me a call."

"I'll do that. Nice dog you've got there."

Dempster turns to stare at the picture on the wall. "*Had*," he says in a stony voice. "He was hit and killed last year by a drunken driver who came over the curb while I was walking King along Central Park South."

"Jesus," Cone says, "that's tough."

"I dragged the guy out of his car," David Dempster goes on, "and kicked the shit out of the bastard."

Again that bonecrushing handshake, and Cone gets out of there. He goes down to the icy lobby, takes off his jacket, and steps out into the steam bath. The heat is a slap in the face, and he starts slogging back to John Street wondering if he'll survive in the office where Haldering & Co. air conditioners, all antique window units, wheeze and clank, fighting a losing battle against the simmer.

. . .

He has an hour to kill before his appointment with Simon Trale, Chief
Financial Officer of Dempster-Torrey, and he knows there are things he
should be doing: checking with Davenport on the homicide investigation;
goosing Sid Apicella to get skinny on the balance sheet of David Dempster
Associates, Inc.; gathering evidence to back up his grand theory on who's
responsible for the campaign of sabotage.

He starts by reviewing his recent conversation with David Dempster.
Timothy knows very well that he himself is a mess of prejudices. For
instance, he'll never believe a man who wears a pinkie ring, never lend
money to anyone who claims to have finished reading *Silas Marner*, never
letch after a woman who, on a bright day, wears sunglasses pushed up in
her hair.

Silly bigotries, he acknowledges, and he's got a lot of them. And the
morning meeting with David Dempster has added a few more. The orotund voice and precise diction. The fanged smile with all the warmth of
a wolf snarl. The showy way he loaded his pipe, as if he was filling a
chalice with sacramental wine. Wearing a vest on the hottest day of the
year and then festooning it with a heavy gold chain from which a Phi
Beta Kappa key dangled.

All minor affectations, Cone admits, but revealing. The man comes
perilously close to being a poof, or acting like one. Whatever he is, Cone
suspects, there is not much to him. Beneath that confident, almost mag-
isterial manner is a guy running scared. Prick him and he'll deflate like a
punctured bladder of hot air.

Except . . . Except . . . In David Dempster's final words, regarding the
drunken driver who killed his dog, he said in tones of uncontrolled sav-
agery, "I kicked the shit out of the bastard." That shocked Cone, not
because of the act or the words describing it, but that it was so out of
character for someone he had tagged as a wimp, and a pompous wimp at
that.

It's a puzzlement, and Timothy decides to put David Dempster on hold,
not that the guy is obviously a wrongo, but only because no one else
questioned up to now has given off such confusing vibes. Like all detectives, Cone tends to pigeonhole people. And when he can't assign them to
neat slots, his anxiety quotient rises.

The interview with Simon Trale is held in the offices of Dempster-Torrey on
Wall Street. Trale elects to meet Cone in the boardroom, a cavernous
chamber with a conference table long enough to sleep Paul Bunyan. It is
surrounded by twenty black leather armchairs, precisely spaced. On the

table in front of each chair is a water carafe, glass, pad of yellow legal paper, ballpoint pen, and ashtray—all embossed with the corporate insignia.

"I brought you in here," Trale says in a high-pitched voice, "because it was swept electronically about an hour ago. The debuggers won't get to my office until this afternoon, so I thought it would be safer if we talked in here."

"Yeah," Cone says, "that makes sense."

He wonders if they're going to sit at opposite ends of that stretched slab of polished walnut and shout at each other. But Trale pulls out two adjoining chairs along one side, and that's where they park themselves.

The CFO is a short guy. In fact, Cone figures that if he was a few inches shorter he'd qualify as a midget. Usually a man so diminutive will buy his clothes in the boys' section of a department store, but Trale's duds are too well tailored for that. He's wearing a dark blue pinstripe with unpadded shoulders and side vents. His shirt is sparkling white, and he sports a paisley bow tie. Small gold cuff links. A wide gold wedding band. A gold Rolex. Black tasseled loafers on his tiny feet.

He's got a full head of snowy white hair neatly trimmed. The white hair is understandable because Timothy guesses that Simon Trale is pushing seventy, if he's not already on the downslope. But his movements are sure, and that reedy voice has no quaver.

"Mind if I smoke?" Cone asks.

"Go right ahead," Trale says. "The doc limits me to one cigar a day, but it tastes all the better for that."

"When do you smoke it—at night after dinner?"

"No," Trale says, smiling. "First thing in the morning. It gets the juices flowing."

"If you don't mind my asking, how old are you?"

"I don't mind. I'll be seventy-three next year."

"I should look as good next year as you do right now," Cone says admiringly. "No aches or pains?"

"The usual," the little man says, shrugging. "But I still got my own teeth, thank God. I use reading glasses, but my hearing is A-Okay."

"How come you're still working?" Cone asks curiously. "Doesn't Dempster-Torrey have a mandatory retirement at sixty-five?"

"Sure we do. But Jack Dempster pushed a waiver through the Board of Directors allowing me to stay on. You know why he did that?"

"Because you're such a hotshot financial officer?"

"No," Trale says, laughing. "There's a hundred younger men who could do my job. But my wife died nine years ago, and all my kids have married and moved away. I don't play golf, and I've got no hobbies. Dempster-

Torrey has been my whole life. Jack knew that, knew how lost I'd be without an office to come to and problems to solve. So he kept me on, bless him."

"Very kind of him," Cone says, looking down at the cigarette in his stained fingers. "But that doesn't sound like the John J. Dempster I've been hearing about."

"Oh, you'll hear a lot of bad things about him," Trale says cheerfully. "And most of them will be true. I'm not going to tell you he was a saint; he wasn't. But do you know anyone who is?"

"I heard he was ruthless and brutal in his business dealings."

The CFO frowns. "Ruthless and brutal? Well . . . maybe. But when you're wheeling and dealing on the scale that Dempster was, you can't afford to play pattycake. He was hard when he had to be hard."

"So he made enemies along the way?"

"Sure he did. The police asked me to make out a list. I told them it wouldn't be a list, it would be a book!"

He smiles at the recollection. He has the complexion of a healthy baby, and his mild blue eyes look out at the world with wonder and amusement. Small pink ears are set flat to his skull, and his lips are so red they might be rouged. It is a doll's head, finely molded porcelain, with every detail from black lashes to dimpled chin painted just so.

"How long have you been with Dempster-Torrey, Mr. Trale?"

"From the beginning. I was the bookkeeper with the Torrey Machine Works up in Quincy, Massachusetts, when John Dempster came to work for us as sales manager. Within a year he had doubled our revenues. And a year after that he married Teresa Torrey and was made vice president."

"Oh-ho," Cone says, lighting another Camel. "He married the boss's daughter, did he?"

"He did. But he'd have been made vice president even if he hadn't. Sanford Torrey knew what a wizard he had in J. J. Also, Sanford and his wife were worried about their daughter. She had plenty of beaux, but they didn't stay around long. Have you met Teresa?"

"Yeah, I met her."

"And what do you think?"

"Off the wall."

"Yes," Trale says sorrowfully, "that's what other young men thought— but John Dempster saw something in her. She's really a dear, loving woman, Mr. Cone. When my wife was ill, she couldn't do enough for us. I'll be eternally grateful. John saw that side of her—the warm affection, the innocent openness. Yes, he married the boss's daughter, but there was more to it than that. I may be a foolish old romantic, but I've always thought that he loved her and married her for the qualities he knew he himself lacked: sympathy, sweet naiveté, absolute honesty."

"But it was also a financial leg up for him."

"Of course. A year after the marriage, the company became Dempster-Torrey—notice that his name came first!—and he started his campaign of acquisitions and mergers, diversifying into areas that had nothing to do with our original business. I went along for the ride, and what a ride it turned out to be!"

"How did this Sanford Torrey like what Dempster was doing?"

"He and his wife were killed in a plane crash a few years after John Dempster began putting the conglomerate together. It turned out that Sanford had left everything he owned, including a majority interest in Dempster-Torrey, to Teresa. But I guess he had some reservations about John Dempster, because he tied up his daughter's inheritance in a trust fund that J. J. couldn't touch. But he didn't have to be afraid of Teresa being left destitute. John took the company public, and it tripled the value of the trust. Provision has been made for the three sons, but she is still a very, very wealthy woman."

Cone stirs restlessly. "This is all interesting, Mr. Trale. Good background stuff. But it really doesn't cut any mustard with what I'm supposed to be doing—finding out who's behind the eighteen cases of industrial sabotage to Dempster-Torrey plants and equipment."

Unexpectedly, Trale smiles. "Those accidents," he says, "they infuriated J. J., but I never could see that they were such a big deal. Every large corporation suffers the same outrages occasionally. But John thought there was a plot against us."

"You don't think so?"

"It's possible, but I doubt it. Insurance covered most of our losses, and they never affected our basic financial structure."

"Did your common stock drop after each of the incidents?"

"Oh, sure. But it came right back up again."

"And what's happened to the stock since Dempster's murder?"

The little man pulls a face. "Not good," he says. "I estimate the total value of our common stock has dropped about thirty percent since his death."

"Still falling?"

"It seems to have stabilized the last few days. Wall Street is waiting to see who'll be named the new CEO."

Timothy punches out his cigarette and takes a deep breath. "Mr. Trale, I'm going to throw a wild idea at you. It's something I've been kicking around ever since I was handed this file. I gotta tell you, I haven't got any hard evidence. But you have a helluva lot more business savvy than I do, so I'd like to get your reaction."

"All right," the CFO says mildly, "let's hear your idea."

"Suppose, just suppose, some corporate raider wants to make a move on Dempster-Torrey. He's got to—"

"Whoa!" Trale protests, putting up a white palm. "Hold your horses. You're talking about a takeover of almost three billion dollars. That's *billion*, with a capital B."

"I know that," Cone says patiently. "And I could name you a dozen pirates—American, English, Australian—who could raise that kind of loot. What if some takeover bandit gets the bright idea that he can force down the price of Dempster-Torrey stock and cut the cost of the raid? So before he starts buying, he engineers a program of industrial sabotage, figuring that he's saving money every time DempsterTorrey stock dips even a point."

"Assuming what you say is true, it didn't work. As I told you, Mr. Cone, the price of the stock didn't decline that much following the incidents, and it came right back up again."

The Wall Street dick stares at him.

Simon Trale returns the stare, then begins biting at his thumbnail. "I see what you're getting at," he says, his voice suddenly bleak. "The acts of sabotage didn't have the desired effect, so the corporate raider, if he exists, murdered John J. Dempster."

"*Had* him murdered. I know a little about violent crime, Mr. Trale, and Dempster's death had all the earmarks of a contract kill. Two wackos on a motorcycle with a submachine gun. They were hired hands. And it worked. You just told me the total value of Dempster-Torrey common stock has dropped about thirty percent. What a bonanza for some bandido who's after your company."

"Wait a minute," Trale says, visibly upset. "First of all, about two years ago we restructured the corporation to make a takeover extremely difficult and expensive. Since then I've heard absolutely nothing about anyone making a move on us."

"The wife is always the last to know," Cone says, but the other man ignores that.

"Second, if anyone has accumulated even five percent of Dempster-Torrey stock, he'd have to file with the SEC informing them of the purchase and stating his intentions."

Cone pauses to light another cigarette. "Come on, Mr. Trale," he says, "you know better than that. Let's say four rich outlaws are sitting around a ginmill somewhere, having a few snorts, and one of them says, 'Hey, what say we put the XYZ Corporation into play.' So they all agree to have a fling. Each man will pick up four percent of XYZ's stock, so no SEC statement has to be filed—correct? But between them they'll be holding sixteen percent. In addition to that, they'll tip off some friendly arbitrageurs to start buying XYZ. And all this time they're trading as individuals. There's nothing on paper to show they're working in cahoots. That'll come later when they figure they've got the muscle to make their move. Then it's goodbye XYZ."

"A very imaginative scenario, Mr. Cone," the CFO says worriedly.

"But possible—isn't it?"

"Yes, it's possible."

"Damned right. It's been done before and it'll be done again."

"And you think that is what's happening to Dempster-Torrey?"

"I don't know," Cone says. "I told you it's just a theory. But I can't spot any holes in it—can you?"

"I just can't believe that any corporate raider would murder Dempster just to inflate his profits."

"You can't believe it because you're a moral man with no more than a normal share of greed. But believe me, there are guys on the Street who'll run a bulldozer over their grandma to make a buck."

Trale is silent. Suddenly he looks even smaller, shrunken and defeated. "Maybe I should retire," he says in a low voice. "Jack Dempster played rough, and I went along with him. That was *business*. But murder? Never! I get the feeling that the world has passed me by. I don't recognize it anymore. I've become obsolete."

"Nah," Timothy says, reaching out to pat the little man's shoulder. "You're not obsolete, and you're not going to resign. I need your help."

"Yes?" Trale says, looking up. "What can I do?"

"You have contacts on Wall Street?"

"Of course. A lot of them. . . . Oh, I understand. You want me to find out if there are any rumors about an attempted takeover of Dempster-Torrey."

"Right," Cone says approvingly. "I've got a few snitches myself, but nothing like what a man in your position must have."

It buoys Trale, and he straightens up in his chair, squares his shoulders. "Yes," he says, "I can do that. I have a number of chits out on the Street, and I'll call them in."

"Just what I was hoping you'd say. How long do you think it'll take?"

"Not long. Probably by tomorrow."

"Good enough. You'll let me know?"

"Of course. As soon as I have anything definite—for or against."

"Thanks," Cone says. "Now I've got a couple of more short questions and then I'll let you off the hook. You told me that John Dempster loved his wife, and I accept that. As a matter of fact, Teresa told me they had a happy marriage. But I also heard that he was playing around."

"What does that have to do with industrial sabotage?"

"Probably nothing," Cone admits. "But I just like to know as much as I can about the people involved. Was John Dempster a tomcat, Mr. Trale?" And then, knowing when to lie, Timothy adds, "Several people have told me he was."

"What people told you that?"

Cone sighs. "You're stalling, Mr. Trale. If you don't want to answer, tell me and I'll accept it. And go on believing what I've heard."

The CFO hesitates a long moment. "It can do no harm now," he says finally. "And besides, too many people know to try to keep it a secret. It's true, Mr. Cone: Dempster was a womanizer. It was almost a carryover from his business methods. When he saw something he wanted, he went after it, regardless of the cost, the risk, or how long it might take. He was that way in his pursuit of women as well. But he always went back to Teresa. I know that for a fact."

"Uh-huh," Cone says, figuring the Security Chief, Theodore Brodsky, was probably right on the button when he implied Dempster and Eve Bookerman were having an affair. "Thanks for the talk; it's been a help. I'll wait for your call on takeover rumors."

They rise, shake hands, start out. But Timothy pauses at the door. "One final question, Mr. Trale: Do you know David Dempster?"

"I've met him," the other man says.

"Do you happen to know if he's married?"

"Divorced. About five years ago, as I recall."

"Has he remarried?"

"I don't know. Why are you interested in David Dempster?"

"I'm trying to figure out the guy," Cone says, leaving the Chief Financial Officer to wonder what that meant.

He slouches into Samantha Whatley's office, and she looks up.

"I'm busy," she says.

"So am I," he says. "Puddling around in this heat, doing God's work. I need a couple of things."

She tosses her pen onto the desk and sighs. "Make it short and sweet."

"That's not what you said the other night."

She looks around nervously. "Keep your voice down." She still believes their co-workers are unaware of their relationship, but he thinks a few of the other dicks guess what's going on.

"I need a rental car," he says. "This Dempster-Torrey thing is spreading out, and I've got to get around. Tell H.H. the client will okay the expense."

"How do you know—did you ask them?"

"No, I didn't ask them. Come on, don't bust my balls, just get me some wheels."

"I'll try. That's it?"

"No, that isn't it. I want you to pull a telephone scam for me. I'd do it myself, but it needs a woman's voice."

"I don't know," she says doubtfully. "Is it important?"

"It's not my main lead, it's sort of a fallback position. You know what that is, don't you?"

"Yeah," she says in a low voice. "I fall back and you jump my bones. All right, what's the scoop?"

He explains: She is to call the office of David Dempster Associates, Inc., and speak only to the secretary. If Dempster answers, hang up. She is to tell the secretary that she's an old friend of Mrs. Dempster but hasn't seen her for years. Now she's in town for a few days and would love to chat with her old school chum. But she understands Mrs. Dempster has been divorced, and she doesn't have her new address and phone number or even the last name she's using now. Could the secretary help her out?"

"What's Mrs. Dempster's first name?" Sam asks.

"Don't know."

"Shithead!" she says wrathfully. "How can I claim to be the woman's old school chum if I don't know her first name?"

"You can finagle it. At least it's worth a try."

He gives her the number and she dials.

"Hello, there!" she carols. "Is this the office of David Dempster? Well, my name is Irma Plotnick, and I'm an old friend of Mrs. Dempster— school pals, you know. I'm in town for a few days—South Bend, Indiana, is my home—and I was hoping to get together with Mrs. Dempster. Well, a mutual friend tells me she's divorced now. I tried her at the number I have for her, but she's no longer there. So I guess she didn't get the apartment as part of the settlement—right, dear? Well, goodness, I don't even know what name she's using now, let alone where she's living. Anyway, dear, I was hoping you'd be able to give me the name she's using, her address—and the phone number if you have it. I so want to get together with her and talk about old times. . . . You do? Oh, that's great! Now just wait half-a-mo until I get a pen. All right, I'm all set now. Uh-huh. Uh-huh. Uh-huh. I've got it. Thank you so much, dear. You've been a love and I'll certainly tell her when I see her. 'Bye now!"

Whatley hangs up and skids the scratch paper she's been scribbling on across the desk. "Name, address, and phone number," she says triumphantly. "How did you like that performance?"

"Not bad," Cone says grudgingly. "But long-winded. When you're pulling a telephone con, keep it as brief as you can. The best lies are short ones."

"I should have known better than to expect thanks from you," Sam says. "Now take off and let me get some work done."

"One final question that's been bothering me," he says. "If a guy who plays around a lot is called a womanizer, what do you call a woman who does the same thing—a manizer?"

Sam points at the door. "Out!" she says.

4

It rains hard that night, breaking the back of the heat wave. When Cone slogs down Broadway to work—only a half-hour late this time—the air is breathable and the sky is clear.

The new receptionist at Haldering & Co. hands him a telephone message on a pink slip: *Call Simon Trale at Dempster-Torrey, Inc.* Cone carries the message and his brown-bagged breakfast into his office. He has a chomp of buttered bialy and a gulp of black coffee before he phones Trale.

"Good morning, Mr. Cone."

" 'Morning. I hope you have good news."

"Good news for us, but I'm afraid you will be disappointed. I spoke to a half-dozen of my most knowledgeable contacts. None has heard a word about anyone planning a raid on Dempster-Torrey. To be quite frank, they thought the idea implausible. The way we're structured would make any pirate think twice before he made a run at us."

"All right," Cone says, "I'll accept that. Thanks for your help, Mr. Trale. I'll be in touch if I get another brainstorm."

He hangs up, lights his third cigarette of the day, finishes his breakfast. So now he's back to square one. That's okay; he's been there before.

But the big question remains: Who would benefit from the death of John J. Dempster? Could his wife have learned of his infidelities and hired a couple of punks to ace him? Unlikely. If she knew about his dedicated search for the perfect bang, she probably didn't give a damn; she had her bonsai—and all the money in the world.

Ditto the underlings at Dempster-Torrey. They might think their boss was a double-dyed bastard, but they had high-paying jobs and weren't about to scratch the fount from whom all blessings flowed. The one exception might be Eve Bookerman: an energetic and brainy lady who was sleeping with J. J. Maybe he threatened to dump her for a younger twist, or maybe she coveted his job. Either one would be motive enough for her to take out a contract on the Chairman and CEO.

A discharged or disgruntled employee? Another possibility. But as Brodsky said, that would narrow the list of suspects to ten thousand. Where do you start digging into something like that?

And then there's David Dempster, that prig. But what reason could he have for putting his brother down? Unless he was hurting for cash and needed an inheritance.

At that moment, as if reading his mind, Sid Apicella comes into his office. He's gripping a sheet of scratch paper.

"You and your lousy 'one phone call,'" he says grumpily. "It took me four calls and almost half a day to get any info on David Dempster. How the hell do you get other people to do your job for you?"

"Boyish charm," Cone says.

"You've got about as much charm as my wife's old poodle—and that monster farts, has fleas, and a breath that would knock your socks off. Anyway, David Dempster Associates, Inc., is a legit outfit that's been in business about twelve years. They do corporate publicity and public relations, and seem to be doing just great. Good cash flow and some heavy clients."

"Bull*shit!*" the Wall Street dick says angrily. "I was up at their place, and it's practically a hole-in-the-wall. Dempster's private office is not much bigger than this latrine."

"So? What do you need in the publicity business? A telephone and a lot of good contacts—right?"

"Maybe. But with all the high-powered PR outfits on the Street, I can't see Dempster attracting any blue-chip clients. How much money they got?"

"The corporation? They keep a minimum hundred-thousand balance. When it gets over that, Dempster pays himself a bonus."

"A sweet setup. And what's he worth?"

"Personally?" the CPA says, consulting his notes. "About four mil, give or take. How does that grab you?"

"It doesn't," Cone says. "You just blew another of my half-assed ideas out of the water. The second time that's happened in the last hour. What a great morning this is. But thanks anyway, Sid; that's one I owe you."

"*One?*" Apicella shouts, rubbing his rosy schnoz furiously. "You owe me so much I'll never get even."

He stomps out after tossing his scrawled notes onto the desk. Cone leans forward to read them, then sits back and lights another Camel. So David Dempster has a personal net worth of four million. That doesn't sound like a man who'd have his brother chilled just to inherit a few more bucks—unless the guy is suffering from terminal greed.

But something smells. Cone well knows that public relations outfits deal with images and perceptions. It's a way of life that carries over into the way the flacks do business: impressive offices, flashy secretaries, a hyperactive staff, and autographed photos on the walls of the boss posing with important people. Dempster has a telephone booth office, one pleasant but plain secretary, and a picture on the wall of his dead hound.

And from this mom-and-pop bodega the cash flow has enabled him to amass a fortune? That just doesn't add up.

He chews it over for a while. Then, groaning, he gets to his feet and wanders down the corridor to the office of Fred Burgess, another Haldering & Co. investigator. Fred is on the phone, but when he sees Cone standing there, he motions him in, points to the armchair alongside his littered desk.

"Marcia," he's saying, "I've already apologized twice, but if you want, I'll do it again. You're the one who picked the Japanese restaurant. I'm not blaming you, but it was the combination of the sashimi and sake that did it. How the hell can you know how much you're drinking when they serve it in thimbles? It didn't hit me until we got up to your place. All that raw fish and rice wine. . . . Marcia, I've already explained I couldn't make it to the bathroom. So your aquarium seemed the best bet. I know it killed all your guppies, but I'll buy you more guppies. Marcia? Marcia?"

He replaces the phone. "She hung up," he says gloomily.

"Have a pleasant evening?" Cone asks.

"Go to hell," Burgess says. "It took me weeks to get this date. She's gorgeous, got a great job on the Street, and beautiful digs up around Gramercy Park. I thought sure last night was going to be *the* night. Then I have to vomit into her goddamned fish tank and kill all her goddamned guppies. I guess I'm on her shit list now."

"Good detecting," Cone says. "Look, I didn't come in here to discuss your love life. You still got that collection of business cards?"

Burgess, a youngish, fattish, liverish guy, stares at him suspiciously. "Yeah, I still got it. And I'm going to keep it."

"One card," Timothy says. "Just one. On loan."

"What's in it for me?"

"I'll tell you how to bring Marcia around."

"Deal. How do I do it?"

"Buy her the most expensive tropical fish you can afford. Something really exotic with big fins. Like a Veiltail Angelfish. Have it delivered to her apartment with a simple, heartfelt note like, 'I'm sorry I puked in your aquarium.'"

"Yeah," Fred says, "that might work. What do you need?"

"The business card of a writer."

"Writers don't have business cards. But I got one from a magazine editor. Will that do?"

"It'll have to."

Burgess pulls out a long file of business cards he's collected over the years at cocktail parties, conventions, and press conferences. He thumbs through them, pulls one out, hands it over.

"'Waldo Sperling,'" Cone reads. "'Feature Editor, *Zebu* magazine.' What the hell does Zebu mean?"

"If you did crossword puzzles, you'd know. It's an Asian ox. But don't worry about it; the magazine is out of business and it can mean anything you want it to."

"Okay," Cone says, rising, "I'll give it a try. Do I look like a Waldo to you?"

"To me," says Burgess, "you look like a schmuck."

Cone goes back to his office and digs out the name, address, and phone number of David Dempster's ex-wife. He dials and waits for nine rings before a woman's voice comes on.

"H'lo?" she says sleepily.

"Am I speaking to Miss Dorothy Blenke, the former Mrs. David Dempster?"

"Yeah," she says, "that's right. What time is it?"

"Almost eleven-thirty, Miss Blenke."

"Jesus! I got a lunch date at noon. Who the hell are you?"

"My name is Waldo Sperling, and I'm the feature editor of *Zebu* magazine. We're planning an article on the life of the late John J. Dempster, Chairman of the Board of Dempster-Torrey, and I'm trying to talk to as many people as possible who knew him."

"I don't want to talk about it."

"You knew John Dempster, Miss Blenke?"

"Of course I knew him. Better than most."

"All I ask is a few moments of your time. To get your personal reactions to the man. His good points and his bad points."

"He didn't have any," she says.

"Didn't have any what?"

"Good points."

"Just a few moments at your convenience," Cone urges. "If you don't wish your name to appear in print, we'll respect that. But we would prefer to use your name in the article and perhaps publish your photograph since you obviously represent a key source for our story."

"Listen," she says, "you got my address?"

"Yes, I do, Miss Blenke."

"Okay," she says. "I got this stupid lunch date I'm late for already, but if you can be here around two-thirty or so, I'll give you some time."

"Thank you very much," Cone says humbly. "The name is Sperling. Waldo Sperling."

He hangs up, grinning, and sees Samantha Whatley standing in his doorway. "I heard that, Waldo," she says. "Kind of long-winded, wasn't it?"

"Up yours," he says.

She growls at him. "Go pick up your rental car," she says, and he winks at her.

So there he is, tooling around Manhattan in a new Ford Escort GT and feeling like King Shit. As usual, traffic is murder, but Cone doesn't care; he's got time to kill, and he wants to get the feel of the car. Even the frustrations of stop-and-go city driving are better than cramming aboard a bus or trying to flag down a cab.

But there is the problem of parking. Cone finally finds a slot on East Eighty-third Street, just west of First Avenue. He locks up and walks back to Dorothy Blenke's address on Third Avenue, north of Eighty-fifth. It's a sliver of a high-rise, faced with alternating vertical bands of precast concrete and green-tinted glass. The doorman is dressed like someone's idea of a Hungarian hussar, with a braided jacket, frogged half-cape, and a purple plume hanging limply from his varnished shako.

"I have an appointment with Dorothy Blenke," Cone tells him.

"Not in," the hussar says. "Try later."

"She said she'd be here at two-thirty. It's past that now."

The doorman looks at Cone's shoddy corduroy suit with some distaste. "I'm telling you," he says, "she's not back yet. Why don't you take a nice walk around the block."

"Splendid idea," Cone says, and does exactly that. He takes his time, looking in store windows and gawking at the construction work going on in the neighborhood. He returns to Blenke's high-rise and looks inquiringly at the doorman.

"Not yet," the hussar says.

So Cone circles another block, smoking a cigarette, and returns to the apartment house.

"Yeah," the doorman says, "she just came in." Then, formally: "Who shall I say is calling?"

"Waldo Sperling from *Zebu* magazine."

"Zebu?" the hussar says. "What's that?"

"It's an Asian ox," Cone says. "I thought everyone knew."

The doorman calls on the intercom, talks a moment, then turns to Cone. "Okay," he says, "you can go up. Apartment Eighteen-A. To your left as you get off the elevator."

"Thanks," Cone says. "I admire your uniform."

"Yeah?" the hussar says. "Try wearing it in the summer. You sweat bullets."

He unlocks the inner door, and the Wall Street dick enters a narrow lobby lined with ceramic tiles. It has all the joyful ambience of an underground crypt, and a couple of desiccated ficus trees add the proper mortuary touch. The automatic elevator is more cheerful, and music is coming from somewhere. Timothy recognizes the tune: "Puttin' on the Ritz."

The woman who opens the door of apartment 18-A is a tall, glitzy blonde with too much of everything: hair, eye shadow, lipstick, bosom, hips, and perfume. And there are three olives in the oversized martini she's gripping.

"You a cop?" she demands.

"Oh, no," Cone says. "No, no, no. Waldo Sperling from *Zebu* magazine." He proffers his business card, but she doesn't even glance at it.

"I hate cops," she says darkly. "Well, come on in. Would you like a drinkie-poo?"

"No, thank you. But you go right ahead."

"I intend to," Dorothy Blenke says. "What a shitty lunch that was. The guy looked like Godzilla, and he's *on salary*, for God's sake. Hey, I like the way you dress. You just don't give a damn—right?"

"Right," Cone says.

"That's the way I am, too," the woman says. "I just don't give a damn. Now you sit in that fantastic tub chair—twelve-hundred from Bloomie's—and I'll curl up here on the couch."

"From Bloomie's?" Cone asks.

"Yep. Three grand." She gives him a vapid smile. "I even got Bloomie's printed on my panties. Wanna see?"

"Not at the moment," Cone says, "but I appreciate the offer. Lovely home you have here, Miss Blenke."

But the living room is like the woman herself—too much of everything: furniture, lamps, rugs, paintings, knickknacks, vases, silk flowers, even ashtrays. The place overflows.

"May I smoke?" Cone asks.

"Why not?" she says with that out-of-focus smile. "This is Liberty Hall. Let it all hang out."

He offers her a Camel, but she shakes her head. So he lights up while she works on her drink. Two of the three olives have disappeared along with half of the martini. Cone figures he better make this fast.

"Miss Blenke," he starts, "as I told you on the phone, *Zebu* magazine is—"

"What the hell is that?" she interrupts. "I've never seen it on the newsstands."

"Controlled circulation," Cone explains. "By subscription only. We go only to top executives in the financial community."

"No kidding?" she says with that bleary smile again. "I don't suppose you want to sell your mailing list."

"I'm afraid not," Cone says, and tries again. "Miss Blenke, as I told you on the phone, we're planning a definitive article on John J. Dempster, and I'm trying to—"

"I don't want to talk about it," she says.

Cone, who's beginning to feel like that hussar-doorman—sweating bullets—plunges ahead. "So we'd be very interested in your personal recollections of the late John Dempster."

"Late," she says gloomily. "The sonofabitch was always late."

"I don't understand, Miss Blenke."

"There's a lot you don't understand," she says portentously. "Just take my word for it."

They sit silently while she takes small, ladylike sips from her giant martini. The third olive has disappeared, and she peers into the tumbler, puzzled.

She's a big, florid woman with shards of great beauty. But it's all gone to puff now. It could be the sauce, but Cone reckons that's only a symptom, not the malady. Thwarted ambitions, soured dreams, chilled loves—all came before the booze. Now her life is tottering, ready to fall. It's there in her glazed eyes and sappy grin.

"You were married to David Dempster for—how long?" he asks, determined to be gentle with this ruin.

"The nerd? That's what I call him: Lord Nerd. Years and years."

"No children?"

"No, thank God. His kids wouldn't have been much anyway. He just hasn't got the jism. But I'll say this for him: The alimony checks are never late."

"And what were his relations to John Dempster?"

"The nerd's?" she says, startled. "He was John's brother."

"I know," Cone says patiently. "I meant their personal relationship. How did they get along?"

"Not like gin and vermouth," she says. "Hey, my drink is gone. Must be evaporation. Have you ever noticed that New York City has a very high rate of evaporation?"

"Yeah," Cone says, "I've noticed."

She heaves herself off the couch, goes into the kitchen. He hears her banging around in there, humming a song he can't identify. He sits hunched forward in the velvet-covered tub chair, hands clasped between his knees, and wonders if there's another line of business he can get into.

She comes back in a few moments, still humming, with a full tumbler. She plops down on the couch again and crosses her knees. Like many heavy women, she's got good legs and slender ankles. "One martini and I can feel it," she says. "Two martinis and anyone can feel it. What were we talking about?"

"David and John Dempster. How they felt about each other."

"Yeah," she says, "that's right. Well, Jack thought Dave was a wash-out—which he is. Dave was always bitching because Jack wouldn't give him the Dempster-Torrey PR account, but Jack knew better than that."

"Oh? When was this?"

"Years ago. Lord Nerd finally gave up. He gave up on a lot of things. Jack never gave up. He'd never take no for an answer."

"He must have been quite a man to build a business like that."

"Jack? He was Napoleon, Hitler, and Attila the Hun all rolled into one. You never knew what he was going to do next. That was the fun of him."

Cone stares at her. "But he always went back to his wife," he says softly.

"That dingbat? She'd blow away in a breeze. I'll never, till the day I die, understand what he saw in her. I'll bet she puts on her nightgown before she takes off her underwear. But I don't want to talk about it."

"If you don't mind my asking, Miss Blenke, why did you divorce David Dempster?"

"Galloping boredom," she says promptly. "You've met the guy?"

"Yes."

"Then you know. He'd have to drink Drano to get his blood moving. Jack had all the get-up-and-go in that family. He could work twenty-four hours and then party for another twenty-four. Dave has to have his nappy-poo every afternoon or he'll collapse. The funny thing was ... What's the funny thing?"

"Something about the brothers?"

"Yeah. Jack was three years younger, but usually it's the older brother who's the big success. Am I right?"

"Usually. But not always. Did you socialize much with John and his wife? When you and David were married?"

"Socialize? Jesus, if we saw them twice a year it was a lot. Those two guys couldn't stand each other, I couldn't stand that ding-a-ling Teresa, and I guess she felt the same way about me. It was not what you'd call close family ties."

Timothy wants to ask her the key questions, straight out, but hasn't the courage. Besides, he has a fairish idea of what had happened.

"Thank you very much, Miss Blenke," he says, rising. "You've made an important contribution to our article. I'll make certain the writer calls you to confirm the accuracy of your quotes."

"You're going so soon?" she says. "Leaving me all alone?"

"Yeah," he says. "I gotta. What was that song you were humming?"

"Song? What song?"

"You were humming it while you were in the kitchen."

"Oh, that . . . 'It Had to Be You.'"

"Uh-huh," he says. "Thanks. Nice meeting you, Miss Blenke."

He figures it's too late to go back to the office. And besides, what the hell would he do when he got there? So, sitting in his rented Escort, he pulls out his tattered list of names and addresses. David Dempster's home is in the Murray Hill section, not out of his way. Cone drives south, planning to eyeball the place—just for the fun of it.

It turns out to be a limestone townhouse on East Thirty-eighth between Park and Madison. A smart building, well maintained, with pots of ivy on windowsills and small ginkgo trees in tubs flanking the elegant entrance. The place looks like bucks, and the Wall Street dick guesses it went co-op years ago.

He double-parks across the street and dashes over, dodging oncoming cars. He scans the names on the bell plate. There it is: David Dempster, third floor. There are only five apartments in the building, all apparently floor-throughs and the top one probably a duplex. Nice. On the drive back to his loft, Cone spends the time stalled in traffic estimating what a floor-through in a Murray Hill townhouse might cost. Whatever, it wouldn't much hurt a guy with a net worth of four mil.

He gets back to his own floor-through to find that Cleo has pawed open the cabinet under the sink, plucked out a plastic bottle of detergent and gnawed a hole in it. Then apparently the demented cat jumped up and down on the punctured bottle. The detergent is spread all over the linoleum. And the cat is sitting gravely in the midst of it, paws together and a "Who—me?" expression on its ugly mug.

"You dirty rat!" Cone yells, and Cleo darts under the bathtub.

It takes twenty minutes to clean up the mess. By this time, Cleo is giving him the seductive ankle-rub treatment along with piteous mews.

"I don't want to talk about it," Cone says.

He's in the kitchenette, opening a beer, when the wall phone jungles.

"Yeah," he says.

"Mr. Timothy Cone?" A woman's voice.

"That's right."

"Miss Bookerman calling. Just a moment, please, sir."

Eve Bookerman comes on the line. "Hello!" she says breathlessly. "Forgive me for calling you at home, but I tried your office and you weren't in. Mr. Haldering gave me your home phone number. I hope you aren't angry."

"Nah," he says, "that's okay."

"I haven't heard from you and wondered if you were making any progress on the industrial sabotage. Simon Trale told me about your suggestion that it might be a corporate raider. That was a brilliant idea. Brilliant!"

"Brilliant," Cone says. "Except it was a dud."

"But it shows you're thinking imaginatively," she says. "I like that. Do you have anything new to report?"

"Nope. More questions than answers. I think you and I better have another meet, Miss Bookerman."

"I'm tied up most of tomorrow, but I'll make time if it's important."

"I think it might be better if we talked outside your office."

Long pause. Then: "Oh? Well, let's see what we can arrange. I'm working late tonight, and then I've got a dinner appointment. I should be home by eleven o'clock. Is that too late for you?"

"I'll still be awake."

She laughs gaily, but it sounds tinny. "You have my home address, don't you? Suppose you come up here at eleven. I'll tell the concierge you're expected. Will it take long?"

"Probably not. Maybe a half-hour."

"Splendid! See you tonight, Mr. Cone."

He hangs up, stares at the dead phone a moment. He figures he'll come down hard on her. She dresses for success; she can take it.

About a week ago he bought a corned beef that weighed almost five pounds. He spent an entire evening boiling it up, spooning off the scum and changing the water to get rid of the salt. While it was cooking, he dumped in more peppercorns, bay leaves, and garlic cloves—just as the butcher had instructed.

When he could dig a fork into it, he figured it was done. By that time the loft was filled with a savory fog, and Cleo was trying to claw up his leg to get at the stove top. Cone chilled the boiled beef for twenty-four hours, then he and the cat began to demolish it. The first night he had it with boiled potatoes, but after that he just had the meat and beer.

He's eaten it every night for almost a week now, except for that one dinner at Sam's, but there's still some left. It's getting a little green and iridescent around the edges, but it tastes okay. It's not too tender, but he's got strong teeth, and so does Cleo.

So that's what the two have that night, finally finishing the beef, with enough crumbs left over to see the cat through the night.

After cleaning up, Cone lies down on his mattress.

"It's called a nappy-poo," he tells Cleo.

He dozes fitfully, wakes about nine-thirty. Then he showers and dons a clean T-shirt that's been laundered so many times it's like gray gauze. He straps on the ankle holster stuffed with the short-barreled S&W .357 Magnum and sallies forth.

Eve Bookerman lives in a high-rise near Sutton Place. Her building makes Dorothy Blenke's look like a pup tent. It seems to soar into the clouds, all glass and stainless steel, and there's a Henry Moore sculpture on a pedestal in front of the splendid entrance.

The concierge is wearing a claw-hammer coat, starched shirt, and white bow tie. He inspects the Wall Street dick and sniffs.

"May I be of service?" he says in a fluty voice.

"Timothy Cone to see Miss Eve Bookerman."

The twit isn't happy about it, but he makes the call, murmuring into the phone.

"You're expected, sir," he reports. "Apartment B as in Benjamin on the thirty-first floor."

"Floor as in Frederick?" Cone says.

"Beg pardon, sir?"

But Timothy is heading toward the elevator bank, wading through a rug so thick and soft he'd like to strip bare-ass and roll around on it.

No music in the elevator this time, but a lingering scent of perfume. The high-speed lift goes so fast that Cone has a scary image of the damned thing bursting through the roof and taking off for the stars.

More plush carpeting in the thirty-first-floor corridor. The door to Apartment B as in Benjamin is open a few inches, and Eve Bookerman is peering out.

"Ah," she says, "Mr. Cone. Do come in."

She swings the door wide, he takes off his cap and follows her into a foyer about as big as his loft, with black and white tiles set in a diagonal checkerboard pattern. She leads him into a living room with floor-to-ceiling windows overlooking the East River.

Some expensive decorator has done a bang-up job. The whole place is right out of *Architectural Digest*, and Cleo would have a ball destroying that collection of Steuben glass. It's all so clean and polished that Cone wonders if he should remain standing.

"Nice place," he offers.

"Thank you," she says lightly. "I've come a long way from Bensonhurst. I'm having a cognac, Mr. Cone. Would you like one?"

"Yeah, that'd be great."

She brings him a snifter and places the bottle on a Lucite table between two rocking chairs. They're in one dim corner of a room that goes on forever. Noguchi lamps are lighted, but it would take a battery of TV floodlights to chase the shadows in that cavern.

She raises her glass. "To your health," she says.

"And yours. How's the ear?"

"My," she says, "you do remember things. It's much better, thank you."

"Any news on who takes over as CEO?"

"No," she says shortly. "The Board appointed a special subcommittee to come up with recommendations, but they haven't reported yet."

He looks at her closely. "Lots of luck," he says.

She giggles like a schoolgirl. "I haven't a prayer."

"Sure you have," he tells her. "You were the person closest to John Dempster, weren't you?"

She stiffens. "What do you mean by that?"

"Listen, Miss Bookerman," he says, "thanks for the brandy, but let's not play games. Okay? I'll ask you questions and you answer. If you don't want to, that's your choice. But it means I'll have to get the answers from someone else. I'm hoping you'll save me time."

"I fail to see what my relationship to John Dempster has to do with your investigation of industrial sabotage."

He sighs. "Look, you have your own way of working—right? And I have mine. You've got to give me wiggle room. All those attacks on Dempster-Torrey property—what do you want me to do: go to eighteen different places around the country and investigate cases that have already been tossed by the local cops and your own security people with no results? I'd just be spinning my wheels. Does that make sense to you?"

She nods dumbly, takes a sip of her cognac.

"So I figure the solution—if there is one—is right here in New York. I also think Dempster's death is tied in with the assaults against your property. His murder was the final act of sabotage."

"But why?" she cries. "For what reason?"

He shrugs. "My first idea about a corporate shark on the prowl got shot down, so now I'm looking for another motive. And all I've got to work with are the people involved—like you. That's why I'm putting it to you straight: Did you have a thing going with Dempster?"

She raises her chin defiantly. "You really go for the jugular, don't you? Incredible!"

"You going to answer my question or not?"

"Yes, I had a *thing* going with John J. Dempster—if that's what you want to call it."

"Okay," he says mildly, "that clears the air a little. You knew he was a womanizer?"

She pokes fingers into her blond curls, then tugs them in a gesture of anger. "You have been busy, haven't you? Of course I knew he played around. I worked closely with the man for years, and we had what you call a *thing* for the past three. He cheated on his wife from the moment he was married. But don't get the wrong idea, Mr. Cone. My balling J. J. had nothing to do with my keeping my job or moving up at Dempster-Torrey. I happen to be damned good at what I do. Besides, that wasn't the way Jack worked. If I had said no, I'd still be Chief Operating Officer because he knew I had earned the title. Also, he could have had any other woman he wanted—younger, prettier, skinnier than I."

"You do all right," he says, and she gives him a faint smile. "Tell me something, Miss Bookerman—and this is just curiosity—how come he was such a hotshot with the ladies? His money? Power?"

She shakes her head. "He could have been a cabdriver or a ditchdigger and he'd still be a winning stud. He had energy and drive and—and a forcefulness I've never seen in anyone before and will probably never see again. Physically he wasn't all that handsome. I mean he was hardly a matinee idol. But when he zeroed in, I don't think there's a woman in the world who could have resisted him. And when he wanted to, he could be kind, considerate, generous, loving."

Suddenly she begins weeping, tears spilling from those big, luminous eyes and down her cheeks. She makes no effort to wipe them away. She reaches out with a trembling hand to pour herself more cognac, but Cone takes the bottle, fills her glass, and helps himself to another belt.

"Sorry about that," she says finally, taking a deep breath. "I thought I was all cried out, but I guess I wasn't."

"That's okay," he says. "You're entitled."

She sits back, takes a gulp of her drink. Tonight she's wearing another suit: glossy black gabardine, with a pale pink man-tailored shirt and a ribboned bow at the neck. She looks weary, and there are lines in her face that Cone didn't spot at their first meeting.

He wonders if she's just a nice girl from Bensonhurst who's suddenly found herself in over her head, her mentor gone, her lover dead, and a lot of business pressures she can't handle. But her next comment disabuses him of that notion; she has spunk to spare.

"What the hell has J. J.'s sexual habits got to do with the sabotage and his murder?" she wants to know.

"Listen, I told you I had more questions than answers. When I work a case, I try to collect as much stuff as I can. Ninety percent of it turns out to be junk, but how do you know what's meaningful when you start? So far you've been very cooperative, and I appreciate that. I hope you'll keep it up. You've got a big stake in this."

"What's that supposed to mean?"

"You're the one who hired Haldering and Company. If I can figure out who pulled the sabotage jobs, and maybe who iced your boss, you'll get brownie points with the Board of Directors, won't you? That should help if they're considering you for the CEO job."

She looks at him in amazement. "You're something, you are," she says. "You think of everything. Fantastic! Well, for your information, Mr. Cone, making CEO comes pretty far down on my anxiety list."

"Uh-huh," he says. "Now can we get back to the Q-and-A for a few more minutes?"

"Sure. Fire away."

"You've met his brother, David Dempster?"

"I've met him."

"What's your take?"

"A neuter."

"How did John Dempster feel about him?"

"Ignored him. He thought David was a joke."

"Did David try to get the Dempster-Torrey PR account?"

"My God, how have you found out these things? Yes, David made a pitch—but that was years ago. Jack turned him down, of course. We set up an in-house publicity and corporate advertising division, and it's worked out very well."

"So there was hostility between the brothers?"

"Not hostility. Just nothing."

"I've talked to Dorothy Blenke, David's ex-wife."

"Have you? I've never met the lady."

"I got the feeling—though she never said yes or no, either way—that maybe John Dempster had a fling with her while she was married to his brother. You know anything about that?"

Eve Bookerman struggles out of the armchair and stands stiffly erect. "Get out!" she yells at him.

"Okay," Timothy says equably. He rises, reaches for his cap.

"No," the woman says, holding up a palm. "Wait a minute. Sit down and finish your drink. I apologize."

They both sit again, stare at each other warily.

"Maybe," she says. "I don't know for sure. But from little things Jack said, it could have been that way."

"There are a lot of 'coulds' and 'maybes' in this file," Cone says. "All right, let's say John and Dorothy had an affair. That was before his thing with you—right?"

She nods.

"And maybe, just maybe, that affair led to David Dempster's divorce. Do you think that's possible?"

"Anything is possible," she says.

"Thank you," he says, "but I knew that when I was four years old." He finishes his drink, rises, takes up his cap. "I appreciate your seeing me."

"I talked too much," she says dully.

"Nah," Cone says. "You really didn't tell me much I hadn't already guessed. Besides, I'm not wired, so who's to know what you did or didn't say. Get a good night's sleep, Miss Bookerman."

"Fat chance," she says bitterly.

Cone rides down in that same scented elevator, flips a hand at the tailcoated gink behind the desk, and exits into a night that's all moon and grazing breeze. He feels loose and restless, and considers his options. He could go directly home. He could drop in at the nearest bar for a nightcap or two. He could call Samantha and see if she's in the mood to entertain a visitor at that hour.

So fifteen minutes later he finds himself double-parked on East Thirty-eighth Street, scoping the townhouse where David Dempster lives. The third-floor lights are on, front windows opened but screened. Cone can't see anyone moving behind the gauzy curtains.

He sits there for almost a half-hour, smoking two cigarettes to make up for his abstinence in Bookerman's apartment. Finally the third-floor lights go out. Now for the moment of truth: Did the guy sack out or is he planning an excursion? Cone waits patiently for another twenty minutes, but no one comes out of the townhouse.

"What the hell am I doing?" the Wall Street dick asks aloud, and then wonders if he's losing his marbles because he hasn't even got a cat there to listen to him.

5

It's a Saturday, and usually he and Samantha spend the day together—and
sometimes the night. But she has shopping to do in the afternoon and
then, in the evening, she must attend a bridal shower for one of the secretaries at Haldering & Co.

"Gonna miss me?" she asks.

"Nah," he says. "I got a lot of things to do."

"Oh, sure. Like smoking up a storm, slopping vodka, and kicking the
cat."

"I wouldn't kick Cleo. Strangle maybe, but not kick."

"How about tomorrow?"

"Let me take a look at my appointment book."

"Keep talking like that, buster, and you'll be singing soprano. Listen,
we haven't had pizza for a long time—maybe a week or so. How's about
you pick up a big one—half pepperoni for you, half anchovies for me—
and bring it over here tomorrow. I've got some salad stuff."

"Sounds good," he says. "Around noon?"

"Make it later," she says. "I've got to read the Sunday *Times*. Unless
you were planning a matinee. Were you?"

"The thought had crossed my mind."

"What mind? How about threeish or fourish?"

"How about twoish?"

"Okay," she says agreeably. "We can read the Real Estate Section in
bed together."

"Whoopee!" he cries.

He really does have things to do—not a lot, but some. He changes
Cleo's litter and damp-mops the linoleum. He takes in his laundry and
decides the corduroy suit will do for another week without dry cleaning.
He goes shopping for beer, vodka, wine, brandy. And he buys a loaf of
Jewish rye (without seeds) and a whole garlic salami. It's about two feet
long and looks like an elephant's schlong.

Back in the loft, he and Cleo have salami sandwiches, two for him, one
for the cat. Cone's sandwiches have hot English mustard smeared on them.
Cleo prefers mayonnaise.

He reads *Barron's* as he eats, marveling at all the reports of chicanery
on Wall Street. Most of them involve inside trading, stock manipulation,

or fraudulent misrepresentation on a company's balance sheet. The Street has its share of gonifs, and the fact that they wear three-piece pinstripes and carry alligator attaché cases doesn't mitigate their corruption.

What never ceases to amaze Cone is how few of these moneyed crooks are stand-up guys. Once they've been nabbed by the Securities and Exchange Commission or the Federal DA, they sing like canaries, happy to squeal on their larcenous associates, willing to be wired or have their phones tapped so old school chums can share the blame. Cone knows that when you drive a BMW and summer on the Cape, you'd be eager to cooperate with the fuzz if it means probation rather than a year in the slammer. But Timothy has known cheap boosters, purse-snatchers, and yeggs with more honor than that.

"It's money," he tells a snoozing Cleo. "Everyone quotes 'Money is the root of all evil,' but that's not what the Good Book says. It says, 'The *love* of money is the root of all evil.' Big difference."

Cleo is not impressed.

Cone finishes his reading and then falls asleep at the table, bent forward with his head on folded arms. He wakes early in the evening, feeling stiff from his awkward position, with pins and needles in both hands. He stalks up and down the loft, jangling arms and legs to get jazzed up again.

There's a greasy spoon around the corner, run by a Greek who can do nothing right but double cheeseburgers and home fries with a lot of onions. So that's what Timothy has, sitting at the counter and wondering if this is the way he's going to die someday, toppling off the stool, OD'd on cholesterol.

He returns to the loft and mooches around for almost an hour, smoking two Camels and buying himself another robust drink. He knows what he's going to do that night, but the prospect is so depressing he puts it off as long as possible. Finally he can postpone it no longer and calls David Dempster.

"Hello?" Dempster says. Cone recognizes that spoony voice.

"Sam?" the Wall Street dick asks.

"No, you've got the wrong number," Dempster says, and hangs up.

So now Cone knows the guy is home, and he has no excuse for stalling. He makes his preparations swiftly: a jelly jar filled with vodka, the lid screwed on tightly; a plastic bag of ice cubes, closed with a metal tie; a fresh pack of cigarettes; a book of matches; a pencil stub; an empty milk carton in case he has to relieve himself.

He gets up to East Thirty-eighth Street at about 8:30 and double-parks across from the limestone townhouse. There's a streetlight right in front of the building, so Cone backs up the Escort to get out of the glare. He still has a good view, and is happy to see the third floor is lighted. In fact, a couple of times David Dempster comes to the front window, pulls the curtains aside, and peers down into the street.

"Waiting for someone, honey?" Cone says softly. He settles down, knowing it's going to be a long night. He figures he'll stay double-parked as long as he can, and if a prowl car rousts him, he'll drive around the block and take up his station again.

One cigarette later, a beige Jaguar Vanden Plus pulls up in front of Dempster's townhouse. It double-parks, a guy gets out, locks up, goes into the building. In a few minutes, Cone sees the shadows of two men moving behind the thin curtains on the third floor.

He hops out of his car, trots across the street, walks purposefully past the Jaguar, and eyeballs the license plate. Back in his Ford, he jots the number on the inside cover of his matchbook. He's no sooner done that when a dark blue, four-door Bentley pulls up behind the parked Jaguar. Guy gets out, locks up, hurries into the townhouse. Then Cone can spot three shadows moving back and forth on the third floor.

He goes through the same drill: crosses the street, takes a long look at the license plate, returns to the Escort to jot down the number. One more and it'll be a poker game, Cone thinks.

But he has to wait almost fifteen minutes before the fourth visitor appears. He arrives in a chauffeured black Daimler that pulls in ahead of the Jaguar. Man gets out, enters the townhouse. Cone doesn't even glance at the third-floor windows; it's a good bet the Daimler owner is going to join the crowd.

But the Wall Street dick has another problem: The chauffeur steps out of the car, slouches against a fender, lights a cigar, and inspects the night sky. Cone decides to give it a try. He crosses the street, glances at the car, then stops as if entranced.

"Wow," he says to the lounging chauffeur. "What kind of a car is that?"

The guy inspects him coldly. He's a big bruiser with shoulders so wide he'd have to go through a door sideways.

"Daimler," he says.

"Expensive?" Cone asks.

"Nah," the guy says. "Just save your bottle caps."

Cone laughs appreciatively. "Mind if I take a look?" he asks.

"Look but don't touch," the guy says.

So the Wall Street dick walks slowly around the Daimler, eyeballing the license plate.

"Beautiful job," he says. "Who's so rich he can afford something like this?"

The chauffeur stares at him. "I thought everyone had one."

Cone knows he's not going to get anything from this tightmouth, so he returns to his car and adds the Daimler's license number to his list. There's no movement behind the third-floor curtains, and he wonders if it really is a poker game, or bridge or tiddlywinks, and the whole night is going down the drain.

He opens his jar of vodka, takes a sip to lower the level, and tips in two cubes and some ice water from the plastic bag. As he drinks, he adds more cubes and more water, stirring with a forefinger until he's got the mix just right. Then he slouches down, keeping an eye on the townhouse entrance and hoping for action.

It doesn't take too long. In about twenty minutes, three men come out. They stand a few moments on the sidewalk, talking, laughing, gesturing. Under the streetlight they all look well-fed, well-dressed, well-fixed. Pinkie-ring guys, Cone figures, or maybe the blow-dried type. They all shake hands, real pals, and go to their cars. The Daimler pulls away first, then the Jaguar, then the Bentley. Cone watches them go.

Now what the hell was that? he wonders. Obviously not a poker game. And too short a time for them all to get fixed by a call girl in a back bedroom or watch a porn flick on Dempster's VCR. Is the guy dealing crack? Just what in God's name is going down to bring three apparent richniks to Dempster's apartment on a Saturday night? Clients on business? If that's what it was, why three of them at one time? And why couldn't they have met in Dempster's Cedar Street office or consulted by phone?

It's getting close to 10:30, and Cone sits patiently, still watching those third-floor windows. Suddenly the lights go out and Timothy straightens up. Too early for beddy-bye; the guy *has* to be on his way out. And he is. He leaves his building, walks swiftly toward Park Avenue. He passes under the streetlight and Cone definitely makes him as David Dempster. He starts the Escort and moves slowly after his target.

David Dempster turns south on Park Avenue. Cone pulls up to the corner and stops as if he's waiting to make a turn. He watches, hoping the guy isn't just out for an evening stroll. He isn't. About halfway down the block he pauses under the marquee of a residential hotel. The doorman comes out. The two men talk a moment. Dempster takes out his wallet, plucks a bill, slips it to the doorman. Then he unlocks and gets into a white Cadillac Seville sitting in the No Parking zone in front of the hotel.

The action is obvious to Cone: Dempster is greasing the doorman to "rent" a convenient parking space. When the Seville pulls out, Cone completes his turn and follows. There's enough traffic so that chances are good Dempster won't spot a tail even if he's looking for one.

They go west, they go north, farther west, farther north. For a few moments Cone fears the Seville might be heading for the Lincoln Tunnel. The prospect of a late-night hegira through the wilds of New Jersey doesn't fill the Wall Street dick with glee. But no, Dempster drives north on Eighth Avenue to Forty-fifth Street, turns west, slows down in the block between Tenth and Eleventh avenues. Awesome neighborhood for anyone in a white Cadillac at night.

But Dempster knows exactly what he's doing. A tenement has been demolished, the vacant area paved, and it now serves as a narrow parking lot. It's completely dark, with a heavy chain across the entrance. Cone stops well back in the shadows and watches. The Cadillac pulls up. A guy comes out of a little hut. Dempster hands him a bill. The chain is unlocked and dropped, the Seville enters.

By the time Dempster comes walking out, Cone has parked alongside a fire hydrant and doused his lights. He isn't worried about a ticket—the client can take care of that—but the possibility of being towed away is a real downer. But he figures he's got no choice. So he gives David Dempster a good lead, then sets off after him on foot.

The tailee walks quickly down the deserted street to Eleventh Avenue. Just as Cone makes the corner, Dempster disappears into a grungy saloon with a spluttery blue neon sign outside: Paddy's Pig.

Cone saunters up, peers through the flyspecked window. He spots David Dempster seated at the bar talking earnestly to a fat guy who's wearing a seaman's watch cap and a T-shirt that was white a long time ago. Cone can't figure Dempster's choice of a drinking companion. Could the guy be a closet faigeleh? Not likely.

There's no way he can enter the bar; Dempster would make him for sure. So Cone spends the next half-hour meandering up and down the block, stopping at Paddy's Pig occasionally to look through the window and make certain his quarry is still inside. There's a faded menu taped to the inside of the window that Timothy finds interesting. It advertises "Turkey dinner with all the tremens." Of the delirium variety, Cone has no doubt.

He's a half-block away, on the corner of Forty-sixth Street, when he sees David Dempster come out of the bar and walk quickly toward Forty-fifth, probably to reclaim his car. The Wall Street dick lets him go, waits a few minutes, then returns to Paddy's Pig. Unexpectedly, it has a fine front door of oak, inset with panels of beveled and etched glass.

But the tavern itself is a swamp. The bar is gouged and burned mahogany. The sawdust on the floor dates from Year One, being liberally mixed with peanut shells and cigar butts.

Cone looks around as if he's trying to locate a pal. The scarred bar is on his left. There's a line of booths on the right, and down the middle is a double row of flimsy wood tables and fragile chairs. The tables are crowded with Saturday night boozers who look like seamen, longshore-men, thieves, and over-the-hill ladies of the evening. Noise slams down from the tin ceiling, and there's a stink of scorched grease and phenol.

The booths on the right are occupied by a different breed. Mostly youngish guys dressed for flash. Some are with women, but all look like hardcases. Cone reckons a few have got to be Attica alumni; they've got the lag look about them: talking without moving their lips, eyes constantly on the qv.

He moves up to the bar, one empty stool away from the fat guy in watch cap and T-shirt. He has faded blue tattoos on his flabby arms and a long, pale scar across his chin as if someone went for his throat with a straight razor and he ducked just in time.

On Cone's right, practically rubbing elbows, is a tall dude with the jits. He's either scratching his acne or probing an ear with a matchstick. Both his little fingers have been lopped off at the second joint, and he's got a greasy black ponytail bound with a rubber band.

A mustachioed bartender wanders up and stands in front of Cone.

"Yeah?" he says.

Cone looks around. Everyone seems to be drinking boilermakers, but he includes himself out.

"Vodka," he orders. "On the rocks."

The mustache looks at him. "Bar vodka?" he asks.

"No, no," Cone says hastily. "What have you got?"

"Bar vodka and Smirnoff."

"Give me the Smirnoff," Cone says. "And there's an extra buck in it for you if you open a fresh bottle."

The bartender stares at him. "We don't water our booze in here, mis-ter."

"Didn't say you did. Do you want the buck or don't you?"

The mustache looks over at the watch cap.

"Give the man what he wants, Tommy," fatso says. "The customer is always right."

Grumbling, Tommy fishes out a fresh bottle of Smirnoff from under the bar and uncaps it in front of Cone.

"Okay?" he says truculently.

"Fine."

He's taking his first gulp when the tall dude on his right leans toward him.

"Hey," he says, "I like the way you handled that. You got class."

Cone shrugs, turns away. He sees tubby is giving him the double-O.

He seems to approve of what he sees because he pushes his boilermaker closer to Cone and shifts his bulk onto the barstool next to him.

"You from around here?" he asks in a raspy voice.

"Used to be," Cone says. "I been away for a while."

"Yeah," the guy says. "Ain't we all. Need anything? Boom-boom? Wanna be a winner? Check it out?"

"Not tonight."

"Merchandise?"

Cone stares at him. "That fell off the truck?"

"That's right. Cassettes, TV sets, VCRs, microwaves. You name it. All in the original cartons. Sealed."

The Wall Street dick considers that a moment, takes another swallow of his drink. "A motorcycle?" he suggests. "I got a buddy looking for a good buy."

"You're talking to the right man. You name it—make and model—and you got it."

"I'll send him around," Cone says. "You hang here?"

"Every night. I own the joint. Name's Louie."

Cone nods, finishes his drink. He slaps a finif on the bar, turns to go. The tall gink has disappeared. Suddenly there's a great crash behind him and he whirls. A wild, drunken fight has erupted between two men and two women seated at the tables. Screaming curses, they go at each other with fists, feet, elbows, weighty handbags. The melee grows more vicious, with bottles swung, tables upset, chairs splintered.

"Tommy," the fat guy calls, and points under the bar. He's handed an aluminum baseball bat. He slides off the stool and waddles into the donnybrook. He starts bouncing the bat off the skulls of everyone within reach. The hard guys in the booths are spitting with merriment. Timothy decides it's time to leave.

He's heading back to his car, walking along Forty-fifth Street, when someone calls, "Hey, mac." He stops and turns slowly. The tall, jittery cat from Paddy's Pig comes up close. He's got a knife in his hand that looks to be as long as a saber.

"Let's have it," he says in a whispery voice.

Cone backs up a step. "Have what?" he asks.

The guy sighs. "Whaddya think? Money, credit cards, whatever you got."

"Oh, my God!" Cone cries, clutching at his chest. "My heart! My heart!" He doubles over as if in agonizing pain, bending low. When he comes up, he has the S&W .357 in his fist. "Here's what I got," he says.

The man looks at the gun. "Hey," he says, "wait a minute."

"Drop the toothpick," Cone says. "Drop it!"

The knife clatters to the sidewalk. The Wall Street dick steps in and kicks the stupe's shin, just below the knee, as hard as he can. The mugger screams, bends, and Cone cold-cocks him behind the ear with the short-barreled Magnum. The guy goes flat out on the pavement, but Timothy takes him with his heavy work shoes, heeling the kidneys and family jewels.

He finally gets control of himself, tries to breathe slowly and deeply. He picks up the knife and drops it through the first sewer grating he comes to. He drives home to the loft, deciding he shouldn't have given the guy the boot. That was overkill, and it wasn't nice.

"Not nice?" he asks aloud, and wonders if he's ready for the acorn academy.

"What did you do last night?" Samantha Whatley asks.

"Nothing much," Cone says. "Had a few drinks, went to bed early."

"Liar," she says. "I called you around midnight; you weren't in."

"Was that you?" he says. "I was sacked out. I thought I heard the phone ringing, but by the time I got up it had stopped."

"Uh-huh," she says.

It's Sunday afternoon, they're lying together in her fancy bed, and she really is reading the real estate section of the *Times*, the rest of the paper scattered over the sheet. She's sitting up, back against the headboard, heavy horn-rimmed glasses down on her nose. Cone is just lying there lazily, not caring if school keeps or not.

"Will you listen to these rents?" Sam says. "A studio for twelve hundred a month. A one-bedroom for fifteen hundred. How does that grab you?"

"It's just money," he says.

"*Just* money? Don't try to be so fucking superior. You like it as much as anyone else."

He turns his head to look at her. "Sure I do. But I wouldn't kill for it. Would you?"

"You're the only one I want to kill, and you don't have all that much gelt."

"Bupkes is what I've got. No, seriously, would you kill for money?"

"Of course not."

"Ever talk to a homicide dick about why people kill?"

"I dated a guy from Homicide for a while, but I had to give him the broom. Whenever he got bombed he started crying. But no, I never talked to him about why people kill."

"I'll tell you why," Cone says. "Subtract the weirdos who murder because God told them to. And subtract the ones who kill because they find

hubby or wifey in the sack with someone else. Those are impulse murders."

"Crimes of passion," Sam says.

"If you say so, Well, subtract those cases and just consider the murders
that are premeditated—sometimes for a long while—and carefully
planned. Now you're dealing with two main motives. One is revenge,
which isn't too important unless you're a Sicilian."

"And the other is money," she says.

"Bingo," Cone says. "I'd guess that greed tops everything else. It may
be for a couple of bucks in a muggee's pocket or for a couple of billion in
a corporate treasury."

"Oh-ho," Whatley says, peering at him through her halfglasses. "Now
I know why I'm getting this lecture on mayhem on a nice, bright, Sunday
afternoon. You're brooding about the Dempster case, and you think greed
was the motive for the industrial sabotage."

"And for John Dempster's murder. What else could it be?" he says
fretfully. "I'm not saying other motives might not be involved, but it was
greed that sparked the whole thing."

"How do you know?" she asks.

"I don't," he says. "And that's what's sending me up the wall. I thought
I had it figured, but I struck out."

Then he tells her about his great inspiration: a corporate raider trying
to put Dempster-Torrey into play, and conniving to reduce the price of
the stock by sabotage and, eventually, assassination.

"Good thinking, Tim," she says.

"Not good," he says mournfully, shaking his head. "Simon Trale, the
CFO, checked it out for me, and there's no evidence at all, not even a
rumor, that some pirate is making a move. So that's that. Ahh, the hell
with it. Let's forget about it."

"Should I heat up the pizza?" Sam asks. "You getting hungry?"

"Yeah," he says, looking at her. "But not for pizza."

"Oh, you sweet-talking sonofabitch," she says. "Can we fornicate on top
of the Sunday *Times*? Isn't that sacrilegious?"

"What's the worst that could happen—you get a headline printed backwards on your ass? Leave your glasses on. I've never balled a woman while
she's wearing specs."

"You're depraved," Sam says.

"Just a mood. It'll pass."

"Oh, God!" she says. "I hope not."

A few hours later, after a lukewarm shower during which they take
turns picking up the soap, they have their pizza, salad, and wine.

Cone gets back to the Dempster case; he just can't get rid of it.

"Of course," he says, "it's garbage to claim anyone kills from one motive alone. Usually it's a tangle of reasons, justifications, and past history."

"Who are you talking about?" she demands.

"Oh . . . just people," he says darkly.

"You're closing up again," she says. "I know that shriveled brain of yours is going 'round and 'round like a Roller Derby, and you're not going to tell me about it."

"Nothing to tell," he mutters, head lowered. "You got any more salad?"

"That's it," she says. "Sorry I ran short."

He raises his head slowly, glares at her.

"Jesus," she says, "what are you looking at me like that for? I just said there's no more salad; so sue me."

"You remember the Laboris case?" he asks. "The guy who was pulling a Ponzi scam so he could launder money from dope and art smuggling?"

"Yeah," she says, "I remember. So what?"

"Without knowing it, you gave me the lead that broke it. Now you've done it again."

"Done what?" she cries desperately. "Just exactly what are you talking about?"

"Forget it," he says, grinning at her. "Have some more wine."

"Up yours," she says grumpily. "Were you labeled 'Most Likely to Fail' in your high school yearbook?"

"I'm a dropout," he tells her.

"I'm willing to testify to that," she says, and they both crack up.

After the pizza is gone, they stay on the floor, sipping the chilled wine, schmoozing about this and that. These are their most intimate moments, the closest. Sex is brutal warfare, but this is gentle peace, and there's a lot to be said for it—though neither would admit it.

Samantha has a choice collection of old 78s, and she puts a stack on her player, selecting the records she knows he likes best. She starts with Walter Houston's "September Song," Bing Crosby's "Just a Gigolo," and Billie Holiday's "Fine and Mellow."

"I've also got her 'Gloomy Sunday,'" Sam says. "I'd play it, but it ain't."

"That's right," Timothy Cone says happily. "It ain't."

He has many illusions about himself. One of the most mundane is that if, before falling asleep, he tells himself exactly when he wishes to arise, then lo! he will awake at that exact hour.

So on Sunday night, curled on his mattress, he instructs himself, "You will wake up at eight o'clock. You will definitely wake at eight." He sleeps soundly and rouses at precisely ten minutes after nine. Cursing, he lights a cigarette, puts water on to boil, and tosses Cleo a small dog biscuit. It's a cat, but not racist.

Still in his underwear, smoking a cigarette and sipping black coffee, he phones Neal Davenport.

"You're up so early?" the city detective says. "Don't tell me you're at the office."

"On my way," Cone says, unshaven and standing there in his Jockey shorts. "How's the Department doing on the Dempster homicide?"

"That's why you called at this hour? To make me feel more miserable? It's a cold trail, sonny boy, and getting icier every day. This one's a pisser. We're getting flak from everyone, and just between you, me, and the lamppost, we haven't got a thing."

"What about the hotshot lieutenant who was running the show? Is he still around?"

"Nah," Davenport says, "he's long gone. Now we got a deputy inspector, and he's feeling the heat, too. Turning into a lush. This goddamned file is going to ruin a lot of careers—mine included."

"Anything on that terrorist group that called the newspapers? The Liberty Tomorrow gang."

"No trace. The thinking now is that it was all bullshit. A stunt pulled by some wild-assed leftists to grab headlines, or maybe by the finks who actually offed Dempster and just wanted to throw us a curve. This is why you called—just to listen to my kvetching?"

"Not exactly," Cone says. "I want to ask a favor."

"No kidding? I never would have guessed."

"Look," Cone says, "you owe me one—right? The Laboris drug deal—remember?"

"Well . . . yeah, I guess maybe. Waddya got?"

"Three license plates. I need to know who owns the cars."

"What for?"

"Neal," the Wall Street dick says softly, "this could involve the Dempster kill."

Long silence. Then: "You shittin' me, sherlock?"

"I swear to God I'm not. It's not definitely connected, but it might be. Come on, take a chance."

Davenport sighs. "Okay, I'll see what I can do. Give me the numbers."

Cone reads off his scrawls from the inside of the matchbook cover. "Push this," he urges. "It really could be something."

"And if it's not?"

"Then you've wasted a phone call. Big deal."

"I'll get back to you," the NYPD man says and hangs up.

Cone, anxious to get things moving, fills his coffee cup again, lights another Camel, and calls Simon Trale at Dempster-Torrey. He has to hold for a few minutes before he's put through. And while he's waiting, he has to listen to music. "Climb Every Mountain," no less.

"Sorry to keep you waiting, Mr. Cone."

"That's okay, Mr. Trale. Listen, I warned you I might contact you again if I needed more poop."

"Poop?"

"Information. Someone accused me recently of using other people to do my job for me. But sometimes it's the only way to get the job done, so that's why I'm calling. All right with you?"

"Of course," Trale says.

"When I talked to you about all those industrial accidents, you said most of the losses were covered by insurance. Have I got that right?"

"Correct."

"Does Dempster-Torrey buy insurance from individual companies or do you use a broker?"

"We use a single broker, Mr. Cone. We've found it more efficient and economical that way."

"One broker for all of Dempster-Torrey's property and casualty insurance?"

"Yes."

"Lucky broker. That must add up to a nice wad."

Simon Trale laughs quietly. "It does indeed."

"So I'd guess that Dempster-Torrey, and you in particular, have got heavy clout with the broker."

"A fair assumption. What are you getting at, Mr. Cone?"

"Here's what I need. . . . There's got to be an association of all the property and casualty insurance companies in the country. Some outfit that lobbies in Washington and also collects statistics on property and casualty losses and the insurance business in general."

"Of course there is. The Central Insurance Association, a trade group."

"The CIA?" Cone says. "That must raise a few eyebrows. But I'll bet they've got all the facts and figures on their industry on computer tapes—right?"

"I would imagine so, yes."

"Well, here's what I'd like you to do: Call your broker, ask him to contact the trade association and get a list of the ten companies in the country that suffered the heaviest property and casualty losses in the last year."

There's a long pause. Then: "You think there may be a connection with our losses, Mr. Cone? That there may be some kind of a conspiracy directed against large corporations?"

"Something like that," Cone says. "Look, Mr. Trale, I wouldn't blame you for thinking I'm a bubblehead after I fell on my face on that corporate raider suggestion."

"Don't apologize for that," the old man says. "It was a very ingenious idea that just didn't work out. Happens to me all the time. But now you feel there may be a link between our accidents and those of other companies?"

"Could be."

"All right," Trale, says without hesitation. "I'll call our broker and ask him to get the information."

"Lean on him if you have to," Cone says.

Trale laughs. "I don't think that will be necessary; I'm sure he'll be happy to cooperate. Shall I have him contact you directly?"

"Yeah, that'd help. I want to move on this as fast as I can, Mr. Trale, but I'm not promising anything."

"I understand that. I'll call immediately."

Cone hangs up, satisfied he's started things rolling. Now he's got to wait for Davenport and the insurance broker to get back to him. He could do it all himself, but it would take weeks, maybe months, of donkeywork. And he has the feeling that something is going down that better be squelched in a hurry.

Having done a morning's labor for Haldering & Co. with two phone calls, he feels no great obligation to occupy his desk at the office. So he has a whore's bath, shaves, and dresses at a languid pace, pausing to make a small aluminum foil ball for Cleo to chase. He even has time for a morning beer to excite the palate and cleanse the nasal passages.

He ambles downtown, frowning at a summer sun that beams back at him. It's a brilliant day, and he might glory in it if he was not a man of a naturally morose nature, a grump still studying joy and how to achieve it. The brimful day is an indignity; he still prefers sleet and wet socks.

The snarly Haldering receptionist gives him a glare for his tardiness, and his cramped office is no great solace. There's a chilly memo from Samantha Whatley on his desk: "Your progress reports for the past three weeks are overdue. Ditto expense account vouchers. Please remit ASAP."

He folds the memo into a paper airplane and sails it up. It flutters, falls. Just like his mood. He wonders if he might not improve his lot in life by learning how to slice Nova thin in a high-class deli. He could force that career switch by marching in and slamming Hiram Haldering in the snout. Attractive thought.

He knows why he is suddenly afflicted with a galloping case of the glooms. Having set the wheels in motion on the Dempster file, there's not a damned thing he can do until Neal Davenport and Simon Trale respond to his requests. The inaction chafes, and he hopes to God his second brain-storm isn't going to prove as big a blunder as his first.

He grimly sets to work on those accursed progress reports, trying not to think of the possibility of another balls-up on the Dempster case. But when his phone rings about 11:30, he reaches for it cautiously as if it might bring news of disaster.

"Yeah?" he says warily.

"Davenport. You got pencil and paper? I got names to go with those license plates you gave me."

"Jeez, that's quick work," Cone says. "I didn't expect you to get back to me so soon."

"Well, you said it might have something to do with Dempster. You know how to jerk my chain. I'll give you the names, but I also got ad-dresses if needed. Ready? Samuel Folger is the first. The second is Jerome K. Waltz. That's W-A-L-T-Z. Like the dance. The third plate is a com-pany car registered to an outfit named Simon and Butterfield, Incorpo-rated. Got all that? Now never say I don't deliver."

"Yeah," Cone says, "thanks."

"Those names mean anything to you?"

"They're all Wall Street guys. They call themselves investment advisers or financial consultants or whatever. But what they really are is money managers—other people's money."

"They're legit?"

Cone doesn't answer directly. "They're all heavyweights," he goes on. "Mostly in trust and pension funds. I mean we're talking about billions of dollars."

"So what's the connection with the Dempster homicide?"

"Well, uh, it's iffy right now."

"You bastard!" Davenport shouts. "I knock myself out getting this stuff, and you clam up on me. You got nothing to trade? What kind of horseshit is that?"

"Calm down, Neal," the Wall Street dick says. "I got something to trade. You ever hear of a scabby joint over on the West Side called Paddy's Pig?"

Silence. It goes on for so long that Cone says, "Hey, are you there?"

"I'm here. You said Paddy's Pig?"

"That's right."

"You think it might be tied to the Dempster kill?"

"Yeah."

"You and I better have a meet," the city detective says.

6

Cone provides the lunch. He's standing outside the office with a shopping bag when Davenport drives up. He double-parks his unmarked blue Plymouth and props up a "Police Officer on Duty" card inside the windshield. Timothy climbs in with the bag.

"Hey, Sherlock," Davenport says, "that smells good. What'd you get?"

"Rare burgers on soft buns with a slice of onion—just like you ordered. Also, French fries, a couple of dills, and a cold six-pack of Bud."

"Sounds good," the NYPD man says, tossing a chewed wad of Juicy Fruit out the window. "You can diddle your expense account?"

"No problem."

"Then let's get at it."

They open up the smaller bags, pop two beers, divide the paper napkins, and start gorging.

"There's mustard and ketchup in those little packs," Cone says.

"I'll skip," the city bull says. "I'm on a diet. Listen, I haven't got much time, so I'll give you the background fast. There's a gang up in Hell's Kitchen—only it's Clinton now—called the Westies. Mostly Irish, and a meaner bunch of villains you never want to meet. I mean they make the outlaws in Murder, Inc., look like Girl Scouts. There's a story that one of the Westies walked into a bar up there carrying the head of a guy he had just popped."

"And the bar was Paddy's Pig?"

"You got it. That's where the Westies hung out. They were mostly into gambling and loan-sharking on the piers. But when the West Side docks dried up, the Westies went into everything else—drugs, prostitution, porn—you name it. Then, about ten years ago, they got into contract killings, including some for one of the Mafia families. We figure they pulled off at least thirty homicides. Most of the victims were chopped up. One guy had his head put in a steel vise, and it was tightened until his skull cracked open like a ripe melon."

"Beautiful. Have some more fries before I eat them all."

They start on their second burgers.

"These onions are hot," Davenport says. "Just the way I like them. But I'll be grepsing all day. Anyway, about three years ago the Department organized a strike force—us and state and federal people. It worked out real good. About a dozen of the Westies were sent up, including some of the bosses, and the rest laid low. Paddy's Pig was closed down for a while, but it reopened with a new owner. And lately our snitches have claimed the gang is back in business again. Now you tell me there's a tie-up between Paddy's Pig and the Dempster homicide. In the first place, what were you doing in that joint?"

Cone wipes his mouth with a paper napkin and opens another beer. "I tailed David Dempster up there."

The NYPD man turns to stare at him. "You shittin' me again?"

"I shit you not," Cone says. "That's where he went, and had a confab with the owner, a fat slob named Louie. Listen, when the Dempster investigation began, did you run everyone involved through Records?"

"Whaddya think? Of course we checked them out. David Dempster's got a sheet—but not much of one. A charge of battery for beating up a drunk driver in Central Park who, Dempster said, killed his dog. And two arrests for assault. Nothing ever came to trial."

"My, my," Cone says. "So the wimp's got a streak of the crude, has he? That figures."

Davenport rattles the windows with a reverberant belch, then unwraps a fresh stick of Juicy Fruit. "It doesn't figure to me," he says. "So David Dempster went slumming and was observed talking to the owner of Paddy's Pig. What does that prove?"

"When I talked to Louie after Dempster left, he tried to push dope. When I wasn't interested, he switched to merchandise that fell off the truck. I told him a buddy of mine was looking to buy a motorcycle. He said sure, send him around."

The two detectives stare at each other.

"Thin stuff," Davenport says.

"You got anything thicker?"

"No," Davenport admits. "We got a lot of doughnuts that are all hole. Look, could you go back to this Louie and see if he can get you a black Kawasaki, Model 650?"

"Well, ah, that might be a problem. To tell you the truth, I got in a slight disagreement with a guy who may be hanging out there."

"A *slight* disagreement? With you that's like being slightly pregnant. Okay, I'll do it myself."

"Neal," Cone says gently, "don't do that. They'll make you for a cop the minute you walk in the place."

Davenport looks down at his stained, off-the-rack brown suit, his belly, plump hands. "You really think so?" he asks.

"Definitely. Why don't you get an undercover guy who can act a scuzz. Bring him around and I'll prep him. He can spend time at Paddy's Pig until he's accepted as just another barfly. Then he can move in on Louie and see if he can get a line on the cycle. I'm betting they didn't drop it in the Hudson or send it to a chop shop. It's too valuable."

"Yeah, that makes sense. If it works out, it'll put David Dempster in the crapper. You know that, don't you?"

"Of course I know it."

"Well, what the hell was his motive? Jealousy? Sibling rivalry?"

"Sibling rivalry? That's fancy talk for a gumshoe."

"I read books," Davenport protests. "Come on—what's the motive?"

"I'm working on that."

"Jesus," the detective says disgustedly, "you always hold back, don't you?"

"You handle Paddy's Pig," Cone says, "and let me go after David Dempster. A guy shouldn't chill his own brother. That's not right."

"You got a brother?"

"No."

"Then what the hell are you talking about?"

"I got my standards," Timothy says.

He carries the two remaining beers up to his office in a brown paper bag. There's a scrawny guy in a seersucker suit waiting in the reception room. He's wearing wire-rimmed cheaters, and there's a straw boater balanced on his knee. He's got the face of a pale hawk, with a droopy nose and a mouth so tight it looks like a lipless slit.

"Man to see you," the antique receptionist snaps at Cone.

The visitor stands and tries a smile that doesn't work.

"Mr. Timothy Cone?"

"Yeah. Who you?"

The guy whips out a business card and proffers it. "Bernard Staley from International Insurance—"

"Whoa," Cone interrupts, holding up a hand. "I'm not buying."

"And I'm not selling. It's International Insurance Investigators. The Triple-I. Have you ever heard of us?"

"Nope."

"Good," the guy says, and this time the smile works. "We like it that way. This concerns Dempster-Torrey. Can we talk?"

"Sure," Timothy says, taking the business card. "This way."

Staley follows him down the corridor and into Cone's littered cubbyhole office.

"This looks like my place," the insurance man says, "but it's bigger."

"Bigger? My God, you must work out of a coffin. Listen, I've got a couple of beers here. They're not too cold, but they're wet. You want one?"

He has the guy figured for a stiff, but Staley surprises him. "Sure," he says. "That'd be good."

They open the cans, take a gulp, stare at each other with cautious interest.

"This Triple-I you work for—" Cone says. "What is it?"

"Claims investigations. Most insurance companies have their own claims department. But some of the smaller ones can't handle anything that's complicated or suspicious. And sometimes the big boys get backed up with a lot of claims at once and need temporary outside help. That's where we come in."

"I follow," Cone says. "But what's your interest in Dempster-Torrey?"

Staley drums his fingertips on the top of his sailor. "The way I get it," he says, "you were hired to investigate their industrial sabotage. Correct?"

"That's right."

"So you call Dempster-Torrey. They call their insurance broker. The broker calls the Central Insurance Association. And they call us."

"There's a helluva lot of phoning going on today," Cone says. "Maybe I should buy some Nynex stock. But how does your company come in on this?"

"About three years ago the computers at the CIA—that's a great name, isn't it—picked up a big increase in property and casualty claims by large corporations. It was a jump that couldn't be explained by normal growth, so the Triple-I was hired to take a look-see."

"So you've been looking into property and casualty losses for the past three years."

"Just for a year. The eye who had the file before me retired, and I inherited it. He got nowhere with it, and that's exactly where I've got."

"Did you investigate this stuff personally?"

"You better believe it," Bernard Staley says. "Traveled all over the country. Spent a lot of the CIA's money—and delivered zilch. And I usually got there a day or two after it happened. Sometimes within hours. Not only torching factories, but sabotage, and vandalism, product tampering, bribery of union leaders, consumer lawsuits, and hiring away or corrupting key personnel—in other words, a complete program to ruin the reputation and profits of the targeted company."

"Any homicides?" Cone asks.

Staley gives him a strange look. "Funny you should ask," he says. "The chief researcher for a biomedical outfit got wiped out in a car crash. Clear night. He wasn't drunk or stoned. The official verdict was that he lost control of his car and drove into a concrete abutment. But the guy was some kind of a genius, and there was talk he was working on a cure for baldness. After he died, the stock of the company went way down, and the new product never did hit the market."

"You think the guy's accident wasn't kosher?"

Staley shrugs. "Just a feeling," he says. "No hard evidence at all. But I keep remembering it. He left a pretty wife and three young kids."

"Yeah," Cone says, "that's hard to forget. And you've gotten nothing from all your digging?"

The other man blinks behind his specs. "Nothing you can take to the bank. Just a crazy notion that all these jobs—different companies, different places—were pulled by the same guy, or the same mob. A lot of similarities. In several of the arson cases, the MO was practically identical. But don't ask me who's behind it or what the motive might be—I haven't a clue. Anyway, I won't bore you with my tale of woe any longer. You wanted a list of the ten companies that had the biggest property and casualty losses. Here it is, with their total claims."

He fishes into his inside jacket pocket, comes out with a folded sheet of typing paper, hands it over.

"You'll notice that Dempster-Torrey is at the top as far as dollar losses go."

Cone scans the list quickly. "I recognize most of the names," he says. "Not all, but most. What do these dates mean?"

"That's when the accidents happened," the Triple-I man says. "I thought it might possibly help. You'll notice some of the dates go back more than a year. I know you asked for losses in the past year, but this thing has been growing for three years now, so I decided to include the biggest losers."

Cone looks at him admiringly. "You know your job," he says.

"No, I don't," Bernard Staley says. "If I did, I'd have closed this file a year ago. I hope you have better luck. I've got a lot more on my plate besides this, but it keeps bothering me."

"Yeah. The pretty wife and three young kids."

The insurance investigator nods, rises, extends his hand. "Nice meeting you, Mr. Cone. I hope that list is what you wanted. I swear to God that something is going down, but what the hell it is, I have no idea."

"Thanks for your help," Cone says, shaking his hand.

"And if you come up with anything you'll let me know?"

"Absolutely. We're both working the same side of the street."

Staley gives him a wan smile. "Some street," he says sadly.

After he's gone, Cone reads over the list again. This sabotage is not piddling stuff; the claims are heavy: millions of dollars of losses. Which means if someone has deliberately planned the damage, he's a professional or, more probably, has hired professionals. Two of the companies on the list suffered arsonous fires on the same day, and they're half a country apart. No one torch could have managed that.

Cone ruminates a moment, searching through the mess in his top desk drawer for the phone number of his contact at the Securities and Exchange Commission. He calls.

"Jeremy Bigelow, please. Timothy Cone calling."

"He's on the phone at the moment, Mr. Cone. Would you care to wait?"

"Yeah, I'll wait."

He waits, and waits, and waits. Finally Bigelow comes on.

"Hiya, Tim," he says.

"What were you doing on the phone so long—trying to explain to your wife why you take off your wedding ring the moment you leave the house?"

"My God," the SEC man says with an empty laugh, "you never forget anything, do you. What's happening?"

"The usual bullshit. Jerry, I need a small favor."

"Well, uh, I'm awfully busy right now."

Bigelow is a nice guy but not too swift. Cone has had to strong-arm him more than once.

"Look," he says in a hard voice, "don't get snotty with me. In the first place, you owe me one for that Sally Steiner scam. Don't think I didn't see your name in *The Wall Street Journal*. But that's okay; I told you to grab the glory. In the second place, if you stiff me on this, you'll be passing up something that could be bigger than the Boesky affair. If you and the SEC don't want a piece of the action, just say so and I'll get out of your hair."

"Bigger than the Boesky affair?" Jeremy repeats. "You just said the magic words. What have you got?"

"A list of ten companies. I need to know the amount of short sales in each company's stock on the dates I'll give you."

"My God," Bigelow says, "it'll take a month of Sundays to dig that out."

"Jerry, stop trying to jerk me around. You've got it all on your computers and you know it. *The New York Times* runs a list of big-board short positions every month. It shouldn't take you more than an hour or two to come up with what I need."

"Well, all right," the other man says grudgingly. "Mail me the list and I'll see what I can do."

"Mail *shit!*" Cone says wrathfully. "I haven't got the time, and if you'd like maybe to see your name in *Business Week*, you'll want to get on this as fast as you can. Have you got a bug on your phone wired to a tape recorder?"

"Well...yeah," the SEC man says hesitantly. "For when informers call."

"I'm the best informer you'll ever have. Switch it on and I'll dictate the names of the companies and the dates."

He hears fumbling, clicking, and then Bigelow says, "Okay, go ahead."

Cone reads aloud the list from Triple-I. He concludes by saying, "That's all for now, folks. Keep those letters and postcards coming."

Jerry gets back on the phone again. "All right," he says, "I'll get it to Research right away. You're sure this is a biggie?"

"Makes the Teapot Dome Scandal look like the Gypsy Handkerchief Switch," Cone assures him. "I'll expect to hear from you tomorrow. If not, look for me at your office with a cast-iron shillelagh. Have a nice day."

"Yeah," Jeremy Bigelow says faintly. "You, too."

Cone disconnects, convinced the pace of the investigation is picking up. He lights a Camel, lifts his work shoes on top of his battered desk, and considers. Where are the flaws? If not flaws, where are the gaps? He spots one, and reaches for the phone again. He calls Mrs. Teresa Dempster.

She answers the phone herself, and he wonders, sorrowfully, if the nubile maid has been canned.

"Hello, there!" she says cheerily. "This is Teresa Dempster speaking."

"How are you, Mrs. Dempster? This is Timothy Cone."

"Mr. Timothy!" she carols. "How nice to hear from you again."

"I was wondering how my bonsai is doing. The Japanese red maple you gave me—remember?"

"Irving! Of course I remember. Well, Irving is doing just wonderfully. Growing enormously. I think we'll have to repot him."

"I was wondering if I might stop by—just for a few minutes—to take a look."

"Of course you may," she says gaily. "Irving will be so happy to see you."

"Be there in a half-hour," he says.

He grabs his cap and starts out. He meets Samantha Whatley in the corridor.

"Where are you going now?" she demands.

"Nutsville," he tells her.

She's wearing a long denim apron over a white linen jumpsuit, but no costume could conceal her feyness. The big azure eyes are widened in constant wonder, and the webby wheaten hair drifts down her back. She greets him at the door and seems genuinely delighted to see him.

"You're the first visitor I've had today," she says breathlessly, taking his hand and drawing him inside. "It's Jeanette's day off, so I've been all by my lonesome—except for my friends, of course."

"Of course," Cone says, figuring she's talking about her trees and plants. "No police guard outside?"

"Not anymore. It was really so unnecessary. Goodness, who'd want to hurt me?"

Cone doesn't answer, but follows her up the stairs and down the hallway to the greenhouse. She stops suddenly and turns to him.

"Would you like a blueberry yogurt?" she asks. "Really delicious."

"Thanks, but no, thanks. I had a heavy lunch."

"I can imagine," she says. "You men with your rare roast beef and Yorkshire pudding—it's not good for you, you know."

"I know," Cone says. "I try to avoid it."

"Well, there's Irving!" she says, pointing. "Isn't he beautiful?"

"He surely is," Cone says, meaning it. "You have a way with growing things, Mrs. Dempster."

"Oh, well, I try," she says, blushing. "I have my share of failures, I do assure you, but I keep trying. Now look at this one, Mr. Timothy. A new arrival. It's a Chinese elm, and it's older than you and I put together. But isn't it magnificent?"

"Very impressive. Have you named it yet?"

She stares at the little tree. It's thick and sturdy—and stunted.

"Yes," she says in a low voice. "I call it John J. Dempster. For my late husband, you know."

"I know," Cone says. "I hope you haven't been lonely since your husband di—since your husband passed over."

"Lonely? Oh, no. I know so many wonderful people who call and visit. I'm so fortunate. And my sons are coming home next month. I don't have time to be lonely."

"Good for you," he says. "And I'm sure your brother-in-law comes by occasionally."

"Occasionally?" she says, and laughs: a high-pitched trilling sound. "Why, he's here almost every day."

"Since you lost your husband?"

"Oh, long before that. David and I are such good friends. Heavens, he practically lives here. John was away so much—on business, you know—and David would take me out to dinner and to the theater."

"So David would know when your husband was leaving on a business trip?"

"Of course," she prattles on. "I'd tell him, we'd plan what we'd do while John was gone. The opera or ballet or just a long walk through Central Park. Once we went to the Cloisters. David is so good to me. And especially since John went on. You know it's difficult for a woman to get around and see things by herself."

"I know," Cone says sympathetically. Then he leans close to her with a viperish smile. "You don't suppose, do you, Mrs. Dempster, that David has a crush on you?"

It's a calculated risk. He knows she is not a total meshuggeneh, and if she resents his question and tells him to get lost, he won't be a bit surprised. But she leans even closer, and her voice is lower than his.

"How odd you should suggest that. You know, it had occurred to me, but I thought I was imagining things. I do that at times."

"No reason why he shouldn't be attracted to you," Timothy says bravely. "You're a fascinating woman."

"Oh, my!" Teresa says, blushing again and putting her long fingers to her cheek. "I thank you, sir. What a nice thing to say."

"The truth," he says. "Well, I'm afraid I must go now, Mrs. Dempster. I hope you won't be alone all evening."

"Oh, no," she says. "I have so much to do, and later David is coming over to take me to dinner and a Mostly Mozart recital at Lincoln Center. Do you like Mozart, Mr. Timothy?"

"Oh, yeah," Cone says. "Can't get enough of him. Thanks for letting me see Irving, Mrs. Dempster."

"He's yours, you know. And you have visitation rights whenever you wish."

He wants to kiss that velvety cheek, but resists. He leaves her home, not proud of what he has done, but telling himself it was necessary. That doesn't help much.

He drives back to the loft, wondering how the possible destruction of David Dempster might affect that sweet, innocent woman. Not a happy thought. But she impresses him as being a survivor, able to endure grief and tragedy. He hopes his appraisal is correct. It's even possible that her wackiness is her salvation. A more rational woman might crack.

When he gets to his building, he finds the front door has been jimmied—again. But it's not yet 6:00 P.M., so the elevator is still working, and he doesn't have to trudge up six flights. Cleo greets him with an ankle rub and a desperate growl that signals starvation.

Cone brings out that length of garlic salami—still plenty left—and whacks off a thick chunk. Cleo takes it under the bathtub to enjoy. Cone opens a cold beer and, on impulse, pours it into an empty jelly jar. Then he sprinkles it with salt.

He can't remember why they did that when he served with the USMC. For the flavor? To raise a head on the brew? But the taste of salted beer brings back old memories, most of which he'd like to forget forevermore.

He slumps at his spavined table, feet up, totally drained by the day's events. All those people, all that pushing and shoving to get what he wants. And then, most recently, duping an ingenuous woman. He's wiped out.

Before he knows it, he's brooding about the victim, John J. Dempster. From what he's heard from everyone, he figures the guy was a hustler—in the boardroom and in the bedroom. With all the chutzpah in the world. Willing to risk his balls in the coliseum. In fact, going from risk to risk because that's where the fun is.

Cone has known a lot of hustlers, on the street, in combat, in the business world. He admires them all, straight or crooked, for their gall and their energy. They play the cards they were dealt to the best of their ability and never whine that they didn't draw a better hand.

Occasionally, but not often, Cone wishes he could be like that. But he hasn't got the temperament, and he knows it. Instead, he seems destined to plod through life armed with a push broom and dustpan, cleaning up after the hustlers.

These melancholy reflections are interrupted by ferocious pounding at the loft door. He slips the magnum out of his ankle holster. Standing to one side of the door, he shouts, "Who is it?"

"The police!" Neal Davenport shouts back. "Open up! Have you got a naked cat in there?"

Cone replaces his revolver, unchains, unbolts, unlocks the door. The city detective lumbers in, followed by a skinny, stooped guy who's wearing a costume so decrepit that he makes Cone look like a candidate for *GQ*.

Davenport jerks a thumb at his companion. "Meet Officer Sam Shipkin," he says.

"You could have fooled me," Cone says, shaking the man's hand.

He's got a black beard that looks as if mice have been at it, and he's wearing shades that are practically opaque. His ragged jeans weren't stone-washed, they were ground between boulders, and his scuffed motorcycle boots look like Salvation Army castoffs. He's got on a sweat-stained T-shirt bearing the legend: ALL THE NUDES FIT TO PRICK.

"How d'ya like this dump?" Neal asks Shipkin. "As ratty as I told you?"

The undercover cop looks around. "I like it," he pronounces. "Poverty chic."

"Listen," the NYPD bull says, "let's not waste time. I've got to get home to Staten Island—and don't ask me why."

"You don't want a drink?" Cone asks.

"Who says so? What've you got?"

"Vodka, beer, wine, some brandy."

"A beer for me. Sam?"

"A little brandy."

They sit at the rickety table, and the host serves them.

"What in God's name is that?" Davenport cries, pointing.

"A garlic salami. Want a hunk?"

"Jesus, no! You want a slice, Sam?"

"I'll pass," Shipkin says. "My ulcer would be infuriated."

"Sam's going up to Paddy's Pig," Neal says, "and see what he can work. I told him you'd prep him."

"Sure," Cone says, and describes the tavern to the undercover man: the physical layout of the place, the patrons, what they drink.

"The hard guys are in the booths on your right," he says. "Down-and-out boozers at the tables in the center. Louie, the owner, is a fat crud with old tattoos. The night I was there he was wearing a watch cap and T-shirt."

"He's dealing drugs?"

"He's dealing *everything*. He offered me Boom-boom. What the hell is that?"

"Gage," Shipkin says. "From Florida. Heavy stuff."

"Screw the drugs," Davenport says. "It's the motorcycle we want."

"I told this Louie I got a buddy looking to buy a bike," Cone says. "He said just tell me the make and model and he'll come up with it."

Shipkin nods, sips brandy from his jelly jar. "I get the picture," he says. He turns to the other detective. "How about this scenario: If I get a lead on the Kawasaki, I'll make a dope buy from Louie with marked bills. Then we'll have him on a drug rap and can lean on him about the cycle. How does that listen?"

"Sounds good to me. How about you, sherlock?"

"Makes sense," Cone says. "We're not going to get anywhere with this unless someone caves. The more clout we have, the better. The way I figure it, this Louie is the broker between David Dempster and the Westies. He arranges the deals and turns over the cash after taking his cut. And once we've got enough to cuff Dempster, even on some shitty charge, I can finger three or four other guys who'll be happy to make deals to save their ass."

Davenport looks at him curiously. "Still holding out on me, huh? Okay, play it your way. Right now, all I want is that motorcycle. Anything else Sam should know?"

"Yeah," Cone says, turning to Shipkin. "If you spot a tall guy at the bar with a black ponytail and a bad case of acne, watch your back. You can't miss him; someone chopped off both his little fingers."

"What's queer about him?" Sam asks.

"He's stretched," Cone says. "Carries a long switchblade and thinks he's a hero."

"Okay," the undercover cop says, "I'll keep an eye out. Thanks for the tip." He finishes his brandy and rises. "Well, I better get to work. The more time I spend up there, the easier it'll be."

"The bartender's name is Tommy," Cone adds. "He's got a big mustache. If that's any help."

"You never know," Shipkin says. He looks around the loft. "It's really getting to me," he tells Cone. "If you ever decide to move, let me know first."

"You kidding?" Davenport says. "This *scroccone* is going to die here. They'll find him under the bathtub someday, OD'd on garlic salami."

"There are worse ways to go," Timothy says.

7

It turns out to be a real nothing morning. The summer sky is somber, and there are rumblings of thunder over New Jersey. The stuffed air smells of turps; there's an ugly ocherous glow over everything.

Grousing, Cone shambles down to John Street, convinced that a day starting so dismally can only end in disaster. He stops at the local deli for black coffee and a bagel with a shmear. He takes his breakfast up to the office, exchanging silent glares with the ancient receptionist. It's that kind of day.

He hasn't slept well, but he doesn't blame the junk food he pigged on the previous night. He's eaten salami, anchovies, and chocolate pudding before, and the mixture never depressed him. But this morning engenders thoughts of making out a will and investing in a cemetery plot.

When his phone rings, he stares at it balefully, convinced it's going to bring him news that he's overdrawn at the bank or the IRS has found another flaw in their annual audit of his return. He finally picks it up.

"Yeah?"

"Tim? This is Jeremy Bigelow. Tell me something: Do you always fall in an outhouse and come up with a box lunch?"

"What the hell is that supposed to mean?"

The SEC investigator is bubbling with excitement. "Those ten companies you gave me—Research says that eight of them had very, *very* high short positions on the dates you mentioned. We got a computer sharpie who loves puzzles like that, and he did some back-checking. He claims that in the month before your dates, the total of shares sold short more than tripled in all eight companies. What in God's name is going on?"

Cone sighs. This time he *knows* he is right, but he feels no elation. "It's a ripoff," he tells Bigelow. "A beautiful swindle that might be funny, but people have been dusted—and there's nothing ha-ha about that. Jerry, I think you better bring the Federal DA in on this one."

"The SEC can handle it."

"No, you can't," Cone says. "This isn't just a civil matter. If it pans out, there are going to be criminal indictments. You got a pet in the DA's office?"

"A pet?"

"A contact. Someone you've worked with before. Preferably someone who owes you."

"There's an ADA named Hamish McDonnell. I've had some dealings with him."

"Hamish McDonnell? Italian, of course."

"No," Bigelow says seriously, "I think he's a Scotsman. He's a hardnose, but he gets things done. You think I should call him?"

"It would be the smart thing to do. Cover your ass. Tell him what I gave you and what your computers came up with. Give him my number. If he wants more skinny, he can give me a call."

"Well, all right," the SEC man says hesitantly. "I'll do it, but don't cut me out of this, Tim."

"Don't worry," Cone says. "You'll see your name in print again."

He hangs up and waits, smoking a cigarette, feet up on his desk. Samantha Whatley, coming along the corridor, stops and looks in.

"Working?" she asks.

"Yes, I'm working," he says irritably. "What the hell do you think I'm doing—fluffing my duff?"

"What a lovely mood you're in," she says. "No wonder the whole office calls you Mr. Congeniality."

"The whole office can go hump," he says angrily. "You think I—"

But she walks away, leaving him with his sour thoughts. He hears the grumble of thunder outside—"The angels are bowling," his mother used to say—and he supposes it'll start pouring any minute now. Or maybe it'll hold off until he goes out for lunch. That'll be nice. When his corduroy suit gets wet, it smells like a Percheron's jockstrap.

His phone shrills, and he lets it ring seven times before he picks it up. Sheer perversity.

"Yeah?" he says.

"Timothy Cone?" A man's voice: sharp, brisk, demanding.

"That's right."

"This is Hamish McDonnell, Assistant DA, Federal. Jeremy Bigelow called, said you had something to talk about."

"He told you about the short sales?"

"He told me," McDonnell says, "but I have to know more about it before I set the wheels in motion. I've got a very busy schedule today, but if you can be at my office at three-thirty this afternoon, I'll give you a half-hour."

That's all Cone needs. "Forget it," he says.

"What?"

"Forget it. Unless you want to drag your ass over to my office within an hour, I'll take it to the FBI. I've got a pal there who loves headlines."

"Now wait just a—"

But Cone hangs up. He gives the guy three minutes to get back to him, but the phone rings again in less than a minute.

"Yeah?"

"Hamish McDonnell here. Listen, I think we got off on the wrong foot."

"Not me," Cone says, "I know the drill: hay foot, straw foot, hay foot, straw foot."

"I don't understand."

"Not important. You interested or aren't you?"

"You really think something is going down with those short sales?"

"Oh, yeah. There's frigging in the rigging."

"All right," the ADA says, "I'll get someone to fill in for me over here, and I'll be at your place in an hour. Now are you happy?"

"Creaming," Cone says.

He's there in a little more than an hour, his rubberized raincoat streaming and his red hair plastered to his skull.

"Aw," Cone says, "did you get caught in the rain?"

McDonnell stares at him. "You're a real comedian, aren't you?"

He's a young guy, broad and beefy. He looks as if he might have been a hotshot in college football but didn't have the moves or speed to make pro. But he's still in good shape: flat belly, hard shoulders, a jaw like a knee, and hands just slightly smaller than picnic hams.

"Where can I hang my raincoat?" he asks.

"Throw it on the floor," Cone says. "That's what I do."

But the ADA sits down in the armchair in his wet coat. He pulls out a clean white handkerchief and swabs his dripping hair. "All right," he says, "let's stop playing games. What've you got?"

Cone takes him through the whole thing: How Haldering was hired to investigate sabotage at Dempster-Torrey factories; how he, Cone, decided the motive was to bring down the price of the common stock so short-sellers could profit; how he suspects that David Dempster might be the knave behind the manipulation.

"David Dempster?" McDonnell says sharply. "The brother of the guy who got scragged?"

"That's right."

"You think he had anything to do with John Dempster's death?"

"How the hell would I know?" Cone says. "I'm just a lousy private eye interested in industrial sabotage."

"What have you got on David Dempster?"

"He runs a two-bit PR operation from a small office on Cedar Street, but his net worth is like four mil. That's got to tell you something—right?"

"Unless he inherited it."

"That I doubt. But you can check it out."

McDonnell looks at him a long time, eyes like wet coal. "It stinks," he says finally.

"Sure it does," Cone agrees. "A dirty way of making a buck."

"That's not what I mean," the ADA says. "I mean your story stinks."

The Wall Street dick jerks a thumb toward the door. "Then take a walk," he says. "Sorry to have wasted your time."

"Jesus, what a hard-on you are! Can you blame me for doubting you? What the hell have you given me? A lot of numbers on a computer tape. Those short sales could have been lucky guesses and you know it. All you've said is that you 'suspect' David Dempster might be finagling it. Where's your hard evidence?"

Cone shrugs. "Take it for what you think it's worth. It's your decision."

McDonnell leans forward to slam a meaty palm down on the desk. "Goddamn it!" he cries. "You're holding out on me and I know it. You want to be charged with obstruction of justice?"

"Be my guest," Cone says. "I'll be delighted to see you make a fucking idiot out of yourself—if you're not one already."

They lock eyeballs, both infuriated. It's Hamish McDonnell who blinks first. "Can't you give me anything to go on?" he says hotly. "Anything at all that will make me think you're just not blowing smoke."

"Yeah," Cone says, "I can give you something. Three names. Two guys and a company. They're all hotshot financial advisers, with pension and trust funds to diddle. They're the weasels who are financing this scam. There may be others, but these three are in it up to their pipiks."

"How do you know?"

"I don't. You want the names or not?"

The ADA groans. "Give me the goddamned names," he says.

It turns out that Cone's ballpoint pen has run dry and he can't find a clean piece of paper to write on. So his triumph is somewhat diminished by having to borrow McDonnell's pen and a sheet torn from his pocket notebook.

"You're a winner, you are," the ADA says. "How do you get across the street—with a Boy Scout?"

Cone jots down the three names provided by Neal Davenport. "You won't have any trouble getting addresses," he tells McDonnell. "They're all well-known operators on Wall Street. And listen, do me a favor and do yourself a favor, get moving on this fast. These bums are planning another trick. It's going down right now."

"Yeah? And how do you know that?"

"You'll have to take my word for it."

"Seems to me I'm taking your word for a helluva lot."

"What do you want—a list of personal references?"

"This is going to take a lot of work, and if—"

"Bull*shit*," Cone says. "You pick up these chiselers, sweat them a little, tell them you've got all the facts and figures on their smelly deals with David Dempster, and I guarantee at least one of them is going to crack. He'll spill his guts to wangle a lesser charge. Wall Street villains are not stand-up guys; you know that."

"If you're scamming me on all this, Cone, I'm going to come back to this shithouse and personally take you apart. And believe me, I can do it."

"Maybe," Timothy says.

Hamish McDonnell rises and buttons his raincoat. He makes no effort to shake hands, and neither does Cone.

"And don't call me," the ADA says. "I'll call you when and if I've got something."

Cone leans back and lights a cigarette. He figures McDonnell for a tough nut who's not afraid to use the muscle of his office to get the job done. That's okay; the pinstriped types will find themselves confronted by a heavyweight with none of the deference of their golf club pros or private nutritionists.

He pulls on his leather cap and leaves the office. He discovers the rain has stopped. But the sky is still leaden with drizzle. He curses his stupidity for not having driven to work that morning. He tries to find an empty cab and fails. Damning the weepy day, he starts the long hike back to his loft, convinced there's no productive work to be done in the office.

It's true that he persuades other people to do his job for him. Neal Davenport, Jeremy Bigelow, and now Hamish McDonnell—all cooperate, but only because they believe it's to their own profit. Everyone acts out of self-interest—right? Because self-interest is the First Law of Nature. You could even make out a case that a guy who devotes his whole life to unselfish service—like spooning mulligatawny into hopeless derelicts or converting the heathen—is doing it for the virtuous high it gives him.

But even assuming that no one acts without an ego boost, there's a very practical problem Cone has in farming out his investigative chores. Once he's done it, all that's left for him is twiddling his thumbs—or anything else within reach. No use leaning on his helpers; that would just make them sore and earn him static. So there's nothing for him to do but be quietly patient—which is akin to asking a cannibal to become a vegetarian.

These rank musings occupy his mind during his sodden toddle back to his cave. There he finds that Cleo, apparently surfeited with garlic salami, has upchucked all over the linoleum.

He spends the remainder of that day futzing around the loft, smoking too many cigarettes and drinking too much vodka. He goes over the caper a dozen times in his mind, looking for holes in the solution. No holes. Then he wonders if another meet with Dorothy Blenke or Eve Bookerman would yield anything of value. He decides not.

In the evening, warned by what happened to Cleo, he shuns the salami and opens a can of pork and beans.

"Beans, beans, the musical fruit," he sings to the cat. "The more you eat, the more you toot."

He finishes the can (eaten cold), leaving just a smidgen for the neutered tom, figuring to give the poor creature's stomach a rest. Then he gets caught up on his financial newspapers and magazines, devouring them with the avidity of a baseball maven reading box scores. Wall Street is his world, and he's long since given up trying to analyze his love-hate feelings about it.

On Wednesday morning, he calls Samantha Whatley at the office.

"I won't be in for a couple of days," he tells her. "I'm sick."

"Oh?" she says. "Don't tell me it's the fantods and megrims again. You pulled that one on me once before."

"No," he says, "this time I think I got coryza and phthisis. With maybe a touch of biliary calculus."

"I'll tell you what you've got, son," she says. "More crap than a Christmas goose. Hiram was asking about you. He hasn't seen you around lately and wanted to know if you still worked here."

"Tell fatso to stuff it," Cone says angrily. "I'm working the Dempster-Torrey file and he knows it."

"How you coming on that?"

"Okay."

She sighs. "I should have known better than to ask. Will you be in tomorrow?"

"Probably not."

"Friday?"

"Maybe."

"It's payday, you know."

"Well, if I don't make it, will you pick up my check?"

"No," she says. "If you want it, do us the honor of stopping by."

"Now you're acting like a shithead."

"Asshole!" she says and hangs up.

He goes out to buy cigarettes, food, cat litter, newspapers, and to replenish his liquid assets. The low-pressure area is still hanging over the city, and the denizens are beginning to snarl at each other. That's all right with Cone; at least it's better than everyone giving him a toothy "Have a nice day."

If it wasn't for the Dempster-Torrey case, he would have enjoyed that solitary day in the loft. The phone never rings—not even a wrong number—and Cleo snoozes away the hours under the bathtub. Cone rations his drinks carefully, just keeping a nice, gentle buzz as he reads his newspapers, takes a couple of short naps, showers with his stiff brushing and cornstarch treatment, and changes his underwear and socks.

Several times he's tempted to call Davenport and McDonnell, but resists. He just hopes to God they're doing their jobs. If not, it'll take him weeks, maybe months, to bring down David Dempster and put that gonzo behind bars.

Late that night, stripped to his briefs, he's ready to sack out. He's got a little high-intensity lamp he uses for horizontal activities. He's also got his copy of *Silas Marner*, which he's been reading for four years now. He's already up to page 23, and has discovered it's a better somnifacient than any flurazepam he can buy on the street.

He reads another half-page and has just enough strength left to put the book aside and turn off his lamp.

Thursday starts in the same lethargic pattern. But then, close to noon, Detective Neal K. Davenport calls, and things start jumping.

"Hiya, sherlock," Neal says breezily. "I called your office but they said you were home sick. I figured that was horseshit, and you're just fucking off."

"You got it," Cone says. "What's doing?"

"Everything's coming up roses. Today is D-Day and H-hour is three o'clock. That's when we're going to raid Paddy's Pig. Sam Shipkin's done a great job. He found the motorcycle, and guess where they've been keeping it."

"In the john?"

"Close but no cigar. There's another building behind the tavern. Like a big shed. Sam says it looks like a department store—everything from condoms to cassettes. All hot. The cycle is the same make, model, and color used in the Dempster kill."

"But you don't know if it's the actual bike?"

"Of course not. But it'll do as corroborative evidence. The icing on the cake is that it's owned by the Ryan brothers, a couple of no-goodniks who got their start as smash-and-grabbers when they were in their teens. They've both done time for strongarm stuff and have sheets that don't end. They fit the witnesses' description of the guys on the motorcycle when Dempster was put down. And to top that, Shipkin says that when he met them, they were both wearing steel-toed boots. How does that grab you?"

"Sounds okay," Cone says cautiously, "but I wouldn't call it an airtight case. Any two-bit shyster could get them off in five minutes if all you've got is a similar motorcycle, descriptions by eyewitnesses, and the boots."

"You think I don't know that?" Davenport says indignantly. "That's why Sam Shipkin made a big drug buy from Louie about an hour ago with marked bills. So we got him cold, and we can lean on him. I figure he'll make a deal and sing. Anyway, we're going to give it the old college try. Listen, the raid on Paddy's Pig is going to be what you'd call a media event. We've tipped the newspapers and TV stations, so it should be a circus. I figured you might want to be there."

"Yeah," Cone says. "Sure. Neal, there's a guy named Hamish Mc-Donnell in the Federal DA's office. I think you should call him and invite him to the bust."

"No way!" the NYPD man says. "This is our party, and we're not sharing the headlines with the Feds or anyone else."

"Now look," Timothy says, "right now you got peanuts. If this Louie is afraid of the Westies and decides to clam up and take his lumps, then where the hell are you? The Ryan brothers waltz away and you guys are left looking like idiots. Is that the kind of headlines you want?"

Silence. Then: "Well, yeah, that could happen. But what's this Hamish McDonnell got to do with the price of tea in China?"

"He's coming at David Dempster from a different angle. Dempster was the brain behind all the industrial sabotage I was assigned to investigate. If McDonnell pins him on that—and I think he will—you'll have insurance in case Louie decides to keep his mouth shut. David Dempster will take a fall either way—or both."

"Goddamn it !" Davenport yells. "Why the fuck couldn't you have told me all this from the start?"

"Because it's outside your jurisdiction," Cone explains patiently. "Granted that the dusting of those three guys on Wall Street is local. And the Department deserves the credit for breaking it. But there's more to it than just those homicides; there's arson, sabotage, bribery, and maybe conspiracy to commit murder. I think David Dempster is up to his ass in all that shit, but they're *federal* raps, Neal. Like crossing state lines to commit a felony. I really think you should invite Hamish McDonnell on the Paddy's Pig raid. You'll make a friend—which might prove a benefit. And you'll have a fallback if you can't nail the Ryan brothers on a homicide charge."

"Well . . . maybe," the city bull says reluctantly. "I'll have to get an okay from the brass. What kind of a guy is this McDonnell?"

"He thinks he's hard-boiled," Cone says, "but I think he's half-baked. But that's neither here nor there. Come on, Neal, once you guys get this thing wrapped up and tied with a ribbon, there'll be enough glory to go around. The Department will get their headlines, and the Feds will get theirs, and everyone will live happily ever after. Will you call McDonnell?"

"I don't like it," Davenport says grumpily. "This is our baby, and I don't want people thinking we can't clean up the garbage in our own gutters. But like you say, it could be insurance for getting an indictment. Okay, I'll see what the higher-ups think about it. If they say go ahead, I'll give the Feds a call. And next time, for Christ's sake, will you try to be a little more open so I know what's going on?"

"I certainly will," Cone says warmly. "See you at three."

But Davenport has already hung up. Cone replaces the wall phone slowly, and his hand is still on it when it rings again. He picks up, wondering if the city dick has already changed his mind.

"Yeah?" he says.

"Tim? This is Jeremy Bigelow. You really sick?"

"Slightly indisposed. What's with you?"

"I got some good news. I went to my boss with the story of the short traders, and he got the Commission to issue a formal order of investigation. That means we can get subpoenas and question the guys who were selling short so heavily before the dates you gave me."

Cone takes a deep breath. "Jerry," he says, "why did you do that? I thought you turned the whole deal over to the Federal DA. You contacted Hamish McDonnell—remember?"

"Well . . . yeah," Bigelow says, "but why should they get all the credit? It was the SEC that uncovered it—right?"

Cone doesn't comment on that. "You'll get your share of the credit," he tells the investigator, and then repeats what he said to Neal Davenport: "There'll be enough glory to go around. Take my advice, Jerry, and give McDonnell a call before you go ahead with your subpoenas. Otherwise you're going to find there are two identical investigations going on, with everyone walking up everyone else's heels, and bad blood between you and the Feds."

"You really think so?" Bigelow says worriedly.

"I really think so. Be smart and play it cool. Call McDonnell and tell him the SEC has launched a formal investigation and can issue subpoenas, but you don't want to do it if it'll interfere with what he's doing. Be nice and you'll score brownie points. And meanwhile, call your favorite re- porters and leak just enough to get their juices flowing. Tell them it's going to be the biggest Wall Street scandal since Boesky. They'll jump at it."

"Yeah," Bigelow says happily; "I could do that."

"Just make sure they spell your name right," Cone says.

He hangs up, shaking his head in bemusement. He can't understand all these headline-hungry guys. Cone couldn't care less about personal ag- grandizement, and he doesn't give a tinker's dam about the reputation of Haldering & Co. In a hundred years, who'll remember all this shit?

But meanwhile it's fun. By three o'clock he's tooled his Ford Escort up to Forty-fifth Street. He finds a parking space around the block and walks back to join the small crowd of rubbernecks that's appeared out of nowhere to watch the police raid on Paddy's Pig.

There's not much to see. No excitement. No wild-and-woolly shoot- outs. The tavern is blocked off by a jam of official and unmarked cop cars. There's also an NYPD truck pulled up in front, flanked by a mobile TV van. Cone edges into the mob and watches.

There's a parade of sweating cops going into Paddy's Pig empty-handed and coming out lugging cartons, crates, unpacked television sets and VCRs. Then two come out wheeling a black motorcycle, and that's hoisted into the truck.

Louie is brought out, cuffed, held firmly between two uniformed mas- todons. He's thrust into a squad car. A younger guy, similarly cuffed, is treated the same way. He's grinning like a maniac. One of the Ryan brothers, Cone assumes. Finally Detective Davenport and ADA Hamish McDonnell exit from Paddy's Pig and stand on the sidewalk, talking rapidly and gesturing.

The vehicles begin to pull away, the rubbernecks disperse. A non-event, Cone figures, and wonders why he bothered to show up. He's about to leave when Hamish McDonnell spots him, yells, "Hey, Cone!" and beckons. Davenport gives him a wise-ass grin and goes back inside the bar.

"You sonofabitch," McDonnell says furiously, "why the hell didn't you tell me the NYPD was after David Dempster for the homicides?"

"Hey," Cone says, "don't get your balls in an uproar. First of all, you had no need to know. Those killings are a Department squeal—correct? I work with the locals just the way I work with you. Everyone gets a piece of the pie."

McDonnell gives him a close look. "I gotta admit you didn't shaft me. Those names you gave me are panning out. All we had to do with one guy was mention the name David Dempster, and he broke. Started blubbering. You know what worries him most? That we'll take his vintage Daimler away from him. How d'ya like that?"

"Beautiful," Cone says. "You got enough on the short-selling and sabotage?"

"We're getting it," the ADA says. "All these guys are going to do time. Maybe not a lot, but some." Suddenly he becomes Mr. Nice. "Listen, Cone," he says, "I'm sorry if I came on heavy. I apologize."

"That's okay. You're entitled. You didn't know me from Adam and probably figured I was handing you a crock."

"Yeah, something like that. Tell me, how did you get onto David Dempster?"

"It was easy," the Wall Street dick says. "I didn't have anyone else."

McDonnell laughs. "And what are you getting out of it?"

"I'll get my reward in heaven."

"Loser!" McDonnell jeers. Then: "Look, I owe you one. We're taking David Dempster tomorrow at four o'clock at his office. Davenport will be there. You want to be in on the kill?"

"I got nothing better to do," Timothy says.

Neal Davenport is waiting in the overchilled lobby of David Dempster's steel and glass office building on Friday afternoon when Cone shows up. They waste no time in greetings.

"How you doing with Louie?" Timothy wants to know.

"We're not ready to dance the fandango yet," the NYPD man says, "but his lawyer sounds like he wants to make a deal. I think we'll nail the Ryan brothers on the kills."

"What about the sabotage?"

"My guess is that David Dempster was directing the whole operation, and paying for it. He gave the orders to Louie, and that shmegegi sent the Westies into action. It was a sweet setup. Louie was Dempster's cutout; he never met the mugs who were doing his dirty work. So naturally they can't finger him."

"Yeah, that's how I see it. But if Louie doesn't talk, Dempster walks away from the homicide rap?"

"Maybe. But McDonnell will get him on the sabotage and conspiracy-to-defraud charges."

"Big deal," Cone says disgustedly. "He'll squirm out of that with a slap on the wrist."

"Don't worry it," Davenport advises. "Louie is going to spill, take my word for it. He's never done time before, and we've been telling him how wonderful Attica is and what a prize his fat ass will be up there."

"You tell him that in front of his lawyer?"

"Of course not. But right now he's being held without bail, and his cellmate is doing us a favor."

"Good," Cone says. "Let the bastard sweat a little."

Then Hamish McDonnell comes marching into the lobby, carrying a scuffed attaché case. He's flanked by two U.S. marshals, both as big as he.

"You three guys look like a half-ton of beef on the hoof," Davenport says to the ADA. "Did you get your warrant?"

"Signed and sealed," McDonnell says, patting his case. "Now we deliver."

"You going to cuff him?"

"Oh, hell yes. You'd be surprised at the psychological effect handcuffs have on these Ivy League types. Takes all the starch out of their boxer shorts." He turns to Cone. "You been up to his office?"

"Yeah. It's a small place; I'm not sure we'll all fit in. There's this little reception room. A secretary at a desk. One door that leads to Dempster's private office."

"Sounds good. Let's go."

They all jam into a high-speed elevator. They exit on the twenty-seventh floor, tramp down the hallway to Dempster's office in a phalanx. The plump secretary looks up from her magazine in amazement when they come crowding in.

"What—" she starts.

"Don't bother announcing us," McDonnell says. "It's a surprise party."

He strides to the inner door, jerks it open. The five men go charging in. David Dempster, crisply clad, is seated behind his desk, talking on the phone. He hangs up slowly, rises slowly, looks slowly from face to face. One of the marshals glides to his left, the other to his right, as if they've performed this ballet a hundred times.

"David Dempster?" McDonnell asks.

"Yes. And who, may I ask, are you?"

"Hamish McDonnell, Assistant District Attorney, Federal." The ADA flaps his ID at Dempster. "I believe you've met Mr. Cone. This gentleman is Detective Neal K. Davenport of the New York Police Department. These two men are United States marshals. I have a warrant for your arrest."

"Warrant?" Dempster says, the plummy voice suddenly dry and strained. "Arrest? For what?"

"Mr. Dempster," McDonnell says, "the charges against you would fill a windowshade. Will you waive the reading of your rights?"

"Now wait a minute..."

"No, Mr. Dempster, you wait a minute. You can waste our time or you can make it easy on us and yourself and just come along quietly. Cooperate—okay?"

David Dempster manages a smarmy grin. "You don't mind if I fill a pipe first, do you?" he asks and, without waiting for a reply, opens a side desk drawer and reaches in.

Surprisingly, it's Davenport who reacts first. The portly detective moves so fast that Cone can't believe it. He launches himself across the desk, grabs Dempster's wrist in both hands, twists in opposite directions. There's a howl of pain, and Neal plucks a nickeled pistol from Dempster's nerveless fingers.

"Nice pipe," the city cop says. "What're you smoking these days—thirty-twos?"

"Cuff him," McDonnell orders, and the marshals bend Dempster's arms behind his back, not gently, and click the steel links on his wrists. They clamp their big mitts on his upper arms.

"Not smart, Mr. Dempster," the ADA says. "What were you going to do, kill all five of us? Or just wave your popgun and make a run for it? It's tough getting a cab on Fridays."

"I wish to speak to my attorney," Dempster says stiffly.

"You'll get your chance," McDonnell says. "Let's go."

Cone stands aside to let the entourage file by. David Dempster pauses a moment, pulling back against the marshals' grip. He stares at Cone.

"You?" he says. "You did this?"

The Wall Street dick nods.

Dempster takes in the rumpled corduroy suit, grayed T-shirt, yellow work shoes.

"But you're a bum!" he says in outraged tones.

"Yeah," Cone says, "I know."

He lets them all go ahead. He dawdles a moment in the reception room where the hennaed secretary has her back pressed against the wall, a knuckle between her teeth.

"I think you can close up now," Cone tells her gently.

"He's not coming back?" she asks.

"Not for a while."

"Shit!" she says unexpectedly. "Best job I ever had."

By the time Cone gets down to the street, the others have disappeared. He glances at the clock over the entrance and figures that if he hurries, he can get back to Haldering & Co. in time to pick up his paycheck. But hurrying anywhere in that heat is not a boss idea.

"Ahh, screw it," he says aloud, causing passersby to look at him nervously and detour around him.

Stripped to their skivvies, they're lazing around the loft on a late Saturday afternoon. The front windows are open, and Cone's antique electric fan is doing its whirry best, but it's still bloody hot.

"When the hell are you going to spring for an air conditioner?" Samantha Whatley demands.

"One of these days," Cone says.

"That's a lot of bull," she says. "You're such a skinflint you'd rather suffer."

It's the truth, and he knows it. Tightwadism is his philosophy, if not his religion, and the thought of shelling out hundreds of dollars for a decent window unit is more than he can bear.

"It's not so bad," he says defensively. "And they say it's going to cool down tonight."

"Yeah," she says, "maybe to eighty. What are we eating?"

"I got nothing in the house. I figured I'd run out to the deli. What do you feel like?"

"Anything as long as it's cold."

"How about a canned ham, potato salad, some tomatoes and stuff?"

"I can live with that," she says. "And see if they've got any Heavenly Hash."

"What the hell is that?"

"Ice cream, you asshole. What world do you live in?"

They're drinking jug chablis poured over ice cubes, and working on a can of honey-roasted peanuts. Occasionally they flip a peanut to Cleo, who'd rather cuff it and chase it than eat it.

"So?" Sam says. "How you doing on the Dempster-Torrey file?"

"Oh, that," he says casually. "It's over. All cleared up. Finis."

Her feet hit the floor with a thump. She bends across the table and glares at him. "You crapping me?"

He raises a palm. "Scout's honor. I'll write up the final report next week."

"Next week sucks," she says wrathfully. "I want to know right now. Who did it—the butler?"

"Nah," he says. "David Dempster."

She draws a deep breath. "David Dempster? The brother?"

He nods, pours them more wine. "Listen, you know what it means when you sell short?"

"Vaguely. It means you sell something you don't own."

"That's about it, kiddo. When you sell a stock short, you don't own it. But it's perfectly legit."

"So how do you sell it if you don't own it? And what's the point?"

"Let's say that the stock of XYZ Corporation is selling at a hundred dollars a share. You don't own any XYZ but you think, for whatever reason, that the stock is going to take a nosedive. So you *borrow* a hundred shares of XYZ and sell them. You get ten thousand bucks—right? Disregarding the broker's commission. Follow?"

"Sure. But who do you borrow the stock from?"

"Your brokerage house—or anyone else willing to lend the shares to you. Anyway, say the shares of XYZ Corporation do just what you figured and go down to eighty. Then you *buy*. Those hundred shares cost you eight thousand. You return the borrowed shares, and you've made yourself two grand."

"Beautiful," Sam says. "How long has this been going on?"

"Since Eve shorted the apple to Adam."

"But what if the stock goes up?"

"Then you slit your wrists and do a swan from your penthouse terrace. Nah, I'm kidding. Selling stock short isn't much chancier than buying it long because you expect it to go up."

"And that's what David Dempster was doing—selling short?"

"I doubt it," Cone says. "He doesn't strike me as being much of a plunger. But he figured out a handy-dandy scheme for the heavyweight short-sellers on Wall Street. I think it started about three years ago. He knew what an emotional, irrational world the Street is. It's really a loony bin. The silliest rumor or statement by some high-muck-a-muck can send the Dow up or down. So the way I figure it, David Dempster worked out a way to depress the price of particular stocks. Maybe he began by just starting rumors. God knows he had the contacts in his PR business to do that. Or perhaps the Tylenol scare in Chicago gave him the idea. He probably reckoned he could sink the value of shares in a drug or food company just by phoning the cops and newspapers anonymously and claiming he had poisoned the product. Then there's a lot of publicity, products are pulled off the shelves—just to be on the safe side—and the manufacturer's stock takes a tumble."

"Jesus," Samantha says, "what a perverted mind to think of that."

"Sure, but it worked. Because Dempster realized that even if the stock slid just a couple of points, you can make a bundle if you're trading thousands of shares. A guy who sold short ten thousand shares of XYZ Corporation at a hundred simoleons a share would receive a million bucks—correct? Then, after a product-tampering scare or some other disaster to the company, the stock falls to ninety dollars a share. He *buys* his ten thousand shares at that price and nets a cool hundred thousand smackers. Nice? Now figure what the profit would have been if he had traded a half-million shares!"

"Disgusting," she says. "You're telling me that David Dempster devised ways to make certain that stocks went *down?*"

"You better believe it. And from anonymous phone calls and product tampering he soon began organizing real sabotage like arson and vandalism—and corrupting key personnel. Anything he could do to damage the company, depress the stock price, and benefit his short-selling clients. The Bela Lugosi of Wall Street."

"And they paid him for the service?"

"Sure. Either a fee or percentage of the take. How do you think he rolled up a personal net worth of four million? He probably had a small list of very greedy customers. Mostly guys who managed OPM—Other People's Money—in pensions and trusts. They'd get together in his townhouse, decide on a victim, and Dempster would get to work. He didn't do the dirty stuff himself, of course; he paid a gang of hoods called the Westies to do that."

"My God," Sam says, "the things people will do for the almighty buck. You think David Dempster arranged his brother's murder?"

"Hell, yes," Timothy says. "He engineered it, even to the extent of using Teresa Dempster to find out when her husband was leaving on a trip so he could set up that Wall Street ambush. And just like he figured, after his brother died the price of Dempster-Torrey stock took a bath, and all his short-selling clients made a bundle."

They sit silently then, sipping their chilled wine and watching Cleo stalk a peanut across the linoleum. Maybe it really is cooling off, a little, but they have no desire for an aerobics session—at least not the vertical variety.

"Tim," Samantha says in a low voice, "he really had his brother put down? His *brother*, Tim?"

"Oh, yes, he did it."

"But *why*? Just for the money?"

"That was part of it, sure. But I told you that none of us acts from a single motive. People aren't that simple. Yeah, David killed his brother for money. But also he did it because John put the horns on him by enjoying fun and games with Dorothy, David's wife. And you've got to figure there was a lot of sibling rivalry as Neal Davenport, of all people, suggested. Listen, just because two guys are brothers doesn't mean they think alike or have the same personalities and temperaments. Ask any horse trainer. Or even people who breed dogs or cats. They'll tell you that every animal in a litter is different, with its own traits and characteristics. John J. Dempster may have played hardball in his business and personal life, but he was genuine. David Dempster is a small, mean, hypocritical bastard."

Sam holds up her palms in protest. "Enough already!" she pleads. "I'll read all about it in your report. Right now I don't want to hear any more about money, greed, and fratricide. It's all too depressing. I just want to think nice thoughts. Give me a couple of more ice cubes and pour me some wine."

The loft is dimming, and a blessed breeze comes sneaking in the front windows. Cone turns off the fan, and that helps. The traffic noises seem muted and far away.

"How you coming with your nice thoughts?" Cone asks.

"Getting there," Samantha says.

"You be nice to me, I'll be nice to you."

"Best offer I've had all day. Did you change the sheets?"

"Of course. It's the last Saturday of the month, isn't it?"

"My hero," she says. She stands, ambles over to the mattress. She peels off bra and panties. Still standing, a pale wraith in the darkling, she begins unpinning her long, auburn hair.

"Maybe I should go get the ham first," Timothy says.

"Screw the ham!" she says, then pauses, arms still raised, tresses half unbound. She looks at him thoughtfully. "You know who I feel sorry for in that whole Dempster mess?"

"Who?"

"Teresa. She sounds like such a nice, nutty lady. But she was married to a rakehell. And then he gets killed, and it turns out her brother-in-law, who's been a real pal, was involved in the murder. My God, what that woman's been through."

"Yeah, well, she's coping. I went up to see her this morning. She's thinking of going to Japan for a while."

"What for?"

"To study Zen. Says she wants to be closer to the cosmos—whatever that means. She told me she thinks everything happens for the best."

Hair swinging free, Sam comes over to stand close in front of him. He bows his head to kiss her pipik.

"But not you," she says, stroking his bristly hair. "You think everything happens for the worst."

"Not everything," Cone says.

Book Three
One from Column A

1

It never occurs to Cone that Samantha Whatley doesn't want to be seen with him in public because he dresses like a refugee from Lower Slobbovia. She says it's because she doesn't want to run the risk of being spotted by an employee of Haldering & Co., and then their rare liaison will be trivialized by office gossip.

So their trysts are limited to her gentrified apartment in the East Village or his scuzzy loft in a cast-iron commercial building on lower Broadway. That's okay with Timothy; he's a hermitlike creature by nature, and perfectly willing to play the game according to her rules.

So there they are in her flossy apartment on Sunday night, August 8, gnawing on barbecued ribs and nattering of this and that.

"When are you going to take your two weeks?" she asks him.

"What two weeks?"

"Your vacation, you yuck. When do you want to take it?"

He shrugs. "Makes no nevermind to me. Anytime."

"Well, I'm taking off on Friday. I'm going home."

He ponders a moment. Then: "You're flying on Friday the thirteenth?"

"Best time. The plane will be practically empty. I don't want you tom-catting around while I'm gone."

"Not me."

"And try to cut down on the booze."

"Yes, mother. Who's going to fill in for you at work while you're gone?"

"Hiram himself."

"Oh, Jesus!" he says, dropping his rib bone. "Don't tell me that while I'm eating."

On Monday morning after Sam leaves, Cone wanders to work an hour late, as usual. He finds two file folders on his desk: assignments to new investigations. He flips through them listlessly; they look like dullsville to him. One concerns a client who's invested a nice chunk of cash in a scheme to breed miniature horses. Now, with his money gone and the phones of the boiler shop operation disconnected, he wants Haldering & Co. to locate the con men and get his investment back. Lots of luck, Charlie.

The second case concerns a proposed merger between two companies that make plastic cocoons for scores of consumer products—the kind of packaging that breaks your fingernails and drives you to stabbing with a sharp paring knife to open the damned stuff. One of the principals wants a complete credit check on the other. Instant ennui.

Cone tosses the folders aside and finishes his breakfast: black coffee and a buttered bialy. He's on his second cigarette when his phone rings. He picks it up expecting a calamity. That's always safe because then a mere misfortune arrives as good news.

"Yeah?" he says.

"Cone? Hiram Haldering. Come here at once, please."

He was right the first time. It's usually a calamity when H.H. says, "Please."

He slouches down the corridor to the boss's office, the only one with two windows. The bright summer sunlight is bouncing off fatso's balding pate, and he's beaming and nodding like one of those bobbing dolls in the back windows of cars driven by morons. But at least his two air conditioners are wheezing away, so the room is comfortably cool.

Which is providential because the visitor, who rises when Cone enters, is wearing a black three-piece suit that looks heavy enough to be woven of yak hair. He's a tall, cadaverous gink with a smile so pained it surely seems his drawers must be binding. The hand he gives to Cone when they're introduced is a clump of very soft, very shriveled bananas.

"This is Timothy Cone," intones Hiram Haldering. "He is one—and I repeat one—of our experienced investigators. Cone, this gentleman is Mr. Omar Jeffreys."

"Of Blains, Kibes and Thrush," Jeffreys adds. "Attorneys at law."

Everyone gets seated, and H.H. turns to the lawyer.

"Mr. Jeffreys," he says, "will you explain to Cone what it is you want."

"It is not what *we* want," the other man says. "Oh, dear me, no. Our desires are of no import. We merely wish to present, to the best of our abilities, the wishes of our client."

"Yeah, well," Cone says, "who's the client?"

"For a number of years Blains, Kibes and Thrush, P.A., has provided legal counsel to an Oriental gentleman, Mr. Chin Tung Lee. He is the Chairman and Chief Executive Officer of a corporation that processes and markets a variety of Chinese foods under the White Lotus label. You are, perhaps, familiar with the products?"

"Oh, hell yes," Cone says. "Lousy grub."

"Cone!" Haldering shouts indignantly.

"Well, it is," he insists. "Take their chicken chow mein, for instance. My God, you can hardly find the meat in it. They must be using the same chicken for ten years. So what I do is buy a small can of boned chicken and add it to the chow mein. That makes it okay. Even my cat loves it."

He ends triumphantly, and the other two men stare at him glassily.

"Very interesting, I'm sure," the attorney finally says. "But I do not believe the ingredients in White Lotus chicken chow mein are germane to this discussion. Mr. Chin Tung Lee is presently faced with a financial problem outside the expertise of Blains, Kibes and Thrush. He wishes to employ the services of Haldering and Company, and I am authorized to conclude an oral agreement, prior to the execution of a written contract that will finalize the terms of the aforementioned employment."

"Why didn't he just pick up the phone and call us?" Cone wants to know. "Or come over here himself?"

"Mr. Lee is an elderly gentleman who, unfortunately, has been confined to a wheelchair for several years and is not as physically active as he would like to be. He specifically asked for your services, Mr. Cone."

"Yeah? How come? I never met the guy."

"He is a close personal friend of Mr. Simon Trale of Dempster-Torrey, and I believe it was Mr. Trale's recommendation that led to Mr. Lee's decision to employ Haldering and Company, and you in particular."

"And I'm sure he'll be happy with our services," Haldering booms. "We guarantee results—right, Cone?"

"Nah," the Wall Street dick says. "No one can do that. Mr. Jeffreys, you said that Lee has a financial problem. What is it?"

"I'm afraid I am not at liberty to reveal that at this particular time. Our client wishes to discuss the matter with you personally."

"Okay," Cone says equably. "If he wants to play it cozy, that's fine with me. How do I get hold of him?"

The attorney proffers a business card. "This is the address on Exchange Place. It is the corporate headquarters of White Lotus. On the back of the card you will find a handwritten telephone number. That is Mr. Chin Tung Lee's private line. Calls to that number will not go through the company's switchboard."

Cone takes the card and stands. "All right," he says, "I'll give him a call and find out what his problem is. I also want to tell him to put more chicken in his chow mein."

He shambles back to his office, digs through the mess in his desk (what's a stale package of Twinkies doing in there?), and finally roots out an old copy of Standard and Poor's Stock Guide. He looks up White Lotus.

The corporation, listed on the OTC exchange, sells packaged Chinese foods to consumers, restaurants, and institutions. It is capitalized for slightly over two million shares of common stock, no preferred. It has no long-term debt. It has paid a cash dividend every year since 1949. What is of particular interest to Cone is that the price range of the stock for the past fifteen years has varied from 31 to 34, never below, never above.

Similarly, there has been little change in the annual dividend rate. White Lotus stock is currently yielding slightly over 5 percent. Its financial position appears exemplary: high assets, low liabilities, and a hefty bundle of surplus cash and cash equivalents.

All in all, it seems to be a solid, conservative outfit, but maybe a bit stodgy. It sounds like the kind of stock Chinese widows and orphans would love to own: a nice five-percent return come wars, inflation, or financial foofarows. No one's going to get rich trading White Lotus, but no one's going down the drain either. So what could their financial problem be?

"Ah so," Cone says aloud in a frightful Charlie Chan accent. "It is written that when icicles drip on the mulch bed, the wise man hides his peanut butter."

He then dials the direct line to the Chairman and Chief Executive Officer of White Lotus. But when Mr. Chin Tung Lee comes on the phone, he sounds nothing like Charlie Chan. And nothing like an invalid confined to a wheelchair. His voice is strong, vibrant, with good resonance.

He says he will be happy to see Mr. Timothy Cone in an hour, and thanks him for his courtesy. A very polite gent.

Cone plods down Broadway to Exchange Place. It's a spiffy day with lots of sunshine, washed sky, and a smacking breeze. Streets of the financial district are crowded; everyone scurries, the pursuit of the Great Simoleon continuing with vigor and determination.

But as he well knows, Wall Street is usually a zero-sum game: If someone wins, someone loses. That's okay; if you can't stand the heat, get out of the kitchen. And thinking that makes him smile because once, not too long ago, Samantha was bitching about how difficult it was for women to rise to positions of power on the Street. To which Cone replied, "If you can't stand the heat, go back in the kitchen." She kicked his shin.

The corporate offices of White Lotus are in a lumpish building that looks in need of steam cleaning. The frowsy lobby is vaguely Art Deco, but the old elevators still have operators—which has become as rare as finding a shoeshine boy or paperboy on the streets of Manhattan.

Timothy, a fast man with a stereotype, figures the offices of any outfit that sells canned chop suey are going to look like a joss house: carved teak furniture, brass statues, and paneled silk screens. But the offices of White Lotus are done in Swedish modern with bright graphics on the walls and, on the floor, a zigzag patterned carpet that bedazzles the eye.

The receptionist—female, Caucasian, young—phones and says Mr. Lee will see Cone in a few minutes. The Wall Street dick spends the time inspecting a lighted showcase in the reception room. It contains packages of all the White Lotus products: noodles, fried rice, chop suey, chow mein, pea pods, water chestnuts, soy sauce, fortune cookies, bean sprouts, bamboo shoots. Cleo would approve.

It really is no more than two minutes before he is ushered into the inner sanctum. Lee's personal office is a jazzy joint with not a hint of any Oriental influence or even the slightest whiff of incense. It's all high-tech with splashes of abstract paintings and clumpy bronze sculptures that look like hippopotamus do-do. There's a mobile hanging from the high ceiling: a school of pregnant pollack in flight.

"You like my office, Mr. Cone?" Chin Tung Lee asks in his boomy voice.

"It's different."

Lee laughs. "My wife decorated it," he says. "I admit it took some time getting used to, but now I like it. My son says it looks like a garage sale."

He presses buttons on the arms of his electric wheelchair and buzzes out from behind the driftwood desk to offer a tiny hand.

"So pleased to make your acquaintance, sir," he says. "Mr. Trale has told me a great deal about you and what a fine job you did for Dempster-Torrey."

"That was nice of him," Cone says, shaking the little paw gently. "You and Trale old friends?"

"Please sit down there. I insisted I have at least one comfortable chair for visitors. As you can see, my chair is mobile, but I must sit on a Manhattan telephone directory to bring me up to desk level."

He laughs again, and Cone decides this guy is the most scrutable Oriental he's ever met. Timothy flops down in the leather tub chair, and Lee whizzes around behind his desk again.

"Oh, yes," he continues, "Simon and I have been friends for many, many years. We play chess together every Friday night."

"And who wins?"

"I do," the old man says, grinning. "Always. But Simon keeps trying. That is why I admire him so much. Mr. Cone, I received a phone call from Mr. Jeffreys of Blains, Kibes and Thrush. He informed me that he has negotiated a satisfactory service contract with Haldering and Company, and that you have been assigned to our case. I was delighted to hear it."

"Thanks," Cone says. "So what's your problem?"

"Before I get into that, I'd like to give you a little background on our company."

"I got all the time in the world," Cone says. "You're paying for it."

"So we are. Well, I'll try to keep it mercifully brief. I emigrated from Taiwan—called Formosa in those days—in 1938, just before the beginning of the war. I had been waiting several years to get on the quota. At that time it was extremely difficult for Asians to enter the United States legally."

"I can imagine."

"However, eventually I did arrive. I came to New York and, with the aid of relatives already here, started a small business on Mott Street. It was really a pushcart operation; I couldn't afford a store. I sold Chinese fruits and vegetables. Well, one thing led to another, and now I own White Lotus. A typical American success story."

"You make it sound easy," Cone says, "but I'll bet you worked your ass off."

"Eighteen hours a day," Lee says, nodding. "In all kinds of weather. Which is probably why I'm now chained to this electric contraption. But the family members I eventually employed worked just as hard. The pushcart became a store, offering poultry and meats as well as vegetables. That one store became four, and we began selling prepared foods. And not only to local residents but to tourists and uptown visitors who came to Chinatown. They wanted mostly chop suey and chow mein in cardboard containers, so that's what we sold. It was merely a small step from that to the canning process. We went public in 1948."

"And the rest is history."

Chin Tung Lee smiles with a faraway look, remembering.

"Do you know, Mr. Cone," he says, "I miss those early days. The hours we worked were horrendous, but we were young, strong, and willing. And you know, I don't think any of us doubted that we'd make it. This country offered so much. If you devoted your life to your business, you would succeed. It seemed that simple."

"Things have changed," Cone offers.

"Yes," Lee says, looking down at the spotted backs of his hands. "I try not to be a boring ancient who talks constantly of the 'good old days,' but I must admit that things have changed—and not always for the better."

He pauses, and Cone has a chance to take a close look. The man has got to be Simon Trale's age or more—well over seventy. And he's even smaller than Trale, though it's hard to judge with him sitting in the wheelchair, propped on a telephone book, short legs dangling.

He's got a polished ivory complexion and sports a faded and wispy Vandyke that makes his face appear truncated and incomplete. His eyes are dark and sparkling—nothing enfeebled about those eyes—but he's wearing what is obviously a toupee, and a hellish one at that: a mustardy mixture of white, gray, black, with reddish strands. The guy who made that rug, Cone decides, should be shot.

"All those relatives," Chin Tung Lee goes on, "who worked so hard with me—brothers, sisters, aunts, uncles, cousins—I'm afraid I've outlived them all. Their portions of the business have passed to the second and, in some cases, to the third generation. But I still think of White Lotus as a family business, Mr. Cone. Not as large as La Choy, certainly, but with a personality and distinctiveness all its own. I am sorry to bore you with all this; you must forgive the maunderings of an old man."

"No, no," Cone says. "I'm getting the picture. But how come you haven't retired?"

"To what?" Lee says, flaring up. "To chess every Friday night with Simon Trale? No, thank you. White Lotus has been my life and will continue to be while life lasts."

"You mentioned the second and third generations—you've brought them into the business?"

"Only my son, Edward Tung Lee. He is my child by my first wife, who died several years ago. The others—nephews, nieces—none showed any interest in White Lotus, other than cashing their dividend checks. Perhaps they all thought devoting their lives to the production of quality canned chop suey was beneath them. However, I must admit that most of them have done very well—doctors, lawyers, musicians. One nephew is doing computer research at MIT. I'm very proud of him."

"And the son who works for the company—what is his position?"

"Edward? I suppose you might call him our Chief Operating Officer. He oversees production, labor relations, marketing, financial planning, advertising, and so on. I want him to be experienced in every department."

"That means you expect him to take over someday."

"Perhaps," Chin Tung Lee says, looking at Cone queerly. "Perhaps not. But enough of these personal details. They really have nothing to do with why you are here."

"Your financial problem?"

"More of a puzzle than a problem. Mr. Cone, have you any idea what price White Lotus common stock closed at on Friday?"

The Wall Street dick shrugs. "I don't know exactly, but I'd guess it was somewhere between thirty-one and thirty-four dollars a share."

Lee stares at him a second, then breaks into a jovial laugh again, tugging at his silky beard. "Ah," he says, "I see you have been doing your homework. I like that. Well, if you had given me that answer six months ago, you would have been exactly right. But as a matter of fact, on last Friday White Lotus stock closed at forty-two and a half."

"Oh-ho," Cone says, "so that's it. How long has this been going on—for six months?"

"Approximately."

"Has the volume of trading increased?"

"Appreciably. And the price of the stock continues to rise."

"Are you planning anything? Like a buyout? A merger? A big expansion? New products?"

"No to all your questions. We are a very well-structured corporation, Mr. Cone. Profitable certainly, but not wildly so. We keep a low profile. We don't dabble in anything in which we have no expertise. As far as I'm concerned, our product line is complete. No increase in the dividend has been declared or even discussed. You may think we are ultraconservative, perhaps dull, but that has been my business philosophy all my life: Learn what you can do, do it as well as you possibly can, and don't take risks trying to conquer new worlds. So I really can't account for the run-up in our stock. As I say, it puzzles me—and it disturbs me. I'm at an age where I don't enjoy surprises—especially unpleasant surprises. I want to know what's going on."

"Yeah," Cone says, "can't blame you for that. Okay, I'll look into it and see if I can come up with something. I'd like to talk to your son if that's all right."

"Of course. Today he's at our factory in Metuchen, New Jersey, but he should be back later this afternoon. I'll tell him to expect a call from you and to cooperate fully."

"Thanks. That should help. All of your stuff is produced in New Jersey?"

"Only the consumer products. The restaurant and institutional sizes are made up at a new facility in the industrial park at what used to be the Brooklyn Navy Yard. We also have several small buying offices around the country to ensure a steady and dependable supply of fresh ingredients."

"That's another thing," Cone says. "Why don't you put more chicken in your chicken chow mein? There's no meat in there."

Chin Tung Lee looks at him with an ironic smile. "Eat more noodles, Mr. Cone," he advises.

"Yeah," Cone says, "I guess that's one solution. Well, thanks for the information. I'll ask around and see what else I can pick up. And I'll get back to you if there's anything more I need."

"Whenever you wish; I am at your disposal. You may think it odd that I should be concerned at this sudden and unexplained increase in our stock price and trading volume. Other companies would welcome such activity, I know. But it's so unusual for White Lotus that I can't help wondering what is going on. And I must admit to a fear that if you discover what it is, it will not be pleasing. I hope you will expedite your investigation, Mr. Cone."

"I'll see what I can do," Cone says. "If I come up with something, you'll be the first to know."

He rises, reaches across the desk to pump the little hand again. He's still in that position when he hears the office door open behind him. He straightens, turns slowly.

A woman has come bursting into the room. She is young (about twenty-five), tall (almost six feet), blond (very), with a velvety hide (tawny), and summer-sky eyes. She is wearing a cheongsam of thin, pistachio-colored silk that clings.

Those jugs have got to be silicone, the Wall Street dick decides, because if they were God-made there'd be a slight sag just so He could remind the public of human imperfection.

"Oh, darling," she carols, "please excuse me. I didn't know you had a visitor. Sorry to interrupt."

"Come in, Claire," Chin Tung Lee says gently. "You're not interrupting at all. Mr. Cone, I'd like you to meet my wife."

Cone nods from where he stands across the room. Which is just as well, he figures, because if he went close to shake her hand he might flop to his knees in humble obeisance.

He meanders back to John Street, inspecting the women he passes and comparing them to Mrs. Claire Lee. She's got them all beat by a country mile.

So stricken was he by her sudden appearance that his impressions are still confused, and he tries to sort them out. He debates if she is the model type, the dancer type, the actress type.

"The goddess type," he says aloud.

He buys a meatball hero and a couple of cold cans of Bud, and goes up to his office. He reflects mournfully that it's a fitting lunch; that's exactly what he is—a meatball hero. Besides, she's the client's wife, and he doesn't dast fantasize depraved dreams about her. A waste of time. Still, a few modest dreams couldn't hurt anyone. Not even Samantha.

He resolutely vanquishes the scintillant image of Claire Lee, and unwraps his oozing sandwich. While he's scoffing, he calls Jeremy Bigelow at the Securities and Exchange Commission.

"Hey, old buddy," Jerry says happily, "that short-trading scam is really panning out. The bad guys are falling all over themselves to squeal and cop a plea."

"Yeah, I read about it," Cone says. "So you owe me one—right?"

"Oh-oh," Bigelow says, instantly worried. "Now what?"

"Very easy. Your secretary could look it up. There's this outfit on the OTC exchange. White Lotus. They sell canned chop suey. I just want to know if anyone has filed a 13-D public disclosure form on them."

"Why would anyone want to buy five percent of canned chop suey?"

"Beats the hell out of me. Look it up, will you?"

"Okay," the SEC man says. "I'll get on it and let you know."

"How soon?"

"As soon as my secretary gets back from lunch."

Cone finishes his hero and starts on the second beer. He leans back in his squeaky swivel chair, puts his feet up on the desk, and broods about what he knows and what he doesn't know.

He knows that a sudden run-up in stock price and an increase in trading volume is frequently—not always, but frequently—a tipoff that someone is going to make a tender offer for the company concerned. Usually the first step is to accumulate sufficient shares to prove you're serious and then make a bid to purchase enough stock from other shareholders—customarily at a premium over the current market price—to give the offeror control.

It can be a friendly takeover in which the company's management cooperates, or unfriendly, during which the company's executives and directors fight tooth and nail to defeat the bidder—and keep their jobs. The benefaction of shareholders is not always the highest good on Wall Street. "Corporate democracy" has all the modern relevance of "Fifty-four forty or fight," and sometimes the poor shareholders have to take their lumps.

One kicker here is that when any entity—individual or corporate—accumulates 5 percent or more of another company's stock, the entity must file a 13-D public disclosure form with the SEC, stating the purpose of the purchase: tender offer or simply an investment.

Jeremy Bigelow's secretary calls in about an hour and tells Cone there is no record of a 13-D form having been filed for White Lotus. He thanks her, hangs up, and goes back to his pondering, demonstrating his enormous physical strength by crumpling an empty aluminum beer can.

The absence of a 13-D form doesn't faze him; it's still possible a tender offer for White Lotus is in the making. There are several ways of getting around the 13-D law, all of them devious. If you like things in black and white, security regulations are not for you. Wall Street prefers grays.

Cone is certain of one thing: If a tender for White Lotus is in the works, it's going to be treated as an unfriendly offer by Mr. Chin Tung Lee. Cone will not soon forget the little man's passion when he spoke of a "family company" and how White Lotus was his entire life. Any hopeful raider is in for a knock-down-and-drag-out fight before Lee surrenders White Lotus—if he ever does.

What Cone can't answer is the question Jeremy Bigelow asked: Why would anyone *want* White Lotus? Admittedly it has a clean balance sheet; the bottom line looks good. But it has no subsidiaries that could be spun off for instant profit. Its product line offers nothing new or different. It would take an enormous infusion of advertising dollars to increase its market share at the expense of La Choy.

Figure White Lotus stock is selling at forty bucks a share. That means, with two million shares outstanding, anyone taking over the company would have to come up with eighty million dollars. That may not sound like much, Cone acknowledges, in this era of megadeals, but it's still a nice piece of change.

And Cone doesn't think White Lotus is worth it. There's little opportunity for growth there, and even with a more dynamic leadership than Chin Tung Lee offers, the company seems fated to amble along at a tortoise pace, paying a nice dividend but with no potential of becoming a real cash cow. Cone can name a dozen companies at the same price, or lower, that would provide a better chance to make a killing.

All this cerebral activity makes him drowsy. His chin sinks onto his chest, and he dozes at his desk for almost an hour. He doesn't even dream of Claire Lee, but he twitches awake when the phone rings. He picks it up.

"Mr. Timothy Cone?"

"Yeah. Who's this?"

"Edward Tung Lee. Mr. Cone, I'm still in New Jersey, but I just spoke to my father and he said you'd like to talk to me."

"That's right. Whenever you have the time."

"Well, I'm about to drive back to Manhattan. I have a business appointment at a restaurant on Pell Street at five o'clock. It shouldn't take long—ten or fifteen minutes. If you could meet me there, perhaps we can have a drink together."

"Sounds good to me," Cone says. "What's the name of the place?"

"Ah Sing's Bar and Grill. They're in the book."

"I'll find it. I better describe myself so you can spot me."

"Don't bother," Edward Lee says, laughing. "You'll be the only honkie in the joint."

He disconnects, and Cone hangs up thoughtfully. The guy sounded high. Maybe he's snorting monosodium glutamate or mainlining soy sauce. Cone shakes his head to rid his still sleep-befuddled brain of such nonsense, and starts flipping through his tattered telephone directory to find the address of Ah Sing's Bar & Grill on Pell Street.

It turns out to be exactly like a hundred other cheap Chinese restaurants Timothy has frequented from Boston to Saigon: all Formica and wind chimes, fluorescent lights and plastic poppies. The walls are white tile, reasonably clean, decorated with paintings of dragons on black velvet and a calendar showing Miss Hong Kong in a bikini.

A small bar is on the right just inside the entrance. Drinkers have a fine view of the frenetic activity on Pell Street through a big plate glass window, though right now the bar is empty. But the remainder of the long, narrow restaurant has plenty of early diners, all men, all Asian, seated at tables and in booths.

Cone has no sooner swung aboard a barstool when there's a slender guy at his elbow. He's dressed like an Oriental yuppie.

"Mr. Cone?" he says in that bouncy voice. "I'm Edward Tung Lee." They shake hands. "Look, why don't you have a drink. I'll be finished in a few minutes and join you here."

"Take your time," Cone says. "No rush."

"Henry," Lee calls to the bartender, "put this on my tab, please."

Cone watches him stride back to a booth. He's tall, about Cone's height, but with better posture. He moves with quick grace: a young executive on the fast track. His jetty hair is blow-dried, and during the few seconds they talked, Timothy noted the gold Rolex, gold chain bracelet, diamond cuff links. Edward Lee doesn't need a fortune cookie to predict a glorious future; he picked the right father.

"Sir?" the bartender asks.

"As long as he's paying for it," Cone says, "I'll have a double Absolut vodka on the rocks. Splash of water. No fruit."

"Very wise," Henry says.

He gets to work, playing a conjuror. Tosses ice cubes into the air. Catches them in the glass. Begins to pour from the vodka bottle. Raises the bottle high without spilling a drop. Sets the glass smartly in front of Cone and adds a dollop of ice water with a flourish.

"Nicely done," Cone says. "If I tried that, I'd need a mop."

"Too much water?" the bartender asks anxiously.

Cone takes a sip. "Just right," he says.

Henry moves away, and Cone works on his drink slowly, looking out the big window at the mob scene on Pell: pedestrians rushing, street vendors dawdling, traffic crawling, a guy carrying a clump of live chickens (heads down, feet trussed), and a young woman strolling in a sandwich board covered with Chinese characters.

He turns to look back into the restaurant. Lee was right; Cone is the only Caucasian in the place. That makes him think the food must be something special. But then he decides that conclusion is probably as stupid as the belief that truckers know where to eat. Follow that dictum and you're in for a humongous bellyache. Those guys are interested only in quantity and low price. Cone figures the patrons of Ah Sing's Bar & Grill have the same needs.

He spots Edward Tung Lee sitting in a booth against the far wall. Lee is leaning over the table, talking rapidly and earnestly to a roly-poly Asian with three chins and a gut that doesn't end. The two have their heads together, which looks funny because Edward has thick, glossy hair and the fat guy is bald as a honeydew melon.

While Cone watches, Lee slides out of the booth, shakes hands with the other man. He comes quickly to the bar, threading his way through the tables, and takes the stool next to Cone. Henry is in front of him instantly.

"The usual, Mr. Lee?" he asks.

"Why not."

They both watch as Henry goes into his act, mixing a scotch sour with all the showy skill of a professional juggler.

"Best bartender I've ever seen," Cone says.

"Henry belongs uptown," Lee says. "I could get him a job like that"— he snaps his fingers—"but Chen would kill me. That's the tubby gentleman I was talking to: Chen Chang Wang. He owns this joint and a dozen others like it around the city. He has enough labor problems without me luring away his favorite bartender."

"Chen Chang Wang is the owner?" Cone says. "What happened to Ah Sing?"

"Long gone," Lee says with his burbling laugh. "But the name lingers on. Ah Sing's is a lot easier to remember than Chen Chang Wang's Bar and Grill."

"A good customer?" Cone guesses.

"A *very* good customer. You'd be amazed at the quantity of White Lotus products he moves. Not exactly gourmet food, but he gives good portions and his prices are reasonable."

"You call on customers yourself? I should think your salesmen would do that."

"Oh, they do, they do. But I like to visit all our wholesale customers myself now and then. Listen to their complaints, make sure they're getting deliveries on time, ask for suggestions on how we can improve our service. Orientals place a lot of importance on close personal relationships, Mr. Cone."

"It makes sense. Listen, I don't want to take up too much of your time. I talked to your father this morning and got most of the information I need. I also met your stepmother," he adds.

Edward Lee makes a face. "There's no fool like an old fool," he says.

Timothy doesn't like that. If Chin Tung Lee wants to marry a dish one-third his age, it's nobody's business but his own. Edward has no call to bad-mouth his father—unless the luscious Claire cut him out of an inheritance he expected.

"I thought she was a nice lady," Cone says, "but that's neither here nor there. I guess your father told you why he hired Haldering and Company."

"The run-up in our stock price? Nothing to it. Much ado about nothing."

"Yeah?" Cone says. "How do you account for it?"

"Easy," Lee says. "With this bull market, a lot of people are getting nervous. There's going to be a huge correction. I don't mean there's going to be a calamitous crash, but what goes up has got to come down. As they say on Wall Street, trees don't grow to the sky. So a lot of investors are getting out of the high-fliers. Lately there's been a stampede to quality. And White Lotus has always been an undervalued stock. My God, where else can you get a safe five-percent return year in and year out from a solid, well-managed company?"

While he expounds all this, Cone has been inspecting him in the mirror behind the bar. In that blued reflection Lee looks older than Cone first thought. His wrinkle-free skin seems more the result of facials and bronzing gel than the placidity of a man at peace with himself and the world.

He's a handsome guy with gently curved lips, cleft chin, and a high unblemished brow. The slant of the eyes is slight but exotic, and the black horn-rimmed glasses with tinted lens give him the appearance of a movie star off camera. He's not wearing a wedding band, but Cone wonders if he's married, and makes a mental note to find out.

His glib explanation of why White Lotus stock is on a rampage disturbs the Wall Street dick. Too much frowning sincerity. The guy seems to be pushing when there's no need to push.

"Well, you may be right," Cone says. "I've just started on this, so I've got no ideas, one way or another."

Edward signals the bartender and points to Cone's empty glass and his own. Henry gets to work.

"Take my advice, Mr. Cone," Lee says, "and don't waste your time. Believe me, it's just a demonstration of normal market forces at work. In another six months or so, I expect the price of White Lotus stock will be back in its usual range."

"Have you told your father this?"

That's when the man's ire becomes apparent. "Tell him? Who the hell can tell him anything? He's always been stubborn, but he's getting worse. Ever since he married that—Well, ever since my mother died and he remarried. Sometimes I wonder if he's getting senile. Let me give you a forinstance. A year ago I went to him with what I thought was a great idea—and everyone in the business I talked to said it would fly. I wanted White Lotus to get into frozen dinners. Packaged gourmet Chinese food. Slide them in the oven or microwave and you'd have a delicious meal as good as anything prepared fresh by the best Chinese chefs. I'm talking about steamed sea bass, salt-baked chicken, mu shu pork, five-fragrant beef, smoke tea duck, and things like that."

"Yeah, well, I don't know much about highfalutin food, but it sounds like a commercial idea."

"Commercial?" Lee cries. "A blockbuster! I spent six months research-ing it. The numbers looked good. I'm not only talking about frozen Chi-nese dinners sold to consumers in supermarkets, but the restaurant trade, too. So a joint like this could expand its menu. The cost would be doable. No chefs to hire. No fresh produce going bad on you. Someone orders, say, twice-fried shredded beef, you just pop the package in the microwave, and that's it. Sensational!"

"And what did your father say?"

"He said no. He wants to stick to the same old crap we've been turning out for forty years. Damn it!" Then, as if ashamed of his vehemence, Edward Tung Lee tries a smile. "Ah, well," he says lightly, "you lose one, you win one—right?"

The owner, Chen Chang Wang, comes waddling by. He gives them a Buddha smile, waves a flabby hand, goes out the door to Pell Street.

"Well," Cone says, "I think I—"

Then the world comes to an end. They hear sharp explosions—more booms than cracks. The plate glass window shatters, comes crashing down. A hole and star appear in the mirror behind the bar. Someone starts shrieking and can't stop. There are more shots.

Cone falls off his barstool and drags Edward Lee to the floor along with him. He goes for the magnum in his ankle holster.

"Stay down!" he orders the other man. "Don't even raise your head."

He looks cautiously to the rear of the restaurant. Tables and booths are empty; the patrons are flat on the floor.

"Keep down," he cautions Lee again.

He rises slowly to a crouch. No more explosions, the shrieking has finally ended. Now there are shouts, and someone is blowing a whistle: short, loud, repeated blasts.

Cone slips the .357 into his jacket pocket. Gripping it, he goes out the front door onto Pell Street. People are coming from doorways, from behind parked cars and pushcarts. A uniformed cop is already there, and another comes pounding up. A circle of gawkers forms.

And in the center, spread-eagled on the sidewalk and leaking blood, lies the body of Mr. Chen Chang Wang, looking like a beached and punctured whale.

Cone goes back inside. Edward Lee is standing, brushing off his black silk suit. Henry rises slowly from behind the bar.

"Sorry I knocked you over," Cone says.

"Glad you did. What the hell happened?"

"I'm afraid," says Timothy, "you just lost a good customer."

Lee stares at him, face twisted. "Chen?"

Cone nods.

"Dead?"

"Very."

Lee's face scrunches up even more. He begins pounding on the bar with a clenched fist. "Bastards!" he spits out. "Oh, the rotten bastards!" Then, calming: "Henry, pour me a brandy, and one for Mr. Cone, and you better have one yourself."

No tricks this time, no wizardry; the bartender fills three snifters with a trembling hand. He drains his glass in one gulp. Cone and Lee right the toppled barstools, sit down, turn to watch the confusion on Pell Street. A squad car, siren growling, has nosed through the mob and parked. They hear more sirens coming closer.

"Ah, Jesus," Lee says, taking a swallow of his brandy, "he was a sweet man."

"Someone didn't think so," Cone says. "Who are the bastards?"

"What?"

"When I told you he was dead, you said, 'The bastards, the rotten bastards.' Who did you have in mind?"

"Oh," Lee says, "that. I meant the man who shot him."

"Uh-huh," Cone says. "Probably more than one. Wang is pretty well perforated. Sounded like forty-fives to me."

Two uniformed officers come into Ah Sing's Bar & Grill. One is Chinese, the other black. They have notebooks and pens ready. The Chinese goes to the back of the restaurant where the patrons, now seated at tables and booths, are again digging into their rice bowls. The black officer stops at the bar.

"Were you gentlemen seated here when the incident occurred?" he asks them.

"Yeah," Cone says. "Having a drink. Then all hell broke loose. We heard shots, and the plate glass window came down."

"Did you see anything that happened outside?"

"Not me," Cone says.

"You?" he asks Edward.

"I saw nothing," Lee says. "We were talking together, facing each other."

"Okay," the cop says. "This is just preliminary. Could I have your names, addresses, and phone numbers, please. And I'd like to see any identification you have."

He copies everything down in his notebook.

"Thank you for your cooperation," he says politely. "Anything else you can tell me?"

"Yeah," Cone says, pointing at the holed and starred mirror. "A wild slug went in there. You'll be able to dig it out if you need it."

The officer looks. "Thanks again," he says gratefully. "I might have missed that."

"Can we leave now?" Lee asks him.

"Sure," the cop says. "Everything's under control." He moves down the bar to question Henry.

"He didn't even search us," Lee says.

"Why should he? They've probably got witnesses who saw the shooters make their getaway. I doubt if killers would pop Mr. Wang and then come into his bar and order drinks."

"If he had searched us," Lee persists, "he'd have found your gun. I saw you take it from a holster on your leg."

"So?"

"You always carry it?"

"Yep. My security blanket. I've got a permit for it."

"You're a valuable man to know," Edward Tung Lee says in a low voice.

What he means by that, Cone has no idea.

2

He wakes in a grumpy mood, hauls himself off the mattress, lights his first cigarette of the new day. He goes growling around the loft, washing and shaving, drinking black coffee and then adding a smidgen of brandy just to get his eyelids up.

"So I tell him a good customer has been scragged," he says to Cleo, who is working on a breakfast of leftover chicken chow mein. "And he says, 'The bastards, the rotten bastards.' So I ask him who the bastards are, and he says he meant the guy who popped Chen Chang Wang. Now I ask you, does that make sense? Of course it doesn't. So he was lying. But why? No skin off my ass. I couldn't care less who ventilated Mr. Wang. Cleo, you dirty rat, are you listening?"

It's a peppy August day, which does nothing for his crusty mood. So the sun is shining. Big deal. That's what it's getting paid for, isn't it? And that mild azure sky with fat little puffs of clouds—it all looks like a sappy postcard. "Having fine time, wish you were here." And when the hell was Samantha coming home?

There's a guy waiting for him in the Haldering reception room. He looks short and squat sitting down, but when he stands up, he's lean and mean, only an inch or two shorter than Cone. He's Chinese, with black hair cut *en brosse*, and he's got a mouthful of too many white teeth.

"Mr. Timothy Cone?"

"That's right. Who you?"

The gink hands him a business card, and the Wall Street dick reads it aloud: "Johnnie Wong. Federal Bureau of Investigation." Cone inspects the card, feeling it between thumb and forefinger. "Very nice. Good engraving. You mind showing me your potsy?"

"Not at all." Wong whips out his ID wallet and displays it.

"Uh-huh," Cone says. "Looks legit. What's with the Johnnie? Why not just plain John?"

"Take it up with my mom and pop," the FBI man says. "I've been suffering from that all my life. The Wong I can live with, but please don't tell me 'Fifty million Chinese can't be Wong.' "

"I wasn't going to," Timothy says—but he was. "You want to palaver, I suppose. This way."

Johnnie Wong follows Cone back to his weeny office and looks around. "I like it," he says. "It's got that certain nothing."

"Yeah," Cone says, and holds up the brown paper bag he's carrying. "My breakfast: coffee and bagel. You want something? I'll call down for you."

"No, thanks," Wong says, "I've had mine. You go ahead."

Cone lights a Camel, starts on the container of black coffee, the bagel with a shmear. "So?" he says to the other man. "How come the FBI is parked on my doorstep?"

"You were in Ah Sing's Bar and Grill on Pell Street when the owner, Chen Chang Wang, was killed."

"Oh-ho," Cone says, "so that's it. Yeah, I was there. But how come you guys are interested? I should think it was something for the locals to handle."

"We're working with the NYPD on this," Wong says. "That's how I got your name. Would you mind telling me what you were doing there?"

"Yeah, I'd mind. There's such a thing as client confidentiality."

"Sure," the FBI man says. "And there's such a thing as obstruction of justice."

The two men stare at each other a moment. Johnnie Wong is a jaunty guy with eyebrows like mustaches. He's a little chubby in the face, but there's no fat on his frame; he looks hard and taut. He grins a lot, flashing all those Chiclets, but it's tough to tell if it's genuine merriment or a grimace of pain.

"Tell you what," Cone says, "you tell me why the FBI is interested in Wang's murder, and I'll tell you what I was doing there."

Wong considers that a moment. "Fair enough," he says finally. "But I trade last."

It's Cone's turn to ponder. "Okay," he says, "I'll deal. I was with Edward Tung Lee, the chief operating officer of White Lotus. You've heard of them?"

Wong nods.

"Haldering and Company was hired by White Lotus to find out why the price of their stock has shot up in the last six months. That's what Edward Lee and I were talking about."

"Interesting," the FBI man says, "but not very."

"Now it's your turn."

"It's a long story."

"I got nothing better to do than listen," Cone says.

"All right then, listen to this: Since 1970 the number of Chinese immigrants in this country has almost doubled. I'm talking about people from Taiwan, mainland China, and Hong Kong. Add to those the immigrants from Macao, South Korea, Singapore, Vietnam, Cambodia, and Thailand, and you'll see there's a helluva lot of Asians here. Ninety-nine percent of the come-ins are law-abiding schnooks who just want to be left alone so they can hustle a buck. The other one percent are dyed-in-the-wool gonifs."

"And that's where you come in," Cone says.

"You got it. I'm a slant-eye, so the Bureau assigned me and a lot of other Oriental agents to keep tabs on the Yellow Peril. What's happened is this: In the past few years the Italian Mafia has taken its lumps. The older guys, the dons and godfathers, are mostly dead or in the clink. The new recruits from Sicily are zips, and the guys running the Families today just don't have the clout and know-how. There's been a vacuum in organized crime. Or was until the Asian gangs moved in. The biggest is United Bamboo. They're mostly from Taiwan but have links with the Yakusa, the Japanese thugs. Their main competitor, not as big but growing fast, is the Giant Panda mob, mostly from mainland China and Hong Kong."

"United Bamboo and Giant Panda," Cone repeats. "Nicer names than La Cosa Nostra. What are these bad boys into?"

"You name it," Wong says. "United Bamboo is in the heroin trade because they've got good contacts in the Golden Triangle. Now they're making deals with the Colombians and pushing cocaine. They also own a string of prostitution rings around the country, mostly staffed by Taiwanese women. Giant Panda does some dope dealing—a lot of marijuana—but most of their money comes from shakedowns: a classic protection racket aimed at Chinese restaurants, laundries, and groceries. Lately they've been trying to take over legitimate businesses."

"Any homicides?" Cone asks.

"Hell, yes! Practically all United Bamboo or Giant Panda soldiers. But a lot of innocents, too. People who refused to pay baksheesh or just had the bad luck to be in the wrong place at the wrong time. Anyway, the reason I'm telling you all this is because Chen Chang Wang, the guy who got chilled yesterday, was an officer in Giant Panda. Not the top general of the New York organization, but a colonel."

"So that's it. You've had your eye on him?"

"Not a tail—we don't have the manpower for that. Just loose surveillance."

"And you think it was United Bamboo who knocked him off?"

"It had all the earmarks of a United Bamboo kill. They use very young punks—guys in their teens—and give them stolen U.S. Army forty-five automatic pistols. They just squat, close their eyes, and blast away. They've got to hit *something*. Then they take off, sometimes on foot, sometimes in a car or on a motorcycle. Get this: Last month there was a murder in Seattle's Chinatown, and the killers made their getaway on bicycles! How does that grab you?"

"Beautiful," Cone says. "So there's no love lost between the two gangs?"

"None whatsoever," Johnnie Wong says with his glittery grin. "They're competing for the same turf. Each wants to take over when the Mafia goes down. Listen, they've got more than a million Asian immigrants to diddle. That can mean a lot of loot."

"No difference between the two?"

"I wouldn't say that," Wong says cautiously. "First of all, United Bamboo speaks mostly the Cantonese dialect while Giant Panda is mostly Mandarin."

"Which do you speak?" Cone asks him.

"Both," the FBI man says, and the Wall Street dick decides his grin is the real thing. Here's a guy who gets a laugh out of the world's madness.

"Also," Wong goes on, "United Bamboo are the heavies. I mean they're really vicious scuts. Burn a guy with a propane torch before they chop off his head. Or take out a victim's family in front of his eyes before they off him. The old Mafia would never touch a target's family—I'll say that for them. But United Bamboo will."

"Like Colombian coke dealers?" Cone suggests.

"Yeah, those guys are savages, too. But the Giant Panda mob is softer. Not saints, you understand. They kill, but it's all business with them. They're putting a lot of their young guys in banks and brokerage houses on Wall Street. Listen, all this bullshit is getting me nowhere. Isn't there anything else you can tell me about your meeting with your client in Ah Sing's?"

"Not a thing," Cone says. "He was talking with Chen Chang Wang when I got there. Then he left Wang in a booth, came over and joined me at the bar. In a little while, Wang walked by, smiled and waved at us, went out—and that's when the fireworks started."

"And that's all you can tell me?"

"That's all."

Johnnie Wong looks at him closely. "You wouldn't be holding out on me, would you?"

"Why would I do that?" Cone says. "I know from nothing about United Bamboo and Giant Panda and who blasted the late Mr. Wang."

"Uh-huh," the FBI man says. "Well, I'll take your word for it—for now. I checked you out before I came over. You add up: the tours in Vietnam, the medals, and all that. Where are the medals now?"

"I hocked them," Timothy says.

Wong flashes his choppers again. "Keep in touch, old buddy," he says. "We haven't got all that many warm bodies assigned to Asian gangs in the New York area, and I have an antsy feeling that something is going down I should know about and don't. So consider yourself a deputy. If you pick up anything, give me a call. You have my card."

"Sure," Cone says, "I'll be in touch. And you've got my number here."

"I do," Johnnie Wong says rising. "And I've also got your unlisted home phone number."

"You would," Timothy says admiringly. "You don't let any grass grow under your feet, do you? We can work together."

"Can we?" Wong says, staring at him. "You ever hear the ancient Chinese proverb: *A freint darf men zich koifen; sonem krigt men umzist.* A friend you have to buy; enemies you get for nothing."

"Yeah," Cone says.

After the FBI man leaves, Cone flips through the morning's *Wall Street Journal.* Then he lights another cigarette, leans back, clasps his hands behind his head. He knows he should be thinking—but about what? All he's got is odds and ends, and at the moment everything adds up to zilch. No use trying to create a scenario; he just doesn't have enough poop to make a plot.

So he calls Mr. Chin Tung Lee on that direct number at White Lotus. The Chairman and CEO picks up after one ring.

"Yes?" he says.

"Mr. Lee, this is Timothy Cone at Haldering."

"Ah, my young friend. And how is your health today?"

"Fine, thanks," Cone says, willing to go through the ceremony with this nice old man. "And yours, sir?"

"I am surviving, thank you. Each day is a blessing."

"Uh-huh. Mr. Lee, the reason I'm calling is that I'd like to get hold of a list of your shareholders and also a copy of your most recent annual report. Is that all right with you?"

"Of course. I'll have a package prepared for you."

"If you could leave it at the receptionist's desk, I could pick it up without bothering you."

"Oh, no," Chin Tung Lee says. "I will be delighted to see you. And there is something I wish to ask you."

"Okay," Cone says. "I'll be there in an hour or so."

He wanders down the corridor to the office of Louis Kiernan, a paralegal in the attorneys' section of Haldering & Co. Cone prefers bracing Kiernan because the full-fledged lawyers give him such a load of gobbledygook that he leaves them with his eyes glazed over.

"Lou," he says, lounging in the doorway of the cubby, "I need some hotshot legal skinny so gimme a minute, will you?"

Kiernan looks up from his typewriter and peers at Cone over his wire-rimmed reading glasses. "A minute?" he says. "You sure?"

"Maybe two. There's this rich old geezer whose first wife has died. Now he's married to a beautiful young knish. He's also got a son by his first wife who's older than his second wife—dig? Now my question: If the codger croaks, who inherits?"

"The wife," Lou says promptly. "At least half, even if the deceased leaves no will. The son would probably be entitled to a third. But listen, Tim, when you get into inheritance law you're opening a can of worms. Anyone, with good cause, can sue to break a will."

"But all things being equal, you figure the second wife for at least fifty percent of the estate and the son for, say, thirty percent?"

"Don't quote me," Kiernan says cautiously.

"You guys kill me," Cone says. "When a lawyer's wife asks, 'Was it as good for you as it was for me?' he says, 'I'd like to get a second opinion on that.' Thanks, Lou. See you around."

He rambles down to Exchange Place, sucking on another cigarette and wondering how long it'll take nonsmokers to have the streets declared off-limits. Then nicotine addicts will have to get their fixes in illicit dens, or maybe by paddling out into the Atlantic Ocean in a rubber dinghy.

Twenty minutes later he's closeted with Chin Tung Lee. The old man looks chipper, and since he's puffing a scented cigarette in a long ivory holder, Cone figures it's okay to light up another coffin nail.

"I know it's too early to ask if you have made any progress, Mr. Cone."

"Yeah, it is. I'm just collecting stuff at this stage. That's why I wanted your shareholder list and annual report."

"Right here," Lee says, tapping a fat package on his desk. "I hope you will guard this well. I would not care to have the list fall into the hands of an enemy."

"I'll take good care of it," Cone promises. "I notice White Lotus stock is up another half-point."

"It continues," the little man says, nodding. "My son believes it is of no significance, but I do not agree."

"By the way," Cone says, as casually as he can manage, "is your son married?"

Chin Tung Lee sets his holder and cigarette down carefully in a brass ashtray made from the base of a five-inch shell. "No, he is not," he says with a frazzled laugh. "It is a sadness for me. Men my age should have grandchildren. Perhaps great-grandchildren."

"He's still a young man," Cone says. "He may surprise you one of these days."

"A very pleasant surprise. Family is important to me. Are you married, Mr. Cone?"

"No," the Wall Street dick says, stirring uncomfortably in the leather club chair. "You said you had something to ask me."

"Ah, yes," Lee says, and now his laugh is vigorous again. "Happy news, I am glad to say. Today is my dear wife's birthday. To celebrate, we are having a cocktail party and buffet dinner in our apartment this evening, and I hope you will be able to join us."

"Hey," Cone says, "that sounds great. What time?"

"From five o'clock until the wee hours," the gaffer says gleefully. "I must admit I am looking forward to it. I enjoy celebrations."

"Fireworks?" Timothy says, grinning.

"Regretfully, no. The popping of champagne corks will have to do."

"Your son will be there?"

"Naturally," Chin says, astonished at the question. "He lives in the apartment. With his own private entrance, I might add. In any event, we are expecting almost a hundred guests, and I trust you will be one of them."

"Sure will," Cone says. "You in the book?"

"We are indeed. But to save you from searching through four pages of Lees in the Manhattan directory, I have written out our address and home telephone number. You will find it in the package. Then we may expect you?"

"Wouldn't miss it," Cone promises. "Should I bring a birthday present?"

The old man waves a hand in protest. "Of course not. Your presence will be gift enough."

A lesson to Cone in grace and civility.

He's down in the lobby carrying the fat package when he realizes what was missing from that conversation. Chin Tung Lee never asked if Cone had spoken to his son. And he had said nothing of the murder of Chen Chang Wang, a good customer of White Lotus products.

Which meant—what? That he considered it of no importance, or that his son had not told him that he and Cone were in Ah Sing's when Wang was sent to join his ancestors.

The Wall Street dick begins to appreciate what is meant by a "Chinese puzzle."

He can go back to the office—but that's not a cheery prospect. Haldering might come nosing around, demanding to know what progress Cone has made on the White Lotus case as well as those other two files, real yawners, he's supposed to be investigating.

So he decides to hike all the way back to his loft, breathing deeply to get the cigarette smoke out of his alveoli. That lasts for six blocks; then he lights up, cursing himself for his weakness as he inhales deeply and wonders which will rot first: lungs, liver, or kidneys.

He doesn't bother picking up lunch, figuring he can last till that buffet dinner. Then he'll gorge and maybe slip something special in his pockets for Cleo. Meanwhile the cat can subsist on refrigerator grub: cheddar and bologna.

In the loft, he strips to T-shirt and baggy Jockey briefs and mixes himself a jelly jar of vodka and water, with plenty of the former, little of the latter, and lots of ice.

"Here's looking at you, kid," he toasts Cleo, who has come out from under the bathtub and is now lying in a patch of diffused sunshine coming through the dirt-encrusted skylight.

The first thing Cone does is phone Eve Bookerman at Dempster-Torrey, something he should have done a week ago.

"I'm so glad you called, Mr. Cone," she says in her ballsy voice. "I wanted to thank you personally for the job you did on our sabotage problem, Marvelous!"

"Yeah," he says, "it turned out okay, and for once the nice guys didn't finish last. Listen, the reason I'm calling is this: When I was working your case, we rented a car for a month. It's a Ford Escort and was charged to Dempster-Torrey. By rights the car should have been turned in when the file was closed. But there's still about two weeks left on the rental, and I wanted to ask if it's all right with you if I keep the car until the month runs out."

She laughs. "Mr. Cone, you keep the car as long as you need it, and don't worry about the billing. It's the least we can do."

"Thanks," he says. "It'll be a big help. Anything new on who's going to be the CEO at Dempster-Torrey?"

"I didn't make it," she says.

"Tough," Cone says. "But tomorrow's another day."

"Thank God for that," she says. "Nice talking to you, Mr. Cone. Let's have a drink sometime."

"You name it," he answers, knowing she never will.

He sits at the kitchen table with his drink and opens the White Lotus package. The first thing he goes through is the annual report, knowing full well that like most corporation reports, it should be submitted for the Pulitzer Prize in fiction.

White Lotus is a four-color, slick-paper job. It doesn't tell him much more than he's already learned except that the number of registered stockholders is slightly over 2,000—which seems high for a company as modest as this chop suey producer. On the opening page are photographs of Chin Tung Lee and Edward Tung Lee, facing the camera with frozen smiles.

The Board of Directors is interesting. Of the ten, three are outsiders, all with Caucasian names. Of the remaining seven, five are named Lee and the other two have Chinese monikers. All seven are officers of White Lotus. Sounds to Cone as if the Chairman and CEO is keeping a very tight rein indeed on his company.

The computer printout of shareholders' names, addresses, and the number of shares held provides more provocative stuff. Cone flips through the list quickly, getting an instant impression that at least ninety percent of White Lotus shareholders are Chinese, or at least have Oriental names. Then he zeros in on the largest holdings, those of Chin Tung Lee, Claire Lee, and Edward Tung Lee.

He does some rough estimates because the battery of his handy-dandy pocket calculator went kaput a long time ago and he hasn't gotten around to replacing it. He figures Chin Tung Lee owns about twenty-six percent of White Lotus, wife Claire eleven percent, and son Edward sixteen percent.

Those numbers add up to some ripe conclusions. The three of them combined hold a majority interest in White Lotus. Chin and Claire can easily outvote Edward. Chin and Edward can easily outvote Claire.

And Claire and Edward can outvote Chin.

The other forty-seven percent of White Lotus is held by the 2,000 shareholders, mostly in odd lots. There are few investors with as many as 1,000 shares. And they, Cone notes, are all Chinese.

"I don't know what it all means," he says to Cleo. "Do you?"

The cat gives him the "I am famished" signal, which consists of ankle rubs and piteous mewls.

So Cone tosses the beast a slice of bologna and mixes himself a fresh drink. He opens a bag of Cheez Doodles and goes back to his arithmetic.

He thinks of it as getting "spiffed up," but no one else would. The thready tweed jacket with greasy leather patches on the elbows isn't quite the thing for a cocktail party in August. The gray flannel slacks, recently laundered, still bear the stains of long-forgotten sausage submarines. The button-down shirt is clean, even if one button is missing. He wears the collar open, of course, and the T-shirt shyly revealed is almost white.

Donning this finery puts him in an antic mood, and on the drive uptown in his red Escort he bangs his palm on the steering wheel and sings as much of the Marine Corps hymn as he can remember—which is not much. Finished with his caroling, he wonders if his frolicsome mood is due to the prospect of free booze and a generous buffet or the hope of seeing Claire Lee again, a woman he wouldn't sully with his dreams.

The Lees live in a Fifth Avenue apartment house just north of Sixty-eighth Street. It is an old building with heavy pediments and carved window casements. It is planted solidly on the Avenue, turning a stern and forthright stare at the frivolity of Central Park. The building is a dowager surrounded by teenyboppers.

The Lees' apartment is something else again. It occupies the entire ninth floor with two entrances and enough space to accommodate a convention of sex therapists. The crowd that has already assembled when Cone arrives is wandering through room after room, seemingly lost in this high-ceilinged, air-conditioned warren. There's enough furniture to equip a small, slightly shoddy hotel.

Three bars have been set up, and two long buffet tables. Repressing his appetites, Cone first seeks out Chin, Edward, and Claire Lee to pay his respects. Duty done, he shuffles off to the nearest bar for a vodka (Finlandia), gulps that, orders a refill, and carries it to an adjoining buffet. There he piles a platter with rare roast beef, sliced turkey breast, cherry tomatoes, cukes, and radishes. He also ladles out a bowl of something that looks Chinese. It turns out to be shrimp in lobster sauce, Szechwan style. It makes his scalp sweat.

He does his scarfing in a corner where he can eyeball the parading guests. They're mostly Orientals, but there's a good representation of whiteys and blackies. All are thin, elegantly dressed and, Cone figures, perform no more arduous chores than clipping coupons from their tax-exempt bonds. But that's okay. Life is unfair; everyone knows that.

He finishes his food but is not ready for seconds—yet. He hands the plate to a passing waiter and joins the wanderers, reflecting that occasionally his job does have its perks. He finds a large room, furniture pushed back against the wall, rug rolled up, where a three-piece combo is playing Gershwin, Cole Porter, and Irving Berlin. It's the kind of toe-tapping music Cone enjoys—he hates any song he can't whistle—and he dawdles there awhile watching a few couples dancing on the waxed parquet floor.

Then he repairs to the closest bar and, since no one is going to hand him a tab, asks for a cognac. He's smacking his chops over that when Edward Tung Lee, wearing a dinner jacket, comes swaying up. It doesn't take a sherlock to deduce that the guy is half in the bag.

"So glad you could make it," he says with a crazed smile.

"I'm glad, too," Cone says. "I wish your stepmother would have birthdays more often."

"Did you see what she's wearing?" Edward demands. "Disgusting!"

The Wall Street dick doesn't think so. Claire is tightly enwrapped in a strapless wine-colored velvet gown with bountiful décolletage. There's a star-shaped mouche stuck to her right clavicle, so adroitly placed that the most jaded observer must become a stargazer, an eager student of heavenly bodies. It happened to Cone.

"It's her birthday," he advises Edward. "Let her enjoy."

But the son's anger will not be mollified. "Let her enjoy," he repeats darkly. "The day will come . . ."

With this dire prediction, he weaves away, and Cone is happy to see him go. His hostility toward his stepmother is understandable—but that doesn't make it right. Timothy just doesn't want to get involved.

He has one final sandwich of smoked sturgeon on Jewish rye (seedless), and a portion of ice cream he can't identify. But it's got cut-up cherries and chunks of dark chocolate mixed in. Cleo would love it.

One more brandy, he decides, and when the black bartender asks, "Sir?" Cone grins foolishly and says, "Double cognac, please."

Working on his drink, he goes back to the buffet table and filches some slices of roast beef, baked ham, and sturgeon, which he wraps in a pink linen napkin and slips into his jacket pocket. And he's not the only guest copping tidbits; a lot of the elegant ladies are loading up their handbags.

He's about to search out Chin Tung Lee and make a polite farewell when he feels a soft hand on his arm. He turns to see that velvety star, the beauty patch adhering to skin as creamy as the ice cream he just scoffed.

"Mr. Cone," Claire Lee says with a smile that buckles his knees, "I'm so glad you could make it."

"Happy Birthday," is all he can manage.

"You already wished me a Happy Birthday," she says, laughing. "When you arrived—remember?"

"So?" he says. "Two Happy Birthdays. A dozen."

"Thank you," she says, suddenly grave. "I know that my husband was delighted that you could come. He likes you, Mr. Cone."

"And I like him. A fine gentleman. I was just about to find him and say goodnight."

"No," she says sharply, "not yet. Have you seen our terrace?"

He shakes his head.

"Let me show you," she says, taking his arm.

It turns out not to be a world-class terrace. First of all, it faces eastward with a dead view of the bricked backs of buildings on Madison Avenue. Also, it is narrow—hardly enough room to swing a cat—and the lawn chairs and tables look like castoffs from a summer place in the Hamptons. There are a few hapless geraniums in clay pots.

Still, it is outdoors, and a number of people have found their way there, carrying drinks and plates of food. They seem to enjoy dining alfresco, and the guy in the white dinner jacket snoring gently in one of the rusted chairs is feeling no pain.

Claire leads Cone down to one end, away from the other guests. They stand at the railing, looking down into a paved and poky courtyard. They'd have been wiser to look up at a cloudless sky made luminous by moonlight. It's a soothing night with a blessed breeze and the warm promise of a glorious day to come.

"Did you see Edward?" she asks in a low voice. "The man is drunk."

"Nah," Cone says. "Just a little plotched. He's navigating okay."

"You don't think he'll make a scene, do you?"

"I doubt it."

"My husband worked so hard to make this party a success. I'd hate to have it spoiled."

"It is a success," he assures her, "and nothing's going to spoil it."

She is silent, still gripping his arm. He is conscious of her softness, her warmth. And her scent. It is something tangy, and he has a terrible desire to sneeze.

She is a lofty woman; in her high heels she is as tall as he. She stands erectly, and he wonders if that's her natural posture or if she's just trying to keep her strapless bodice secure. The moonlight paints a pale, silvery sheen on her bare shoulders, and her long, slender arms are as smooth and rounded as if they had been squeezed from tubes. The wheaten hair is braided and up in a coil.

"He hates me," she says quietly. "Edward. I know he does."

Cone doesn't like this. He's a shamus and doesn't do windows or give advice to the lovelorn.

"He's an awful, awful man," Claire Lee goes on, "but I can understand the way he feels. I'm so much younger than Chin. I'm even younger than Edward. Naturally he thinks I'm a gold digger. But I happen to love my husband, Mr. Cone; I swear I do."

"Yeah," he says, acutely uncomfortable.

She takes her arm from under his and turns suddenly to face him. He is proud that he can return her stare and not let his eyeballs drift downward into the valley of the damned.

"You're a detective, aren't you?" she asks, her voice still low but steady and determined.

"Well, my boss calls us investigators. Most of our work is financial stuff. Wall Street shenanigans. I mean, we don't handle burglaries or homicides or crimes like that—"

"But you know *about* them, don't you?"

"Some," he says, totally confused now and waiting to hear what she's getting at.

"Listen," she says, "I need your advice."

"Not me," he says hastily. "If it's something personal, I'm just not qualified. Sorry."

She turns away to peer down into the concrete courtyard again.

"I've got no one else I can talk to," she says.

"No one? What about your husband?"

"No."

"A girlfriend? Family?"

"No one," she repeats.

The wine-colored velvet gown has no back. He can see gently fleshed shoulders, the soft channel of her spine. His weakness makes him angry.

"Just what the hell are you talking about?" he says roughly, then finishes his drink and puts the empty snifter in his pocket.

"I need help," she says, turning her head toward him, the big baby-blues widened and softened with appeal.

He realizes it's a practiced come-on, but he can no more resist it than he could resist that final double cognac.

"What's the problem?" he says in a croaky voice.

"I can't talk about it now," she says, speaking more rapidly. "Not here. You know Restaurant Row?"

"Forty-sixth Street between Eighth and Ninth? Yeah, I know it. Some good take-out joints."

"There's an Italian place called Carpacchio's on the north side of the street, middle of the block. They've got a small bar in the back. It can't be seen from the street. Can you meet me there at three o'clock tomorrow afternoon? The lunch crowd will have cleared out by then."

So she had it all planned, he reflects mournfully, and knew I'd jump. Sucker!

"Sure," he says, "I could do that. Carpacchio's at three tomorrow. I'll be there."

"Oh, thank you," she says breathlessly. "Thank you so much." She leans forward to kiss his cheek fleetingly. "You stay here a minute; I'll go in alone."

"Yeah," he says, "you do that."

He waits a few moments after she's gone, then leaves the Lees' apartment without saying goodnight to the host.

On the drive back home, he tries to con himself by reasoning that all he's doing is helping a damsel in distress. But that won't wash. He wonders if he would have agreed to the meet if Claire was ugly as a toad and caused warts. He knows the answer to that one.

Then he figures that it's possible that whatever her problem is, it just might have something to do with what he's supposed to be investigating: the run-up in the price of White Lotus stock. There's no way he can deny that possibility and no way he can confirm it except by appearing at Carpacchio's at three o'clock tomorrow.

Feeling better about his decision, telling himself it's all business, just business, he climbs the six floors to his loft to find Cleo in an agony of hunger. When he pulls the napkin-wrapped package from his pocket and opens it, the demented animal, sniffing the odors, begins leaping wildly at him, pawing his legs.

Cone tears off bite-sized pieces of beef, ham, and sturgeon and puts them in the cat's dish, a chipped ashtray. Cleo starts gobbling, then stops a moment in the ingestion of these rare delicacies to look up at him in astonishment, as if to say, "How long has *this* been going on?"

He pulls the empty snifter from his other pocket and pours himself a jolt of harsh Italian brandy for a nightcap. He sucks on it slowly, sitting at his table, feet up, trying to imagine what the lady could want. He thinks about possible motives for a long time, and then realizes his primal urge has cooled.

There's something more, or less, to Claire Lee than a goddess. She was rehearsed and knowing. Very sure of her physical weapons and how to use them. Nothing wrong with that except his vision of her is shattered. But it's not the first time his hot dreams have been chilled. He can endure it.

But what, in God's name, could Claire Lee *want*? Considering that, he looks down to see Cleo crouched at the table. The cat's dish is empty, and the ravenous beast, mouth slightly open, is staring at him with a feral grin that seems to be saying, "More, more, more!"

3

He spends the morning at the office, groaning over the composition of the weekly progress report that each of the five Haldering & Co. investigators is required to submit. With Samantha on vacation, the reports will go to Hiram Haldering himself, known to his employees as the Abominable Abdomen.

Cone composes what he considers a masterpiece of obfuscation. It hints, it implies, it suggests, and is such an incomprehensible mishmash that he figures it'll send Hiram right up the wall. The report ends: "Will the White Lotus investigation be brought to a successful conclusion? Only time will tell."

Satisfied with his literary creation, he tosses it onto the receptionist's desk and flees the office. He stops at a nearby umbrella stand for a Coney Island red-hot with mustard, onions, and piccalilli, washed down with cherry cola. Eructing slightly, he pokes back to his loft. But instead of going up, he finds his Ford Escort, unticketed and with hubcaps intact, and drives uptown.

Parking anywhere near the Times Square area is murder, and he has to go over Forty-fourth Street and Tenth Avenue before he discovers an empty slot. He walks back to Restaurant Row, pausing en route to buy a lemon ice from a sidewalk vendor and watch the action at a three-card monte game. The dealer is really slick, and Cone, making mental bets, loses fifty imaginary dollars.

He gets to Carpacchio's on West Forty-sixth Street about twenty minutes early, figuring it'll give him a chance to have a drink and scope the place. But when he enters and walks to the back, Claire Lee is already there, sitting alone at the little bar and working on something green in a stemmed glass.

The only other people in the dim restaurant are six waiters having their late lunch at a big table up front. Cone takes off his cap and slides onto the barstool next to Claire. She gives him a thousand-watt smile.

"I was afraid you wouldn't show up," she says.

"I told you I would," he says gruffly. "What do I have to do to get a drink in this joint?"

She swings around to face the table of waiters. "Carlos," she calls. "Please. Just for a minute."

One of the guys rises, throws down his napkin, comes back to the bar. He isn't happy at having his lunch interrupted.

"Yeah?" he says.

"Could I have another of these, please. And my guest will have— what?"

"Vodka rocks," Cone says. "And you better give me a double so you don't have to stop eating again."

Carlos shoots him a surly look but serves them, then returns to the noisy table up front.

"A real charmer," Cone says.

"Carlos isn't angry at waiting on us during his lunch. He just doesn't like seeing me with another man."

"Oh-ho," Cone says. "It's like that, is it?"

She takes a cigarette from a platinum case. He holds a match for that and his own Camel, noticing that her fingers are trembling slightly.

She looks smashing in a printed silk shirtwaist with a rope belt. Her hat is enormous: a horizontal white linen spinnaker. It would look ridiculous on a smaller woman, but she wears it with all the aplomb of a nun in a starched wimple.

"Lovely day, isn't it?" she says.

"Oh, my, yes," Cone says. "And here it is Wednesday, and don't the weeks just fly by."

She stares at him, outraged, then tries a weak grin. "I guess I deserved that. But it's hard to explain why I asked you to meet me."

"Just say it. Get it over with."

"Yes, well, I'm afraid it's a confession. I hope I can trust you, Mr. Cone. If not, I'm dead."

"I don't blab."

"First of all, I want to hire you, Mr. Cone."

"I told you," he says patiently, "I've got a job. Financial investigations. If what you want comes under that heading, then you'll have to make a deal with my boss."

"Then I want your advice," she says, looking at him directly. "Will you give me that?"

"Sure. Advice is free."

"Before I married my husband, I was living in California. I was very young and hadn't been around much. I went to Los Angeles hoping to get in the movies or television."

"You and a zillion others."

"I found that out. Everyone told me I had the looks. I don't want to sound conceited, but I thought I did, too. Prettier than a lot of girls who made it. And a better figure."

"I'll buy that," he says.

"What I didn't have," she goes on, "and don't have, is talent. I did one test and it was a disaster. My aunt, my closest relative, sent me the money for acting school. I tried, I really did, but it didn't help. I just couldn't act or sing or dance. Have you ever been to southern California, Mr. Cone?"

"Yeah, I spent some time there."

"Then you know what it's like. Life in the fast lane. Sunshine. Beaches. Partying. Twenty-four-hour fun."

"If you've got the loot."

She drains her first green drink and takes a little sip of the second. "Exactly," she says. "If you've got the loot. I ran out. And I couldn't ask my aunt for more."

"Why didn't you go home?"

"To Toledo? No, thanks. No surfing in Toledo. And it would have been admitting defeat, wouldn't it?"

"I've done that," he tells her. "It's not so bad."

"Well, I couldn't. So, to make a long story short, I ended up in a house in San Francisco. Not a home—a house. You understand?"

"I get the picture," he says.

"Don't tell me there were a lot of other things I could have done: sell lingerie in a department store, marry a nebbish, go on welfare. I know all that, and knew it then. But I wanted big bucks."

He doesn't reply.

She is silent a moment, and he stares at her, wondering how much of her story is for real and how much is bullshit. Her face reflects the innocence of Little Orphan Annie, but he suspects that inside she's got a good dollop of Madame Defarge.

Her nose is small and pert. A short upper lip reveals a flash of white teeth. The complexion is satiny, and if she's wearing makeup it's scantily applied. He finds something curiously dated in her beauty; she could be a flapper: She's got that vibrant look as if at any moment she might climb atop the bar and launch into a wild Charleston that would shiver his timbers.

"So?" he says, wanting to hear all of it. "Now you're in a house in San Francisco. A cathouse."

"That's right," she says, lifting her chin. "In Chinatown. It was called the Pleasure Dome. Very expensive. It catered mostly to Oriental gentlemen. It was run very strictly. No drugs, believe it or not, and no drunks tolerated. We accepted credit cards."

"Beautiful. Were you the only white in the place?"

"There were two of us. The other girls were mostly Chinese, some very young, from Taiwan."

"And you made the big bucks?"

"I surely did. I had my own apartment, a gorgeous wardrobe, and for the first time in my life I had money in the bank. I even filed a tax return. In the place where you have to put in your occupation, I wrote Physical Therapist."

"I'll drink to that," Cone says, and does. "How long were you there?"

"Almost two years. Then the place was raided and closed down."

"Oh? Local cops?"

"No, FBI. According to the newspaper stories, the Pleasure Dome was part of a chain of fancy houses owned and operated by some Chinese gang."

"Uh-huh. Were you charged?"

"I wasn't caught. I lucked out. On the weekend the place was busted, I was up in Seattle with a Chinese gentleman who was on a business trip. They let us do that occasionally—take short trips with some of the wealthier clients. The tips were great. Anyway, I got back to Frisco on Monday and discovered I was out of a job. More important, the other girls who had been picked up during the raid were still in jail. It turned out that most of them were here illegally and would be deported. I decided the smart thing would be to put distance between me and the Pleasure Dome. In one day I closed out my bank account, packed my favorite clothes, and got a plane to New York."

He looks up at her admiringly. "No flies on you," he says.

"I've learned," she says. "The hard way. But I did all right. I had some names to look up in New York."

"Chinese gentlemen?"

She looks at him sharply but can see no irony in his face or hear sarcasm in his voice. "That's right," she says. "Old friends. Then, about three years ago, I was introduced to Chin Tung Lee. He was and is the sweetest, dearest, most sympathetic and understanding man I've ever met. His wife had died, and he didn't want to live out his life with just that miserable son of his for company. Chin is almost three times my age, but when he asked me to marry him, I said yes,"

"You were tired of the game?" Cone guesses.

"Yes, I was tired."

"And Chin was wealthy."

She shows anger for the first time. "What the hell did that have to do with it? All my friends were wealthy, but I had enough money in the bank to tell any one of them to get lost—and I did it, too, on a couple of occasions. I don't care what you may think; I didn't marry Chin for his money."

"Okay, okay," Cone says, "I'll take your word for it. Did you tell him any of your past history before you married him?"

"No."

"Did he ever ask?"

"Once. I made up some stuff about teaching school in Ohio."

"Sounds like a happy ending to me," the Wall Street dick says. "So what am I doing here listening to your soap opera?

What's your problem?"

She sighs and opens an alligator handbag that probably cost more than Cone makes in a week. She pulls out an envelope and hands it over.

"I got this in the mail last Friday," she says. "Take a look."

He inspects the long white envelope. Addressed to Mrs. Claire Lee at their Fifth Avenue apartment. No return address. Postmarked New York. Cone looks at her. "You sure you want me to read this?"

"That's why I'm here," she says determinedly.

It's a single sheet of white paper folded in thirds. Two lines of type-writing: "Remember the Pleasure Dome? We have the photographs."

Cone reads it again and looks up at her.

"Blackmail?" she asks.

"Sounds like. What photographs do they mean?"

"No porn, if that's what you're thinking. But on the Chinese New Year we always had a big party at the Pleasure Dome. Free food and booze for our best clients. All of us girls would be there. Fully clothed, of course. Maybe our gowns would be low-cut or very short, but all our bits and pieces were covered. It was just a big, noisy party, and pictures would be taken as souvenirs for the clients. Those were the only photographs taken in the Pleasure Dome as far as I can recall."

Timothy stares at her. "You may have learned the hard way, as you say, but I wonder if you learned enough. When you had a scene with a customer at the Pleasure Dome, where did you take him?"

"Upstairs. To one of the bedrooms. They were beautifully decorated and furnished."

"I'll bet. Mirrors on the walls?"

"Of course."

He gives her a cold smile. She returns his stare, her face becoming as white and stiff as her hat. "Jesus!" she gasps. "You don't think they took photos through the mirrors, do you?"

Cone shrugs. "It's been done before. It's a smart move for any guy who runs a kip. First of all, it helps keep his girls in line. Second, he can always sell the photographs or videotapes to jerks who get their jollies from that kind of stuff. And third, the possibility of blackmail is always there. So he shoots the action through a two-way mirror and builds up a nice file that his girls and clients don't know about. He can lean on them anytime he wants."

"Oh, my God," Claire Lee says despairingly, "what am I going to do?"

"Right now? Nothing. This is just the opening move. A blackmailer wants the victim to sweat a little first, lose sleep, think of nothing but what it's going to cost to keep the secret hidden. Have you been sleeping since you got the letter?"

"With pills."

"There you are. You're getting nervous already, anxious enough to tell me about it, and you don't even know what the blackmailer's got and what he wants for it. You'll get another letter, Mrs. Lee, with maybe a sample photograph attached. Then you'll get more letters, spelling out exactly what you'll have to pay. You have any idea who might be pulling this?"

"No. Not the slightest. Isn't there anything you can do to stop it?"

"Nope. This first letter is completely innocent. Take it to the cops and they'll laugh. You haven't been threatened—yet. This is only the opening move in a dirty game. You'll just have to play it out. Mrs. Lee, why don't you let me keep this letter."

"Why do you want it if you can't do anything?"

"So you don't keep reading it and driving yourself nuts. How many times have you looked at it already? A dozen? A hundred? A thousand times?"

"At least," she says with a wan smile. "All right, you take it."

"Let me know when the second letter arrives," Cone says. "Because you're going to get another; I guarantee it."

She finishes her drink. "You know, Mr. Cone," she says, "I feel better just telling you about it. I guess confession really is good for the soul."

"Is it?" he says. "I wouldn't know."

He drains his vodka and stands up. "Keep in touch," he says, trying to keep it light. "And thanks for the drink."

He walks slowly toward the outside door and pauses to pull on his cap. He glances back. Carlos, the waiter, is already at her side. The two are talking earnestly, their heads so close together that the guy is practically standing under her broad-brimmed hat.

He's back in the loft before five o'clock, nods at Cleo, and immediately gets on the horn to Johnnie Wong at the Federal Bureau of Investigation.

"Can I buy you a drink?" he asks.

"Hey, old buddy," Wong says, "that's the best bribe I've had all day. Where?"

"How about my place?"

"Sounds good. How do I find it?"

Cone laughs. "If you've got my unlisted phone number, you've got to have my address. If you can get here before six, the downstairs door will be open and the elevator will be working. I'm on the top floor, a loft."

"I'll find you."

Cone gives Cleo fresh water, half a can of human-type tuna, and sits back to review that wacky conversation with Claire Lee.

He can't for the life of him think of any reason why she would make up a history like that. And after all, it wasn't so unusual that it couldn't be true. But what was her motive for telling Cone, practically a stranger, all the squalid details of her past when, according to her, she hadn't even told her husband?

Cone decides he'll buy her story. The lady is terrified—or at least badly spooked. She can't ask help from Chin or Edward Lee, and apparently has no close friends she can consult. So she picks the only guy in the law enforcement business she knows. Looking at it from that angle, her confession makes a crazy kind of sense.

He pulls the letter from his pocket and reads it again. "Remember the Pleasure Dome? We have the photographs." That tells him exactly nothing, unless Claire's horror was feigned when he told her about a camera clicking away through a two-way mirror. Maybe she had willingly posed for centerfolds with men, women, donkeys, and dalmatians. That would account for her fear of a letter that apparently said zip.

He is still trying to puzzle out what's going on in that beautiful head, and wondering about the extent of her chicanery or absence thereof, when there's a sharp rapping on the door. He moves to one side of the jamb.

"Yeah?" he calls. "Who is it?"

"Johnnie Wong."

Cone unchains, unbolts, unlocks the door. The FBI man comes in, flashing his toothy grin. He takes a look around the place.

"Holy Christ!" he says. "You live here? If I were you, I'd sleep in the office. What's that thing under the bathtub?"

"Cleo, my cat," Cone says. "Listen, this joint's not so bad. It was neat and clean when I moved in, but I grunged it up a little to make it livable."

"You call this livable? It's the biggest Roach Motel I've ever seen. Where's that drink you promised me?"

They sit on opposite sides of the table. Wong has a beer. "No, thanks," he says when Cone offers a jelly jar. "I'll drink it right out of the can. That way the worst thing that can happen to me is a cut lip." He takes a gulp, then looks at the Wall Street dick thoughtfully. "Okay, you didn't ask me up to admire the interior decoration. What do you want?"

"I told you Haldering was hired to investigate the run-up in the price of White Lotus stock. I've got a list of the shareholders here. There're more than two thousand names, so I don't expect you to study the whole printout. But would you take a quick look and see if you recognize any of the names."

"Oh, God," Johnnie Wong says, sighing. "This I've got to do for a free beer? All right, let me see the damned thing."

He flips through the pages swiftly, then goes back to the first and starts again, slower this time. Cone sits silently until Wong tosses the list aside.

"Interesting," the FBI man says. "The second time I went through it, I looked for people with big holdings, a thousand shares or more."

"You recognize any of the names?"

"About a half-dozen. They're all members of the Giant Panda gang."

The two men stare at each other a moment.

"What does that mean?" Cone asks.

"Beats the hell out of me," Johnnie says. "I guess it means that Giant Panda is assembling a heavy position in White Lotus stock. But for what reason, the deponent knoweth not. Got any ideas?"

"Not a one," Cone says fretfully. "They're a long way from having control of the corporation. And the stock pays five percent. That's a nice return for legitimate equity investors, but it's bupkes for a criminal gang."

"Well," Wong says, "it's your problem. Now do you figure I've paid for my brew, or have you got something for me?"

Cone admires the guy. He's a no-horseshit operator, cards on the table, everything up front. Timothy figures he better give him something if he wants the agent on his side.

"I've got a weirdie for you," he says. "It may be a bone or there may be some meat to it. Ever hear of a cathouse in San Francisco called the Pleasure Dome?"

Wong is about to take a swallow of his beer, but he stops and puts the can back on the table.

"The Pleasure Dome," he repeats. "How in God's name did you come up with that one? Have I ever heard of it? You bet your sweet patootie I have. I was stationed in Frisco when we busted the joint. What a palace that was! White girls, blacks, Chinese, Koreans, Hispanics, Japanese. It was a House of All Nations. Very exclusive. Very expensive. No sailors allowed. How do you know about the Pleasure Dome?"

"It just came up in conversation," Cone says. "Who owned the joint?"

The FBI man shoves his beer away and stands up. "Okay," he says, "you wanna play hard to get, so be it. Don't call me again."

"Wait a minute," Cone says. "Let me think."

"Yeah," Wong says, sitting down again, "you do that."

He is quiet then, sipping his suds slowly, his eyes on Cone.

The Wall Street dick knows that he needs this guy. He's got a pipeline into the Asian underworld that Cone could never match. Secretiveness is Cone's nature, but here's a case where it could work against him, make his job twice as hard, if not impossible. He ponders a long time, trying to decide where his loyalties belong. How much does he owe the client? And the client's wife?

"Who owned the Pleasure Dome?" he asks again, trying one last time.

Wong gives him a mocking grin. "Trade last," he says. "Who told you about the place?"

Cone gives up, figuring he's got no choice. "A woman named Claire," he says. "Ring any bells?"

"Good God, this is like pulling teeth. What's Claire's last name?"

Cone hesitates a beat or two, then realizes he's in for a penny, he might as well be in for a pound. "Lee," he tells Wong. "Claire Lee. She claims she worked in the Pleasure Dome."

"So? She might have; a lot of women worked there. What's your interest?"

"She happens to be the wife of Chin Tung Lee, the CEO and largest shareholder of White Lotus."

"Oh, boy," the FBI man says with a grin. "The shit is beginning to hit the fan, old buddy."

"How so?"

"Because the Pleasure Dome was owned by the United Bamboo mob. It was one of the string of whorehouses they operated up and down the West Coast. So now let's recap . . . Giant Panda is buying into White Lotus. And the wife of the bossman at White Lotus once worked in a crib owned by United Bamboo. What do you make of that?"

"Nothing," Cone says. "I can't figure it."

Johnnie Wong leans across the table, thrusting his face close to Cone's. "You wouldn't be holding out on me, would you?"

"Not me. I'm just as flummoxed as you are."

The FBI man sits back, then slaps the tabletop with a smack of his palm that brings Cleo growling out from under the tub.

"Damn!" Wong says angrily. "I told you I felt in my stones that something is going down. I pick up rumors and get tips from my snitches. The big guns of United Bamboo and Giant Panda are in town. A lot of meetings. A lot of comings and goings. That murder of Chen Chang Wang. And now this business with White Lotus. Something's cooking. Maybe a full-scale gang war. Maybe just a fight for the New York territory. Who the hell knows? Listen, if you get anything, give me a shout. Even if you think it's not important. I'll do the same with you. I'd like to stop these assholes before they start shooting up Manhattan. Keep in touch, and thanks for the beer."

"Anytime," Cone says.

After Wong leaves, Cone goes into the kitchenette and starts heating up a can of corned beef hash. He wonders if he spilled too much in revealing the identity of Claire Lee. He decides not. After all, he didn't say a word about the blackmail letter.

Because the FBI agent has no need to know. Not yet.

Cone spends Thursday morning in the office making a series of desultory phone calls on those two tedious files he was assigned. It's donkeywork, and while he's talking to people and scribbling notes, he's thinking about the White Lotus affair and remembering how great Claire Lee looked in her spinnaker hat. The life she's led hasn't raddled her beauty; she looks untouched by human hands.

Maybe, Cone imagines, she sold her soul to the Devil in exchange for eternal youth. He'd be willing to sign a contract like that, but the Devil has never asked him.

He finally gets all he needs to close out the two cases. The shlumpf who fell for the miniature horse scam ain't going to get his money back. And the two plastic manufacturers can merge with confidence and live happily ever after. *Sic transit* . . .

He's smoking his fourth cigarette of the day, scanning the stock tables in *The New York Times*, when his phone rings. He stares at it a moment, then puts his newspaper aside and picks it up, thinking it might be the Devil calling, ready to make a deal.

"Yeah?" he says.

"Mr. Cone, this is Edward Tung Lee. How are you this morning?"

"Surviving."

"I'm going to be in your neighborhood shortly and wondered if I could stop by your office for a few minutes. There's something I'd like to discuss with you."

"Sure," Cone says, "come ahead. I'll be here."

Lee arrives in less than ten minutes, which makes Cone think the guy called from around the corner; there's no way he could have made it from Exchange Place that quickly.

He's dressed as dapperly as he was at Ah Sing's Bar & Grill, this time in a gray silk suit that glints like a newly minted silver dollar. But the breezy self-confidence is dented; he's got the jits. That high, broad brow is sheened with sweat, and he can't stop twisting his gold bracelet around and around.

He slumps into the chair facing Cone's desk with no digs about the claustrophobic office.

"First of all," he starts off, "I want to thank you for not telling my father that you and I were at Ah Sing's when Chen Chang Wang was killed."

"Yeah, well, since you hadn't told him, I figured you must have a good reason."

"I didn't want to upset the old man," Lee says earnestly. "He and Chen were friends from way back."

"Uh-huh," Cone says. "But he must have read about it; all the papers carried it. And I suppose it was on local TV."

"Oh, he knows about it, but I didn't want to be the one to tell him."

"Sure," Cone says.

"About your investigation," Lee goes on. He plucks a white handkerchief from his breast pocket and dabs at his forehead. "Hot day."

"Yeah," Cone says. "Usually is in summer."

Lee ignores that. "About your investigation," he continues. "Have you been getting anywhere?"

"Not really," Cone says. "I had a couple of other files I had to work on."

"Well, I'm sure you'll find it's just the way I explained at Ah Sing's: normal market activity, a flight to quality."

"Could be," Cone says. "I see where White Lotus was up another seven-eighths yesterday. Heavy volume for a stock with your capitalization."

"Just a blip," Edward says. "Nothing to it."

The Wall Street dick makes no reply, waiting for this Nervous Nellie to speak his piece.

"Actually," Lee says, swabbing his brow again, "what I wanted to talk to you about has nothing to do with White Lotus. It's more of, ah, a personal matter."

"Oh?" Cone says, wondering when he was ordained and became a father confessor. "What's that?"

"It's silly, really," the man says with a shaky smile. "Probably nothing to it."

Cone waits silently, giving him no help at all. If this guy, he thinks, tells me he once worked at the Pleasure Dome, I'm going to toss his ass out of here.

"As you probably know," Lee plunges ahead, "I live in my father's apartment. But I have my own suite with a private entrance. I also have my own phone, an unlisted number. Last Friday night, at about eleven o'clock, I was reading when the phone rang. A man's voice asked, 'Edward Tung Lee?' I said yes, and he said, 'We know about the Bedlington.' And then he hung up. Well, naturally I thought it was just a crank call. But it did worry me that he had my unlisted number and called me by my full name."

"Recognize the voice?" Cone asks.

"No," Lee says. "A BBC English accent, but beneath that I thought I heard something else. Perhaps a Chinese educated in England. A singsong quality you learn to recognize."

"I get it," Cone says. "Instead of emphasizing a syllable, you change the pitch of your voice."

Lee looks at him in astonishment. "How on earth did you know that?"

"I remember a lot of useless stuff," Cone says. "So the guy said, 'We know about the Bedlington.' Then he hung up. Right?"

"Yes, that's correct. Then, last night, he called again. Same voice. He said, as nearly as I can recall, 'About the Bedlington, you'll be hearing from us.'"

"You're sure he said 'us' and not 'you'll be hearing from 'me'?"

"No, he said 'us.' And on the first call, he said, 'We know about the Bedlington.'"

"Uh-huh," Cone says.

"Does the name Bedlington mean anything to you?" Edward asks.

"Sure," Cone says, all wide-eyed innocence. "It's a dog, a terrier."

Lee gives a short honk of laughter. "True," he says. "It also happens to be a hotel on Madison Avenue. About three blocks from my apartment. From my father's apartment."

"So?"

"Well, ah, as you probably know, I am not married. But, hah!—that doesn't mean I must live like a monk—right? So, on occasion, I have taken a woman to the Hotel Bedlington. You've shacked up with women in a hotel or motel, haven't you?"

"Not recently," Cone says.

"Well, I do. I have an understanding with the desk clerk at the Bedlington. Everything is handled very discreetly. I mean, I have no wild parties or anything like that. I've had absolutely no problems until I got those stupid phone calls."

"How long you been using the Bedlington for fun and games?"

"Oh, about two years now."

"You trust the desk clerk?"

"Completely. He'd never try to blackmail me."

"What makes you think it's blackmail? You're over twenty-one. So you're having a toss in the hay with a consenting adult. Big deal. Your playmates *were* adults, weren't they?"

"Of course," Edward says, offended.

"Well, then? How can anyone blackmail you? What are you worried about?"

Lee shifts uncomfortably in the creaky armchair. "It's my father, d'ya see," he says. "He's from the old school. Very straitlaced. I know that if he found out, there'd be hell to pay."

Cone shrugs. "Sounds thin to me," he tells Lee. "You've got a right to live your own life. If those phone calls are having you bananas, why don't you go to your father, confess all, ask for his forgiveness, and promise to be a good little boy in the future. He impresses me as being a very shrewd, intelligent man. He's lived a long life, and I'd guess he's seen everything and probably done more than you realize. I just can't see him making a federal case out of your occasional bangs at the Bedlington."

"You just don't know him," Lee says in a low voice. "He can be a very vindictive man when he's angered."

"Well," Cone says, "I don't see that there's a helluva lot you can do about it. You could have your private number changed, but they'd just call you at the office."

"And there's nothing *you* can do about it?"

"Like what?"

"Find out who's behind it."

Cone shakes his head. "Not on the basis of what you've told me. I could get someone to put a tap on your phone and record the calls—but what good would that do? If the guy only talks for a minute or two, the chances of tracing the call are zero. The only thing I can suggest is this: If it *is* blackmail, sooner or later your mystery caller is going to tell you how much he wants and how it's to be delivered. If it's a person-to-person payoff, I can handle it for you and maybe collar the guy or at least get a line on him. If the payoff is to be made by drop or by mail, it'll still give a possible lead. Right now we've got nothing."

"Then if I do get another call and I let you know, can I depend on your help?"

"Sure."

"Thank you!" Edward Tung Lee cries fervently. He rises and leans across the desk to pump Cone's hand. "I can't tell you what a load you've taken off my mind. Thank you!"

After he's gone, Cone lights another Camel, leans back, parks his feet on the desk. That had to be, he reflects, one of the sleaziest stories he's ever heard in his life. It's got more holes than a wheel of Emmentaler. The only reason he's giving it a second thought is that the guy who called Edward Lee said, "*We* know about the Bedlington." And the guy who sent the letter to Claire Lee wrote: "*We* have the photographs."

That's interesting.

4

On Thursday evening Timothy Cone ambles up Broadway at a leisurely pace, stopping in bars twice en route to have a beer and smoke a cigarette. He can't get Edward Lee's fish story out of his mind. It may have elements of truth in it, but it also has gaps big enough to drive a Mack truck through.

For instance, if Edward wants to make nice-nice with a tootsie, why doesn't he invite her up to his apartment? He's got a private entrance, hasn't he?

And that business of dreading his father's wrath is so much kaka. Chin Tung Lee may be old and straitlaced, but Cone can't believe he'd go into an Oriental snit upon discovering that his Number One son likes to get his ashes hauled occasionally.

No, Edward isn't Telling All. His report of the phone calls may be legit, but Cone would bet the family farm that those calls are making Edward sweat for a more significant reason than fear of shocking dear old dad.

It's a creamy night, pillow soft, with a clear sky and a teasing breeze. Stars are beginning to pop out, and a waning moon is still strong enough to silver the city. Cone hates to go up to the loft, but figures he'll eat, feed the cat, and later do a little more pub crawling if the mood is on him.

His phone is ringing when he enters, and he kicks Cleo out of the way to get to it.

"Yeah?" he says.

"Hello, asshole," Samantha Whatley says. "I figured I better call you early before you started pub crawling."

"Nah," he says. "Farthest from my thoughts. How are you?"

"Eating up a storm. Mom is stuffing me. I've gained three pounds so far, all in the wrong places. How are things at the office?"

"Okay."

"Hiram giving you any problems?"

"Not me. I'm keeping out of his way."

"I spoke to him this afternoon. He says you're working on some Chinese thing."

"Yeah, I'm up to my tail in chop suey."

"Anything exciting?"

"Not very," Cone says.

"Jesus, you're a chatty sonofabitch," Sam says. "Cutting down on your smoking?"

"Trying to," he says, fumbling the pack out of his jacket pocket and shaking a cigarette free.

"And how's that miserable cat?"

"Hungry. When are you coming back?"

"A week from tomorrow. But I'll be in late. See you on Saturday?"

"Sure," he says, "sounds good."

"Take care," she says lightly.

"Yeah," he says. "You, too."

"That was Sam," he tells Cleo after he hangs up. "She says to give you her best."

He inspects the contents of the refrigerator. It's famine time. There's a half-can of tuna, a couple of odds and ends of this and that, but nothing to *eat*. He gives Cleo the tuna and fresh water, then heads out again.

"Be back soon," he promises the cat, "but don't wait up."

There's a Greek joint around the corner that's usually open till nine o'clock. Cone calls it the Ptomaine Palace. "The food is poisonous," he once told Samantha, "but the portions are big."

He sits on a stool at the Formica counter and orders a bowl of lamb stew with rye bread and a bottle of Heineken. He finds a few shreds of lamb floating in the viscid gravy, but there are chunks of potatoes, carrots, celery, and onions. He uses a lot of salt and pepper and fills up, which is all he asks of any meal.

He finishes by sopping puddles of gravy with pieces of bread. Before he leaves, he orders another lamb stew to go, figuring it'll keep Cleo happy for at least a couple of days. It's poured into a Styrofoam container and put into a brown paper bag.

Carrying that, he heads back for the loft. He's on Broadway, close to home, when two short guys step out of a doorway and crowd him. They're both wearing black trousers and gray alpaca jackets. He makes them as young Chinese.

"You are Mr. Timothy Cone?" one of them asks.

"Not me, friend," Cone says. "I'm Simon Legree from Tennessee."

There's a rapid jabber of Chinese, then the other man stoops swiftly and runs his hands down Cone's shins. He plucks the .357 magnum from the ankle holster and hands it to his partner.

"So you are Timothy Cone," the speaker states. "Come this way, please."

Since he's now waving the S&W, Timothy goes along, still carrying the lamb stew. They lead him to an old, black, bulge-bodied Buick, a real doctor's car. There's a third Chinese sitting behind the wheel. They get Cone in the wide back seat, between the two men who took him.

"I must blindfold you now," the leader says. "So sorry."

The blindfold is white, padded, and is put on so slickly that Cone figures it's got to be fastened with Velcro. The car starts up.

"Nice night for a drive," he offers, but no one answers, and after that he doesn't try any chitchat.

He lets his body go slack, feeling gravity and momentum, swaying slightly when the car takes a corner. He tries to imagine the route. A right-hand turn, a straightaway with the Buick accelerating, then slowing to make another right. Now we're around the block and heading uptown, he guesses.

He can't get a glimmer through that thick bandage over his eyes, but he can hear traffic noises change as they pass crossstreets. He counts the number of blocks, and when the Buick veers slightly to the left, he estimates they're about at Fourteenth Street. They pause awhile, probably for a traffic light, then make a left turn. Heavier traffic noise now, and Cone thinks it's got to be a wide east-west street, either Fourteenth or Twenty-third.

The car slows after traveling for about four minutes, and Cone sways as it turns to the right. They go down an incline, and the Buick's engine takes on a reverberant sound, almost like an echo. An underground garage, Cone decides. The car comes to a stop, a back door is opened. He's helped out, gently, no rough stuff, and still carrying his lamb stew, is led about twenty feet, hands gripping both his arms. He scuffs his work shoes on concrete and smells gas and oil fumes. Now he's convinced it's an underground parking garage.

The men holding him press closer, and the three of them slow, stop, wait a minute. Sound of elevator door opening. Forward, with a smoother floor under his feet: tile or linoleum. Metallic sound of elevator door closing. Then they go up, and Cone silently counts off seconds: A hundred and one, a hundred and two, a hundred and three... He's figuring two seconds per floor; the elevator stops at 118. The doors swish open, he's ushered out.

Now he's walking on a rug, springy beneath his feet. A long walk and Cone, counting his paces, estimates forty feet at least. His captors are no longer pressing him, so it's got to be a wide corridor. A hotel maybe? No, they wouldn't run the risk of bumping into guests while hustling a blindfolded man.

They halt. Three sharp raps on wood. Small squeak of a door opening. Cone's pulled forward, stumbling a bit on thicker pile carpeting, maybe a deep shag. Around a corner. He's thrust forward, hands on his back. Stop. A fast spatter of Chinese. Then...

A precise voice: "Mr. Cone, what is that you are carrying?"

"Lamb stew," he says. "You can have some if you like."

There's a snap of fingers. The brown paper bag is taken, and Cone hears the crinkle of paper, the pop of the lid coming off the Styrofoam container.

"You are right," the voice says, "it is lamb stew. It looks and smells dreadful."

"It's not so bad," Cone protests. "It's filling."

"Mr. Cone, I must apologize for this unconventional method of making your acquaintance. I trust you were not physically harmed."

"Nah," Cone says, "your guys did a nice job. Can you take the blindfold off now?"

"I fear that would be most unwise. And please do not try to remove it yourself. There are two very quick men standing behind you, both of them armed."

"Okay," Cone says, "I'll be good."

"Excellent. This will only take a few moments, and then you will be returned to your home. Mr. Cone, I understand you are investigating the increase in the price of White Lotus stock."

"Where did you hear that?" Cone says. Then: "Listen, if we're going to have a confab, could I sit down?"

"I prefer you remain standing," the voice says sharply. "I am not going to ask you to terminate your investigation, Mr. Cone. I know you are an employee of Haldering and Company, and have been assigned to the case. All I am asking is that you delay your inquiries for perhaps another week. Two weeks at the most. Surely you could do that without insurmountable objections from your employer."

"Maybe I could," Cone says. "But why should I?"

"Because I request it," the voice says with a silky undertone. "In return, naturally, you may expect to profit."

"Yeah?" Cone says. "How much?"

"Five thousand dollars. In small, unmarked bills."

"Forget it. I work for a salary. It's not king-sized, but it's enough."

"Come, Mr. Cone," the voice says softly, "it is never enough. We all want more, do we not?"

"I got enough," Cone insists stubbornly.

"And there is nothing in this world you want?"

"Yeah, I've always wanted to screw a contortionist. It's something I've dreamed about for a long time."

The voice gives a chuff of laughter, then rips off some Chinese, and the two men standing behind Cone also laugh.

"That could be arranged, Mr. Cone," the voice says dryly.

"Just kidding," Cone says. "Listen, I don't like standing here with this shmatteh over my eyes, so let's get down to the nitty-gritty. If I refuse to stall on this White Lotus thing, what happens then?"

"Please do not ask me to say it."

"Go ahead; say it."

"Then I am afraid we shall have to kill you, Mr. Cone."

"Okay," the Wall Street dick says cheerfully. "As long as I know where I stand. Give me a chance to think about your cash offer—all right?"

"How long?"

"A week."

"Three days," the voice says sternly. "Then we must come looking for you. You can run, but you cannot hide."

"Good line," Cone says, "but it's not yours. Joe Louis. Can I go home now?"

"We shall contact you on Monday, and expect your answer at that time. Yes, you may go now."

"Can I take my stew?"

"Please do."

"And how about my piece?"

"Your piece?"

"My gun. Revolver. Your guys lifted it."

"Your weapon will be returned to you, Mr. Cone. Thank you for your kind cooperation."

There's a long chatter of Chinese. The brown paper bag is thrust into his hands, he is gripped, and the film starts running in reverse: Around the corner, across the shag rug, through the door, along the corridor, down in the elevator to the garage, into the car, and then the drive back. Cone, counting to himself, figures it takes about fifteen minutes.

The car stops, he's helped out, still carrying his lamb stew. The blindfold is whisked away. He stands there, blinking.

There's another rat-a-tat of Chinese between the two alpaca jackets. One turns and starts walking south on Broadway toward the corner. The speaker is now armed with a sleek 9mm Luger, which he waves at Cone.

"Your revolver will be left on the sidewalk," he explains. "Please do not attempt to reclaim it until we have left, or we will be forced to return."

Through bleary eyes Cone watches the other guy place his magnum on the pavement near a fire alarm box. Then he returns, and the two young Chinese climb into the car.

"Good night, Mr. Cone," the leader calls, and the Buick accelerates, turns the corner with a chirp of tires, and is gone.

Cone goes down to the corner and reclaims his iron. He inspects it quickly under a streetlight. It looks okay. Still loaded. He slips it into his jacket pocket. Then he walks slowly back to his building. But before going upstairs, he stands a moment on the deserted street.

It has been a scarifying experience, being blind. He doesn't want to go through that again. Now he can see the haloed glimmer of the streetlight, see the gleaming gutters of his city and, looking upward, see the glittering stars whirling their ascending courses. A blessing. More than that: a physical delight. Almost a thrill.

Up in the loft, he pours some of the gelatinous stew into Cleo's dish. The happy cat goes to work on it immediately. Cone goes to work on a stiff shot of brandy while he undresses, staring with new eyes at Cleo, the loft, furniture, everything.

He strips to his skivvies, turns out the lights, and rolls onto his floor mattress.

"Now for a lot of Z's," he calls to the cat, but all he gets in reply is the noisy slurping of lamb stew.

He's still in his skivvies when he phones Johnnie Wong on Friday morning.

"Don't tell me you're in the office already," the FBI man says.

"On my way," Cone says. "Listen, you told me to contact you if anything happened, even if I didn't think it was important. Okay, something happened; I got taken for a ride."

"Well, you're talking to me so it couldn't have been a one-way trip."

Timothy describes the events of the previous evening. Wong listens without interrupting. Then, when Cone is finished, he says, "Could you ID the two foot soldiers who picked you up?"

"I doubt it."

"I know," Johnnie says. "We all look alike to you blue-eyes."

"Not me; my eyes are shit-brown."

"What about the boss?"

"I'd make him for a Chinese. He speaks English like a professor or like it's his second language. I mean he never uses contractions. Never 'I'm' or 'You're' but always 'I am' or 'You are.'"

"I know what contractions are. Anything else about him?"

"An iron fist in a velvet glove kind of guy. Very polite. He'd apologize before he had your head blown off. He talked about me stalling for two weeks, so you're right; something's going down soon."

"And that's all you can give me on him?"

"I told you I was blindfolded the whole time."

"Any idea where you were?"

"I figure I was in an apartment house on West Fourteenth Street, somewhere around Tenth Avenue. It's on the north side of the street. At least nine stories high. It's got an underground garage and automatic elevators. The corridors are wide and carpeted. The apartment I was in had a wood door and a thick shag rug."

"I thought you said you were blindfolded."

"I was, but I could hear and smell, and feel things under my feet. Also, I counted seconds and minutes."

"You're something, you are," Johnnie Wong says. "Well, you've given me enough to make an educated guess. You were in a twelve-story apartment house owned by the Giant Panda mob. It's on West Fourteenth Street like you said, but it's between Eighth and Ninth. It's all rentals, but the entire tenth floor is the East Coast headquarters of the Pandas. The bossman you talked to was probably Henry Wu Yeh. He's the warlord of the New York branch. From Hong Kong. Educated at UCLA. A very flinty customer. And a real tycoon type. He's the guy who's trying to muscle Giant Panda into legitimate businesses. You will turn General Motors over to us—or else! That kind of guy."

"Yeah, that sounds like him," Cone says. "One minute he's Mr. Nice and the next he's the Voice of Doom."

"By the way," Wong says, "you'll find Henry Wu Yeh on that list of White Lotus shareholders you showed me."

"No kidding?"

"No kidding. I forget how many shares he owns, but it's more than a thousand. Listen, do you want protection?"

"What for?"

"Well, Yeh said they're going to come looking for you on Monday, didn't he?"

"So? That's Monday. I got three days before they yank my chain."

Johnnie Wong laughs. "As we Chinese say, 'Rots of ruck, old buddy.'"

After he hangs up, Cone stands a moment, staring at the wall. It comes as no surprise to him to learn he was rustled by the Giant Panda gang. His reasoning goes like this:

He meets Edward Tung Lee at Ah Sing's Bar & Grill on Pell Street.

He sees Lee and Chen Chang Wang in deep conversation.

Wang gets blown away and is later revealed to be an officer in the Giant Panda organization.

During the excitement, Edward Lee notices that Timothy Cone carries a shooter in an ankle holster.

When the Giant Panda soldiers pick Cone up, the first thing they do is dust him down for an ankle holster. It was no normal frisk; the alpaca jackets went directly to his shins.

Ergo: Edward Tung Lee is a member of, or working closely with, the

Giant Panda mob and tipped them off that Cone was carrying on his leg bone.

So, if Edward Lee is buddy-buddy with the Giant Pandas, those phone calls he received must have come from someone else. The United Bamboo gang maybe? And are they also responsible for the letter to Claire Lee? United Bamboo owned the San Francisco kip where she worked, and could easily have taken the photographs.

Musing on all these permutations and combinations, Cone lights his first cigarette of the morning, coughs, and wanders over to his desk to consult the White Lotus shareholder list. He's curious about how many shares are owned by Henry Wu Yeh, the pooh-bah of the Giant Pandas.

No list. He can't find it. He searches, even in such unlikely places as the cabinet under the kitchen sink. No list. He gets down on hands and knees and peers beneath the claw-footed bathtub, thinking Cleo might have dragged it there. No list. The White Lotus annual report is still on his desk, but that confidential record of shareowners has disappeared.

He inspects the locks on the loft door. No signs of a break-in. But that doesn't mean shit. A good picklock could open almost any door and never leave a trace. And no use wondering when it was done. Last night or yesterday afternoon while Cone was at work. Whenever, the White Lotus shareholder list has been snaffled.

Cone glares accusingly at Cleo.

"What a lousy attack cat you turned out to be," he says to the beast. "What'd the gonif do—toss you a fish head? You fink!"

He's in his office in a sour mood and telling himself he's got a lot to be sour about.

That missing list bothers him, mostly because he promised Chin Tung Lee he'd take good care of it. It would be easy to assume it had been glommed by the Giant Pandas while they had him in custody, but that just won't wash. If Edward Lee is snuggling up to the Pandas—and Cone believes he is—he could easily provide a shareholder list anytime it was wanted.

That probably means the guy who burgled the loft was a paid-up member in good standing with the United Bamboo mob. But what would that gang of cutthroats want with a list of White Lotus investors? Unless they were going to put the company into play.

Three days, he reflects: that's how long he's got before he faces the long knives. The prospect of his immediate demise doesn't dismay him as much as fears for Cleo's future without him. He wonders if he should leave

Samantha Whatley a letter, willing the cat to her. Unless, of course, when he is knocked off, Cleo is also sent to the great litter box in the sky.

Engrossed with these morose musings, he suddenly becomes aware that his phone is ringing. He picks up, wondering if it's Mr. Yeh, calling to remind him that the clock is ticking.

"Yeah?" he says.

"Mr. Cone? This is Claire Lee. I'm calling from home. My husband is with me and would like to see you as soon as possible."

She sounds breathless. Maybe distraught.

"At your Fifth Avenue apartment?" he asks.

"Yes. Please. As quickly as you can, Mr. Cone."

"Okay," he says, "I'll be there."

He has no idea what it's all about, but figures that maybe it would be smart if he had wheels. So he grabs a cab back to his neighborhood, reclaims the red Ford Escort from a parking lot on Wooster Street, and heads for the Lees' Fifth Avenue apartment.

Finding a parking space in that area is like the search for the Holy Grail. Finally Cone gives up, double-parks on East Sixty-eighth Street, and locks up. If the Escort is towed, so be it; the client will pay the ransom to get it out of hock.

Claire meets him at the door of the apartment. She looks yummy in a white linen jumpsuit with an alligator belt. But her face is drawn, and when she clasps Cone's hand in both of hers, her skin feels moist and clammy.

She draws him into the apartment, closes and bolts the door, then turns to face him. He wonders if she's been weeping; her eyes are lost in puffy bags. She leans close, and he catches a whiff of eighty-proof something.

"My husband is ill," she says in a low voice. "Maybe not ill, but very upset. Troubled."

"Sorry to hear that," Cone says. "What's he troubled about?"

"You better hear it from him."

She leads the way through a maze of hallways, corridors, empty rooms, up two steps, down two steps, until they finally reach what is apparently the master bedroom.

It is a huge, high-ceilinged chamber dominated by an enormous oak four-poster that could sleep the Celtics, spoon fashion. And there are armoires, dressers, escritoires, cabinets, chests, cupboards, étagères—all in dark, distressed woods, looking as if an entire Scottish castle had been denuded to furnish this one melancholy room.

In the center of the immense bed is Mr. Chin Tung Lee, shrunken under a sheet and light blanket drawn up to his scrawny neck. His complexion is tallowy and his eyes are dimmed. Even his little beard seems limp. He withdraws a hand from beneath the covers and offers it to Timothy. The skin is parchment, the bones as thin and frail as a chicken's wing.

"Thank you so much for coming," he says in a wispy voice. "Please, pull up a chair."

Cone wrestles one as heavy as a throne to the bedside and sits, leaning forward.

"Sorry you're feeling under the weather, Mr. Lee. Is there anything I can do?"

Claire Lee is standing on the other side of the bed, opposite Cone. Her husband turns his head slowly in her direction.

"The first letter, dear," he says, and there's no vigor in his voice. "Please show it to Mr. Cone."

She plucks a single sheet of paper from a bedside table and brings it around to him. It's heavy stationery, thrice folded. The letterhead is embossed. Cone scans it, then looks up at Chin Tung Lee.

"Yangtze International, Limited," he says. "On Pine Street. Never heard of them. Have you?"

"Oh, yes, I've heard of them. My countrymen." Then, bitterly: "I understand criminal elements are involved."

"Uh-huh," Cone says, and reads the letter. It's in polite legalese, but the meaning is clear. Yangtze International has accumulated sixteen percent of all White Lotus stock, with the pledge of proxies by "many other shareholders" and requests a personal meeting with Mr. Chin Tung Lee with a view toward "proper representation" on the Board of Directors.

Cone reads it twice, then folds it and taps the letter on his knee.

"I checked with the SEC early this week," he says. "No one has filed a 13-D notifying an investment in White Lotus of five percent or more and declaring intent. But that doesn't necessarily mean anything; there's a ten-day delay allowed."

"But what does it *mean*, Mr. Cone?" Lee asks.

"You know what it means," Cone says harshly. "They're making a run on your company. Now we know why the stock has been going up, up, up."

"I'll never sell out," the old man wails. "Never!"

"You won't have to," Cone says, "if you play your cards right. You've got options. You can pay them greenmail—more than the market value of the stock—and buy *them* out. You can start a poison pill defense to make it so expensive to take over White Lotus that they'll just go away. You can look for a friendly buyer. You can consider a leveraged buyout: You buy everyone's shares and go private. You'll have to take on debt to do that. But then, in a couple of years or so, depending on what the Dow is doing, you can go public again. It could make you a zillionaire. But I'm not the one to be giving you advice on this. Have you got an investment banker?"

"No. I've never had the need for one."

"Well, you've got the need for one now. Mr. Lee, you're in a war, and you better have the best strategist money can buy. Ask around, then pick one. If you want a tip from me, try Pistol and Burns on Wall Street. It's an old outfit. Very conservative. Talk to G. Fergus Twiggs. He's a full partner and a smart apple."

Lee looks imploringly at his wife. "Claire, will you remember that?"

"Yes, daddy," she says. "Pistol and Burns. G. Fergus Twiggs."

"Thank you, dear. Now show Mr. Cone the second letter."

She goes back to the bedside table, returns with a sheet of white foolscap. She hands it to Cone with fingers that are trembling even more than they did at Carpacchio's bar.

Timothy unfolds the paper and reads. No letterhead on this one. Just two typed lines: *We have Edward. Do not go to the police if you wish to see your son alive again.*

He looks up in astonishment. "What the hell is this?" he demands. "Has someone grabbed him?"

"I checked," Claire says, gnawing at a knuckle. "He didn't sleep in his bed last night. No one's seen him or heard from him since yesterday afternoon."

"Oh, Jesus," Cone says. "No wonder you're in bed, Mr. Lee."

The oldster sighs. "As the Good Book says, 'Man that is born of a woman is of few days and full of trouble.'"

"I'll buy that," Cone says. "This is the only letter you've received?"

"The only one," Claire says. "It came this morning."

"Phone calls?"

"About Edward? No, none."

"Well, if he's been snatched, you'll be hearing from the people holding him. They'll either phone or send you another letter. I think you should bring the cops in on this, Mr. Lee."

"No," the gaffer says in an unexpectedly firm voice. "Absolutely not. I'll pay anything to get him back, but I won't endanger his life."

"You've got no guarantee," Cone argues. "You could pay off and they still might croak—they still might do away with him because he can identify them. But listen, this is a rough decision and you have to make it yourself. Don't listen to me."

"I want to do the right thing," the septuagenarian says, his voice faint again.

"Sure you do."

"You won't tell the police, will you?"

"If you don't want me to, I won't."

"But is there anything you can do to help?"

"Very iffy," Cone says. "Right now they're just letting you sweat a little. You'll be hearing from them again. Then we'll know where you stand."

He looks at Claire to see if she picks up on that: practically the identical language he used at Carpacchio's. But she won't look at him.

"Tell me something," Cone says. "How did this letter arrive? In your regular mail delivery?"

"No," Claire says, "it wasn't mailed. A messenger left it with our concierge this morning. The other letter—the one from Yangtze International—that was hand-delivered, too."

"Uh-huh," Cone says. "Both letters came at the same time by the same messenger?"

"No," she says. "I asked. They both came this morning but at different times. About an hour apart. The letter from Yangtze came first, delivered by a commercial service. Then, an hour later, the letter about Edward was brought by a young Chinese boy. The concierge says he dropped the letter on his desk and ran out."

"I get the picture," Cone says. "Look, I'm going to leave you folks now. I've got some calls to make to people who may be able to help." Then, when Chin Tung Lee glares at him, he adds hastily, "Not the cops. Just some guys who might have heard some talk. It's worth a try. Listen, do you mind if I take this letter about Edward along with me? I got a pal in the typewriter business. He'll be able to identify the machine used. That might help; you never know."

"Take it," Lee says wearily.

"And call me if you hear anything more. Either by letter or phone. And don't forget to contact an investment banker. I know that your son's disappearance is enough troubles, but you've got to start moving to protect your business, too."

The old man nods and holds out his hand. Cone shakes it gently, afraid the wrist bone might snap.

"I'll be in touch, Mr. Lee," he says as lightly as he can. "I'm not going to tell you not to worry because I know you will. But you've lived a long life and had a lot of problems, and you solved them all, didn't you?"

"Yes," Chin Tung Lee says, straightening up a little and raising his head from the pillow. "That is true."

"So? I'm betting you'll grab the brass ring on this one, too."

Claire Lee leads the way to the front door. Cone appreciates that or he'd be lost in the warren.

"First that letter I got," she says in a low voice, "and now this. I think I'm going nuts."

"Nah," Cone says. "You're a survivor. And your husband needs you. Got any ideas who might have snatched Edward?"

"Anyone out to make a lot of fast bucks," she says bitterly. "But no, I have no idea who it might be."

"How about your problem? Did you get another letter or phone call?"

"No."

"Okay," Cone says at the door, "hang in there and take care of your husband. He looks shvach."

"Just the way I feel," she says. She puts a hand on his arm. "Please, Mr. Cone, help us."

"I'll see what I can do," he says gruffly.

Mercifully, the Ford Escort is still peaceably double-parked, which Cone considers a good omen—but of what he cannot say. He drives back to the loft, his brain whirling like one of those spheres of ivory intricately carved by Chinese artists. Within the outer ball, the size of a softball, is a smaller one, turning freely; within that a golf ball; within that something smaller, the balls dwindling down to a carved pea, and all these nesting globes are perforated with ornate designs and revolve dizzily like Timothy's brain.

The first thing he does in the loft—even before he pours a vodka—is to compare the letter from Edward Lee's kidnappers with the letter from Claire Lee's blackmailers. Even to his inexpert eye it's obvious the two letters are of different sizes and grades of paper and were typed on different machines.

"Shit!" he says aloud.

Then he mixes a vodka and water.

He works on that, smokes a butt in short, angry puffs, and ponders his next move. First things first, he finally decides, and calls Johnnie Wong at FBI headquarters on Federal Plaza. A real grouch of a guy tells him Wong is not available, but he can leave a message if he wants to. Cone wants to, and does.

It's one hour, two drinks, and three cigarettes later before Johnnie gets back to him.

"The office told me you called," he says breezily. "Second time today we've talked. When are we going to start living together?"

"God forbid," Cone says. "Where are you—can you tell me?"

"Sure," Wong says, laughing. "I'm calling from my car. I was over in Jersey on a job, and just came through the Lincoln Tunnel. Traffic is murder! Right now I'm heading south on Ninth Avenue. What's up?"

"Listen, I think we better meet as soon as possible. The pasta fazool just hit the fan."

"Yeah? Well, don't say any more about it. Too many big ears on these mobile circuits."

"So I've heard," Cone says. "How's about you stopping by my place? Don't come up; I'll wait for you downstairs. Double-park and we can talk in your car. How does that sound?"

"Okay by me," Johnnie Wong says. "Give me fifteen minutes or so. I'm driving a black Chrysler two-door."

Cone's waiting on the sidewalk when the Chrysler pulls up about twenty minutes later. He slides into a leather bucket seat.

"Nice yacht," he says to Wong. "So this is where the taxpayers' money goes."

"This is where," the FBI man agrees. "What've you got?"

"The first thing I got is a question. Then I'll trade. Ever hear of Yangtze International, Limited?"

Johnnie turns sideways to stare at him. He's not smiling. "You really come up with some doozies," he says. "Yeah, I've heard of that outfit. It's the business arm of the Giant Panda mob. Handles all their purchases, leases, rentals, and investments. How did you hear about it? And don't tell me it was in idle conversation."

"Chin Tung Lee, the boss of White Lotus, got a letter from Yangtze this morning. They claim they now own sixteen percent of White Lotus stock and want to put their people on the Board of Directors. Sounds like the start of a takeover to me."

"I'll be damned," Wong says thoughtfully. "But then I shouldn't be surprised. I see the fine Italian hand of your old pal Henry Wu Yeh behind that deal. Did I tell you the guy's an MBA? It fits the pattern of the Pandas trying to muscle into legitimate businesses. What's Lee going to do?"

"Fight it, of course. I gave him the name of a good investment banker. The old man really loves that company; it's his whole life, and he's not going to fold because of one letter from Yangtze. But all that is just an appetizer. Here's one from Column A: it's a letter that was delivered to Lee's apartment house this morning."

He hands over the two-sentence note from the kidnappers. Wong scans it, then looks up in shock.

"Jesus," he says, "they grabbed his son? The guy you were with at Ah Sing's?"

"That's what it says. Listen, Johnnie, you've got to cover my ass on this. I promised the father I wouldn't go to the police."

"So? We're not the police—exactly."

"I know, but if you guys go charging up there, install phone taps and tape recorders, put on around-the-clock guards and all that crap, Chin Tung Lee will know for sure I tipped you, and my name will be mud. He'll probably send a hatchetman after me, and I got enough problems with Henry Wu Yeh."

"Maybe you should read *How to Win Friends and Influence People*. You figure Giant Panda pulled the snatch? It makes sense. They put more pressure on Lee to make him turn over White Lotus to them. And if he pays a hefty ransom, they use the money to buy more White Lotus stock. It's neat."

"Too fucking neat," Cone says angrily. "And it doesn't listen. Because Edward Lee is palsy-walsy with the Pandas."

Then he tells Wong the story of how, when he was frisked by Giant Panda foot soldiers, they went directly to his ankle holster. Only Edward could have told them about that. Also, Lee and Chen Chang Wang were thick as thieves at Ah Sing's Bar & Grill before Wang got popped.

"Yeah," the FBI man says, "I see what you mean. It sure sounds like Edward is sleeping in the Pandas' bed. Maybe he's in so deep that he gaffed his own kidnapping. It wouldn't be the first time the so-called victim was working hand in glove with the so-called kidnappers."

"That's possible, too. But look, you told me the United Bamboo and Giant Panda gangs hate each other's guts—right?"

"You better believe it. Like Cain and Abel, the Yanks and Red Sox, Texaco and Pennzoil."

"You think they both got spies in the other's camp?"

"You believe there's honor amongst thieves? Of course they do. About a month ago we found two Giant Panda thugs sliced to linguine in a Jersey pig farm. Only it turned out they weren't really Pandas; they were actually United Bamboo undercover guys. Their cover was blown, and they ended up feeding the pigs—personally."

"So you've got to figure both mobs have a pretty good idea what the other one is up to. How's this for a scenario: Giant Panda starts buying White Lotus stock through Yangtze International, planning a takeover. United Bamboo hears about it, takes a look at White Lotus, and decides they want a piece of the action. But Giant Panda has already accumulated sixteen percent of the stock, so United Bamboo has got to move fast. That they do. They kidnap the son of the CEO and biggest shareholder in White Lotus. You want to see Edward alive again? Okay, the ransom will be all your stock in White Lotus. And that amounts to about twenty-six percent of all outstanding shares. So by snatching Edward, United Bamboo ends up with a bigger hunk of the company than Giant Panda assembled by buying shares on the open market."

Johnnie Wong, frowning, considers it for a moment. Then: "I'll buy that. Mostly because it's the way United Bamboo operates: they're tough, direct, violent. They prefer physical action to reading SEC regulations before they move."

"Have you guys got snitches in United Bamboo?"

The FBI man gives him a blazing grin. "You don't expect me to answer that, do you? I will neither confirm nor deny."

"Okay, then I reckon you do," Cone says. "How about contacting your plants and find out if United Bamboo is holding Edward Tung Lee."

"I'll try," Wong says cautiously.

"You've got to do better than that," Cone urges. "This thing has to be wrapped up by Monday, or I may end up in a pig farm."

"All right, I'll move on it as soon as I get back to the office."

"When will I hear from you?"

"Depends. You'll be home tonight?"

"Oh, yeah," Cone says. "With the door locked, bolted, and chained."

"Why don't you teach Cleo karate?" Johnnie Wong suggests.

After the black Chrysler pulls away, Cone goes around the corner to a deli and buys a whole barbecued chicken, a container of potato salad, and two dills. He carries the fragrant bag back to the loft, rips it open, and starts on his dinner, after twisting the tail off the chicken and tossing it to Cleo.

He eats slowly and methodically because he's got a lot to brood about. He figures he's done all he can on Edward's kidnapping; now it's up to Johnnie Wong. But that's not what's bothering him; it's the threatening letter Claire Lee received and those phone calls to Edward Lee.

Cone's first idea had been that the United Bamboo mob was behind both letter and calls. But that no longer makes sense. You don't act like a blackmailer on the phone and then kidnap your intended victim. And it couldn't have been the Giant Pandas for the reason he had given Wong: Edward Lee is playing kneesy with that gang.

Which means, if Cone's reasoning is half-assed correct, there's a wild card in the deck: some free-lancer out to make a nice score by leaning on Claire and Edward. Timothy can't totally buy that notion, but it's the best he can come up with.

He gives the wingtips to Cleo and starts on the second leg, pausing occasionally to gulp potato salad or chomp on a pickle. He's drinking a beer with his meal and making it last because he only wants a single before getting back to vodka.

Vodka, he sincerely believes, is a great aid to mental labor because it frees the mind of discipline and diminishes linear thinking. You can fly on vodka, and if ever a case demanded an unfettered, soaring brain, the White Lotus caper is it.

He bundles up the de-winged, de-legged, de-tushed carcass of the bird and puts it in the fridge along with the remains of the potato salad and the second pickle. He reckons it'll make a nice Saturday morning brunch. Cleo can have the neck and back.

Then he goes back to his cigarettes and vodka. He runs out of ice cubes, but that doesn't annoy him. What nags is a feeling that he's missing something in this whole cockamamy jumble. He's missing something or someone is jerking him around. Either way, he doesn't like it.

Johnnie Wong hasn't called by 11:00 P.M., or midnight, or 1:00 A.M. Finally Cone gives up and undresses. He checks the door, turns off the lights, rolls onto his mattress. The magnum in its holster is close at hand. Cleo comes padding up to curl into the bend of his knees. The two of them sleep, both snoring gently.

When the phone rings, Cone comes groggily awake. It's still dark. He stumbles over to the wall phone, cursing when he stubs his toe on the refrigerator.

"Yeah?" he says, his voice thick with sleep.

"Aw," Johnnie Wong says, "I didn't wake you up, did I?"

"What time is it?" Cone asks.

"After five. But don't complain; I've been up all night."

"Any results?"

"Oh, yeah. I think we got a world-class flap on our hands. Listen, can you meet me down on the street in front of your place in about twenty minutes?"

"Sure. What's going on?"

"I want to drive you somewhere, and I'll tell you about it on the way."

Cone dresses quickly, straps on his shin holster, makes sure he's got cigarettes and matches, waggles his fingers at a drowsing Cleo, relocks the door, and clatters downstairs to an early morning that's just beginning to break over Brooklyn.

Timothy hasn't been out at that hour in a long time, and it's nice. The air is fresh—it hasn't yet been breathed by a million other people—and the sky is a patchwork of grays and violets. Stars are fading, and an unexpectedly cool August breeze is coming from the northwest. Sprinkler trucks have wet down Broadway; the pavement gleams in the pearly light.

Johnnie Wong is late, but Cone waits patiently, walking up and down slowly, smoking his first Camel of the new day. When the Chrysler arrives, Cone slides into the passenger seat.

"Hey, old buddy!" the FBI man cries, clapping him on the shoulder. "Sorry to interrupt your beauty sleep."

Cone looks at him closely. "Christ, you're wired," he says. "Haven't been popping bennies, have you?"

"Nah, I'm just hyper. A lot going on, and it could make me a hero or leave me looking like a putz."

He starts up, turns eastward, accelerates down a deserted street.

"Great morning," he says. "Best time of the day. No traffic. No pollution. Everything fresh and clean."

"That's what you wanted to tell me?" Cone says. "How wonderful the world is at six o'clock in the morning?"

Wong laughs: "Not exactly. Listen, you were right; the United Bamboo pirates are holding Edward Lee. They grabbed him late Thursday afternoon. It took me all night to authenticate that, and I had to call in a lot of chits."

"Where have they got him?"

"Where we're heading: Doyers Street in Chinatown. The Yubies' headquarters. That's what I call them—the Yubies. From the 'U' and 'B' in United Bamboo."

"You don't have to draw me a diagram," Cone says.

"God, you're grouchy early in the morning."

"I'm always grouchy."

"Well, the Yubies have three or four hangouts that we know about. Mostly in Manhattan, but one in Queens. Anyway, their headquarters is on Doyers Street in a five-story tenement. They've got the whole building except for a ground-floor restaurant, which happens to be the best dim sum joint in Chinatown. Edward Lee is being held in a third-floor office. He's been roughed up a little, but he's alive and okay. At least he was a couple of hours ago."

"You guys going in for him?"

"Ah, there's the rub. That's why I'm taking you to see the place. It's a fucking fortress."

Even at that early hour Chinatown is bustling. Merchants are taking down their shutters, street vendors are setting up their stalls, the narrow streets are crowded with men and women carrying live ducks, dead mackerel, and net bags filled with fruits and vegetables. Tea houses are already open for business, and the whole area has a raucous vitality.

Wong finds a parking space on Chatham Square. As they walk back to Doyers, he describes the setup.

"The entrance to the Yubies' headquarters is alongside the dim sum restaurant. There's an iron grille door on the street, kept locked, a small vestibule, and then a steel door painted to look like wood. Also kept locked. And if that wasn't enough, there are always two United Bamboo soldiers on the sidewalk outside the entrance. Twenty-four hours a day. I figure they're carrying. They don't let anyone inside the iron grille or the steel door unless they're recognized or expected. There's an intercom to the upper floors and also an alarm bell the guards can sound in case they get jumped."

"Beautiful," Cone says. "Back entrance?"

"Nope. Just a small blind courtyard. Fenced and topped with razor wire. There it is; take a look."

They saunter along on the other side of Doyers Street, pausing while Cone lights a cigarette, giving him a chance to eyeball the place. Three red-brick tenements in a row. The center building has the ground-floor restaurant. He spots the guards lounging near an iron gate. They look like kids to him: short and wiry.

Cone and Wong continue their slow stroll, turn onto Pell and then Mott Street.

"There's a place up near Canal where we can get coffee and a nosh," Johnnie says. "It's probably open by now."

"Yeah," Cone says, "that sounds good. My treat."

They sit at a table against a white-tiled wall. Wong tucks into a down-home breakfast of buttermilk pancakes and pork sausages with a side order of hush puppies. Cone has a bagel with cream cheese, lox, and a slice of onion. Both swill black coffee.

"You were right," Timothy says. "A fucking fortress. You guys thinking of hitting it?"

"Our legal eagles say we don't need a warrant; we've got probable cause: a kidnap victim being held against his will on the third floor. But how do we do it? We rush the place like gangbusters and already we're in deep trouble. Those two jerko guards will probably draw and start blasting away; you know that. And if they don't, they'll push the alarm button. That's what scares me most, because if the alarm goes off before we get upstairs, the guys in the third-floor office are liable to pop Edward Tung Lee just so he can't testify against them. I told you they were savages, didn't I? Real primitive types."

Cone continues munching his bagel sandwich and gulping black coffee. "So what do you want from my young life?"

"We can't let Edward Lee rot in there, can we? We've got to make a try at getting him out as long as it doesn't endanger his life."

"You could surround the front of the building and make a big show of force. Then bring in your hostage negotiation team."

"You think that would work?" Wong says, pouring more syrup on his pancakes.

"No," Cone says. "Because if they cave and hand you Lee, they'll know you've got them on a kidnap rap."

"Right. Well, you were an infantryman. Vietnam and your medals and all that shit. So what do you suggest?"

Cone pushes back from the table, lights another cigarette. He finishes his coffee and signals for a refill.

"You got some cowboys in your office?" he asks.

"You mean like a SWAT team? Sure, we got guys like that. An assault squad. Specially trained. Real hotshots. They just don't give a damn."

"Uh-huh," Cone says. "Listen, you know anything about the tong wars back in the twenties and thirties?"

"A little. I know the area bounded by Mott, Pell, and Doyer streets was called the Bloody Triangle."

"That's right. Well, during one of those wars the boss of a tong was threatened by an opposing gang. They swore they were going to top him. So he surrounded himself with bodyguards. On the street outside his head-quarters. In the room where he worked. Even in his bedroom. But he got slammed just the same. You know how?"

"How?"

"The enemy went up on the roof of the building next to the tong headquarters. Same height. They crossed over and let a shooter down in a bosun's chair. He popped the bossman through a front window."

Johnnie Wong stares at him. "Son of a bitch," he says softly.

"Probably the world's first demonstration of vertical envelopment," Cone goes on. "When you're in a firefight, or going into one, you tend to think horizontally. You figure the enemy will be on the same level. You never expect to get a load of crap dumped on your head. In World War Two it took a while for our guys in the South Pacific to learn the Nip snipers were up in the trees."

Wong leans forward, interested. "You think it would work here?"

"You've got buildings on both sides of the United Bamboo headquarters. All the buildings are tight together and the same height. Crossing to the middle roof should be a cinch. You couldn't lower just one guy; you need more firepower than that. The Yubies' headquarters are three windows wide. You make sure your lines are secure, and then three guys rappel down the face of the building, one guy to each stack of windows. They're armed with Uzis or maybe Ingrams or whatever lightweight choppers you guys are using these days. They rappel down to the third floor and start blasting the bejesus out of everything in sight, keeping their shots high because you don't want Edward Lee cut in two. If you think all that shooting is too risky, then have your hotshots kick the windows out with their boots and toss in stun grenades."

"Or tear gas," Wong says. He's getting excited now.

Cone shakes his head. "Gas would take too long to knock out Lee's guards. And besides, while this is going on, you're going to have a squad charging up the stairs to the third floor. And unless they're wearing masks, the gas will take them out, too."

"And how does this squad get past the guards, inside the two locked doors, and go galloping up to the rescue?"

"When the guys come down from the roof and the party begins, those two guards are going to run out into the middle of the street and look up, to see what's going on. That'll be your chance to grab them—while they're still peeing their pants. As for those locked doors, they shouldn't take more than a minute or two to pry open if you've got the right tools. My advice would be to blow them. Look, I haven't been in the war business for years, so I don't know what new goodies you guys have in your armory. But I'll bet you've got gizmos to get you through locked doors in seconds. Then you go hotfooting up to the third floor where the bad guys are still spooked."

"You really think that meshugass would work?"

Cone shrugs. "Fifty-fifty," he says.

"Come on," Johnnie Wong says angrily, "give it to me straight. If you had to make the top decision, would you say go or no-go?"

"Go," Cone says.

Wong sighs. "All right," he says. "I'll give it the old college try. We'll have to buck this one all the way up the line, probably to D.C. It's the time factor that worries me. I want to get Edward Lee out of there before the media gets wind of it or we'll have a three-ring circus on our hands. By rights, we should have conferences on this, liaise with the NYPD, and maybe even run a rehearsal down at Quantico. But we just don't have the time. Listen, are you going to be home this weekend?"

"I'll be in and out."

"I'll try to keep you up to speed on what's going on. I owe you that; it's your idea."

"Look," Cone says, "if you can't get enough guys to jump off the roof, I could do that. I know how to rappel."

Wong looks at him with amusement. "Smell action?" he asks. "Can't get it out of your system, can you? Thanks for the offer, but we've got weapons you haven't even heard about."

"Guns are guns," Cone says. "You point and pull the trigger."

"Forget it," the FBI man advises: "My God, you're just a lousy civilian."

Johnnie says he wants to get back to his office as soon as possible, so Timothy decides to walk home—a nice hike that'll get his juices flowing. The sun has popped up, but the air is still cool enough. It promises to be a hot, beamy day, not a rain cloud in sight. There's a skywriting plane at work over Manhattan, and Cone wonders what would happen if a berserk pilot spelled out FUCK YOU for all the city to see and ponder.

He buys a morning *Times* and a *Barron's* from a sidewalk kiosk. Then, nearing home, he begins stocking up on groceries and potables, figuring he'll spend the weekend in the loft; he doesn't want to be out if Johnnie Wong calls.

The elevator works until noon on Saturdays so Cone doesn't have to lug all his bundles up six flights of steep stairs. He gets everything stowed away, gives Cleo fresh water, fresh litter, and a Twinkie. Then he undresses and sacks out on the floor mattress to complete his night's sleep.

He awakes a little after noon, feeling grungy and tasting that onion from the bagel sandwich. So he brushes his teeth, showers, shaves, and pulls on fresh skivvies. Then he pops a beer, lights a cigarette, and eats two Mallomars.

He figures the action he suggested to the FBI man has a reasonable chance of success. It's got surprise going for it, and if the guys on the roof and the guys on the street can coordinate, it should go like silk. If their timing is off, it could be the biggest foozle of all time.

What it requires, of course, is luck. Cone has seen perfectly plotted combat operations go awry because of accidents, breakdowns of equipment, or acts of God. Other rumbles, planned by wetbrains who didn't know shit from Shinola about fighting a war, went off without a hitch because they had luck going for them.

He hopes Johnnie Wong has luck, or a lot of good men could get their butts shot off. Still, he reflects, that's what they're getting paid for, and if they don't like the odds, they should get into another line of business—something a frontline grunt in Nam would have found a wee bit difficult.

He resolutely puts memories of that time and that place into the farthest, dimmest corners of his mind, and tries to concentrate on today's trials and tribulations. He wishes Samantha wasn't a thousand miles away. Not that he would ever ask her advice or cry on her shoulder, but her physical presence is spice in a world he finds flat and tasteless without her.

He wonders how he ever got diddled by the fickle finger of fate and ended up an investigator, prying into other people's lives and sticking his nose into financial brannigans. Because, he ruefully admits, his own life is so dull. He's living vicariously, and if it wasn't for Cleo, he could go nights without speaking to a living soul—assuming cats have souls. And why not?

It's that kind of a moony weekend, with a lot of reading, drinking, smoking, and pigging out on food that comes in plastic wrappers. Not a phone call, from Wong or anyone else, and his cabin fever is just about to drive him to a seizure of pub-crawling when his phone rings late Sunday night, and he kisses it for luck before he says, "Yeah?"

"It's on," Johnnie Wong says. "And if I sound whacked-out it's because I haven't slept for forty-eight hours. I can't talk about it on the phone. You remember where I parked my car on Saturday?"

"Sure."

"Can you meet me there at two-thirty?"

"I'll be there. Anything I can do to help?"

"Pray," Wong says, and hangs up.

Cone's got about three hours to kill and figures it's too risky to take a snooze; he might not wake up in time to witness the fireworks. So he spends a half-hour cleaning his S&W .357 magnum and oiling the ankle holster.

Since it's going to be a night operation, he debates the wisdom of wearing a black turtleneck sweater and dark gray slacks. But then he realizes he's just conning himself; he's going to be a spectator, not a combatant, and his costume is of no importance. So he wears a navy blue T-shirt under the usual corduroy jacket, and stuffs his cap in the pocket.

He spends the last hour reviewing the plan again, trying to spot flaws. He can't find any; the plot still looks good to him. If everyone does his job, and Lady Luck is smiling, Edward Tung Lee should be sleeping in his Fifth Avenue apartment by dawn.

He exits his building to find a low-hanging cloud bank over the city. If there are moon and stars up there, they can't be seen—which Cone takes as a promising portent for night action. Also, there's no wind to speak of, nothing strong enough to bother those cowboys rappeling down from the roof.

He drives the red Escort over to Chatham Square, finds a place to park on the Bowery, and walks back. Johnnie Wong is waiting for him. The FBI man is wearing camouflaged combat fatigues and looks unexpectedly bulky. Cone digs a finger into his ribs and feels the armor beneath the cloth.

"Bulletproof vest?" he asks.

"I hope so," Wong says, grinning.

"Don't tell me you're flying off the roof?"

"Hell, no; I'm no bird. I'm leading the squad up the stairs after we blow the outside doors."

"Then it's going down like we said?"

"Pretty much," Wong says. "With a few minor refinements. The guys going off the roof will be carrying Ingram Mark Tens. Plus stun grenades."

"What are you carrying?"

"Old Faithful: a Thompson forty-five with drum magazine."

"How do you blow the doors?"

"Our boffins have come up with a cutie. It's a high-energy explosive made to look like a credit card, and just as thin. You slide it between the door and jamb, pull the friction snapper, and run like hell because it's got a five-second fuse—if you're lucky. Listen, I haven't got much time so let me give you the scoop. We had to liaise with the NYPD, and in about fifteen minutes they're going to close off Doyers Street at both ends with barricades and unlighted, unmarked police cars. They'll position flatbeds at each end loaded with floodlights and searchlights. And portable generators, of course.

"Our combat control is on the roof of the building across the street from the Yubies' headquarters. You get up there by going through a courtyard and climbing six flights of stairs. We've got men posted on every floor to keep tenants inside their apartments. Everyone's connected by walkie-talkies—and let's hope they work."

"What about the guys on the roof of the United Bamboo building— did they get there okay?"

"No sweat. They've been up for about a half-hour now, moving around on felt boots so they don't spook the bandidos downstairs. They report they've got their lines securely anchored—one around a chimney and the other two with grappling hooks. Time's getting short; let's go."

Johnnie leads the way to Doyers, and they begin passing men in dark suits, some of them talking quietly into their radios.

"How many guys you call in on this caper?" Cone asks.

"Almost a hundred. The controller flew up from Quantico. He's run operations like this a dozen times before. He's got a good score, but he's a bastard to deal with. It took me a while to persuade him to let you watch the action. After all, it was your idea."

"I know," Cone says. "But I'm just a lousy civilian."

They go across a bleak courtyard, through the back door of a tenement, and climb the stairs to the top floor, where there's an iron ladder leading through an opened skylight to a tarred roof. There are two brick chimneys and a number of vent pipes protruding from the roof. Cone spots a waist-high wall with a coping of slates facing Doyers Street.

There are five men up there. One has what appears to be a four-by-five Speed Graphic, another has a shoulder-mounted video camera.

"We're recording all this for posterity," Wong says dryly. "I'm not going to introduce you to anyone; they're too tense for politeness."

"Yeah," Cone says, "I know the feeling."

Two of the other FBI men are using their walkie-talkies. The fifth man, apparently the controller, is standing well back from the wall, hands jammed into his pockets. He's staring up at the dark sky, his mouth half-open. Johnnie goes up to him, speaks a few words, and jerks a thumb in Cone's direction. The controller turns to look, nods, then says something. Wong comes back to Cone's side.

"Keep back from the roof edge until the action starts," he says. "And no lighting matches, no smoking. Okay?"

"Sure," Cone says. "Listen, I don't want to put the whammy on this, but have you made plans for casualties?"

"Two ambulances and medical evac teams standing by on Mott Street. And paddy wagons. Only they're buses. Well, I've got to leave now and get on station."

"Look," Timothy says, "do me a favor, will you? Remember that White Lotus shareholder list I showed you at my place? Someone copped it from my loft, and I think it was a United Bamboo picklock. When you get up to their offices, and this whole thing is winding down, will you take a look around and see if you can find it? I promised Chin Tung Lee I'd take good care of it. It's confidential information."

"Sure," Johnnie says, "I can do that. See you soon, old buddy."

"You bet," Cone says.

Wong leaves, and the Wall Street dick reaches into his pocket for a cigarette, then pulls his hand guiltily away. He notices the five FBI men on the roof are inching closer to the wall overlooking Doyers Street. Cone inches right along with them.

The controller is holding what appears to be a stopwatch, big as an onion. He consults it and says quietly to his talkers, "Coming up to one minute."

They murmur into their radios.

"One minute...mark," the controller says in dullish tones.

The talkers repeat.

They all wait in silence.

"Forty-five seconds," the controller says. His voice is sluggish. "Thirty seconds...twenty...ten...five, four, three, two, one. Go."

The talkers begin shouting into their walkie-talkies. Everyone moves to the edge of the roof. They grip the wall coping, stare across the street.

Three men drop on lines from the top of United Bamboo headquarters. They rappel swiftly downward. They use leg kicks to keep themselves bouncing off the brick front of the building.

They come to a stop facing the third-floor windows. They smash the glass with their boots. They toss in grenades. The three explosions are almost simultaneous: one titanic *boom!*

"Lights," the controller says in his listless voice.

Searchlights and floods make day of night. The street is frozen in a harsh, greenish glare.

"Go with Unit Two," the controller says.

Cone figures no one is going to send him to Leavenworth for smoking a Camel now. He lights up, leans over the wall, peers down.

One of the Yubie guards has run out into the street, is staring upward. The other has his back against the iron grille door. He's fumbling at his belt.

Wong's squad comes spilling out of tenement doorways. They rush the guards. Grab them. Johnnie works at the iron grille. Motions everyone back, then ducks away. Sheet of flame brighter than the floodlights. Sparks. The grille hangs crazily from one hinge.

Same thing with the inner door. It's blown completely inward. The attackers cram into the entranceway, Wong leading.

Now the three rappelers have disappeared. They're inside, through the shattered windows. Gunfire. Single shots. Then short bursts from automatic weapons.

"Unit Three," the controller says stolidly.

Cone wonders if a reserve has been put on standby. It has. A dozen men come charging down Doyers. These are New York City cops, wearing helmets and flak jackets. Following them is a platoon of uniformed police who set up a cordon around the United Bamboo building.

More gunfire. A lot of it.

"Medics," the controller mentions. Then: "Let's go."

He leaves first, climbing carefully down the iron ladder. Followed by his two assistants. Then the photographers who have been working steadily since the action started.

Cone lights another cigarette and follows them. By the time he hits the street, the small-arms fire is dwindling; just single shots or brief chatters of submachine guns.

An ambulance comes slowly up the street, siren growling. Cone stands in the doorway, watches the stretchers and body bags unloaded. Then an armored bus pulls up.

By this time every building on Doyers Street is lighted. People are leaning out windows; some have gone to their roofs for a better view.

The shooting stops. Cone lights another cigarette and realizes he's got two going at once. He finishes the butt with quick drags and starts on the other.

Two FBI men come out of the United Bamboo building. They're gripping Edward Tung Lee by the arms. His knees are buckling, but he can walk. They help him into the ambulance. Then more cops come out, FBI and NYPD. They're herding a long file of prisoners, some dressed, some in pajamas and robes, some wearing shorts. All have hands clasped atop their heads. They're stuffed into the bus. It pulls away; another takes its place.

Johnnie Wong comes out, helping to carry a stretcher. The supine body is covered to the chin with a blanket. A medic walks alongside, holding a plastic bag high, the connecting tube disappearing under the blanket.

The ambulance pulls away. A second comes purring up. Wong stands dazedly, looking around. The Thompson dangles from one hand.

Cone crosses the street, goes up to him.

"Johnnie," he says gently.

The FBI man turns slowly to stare, not recognizing him at first. Cone knows the symptoms: shock, flood of adrenaline, postaction shakes.

"You okay?" he asks Wong.

"What? Oh, yeah, I'm all right. One of my guys caught it."

"Ah, Jesus," Cone says. "Bad?"

"I think so. It looked bad. Chiang Ho. He's been with the Bureau almost ten years. A sweet man. Oh, God, what am I going to tell his wife?"

"Maybe he'll make it."

"No," Wong said, "he won't." Then, savagely: "But I got the fucker who chilled him. We grabbed Edward Lee out of there—did you see?"

"I saw. It was a beautiful job, Johnnie."

"I guess. Yeah, it was. It went real good. We're taking everyone in. You know, after Chiang went down, I wanted to dissipate all those guys. I never felt like that before in my life. Not a nice feeling."

"I know. But what the hell, you'll get an 'I love you' letter from the Director for all this."

"Maybe," Wong says. "Hey, I found your fucking list. It was right on top of the desk in the office."

He reaches into his fatigue jacket, pulls out the White Lotus computer printout.

"Thanks," Cone says. "I owe you a big one, payable on demand."

"I'll remember that, old buddy," the FBI man says. "Keep in touch."

By all rights, he should zonk out the moment he hits the loft and sleep until late Monday morning. But he is too wired. Granted he has been a sideliner, not an active player in that raid on United Bamboo headquarters. But the tension and suspense have clutched him. He can still hear the controller's phlegmatic "Go" and then the eruption of gunfire.

It takes a stiff vodka to soothe the jits, and by that time he's concentrating on the remainder of the puzzle—the reason he was dumped into this mishmash in the first place.

Why the run-up in the price of White Lotus stock? Obviously because the Giant Panda mob has been buying up shares through Yangtze International with the aim of taking over the company. That's a perfectly legitimate ploy. So why did Henry Wu Yeh have Cone kidnapped and tell him to stall his investigation or be prepared to knock on the Pearly Gates? That doesn't make sense.

And where do the blackmailing letter to Claire Lee and phone calls to Edward Lee fit into the jumble?

Groaning, he starts flipping through the White Lotus share holder list. He pays particular attention to investors owning more than a thousand shares—the people Johnnie Wong said were associated with Giant Panda.

Revelation comes slowly, not in a sudden inspiration. No light bulb flicks on over his head as in a cartoon strip. The answer comes from dry numbers which, the Wall Street dick well knows, can relate a tale as gory as bloodstains, a wet knife, or brain-splattered hammer.

The first step is adding up the holdings of all those thousand-share investors and realizing that no way, *no* way can they represent 16 percent of the outstanding shares of White Lotus. Yet that is what the letter from Yangtze International claimed—that they owned 16 percent of the stock, with the pledge of proxies by "many other shareholders."

So how did they come up with that magic number of sixteen percent? Timothy knows how. Edward Tung Lee personally owns sixteen percent of White Lotus. What a beautiful coincidence. And if you believe that, try the Tooth Fairy on for size.

What it means, Cone realizes, is that Edward Lee is conniving with Giant Panda to make a run on his father's company. But for what reason? Cone thinks he has the answer to that one, too.

He turns to the first page of the glossy White Lotus annual report. There is the photograph of Edward Tung Lee, Chief Operating Officer. Even with his frozen smile he's a handsome devil: curved lips, cleft chin, high brow, blow-dried hair.

He could be a matinee idol. And Cone decides that's exactly what he is.

"Cleo," he calls, and the slumbering cat lifts its head.

"I've been snookered," Cone says.

He wakes late on Monday morning, sits up on his mattress, yawns, roughs his scalp with his knuckles. He thinks of that punky saying: "Today is the first day of the rest of your life." If he doesn't get to work, he reflects sourly, it may be the last day—courtesy of Henry Wu Yeh.

It's almost ten o'clock before he gets his act together; two Camels, two cups of black coffee, and a tot of brandy bring the roses to his cheeks.

He gives Cleo fresh water and a pickled pig's foot to chew on. He checks the revolver in his shin holster, makes sure his wallet is stuffed with lettuce. Then he tears the photograph of Edward Lee from the annual report and sticks it in his jacket pocket. He sallies forth, feeling full of piss and vinegar, and not a little vindictive.

He drives directly to the Upper East Side and spends ten minutes wedging the Escort into a parking space that would be jammed with a moped. He walks back to the Hotel Bedlington on Madison Avenue, a few blocks away from the Lees' apartment on Fifth.

He knows this joint; it's figured in other cases he's handled. It's a staid, almost mousy establishment, with a lot of over-the-hill permanent residents, a cocktail bar that is proud of its Grasshoppers, and a lobby that smells faintly of must and has a magnificent framed lithograph of Grant's Tomb over the desk.

Cone wanders around a few moments before he spots a bellhop. The guy is short, squat, and has a heavy blue jaw. He looks one year younger than God. Cone figures he belongs in an OTB with a cigar butt stuck in his kisser. He's got that New York wisenheimer look, and Timothy knows it's going to cost him.

"Can I talk to you a minute?" he asks.

The bellhop gives him the up-and-down, taking in the black leather cap, ratty corduroy suit, scuffed work shoes.

"Talk is cheap," he says.

"I hope so," Cone says. "Anyplace where we can have a little privacy?"

"What's in it for me?" the guy says. He looks like a tall midget, and his gut is busting the brass buttons on his waistcoat.

"A couple of bucks?" Cone says hopefully.

"G'wan. I don't even say hello for a deuce."

"A fin," Cone says.

The bellhop jerks a thumb toward the door of the men's room. "In there," he says. "And make it snappy. I got a job to do, you know."

They lean on urinals in the empty loo. Cone hands over a fiver.

"You ain't no cop," the guy says. "That I guarantee. A private eye? Bill collector? Maybe a reporter for a scandal sheet?"

"Something like that," Cone says. "What's your name?"

"Max."

"Listen, Max, I'm going to show you a photograph. I want to know if you've ever seen the guy before. Just a simple yes or no. That's easy enough—right?"

"Let's see it."

Cone pulls out the photograph of Edward Tung Lee and holds it up. The bellhop stares at it.

"Never saw him before in my life," he says, but meanwhile he's rubbing a thick thumb against a bent forefinger.

The Wall Street dick sighs, pulls out his wallet. "You already got a Lincoln," he says.

"It'll cost you a Hamilton," Max says. "Look, you're making a nice couple of Washingtons on your job, aintcha? What am I—chopped liver?"

Cone fishes in his wallet, hands over a ten-dollar bill.

"Yeah, I make the guy," Max says. "He checks in two, three times a week. Always in the afternoon. Stays maybe a couple of hours."

"Since when has this been a hot-pillow joint?" Cone asks.

"Since day one," the bellhop says. "Whaddya think, every hotel in the city don't do it? It's easy money—and fast turnover."

"And how long has this guy been checking in for a few hours of fun and games?"

"Oh, maybe a couple of years now. That's it; you got your money's worth."

"Not yet," the Wall Street dick says. "Different women—or always the same woman?"

Max makes the same gesture, rubbing his thumb on a crooked forefinger.

"You're going to wear out your thumb," Timothy says. "How much?"

"I figure it's worth a Jackson."

"A double-sawbuck?" Cone says, outraged. "Are you sure your name's not Jesse, as in Jesse James?"

"Listen, I know and you want to know. It's supply and demand—get what I mean?"

Groaning, Cone gives him a twenty-dollar bill.

"Always the same woman," Max says. "The guy calls the desk before he shows up so he's got the room number—you cappish? The Hitler on the desk is on the take. So the guy shows up, no luggage, and goes directly to his room. Then fifteen, twenty minutes later, the dame shows up. She's got the room number from him, sails through the lobby, and goes straight upstairs. Nice people. Good tippers. They spread it around like they should."

"Uh-huh," Cone says. "And I guess she's a short, dumpy broad with dark hair—right?"

The bellhop looks at him with disgust. "Whaddya think," he says, "I was born yesterday?"

"All right," Cone says, sighing. "How much?"

"A Grant. But I won't testify in court if this is a divorce thing like I figure it is."

"This better be good," Cone says, handing over a fifty-dollar bill.

Max slips the folded bill into a waistcoat pocket. "She's a beauty, a real sparkler. Tall as you. Young. Blond. Great jugs. Wears expensive clothes. Once I heard the guy call her Claire. Is that what you wanted?"

"It'll do," Cone says, nodding. "Now can you tell me where the public phone is—or are you going to hold me up for that, too?"

"Nah, that's a freebie. It's on the mezzanine."

Cone finds the phone in an old-fashioned booth with a folding door. It's even got a little wooden seat. He calls the corporate offices of White Lotus on Exchange Place.

"Is Mr. Chin Tung Lee in this morning?" he asks the operator.

"Yes, he is, sir. May I ask who's calling?"

"I have a personal delivery to make to Mr. Lee and just wanted to make sure he's there. Thank you."

He hangs up, leaves the Hotel Bedlington, heads for the Lees' apartment on Fifth Avenue.

There's a monster standing in front of the Lees' door with his arms folded. He looks like a young Genghis Khan, with slit eyes and mustachios bushy enough to sweep out a parrot's cage. Cone decides to play it safe, not knowing if this muscle is FBI, NYPD, or a hired janissary.

"Timothy Cone to see Mrs. Claire Lee," he says. "She's expecting me."

The mastodon unfolds his arms, and the Wall Street dick wonders if he's going to get a karate chop that will decapitate him.

"You wait," the guy says in an unexpectedly high-pitched voice.

He disappears and Cone waits in the corridor. In a few moments the door is opened again by the juggernaut.

"You come," he says.

Timothy follows him through that maze of rooms and hallways. He's finally ushered through a double set of doors, into a small living room, and then into an adjoining bedroom. The woolly mammoth withdraws.

Edward Tung Lee is seated in a leather club chair. He's wearing cerise silk pajamas under a brocaded dressing gown. There's a white handkerchief neatly peaked in the breast pocket of the robe. His feet are bare. Claire Lee is standing next to him. She looks like a pom-pom girl in a middy, short pleated skirt, bobby socks and white Reeboks.

"Mr. Cone!" she carols. "What a pleasant surprise!"

"I was in the neighborhood," he says, "and thought I'd drop by to see how your husband is doing."

"Much better, thank you," she says. "So well, in fact, that he insisted on going into the office this morning."

"Silly thing to do," Edward says. "He just won't slow down."

They all look pleasantly at each other.

"Now listen," Claire says, "I really don't think it's too early in the morning for a drink. Do you, Mr. Cone?"

"It's never too early," he tells her.

"And I know what you like," she says archly. "Vodka on the rocks with a splash of water. Right? Edward, I think you should have something. Perhaps a brandy. The doctor said it would do you good."

"A small one," he says.

"And perhaps a small something for me," she says gaily. "Be back in a jiff."

She sashays out the door and Edward says, "Pull up a chair, Mr. Cone."

But he sits on the edge of the unmade bed. Now he's facing Lee and the other armchair. He wants them both in his sights when the woman returns.

"You look a little puffy around the gills," he says, "but none the worse for wear. They give you a hard time?"

Edward is startled. "You know what happened to me?" Cone nods.

"How did you find out? It hasn't been in the papers."

"The grapevine," Cone says. "The FBI did a helluva job grabbing you out of there."

"They saved my life. And one of them was critically wounded in the shoot-out—did you know that?"

"I heard."

"I'll never forget that," Edward says somberly. "Never in my life."

"Yeah," Cone says.

Claire comes bustling in, carrying a silver tray of drinks. She hands them around: vodka rocks to Cone, small snifter of brandy for Edward, and something green in a stemmed glass for herself.

"Cone knows what happened to me," Edward tells her.

"Oh, Mr. Cone knows *everything*," she says lightly. "Don't you, Mr. Cone?"

"Just about," he says.

She takes the armchair, and now he can look at both of them without turning his head from side to side. They lift their glasses in a silent toast, then sip their drinks delicately. Very civilized.

"You two are a nice couple of bums," Timothy says.

Their faces congeal. Edward's hand begins trembling. He sets the snifter down on the floor next to his chair.

"What?" Claire Lee says, voice strangled. "What did you say?"

"Bums," Cone repeats. "Cruds. Both of you. How long did you think you'd be able to have those matinees at the Bedlington? Forever and ever?"

"I don't know what you're talking about," she says hotly; "And I think you better leave right now."

"Oh, stuff it," he says angrily. "I couldn't care less if you rub the bacon every day of the year. What I don't like is that you both played me for a fool, each telling me how much you hated the other. I fell for it because it was a classic setup: younger stepmother, older son, both competing for an old man's inheritance. Only you've been rumpling the sheets together for two years."

"You're a dirty, filthy man," Claire says, glaring at him.

"You better believe it," he tells her, taking a gulp of his drink. "Look," he says, addressing Edward, "if you want to put horns on your pop, that's your business. *My* business is finding out why the price of White Lotus stock has been going up, up, up. Do you want to hear my scenario? It's a cutie."

Neither replies.

"It goes like this," Cone continues. "And don't interrupt to tell me I'm wrong—because I don't think I am.

"One: Claire and Edward are shacking up and making jokes in the sack about what a senile old fart Chin is. Two: Edward is still steaming because his father wouldn't finance his great idea of having White Lotus market a line of frozen gourmet Chinese dinners. Oh, yeah, I saw how riled you got at Ah Sing's when you told me about it. Three: During those tosses in the hay, Claire eggs you on, and you decide to cut loose from White Lotus, go off on your own, start a new business and make a zillion."

"Now see here—" Edward starts.

"Shut up, you," Cone says savagely. "Nothing wrong with your plan, but it's the way you went about it that sticks in my craw. Your sixteen percent of White Lotus stock at the old price of thirty bucks a share would be worth a nice piece of change if you sold your stock on the open market. But it would take that to open a pizza parlor these days. You needed a lot more loot to start a frozen food operation."

"Claire," Edward says stiffly, "maybe you better phone the police."

"Go ahead and call them," Cone says. "And tell them to bring along reporters and photographers—you jerk! So your problem was how to increase your capital. The answer? Greenmail! You make a deal with Giant Panda. Those thugs play along because they're anxious to get into a legitimate business and put all that money to work they've made from dope and shakedowns. The scam is this: Fronts for Giant Panda start buying White Lotus stock. The price goes up. When it's high enough, as it was last week, Giant Panda makes a play for White Lotus, working through Yangtze International.

"Look, both of you know how much Chin Tung Lee loves his company. It's his whole life. You figured he'd pay a premium to keep control. So Yangtze pretends they want to take over when what they really want is for Chin to pay greenmail—buy their shares at more than the market price. That would yield enough dough for you to start your frozen dinner business."

"You're insane," Edward Lee says in a low voice.

"Sure I am," Cone admits cheerily. "But I'm also right. Almost everything fits: Your father's need to hang onto the company he created. Your need to get your new business started and prove you're as smart an operator as your old man. And Giant Panda's need to get into a legitimate moneymaker. What was the deal? Were they going to give you a controlling interest? Like shit they were! Those guys are gangsters, even if they work through a financial front on Pine Street. You'd be lucky to end up with thirty percent. Am I right or am I right?"

Edward Lee, stunned, makes no reply, but Claire does. "You said 'almost everything fits.' What doesn't fit?"

"You don't," he tells her. "You and Edward could have taken over White Lotus anytime you wanted. Between the two of you, there's enough stock to elect your own Board of Directors and put the old man out to pasture. But you didn't go that route. Why not? Mrs. Lee, I make you for a streetwise lady who's always had an eye on the main chance. You're a nice-looking woman, no doubt about it, but when it comes to spine, you got short-changed.

"I figure your thinking went something like this: Yeah, I could go in with Edward on his greenmail scheme, but would it really be smart? What if Chin conks out tomorrow from a stroke or cardiac arrest and I inherit? It's more than possible at his age. So maybe I should play my cards cautiously. If Edward's plot comes off, and his business is a big success, then I'll think about dumping the father and going with the son. But meanwhile I'll play it cozy, let Edward carry the ball and see how far he gets. I'm young; I can afford to wait. If Edward's a winner, I'll go with him. If he takes a pratfall, it's ta-ta, Eddie darling."

"You're disgusting," she says, spitting it out.

"Oh, yeah," Cone says, draining his drink. "Almost as disgusting as you two upright citizens." He rises, places his empty glass on a bedside table. "Thanks for the belt. I've got to run along now. So much to do, doncha know."

"Mr. Cone," Edward Lee says nervously, "you're not going to tell my father about the Bedlington matter, are you?"

"Like the lawyers say," Cone tells him, "I'll take it under advisement. Meanwhile, sweat a little. Now will someone show me how to get out of this damned place?"

Claire Lee leads the way in silence. But at the outside door she pauses and turns to face him.

"You had eyes for me, didn't you?" she says.

"Yeah," Cone says. "At first. Until I remembered I've got a lady who makes you look like a Barbie Doll. And she's got spine to spare."

"I'm not so bad," Claire says defensively.

"Compared to whom?" Cone asks.

He gets to Exchange Place by one o'clock, after stopping at a Lexington Avenue saloon for a cheeseburger and a bottle of dark Heineken. And another cheeseburger and another bottle of dark Heineken. He's famished because he's coming off a high after that confrontation with Claire and Edward. Feeding his face brings him down, and he can plan what he's going to say to Chin Tung Lee.

But he has to wait in the White Lotus reception room. "Mr. Lee is busy at the moment, sir, but he'll be with you shortly." That's okay; it's still Monday, Cone's still breathing, and if Henry Wu Yeh's hatchetmen are on his tail, Timothy hasn't spotted them.

When he's conducted into Lee's garish office, the old man appears chipper enough. He's got his long ivory holder with a scented cigarette clamped between his plates at a jaunty FDR angle. The mustardy toupee is slightly askew, giving him a raffish look. Even the wispy Vandyke is alive and springy.

"So happy to see you, Mr. Cone," he says in his boomy voice, offering his tiny hand across the desk. "I meant to call you, but this is the first day I've been out of bed. Please, sit down and tell me what you've been doing."

The Wall Street dick slumps into the leather tub chair. He shakes a Camel from his pack and lights it. "Glad you're up and about," he says. "I went to see your son this morning."

"I know," Lee says. "He called right after you left. He said you knew about his rescue."

"That's right."

"What a happy ending to an unfortunate affair. You had nothing to do with it, did you?"

"Not me."

"In any event, all's well that ends well, as your Shakespeare said."

"He's not my Shakespeare," Cone says, "and a lot of other guys said it first."

Then they sit in silence a moment. Lee seems to sober under Cone's hard stare; the sprightliness leaks away, the smile fades. He sets holder and cigarette down carefully in the brass ashtray.

"Is something troubling you, Mr. Cone?"

"Yeah," Timothy says, "something is. You suckered me good, didn't you?"

"What? What are you saying?"

"I thought you were a cocker spaniel, and you turn out to be a pit bull. How long have you known about your wife and son?"

Chin Tung Lee doesn't answer, but he seems to shrivel and slide down in his wheelchair.

"Any other man would have kicked their butts out the window," Cone goes on. "But that's not your style. You're a chess player with a habit of winning. You prefer to think five plays ahead—at least. You like to move people around the way you maneuver chess pieces. So you got a friend or employee to type up a scary letter to your wife and make threatening phone calls to your son. For a man in your position that would be duck soup. You figure to spook them into ending those matinees at the Hotel Bedlington. Then you'd forgive and forget."

"What my son did to me," Chin says stonily, "I can never forgive or forget."

"Come on," Cone says. "If it wasn't Edward, it would be someone else—and you know it. Would you prefer a stranger? Would that make it better?"

"You are a very cynical man, Mr. Cone."

"Nah. Just realistic. How old are you—late seventies?"

"Eighty next year."

"So you're more than three times her age. What did you expect? You probably knew her history when you married her; you must have figured something like this would happen."

"Yes, I anticipated it. But not my son!"

Cone shrugs. "The family that plays together stays together."

That, at least, earns a wan smile. "Tell me, how did you find out I was responsible for the threats?"

"No great job of detecting. Just elimination. It couldn't have been the United Bamboo mob, because they kidnapped your son, and you don't kidnap a potential blackmail victim. And it couldn't have been the Giant Panda gang, because Edward is practically in bed with them."

Then the old man straightens up on the telephone directory he's sitting on. He glares wrathfully at Cone.

"Are you certain of what you're saying?"

"As sure as God made little green apples. Look, this thing between Claire and Edward is a sideshow. It's none of my business. My job was to find out why the price of White Lotus stock has been galloping. All right, here's the answer: Your son and Giant Panda, working through Yangtze International, have been shafting you by driving up the price. Edward has probably pledged his shares to the Pandas to give them more clout."

"My own son? He wants to force me out?"

Cone sits back, lights another cigarette slowly. He sees Chin's hands are trembling, and he gives the geezer a few moments to settle down.

"You got it wrong," Cone tells him. "Your son couldn't care less about taking over White Lotus. He thinks it's got no pizzazz. He wants to start his own company, to market frozen gourmet Chinese dinners—the idea you turned down. The only way he can get enough capital to swing that is to force you to buy him out at an inflated price. And give Giant Panda a nice profit at the same time, of course. It's greenmail, Mr. Lee. They know you'll pay a premium over the market price of the stock to keep control of White Lotus."

The old man tugs gently at his wispy beard. "So other people play business chess, too," he says.

"On Wall Street? You better believe it."

"Mr. Cone," Lee says, "in that ugly commode across the room you will find a bottle of sake. A Japanese drink, but tasty. Rice. Also some crystal sake shot glasses from the Hoya Gallery. Very handsome. I suggest this might be the right time for a drink."

"I'm game," Cone says.

He brings bottle and glasses back to the driftwood desk. He pours the miniature tumblers half-full. Chin drains his in one gulp and holds it out for a refill. Cone pours again, filling both. He's glad to see Lee's hand is now steady.

They settle back, smiling at each other.

"Do you play chess, Mr. Cone?"

"Nope. I don't play anything."

"Ah. Too bad. I think you may have the gift. Tell me, how do you suggest I react to this extortion?"

"Have you contacted an investment banker?"

"Yes, I have an appointment tomorrow with Mr. Twiggs of Pistol and Burns."

"Good. He's a smart man. Well, if this was a purely business decision, there are a lot of things you could do to fight off the greenmailers. Restructure your company. Take on heavy debt to buy up your stock on the open market. Look for a white knight to take over with your approval.

Use the poison-pill defense and put in golden parachutes to defend your personal position and your closest buddies."

"I have the feeling you don't support these methods wholeheartedly."

"I would if it was purely a business decision. But it's not. It's Edward, your only son. We're talking about family here, Mr. Lee, and I know how much that means to you."

"Yes. So what do you suggest?"

"How about this: You call in your son and make him an offer. You'll pay him whatever he wants, within reason, for his sixteen percent of all White Lotus shares. In addition, you'll help finance his new business up to X dollars. The exact amount you're willing to gamble on him is up to you. The important thing is that your offer will get him off the hook with Giant Panda. If he goes in business with them, he'll be lucky to keep the fillings in his teeth. But if you promise him majority control of his new company, he'll jump at it—unless he's an idiot, which I don't think he is. You follow?"

"I follow."

"Now in addition to getting your son out from under Giant Panda, this plan will also give you such a heavy block of White Lotus stock that no takeover pirate will even think of making a run at your company."

"You believe Giant Panda will accept defeat gracefully?"

"Of course not," Cone says. "They'll squeal like stuck pigs. You can tell them to go screw, but I think it would be wiser to make a deal with them. You know Henry Wu Yeh?"

"I've met the gentleman."

"Is that what he is? Well, I hear he's got the smarts. First, sew up your deal with Edward. Then go to Yeh and offer him the same share price you gave your son. He'll go for it. What other choice has he got? Fronts for Giant Panda have been buying up White Lotus stock in lots of a thousand shares or more. They should be happy to unload at a premium over the market price. That's why they got into this scam in the first place. The only thing they'll be losing will be majority control of Edward's new company—an iffy proposition."

"This is going to cost me a lot of money, Mr. Cone."

"You bet your sweet ass it will," Timothy says cheerfully. "I don't know what your personal net worth is, but I'd guess you may have to take on some heavy debt to finance the greenmail and investment in Edward's venture. But what's your alternative? Complete estrangement from your son. You don't want that, do you?"

"No. In spite of what he's done, he is still my flesh and blood. More sake, please."

Cone fills their crystal glasses again. The vodka at the Lees' apartment, beers at the Lexington Avenue saloon, and now two shots of rice wine. . . . He figures if he keeps this up, his liver will look like a cellulose sponge.

"So tell me, Mr. Lee—what do you think of my scenario?"

"It has much to recommend it. I will give it very careful consideration."

"Yeah, well, I've got to level with you; I have a personal interest in your going for it. Mr. Henry Wu Yeh isn't happy about my sticking my schnoz in his affairs, and he's suggested his world would be a brighter place without me—permanently. So if you could speed up your decision and, if you decide to go for it, give Yeh a call today, I'd appreciate it. I don't want to lean on you—the choice is yours—but I don't want you to hear from someone else that I suggested this plan just to save my own cojones. I happen to think it would be best for you, your son, and just incidentally for me."

"Thank you for your honesty, Mr. Cone. Now I hope you will be equally honest about another matter. Was my wife a party to this green-mail scheme?"

"I don't know. All I can do is guess. And my guess is that she may have encouraged Edward to break with you. But that could have been just pillow talk—you should excuse the expression. I don't think she made any commitment or actually pledged her stock. I think she decided to wait and see how the cards would fall—and then go with the winner."

"Yes," Chin Tung Lee says sadly, "she is capable of that. My wife has a certain peasant shrewdness."

"That she has. Here's a thought: If you decide to cut a deal with your son and help finance his new business, why don't you stipulate that he relocates in California and starts the company out there."

"Ah, you think that will effectively end their affair?"

Timothy shrugs. "There's always the chance that she'll follow Edward to the West Coast. But I'm betting she sticks in New York. You've got more money than your son."

"Yes," Lee says, "and I'm an old man with not too much time to go. Is that what you're thinking? You *are* realistic."

Then, emboldened by the second sake, Cone says, "Look, Mr. Lee, why don't you say to your wife, 'Hey, baby, straighten up and fly right. Stop playing around or you're out on your ass.' Have you got the gumption to talk to her like that?"

"I may speak to her," the old man says cautiously, "but perhaps not in those exact words."

"Whatever," Timothy says. "You're the chess whiz." He rises, takes up cigarettes, matches, leather cap, and prepares to leave.

"Another sake?" the oldster suggests.

"No, thanks. I know a guy who drank a lot of that stuff and then threw up in his girlfriend's aquarium."

"You know some odd people, Mr. Cone."

"Everyone's odd—including me. You still love your wife, don't you?"

"Yes," says Chin Tung Lee.

They're humping away as if the Bomb is en route and they've only got minutes to wring the last twinge of joy from sentient life.

"Oh," Samantha Whatley says. "Oh oh oh."

Maybe it's because she's been away so long or because he's missed her so much. But they're playing the brangle buttock game with brutal intensity, perhaps meaning to punish each other for their separation. They couple with the desperation of survivors.

In her bouncy bed, with the pink mattress flounce all around, French dolls tossed to the floor to stare at the ceiling with ceramic eyes, they joust with grunts and fervor, reclaiming their intimacy with groans and curses. No delicacy or gentle caring here, but naked warfare and the fury of combat.

"Ah," Timothy Cone says. "Ah ah ah."

These two demons never have figured out if they're lovers or antagonists—and have no interest in finding out. All they seek is the resolution of their wants. And if the end doesn't justify the means, what the hell does?

So they slide slickly over each other, prying ferociously, grappling, twisting, biting, and losing themselves in a quest they cannot define. There is anguish in their lovemaking as if they mean to perish when all is complete. But meanwhile they practice the age-old tricks and skills that came out of the cave, or might have been perfected by hairy primates swinging from trees.

Neither will surrender, but both must. They end with a duet of moans and yelps, singing a song of longing and need deferred. Then, slackening, they stare at each other wide-eyed, fearful of their release, wondering if the world still turns.

Cone lurches off the sheets, stands a moment until his knees solidify. Then he pads over to Samantha's refrigerator and returns with the chilled California chablis he brought to celebrate her homecoming. He fills their glasses, then sets the jug down on the floor alongside the bed.

They sit up with their backs against the headboard, sipping their wine and content to laze away the late Saturday afternoon.

"Did you miss me?" Sam asks.

"Sure."

"Don't tell me you didn't cut your eyes at another woman while I was gone."

"I might have looked," Cone admits, "but I didn't touch."

"Fair enough," Sam says. "And what have you been up to at the office?"

"Nothing much. The usual bullshit."

She turns her head to glare at him. "Come on, asshole, give me a break," she says. "I'll read your reports on Monday anyway."

"Yeah, well, mostly I was working the White Lotus file."

"Tell me about it."

He gives her a condensed account of his adventures with Chin, Claire, and Edward Lee, with Johnnie Wong and Henry Wu Yeh, with the United Bamboo and Giant Panda gangs. By the time he finishes, they've polished off the wine. Cone refills their glasses. The light is muted now, the apartment mellow with dusk.

"Jesus," Sam says, "you really get the crapolas, don't you. Did the Giant Panda baddies ever come after you?"

"Nah. I got a call on Wednesday from Chin Tung Lee. He made a deal with Yeh—bought back Giant Panda's shares of White Lotus stock at a premium. And Edward is moving to the coast to start his new business."

"Was Chin happy at how it all turned out?"

"I guess so. He sent me a great big carton of White Lotus products. I've got enough Chinese food in the loft to give Cleo slanted eyes."

"Tim," she says thoughtfully, "that Claire Lee—was she the one you had the hots for?"

"She's something. I thought at first she was gold, but she turned out to be tin."

"But her husband loves her."

"Everyone's got problems," Cone says.

"Yeah? What's your problem, sonny boy?"

"I'm horny again."

"Thank God!" Samantha cries.

Sullivan's Sting

1

He was a perfect gentleman, attentive, eager to please. There was something balletic in his movements: a swoop to light Mrs. Winslow's cigarette with a gold Dupont, a bow to place the black mink stole about her fleshy shoulders, a pirouette as the maître d' came bustling up.

"Was everything satisfactory, Mr. Rathbone?"

"Everything was excellent, Felix," he said, and pressed a folded twenty into the waiting palm.

"The zabaglione was *divine,*" Mrs. Birdie Winslow said. "Something extra, wasn't there?"

"Just a few drops of rum, madam. For flavor."

"Marvelous idea. We must come again."

"Please do," Felix said, escorting them to the door. "On Friday we shall have baked pompano with a champagne sauce."

Outside, they stood a moment staring up at a lucid sky sown with rows of stars. But the easterly wind had an edge, and Mrs. Winslow wrapped her stole tighter. Rathbone slipped an arm lightly about her thick waist.

"Chilly?"

"Not really."

He leaned closer. "Love your perfume. Obsession, isn't it?"

"Oh, David," she said, "you know everything."

"Yes," he said solemnly, "I do." And then laughed, hugging her to share the joke. "All right, now let's test your sense of direction. We're in Boca Raton. Which way do we go to get back to Lauderdale?"

She looked around a moment, then pointed. "That way?"

"And end up in Palm Beach? Nope, we go south."

He handed the ticket to the waiting valet, and they stood in comfortable silence until the black Bentley was brought around.

"Thank *you*, Mr. Rathbone," the valet said, pocketing his tip. "You folks have a nice evening now, y'hear."

"Everyone in Florida is so polite," Mrs. Winslow said as they drove southward on A1A.

"Uh-huh," David Rathbone said. "The last outpost of civility. All you need is money. Birdie, I hope you don't mind dropping in at this party."

"Of course not. I'll be happy to meet your friends."

"Not friends—clients. I don't socialize much with them. I prefer to keep our relations on a professional level. But I thought it would give you a chance to chat with them, find out for yourself if they're satisfied with my services. That's the best way to select an investment adviser: talk to the man's clients and get their opinions."

"Are they all wealthy?"

"None of them is hurting. And Sidney Coe is *rich* rich. He keeps a yacht down at Bahia Mar that's just a little smaller than the *QE2*. Crew of five live aboard, but Coe never takes it out. Just uses it for partying."

"And you handle all his funds?"

"Oh yes. Up about forty percent last year. But all my clients have done as well. At that rate you can double your money in less than two years."

"I'd like that. Poor Ralph used to handle all our investments and after he died I just turned everything over to the bank."

"Banks are all right," Rathbone said, "but too conservative. They're so heavily regulated that there are a lot of aggressive investment opportunities they're not allowed to touch."

"How long will it take the bank to double my money?"

"Probably about ten years—if you're lucky."

"And you can do it in two?"

"Or less," he said. "You won't object if we only spend an hour at the party? Then I'll drive you home. I've got to get back to my office. I have a client in Madrid who's phoning at midnight."

"Madrid? Oh my. Do you have many foreign clients?"

"Five. One in Spain, two in England, one in France, one in Germany. I usually get over there several times a year and visit them all. And of course they frequently come to Florida. Especially in the winter!"

"I can understand that," Birdie Winslow said. "The climate is *divine*. I'm so glad I moved here."

"So am I," David Rathbone said, and placed a hand gently on her plump knee.

The home was on the Intracoastal Waterway at the Hillsboro Inlet. They parked on a circular driveway of antique brick, along with a Cadillac, BMW, and Jaguar XJ-S. They sat a moment, staring at the glittering mansion.

"David," she said, "it's *divine!*"

"Is it? Four bedrooms, three baths, marble floors, pool, sauna, private dock. It's listed, fully furnished. They're asking a million five. Interested?"

"Oh heavens, no! Too big for just little old me."

"Of course it is. You have better things to do with your money."

"But why are they selling?"

"They're building on the beach. A larger place with a guest house. Before we go in, let me brief you on what to expect. The host and hostess are Mortimer and Nancy Sparco. He was in sewer pipe in Ohio. Retired now. The guests will be Sidney Coe, the yacht owner I told you about, and his third wife, Cynthia. He made his money in natural gas. Oklahoma. The third married couple are James and Trudy Bartlett. He was a neurosurgeon. Then there's Ellen St. Martin. You already know her. A divorcée. And Frank Little, who may or may not be gay. He's an importer. Mostly sports equipment. The butler's name is Theodore, and the maid is Blanche."

"I'll never remember all that."

"Of course you won't," he said, taking her arm as they strolled up the chattahoochee walk. "But you'll sort them out eventually. Don't forget to ask what they think of the job I'm doing for them."

Mrs. Winslow was happy she'd worn her basic black and pearls, for all the women were in evening gowns and the men, like Rathbone, were spiffy in white dinner jackets and plaid cummerbunds. She was introduced around, and everyone was just as nice as they could be. Champagne was served in crystal flutes.

Rathbone drew aside and let Mrs. Winslow mingle with the other guests. They spoke of planned cruises, a new restaurant in Miami, the polo season at Wellington, and an upcoming charity ball in Palm Beach for British royalty. It was all easy talk, moneyed talk, and Mrs. Winslow was dazzled.

"If you don't mind my asking," she said to Cynthia Coe, "what do you think of David Rathbone? I mean as an investment manager. I'm thinking of going in with him."

"Do it," Mrs. Coe said promptly. "The man's a wizard. The best in the business."

"He's got the Midas Touch," James Bartlett said. "Doubled my net worth in two years. You can't go wrong."

"A financial genius," Mortimer Sparco said. "Absolutely trustworthy. He'll make you a mint."

"Divine," Mrs. Winslow kept breathing. *"Divine."*

The hour passed swiftly. Finally, goodbyes were said, with all the women vowing to call Birdie for lunch or a shopping tour of the malls. Then Rathbone drove her home to her rented condo.

"Nice people," he said, "weren't they?"

"*Very* nice. So friendly. Nothing standoffish at all. David, I've decided I'd like to have you manage my money."

"I think that's a wise decision," he said. "You won't have the nuisance of watching your investments every day. You'll get a monthly statement from me detailing exactly how much you've made. My fee will be deducted automatically from the profits. Suppose I stop by around eleven tomorrow morning with the papers. Just a simple power of attorney and a management contract. It won't take long. And then perhaps we could have lunch at the Sea Watch."

"I'd like that," Birdie Winslow said.

He stopped in front of the lobby, got out of the Bentley, came around and held the door open for her. Before they parted, he kissed her cheek lightly.

"Thank you for a lovely evening," he said. "I'm looking forward to a long and mutually profitable relationship."

"Friendship," she said with a tinkly laugh, touching his sun-bleached hair.

"Of course," he said.

He drove swiftly back to the house on the Hillsboro Inlet. The others were still busy cleaning up, wiping out ashtrays, plumping cushions, arranging the chairs precisely.

"Come on, gang," Ellen St. Martin was saying. "Everything's got to be spick-and-span. I'm showing this dump tomorrow."

They all looked up expectantly when Rathbone entered. He lifted a hand, thumb and forefinger making a circle in the A-OK sign.

"Got her," he said, and they applauded.

He moved amongst them, taking out a gold money clip in the shape of a dollar sign. He gave each of them a fifty, not forgetting Theodore and Blanche, washing glasses in the kitchen.

"Now let's adjourn to the Palace," Rathbone said. "The booze is on me, but you guys will have to buy your own macadamia nuts."

Laughing, they all moved outside to their cars. Frank Little grabbed Rathbone's arm.

"Where did you find that mooch?" he asked. "My God, she's as fat and ugly as a manatee."

"Really?" Rathbone said with a smile. "I think she's *divine*!"

2

His name was Lester T. Crockett, and he was an austere man: vested, bow-tied, thin hair parted in the middle. He raised his eyes from the open file on his desk, looked at the woman sitting across from him.

"Rita Angela Sullivan," he said. "Unusual name. Spanish and Irish, isn't it?"

"You've got it," she said. "Puerto Rico and County Cork."

He nodded. "That was a fine operation in Tampa," he said.

"I didn't get much credit for it."

"Not in the newspapers," he agreed with a frosty smile. "You can blame me for that. I didn't want your name or picture used. I wanted you down here for an undercover job."

"But it was me who roped the banker," she argued. "Without him, they'd have no case at all."

"I agree completely," he said patiently, "but I assure you that your work did not go unnoticed. That's why you're here."

"And where the hell is *here*?" she demanded. "All I know is that my boss in Tallahassee put me on a plane for Fort Lauderdale and told me to report to you. What kind of an outfit is this?"

He sat back, twined fingers over his vest, stared at her. "Let me give you some background. About a year ago it became obvious that the war against so-called 'white-collar crime' in Florida was being mishandled. I'm speaking now not of the drug trade but money laundering, boiler room scams, stock swindles, and tax frauds. There are a lot of elderly people in Florida, *rich* elderly people, and along with the retirees came the sharks."

"So what else is new," she said flippantly, but he ignored it.

"The Department of Justice sent me down to study the problem and make recommendations. I found that it wasn't so much a lack of money or a lack of manpower that was hurting law enforcement in this area, it was the number of agencies involved, overlapping jurisdictions, and a competitiveness that frequently led to inefficiencies and rancorous dispute."

"Everyone hunting headlines?" she suggested. "Big egos?"

"Those were certainly factors," he acknowledged. "The FBI, SEC, State Attorney's Office, IRS, and local police, to name just a few, were all involved. Investigators from those agencies were walking up each other's heels, withholding evidence from each other, and planning sting and undercover operations with absolutely no coordination whatsoever."

"I believe it," she said. "I heard of a case in Jacksonville where a local undercover narc set up a big coke buy. Only the seller turned out to be an undercover FBI narc."

"Happens more often than you think," Crockett said, not smiling. "My recommendation was to set up an independent supra-agency that would draw personnel from all the others, as needed, and work with absolutely no publicity or even acknowledgment that such an agency existed. My recommendation was approved with the proviso that such an organization would be allowed to function for only two years. At the end of that time, an evaluation would be made of the results, if any, and it would then be determined whether or not to allow the supra-agency to continue to exist. I was appointed to direct the agency's activities in south Florida."

"Lucky you," Rita Sullivan said. "What's the name of this agency?"

"It has no name. The theory is that if it's nameless it is less likely to attract attention."

"Maybe," she said doubtfully. "And where do I fit in?"

"You'll be working with a man named Anthony Harker. He's on loan from the Securities and Exchange Commission."

"A New Yorker?" she asked.

"Yes."

"That's one strike against him," she said. "He's my boss?"

Crockett gave her his wintry smile. "I prefer the word 'associate.' He's waiting in his office, down the hall. He'll brief you."

"If I don't like the setup, can I go back to Tallahassee?"

"Of course."

"But it'll go in my jacket that I bugged out. Right?"

"Right," Lester T. Crockett said, rising to shake her hand.

Instead of names painted on the doors, there were business cards taped to the frosted glass. She found one that read Anthony C. Harker and went in. The man seated behind the steel desk had an inhaler plugged up one nostril. He looked at her, blinked once, pocketed the inhaler.

"For an allergy," he said. "You might have knocked."

"Sorry."

"You're Rita Angela Sullivan?"

"That's right. Anthony C. Harker?"

"Yes." Then, stiffly, "You can call me Tony if you like."

"I'll think about it," she said and, unbidden, slid into the armchair alongside his desk.

"When did you get in?" he asked.

"Last night."

"Where you staying?"

"The Howard Johnson in Pompano Beach."

"Using your real name?"

"Yes."

"Good. What address did you give when you registered?"

"My mother's home in Tallahassee."

"That's okay. When you check out, pay cash. No credit cards."

"When am I going to check out?"

"We'll get to that. Have you got wheels?"

"No."

"Rent something small and cheap. By the way, I heard about the bust in Tampa. Nice work."

"Thanks."

"They were flying the stuff in from the Bahamas?"

"That's right. Using an old abandoned landing strip out in the boon-docks."

"How did you get the banker to sing?"

She lifted her chin. "I persuaded him," she said.

Harker nodded. "This thing we're on isn't drugs. At least not the smuggling or dealing."

"Money laundering?"

"That may be part of it. The key suspect is a guy named David Rath-bone. No relation to Basil."

"Who's Basil?"

"Forget it," he said. "You're too young. This David Rathbone is a wrongo. No hard stuff, but he's a con man, swindler, shark, and world-class nogoodnik. You hungry?"

"What?" she said, startled. "Yeah, I could eat something."

"Here's the subject's file. Read it. Meanwhile I'll go get us some lunch. Pizza and a beer?"

"Sounds good. Pepperoni and a Bud for me, please."

He was gone for almost a half-hour. When he returned, they spread their lunch on his desktop.

"No pepperoni for you?" she asked.

"No, just cheese. I've got a nervous stomach."

"I read the file on Rathbone," Sullivan said. "A sweet lad. Where did you get that photo? He's beautiful."

"From his ex-wife. If she had her druthers, she'd have given us his balls, too."

"What's he into right now?"

"He's set himself up as an investment adviser or financial planner—whatever you want to call it. I estimate—and it's just a guess—that's he's got at least fifteen mooches on his list, and he's handling maybe twenty million dollars."

"Oh-oh. Who are all these lucky victims?"

"Widows and divorcées plus a choice selection of doctors and airline pilots—the biggest suckers in the world when it comes to investments."

"What's his con?"

"He gets them to sign a full power of attorney plus a management contract. Then he's home free. His fee, he tells them, is three percent annually. If he's handling twenty mil like I figure, it would give him a yearly take of six hundred thousand. But I don't think he's satisfied with that. A greedy little bugger, our Mr. Rathbone. And with his record, he's got to be dipping in the till. But he sends out monthly statements, and no one has filed a complaint yet. About two months ago I convinced one of his clients, a divorcée, to demand all her money back from Rathbone, including the profits he claimed he had made for her. She got a teller's check for the entire amount the next day. She was so ashamed of doubting Rathbone that she returned the check and told him to keep managing her money."

"If Rathbone is looting the assets, how was he able to return the divorcée's funds?"

"Easy. The old Ponzi scam. He used other investors' money to pay off. He came out of it smelling like roses, and it made me look like a shmuck. Why are you staring at me like that?"

"How long have you been in south Florida?" Sullivan asked.

"Almost eight months now."

"How come you're so pale? Don't you ever hit the beach?"

"I'd like to but can't. I get sun poisoning."

"Allergy, nervous stomach, and sun poisoning," she said. "You're in great shape."

"I'm surviving," Harker said. "You look like you toast your buns every day."

"Not me," she said. "This is my natural hide. I can get a deeper tan just by walking a block or two in the sunshine."

"Count your blessings," he said. "Now let's get back to business. Rathbone hangs out with a crowd of wiseguys who are just as slimy as he is. I've only been able to make one of them: an ex-con named Sidney Coe, who did time for a boiler room operation in Kansas City. I don't know what the others are into, but you can bet it's illegal, illicit, and immoral. They all meet in the bar of a restaurant on Commercial Boulevard in Lauderdale. It's called the Grand Palace."

"Great," she said. "Now let me guess. You want me to start hanging out at the Grand Palace and try to cozy up to this gang of villains."

"That's about it," he agreed. "Especially David Rathbone. I'm the guy who racked him up on that insider trading charge in New York. But he waltzed away from that with a slap on the wrist. That's one thing to remember about this man: He's been charged three times, to my knowledge, and never spent a day in chokey. You know why?"

"He cut a deal?" Rita suggested.

"Right. By ratting on his pals. This is not a standup guy. The other thing to remember about him is that he's a womanizer. It helps him hook those female mooches, but he also plays around when there's no profit involved."

She stared at him a long moment. Finally: "I'm beginning to get the picture. You expect me to ball this guy."

Harker slammed a palm down on the desktop. "I expect you to do your job," he said angrily. "How you do it is up to you. I want to know how he's rolling his victims and I want to know what his buddies at the Grand Palace are up to. You want out?"

She considered for two beats. "Not yet. Let me make a few moves and see what happens. Do I call you here?"

"No," he said. "And don't come back to this building again. These people we're dealing with are bums but they're not stupes. You could be tailed. Here's a number you can call, day or night. Leave a message if I'm not in. One other thing: What are you carrying?"

"Thirty-eight Smith and Wesson. Short barrel."

"A cop's gun," he said, holding out his palm. "Let me have it."

She hesitated, then took the handgun from her shoulder bag and handed it over. Harker put it in his desk drawer and gave her a nickel-plated Colt .25 pistol. She examined it.

"What am I supposed to do with this peashooter?" she asked.

"Carry it," he said. "It's more in character. And leave your ID and shield with Mr. Crockett's secretary on your way out. Here's something else."

He withdrew a worn, folded newspaper clipping from his wallet and passed it to her. It was a two-paragraph story about Rita Angela Sullivan being arrested in a Tallahassee specialty shop for shoplifting. According to the clipping, charges were dropped for lack of evidence.

She read the story twice, then looked up at him. "How much did it cost to have this thing printed up?" she asked.

"Plenty," he said. "It looks like the real thing, doesn't it? Don't lose it. It might come in handy."

"How do you figure that?"

"If Rathbone goes through your purse, he'll find your dinky little gun and this clipping. It'll help you con the con man."

"Uh-huh," she said. "Pretty sure of me, weren't you?"

"I was hoping," Harker said.

She tucked pistol and clipping into her shoulder bag and stood up.
"Thanks for the lunch," she said.

"My pleasure."

She paused at the door. "You can call me Rita if you like," she said.

"I'll think about it," he said.

3

The Grand Palace was located on the north side of Commercial Boulevard between A1A and Federal Highway in an area known to local law enforcement agencies as Maggot Mile. The restaurant advertised Continental Cuisine, which in south Florida might include broiled alligator and smoked shark.

The main dining room, decorated in Miami Hotel Moderne, attracted a regular clientele of well-heeled retirees and tourists during the season, October to May. The shadowy back room, called the Palace Lounge, had its own side entrance opening directly onto the parking lot. The Lounge was decorated with fishnets, floats, lobster traps, and a large preserved sailfish over the bleached pine bar.

David Rathbone left his black Bentley in the care of the parking valet in front of the Grand Palace, then walked around to the Lounge entrance. He was wearing a suit of raw white silk with a knitted mauve polo shirt, open at the throat. His white bucks were properly scuffed. His only jewelry was an identification bracelet of heavy gold links, a miniature anchor chain.

The Lounge was empty except for Ernie polishing glasses behind the bar. Ernie was an ex-detective of the NYPD, cashiered for allegedly shaking down crack dealers. In addition to his barkeeping duties, he booked bets and served as a steerer for pot and coke dealers. He could also provide the phone number of a young call girl who happened to be his daughter.

"Good evening, Mr. Rathbone," he said. "How you doing?"

"Surviving," Rathbone said, and removed a five-dollar bill from his money clip. "Will you do me a favor, Ernie?"

"You name it."

"Put this fin in your cash register. Later in the evening I'll ask you for a five. Be sure to bring me this one. Got it?"

Ernie examined the bill, running his thumb across the surface. "Queer?"

"No," Rathbone said, "it's the real thing."

The bartender stared at him. "Is this a scam?"

"Nah, just a little joke."

"Uh-huh. What's in it for me?"

"The five."

"Okay," Ernie said, "I'll play. You want the usual, I suppose."

"You suppose correctly. With a wedge of lime, please."

The Lounge had tables of fake hatch covers polyurethaned to a high gloss. Most of them seated two or four patrons comfortably. But in the most shadowed corner was a giant table set about with nine mate's chairs. This table bore a small card, RESERVED, and it was there Rathbone carried his vodka gimlet. He lighted his first Winston of the day and settled down.

He didn't wait long. Ten minutes later Mortimer and Nancy Sparco came in, stopped at the bar, then brought their Scotch mists over to the big table. Rathbone stood up.

"Nancy," he said, "you look ravishing, and if Mort wasn't here, I would."

"Be my guest," Sparco said and flopped into the chair next to Rathbone's.

"Mort's in a snit," Nancy said. "He didn't win the lottery—again."

"You still playing that?" Rathbone asked. "It's a sucker's game; you know it. Look at the odds."

"Look at the payoff," Mortimer said. "Millions! It's worth a hundred bucks a week."

"What numbers do you play?" Rathbone asked idly.

"He plays anything with a seven in it," Nancy said. "Claims it's his lucky number. Some luck!"

"It'll hit," Mort said. "Seven has always been very good to me."

"That's where you're making your mistake," Rathbone said. "Look at the winning numbers over the past year. You'll find that most of them have five in them. Like five, fifteen, twenty-five, and so on."

Sparco looked at him. "You're kidding."

Rathbone held up a palm. "Scout's honor. I've studied random number frequency on my computer and believe me, five turns up more often than seven or any other number."

"I don't believe you," Mortimer said.

Rathbone shrugged. "It's even true for the serial numbers on five-dollar bills. You'll find that the digit five occurs most frequently."

"David, you're nuts."

"Am I? Would you like to make a small bet?"

"Mort," Nancy said, "don't do it."

"I'll make it easy on you," Rathbone said. "I'll bet you twenty bucks that the first five-dollar bill we examine will have more fives in the serial number than any other digit."

"All right," Sparco said, "I'll take your bet." Then, when he saw Rathbone reach in his pocket for his money: "Oh no, not your five! You've probably got a ringer all ready for me."

Rathbone shook his head. "What a suspicious bastard you are. You're my friend; I wouldn't cheat you. All right, we'll do it this way." He called over to the bar: "Ernie, you got any fives in the register?"

"Sure, Mr. Rathbone," the bartender said. "How many you want?"

"Just one. Pick out any five-dollar bill you like and bring it over here for a moment, will you?" Then, to Sparco: "Satisfied it's on the up-and-up now?"

"I guess so."

Ernie brought the bill to their table. They bent over it and examined the serial number.

"There you are!" Rathbone said triumphantly. "Three fives. Now do you admit I'm right?"

"Son of a bitch," Mortimer said, and handed a twenty to the other man. "You've got the luck of Old Nick."

"It's the science of numbers," Rathbone said. "You can't fight it."

"Mort, I told you not to bet," Nancy said morosely. "David always wins. I need another drink."

James and Trudy Bartlett joined them, and a few regulars came through the side entrance to sit at the smaller tables. A noisy party of four tourists entered from the dining room, headed for the bar. Sidney and Cynthia Coe arrived, and then Ellen St. Martin and Frank Little. More regulars came in; the tables filled up; someone fed the jukebox; the joint began to jump.

At the big table, the talk was all about a three-year-old filly, Jussigirl, who had won all her eleven starts. Then the conversation turned to the recent run-up in the price of precious metals. Sid Coe, who owned a boiler room on Oakland Park Boulevard, announced his intention of switching his yaks from gemstones to platinum.

Ernie came from behind the bar, leaned over Rathbone, whispered in his ear.

"That guy at the end of the bar, dressed like an undertaker, he says he's a friend of yours, wants to talk to you. Okay, or should I bounce him?"

Rathbone turned his head to stare. "Yes, I know him. Is he sober, Ernie?"

"He's had a few, but he's holding them."

Rathbone excused himself and joined the man standing at the bar. He was tall, skinny, almost cadaverous, wearing a three-piece black suit of some shiny stuff. The two men shook hands.

"Tommy," Rathbone said, "good to see you. When did you get out?"

"About a month ago."

"Hard time?"

"Nah. I can do eighteen months standing on my head. Just the cost of doing business."

"They sure as hell didn't fatten you up."

"The food in that joint is worse than hospital slop. The warden's on the take."

"Need some green?"

"No, thanks, David; I'm doing okay. I had a safe deposit box they never did find. You got anything going?"

"This and that."

"I got something that could be so big it scares me. But I don't know how to handle it. You interested?"

"Depends," Rathbone said. "What is it?"

Tommy leaned closer. His breath was 94 proof. "I shared a cell with an old Kraut who was finishing up five-to-ten. He was in for printing the queer. Not pushing it, just manufacturing fifties and hundreds and selling them to the pushers. He told me a lot about papers, inks, and engraving. The guy really knows his stuff. He claimed that when he was collared, he had just come up with an invention that could make a zillion if it was handled right. Well, you know how old lags talk, and I thought he was just blowing smoke. He got out a couple of months before I did and told me to look him up and maybe we could work a deal together. So when I was sprung, I decided to do it. Right now he's got a little printshop in Lakeland. We killed a jug one night, a bottle of schnapps that tasted like battery acid, and he showed me his great invention."

"And?" Rathbone said. "What was it?"

Tommy withdrew a small white envelope from his inside jacket pocket, lifted the flap, took out a check. "Take a look at that."

Rathbone examined it. It appeared to be a blank check printed with the name and address of a California bank. "So?" he said.

"Got a pen?"

Rathbone handed over his gold Montblanc ballpoint. Tommy made out the check to David Rathbone for a thousand dollars, dated it correctly, then signed "Mickey Mouse." He slipped the check back into the white envelope, sealed it, handed it to Rathbone.

"Keep it for a week," he said, "then open it. I'll come back here in ten days or so and we'll talk about it. Okay?"

"If you say so, Tommy, but why all the mystery?"

"You'll see. Just leave the check in the envelope for a week and then open it. David, this could be our ticket to paradise. See you around."

Tommy left a sawbuck on the bar, then went out the side entrance.

Rathbone put the sealed white envelope in his side pocket and rejoined the crowd at the big table.

"Who was that?" Jimmy Bartlett asked. "The guy you were talking to at the bar."

Rathbone laughed. "You didn't recognize him? That was Termite Tommy."

"Never heard of him."

"He organized a great gig in south Florida. Guaranteed termite extermination. Traveled around in a van offering free termite inspection to homeowners. He also carried a jar of live termites and a bag of sawdust. After he made his inspection, he showed the mooch how his house was about to collapse unless he signed a contract for total termite control. Then Tommy would pocket the up-front deposit and take off. He had a nice thing going for almost three years until the gendarmes caught up with him. He drew eighteen months. But as he said, it's just part of the cost of doing business."

"What's he up to now?" Cynthia Coe asked.

"Who knows?" Rathbone said. "Probably selling earmuffs to south Floridians. The guy's a dynamite yak."

Frank Little leaned across the table. "Hey, David," he said, "catch who just came in. Ever see her before?"

4

Rita Sullivan figured that if she dressed like a flooze, Rathbone would make her for a hooker arrived in south Florida for the season, and he'd be turned off. At the same time she didn't want to look like Miss Priss. So she settled for a rip-off of a collarless Chanel suit in white linen with a double row of brass buttons. The newly shortened miniskirt showed a lot of her long, bare legs. Her white pumps had three-inch heels.

When she got out of her rented Honda Civic, the parking valet caught a flash of tanned thigh and said, in Spanish, "God bless the mother who gave birth to you."

"Thank you," Rita said and, chin high, marched into the Grand Palace.

The maître d' came bustling forward, giving her an admiring up-and-down. "Ah, madam," he said, "I am so sorry but the kitchen is closed."

"That's all right," she said. "I just wanted a nightcap. You have a cocktail bar?"

"But of course!" he cried. "The Palace Lounge. Through that back doorway, if you please."

The Lounge was jammed, noisy, smoky. Rita swung onto a barstool, turned sideways, crossed her legs. She ordered a vodka stinger from the baldy behind the bar. It was served in a glass big enough to float a carp. She took a sip.

"Okay?" Ernie asked.

"Just right," she said. "Busy night."

"It's always like this. On Saturday we have a three-piece jazz combo."

"I'll have to catch that."

"You can't go wrong," he told her.

"In that case I'll skip it," she said, and he gave her a knowing grin.

She turned and surveyed the Lounge casually. It wasn't hard to spot David Rathbone. He was seated at the head of a big table in the corner. He was even better-looking than his photograph, a golden boy, and he was staring at her.

She turned back, waited until baldy was down at the other end of the bar, then opened her shoulder bag and took out a pack of Virginia Slims. She kept rooting in her bag as if looking for a match. It was a corny ploy, but she reckoned if the guy was on the make he'd catch the signal and come running. He did. A gold Dupont lighter was proffered.

"May I?" he said.

She liked his voice. Deep, throaty, with a burble of laughter.

"Thank you," she said, and lighted her cigarette.

He looked at the pack. "You've come a long way, baby," he said.

"So they tell me," she said.

"Can I buy you a drink?" he asked.

"I've hardly touched this one."

"So? The night's young. May I join you?"

"If you like."

He took the barstool alongside her, not too close.

"First time here?"

She nodded.

"You'll like it. Good crowd. Big drinks."

"Uh-huh. And not exactly cheap."

"They're expensive," he acknowledged. "But there are a lot of fringe benefits." He gave her a dazzling smile. "I'm one of them."

She laughed and worked on her stinger.

"Where are you from?" he asked her. "I've been in Florida for years and I've never met anyone who was born here. Everyone's from somewhere else. I'm from Boston originally, then New York. You?"

"New Orleans originally, then Tallahassee."

"Work down here?"

"Hope to. I just arrived. I'm a schoolteacher."

"Oh? And what do you teach?"

"Spanish."

"A otro perro con ese hueso."

Rita laughed again. "Do you know what that means?"

"Not really. But I once told a Spanish lady that I loved her, and that's what she said. I always thought it was the Spanish equivalent of 'And I love you, too.'"

"It's the Spanish equivalent of 'Tell it to the Marines.'"

Then *he* laughed. "I better stick to English. Ready for a fresh drink? I am."

"Sure," Rita said. "Why not."

Ernie brought them a vodka gimlet and a stinger and left them alone.

"I love your Chanel suit," Rathbone said.

"It's a cheap copy."

"You're joking." He examined one of the brass buttons. "It even has the insignia." He shook his head. "Those rip-off artists are really something. Do me a favor, will you?"

"What?"

"Never cut your hair. It's glorious."

"Thank you. But it's a pain in the ass to wash."

"I'll help," he said, and they stared at each other.

"My name is David Rathbone," he said.

"My name is Rita Sullivan," she said, and they shook hands.

"Where do you live, Rita?"

"I just got in a few days ago. I'm staying at the Howard Johnson in Pompano Beach."

"You want to go back to HoJo tonight?"

"Not particularly."

"You have a car?"

"Yes."

"So do I. I also have a town house on the Fourteenth Street Causeway. The drinks are free. Will you follow me there?"

"All right," she said, "I'll follow you."

They rose to leave. Ernie, watching covertly from the end of the bar, wondered who was hustling whom.

Rathbone's home was between A1A and the Waterway. They stood on the lawn and looked up.

"It's enormous," Rita said.

"Not really," he said. "Two bedrooms and a third I use as an office. Three and a half bathrooms. Florida room. Terrace. The pool is for the entire development, but no one uses it; they walk to the ocean."

"You live alone?"

"I have a houseman and a cook-housekeeper. Theodore and Blanche. Jamaicans. Nice people. But they don't live in."

The vaulted living room was all white, beige, gold. There was a forty-one-inch rear projection TV. The kitchen was white with black plastic panels on the appliances. A restaurant range, microwave, overhead rack of coppered pots and pans.

"You know how to live," Rita said.

"Everyone knows how to live," he said. "There's no trick to it. All you need is money. Want to stick to the stingers?"

"Please."

"I'll have one, too."

They took their drinks into the living room, sat on the couch, kicked off their shoes.

"What do you do to afford all this?" Rita asked. "Rob banks?"

"No," he said with a tight smile. "I manage O.P.M.—Other People's Money. I'm an investment adviser."

"I'd say you're doing all right," she said, looking around.

He shrugged. "I work hard. And I've been lucky. Luck is very important."

"It's been in short supply with me lately."

"Married? Separated? Divorced? Or widowed?"

"No, no, no, and no," she said. "Just a single lady. Disappointed?"

"Of course not."

"What about you?"

"Married," he said. "Once. And now divorced. Thank God."

"And never again—is that what you're saying?"

"That's what I'm saying. Today. Tomorrow I might feel differently."

"You might," she said, "but I doubt it. You know, if I was a man, I'd never get married. What for? Sex? Companionship? A nurse if you get sick? A housekeeper when you get old? You can buy all that."

"If you've got the money," he reminded her. "You have a very cynical outlook, Rita."

"Not cynical, just realistic. Am I going to spend the night?"

"I want you to, but it's your decision."

"The bedrooms are upstairs?"

"Yes."

"Mix us another and let's take them upstairs."

"Wise decision," he said.

"You want me out of here tomorrow morning before your servants show up?"

"That's the first dumb thing you've said tonight."

Upstairs, she looked around the master bedroom and whistled. "I like everything about it except for the engraving over the bed. Who the hell is *that*—your grandfather?"

Rathbone laughed. "Big Jim Fisk. I'll tell you about him someday. A romantic story. He was murdered at the age of thirty-eight."

"Oh? How old are you, David?"

"Thirty-eight."

"Whoops!" she said. "Can I use the john?"

She did, and then he did. When he came out, she was lying naked atop the silver coverlet, black hair spread over the pillows. He stood looking down at her long body, dusky, with raspberry nipples.

"Ah, Jesus," he breathed.

She watched him undress. "You really are a golden boy," she said. "Where did you get that allover tan?"

"Show you tomorrow," he said, and joined her.

He was very good. She was better.

The morning sun was hot, bright. She roused slowly, staring at the ceiling, wondering where she was. Then Rathbone was at the bedside, looking down at her without smiling. He tossed a yellow terry robe onto the coverlet.

"Breakfast on the terrace in fifteen minutes," he said, no laughter in his voice now.

She came out into the sunlight, wearing the robe, toweling her hair.

"Glorious day," she said.

"It may be," he said. He was wearing a short-sleeved shirt of cotton gauze, pale linen slacks belted with a neck tie, espadrilles.

She glanced around the terrace. Glass-top table and chairs of verdigrised cast iron. Canvas slings. Two redwood lounges with flowered mattresses.

"Now I know where you get your allover glow," she said.

"Right. The only ones who can see you are helicopter pilots."

Theodore served freshly squeezed grapefruit juice, honeydew melon with wedges of lime, hot miniature croissants with sweet butter and mango jam, black coffee laced with chicory.

"You eat like this every morning?" she asked.

"Uh-huh. Why do you carry a gun?"

She continued buttering her croissant. "Self-defense," she said. "Everyone in Florida carries a gun."

"Maybe everyone in Florida *has* a gun," he corrected. "I do. But not everyone *carries* a gun."

"Since you obviously tossed my bag," she said, looking at him directly, "you probably found the newspaper clipping, too. Why the search?"

"You know what Barnum said?"

"There's a sucker born every minute?"

"And two to take him. I prefer being a taker rather than a takee. I like to know the people I deal with. And you're no schoolteacher."

"So now you know: I pack a popgun and I was charged with shoplifting. You want me gone?"

"No, I don't want you gone," he said. "Do you want to move in?"

She was astonished. "For how long?"

"Until I want you gone."

She took that. "What do I do for walking-around money?"

He took out his gold clip, extracted five hundred in fifties, handed them across the table.

She took the bills, then looked at him with a crooked grin. "What's this for?" she said. "Fun and games?"

"Check out of your hotel," he told her. "You can take the guest bedroom. Then go buy some clothes and lingerie. That stuff you're wearing is a disgrace. Get things that are simple and elegant—whites and beiges, blacks and grays. Forget about the wild colors. Tone down."

"Yes, boss," she said. "You wouldn't be putting a hustle on me, would you?"

Then he smiled for the first time that morning, displaying his sharp white teeth. "Call it love at first sight."

"The L-word?"

"You got it," he said.

5

The meeting ended precisely as 2:45 P.M. (Lester T. Crockett ran a tight ship), and the staff filed out carrying case folders and notebooks. The air was still fumy with cigarette smoke and the odors of hamburgers and french fries they had ordered in for lunch. Crockett switched his window air conditioner to Exhaust and turned back to his desk. Anthony Harker was still sitting in a folding metal chair.

"Fifteen minutes, chief?" he asked.

"Can't you put it in a memo?" Crockett said.

"No, sir."

"All right. Ten minutes."

Harker hunched forward. "Sullivan called yesterday and left a message on my machine. She's made contact with David Rathbone."

"Made contact?" Crockett said. "What does that mean?"

"She's moved in with him."

The chief laced fingers across his vest and stared up at the ceiling. "Yes," he said, "I would call that making contact. What else did she say?"

"Not much. He was in a unisex beauty salon getting his hair trimmed and styled, plus a shampoo, facial, manicure, and pedicure."

Crockett grunted a laugh. "He lives well."

"Anyway, Rita left him there while she did some shopping with money he gave her. That's when she made her call."

"So? What's your problem?"

"Communications. Chief, there were a lot of questions I wanted to ask, but she had to leave her message on my machine. I want to give her permission to call me here anytime during the day."

Crockett frowned. "Including from Rathbone's home?"

"Yes, sir."

"Chancy. She might be overheard. No, she's too smart for that. But he might notice the higher phone bills and ask for itemization of local calls. That could blow the whole thing."

"I realize that," Harker said. "What I'd like is an unlisted phone in my office for Sullivan's use only. We'd arrange with the phone company that all incoming calls on that line would be billed to us. That way she could call me here during the day and, in case of emergency, my motel at night."

"All right," Crockett said, "set it up." He unlaced his fingers, leaned forward over the desk. "Something else bothering you?"

"Chief, Rathbone and his pals are not tough guys. I mean they don't go around knocking people on the head or robbing gas stations. They live relatively normal lives; they're just nine-to-five crooks."

"Get to the point."

"Admittedly Rathbone isn't Billy the Kid, but if he finds out Rita is a plant, he might turn vicious."

"He might. But you spelled out the deal to her, didn't you? And she didn't back off. She's a cop, and a good one."

"Still . . ."

"Listen, Harker, you're accustomed to stock swindles and inside trading. White-collar crime. Sullivan's expertise is drug smuggling, homicide, and rape. So don't tell me she won't be able to handle a flimflam artist like

Rathbone if he turns nasty." He paused a moment, then: "Worried about her, are you?"

"Yeah."

"Want to pull her off the case and go at Rathbone from a different angle?"

"No."

"Then stop worrying. If anything happens to Sullivan, I'll take the rap, not you."

Harker stood up. "This is the first time I've asked a woman to put out to help me make a case. I don't like this business."

"You'll get used to it," Crockett said.

6

The door to David Rathbone's office was equipped with a Medeco lock and a dead bolt. Only Blanche was allowed in once a week to clean, and then Rathbone was always present.

It was an austere chamber with a tiled floor: black and white in a checkerboard pattern. The desk, chairs, file cabinets, coat tree, and glass-fronted bookcases were all oak. Even the Apple Macintosh Plus was fitted into an oak housing. The room was dominated by an old-fashioned safe, a behemoth on casters, with a handle and single dial, painted an olive green and decorated with a splendid American eagle.

Rathbone sat in his high-backed swivel chair, an antique that had been reupholstered in black leather with brass studding. He stared at the sealed white envelope Termite Tommy had given him, containing the thousand-dollar check.

He had known from the start that he'd never be able to wait the week Tommy had requested; he couldn't endure unsolved riddles, puzzles, mysteries. He took a sterling silver letter opener from his top desk drawer and slit the flap. He peered inside.

The check had disappeared. In its place was a fluff of white confetti, no piece larger than a quarter-inch square.

"Son of a bitch," Rathbone said aloud.

He dumped the confetti onto his palm. It felt slightly oily and smelled oily, too. That wasn't important. What counted was that a thousand-dollar check had disintegrated. That old German forger had developed a paper that self-dissolved into worthless chaff. Except, as Termite Tommy had said, if handled right, it could be a ticket to paradise.

He spun the dial of the big safe: 15 left, 5 right, 25 left. He heaved up on the handle and the heavy door swung silently open. He put the white envelope and confetti inside, closed the door, spun the dial. Then he left the office, locked up, went out onto the terrace.

Rita Sullivan was lying naked on one of the lounges, hair bound up in a yellow towel. On the deck alongside her were a bottle of suntan oil, a thermos and plastic tumbler of iced tea. Rathbone pulled a chair close to the lounge.

"You know how to live," he told her.

"I'm learning," she murmured.

"I have to go pick up my tickets," he said. "I'm flying to London tomorrow, then on to France, Germany, and eventually to Spain. I have clients over there and have to discuss their investments."

She raised up on an elbow, back arched, and he caught his breath.

"How long will you be gone?" she asked.

"Three days. I'll fly back from Madrid."

"Can I go?"

He smiled and handed her the tumbler of iced tea. "Not this time. Maybe next trip. I go four or five times a year. Clients need stroking."

"What airport are you leaving from?"

"Miami. Will you drive me down?"

"Of course."

She put the tumbler aside and lay prone again.

"More oil?" he asked.

"Please," she said. "My legs."

He loved it, and she knew it: smoothing the oil onto her hard, muscled thighs, onto the dark satin behind her knees, her smooth calves.

"Will you be faithful while I'm gone?" he said in a low voice.

"Uh-huh."

"I know you will be. Or I'll find out about it. My spies are everywhere. I thought we'd drive up to Boca tonight for dinner. Then meet some people at the Palace for a few laughs."

"Sounds good."

"Happy?" he asked her.

"If I was any happier I'd be unconscious."

He laughed, slapped her oiled rump lightly, and left to pick up his tickets.

That night, at a Spanish restaurant in Boca Raton, they had a pan of paella in the classic version, made with chicken, rabbit, and snails. And they shared a bottle of flinty muscadet. Then they drove back to Fort

Lauderdale singing "I Can't Give You Anything But Love." They both had good voices.

The Lounge at the Grand Palace was bouncing: tables filled, the bar two-deep, and waitresses hustling drinks. David's friends were already at the big table, and Rita Sullivan was introduced around. No chair was available for her, but Frank Little offered his lap, and she accepted with great aplomb.

Rathbone excused himself and went over to the bar. He waited patiently and was finally able to grab Ernie's arm.

"That man I was talking to the other night," he said. "The one dressed in black. If he comes in, tell him I'll meet him here Tuesday night. Got it?"

"Got it, Mr. Rathbone," the bartender said. "Tuesday night."

Rathbone slipped him a fin and went back to the gang. After he took his chair at the head of the table, Rita came and sat on *his* lap. She was drinking vodka gimlets now: the way David liked them, with a lime wedge and just a drop or two of Triple Sec.

After a while Ellen St. Martin waved goodnight and departed. Rita took her chair, sitting between Frank Little and Mortimer Sparco. She asked how long they had all known each other.

"Too long," Sparco said, laughing. "Years and years."

"We're a troop," Little proclaimed, "and David is our scoutmaster. Watch out for him, sweetie; he has merit badges for loving and leaving."

She listened to the idle chatter at the table for a while, then excused herself to go to the ladies' room. She made her phone call from there.

She returned to the big table, finished her gimlet, ordered another. She listened to the bright talk, marveling at how nonchalantly these people spoke of their swindles: of mooches taken, the naive conned, the gullible defrauded and plucked clean. David and his friends dressed nicely, drove Jaguars, and rarely used profanity. But they were a bestiary of thugs.

The gathering broke up shortly after midnight. Rita and David drove back to his town house, laughing at the new business card Frank Little had distributed. It read: "FL Sports Equipment, Inc. Baseball, Football, Basketball, Soccer, Softball, Volleyball." And at the bottom: "We have the balls for it."

Rathbone took a chilled bottle of Asti Spumante and two flutes from the fridge.

"Oh my," she said, "are you trying to get us drunk?"

"No," he said. "Just keep the glow."

They went up to the terrace. The moon was not full, but it was fat enough. A few shreds of clouds. A balmy easterly wind. Scent of salt sea and bloomy things.

"Be back in a minute," David said. "Don't go away."

He returned with a portable recorder, inserted a cassette, switched it on.

"I swiped this off a radio station that plays Golden Oldies," he told her. "I was born too late. I should have been around in the 1920s and '30s. Cole Porter. Fred Astaire. Gershwin."

They drank a little wine. They danced to "You're the Top." They drank a little wine. They danced to "I Get a Kick Out of You." They drank a little wine. They danced to "Let's Fall in Love." They drank a little wine. They danced to "Anything Goes," and stopped.

They went to his bedroom. The sheets were silk, and he couldn't get enough of her.

7

Anthony Harker was living on the second floor of a motel on A1A in Pompano Beach. It was on the west side of the highway, but his suite was in the rear so most of the traffic noise was muted.

Rita Sullivan showed up a little after nine P.M. She was wearing a pink linen jumpsuit, her long hair tied back with a dime-store bandanna. There was a chunky silver bracelet on her right wrist.

"I hope you didn't drive his Bentley," Harker said. "Someone might spot it parked outside."

"No," she said. "He bought me a Chevy Corsica. White."

"Oh?" Tony said, looking at her. "Generous scut, isn't he?"

"Yes," she said, "he is. I hope his flight to London got off okay. If not, and he calls home and I'm not there, I'm in *deep* shit."

"He took off," Harker said, "but he's not flying to England. I had a CIA tracker standing by at the airport. But Rathbone went to Nassau in the Bahamas. And from there he's going to the Cayman Islands, then on to Limón in Costa Rica, and returning home from there. We checked his ticket after he left, but it was too late to set up a tail."

Rita sighed and looked around. "Got anything to drink in this dump?" she asked.

"Some cold Bud."

"That'll do me fine. How're the allergy and nervous stomach?"

"I'm surviving. Mind drinking out of the can?"

"That's fine," she said. "Pop it for me, will you? The government can't afford better digs for you than this shithouse?"

"It suits me," he said. "I'm only on loan for a year. Then back to New York. I can stand it for a year."

"If you say so. Got a tape recorder?"

"Sure."

"Let me put my report on tape. Then we can talk."

Twenty minutes later she finished dictating the names and descriptions of Rathbone's friends, plus what little she had learned of their activities.

Harker switched off the recorder. "Nice job," he said. "Let's take them one by one. First, have you any glimmer of what Rathbone is up to?"

"Nope. He keeps his office double-locked. He claimed he had to go stroke clients in England, France, Germany, and Spain."

"Uh-huh. But he's heading for places where it's easy to hide money if you pay off the right people. Well, I'll start a search in Nassau, the Caymans, and Costa Rica, but he's probably using a fake name and phony IDs. What about this Ellen St. Martin?"

"Apparently a legit real estate lady," Rita said, "with a small-time scam going on the side. She owns a house-sitting outfit for rich clients who go north from May to November. She gets paid to inspect their homes or condos weekly and make sure the air conditioning is working and the place hasn't been trashed. What the owners don't know is that she's also renting out their homes to tourists. In fact, some of the places are probably hot-pillow joints. But she makes a nice buck."

"Beautiful. And Frank Little?"

"Here's his business card. Notice the last line."

Tony read aloud: " 'We have the balls for it.' It doesn't double me over with laughter. You think he's legit?"

"And playing around with that crowd? I doubt it."

"All right," Harker said, "I'll have him checked out. Sparco?"

"A discount broker on Commercial. I think he deals in penny stocks. He also handles Rathbone's Wall Street investments."

"Then he'll be registered with the SEC, and I can get a look at his books. Sidney Coe?"

"He's got a boiler room on Oakland Park Boulevard. Right now his yaks are pushing precious metals."

"We can't do much on that until someone files a complaint. But mooches are funny; they'll take a big loss and immediately fall for another sucker deal, trying to recoup. They never do. What about James Bartlett?"

"A pleasant roly-poly guy. Something to do with banking. He seems to know every bank in south Florida."

"Laundering drug money?"

"Could be," Rita said. "He and David had a long, whispered conversation last night before the party broke up. Bartlett was doing most of the talking. And that's all I've got so far. I should be able to fill in some of the blanks as I get to know these people better."

"What's your take on Rathbone?" Tony said. "The honcho?"

"Well, I get the feeling that they're all independent operators, but they do look up to him. He sits at the head of the table. 'Our scoutmaster,' Frank Little called him. They seem to respect his opinions, but I don't think he bosses them."

"Good start, Rita," Harker said. "You've given me enough to requisition some more warm bodies from Crockett and get the wheels turning. Now I suppose you want to go home."

"Why do you suppose that?" she asked. "Is the beer all gone?"

"No, I have another six-pack."

"Break it out, sonny boy, and let's kick off our shoes and Confess All."

They slumped with feet up on a scarred Formica cocktail table, sipped their beers, stared at each other.

"Listen, Tony," she said, "I want you to know you were right on target with that dinky little pistol and the fake newspaper clipping. Rathbone did go through my bag, and I think those decoys convinced him I was in the game."

Harker shrugged. "Con men are easy to con. Their egos are so big they just can't conceive of being diddled. But don't relax. I had a talk with the boss about you. I told him I was afraid that if Rathbone ever discovers you're a plant he might turn physical."

"What did Crockett say?"

"He said you can take care of yourself."

"He's right; I can."

"Just be careful, will you?"

"Yes, mommy. And I'll look both ways before I cross the street."

Harker stirred restlessly. "You never know how a rat is going to act when he's cornered."

"David's no rat; he's a pussycat. I can handle him."

Tony took the inhaler from his shirt pocket, turned it in his fingers. Then he put it away without using it. "There's something else."

"What's that?"

He sighed. "You might as well know. I don't like the idea of you—or any other woman—putting out just to help me make a case."

"Well, aren't you sweet," she said, and leaned forward to pat his cheek. "Don't give it a second thought. I worked a drug case in Gainesville last year. My partner was a local cop everyone called King Kong. He was six-six and must have weighed three hundred. He used to be a second-string linebacker for the Dolphins. Anyway, when King Kong questioned a suspect, he'd never touch the fink with his hands, but he'd crowd him, coming in close and pushing his big chest against the guy. The suspect would look up and see this monster towering over him, and he'd start singing. King Kong was using his body to get the job done. I use my body in the same way."

"Not exactly," Harker said in a low voice.

"Look, Tony, I don't have the muscle of a male cop, so I use what I do have. If we rack up Rathbone and his pals, it'll go into my jacket and eventually I'll get a raise or promotion. I'm doing it for myself as much as I am for you."

"I don't know," he said, shaking his head. "It just doesn't seem right."

"Right? What the hell is *right*? You're talking like a Boy Scout."

"I suppose," he said. "Maybe I'm a closet puritan."

"Married?"

"No."

"Ever been?"

"No."

"Me neither," she said. "I've been too busy having fun."

"You call being a cop having fun?"

"It is to me. I like the challenge."

He looked at her directly. "And the danger?"

She thought a moment. "Maybe," she said finally.

She reached up and untied the bandanna. Shook her head and let her long hair swing free. She toyed with the zipper tab on her jumpsuit.

"I haven't got a thing on underneath," she said. "Interested?"

"Yes," Tony said.

"I'd be deeply, deeply wounded if you weren't. Does this dump provide clean sheets?"

"They were supposed to change them today."

She rose. "Let's go see if they did."

She sat on the edge of the bed, watched him undress.

"My God," she said, "you look like an unbaked breadstick."

"I know," he said. "A golden boy I ain't."

"That's all right," Rita said, inspecting him. "You've got all the machinery."

She stood, unzipped the jumpsuit, wriggled out of it. She flopped back on the bed, bouncing up and down a few times.

"Come on," she said, holding out her arms to him. "Everyone deserves a little joy."

"I suppose," he said.

8

David Rathbone waved the valet away and parked the Bentley himself. "What time have you got?" he asked.

Rita held her new gold Seiko under the dash light. "About a quarter to eleven."

"Don't give me *about;* what time exactly?"

"Ten forty-three."

He consulted his own Rolex. "Okay, I've got it. Now you sit out here and don't come into the Lounge until exactly eleven o'clock. You've got to be on the dot. Understand?"

"Sure. What's this all about?"

"Tell you later."

He picked up his gimlet at the bar and sauntered over to the big table. Trudy and Jimmy Bartlett were there, and Cynthia and Sid Coe. They all waved a greeting.

"Where's Rita?" Trudy asked. "You haven't ditched her already, have you?"

"Not yet," Rathbone said, smiling. "She had some things to do. Said she'd meet me here at exactly eleven." He glanced at his watch. "In seven minutes. She's very prompt."

Sid Coe rose to the bait.

"A prompt woman?" he said. "That's like a fast turtle. Ain't no such animal."

"Rita is prompt," David insisted. "If she said she'll be here at eleven, she will be."

"Ho ho ho," Coe said. "She'll be late; you can count on it."

"A little wager?" Rathbone said. "I'll bet you twenty Rita will show up here at eleven, within a minute either way."

"You're on," Coe said. "Easiest twenty I ever made. I know women."

They sat comfortably, smiling pleasantly at each other, occasionally glancing at their watches. At precisely eleven o'clock Rita came sailing through the side door of the Lounge.

"Hi, everyone," she said.

Rathbone held out his hand to Coe. "Twenty," he said. "Clean bills, please."

"Tell me something, dimwit," Cynthia said to her husband, "have you *ever* won a bet with David?"

"And no one else has either," Trudy Bartlett said. "Our David has the luck of the devil."

"You make your own luck in this world," Rathbone said.

"Ernie's waving at you, David," Rita said.

He turned to look. Ernie gestured toward the end of the bar where Termite Tommy was standing.

"Please excuse me," Rathbone said, rising. "Keep the party going. I'll be back in a few minutes."

He took Tommy out to the parking lot. They sat in the back of the Bentley and lighted cigarettes.

"You're right," David said. "It's got possibilities—but it needs managing."

"That's why I came to you."

"How much does that German printer want for the paper?"

"He wants a piece of the action. But I figure we can always cook the books. Besides, he's usually half in the bag."

"Uh-huh. That check you gave me dissolved in about four days. Is that the usual time?"

"Three days to a week. It's not exact."

"That's even better," Rathbone said. "I've been talking to Jimmy Bartlett. You know him?"

"No."

"He's in the game. He knows everything about banks. He should; he owned one up in Wisconsin until the examiners moved in. He did a year and nine, and he was lucky. Anyway, he knows how banks move checks. I asked a lot of questions—without mentioning the self-destruct paper, of course—and Jimmy gave me some good skinny on how to hang paper with minimum risk."

"How do we do that?" Termite Tommy asked.

Rathbone turned to look at him in the gloom. "I figure the best is to print up government checks."

"Holy Christ!" Tommy cried. "That's a federal rap."

"So is mail and wire fraud. No matter how you slice it—queer civilian checks or government checks—the bottom line is Leavenworth. But I think it can be fiddled. The risk-benefit ratio looks good to me. The big plus in using fake checks from Uncle Sam is that, according to what Jimmy told me, you can draw against them in one day. Sometimes immediately if the bank knows you."

"I don't get it."

"Look, if you write a forged check against someone who lives, say, in California, that crazy paper would be sawdust before the check clears. That means the California bank will never debit it to the mooch's account because all they've got is a handful of confetti. But if a local bank will credit a U.S. Treasury check within a day, then you can draw on it and waltz away whistling. By the time the blues catch up with the scam, that fake check is little bitty pieces of nothing, and they've got no evidence. No fraud. No counterfeiting. No forgery. Nothing."

"Yeah," Tommy said slowly, "I can see that."

"What I figure is this: We'll make a trial run. Have the Kraut make up a fake U.S. Treasury check, complete with computer code. Make it look like an IRS refund or something. Then we'll get the pusher to set up a checking account in a local bank. After the account is established, the fake government check is deposited. The next day the pusher takes out the money and disappears."

Tommy lighted another cigarette. "The way you explain it makes sense. Let's try it and see how it works. But don't expect me to do the pushing. I've done all the time I want to do."

"No," Rathbone said, "not you and not me. I think I've got the right player for the part. As soon as you have the check ready, let me know."

"How much you want to make it for?"

"Some odd number. Like $27,696.37. Not over fifty grand. We'll start small and see how it goes."

Termite Tommy nodded and got out of the car. Then he leaned back in. "You'll have to give me the name of the pusher. It's got to be printed on the check."

"I'll let you know," Rathbone said, and took a business card from his Mark Cross wallet. "Here's my front; it's legit. David Rathbone Investment Management, Inc. Call me there when you're set."

"Will do," Tommy said, and walked away.

Rathbone went back into the Grand Palace Lounge. All the gang had assembled, and everyone was laughing up a storm. David took his chair at the head of the table and winked at Rita. She rose and came behind him, leaned down and nuzzled his cheek.

"Where have you been?" she asked.

"Business," he said.

"Monkey business?"

"Something like that. How would you like a job?"

"I've got a job: keeping you happy."

"And you succeed wonderfully. This is just a little errand with a super payoff."

"Lead me to it," she said.

9

Knowing the ways of officialdom, Harker asked Crockett for ten more warm bodies. He got four, which was one less than he had hoped for. They were reportedly all experienced investigators from agencies lending personnel to Crockett's operation.

Tony started with a local from the Broward County Sheriff's Office. He was a tall black named Roger Fortescue.

"That's an unusual moniker," Harker said. "English, isn't it?"

"Beats me," Roger said. "Could be. My folks come from tidewater Virginia. I got a grandpappy still alive. When he talks, I catch about every third word he says. What kind of an outfit is this?"

"Mostly white-collar crime."

"Nobody in south Florida wears white collars. We got red, green, yellow, all-colored golf shirts. Call it purple-collar crime and you'll be closer to the mark."

"I guess," Harker said. He passed Frank Little's business card across the desk. "This is your subject."

Fortescue held the card a moment without reading it. "What's his problem?"

"Unsavory associates."

"Sheet," the investigator said, "they could rack *me* up on that charge. I guess you want the inside poop on this guy."

"You've got it. He may turn out to be clean, but I want him checked out."

"No strain, no pain. I report to you?"

"That's right. Here's my night number. If I'm not in, you can leave a message."

"This Frank Little—is he a heavy?"

"You tell me."

Fortescue nodded and rose lazily. "I'll take a look at him. Keep the faith, baby."

Harker said, "They stopped saying that twenty years ago."

"Did they? Well, I still say, 'That's cool,' but I always was old-fashioned."

Fortescue ambled down to his four-year-old Volvo and took another look at Frank Little's business card. The guy was out on Copans Road. The snowbirds were beginning to flock down, and Federal Highway would be crowded. But the investigator figured he had all the time in the world. That Harker seemed laid-back; not the type to crack a whip.

He found FL Sports Equipment, Inc., sandwiched between a shed that sold concrete garden statuary and a boarded-up fast-food joint that still had a weather-beaten sign: OUR GRITS ARE HITS. Fortescue parked and eyeballed Little's place.

Not much to it. A cinderblock and stucco building, painted a blue that had been drained by the south Florida sun. Behind it was what appeared to be a warehouse surrounded by a chain-link fence with a locked gate. A wide blacktop driveway led from the road past the office to the warehouse. And that was it—except for an American flag on a steel flagpole in front of the blockhouse.

Roger locked the Volvo and shambled up to the office. The door was unlocked. The inside was as bare and grungy as the exterior. There was a cramped reception room with one desk, one chair, one file cabinet, one coat tree. No inhabitant. An open door led to an inner office.

"Hello?" Fortescue called. "Anyone home?"

A man came out of the inner office. He had hair as fine and golden as corn silk. He was wearing a sharp suit that Roger recognized as an Armani. His embroidered shirt was open to the waist, and he wore a heavy chain supporting a big gold ankh. It lay on his hairless chest.

"Yes, sir," he said briskly. "Help you?"

"Hope so," Fortescue said. "I'd like to buy a dozen baseballs."

The man's smile was cool and pitying. The investigator didn't like that smile.

"Oh, we don't sell retail," he said. "We're importers and distributors."

"I was hoping maybe you could sell me a dozen baseballs wholesale. Give me a break on the price."

"We don't even sell wholesale. As I said, we're distributors. We sell *to* wholesalers."

"Sheet," Fortescue said. "Well, can you tell me any local place that carries your stuff?"

"Sorry, we have no wholesale or retail outlets in south Florida. All our sports equipment goes north."

"You sure?"

The flaxen-haired man gave him that irritating smile again. "I'm Frank Little. I own the business, so I should be sure. I think your best bet would be Sears or any sporting goods store on the Strip in Lauderdale."

"I guess so," Fortescue said. "Thanks for your trouble. Sorry to bother you."

"No bother," Little said. "I wish I could help you out, but I can't. Tell me something: Why do you want a dozen baseballs?"

"I coach an inner-city Little League," the investigator said. "We haven't got all that many bucks. That's why I was trying to shave the price."

Unexpectedly Little took out a fat wallet and handed Fortescue a crisp fifty. "Here," he said. "For your kids."

"That's mighty kind of you," Roger said, "and I do appreciate it."

Back in the Volvo he slipped the fifty into his pocket and decided he liked the way this case was shaping up.

He drove to Federal Highway and stopped at a discount liquor store. He shot the fifty plus on a liter of Absolut, a bottle of Korbel brut and another of Courvoisier cognac. His twin sons were still awake when he arrived home, and he roughhoused with them awhile until Estelle packed them off to bed. She returned to the kitchen to find her husband had mixed a pitcher of martinis with the Absolut. The other bottles were on the countertop.

"What's the occasion?" she asked.

"A nice man gave me a tip," he said. "A nice, freaky man."

They each had two martinis and drank the champagne with a fine dinner of broiled grouper, corn on the cob, and creamed spinach. Then they took cognacs and black coffee into the living room to watch TV.

"I wonder what the poor folks are doing," Fortescue remarked.

"I don't want to know," his wife said.

It was close to midnight when he rose, strapped on a hip holster with a .38 Police Special, and checked a little two-shot derringer he carried in an ankle pouch. Estelle watched these preparations without asking questions.

"A little business," he told her. "Should be back in an hour or two. You go on to bed."

"You know I won't," she said. "Listen, you get yourself killed, and I'm not going to bury you, I swear it. I'll prop you up on the couch in front of the TV until you just turn to dust. Then I'll sweep you out—y'hear? You remember that."

"I surely will, mommy dearest," he said, grinning.

He drove back to Copans Road, past the FL Sports Equipment layout. He parked on the shoulder across the street and sauntered back. He stood in the shadow of a big bottle palm, watching the activity.

Floodlights were on, the gate of the chain-link fence was open, and a big white semi was parked alongside the warehouse. At least four men were carrying cardboard cartons from the warehouse and loading them into the trailer. Frank Little and another guy, a mastodon, stood to one side watching the loading. Little had a clipboard and was apparently keeping a tally.

Slumped against his tree, Fortescue observed the action for almost an hour. He counted at least fifty cartons. Then the truck doors were slammed and locked. Three men got into the cab, and the semi began to back slowly onto Copans Road. That's when Fortescue got a good look at the legend painted on the side: SIENA MOVING & STORAGE. NEW YORK-NEW JERSEY.

The investigator strolled back to his Volvo and drove home. Estelle was still awake, watching an old movie on TV. She looked up when he came in.

"You again?" she said. "Have a good time?"

"A million laughs," he assured her.

He went into the kitchen and called the night number. It was after two in the morning, but the phone was picked up almost immediately.

"Harker. Who's this?"

"Fortescue. Look, you're from New York, aren't you?"

"That's right."

"Ever hear of Siena Moving and Storage? They operate in the New York-New Jersey area."

There was a brief silence. Then: "I've heard of them. The outfit is owned by one of the Mafia families in Manhattan."

"My, my," Roger Fortescue said. "Those bentnoses must play a lot of baseball."

10

It was starting out to be a great season: balmy days and one-blanket nights. The tourists lolled on the sand, groaning with content, and later showed up at Holy Cross Emergency with second-degree burns. That noonday sun was a tropical scorcher, but the snowbirds bared their pallid pelts and wanted more.

Rathbone took the sun in small, disciplined doses, before eleven A.M. and after three P.M. And he spread his body with sunblock. Rita Sullivan was out on the terrace every chance she got, slick with baby oil, getting darker and darker.

"The back of the bus for you," David said, laughing. But he loved it, loved the contrast between her cordovan and his bronzy gold.

Then, one day at breakfast, he said to her, "Ready for that little job I told you about?"

"I'll never be readier."

"We'll leave at ten-thirty."

She showed up in the same pink linen jumpsuit she had worn to Tony Harker's motel.

"Nice cut," Rathbone said, inspecting her. "But I told you I don't like those sorbet colors on you."

"Want me to change?"

"No. Where did you buy it?"

"At Hunneker's."

"How much?"

"About two hundred with tax," she said.

"You still have the sales check?"

"I guess so. Why? Are you going to return it?"

"Not exactly. How did they wrap it when you bought it?"

"What's this—Twenty Questions?"

"Come on," he said, "how was it wrapped?"

"In tissue paper and then put in a Hunneker's bag. A plastic bag."

"Still got the bag?"

"Yes."

"Get it and the sales check. I'll meet you downstairs and we'll get this show on the road. We'll take your car."

They drove over to Pompano Fashion Square and found a slot in the crowded parking lot.

"Stay in the car," Rathbone ordered, "but keep the doors locked. I shouldn't be more than twenty minutes or so. What floor did you buy the jumpsuit on?"

"The second. Sportswear."

He headed directly for Hunneker's, the plastic bag and sales check folded flat in his jacket pocket. The store had big plate-glass windows with gilt lettering:

J. B. HUNNEKER'S. SATISFACTION GUARANTEED OR YOUR MONEY CHEERFULLY REFUNDED.

He took the escalator to the second floor and wandered about until he located the Sportswear department. It didn't take long to find a rack of jumpsuits exactly like the one Rita was wearing. He looked about casually. Then, finding himself unobserved, he took a pink jumpsuit off the rack, folded it into the plastic Hunneker's bag, and approached the service desk.

"I'm sorry," he said to the woman behind the counter, "but I bought this for a birthday gift, and my wife doesn't like the color."

"What a shame," she said. "Would you like to exchange it for another color?"

"No, I think I better let her come in and pick out what she wants. Could I get a refund, please. Here's my sales check."

He was back in the car in fifteen minutes. He told Rita what he had done, and she laughed.

"You don't miss a trick, do you?"

"Not if I can help it. I'm certainly not going to shell out two hundred for something I don't like."

"Do I get the money?"

"I think not," he said. "You keep your jumpsuit and I'll keep my money. It's a win-win game—the kind I like. Now move over and let me drive."

He maneuvered the Chevy out of the parking lot and turned northward on Federal Highway.

"We're going to a bookstore on Sample Road near I-95," he told her.

"Oh? Going to shoplift a couple of books?"

"No," he said, "I'm not into boosting. This is an interesting place. It's owned by a man named Irving Donald Gevalt. He deals only in rare books and antique manuscripts."

"And he makes a living from this?"

"He owns two motels, a fast-food franchise, and three condos on the beach. But he didn't get all that from pushing rare books; he's got a very profitable sideline. He's in the game, and all the sharks call him ID Gevalt. He's the best paperman in south Florida. Social Security cards, driver's licenses, military discharges, voter registrations, passports, visas—you name it and ID can supply it. That's why we're going to visit him, to fix you up with an identification package for that little job you're going to do for me."

She turned to look at him. "Hey, wait a minute. You didn't say anything about forged papers. I don't like that."

"They're not forged," Rathbone said. "Everything ID Gevalt handles is strictly legit. That's why he gets top dollar."

"So where does he get the documents—from stiffs?"

"Sort of. He's got freelancers working for him in a dozen cities. They go through old newspapers in their hometowns and clip out items about infants and little kids who died twenty, thirty, forty years ago. They send the name, address, and date of birth to Gevalt. He writes to the Department of Birth Records in those cities, requesting a copy of the dead kid's birth certificate. Costs him from two to ten bucks, and they never ask what he wants it for. So now he's got a legitimate birth certificate of someone who's been dead for years. The certificate is the key. With that Gevalt can get a Social Security card, voter's registration, even a driver's license, by hiring someone to take the test under the name on the certificate."

"A slick operation."

"Like silk. How old are you, Rita—about thirty-five?"

"That's close enough."

"So we'll buy you a package of identification for a white female about thirty-five years old."

"And what do I do with that?"

"Tell you later. Here we are."

The Gevalt Rare Book Center was located over a shop that installed domed plastic ceilings for condo kitchens and bathrooms. There was a steep outside staircase leading to the second floor. The center was a dusty jumble of books, magazines, newspapers. It was comfortably air-conditioned, but smelled mildewy.

"David!" the old man said, coming forward with an outstretched hand. "Good to see you again!"

"ID," Rathbone said, shaking the proffered paw gently. "You're looking well."

"Liar," the geezer said. "But I'm surviving. And who is this lovely lady?"

"A dear friend. Rita, meet the famous Irving Donald Gevalt."

The gaffer bent creakingly to kiss her hand. "Famous, no," he said. "Notorious, possibly. Rita, you are a sylph."

"I hope that's good," she said.

"The best," Gevalt assured her. "The very best. David, this is a social call?"

"Not exactly. I need a package for Rita. Birth certificate, Social Security, driver's license. And any extras you might have."

The old man pushed up his green eyeshade and stared at Rita through rheumy eyes. "Middle-thirties," he guessed. "Could be Hispanic. I think I have something that will just fit the bill. Excuse me a moment, please."

He shuffled slowly into a back room, closing the door carefully behind him.

Rita looked around at the stacks of books and journals. "Does he ever sell any of this stuff?"

"Occasionally," David said. "Mostly by mail order. It's a good front. And he knows the rare book business. I heard he's got the world's best private collection of Edgar Allan Poe first editions and original manuscripts."

Gevalt was back in a few minutes with a worn manila envelope. "Gloria Ramirez," he said, "from San Antonio, Texas. I think Gloria will do splendidly. Would you care to inspect?"

"Of course not," Rathbone said. "I know the quality of your work. The usual, ID?"

"Ah, I am afraid not. With this dreadful inflation, I have been forced, regrettably, to raise my fees. Two Ks, David."

Rathbone took out his stuffed money clip and extracted the two thousand in hundred-dollar bills. "A business expense," he said, shrugging. "I'll write it off as entertainment."

"Of course," Gevalt said with a gap-toothed grin. "That is what life is all about—entertainment. Am I right?"

The door to the back room opened, and a young blonde, no more than nineteen, stood posed, hip-sprung. She was wearing a tiny black bikini that seemed to be all fringe.

"Lunch is ready, daddy," she said.

"In a moment," Gevalt said, and led the way to the outside door. "Do come back again, David, and you also, Rita. Not only for business, but just to visit."

In the car, Rita looked at him with a mocking smile. "You certainly didn't miss the daughter," she said.

"I noticed her," David admitted. "But she's not his daughter; she's his wife."

"You're kidding!"

"Scout's honor. That's what life is all about—entertainment. Am I right?"

On the drive back to the town house, he explained to Rita what the first part of her new job would entail. She would drive up to Boca Raton and, at the Crescent Bank on Glades Road, open an interest-bearing checking account under the name of Gloria Ramirez, depositing the minimum required.

"The bank officer to see is Mike Mulligan," Rathbone told her. "Give him a phony home address in Boca and say you work at the Boca Mall. Jimmy Bartlett has this Mulligan on the pad, and he'll be tipped off to approve your application without investigating your references. Got it?"

"Sure," Rita said. "See Mike Mulligan at the Crescent Bank on Glades Road in Boca and open a checking account in the name of Gloria Ramirez. That's all?"

"For now."

"I don't suppose you want to tell me what this is all about?"

"You're right; I don't. But it's for your own protection. If the deal turns sour, you can always claim you know nothing about it and were just doing a favor for a friend."

"Uh-huh. Why do I have a feeling you're playing me for a patsy?"

"I'd never do that," David said. "If I thought there was any real risk, I'd never ask you to do it. I want you around for a long time. And now I'm going to drop you at the town house and switch to the Bentley. I have a lunch date with a potential client."

"He or she?"

"He. A retired professor who I hear has more bucks than brains."

"David, how do you find these mooches?"

"I have steerers all over south Florida. Sometimes Jimmy Bartlett hears of a good prospect through his bank contacts. Sometimes Ellen St. Martin gives me the name of someone who's just moved down here and is looking to spend big money on a house or condo. If I land the fish, I always pay a finder's fee. What are you going to do this afternoon?"

"I don't know. Maybe I'll go down to the beach for a few hours."

"I wish you wouldn't," he said. "There are a lot of sleazes cruising the beach looking to score off a single woman."

"David! You're worried about me! Don't give it a second thought, honey; I can take care of myself."

"Just carry your gun—all right?"

"Okay, I'll carry my gun, and I won't talk to beach bums. I'll even wear a one-piece suit. Satisfied?"

"With your body it doesn't matter if you wear a bikini or a raincoat; you're still going to attract attention."

"David, do you think I have a better body than Gevalt's wife?"

"You make her look like a boy."

"Flattery will get you everywhere. Hurry back from your lunch and we'll have us a matinee."

"Yes," he said, "I'd love that."

After Rathbone took off in the Bentley, Rita went into the kitchen and had lunch with Blanche and Theodore. They all shared a big shrimp salad and drank beer. Theodore told her how David landed Birdie Winslow as a client by staging a fake cocktail party with the Palace Lounge crowd masquerading as richniks. Everyone had a good laugh.

Rita put on a white maillot and used one of David's shirts as a coverup. She took her beach bag and told Blanche she'd be back in an hour or so. She walked eastward, crossing A1A. But she didn't join the crowd heading for the beach. She went into a hotel lobby, bought a pack of cigarettes and asked for two dollars' worth of quarters.

She found a public phone and called her special number. Tony Harker answered and had her wait a moment until he connected a tape recorder to his phone. Then she started talking.

11

Crockett gave the new man the orientation lecture on the need and purpose of the supra-agency. Henry Ullman, borrowed from the Treasury Department, listened politely, his meaty features revealing nothing. Then, when Crockett finished, he said, "Why me?"

"Because," the chief said, "the personnel computer spit you out. You did time with the Federal Home Loan Bank Board, didn't you?"

"That's right. Six years as examiner. Working out of San Francisco. But I got tired of crunching numbers and wangled a transfer to the Secret Service."

"Counterfeiting?"

"No," Ullman said with a sour grin, "jogging. I was assigned to the Vice President, and that guy never stops jogging. Rain, sleet, snow—he's out there at seven every morning, with me puffing along behind him."

Crockett stared at him. "You look like you could keep up. Ever play any football?"

"Nah. I was big enough but not fast enough. I'll be reporting to you?"

"Not directly. Your immediate supervisor will be Anthony Harker. He's right down the hall. You better check in with him now; he's expecting you. Good luck."

"Sure," Ullman said, hauling his bulk off the little folding chair.

In Harker's office the two agents introduced themselves and shook hands. Tony looked up at the Treasury man.

"About six-four and two-fifty?" he guessed.

"More or less," Ullman said. "I call you Mr. Harker?"

"Tony will do."

"Hank for me. What's this all about?"

Harker took several clipped pages from his top desk drawer and handed them over. "Take a look at this. It's a transcript of a taped telephone conversation called in by an undercover agent, a woman, we planted with the main villain, a guy named David Rathbone."

Ullman scanned the pages swiftly, then tossed them onto the desktop.

"You read it?" Tony said, amazed.

"Yeah. I took a speed-reading course. It's a big help. You want me to get the poop on this David Rathbone?"

"No, he's covered. Your target is James Bartlett, a man who seems to know a lot about banks. I want a complete rundown."

"Shouldn't be too difficult. I still have some good contacts in the bank biz. Do I get an office?"

"Afraid not. We're cramped for space as it is. You'll have to settle for a desk and phone in the bullpen."

"I'll manage," the investigator said.

The first thing Henry Ullman did was to go shopping for clothes. He had come down from D.C. wearing a three-piece navy-blue pin-striped suit, and he saw at once it might attract a lot of unwanted attention in south Florida. So he bought four knitted polo shirts in pink, lavender, kelly green, and fire-engine red; two pairs of jeans, khaki and black; and a polyester sports jacket in a hellish plaid.

He went back to his motel room to change and inspected himself in a full-length mirror. "Jesus!" he said. Then he went back to the office and started making phone calls. He worked until almost midnight, then found a steakhouse on the Waterway and treated himself to a twenty-four-ounce rare sirloin, baked potato, double portion of fried onion rings, and two bottles of Molson ale.

On the second day he looked up James Bartlett in the Pompano Beach phone directory. None listed. But there was one in the Fort Lauderdale directory and Ullman hoped that was his pigeon. To make sure, he changed back into his vested pinstripe and drove out to Bayview Drive in his rented Plymouth.

He whistled when he saw the homes in that neighborhood: big, sprawling places with a lot of lawn, palm trees, and usually a boat on a trailer sitting in front of a three-car garage. There were gardeners and swimming-pool maintenance men at work, and the parked cars Ullman saw were Cadillacs, Mercedeses, and top-of-the-line Audis. He figured no one who lived on that stretch of Bayview was drawing food stamps.

He parked, locked the Plymouth, and marched up to the front door of the Bartlett residence. When he pushed the button, there was no bell, but melodious chimes sounded out "Shave and a haircut, two bits."

The man who opened the door was a short roly-poly with a wispy mustache that didn't quite make it. He was wearing Bermuda shorts that revealed pudgy knees, and his fat feet were bare.

"Mr. James Bartlett?" Ullman asked.

He got no answer. "Who're you?" the guy said, giving him a slow up-and-down.

"Sam Henry from Madison, Wisconsin, sir. I'm with the First Farmers' Savings and Loan up there. I'm sure you don't remember me, but I met you at the Milwaukee convention years and years ago."

"Oh? The one where I gave the keynote speech?"

Ullman wasn't about to get tripped up by a trick question like that.

"To tell you the truth," he said, laughing, "I was so smashed for the entire convention, I don't remember who gave the speeches or what they talked about."

The man smiled. "Yes," he said, "it was rather wet, inside and out. Sure, I'm Jim Bartlett. What can I do for you?"

"The wife's got arthritis bad, and the doc thinks she'd do better in a warm climate. So I came down to south Florida to scout the territory. I hear it's booming."

"It's doing okay. This year."

"Well, I heard you had relocated here, and I thought I'd look you up and chew the fat awhile."

"I'd ask you in," Bartlett said, "but the house is full of relatives down for the season."

"That's okay," Ullman said. "This won't take but a minute. If we move down here, I'll have to find a slot. I was wondering if you know of any local banks looking for experienced officers."

"What's your specialty?"

"Home mortgage loans."

Bartlett shook his head. "I don't know of anything open at the moment, but I'll ask around. If I hear of anything I'll let you know. How do I get in touch with you?"

Ullman fished in his pocket. "Here's the card of the motel where I'm staying. It's a ratty place, and I'm looking for something better. If I leave, I'll give you a call. All right?"

"Sure," Bartlett said, taking the card. "Sam Henry of the First Farmers' S-and-L in Madison—right?"

"You've got it," Ullman said.

Bartlett nodded and pumped the big man's hand. "Nice to see you again, Sam," he said, and closed the door softly.

Ullman drove back to the office and asked Tony Harker for ten minutes. He related the details of his meeting with James Bartlett.

"He's a cutie," he said. "I'll bet he's on the phone right now calling First Farmers' in Madison. But that's okay; I set up my cover with them. They were happy to cooperate with the Secret Service. Here's what I've got on Bartlett so far: He did a year and nine for bank fraud. He's only been in south Florida for seven years, but his most recent tax return shows an adjusted gross of more than eight hundred thousand, and that house he lives in has got to go for a million, at least. He lists himself as a bank consultant, but no one in banking down here has ever heard of him. Or so they say. Something ain't kosher."

"Yeah," Tony said, and pondered a moment. Then: "Hank, that business of Rathbone having our agent open a phony account at the Crescent Bank in Boca—how do you figure that?"

"I don't. A scam of some kind, but it's hard to tell what's going down."

"So what's your next move?" Harker asked. "Tail Bartlett?"

"I don't think so," Ullman said. "In that neighborhood he'd spot my dusty Plymouth in a minute. How about if I take a different angle. According to that transcript, Bartlett has Mike Mulligan of the Crescent Bank in his hip pocket. Suppose I drive up to Boca and get a look at this Mulligan. I'd like to know what the connection is."

"Sounds good to me," Harker said. "Maybe you can turn Mulligan. The only way we're going to flush this gang is by getting someone to sing."

"I'll give it the old college try," Hank said, rose to leave, then paused at the door. "By the way, Bartlett is married. Three kids. The oldest, a girl of nineteen, OD'd on heroin about two years ago."

They stared at each other.

"You better get up to Boca as soon as possible," Tony said.

"I think so," Ullman said.

12

He explained to her that once a month the five men in the Palace gang met for a night of poker. The party was held in their homes, on a rotating basis, and tonight was Rathbone's turn.

"It's strictly stag," he told Rita. "No women allowed. I had Blanche make up a dozen sandwiches, and we'll mix our own drinks. The guys will be over around six o'clock. The rule is that no matter who's winning or losing, or how much, the game ends promptly at midnight. So I want you to take off at six and don't come back until after twelve. All right?"

"And what am I supposed to do for six hours?"

"Go shopping. Have dinner at some nice place. Take in a movie. Spend! You like to spend, don't you? Here are two yards; go enjoy yourself."

"Okay," she said. "Have a good time and win a lot of money, hon."

"I intend to," he said.

After she left, he put all the bottles of booze out on the countertop in the kitchen, along with containers of lemon peel, lime wedges, pearl onions, and some fresh mint for Jimmy Bartlett, who had a fondness for juleps. Glasses were lined up, and there was a big bucket of ice cubes with more in the freezer.

The doorbell rang a little before six o'clock, and Rathbone put on a pair of rose-tinted sunglasses before he opened up.

"Good evening, girls," he said, giving them his high-intensity smile. "Thank you for being so prompt."

Their names were Sheila and Lorrie, and both were dancers at the Leopard II, a nudie joint on Federal Highway. They were in their early twenties. Sheila did two lines of coke a day, and Lorrie had a four-year-old dyslexic son.

David took two envelopes from the inside pocket of his suede sports jacket and handed one to each woman. "Payable in advance," he said, still smiling. "And a nice tip before you leave if you do a good job."

"But no push?" Lorrie said.

"Absolutely not. If you want to make dates with these guys to meet them later, that's your business. But not in my home. Now come with me and I'll show you where to undress."

The two women stripped down in the pantry and left their jeans and T-shirts in a jumbled heap on the floor. Rathbone led them back into the kitchen and showed them the bar, the sandwiches in the fridge.

"You told me you could mix drinks," he said, "but if you have any problems, ask me. Help yourself to a sandwich if you get hungry."

"How about a drinkie-poo?" Sheila said.

"Of course," Rathbone said. "Just don't get plotched. That I don't need."

Frank Little was the first guest to arrive. He immediately pointed at David's sunglasses. "What's with the shades?" he asked.

"A mild case of conjunctivitis," Rathbone said. "The doc says I've got to avoid bright light."

"Tough shit," Little said. "Hey, I could use a drink."

"Why don't we wait for the others to show up. I've got a surprise for all of you."

James Bartlett and Sidney Coe arrived together. Then Mortimer Sparco came bustling in. When they were all seated in the living room, Rathbone told them he was tired of serving himself food and mixing his own drinks at their monthly get-togethers, so he was going to try something new.

"Sheila!" he called. "Lorrie! You can take our drink orders now."

The naked women came smiling out of the kitchen. The guests, startled, stared at them, then looked at their host, burst out laughing and climbed awkwardly to their feet.

"Sit down," David said. "These ladies are here to wait on us."

"David," Frank Little said, "you're too much."

"What would you like, sir?" Lorrie asked, bending over Mort Sparco, her pointy breasts almost touching his beard.

"If I told you," he said, "you'd slap my face. So I'll settle for a Scotch mist."

Everyone gave their drink orders, interspersed with ribald comments.

"The hell with poker," Sid Coe said after the waitresses went back to the kitchen. "I know a better game."

"Not in my home," Rathbone repeated. "What you do after midnight is up to you."

"Hey, David," Jim Bartlett said, "what's with the cheaters?"

He explained again about his mild case of conjunctivitis and how he had to avoid bright light. Everyone bought the story.

After the second round of drinks, the men moved into the dining room and sat at a big round table of bleached pine covered with a green baize cloth. Rathbone had set out two new decks of Hoyle playing cards.

"Dealer's choice," he said, shoving a deck at Sidney Coe.

"Five-card stud," Coe said. "Jacks or better to open. And just to separate the men from the boys, spit in the ocean."

He took out his wallet and dropped a hundred in the center of the table. The others followed suit. Coe broke the seal on the deck of cards, discarded the two jokers, and shuffled, shuffled, shuffled. Then he slapped the deck in front of Sparco.

"Cut your heart out," he said.

The playing cards were a forged deck and so cleverly marked that it required rose-tinted glasses to read the code printed on the backs. Rathbone bought them from a talented artist in Miami who also supplied the sunglasses. David knew that with his wiseguy pals, it was strictly a one-time gimmick, but worth the risk. The naked waitresses were his edge—to keep his guests distracted enough not to question his incredible luck.

He played craftily, folding when he saw he couldn't win, plunging when he held a winning hand. He deliberately lost a few small pots, but as the evening progressed the stack of bills in front of him grew steadily higher.

Meanwhile, the naked girls hustled drinks and sandwiches and held lights for cigars. Their presence had the desired effect; even Mort Sparco, the best poker player of the group, found it difficult to concentrate on his game. And, Rathbone noted, his guests were drinking a lot more than usual.

The session ended at midnight with David ahead almost four thousand, and all the others losers.

"You did all right," Jimmy Bartlett said, watching him pocket his winnings.

"It's about time," Rathbone said. "I've been a loser all year. Now I'm just about breaking even."

The other three men went into the kitchen to schmooze with the women. Bartlett and David stayed at the table, smoking cigars and sipping their drinks.

"How did you make out with Mike Mulligan at the Crescent in Boca?" Jimmy asked. "Any problems?"

"Not a one. Thanks for setting it up."

"I don't suppose you want to tell me what's going down."

"Not yet," Rathbone said. "If it works, I will. It could be a sweet deal, and I'll cut you in. Is Mulligan one of your laundrymen?"

"On a small scale—so far. Things are getting a little warm in Miami, so I've been trying to expand: Lauderdale, Boca, Palm Beach."

"Business good?"

"So-so. The demand is always there, but right now the supply is so plentiful that prices have dropped. One of these days my clients will get smart and set up a cartel like OPEC, just to stabilize prices."

"Is it all coke?"

"Coke, pot, heroin, hash, mescaline—you name it. I've even got one guy handling nothing but opium. With all the Asian immigrants in the country, he's doing all right. David, why are you staring at me like that?"

"I just had a wild idea," Rathbone said. "So crazy that it might work. Look, what you're talking about are commodities—right? The prices rise and fall just as they do with grains, metals, livestock, foods, and everything else they trade in the Chicago pits."

"That's correct."

"Well, what if we set up a commodity trading fund that would deal only with drugs, buying and selling futures and options?"

Bartlett drained his drink and set the empty glass down with a thump. "You're right: It is a wild idea. What are you going to do—advertise the fund in *The Wall Street Journal*?"

"Of course not. But what if we have Mort Sparco set up a penny stock in the fund, and have Sid Coe push the shares in his boiler room."

Jimmy rubbed his chin. "Now it doesn't sound so crazy. You could organize it for peanuts, and there's a possibility it could actually turn a profit on the fluctuation of drug prices. Some of my clients would probably be willing to sell kilos for future delivery in three months or six months at a set price. David, let me think about this awhile and talk to a few people."

"If there's a Ponzi payoff up front," Rathbone pointed out, "you know the mooches will be fighting to buy stock. They don't have to know what the fund is dealing in; just that it's commodities."

"It might go," Bartlett agreed. "Don't say anything yet to Coe or Sparco. Let me figure out how we can finagle it."

"Don't take too long," David warned, "or some other shark will think of it and get it rolling. It could be a world-class scam."

"You're right," Jimmy said. "And the best part is that you're not dealing with the drugs themselves. Just with contracts: pieces of paper using code names for coke, heroin, and so forth. David, I'm beginning to think it's doable. Now I need a drink."

"Let's go in the kitchen and see how my waitresses are making out."

"How much did you pay them?"

"An arm and a leg," Rathbone said. "But it was worth it."

"That Sheila turns me on. Great boobs."

"Come on, Jimmy; you're married."

"My wife is," Bartlett said. "I'm not."

13

They were walking on the beach, carrying their shoes. A gleaming crescent cast a silver dagger across the sea. The breeze was from the southeast, smelling strongly of salt. There were a few night swimmers splashing about, yelping in the chilly surf.

"He's having his pals over for a poker party," Rita reported. "Strictly stag. I can't go back till midnight so we have plenty of time. Did you eat?"

"I worked late," Tony said, "and had a pizza sent in. How about you?"

"I did some shopping at the mall and then grabbed a Caesar salad. Lots of garlic. Can't you smell it?"

"Smells good. These guys Rathbone's having over—the gang from the Grand Palace?"

"That's right. They're as thick as thieves, that bunch."

"Rita, they *are* thieves. Has he sent you back to the bank in Boca?"

"Not yet. I haven't the slightest idea what's going on there."

"Anything else?"

"Not much. He's got a new client, a retired professor with *mucho dinero*."

"Damn!" Harker said. "I can't get a handle on how his swindle works. I had the SEC take a look at his accounts with Mortimer Sparco, who's a discount broker. Sparco runs a lot of penny stocks, but so far he's clean. Anyway, Rathbone has accounts for all his clients. But they're all holding blue chips like IBM and AT&T. But I know, I *know* Rathbone is skimming. I just don't know how."

She told him the story of how David got a refund from Hunneker's on a jumpsuit he didn't like. Tony laughed.

"A crook is a crook is a crook," he said. "The guy is making at least six hundred thousand a year, but he can't stand the thought of someone taking him, even for two hundred."

"In some ways," she said, "he's very generous."

"You already told me that."

"Well, he is! I bet if I asked him for a thousand, he'd hand it over and not even ask what I wanted it for."

"He's getting his money's worth," Harker said in a low voice.

She stopped walking, making him stop, and turned to stare at him. "That was a shitty thing to say. Let's you and I get something straight, buster. I'm not a total bubblehead, you know. I have very good instincts about people, especially men. I know David is a conniving thief and belongs in the pokey, but I happen to like the guy. Okay? I happen to think he's sweet."

"Sweet?" Harker said with an explosive snort. "He's a bum!"

"So he's a sweet bum. All right?"

They turned around and continued their stroll back to his motel.

"You claim you have a good instinct about men," he said. "What about me?"

"You? A straight arrow. Uptight. If you could learn to relax, you could be quite a guy."

"Well, if it'll make you feel any better, since I met you I've stopped using my inhaler and tonight I had a pepperoni pizza."

"Bed therapy. Stick with me, kiddo, and you'll be tanning your hide in the sun." She hugged his arm, adding, "We've got till midnight."

His bedroom window was open wide, and they could smell the sea. The ghostly moonlight was all the light they needed. Her body was a hot shadow on the white sheet.

"Hand and glove," she said dreamily.

"What?"

"That's how we fit."

He was enraptured, lost and gone. He surrendered totally. I must never lose this woman, he vowed. Never.

Later, she took his face between her palms. "You're getting there," she said.

"Thank you, Dr. Sullivan," he said. "Would you like a cold beer?"

"I'd love a cold beer."

They sat up in bed, sipping. She rested the dripping can on his belly, and he winced.

"Mama told me," she said, "that I should never talk to a man about another man—especially in bed—but this is part of our job, so I figure it's okay."

"What is?"

"David Rathbone. You said he's a bum, and he is. He cheats his friends; I know that for a fact. But I've had a lot of experience with hard cases, and I've learned one thing about them: none are completely bad. A rapist can be devoted to a sick mother. A safecracker can help support his church. Even a murderer can drag a kid out of a burning house. None of us is one-dimensional. So when you call David a con man, a swindler, a thief, I know you're right. But he's more than that."

"If you say so," Tony said.

She left a little before midnight, and he went to sleep smelling the garlic on his pillow and smiling.

The next morning he gave Crockett an update. The chief listened intently, fingers laced across his vest. He looked as broody as an Easter Island statue. Harker knew he was bossing a half-dozen concurrent investigations; the man's brain must be churning.

Crockett stirred when Tony finished his recital. "Can't you move any faster on this?" he asked.

"No, sir. The two new men are coming in today. But I had to set up their legends first. I've established cover stories that'll back them up. I'll put one on Sidney Coe and one on Mortimer Sparco."

"Which on which?"

"I want to talk to them first."

Crockett nodded. "So all we've got at the moment is that paperman, Irving Donald Gevalt. You want to pull him in?"

"I don't think so, sir. He's small-fry. If we take him now, it might tip our hand and blow the whole investigation. We can pick him up anytime we want."

"I suppose so," Crockett said. "But Washington is screaming. They want to see some results from all the money they've been spending. Well, they'll just have to be patient. Like me. Anything else?"

"Yes, sir. I'd like you to authorize a black-bag job on Rathbone's town house."

"Tap his phone? We could do that at the central exchange if you think it would yield anything."

"I doubt if it would. He's too clever for that. What I had in mind was to bug the whole apartment. He had the whole gang over for a poker session. I would have loved to hear what they talked about."

Crockett shook his head. "Too risky. If he has the place swept electronically, and the bugs are discovered, there goes your ball game."

"I don't think he has the place swept. I don't think it would occur to him that he could be a target."

"What would you bug?"

"Everything, though we may have trouble getting into his office. But certainly the living room and bedrooms."

"Bedrooms? And would you tell Rita Sullivan about the bugs?"

"Oh no, sir. Why would we want to do that?"

"Why indeed," said Lester Crockett, staring at him. "I'll think about it, Tony."

14

Manny Suarez was a feisty little man with a black walrus mustache and a habit of snapping his fingers as he walked. In fact, his walk was almost a dance step, and as he bopped along, he smiled at all the passing women. Most of them smiled back because he looked like fun.

Manny was with the Miami Police Department, where he was called "Bunko" Suarez because that was his specialty: breaking up flimflams and swindles, especially those preying on newly arrived immigrants. He spoke Spanish, of course, but a lot of his success was due to his warm grin and ingratiating manner. The bad guys couldn't believe he was a cop until he snapped the cuffs on them.

He bade an emotional farewell to his wife and six children in Miami and, following orders, drove up to Fort Lauderdale in his new Ford Escort for what he was told was a "special assignment."

In Lauderdale, he reported to Tony Harker and got a two-hour briefing. Manny thought Harker was a typical Anglo: cold, starchy, and not the kind of guy you'd want to have over for a pig roast and a gallon of Cuba Libres.

But he had to admit his new boss was efficient; Harker had already set up his cover: Manny had done eighteen months in a San Diego clink for an aluminum-siding fraud, and had decided to come east to put as much distance as possible between himself and his irate victims.

His target was a man named Sidney Coe, who ran a boiler room on Oakland Park Boulevard. Manny was to apply for a job as a phone salesman, a yak, and since yaks worked only on commission, the chances were good that Coe would take him on for a trial period to see if he could fleece the mooches.

Suarez knew all about bucket shops and assured Harker that, if he was hired, he'd be handed a script to follow. It really was an acting job, Manny said, and if he could deliver a convincing performance, he'd be in like Señor Flynn.

"What I want out of this," said Harker, "is an inside report on Coe's operation, what he's pushing right now, how much money you figure he's stealing. Also, Coe has a good friend, a man named David Rathbone. I want to know if Rathbone has a piece of Coe's action, or what his connection with Coe might be. Got all that?"

"Don't worry," Manny said, grinning. "I can do it. Tell me something—do I get to keep the moaney I make?"

Tony was startled. "I never thought about that," he admitted. "I'll have to check it out with the chief. Meanwhile you try to land a job at Coe's place. Here's the address."

"Hokay," Suarez said cheerfully.

He already had a place to stay: a room in the home of a nice Cuban lady, a friend of his aunt's, who was happy to have a cop in the house and someone to cook for. So he drove directly to Coe's boiler room on Oakland Park Boulevard.

It looked no different from the legit places on the wide boulevard. The sign over the door read: INSTANT INVESTMENTS, INC. The sign was on a board, hung on a chain from a nail pounded into the stuccoed wall, and Manny wondered how often that sign had been changed.

"Good morn'," he said to the receptionist, flashing his big white teeth.

"Good morning, sir," she said, returning his smile. "May I help you?"

"Could I speak to the boss man, pliz. I am looking for a job."

"Just a moment, sir. I'll see if he's in."

She spoke softly in a phone, listened a moment. Then, to Manny: "Please sit down, sir. He'll be with you in a few minutes."

The investigator sat in an orange plastic chair and picked up a month-old copy of *Business Week*. He read a short article on inside trading, then tossed the magazine aside. He stared at the receptionist, who was typing away busily. She had short brown ringlets, and Manny thought her ears were *exquisito*. The lobes were flushed and plump. He could go *loco* nibbling on one of those lobes.

Finally a skinny, suntanned guy came out of a back door and beckoned. Suarez followed him into an inner office. It was a square chamber, sparsely furnished. The desk, chair, and file cabinet looked ready to collapse, and the tiled floor was stained and scarred with cigarette burns. The man didn't sit down and didn't ask Manny to sit.

"Looking for a job?" he asked. Cold voice.

"Tha's right."

"How did you hear about this place?"

Suarez shrugged. "You know how word gets around. Maybe some of your yaks are mouthy guys. That's why they're yaks—am I right?"

"Uh-huh. Well, I'm Sidney Coe. I own the joint. What's your name?"

"Manuel Suarez."

"Cuban?"

"Mexican," Manny said, figuring this Anglo would never know the difference in the accents.

"You live in south Florida?" Coe asked.

"Now I do."

"Where you from?"

"San Diego."

"How come you left?"

"I had a little trouble."

"Yeah?" Coe said. "How little?"

Manny hung his head and shuffled his feet. "Eighteen months," he said in a low voice.

Coe nodded. "That's a little trouble, all right. What were the eighteen months for?"

"I was selling aluminum siding."

Coe laughed. "That scam will never die. You ever sell by telephone?"

"No, but I know I can do it. I can talk fast and hard."

"I don't know," Coe said doubtfully. "You *sound* Spanish. I'm not sure the mooches will go for that."

"Look, mister," Manny said, "you got Hispanic names on your sucker list—am I right? There are plenty of rich Cubans, Mexicans, Salvadorans, Nicaraguans in the country. Let me talk to the Hispanics in their own language. I ask how is their health, are their families well, how do they like the United Sta'. Hispanics like that: the personal touch. Right away they trust me. Then, when we're friends, *compañeros,* I give them the hard sell."

Coe stared at him a moment. "Yeah," he said finally, "that might work. Let's try it. Come with me."

"Wait, wait," Suarez said hastily. "How much you pay?"

"Strictly commish. Ten percent. The harder you work, the richer you get. Some of my yaks clear a grand a week. How does that sound?"

"Hokay," Manny said.

15

Rathbone rose early and showered, shaved, dressed. He went downstairs where Blanche and Theodore were laughing in the kitchen. David had a small tomato juice and told them he'd be back soon to have breakfast on the terrace.

There was a heavy morning fog, but he knew that would burn off as the sun strengthened. He drove to a nearby mini-mall that included a drugstore selling out-of-town newspapers. He parked and noticed, on the other side of the mall, a newly installed line of newspaper-vending machines. One was the distinctive blue box of *The New York Times*' national edition.

Rathbone walked over, fishing two quarters from his pocket. He dropped them in the slot, pulled down the front lid. Glancing around to make certain no one was watching, he took two copies of the *Times* from the box and let the lid slam shut.

One newspaper he tossed onto the front seat of the Bentley. The other copy he carried into the drugstore.

"My wife bought this," he said, smiling at the clerk. "It's today's paper. But she didn't know I had already bought a copy. I wonder if I can get a refund."

"Sure," the young man said. "No problem."

He took the newspaper and handed David two quarters.

"Thank you very much," Rathbone said.

He drove home, noting the fog was already thinning. It promised to be a warm, sunny day, but maybe a little humid. Rita was still sleeping, so he breakfasted alone on the terrace. Theodore served California strawberries, a toasted bagel with a schmear of cream cheese, and black coffee. Rathbone read the Business Day section of his newspaper as he ate—paying particular attention to activities in the Chicago commodity pits—and had a second cup of coffee.

He was just leaving when Rita came straggling out, wearing his terry robe.

"I guess I overslept," she said.

"Not really," he said, kissing her cheek. "It's still early. But I'd better get to my office. Work, work, work."

"Rather you than me," she said, and yawned.

He sat before his computer screen and took a look at balances in his checking accounts. He maintained both personal and corporate accounts. But because the government provided deposit insurance of only $100,000, he used several banks with no account in excess of the cap.

He was working on a schedule of deposits and withdrawals when his phone rang.

"David Rathbone Investment Management," he said. "David Rathbone speaking."

"This is Tommy."

"How're you doing, Tommy?"

"Okay. Can we meet?"

"Sure. When?"

"Soon as possible."

"How about a half-hour. Same place we met before."

"Suits me," Termite Tommy said. "I'll be there."

Rathbone locked his office and went back to the terrace. Rita was finishing her breakfast and reading his newspaper.

"I have to run out for a few minutes," he told her. "Stick around for a while, will you? I may have a job for you later."

"I'll be here," she promised. "Knock us a kiss."

He bent to kiss her lips. "Last night was super," he said.

"They're all super," she said. "I love being pampered."

"Is that what you call it?" he said, laughing. "Slavery is more like it."

The Grand Palace hadn't opened yet; the parking lot was empty except for a decrepit pickup truck. Rathbone parked, and Termite Tommy got out of the pickup and came over to join him in the Bentley.

"Going to be a hot mother," he said.

"I guess," David said. "Got something for me?"

Tommy handed over a white envelope. "I hope we got the name spelled right," he said.

Rathbone examined the forged U.S. Treasury check. It was made out to Gloria Ramirez in the amount of $27,341.46. It looked very official, with seal, numbers, computer coding.

"A work of art," David said. "It still feels a little oily, but not so much that a busy teller would notice. How much time do we have before it dissolves?"

"Three days. Maybe four."

"I'll have the pusher deposit it today, and we'll draw on it tomorrow."

"You'll let me know?" Tommy asked.

"Of course."

"That crazy German wants a third."

"Let's wait till we see how this goes. When we have the money, we can talk a split. Except that the pusher wants her cash off the top. I promised her two grand. Okay?"

"Sure," Termite Tommy said. "If this goes off without a hitch, maybe we can use her again. Have a nice day."

"You, too," Rathbone said.

He drove home and found Rita in her bedroom, painting her toenails vermilion. David sat down on the bed next to her and held up the check for her inspection.

"Don't touch it," he warned. "You might get polish on it."

She stared long and hard at the check.

"Queer?" she asked.

"As a three-dollar bill. But it's beautifully done. It'll pass. As soon as your toenails dry, I want you to endorse it as Gloria Ramirez. Then drive up to Boca and deposit it at the Crescent."

"And then?"

"Tomorrow you go back to the bank. Draw this out plus your original deposit. Close out the account."

"What if they ask why I'm closing an account I just opened a few days ago?"

"Death in the family, and you've got to go home to San Antonio. Tell them anything. If you have any problems, Mike Mulligan will okay it."

She bent down to remove the wads of cotton from between her toes. Then she straightened up to stare at him.

"I don't like it," she said. "It's a federal rap. They'll lock me up and throw away the key. What if they lift my prints off the check?"

"They won't," he assured her. "Trust me."

She stood, naked, and began to pull on white bikini panties. "Seems to me you're asking for a whole bunch of trust. It's my ass that'll be on the line, not yours."

"In the first place," he said, "if I thought there was any real risk, I wouldn't ask you to do it. I don't want to lose you; I already told you that. In the second place, I want to find out just how much I can trust *you*. If you turn me down on this, I'll know."

"And then it's goodbye Rita?"

"You better believe it," he said, nodding. "But if you do it, there will be other jobs, bigger jobs. So it's your future you've got to consider."

She looked again at the check he was still holding. "What's in it for me?" she asked.

"Now you're talking like a mature adult," he said, giving her his 100-watt smile. "A grand for this job. And much more to come if you play along."

"All right," she said. "I'm game."

"That's my girl," he said, pulling her close.

He watched her endorse the check "For deposit only" and the account number. Then he went back to his office. Rita dressed and drove her Chevy up to Boca Raton, where she deposited the Gloria Ramirez check at the Crescent Bank. Then she called Tony Harker.

"A counterfeit Treasury check?" he said. "I can't believe it. Most yobs are specialists. A bank robber does nothing but hit banks. A strong-arm guy mugs people. They very rarely go outside their field. Like a gynecologist doesn't do tonsillectomies. Now we've got David Rathbone, a con man, going in for forgery. It doesn't make sense."

"I'm just telling you what he told me."

"I know," Harker said. "All right, do exactly what he wants. Go back to Boca tomorrow and close out the account. I'll take it from there. We'll let the Ramirez check clear so we have evidence of counterfeiting and bank fraud."

"I suppose I'll have to testify."

"Of course," he said. "That doesn't scare you, does it?"

"No," she said.

"Listen," he said in a low voice, "when am I going to see you again?"

She laughed. "Anxious?" she asked.

"Not anxious," he said. "Eager."

"That's nice," Rita said.

16

The fourth man assigned to Anthony Harker's staff came from the U.S. Attorney's office in Chicago. He had helped investigate and prosecute a stock-rigging fraud that had sent a half-dozen brokers and financiers to jail. His name was Simon Clark, and Harker disliked him on sight.

There was nothing wrong with Clark's appearance, although he could have lost twenty pounds, but he had a supercilious air about him and made no effort to hide a patronizing attitude toward Lester Crockett's supra-agency. Obviously, he thought Fort Lauderdale was no Chicago, and nothing that might advance his career could possibly come out of this rinky-dink operation.

He listened, expressionless, when Harker explained that his target was Mortimer Sparco, a discount broker with offices on Commercial Boulevard. Sparco was suspected of possible fraud and criminal conspiracy in the trading and manipulation of penny stocks, thinly traded securities that usually sold for less than $1 a share. In addition, Sparco was a close friend of David Rathbone, who called himself an investment manager but was quite possibly a con man swindling his clients with a variation of the Ponzi scheme.

"What I want you to do is—" Harker started.

"I know what you want," Clark interrupted. "You want me to pose as a new client, find out what Sparco is pushing and promising, and if this Rathbone is in on it."

The fact that he was completely correct didn't make his superior manner any easier to endure. "That's about it," Harker admitted, and couldn't resist adding, "Think you can handle it?"

The other man gave him a glare that might have chilled defendants in a courtroom, but had absolutely no effect on Tony.

"You don't need an assistant DA for a job like this," Clark said. "Any gumshoe could do it."

Harker shrugged. "You want out? Planes leave for Chicago all the time. It'll go in your file, of course."

That rattled the attorney. "I'll look into it," he said. "Besides, it's getting cold in Chicago." His smile was stretched.

"Uh-huh," Tony said. "Keep me informed. Calls every day, and a written report every week. I'll try to find you a desk and chair in the bullpen."

Cursing his luck at being dumped in what he considered a backwater, Clark returned to his hotel on the Galt Ocean Mile and changed from his heavy tweed suit to polyester slacks and a lightweight sports jacket. He stopped at the hotel bar for a quick gin and bitters, then got into his rented Olds Cutlass and drove back to Commercial Boulevard.

Sparco's place of business was located in a long, low building that also housed a unisex hairdresser, a real estate agency, a women's swimwear shop, and a store that sold and shipped Florida oranges "Anywhere in the World!"

The brokerage itself looked legit enough. There was a small anteroom with wicker armchairs and a table piled with financial periodicals. There was also a TV set with the stock tape jerking across the screen. Two old geezers wearing Bermuda shorts and sandals stood in front of it, transfixed by the moving price quotations.

There was a receptionist's desk at the open doorway to a spacious room in which several men sat at littered desks equipped with computer terminals. Most of the brokers, Clark noted, were on the phone or busily writing on order pads. The place seemed prosperous enough, but so did betting shops and boiler rooms.

"May I speak to the manager, please," Clark asked the middle-aged receptionist. "I'd like to open an account."

"Just a moment, please, sir," she added, and spoke into her phone.

The man who came forward a few moments later was tall, stooped, and had a neatly trimmed beard so black and glossy that Clark figured it had to be dyed and oiled.

"I'm Mortimer Sparco," he said, smiling and holding out his hand. "How may I be of service?"

"Simon Clark," the attorney said, gripping the proffered hand briefly. "I'm in the process of moving to Fort Lauderdale from Chicago and thought I'd open a brokerage account."

"You're too young for retirement," Sparco said, still smiling. "Your company transfer you down here?"

"Not exactly. My parents live in Lauderdale, and I thought it would be nice to be closer to them. I'm a freelance writer for how-to magazines— you know, like *Home Mechanics*—and you can do that from anywhere."

"Fascinating," Sparco said. "Why don't you come back to my office and talk about your investment aims."

"My aim is to make money," Clark said.

"You've come to the right place," Sparco said. "This way, please."

The office was all leather, chrome, and glass, and smelled of cigar smoke. The entire rear wall was covered with a mural: a Florida beach scene with sand, palm trees, sailboats on the ocean, pelicans in the sky. The painted sun looked like a toasted English muffin.

The two men sat at either end of a tawny leather couch and turned to face each other.

"I'll be honest with you, Mr. Sparco," Clark said. "I've never bought a share of stock in my life. I know zilch about the market. But I've become dissatisfied with the rates I'm getting on my savings account and CDs."

"Completely understandable," the broker said.

"I've been doing some reading on stock investing and learned that discount brokers may charge as little as half the commissions of the big brokerage houses, but they don't provide a full range of services."

"Generally that's true. But at Sparco, while our fees are competitive with those of other discount brokers, we pride ourselves on offering services the others don't. Most of them are merely order-takers. But at Sparco we believe in personalized service, tailored to our clients' needs. Tell me, Mr. Clark, how much were you thinking of investing?"

"Well, I thought I'd start slow, sort of dip my toes in the water. I'm sure you'll think it's chicken feed, but I'd like to begin with ten thousand dollars."

The broker leaned forward, very earnest. "Let me tell you something:

At Sparco we treat a client with ten thousand exactly the same way we treat one with ten million. We take our responsibility to *all* our clients very seriously, and provide the most up-to-date information and the best advice we possibly can. You say you are dissatisfied with the current rates on your CDs. Does that mean you're willing to assume a limited amount of risk to increase your yields?"

"Well . . . not *too* much risk."

"Of course not. Sparco wouldn't put you in anything where the risk-benefit ratio is not in your favor. But occasionally we learn of special situations that demand fast decisions. I would advise you to open a discretionary account with us. That will authorize Sparco to buy and sell in your name, on your behalf. It relieves you of the need to watch your portfolio every day. After all, you're just interested in results. Am I correct?"

"That's right."

"And, with your approval, we can trade on margin in your account. That will give you a lot more leverage; your ten thousand can have the clout of fifteen or even more."

"Sounds good to me," Clark said.

Mortimer Sparco leaned closer and lowered his voice. "In addition," he said, almost whispering, "we help make the market in certain specialized stocks that are not listed on the exchanges. They customarily sell for less than a dollar a share and represent ownership in new companies with an enormous potential for growth. Sparco has a select group of clients who have done very well with these little-known equities. I think you'd be amazed at how fast your money can double, even triple, with stocks that most investors never even heard of."

"With no risk?" the attorney asked.

"There is risk in every investment, even government bonds. But in this case the risk is minimal and the possible profits simply unbelievable."

"Then let's do it."

"You're making a wise decision, Mr. Clark. Now if you'll just step over to my desk, there are a few documents I'd like you to sign."

17

She loved to drive the Bentley.

"It's so *solid*," she said. "And it even smells of money."

So she was at the wheel as they headed up A1A to Boca Raton. Traffic was surprisingly light going northward, but out-of-state cars, jammed with vacationers, were flocking south.

Rathbone sat relaxed, smoking his first cigarette of the day.

"After you finish at the bank," he said, "let's have lunch in Boca, maybe do some shopping. We'll get back in time to catch some sun on the terrace."

"Sounds good to me."

"Nervous?" he said.

"Nah. You said it will be a piece of cake."

"Sure it will," he said. "Just sail in, pick up the money, and sail out. You'll do fine."

They parked in front of the bank. Rita got out, and David slid over behind the wheel.

"I'll be right here," he told her. "I'm not going anyplace."

She nodded and marched into the bank. Rathbone spent the next twenty minutes making "air bets," declaiming them aloud:

"I'll bet fifty that the next woman to come out of the bank will be wearing blue.

"I'll bet a hundred that the next man to come around the corner will have a mustache.

"I'll bet a thousand that the next car to park will be a white two-door."

And so on.

By the time Rita returned, he was two hundred dollars ahead, which he took as a good omen.

She opened the door on the passenger side, slid onto the leather seat. She tossed a fat manila envelope into his lap. "Bingo!" she said.

He smiled and leaned to kiss her lips. "Any problems?" he asked.

"Nope. They wanted to give me a bank check, but I told them I was flying home to San Antonio tonight and needed the cash. So they came across."

"Beautiful," he said.

He took a thousand in hundred-dollar bills from the envelope and handed them to her.

"Invest it wisely," he said.

"With you?"

"You could do worse," he said. "Now let's go eat. I know a place that makes a great chef's salad."

"Can I have a hamburger instead?"

"You can have anything you want," he said, and kissed her again. "Partner," he said.

They had a nice, relaxed lunch, did a little shopping at the Town Center, then headed home.

"Can we pull that bank dodge again?" she asked him.

"Oh-ho," he said. "Getting ambitious, are you?"

"It's so *easy*," she said.

"Sure it is. The problem is whether or not to use the Gloria Ramirez ID again, and if we do, hit another Boca bank or try somewhere else. I'll have to think about it."

"Who printed up that queer check?" she asked idly, staring out the side window.

"A genius," he said, and she didn't push it.

An hour later they were lying naked on the terrace lounges. The sun was behind a scrim of high cloud cover, but it was strong enough to cast shadows and hot enough to make them sweat. They drank iced tea from a thermos.

"I'm going to have to change my plans," he said.

"What plans?"

"A schedule I had mapped out. I was going to give it maybe another six months and then retire, get out of the game."

She raised her head to look at him. "What about me?"

"Not to worry," he said. "I'll take care of you; you know that. But this check scam changes things. The possibilities are tremendous if it's handled right. Also, something else came up the other night that could be a gold mine. So I think I'll stick around for a while."

"Where were you going?"

"Oh . . . there are a lot of places in this world I haven't seen yet."

"When you decide to go, can I go with you?"

"We'll see. Let's take another half-hour of sun and then go shower."

"And then what?"

"You know what," he said.

That night they dined at an Italian restaurant on Atlantic Boulevard, and David ordered a bottle of Dom Perignon to celebrate their triumph at the

Crescent Bank. Then they drove to the Grand Palace and found the gang already assembled at the big table in the Lounge. Rita sat in one of the mate's chairs and watched as Rathbone beckoned James Bartlett over to the bar. The two men stood close together, talking with lowered heads.

"Jimmy, have you given any more thought to what I suggested on poker night?"

"The commodity trading fund? Yes, I've talked to several clients about it. You know, David, these guys are shrewd. They've got all the street smarts in the world, but they don't understand options and futures. Finally, I stopped trying to explain, and just told them it would mean money in their pockets. That, they could understand. Four of them definitely will sign contracts for delivery in three, six, nine, and twelve months at preset prices."

"They'll trust you?"

"On the first delivery. If I welsh, I'm dead; you know that."

"So actually we have three problems. One is to analyze the market for the coming year and determine prices that'll yield a profit. The second is to make sure funds are available to take delivery. And finally, we've got to line up markets and sign contracts with buyers."

"You've got it."

"Jimmy, I think now is the time to bring Sparco, Coe, and Little in on this. It's too big for the two of us to swing alone."

"I agree."

"Then let's talk to them. I think they'll go for it."

"They'd be idiots not to."

"Who were the four clients who agreed to play?"

"Three Colombians and one American. These are not men you'd want to introduce to your wife, David—if you had a wife."

"Hard cases?"

Bartlett rolled his eyes. "Last year one of the Colombians murdered his younger brother because the kid lost a shipment to the Coast Guard. You know how he killed him?"

"No, and I don't want to know. Let's get back to the table."

"Rita is looking especially sexy tonight, David. She's not beautiful, but she's striking."

"I know."

"You serious about her?"

"I don't know how I feel about her. All I know is that she's got me seeing pinwheels."

"That sounds serious. Does she know what you do?"

"I'm letting her in on it, little by little. It doesn't turn her off. I think she likes it. Maybe it's the risk, the danger."

"Uh-huh," Jimmy said, staring at him. "And maybe it's fear. With some women fear can be an aphrodisiac."

Rathbone laughed. "And what's an aphrodisiac to men?"

"Guilt," Bartlett said.

18

"Mr. Harker," the secretary said on the phone, "will you come to Mr. Crockett's office, please."

Tony pulled on his jacket, straightened his tie, walked down the hall. There was a somber man seated alongside the chief's desk. He wore wire-rimmed spectacles with lenses so thick they made him look pop-eyed.

"Tony," Crockett said, "this is Fred Rabin from the Federal Reserve. Mr. Rabin, this is Anthony Harker, who spoke to your office."

Rabin didn't stand up or offer to shake hands, but at least he nodded. Tony nodded back. No one asked him to sit down, so he remained standing, looking down at the two men.

"Mr. Rabin," Crockett said, "will you please repeat what you told me."

The Federal Reserve man stared at Tony through those thick glasses. "You asked us to put a trace on a U.S. Treasury check in the amount of $27,341.46, issued to a Gloria Ramirez and deposited at the Crescent Bank in Boca Raton. Is that correct?"

"Yes."

"Why did you ask for a trace?"

"Because I had good reason to believe the check was counterfeit. Allowing it to clear the Crescent Bank and then recovering it would give me hard evidence of bank fraud. Did you find the check?"

"Oh, we found it," Rabin said. "Would you like to see it?"

He took a long glassine envelope from an attaché case and held it up for Harker to inspect. It appeared to be filled with greenish-blue confetti.

"What the hell is that?" Tony said, bewildered.

"That's the check you wanted."

"What happened? Did it get chopped up in a canceling machine?"

Rabin sighed. "The intact check was retrieved in Atlanta, on its way to Treasury. It was put aside to be mailed to you the next morning. But in the morning, this was all that was left of it. It just shredded away, disintegrated. We have our lab working on it now."

Harker turned to Crockett. "There goes our case," he said.

"Your case may be important," Rabin said, "but not as important as finding the source of this paper that self-destructs. Do you realize what this could do to the banking system? Chaos! We are now in the process of preparing a letter of warning to every bank and savings and loan in the country."

"Mr. Rabin wants the Secret Service to take over the whole investigation," Crockett said, lacing his fingers across his vest. "He feels they have more manpower and resources than we have."

"We already have a Secret Service man working on it," Harker said. "Henry Ullman, a good investigator."

Rabin shook his head. "One man is hardly sufficient to assign to a problem of this magnitude. I must ask that you turn over to us all the information you have in your possession, such as how you knew the check was forged, who deposited it, and any other evidence you may possess bearing on the case."

Silence in the room. Finally, Crockett shook his head.

"No, Mr. Rabin," the chief said, "I don't think so. I am sure you'll go over my head and file your request with my superiors. If they order me to turn the case over to you, then I have no choice. But at the moment I do have a choice, and I choose to have this organization retain control of the investigation."

Rabin looked at them, eyes blinking furiously. "I shall certainly inform Washington of your refusal to cooperate. You are making a very, *very* serious error of judgment."

He stood, gathered up hat and attaché case, stalked out. He didn't exactly slam the door behind him, but he didn't close it gently either.

"Thank you, sir," Tony said.

Crockett shrugged. "Calculated risk. I have some chits in Washington I'll have to call in on this, but I think we're safe for a time. I'll ask for six months. Can you do it?"

Harker drew a deep breath. "Sure," he said. He left the office and went directly to the bullpen. He found Henry Ullman at his desk, writing on a yellow legal pad.

"I know," Ullman said, looking up. "You want my report. You'll have it this afternoon."

"No, Hank," Tony said, "it's something else. Will you come to my office, please."

There he told the investigator about the disintegrating check.

"Son of a bitch," Ullman said. "That's a new one. Going to pick up Rathbone?"

"What for? The evidence is destroyed. And I want to give our plant a chance to track the source of the paper. Rathbone isn't the forger; he's the pusher, once removed. And I still want to know what part Mike Mulligan is playing. He was Rathbone's contact at the Crescent Bank. What have you got on him?"

"Apparently a fine, upstanding citizen. No rap sheet. He's clean with the IRS. Been with the bank almost thirty years. Divorced. No children. Lives in a one-bedroom condo in a plush development. Drives a two-year-old Buick. Goes to church. Nothing in his lifestyle to indicate he's on the take."

"What kind of a guy is he?"

"You'd think, wouldn't you, that with a moniker like Mike Mulligan he'd be a big, brawny, red-faced Irishman. Actually, he's a scrawny little guy, a real Caspar Milquetoast. Elderly. White-haired. Wears horn-rimmed cheaters and carries an umbrella on cloudy days. He's got a schedule during the week that never varies. People say they can set their watches by him. For instance, every working day he leaves the bank at precisely five o'clock, walks three blocks to a bar called the Navigator. Mulligan sits in a back booth by himself and has two extra-dry gin martinis straight up, no more, no less. Then he goes home by cab. I got most of this personal stuff from the barmaid, a mouthy broad. She says she's never seen him drunk or with a woman."

"Have you been able to make contact?"

"Not yet. I've been hanging out at the Navigator, so now I'm considered a regular. But the guy sits by himself way in the back and doesn't talk to anyone. I'm afraid a direct approach might spook him. I've got a way to get to him, but I'll need a partner. You have anyone I can borrow for an afternoon?"

"Sorry," Harker said, "all my guys are out. What's your idea?"

Ullman described it to him. "It's a neat scam," he finished. "A variation of the good cop-bad cop routine. I've used it before, and it works. But I need someone who can put on an act."

"I think I could do it," Tony said.

"You sure?" Hank said. "If you blow it, I never will be able to get close to the guy."

"I won't blow it," Harker said. "Come on, let's do it today."

"Okay," Ullman said. "We both better take our cars because if this thing goes down, we won't be coming back together."

They discussed the details, and the Secret Service man drilled Tony on the role he was to play. Then they went out for hamburgers and fries before heading up Federal Highway.

They got to Boca Raton about three-thirty, Ullman leading the way in his dusty Plymouth. He pulled up in front of the Navigator Bar & Grill, signaled by waving an arm out the window, then drove away. Harker parked nearby, locked up, and walked back to the bar.

It was a long, narrow room, bar on the right, booths on the left. There were no customers. When Tony entered, the tall, rawboned barmaid put down the supermarket tabloid she was reading and gave him a gap-toothed smile.

"Am I ever glad to see *you*," she said. "I was beginning to wonder if we had a quarantine sign on the door."

As instructed by Ullman, Harker went to the rear and took the last barstool.

"Want to be by your lonesome, huh?" the barmaid said, coming down to stand before him. "What can I get for you, honey?"

"Vodka on the rocks. Splash of water."

"Any special brand?"

"Nah," he said. "The house vodka will do. They're all alike."

"If you say so," she said, made his drink, and put it on a cork coaster in front of him.

He drank it off in four deep swallows and set the empty glass down.

"Another," he said.

"Hoo, boy," she said, "someone was thirsty. Take it easy, honey; the day is young."

He made no reply and she gave up on him, going back to her tabloid. After he finished his second drink, he deliberately knocked over the glass, spilling ice cubes onto the bar.

"Clean this up, will you?" he said.

"Sure," the barmaid said, mopping up. "Happen to anyone. Another?"

"Yeah," Harker said. "Make it a double. This lousy vodka's got no kick." He threw a twenty on the bar.

"You're the boss," she said, but she was no longer smiling.

As he worked on his drink, patrons began to straggle in, taking seats at the bar. Two couples arrived and took a booth. At four-thirty Henry Ullman came in and stood near the center of the bar.

Harker signaled the barmaid. "Another double," he said in a loud voice. "You sure you're not watering this booze?"

She didn't reply but poured him a refill. Then she went back to where Ullman was standing. She leaned across the bar and whispered to him, jerking her head in Tony's direction.

At five after five, precisely, a white-haired man entered the Navigator. Harker figured he had to be Mike Mulligan. He was small, skinny, in a three-piece suit of gray tropical worsted. And he was wearing horn-rimmed specs. He went directly to the last booth and slid in. The barmaid was at his side almost instantly with a martini in a stemmed glass.

In about fifteen minutes, Tony glanced at Henry Ullman, and the big man nodded once. Tony got off his barstool and staggered slightly. He didn't have to fake that. He looked around a moment, then carried his drink over to Mike Mulligan's booth.

"Mind if I join you?" he said in a voice he hoped was suitably drunken.

"Yes, I would," Mulligan said. "I prefer to enjoy my drink alone."

"What're you, a goddamn hermit or something?" Harker said boozily. "Wassamatter, I'm not good enough for you?"

"Please," Mulligan said, staring straight ahead. "I just want to be left alone. All right?"

"Well, screw you, buster," Harker said in a loud voice. "I could buy and sell you any day of the week."

Now the bar had quieted, and all the customers were looking in their direction.

"I have to go now," Mulligan said, and tried to get out of the booth. But Harker blocked his way.

"I don't like your looks," he said. "You look like a real wimp to me."

The barmaid was heading toward the booth, hefting an aluminum baseball bat. But Henry Ullman got there first. He put a meaty hand on Tony's shoulder, spun him around.

"Okay, buddy," he said, facing Harker toward the door. "Out!"

"What?" Tony said, wavering on his feet. "Who're you to—"

"You heard what I said. *Out!*"

Tony hesitated, then looked up at the big man. "Lissen," he said. "I was only—"

Ullman pushed him toward the door. "On your way," he said. "Go sober up."

Harker stumbled toward the street, mumbling to himself, not looking at the people he passed. The joint didn't relax until he was gone.

"Thank you, sir," Mike Mulligan said to Ullman. "What a nasty fellow that was."

"He's drunk," Hank said. "But there's no excuse for acting like that."

"You're absolutely right," Mulligan said, "and I appreciate your assistance. May I buy you a drink?"

"Only if you let me buy the next round."

"Why not?" said Mike Mulligan.

19

The best thing about this job, Roger Fortescue decided, was that his boss, Tony Harker, was letting him run free. None of this "Call me every hour on the hour" bullshit. Harker seemed to feel Roger was capable of figuring out what had to be done and then doing it. The investigator appreciated that. Maybe he moved slowly, but sooner or later he got there.

The *worst* thing about the job was that Estelle kept busting his balls about the hours he was keeping.

"I never know when you're coming home for dinner," she complained. "Or if you're coming home at all."

"It's my job, hon," he explained patiently. "It's what puts bacon on the table."

He looked up Frank Little's home address. It was way out in the boondocks, in Parkland north of Sample Road. Roger drove by slowly, but when he saw a sign on the fence, UNLEASHED PIT BULLS, he decided not to stop. It was flatland with no cover or concealment, and Fortescue knew a stakeout would be impossible.

Little's home was really a ranch with a separate garage, outbuildings, and what looked big enough to be a three-horse stable. Roger figured the spread for maybe five acres. There was a guy on a sitdown power mower working one of the fields, and another guy with a long-handled net fishing dead palm fronds from the surface of a big swimming pool.

"Two million," Fortescue said aloud. "Sheet, *three* million!"

He drove back to Copans Road and cruised by the FL Sports Equipment layout. No activity. Just a car parked outside the office. And what a yacht that was! A 1959 white Cadillac convertible that appeared to be in mint condition. That grille! Those tailfins! Roger's Volvo seemed like a pushcart.

He noted again the boarded-up fast-food joint next to Little's place. That would be it, he suddenly decided; his home away from home.

He was right on time for dinner that night, bringing a five-pound boneless pork loin as a peace offering to Estelle. They put the pork in the fridge for the next day because she had already baked up a mess of chicken wings with hot barbecue sauce. They had that with home fries and pole beans. Beer for the adults, Cokes for the kids.

After dinner, Roger went upstairs, kicked off his loafers, and crashed for almost two hours, sleeping as if he had been sandbagged. Then he rose, changed to dungarees, checked his armament, and began assembling his Breaking & Entering kit: small crowbar, set of lockpicks, penlight, bull's-eye lantern, a shot-filled leather sap, binoculars, small transistor radio, and a cold six-pack of beer.

At about nine P.M. he drove back to Copans Road, past FL Sports Equipment, looking for a place to park. He finally located a likely spot, alongside a darkened garage that did muffler and shock replacements. He loaded up with his gear and trudged back to the deserted fast-food joint.

Traffic on the road was light, but he tried to stick to the shadows during his amble. In the rear of the derelict restaurant he found a weather-beaten door secured with a rusty hasp and cheap padlock. He could easily have wrenched it away with his crowbar but didn't want to leave evidence of an illegal entry. So he spent five minutes picking the lock, holding the penlight between his teeth. Then he pushed the creaking door open.

It was unexpectedly warm inside, and smelly. He heard the rustle of wildlife which he hoped was just rats and not snakes. He made a lantern-lighted tour through what had been the dining area, kitchen, lavatory, and a small chamber that had probably served as an office.

It was this last room he selected for his stakeout because it had a boarded-up window facing FL Sports Equipment, Inc. Prying two of the boards farther apart gave him a good view of the blockhouse, driveway, and warehouse. He dragged a rickety crate in from the kitchen to use as a chair, turned on his radio with the volume low, and popped a beer. Then he settled down to wait.

He was still waiting at four in the morning, peering out the window every few minutes and walking up and down occasionally to stay awake. The beer was finished, and his favorite radio station had gone off the air. He packed it in then, and lugged all his gear back to the Volvo. He left the padlock in the hasp, seemingly closed but actually open. He drove home, and when he went up to the bedroom, Estelle roused and said sleepily, "When do you want to get up?"

"Never," he answered, undressed, and rolled into bed.

But he was back at his hideout the following night, and for three more nights after that. Estelle stopped complaining about his crazy hours, and his sons seemed to like the idea of Daddy being home during the day.

By the time he decided to end his vigil, he had compiled four pages of notes on ruled paper he swiped from one of the kids' notebooks. He read over his jottings on what he had observed and tried to make some sense out of it all.

1. Deliveries were made to FL Sports Equipment, usually well before midnight, by trucks and vans with familiar names lettered on the sides. They were carriers working out of Port Everglades and the Fort Lauderdale-Hollywood Airport.

2. These deliveries were packed in wooden crates, some secured with steel bands. The boxes were long enough to hold smuggled AK-47s or other weapons, Roger reckoned, but he doubted if they did; each crate was handled easily by two men.

3. Pickups were made after midnight by an assortment of trucks, flatbeds, and vans, all with out-of-state license plates. Most of them were unmarked, although once the big Siena Moving & Storage semi showed up.

4. The pickups were cardboard cartons, and there was little doubt what they contained; one of them broke open and white baseballs went rolling all over the place. The loaders carefully collected every ball, and Frank Little, standing nearby with his clipboard, seemed to be verifying the count.

Fortescue, reading over his notes, concluded that for some reason the big wooden crates of baseballs were unpacked in the warehouse and their contents repacked into the smaller cardboard cartons.

One thing he couldn't understand was why the pickups, presumably by those wholesalers Frank Little had mentioned, were always made at go-dawful hours like two, three, and four o'clock in the morning. And why weren't the wholesalers' trucks painted with their names and addresses?

Most perplexing were the deliveries of imported baseballs from Port Everglades and the Lauderdale airport. After all, baseball was the National Pastime, the Great American Game. Surely baseballs would bear the stamp MADE IN THE USA.

"Hey, hon," Roger called to his wife, "you know that girlfriend of yours who works in the main Broward Library. The lady with the big teeth."

"You talking about Claire?" Estelle said. "Her teeth aren't so big. She's just got a lot of them is all."

"I guess. Well, will you give her a call and ask if she can look up where baseballs are made. Tell her I need the information as part of a crucial law enforcement investigation."

"Oh sure," Estelle said. "Baseballs are real crucial."

But she went into the living room to make the call, leaving Roger reading his notes in the kitchen, trying to see if he had missed anything.

Estelle came back in a half-hour. "Claire has a cold," she reported. "She's afraid it might be the flu."

"That's a shame," Fortescue said. "Did she say she'd look up where baseballs are made?"

"She didn't have to look it up," Estelle said. "She knew right off. Most baseballs are made in Haiti."

Roger stared at her. "Haiti?" he said. "That's amazing."

20

Rita arrived with a chilled bottle of premixed strawberry daiquiris and two plastic glasses. Harker took a blanket from his bed, and they went down to the beach. They sat close together, knees drawn up. It was a cool night, but there was no wind and there were so many stars that the cloudless sky looked as if it had been ordered from Tiffany's.

"How come you got out tonight?" Tony asked. "Don't tell me he's playing poker again."

"No," she said, "he told me he had a business conference. I said maybe I'd stop by the Palace and have a drink with the gang, but David said no one would be there. So I guess he's meeting with the other sharks."

"You know that check scam at the Crescent Bank?" Harker said. "Well, you're off the hook. There's no case against Rathbone. No evidence."

He told her how the Treasury check had disintegrated.

"Son of a bitch," she said. "No wonder he told me there was no risk. What do we do now?"

"We're working a couple of angles," Harker said. "Starting with Mike Mulligan at the Crescent. Listen, do you think you could find out where Rathbone got the check? We need to find the source of that trick paper."

"I asked him straight out, but no soap, he wouldn't say. I'll try again, but he's awfully closemouthed when his own neck is on the block. Tony, it's going to be tough to rack up this guy; he's smart."

"I know," Harker said, "but I'll get him. Sooner or later his greed will trip him up."

"Maybe," Rita said. "Pour me another, will you, baby?"

"I like your white pants," Tony said, filling her glass. "Real leather?"

"You better believe it."

"Rathbone buy them for you?"

"That's right. Any objection?"

"No," he said, "you're entitled. Rita, I don't want you to push him so hard he gets suspicious, but could you suggest that maybe he needs a secretary? A private secretary. You. The aim is to get into that locked office, take a look at his records, find out exactly how he's clipping the mooches."

"I don't think he'll go for it."

"Look, the way to manipulate this guy is through his love of money. He's got a corporation. Suggest to him that he could put you on the payroll legitimately. The corporation will pay your salary, and it'll reduce his corporate tax. The cash you get won't come out of *his* pocket; Uncle Sam will be financing your relationship."

She was silent a moment. "Yeah," she said finally, "that might work. He surely does worship the green."

"Give it a try," Harker urged. "Don't make a big deal out of it; just throw him the bait and see if he bites. I think he will."

"But putting me on salary as a secretary is no guarantee that he's going to let me in on his secrets."

"No, but it's a start. Maybe he'll like the idea of having someone answer the phone, do his typing, go to the banks and post office for him. It'll make him feel like a tycoon."

Rita laughed. "You know," she said, "you just may be right. He thinks he's pretty important people. Okay, I'll see if I can grift the grifter. Hey, I'm getting goose bumps. Let's go to your place."

Back at the motel, Rita climbed into bed fully clothed. Still shivering, she pulled sheet and blanket up to her chin. Tony made her a cup of black coffee and brought it to her with a pony of cognac.

"Can't have you getting sick," he told her. "You're too valuable."

He sat on the edge of the bed and watched as she sipped coffee and brandy.

"That's better," she said. "I'm beginning to thaw. I really got a chill. I've never been sick a day in my life, and I sure don't want to start now."

He leaned back against the footboard. "Rita, how come you joined the police? Was your father a cop, or maybe a brother?"

"Nah, I'm an only child. And my father was a carpenter. He died five years ago. What happened was that a girlfriend was going to take the police exam and talked me into going along with her and taking it, too. Well, she flunked, and I passed. So then I thought, why not? It sounded more exciting than a typing job or working at K-Mart."

"Ever regret it?"

"Never. It's been a hoot. Something new and different every day. I love it. Honey, turn off the light, will you. It's shining in my eyes."

He switched off the overhead light. When the brightness faded, their voices lowered, almost becoming murmurs.

"Do you plan to get out of it someday?" he asked. "Marry, settle down, have kids?"

"Who can plan a life? Looking ahead is a drag. I just take it day by day. When it gets routine, maybe I'll look around for a change. But right now I'm having a ball. How about you?"

"I like what I'm doing, and I happen to think it's worthwhile. There are worse ways to earn a living than putting crooks behind bars. Listen, Rita, I'd like to ask you something, but I'm afraid you'll get angry."

"Why don't you ask and find out."

"You're not falling for Rathbone, are you?"

She finished coffee and cognac, and leaned out of bed to put cup and glass on the floor. "I honestly don't know how I feel about him," she admitted. "Sometimes he can be so sweet and considerate that I have to keep reminding myself that he's an out-and-out thief. Also, he knows how to treat a woman. He washes my hair, gives me a super massage, goes shopping for clothes with me. And he's always giving me unexpected gifts. It's hard to hate a guy like that."

"I can imagine," Tony said.

"But I know I've got a job to do," she went on. "If I ever get to the point where the way I feel about him interferes with that job, I'll tell you and ask you to pull me out. Okay?"

"Sure," he said. "And not only for the sake of the job. Getting involved with that guy could be dangerous for you."

"I can handle it," she said. "Hey, I'm all warmed up now. So what I'm going to do is get undressed. And let nature take its course. How does that grab you?"

Just before nature took its course, she held his face between her palms, peered closely into his eyes.

"Are you sure you're not jealous?" she whispered. "Of David?"

"Maybe," he said. "Maybe I am. Because he spends so much more time with you than I can."

"That's sweet," she said. "Which means we'll have to make the most of the time we do have. Right?"

"Right," he said, and gently pulled her closer.

"Don't be afraid, honey," she said. "I bend, but I don't break."

21

The living room of Frank Little's ranch was decorated in *faux* Texan: Indian rugs on the polished wood floor; deer antlers on the whitewashed walls; exposed beams overhead; a gun rack; sling chairs covered with pony hides. Looking at this set for a Western movie, and then inspecting Little in his silk slacks and sports shirt unbuttoned to the waist, hairless chest festooned with gold chains and amulets, David Rathbone could only think of the classic definition of a would-be Texan: "All hat; no cattle."

The five men were served drinks and cigars by Jacques, Little's Haitian houseboy. Jacques was nineteen, olive-skinned, sloe-eyed. He would last a year. Little replaced his houseboys annually, all clones of Jacques.

Rathbone waited until all five had drinks and Jacques had left the room. Then he said, "Here's what this is all about."

He outlined the proposed commodity trading fund, dealing only in "controlled substances," meaning marijuana, cocaine, heroin, and other illicit drugs. The fund would buy and sell options and futures, making a profit by the spread between buy and sell orders, and from the investors, who would, of course, be unaware of the true nature of the commodities being traded.

Bartlett would sign buy contracts with his clients. Little would sign sell contracts with his customers. Mort Sparco would organize the fund and peddle shares of the penny stock to his local accounts. Sid Coe would push the shares in his boiler room. Rathbone would serve as comptroller and chief executive officer.

"But none of us risks his own money," he said. "Start-up cash comes from Mort's suckers and Sid's mooches. We start out small and see how it goes. If it looks like a winner, we tie up with bucket shops all over the country and with penny stock brokers in Denver, giving them a piece of the action. All profits are split evenly five ways. How does it sound?"

"Let me get this straight," Frank Little said. "You want me to get my customers to sign contracts to buy?"

"Right," Rathbone said. "The drugs will be given code names, and you'll set a price for delivery in three, six, nine, and twelve months. Jimmy will do the same with the imports. The only way this is going to work is by analyzing what the future market will be like: how big the supply, how big the demand."

"I think you got a hot idea," Sparco said. "But take my advice and forget about trying to push options and futures. My pigeons just don't understand them. Buy low and sell high—that they can understand. But not the mechanics of future and option trading."

"Ditto the suckers on my lists," Coe said. "My yaks have a limited time to close a deal. They've got to keep their pitch short and sweet."

"That's what I told David," Bartlett said. "My clients work on a simple business principle: make a sale, get cash on delivery. They're willing to sign contracts at preset prices, but they know nothing about options."

"All right," Rathbone said, "then let's stick to basics. We set up the fund financed by sucker money. We pull a Ponzi to keep the early investors eager. But we invest the bulk of the cash in purchases for future delivery. Jimmy, can you trust your clients to honor signed contracts?"

"Some of them, sure. I know which ones we can trust. But buying the stuff is less a risk than selling it. Frank, will your customers honor a signed contract if, say, the price drops before you deliver? You follow? I mean if you promise H at 18K a kilo in six months, and then in six months the going price falls to 16K a kilo, will your guys ante up the 18K or will they renege?"

"Some of them will welsh," Little said. "But some I deal with have this big macho honor thing; they'll pay what they agreed on even if they have to take a bath."

They all fell silent as Jacques padded in with a tray of fresh drinks. They waited until he left the room before resuming their discussion.

"What about timing on this?" Rathbone asked. "Mort, how long will it take to set up the fund and get the shares printed?"

"A week or ten days. No more than that. My paperman works fast, and he turns out beautiful stuff. Old engravings on the shares. They really look legit."

"And what about you, Sid?" David said. "It shouldn't take long to write a script for your yaks on the new fund."

"I could do it tonight," Coe said, "if I knew what the name was. What are we going to call this thing?"

They stared at each other a moment.

"How about the Croesus Commodity Trading Fund?" Bartlett suggested.

Rathbone shook his head. "It won't fly," he said. "The mooches aren't going to know who Croesus was."

"How about this," Frank Little said. "The Fort Knox Commodity Trading Fund."

Everyone smiled.

"A winner," Sparco said. "And if the suckers think we're dealing in gold, so much the better."

The name decided, they then discussed their first deal. Bartlett urged that they start small with limited contracts for the purchase and sale of cocaine in three months' time.

"You've got to remember that I've never bought on my own," he said. "I just provide banking services. Being an importer is new to me, and I want to go easy at first."

"Same with me," Little said. "I'm just a transshipper and live off fees. My customers do their own buying."

"But if you can shave the price and deliver high-quality stuff," Rathbone said, "they'll buy from you, won't they?"

"No doubt about it. These are bottom-line guys."

"Good," David said. "I'll get to work on a standard contract and draw up a list of code names for the commodities we'll be handling. I'll also get some new software for my computer. Maybe a spreadsheet. If we're going to do this thing, let's do it right."

"The way I figure is this," Mort Sparco said. "What's the worst thing that could happen? That we lose all our money—right? Only it's not our money. So we've really got nothing to lose, and everything to gain. If we call the prices right and make a nice buck, we'll just pay the investors enough to keep them coming back—and pocket the rest. This could be a sweet deal."

"Yeah," Coe said, "even better than the Gypsy Handkerchief Drop." And they all laughed.

They had another round of drinks and discussed where and how to set up a checking account for the Fort Knox Commodity Trading Fund. They talked about the advisability of renting a small office, hiring a secretary, and having letterheads and business cards printed. Then the gathering broke up. Before they separated, they all shook hands as serious entrepreneurs starting a daring enterprise with exciting possibilities.

Rathbone had picked up James Bartlett at his home and had driven him to Frank Little's. Now, on the ride back to Bayview Drive, the two men briefly discussed the meeting.

"I was surprised at how easily it went," Rathbone said. "I didn't have to use the hard sell at all. Well, they're shrewd guys and could see the potential. Jimmy, it could be a bonanza if we have luck analyzing the future market."

"I think I know the man who can evaluate the supply and demand picture for us," Bartlett said. "He knows the drug scene inside out, from Bogotá to the South Bronx."

"Sounds good," David said. "Is he a dealer?"

Bartlett laughed quietly. "No," he said, "he's a federal narc who turned sour about four years ago. Now he's got accounts in Switzerland and the Cayman Islands I helped him set up. He'll be happy to help us."

"You sure? If he turned once, he can turn again."

Jimmy shrugged. "That's a risk we'll have to take. But I don't think it'll happen. He's in too deep."

"Well, tell him what we need and see what he comes up with. If he works out, we can always cut him in for a point or two. Jimmy, there's something else I want to talk to you about. You'll love it."

"Will I?" the other man said. "Try me."

Rathbone told him all about Termite Tommy, the old German printer in Lakeland, the self-destruct paper, and how he had passed a forged check at the Crescent Bank.

Bartlett didn't speak for a moment after David finished. Then: "You saw Termite Tommy's sample check after it had disintegrated?"

"With my own eyes. Believe me, it turned to confetti in about four days."

"No way he could have pulled a switch on you?"

"Come on, Jimmy; I'm no rube. That check just fell apart."

"And since Rita deposited the fake Treasury check, you've heard nothing about it? No cops knocking on your door at midnight?"

Rathbone rapped his knuckles on the walnut dash of the Bentley. "So far, so good," he said. "We got the cash, and Treasury has a handful of fluff."

"So what's your problem?"

"How to capitalize on this. I could keep buying new ID for Rita—or anyone else—and pulling the same scam on other Florida banks. But the take wouldn't be big enough. I thought of franchising the whole operation: selling pads of blank checks to paperhangers all over the country. But that wouldn't work; the checks would destruct before they got through the mail. You got any ideas?"

"I know a little about counterfeiting," Bartlett said, "and I can tell you one thing: That German never *made* the paper. Making paper is just too difficult and complex an operation for one guy. It would take forever. So counterfeiters buy standard grades of paper and doctor them to suit their needs. A lot of them soak paper in black coffee to give it a weathered look, like their fake bills have been handled. I knew a hustler who spent hours with a one-hair brush painting his paper with those tiny threads you see in U.S. currency."

"Well, if the German didn't make the paper himself, how did he get the checks to fall apart?"

"My guess is that he bought paper of Treasury check weight and stiffness, and then treated it with chemicals. Probably an acid. You know, David, the wood-pulp paper used in most books and magazines is acidic and will crumble to dust in about thirty years. I think the Kraut found a chemical that speeds up the process."

"Well, all I know is that it works, and I've been racking my brain trying to figure how to make the most of it."

"David, why did you use the trick paper in a check?"

"Why? I guess because Termite Tommy gave me a sample of the stuff in check form, and that got me thinking of how to turn a profit from self-destroying checks."

Bartlett sighed. "You know, you're one of the best idea men in the game. You've got a lot of creative energy. Like that commodity trading fund you came up with. But sometimes you go sailing ahead without thinking things through. You're so eager to cash in, you don't stop to wonder if there might be a less risky or more profitable way. One of these days your love affair with lucre is going to do you in."

"I don't see you passing up any surefire rackets, old buddy."

"I don't—if they *are* surefire. But I spend a lot more time than you do calculating the risk-benefit ratio. Look, David, you can go on hanging queer checks, hiring more pushers, buying more fake ID, but as far as I'm concerned, the risk outweighs the benefit. The banks are sure to be alerted by the Federal Reserve, and sooner or later they'll get to you."

"So you think I should just drop it?"

"I didn't say that. But there's a better way. You said this Lakeland printer did time for counterfeiting?"

"That's what Termite Tommy told me. He met the guy in the pokey. The German was doing five-to-ten. Tommy said he had been printing and wholesaling the queer, not pushing it."

"Well, there's your answer. Get him back to making twenties and fifties, using the self-destruct paper. Then anyone—you, me, the man in the moon—can deposit the queer cash in any bank account. If it gets by the teller, you're home free because in a couple of days those bills are going to be gone, and there'll be nothing to point to who made the deposit. How are they going to arrest you for pushing forgeries if there's no evidence? The only things left will be your deposit slip and the credit to your account."

Rathbone lifted one palm from the steering wheel to smack his forehead. "Now why didn't I think of that? It's a great idea. But maybe we should wholesale the stuff instead of pushing it ourselves. How do you feel about that?"

"Wholesaling is what put the Kraut behind bars, and he might be a little gun-shy about trying it again. There's another possibility that occurs to me. You know, in my laundering deals, the cash is brought to the banks' back doors in shopping bags or suitcases. Sometimes the banks don't even bother counting; they weigh it. And they certainly don't inspect every bill to make sure it's legit."

By that time they were parked in the brick driveway of Bartlett's home. Rathbone switched off the engine and turned to stare at the other man.

"Jimmy," he said, "let me guess what you're thinking. If we wholesale the queer self-destruct bills, we'll be lucky to get twenty percent of the face value. But if you can switch the fake bills with your clients' genuine bills, we'll get full face value."

"That's right," Bartlett said, "and so will my clients. They'll be credited for the correct total deposited. It's the banks that'll take the loss when the queer turns to dust."

"But won't the banks scream when their twenties and fifties fall apart?"

"Scream to whom?" Jimmy asked. "If they call in the law, they'll have to explain why they were accepting shopping bags full of cash at the back door. No, they'll take the loss and keep their mouths shut. They'll figure it's just the cost of doing business, and the profits are so enormous they'll keep on dealing. So it really ends up a win-win game."

"Brilliant," Rathbone said.

22

The bullpen was on the second floor of Sidney Coe's office building, and although the ceiling and walls were soundproofed, the place was bedlam.

Almost twenty yaks worked in that madhouse, their splintery desks cramped side by side. On each desk was a telephone, script, sucker list, and overflowing ashtray. The air conditioner was set at its coldest and operated constantly, but the smoky air in that crowded room rarely got below 80°, the humidity was a fog, and some of the men stripped to the waist.

The yaks were currently hawking platinum, selling ounce bars of the metal with "free insurance and storage" included in the sales price. At the moment, the price was $500 per troy ounce (ten ounces minimum purchase), and any mooch could consult the financial pages and see he was buying at $23 per ounce under the market price.

"Because we have an exclusive source of supply that's liable to dry up any minute, the demand is so great. Now's the time to get in on the greatest money-making opportunity we've ever offered. Here's the chance of a lifetime, but you've got to get in on it NOW! Tomorrow may be too late. How much can I put you down for? Mail in your check today, and then go shopping for a new Cadillac because you're going to be rich, *rich*, RICH!"

Twenty yaks made this pitch, talking into their phones as rapidly and loudly as they could so the mooch was confused, didn't have time to think, heard only the shouted NOW! and RICH!, and decided he better get in on this bonanza before the exclusive source of cheap platinum was exhausted.

Checks arrived daily from all over the country, so many in fact that Sid Coe made two trips to the bank every day, hoping the checks would clear before the mooches had second thoughts and stopped payment. Few did. Even more remarkable, suckers who had lost money with Instant Investments, Inc., on precious gems, uranium, rare coins, and oil leases, sent in checks for platinum, hoping to recoup their losses.

"They like to suffer, Cynthia," Sid opined to his wife. "I tell you it's pure masochism. For some reason they feel guilty and want to be punished."

"Thank you, Doctor Freud," she said.

Coe stalked the boiler room like a master lashing on his galley slaves. "Close the deal!" he kept yelling. "Close the deal, get a meal! Get the cash, buy the hash! Get the dough or out you go!"

He hung over their sweaty shoulders, nudging them, spurring them on. Occasionally he grabbed the phone from their hand and demonstrated his version of the hard sell: raucous, derisive, almost insulting.

"Go ahead," he'd shout. "Put your money in CDs and savings accounts. Take your lousy eight percent. Haven't you got the *guts* to be rich? Does it scare you to make real money? I'm offering you a chance to get out of that rut you're in. Do you want to live like a man or do you want to play kids' games all your life?"

Invariably he closed the deal.

Manny Suarez loved the place, couldn't wait to get to work in the morning. It was eight to twelve hours of noisy action, right up his alley. Coe assigned him one of the few vacant desks, gave him a script and sucker list, and turned him loose. Manny imitated the other yaks, with a few significant changes.

He picked out the Hispanic names on his list, and although he made the pitch rapidly in Spanish, he never shouted. Instead, his voice was warm, friendly. Their health? The health of their family? And how did they like the United Sta'? Then, after a few moments of his intimate chitchat, he launched into the spiel.

He discovered he had a real talent for bamboozling. He closed the deal on almost half his calls, a percentage that rivaled that of the most experienced yaks. And during the second day he was on the job, he sold $25,000 of nonexistent platinum to a mooch in Los Angeles, a coup that impelled Sid Coe to give him a $500 bonus on the spot.

Payday was Saturday afternoon. The yaks filed into the ground-floor office, one by one, and were paid their commissions in cash from a big stack of bills on Coe's desk, alongside a brutal .45 automatic. For his first week's work, Manuel Suarez earned over $900, including his five-yard bonus.

"You're doing real good," Coe told him. "You like the job?"

"It's hokay," Manny said. "But I need more Hispanic names."

"You'll get them," the boss promised. "I buy our sucker lists from a guy in Chicago who supplies most of the boiler rooms in the country. I called him, and he's going to run his master list through a computer and pull every Spanish-sounding name for us. He says it's a great idea, and he's also going to get up an Italian list, a French list, and a Polish list. Apparently no one ever thought of ethnic sucker lists before. It could help the whole industry."

Suarez pocketed his earnings and drove down to headquarters. It was then late Saturday afternoon, but Anthony Harker was still at his desk, working on a big chart that he covered up when Manny came into his office.

"Hey, man," Suarez said, flashing a grin, "I got a small problem."

"Yeah?" Tony said. "How small?"

"I just got paid at Coe's boiler room. Do I gotta turn in the moaney to this organization or what?"

"I asked Crockett. He says you'll have to turn in the money. Sorry."

"Hokay," Suarez said.

"By the way," Harker said, "how much did you make?"

"Almost three hundred," Suarez said, and bopped out to his car, snapping his fingers and smiling at all the women he passed.

He stopped at a few stores before returning to the home of the Cuban lady where he was staying. She was nicely put together. And she seemed *muy simpática*. Manny bought five pounds of barbecued ribs, a liter of light Puerto Rican rum, and drove homeward whistling "Malagueña."

On Monday morning there were new scripts on all the yaks' desks. They were no longer peddling platinum. Now they were to push shares of stock in something called the Fort Knox Commodity Trading Fund. One dollar per share; 1,000 shares minimum. Suarez picked up his phone and went to work.

23

On his way to Birdie Winslow's condo, David Rathbone stopped at a florist on Atlantic Boulevard. The place was crowded, with two clerks trimming and wrapping flowers at a back counter.

Just inside the door was a display of lavender mums. They were bunched by the dozen with maidenhair, each bouquet held by a rubber band. The sign read: $20 PER DOZEN. Glancing at the busy clerks to make certain he was unobserved, Rathbone selected a bouquet, then slipped a single mum from another bunch and added it to his selection. He took the thirteen flowers to the desk, had them wrapped in green tissue, paid the $20 plus tax, and was on his way.

Mrs. Winslow met him at the door of her apartment clad in a paisley muumuu that hid her lumpish body. David proffered his bouquet.

"A dozen mums!" she cried. "How *divine*!"

"Baker's dozen," he said, smiling. "About an eight-point-four percent return on investment."

"What?" she said, puzzled. "Well, they're lovely, and I thank you for them. But you've been a naughty, naughty boy. You haven't called me once, and I thought you had just forgotten little old me."

"No chance of that," he said, touching her cheek. "But I've been to Europe since I saw you last and came home to a deskful of work."

She motioned toward the couch, then took the mums into the kitchen. She returned with the flowers in a crystal vase half-filled with water.

"Don't they look *divine*?" she said. "Lavender is one of my favorite colors. Now where shall I put them?"

He glanced around. He couldn't blame her for the way the apartment was furnished since it was a rented condo, but the decoration was really horrendous, the upholstery and wallpaper all fuchsia poppies and bilious green palm fronds.

"Perhaps on top of the TV set," he suggested.

She placed the vase there and stood back to admire the effect. "Sooo pretty," she murmured. Then: "I made a pitcher of your favorite—vodka gimlets."

"Just what I was hoping for."

She brought him a warm drink in a small glass with one lone ice cube. He sipped and decided it had to be the worst vodka gimlet he had ever tasted, so limey that it puckered his lips.

"Delicious," he said. "Aren't you having any?"

"A diet cola for me," she caroled. "I've been trying so hard to lose weight."

"Oh Birdie," he said, "you're not too heavy. You're like my gimlet— just right."

"Thank you, kind sir," she simpered, brought her drink and sat close to him on the couch.

He lifted his glass in a toast. "Here's to health and wealth," he said.

"And love," Mrs. Winslow said, looking at him through her false lashes. "Don't forget love."

He set his drink on the glass-topped cocktail table. "Birdie, I hope you've been getting your statements regularly."

"Yes, I have, and that's something I want to talk to you about."

"Is anything wrong?"

"Well, my next-door neighbor has an account with Merrill Lynch, and he says that every time he buys something or sells something he gets a confirmation slip. Should I be getting confirmation slips, David?"

"None of my clients ask for them, but you can certainly have them if you wish. I just didn't want to flood you with a lot of unnecessary paper. After all, the purchases and sales I make on your behalf show up every month on your statement."

"That's true. So you don't think I need confirmations?"

"Not really. Just more paper to file away and forget."

"I suppose you're right. I can't tell you how pleased I am with the way my money has grown."

"And it's going to do even better," he said. "Why, just this morning I got a tip from a friend on Wall Street about a new commodity trading fund that's being organized. If we get in on the ground floor, I can practically guarantee a fifty-percent return."

"Oh David, that is exciting!"

He finished his drink manfully. But it did him no good; she brought him another.

"Now let's forget about business for a while," she said, "and just relax. It's been so long since we've been together. I hope you don't have to rush off."

"Not immediately," he said. "But I do have an appointment in about an hour."

"Plenty of time," she assured him. She rose, held her hand out to him. "I bought a new clock-radio for the bedroom," she said. "Would you like to see it?"

She was naked under the muumuu and smelled of patchouli. But in situations like this—and he had experienced many—he resolutely closed his mind to physical stimuli, or the absence thereof, and concentrated only on the profits this suppliant woman represented. Then he was able to perform competently, his mind detached and calculating.

He left her lolling on the rumpled sheets. He dressed swiftly, kissed her cheek, and murmured, *"Divine!"* Then he drove home, windows open, gulping the salty sea air. Back in the town house, he gargled, brushed his teeth, and showered. He hoped he merely imagined that the scent of patchouli still clung to him.

He mixed a decent vodka gimlet, a double in a tall tumbler with plenty of ice and fresh lime. He carried it upstairs to the terrace. It was a warm day but cloudy, with rumblings of thunder westward. He hoped for a driving rain that might wash everything clean and leave the world shining.

He was still on the terrace, a few fat drops beginning to splatter, when Rita returned.

"You're going to get soaked," she warned. "It was pouring at the Pompano Mall."

"I won't melt," he said. "Did you ever walk through puddles when you were a kid?"

"No, and I never toasted marshmallows. I had a deprived childhood. I'm going to take a shower."

"I'll mix us drinks and bring them to your bedroom."

"That's a good boy," she said.

When he brought the drinks up from the kitchen she was still in her bathroom, the shower running. He sat on the edge of her bed, sipped his gimlet. He knew that in a few moments he would be the supplicant, a reversal of the roles he and Mrs. Winslow had played, and he wondered idly if love might be a lose-lose game.

Rita came out of the bathroom dripping, wiping her shoulders and arms. She handed him the towel and turned. Obediently he dried her back, with long, slow strokes.

"Guess what," she said. "I was wandering through the Mall, just looking around, and I bumped into an old girlfriend I haven't seen in years. Claire McDonald. We used to party together in Tallahassee. We had lunch together and talked over old times."

She took the damp towel from his hand and tossed it onto the floor. Then she sat down next to him on the bed, picked up her drink, took a sip.

"Claire looked like she had won the lottery: dressed to kill, her fingers covered with rocks. The real stuff, too. She told me this older guy was sponsoring her. 'Sponsoring.' I never heard it called that, did you?"

"Never did," Rathbone said, smiling.

"Anyway, her guy owns two restaurants in the Orlando area, so I guess he's got *mucho dinero*. They drove down to scout a location in Lauderdale for a new restaurant. She says he put her on the payroll of his company as a secretary; the corporation pays her salary. So the money he gives her doesn't come out of his pocket, it just reduces his corporate income tax. David, could you do that? Make me a secretary in your company? That way you wouldn't have to give me your own money. It would just be a business expense."

"Well, that's one way of looking at it," Rathbone said. "But by paying her a salary, he's also reducing his corporation's after-tax income. So one way or another, she's costing him."

"So you don't want to hire me as your private secretary?"

"Afraid not," he said, laughing. "But I'm willing to sponsor you."

They put their drinks aside. He took off his robe and they slid into bed. The thunder was closer, then overhead, then dwindling away. But it was raining heavily, streaming down the windows. The room was filled with a faint ocher light, dim and secret.

She let him do all the things that she knew pleasured him. She lay almost indolent, staring at the fogged windows, until her body roused. Then she closed her eyes, listened to the rain and the sounds he was making. Finally she heard nothing but the thump of her own heart, and cried out. But he would not stop, or could not, and she suffered him gladly.

At last he emerged panting from under the sheet, his hair tousled, a wild, frightened look in his eyes.

"Are you all right?" he asked anxiously.

She smiled, took his face in her hands, kissed his smeared lips.

"Let's do it again, lover," she said.

He managed a small smile, then got out of bed and stalked naked about the darkened room, hands on his hips.

"I thought I might die," he said.

"Die? From what?"

"It was too much. I couldn't stop."

"No one dies from too much love."

"I was afraid I was hurting you."

"You didn't. I'm a tough girl."

"I know. Do you need anything?"

"Like what?"

"Kleenex? A washcloth?"

"Nope. I like the way I feel. Now, stop pacing and come over here."

He stood alongside the bed. She leaned to him.

"Now it's my turn," she said.

Within minutes he was shuddering and sobbing. She was tender-cruel and would not let him move away until he surrendered, his mouth open in a silent scream. Then he collapsed facedown across the bed.

"I died and I was born again," he said. "And then I died and was born again."

"That's the way to do it," she said. "Don't ever stop halfway."

He reached under the sheet, grasped her left foot, pulled it to his lips, kissed the instep. Then he looked up at her. "Don't ever leave me, Rita."

"Why should I do that? It's hard to find a sponsor like you." She saw the focus in his eyes change. "Why are you looking at me like that? A penny for your thoughts."

"They're worth more than that. I just had a great idea. I don't want to put you on my payroll, but I know how you can make a steady salary."

"Pushing your queer checks?"

"No, that scam's on hold. But the Palace gang and I are starting a new business, and we'll need a secretary."

"Yeah? What kind of business?"

"It's an investment company. Ellen St. Martin is looking for office space for us. We'll need someone to answer the phone and type a few letters. You can type, can't you?"

"Oh sure. Hunt and peck."

"Good enough. How about it? Would you like an office job?"

"Does it mean I'll have to sit behind a desk eight hours a day?"

"Nah. We'll get you an answering machine, so you can come and go as you please."

"Sounds good," she said.

"To me, too. Because your salary won't be coming out of my pocket; just one-fifth of it."

"You think the other guys will go for it? Hiring me, I mean."

"Sure they will. We'll have an office and a secretary; everything on the up-and-up."

"What's this new business called?"

"The Fort Knox Commodity Trading Fund. Like it?"

"Love it," she said.

24

Simon Clark still resented what he considered a demotion to Florida. In the Chicago office of the U.S. Attorney he had been an executive, a man of substance. He rarely had been personally involved in outside inquiries. He sat at a desk, collected and assimilated reports from detectives, analyzed evidence, prepared briefs, obtained arrest warrants, and finally represented the DA's office in court.

Now he was being called upon to assume the role of what he had scathingly called a "gumshoe." But to his surprise, he found he was enjoying it. The investigation of Mortimer Sparco's discount brokerage required the talents of an actor, and nothing in Clark's education or experience had prepared him for the job. But his ego was not small, and he grudgingly accepted the fact that to nail Sparco, he had to prove himself the more accomplished liar.

There was no difficulty in obtaining sting money from Lester Crockett's office. The $10,000 was deposited in a local bank suggested by Crockett. It took less than a week to obtain a book of blank checks imprinted with Clark's name.

Meanwhile, he had another meeting with Sparco, and on his recommendation bought two different dollar stocks, neither of which was listed on any exchange. One company, according to the broker, had developed an electronic booster for solar cells, and the other, Sparco claimed, was about to market a revolutionary remedy for baldness. The purchase of the two stocks almost depleted Clark's bank account.

Then Sparco called his hotel and asked him to drop by to hear "some really sensational news." When Clark arrived, the broker took him into his private office and announced he had sold out both stock positions, and Clark had a profit of slightly more than $3,000.

"Why, that's wonderful!" the investigator said. "You're certainly doing a bang-up job. I had no idea I could make so much money so quickly. I hope you have more suggestions as good."

Sparco looked about cautiously, then lowered his voice. "I have a special deal I'm restricting to a select list of clients. Even my account executives don't know about it. Look, there's a restaurant across the street called the Grand Palace. It has a bar in the back that should be deserted this time of day. Why don't we go over there for a drink and a private talk. This investment opportunity is so hot I don't even want to mention it in the office. The walls have ears, you know."

Sparco told the receptionist he'd be right back, and then they dodged through traffic on Commercial Boulevard and entered the Palace Lounge through the side door. They were the only customers, and Ernie brought their drinks to a rear table tucked into a shadowed corner.

"Do you know anything about commodities?" Sparco asked in a conspiratorial whisper.

"Commodities?" Clark said. "You mean like corn, wheat, soybeans?"

"Exactly. Well, about a week ago, a new, SEC-approved investment vehicle was organized on Wall Street. It's called the Fort Knox Commodity Trading Fund. I heard about it through a close friend. The man running the Fund is a genius in commodity trading. A *genius*! He's made a lot of people multimillionaires, and now he's decided to do the same thing for himself. He's keeping a controlling interest, of course, but through my friend I was able to tie up a limited number of shares. Not as many as I wanted because when this fund is announced publicly, the share value will double overnight. At least! It's your chance to get in on the ground floor."

It was an impressive spiel and, Simon Clark reflected, shattered at least three regulations governing the sale of securities.

"The only problem," Sparco went on, "is that because of the limited number of shares I was able to get at the initial offering price, I had to set $50,000 as a minimum investment. I have one package left. Do you think you can swing it?"

"Gee, I don't know," Clark said. "I really don't have that much ready cash."

"Uh-huh," Sparco said, glancing at his watch. "Didn't you tell me your parents live down here?"

"That's right. They have a home in Plantation."

"Think your father would be willing to loan you the money? Just for a short time until you take your profits."

"To tell you the truth, I don't think he has that much cash available. Everything he owns is tied up in his home and long-term government bonds."

"He could get a home-equity loan," Sparco said, looking at his watch again. "The bank doesn't have to know what it's really for. He can tell them home improvements, and they'll accept that."

"I can ask him," Clark said. "You're positive this is a sure thing?"

"Can't miss," Sparco said. "I've been in business fifteen years, and this is the hottest—"

The side door of the Lounge banged open, and a short, stout man came bustling in. He paused until his eyes became accustomed to the darkness.

Then he looked around, spotted the two men at the rear table, and rushed over.

"Mort," he said, "you've got to get me another 50K of that commodity fund. I just heard that the price of shares in the secondary market is already up thirty percent and—"

Sparco rose and put a finger to his lips. "Shhh, Jimmy," he said. "Not so loud. Mr. Clark, this is James Bartlett, a valued client. Jimmy, this gentleman is Simon Clark. We were just discussing the Fund."

"Grab it," Bartlett said to Clark, shaking his hand. "And if you don't want it, I do. Mort, you've got to get me more."

"I'll do my best," Sparco said. "Call me in the morning and I'll let you know."

"I'm depending on you!" Bartlett cried. "Nice to have met you, Mr. Clark." And he scurried out.

Sparco smiled. "Jimmy's a banking consultant and knows a good deal when he sees one. How about it, Mr. Clark? Think you can get your father to take out a home-equity loan? It's the last package of Fund shares I have available, and I'd hate to see you miss out on a dynamite opportunity like this."

Clark considered a moment. "I'll convince my father," he said finally. "Can I call you later today?"

"Anytime before five o'clock. If you haven't called by then, I'll have to give it to someone else. Bartlett isn't the only client begging for more."

They left the Palace Lounge, shook hands, and separated. Sparco returned to his brokerage. When he walked into his office, James Bartlett was seated on the leather couch smoking a fat cigar.

While the two men had a drink from Sparco's office bottle of Chivas, Simon Clark sat in his rented Cutlass, pausing a moment before he drove to headquarters to request additional sting money.

He found it hard to believe the crudeness of south Florida swindlers. Sparco's claiming a profit on Clark's first two investments was an ancient technique used by con men of all stripes, from pool hustlers to bait-and-switch retailers: Let the mark win, or *think* he's winning. Then, when he plunges heavily, overcome by greed, cut his balls off.

Even more primitive was Sparco's use of a shill. That Jimmy Bartlett was no more a legitimate investor than Clark himself. The two slickers had staged the scene in the bar, confident it would convince the pigeon that he *had* to invest in a get-rich-quick deal and do it *now*.

Compared to the sharks on Wall Street and in Chicago's commodity pits, these south Florida chiselers were pilot fish. And yet, for all their dated tricks, they seemed to be thriving. Probably, Clark decided, because they were preying on an ever-growing population of financially unsophisticated retirees trying desperately to augment their Social Security and pension incomes during a time of horrendous inflation.

But if mutts like Sparco and Bartlett could flourish, Clark thought, what might an operator do who knew all the latest methods of duping money-hungry suckers? There was a fortune to be made, and if you knew the law, as Clark did, the risk was negligible.

It was, he decided, a prospect he'd have to consider seriously. The climate of south Florida was super, and there were more than oranges to be plucked.

25

"What exactly *is* the Fort Knox Commodity Trading Fund?" Lester T. Crockett asked. "Do you know?"

"Negative, sir," Harker said.

They were standing in Tony's office, looking down at the chart spread across his desk. It was an organization diagram with a box at the top labeled David Rathbone. Straight lines led to four smaller boxes: Mortimer Sparco, Sidney Coe, James Bartlett, Frank Little. The boxes also contained the names of the assigned investigators: Rita Sullivan, Simon Clark, Manuel Suarez, Henry Ullman, Roger Fortescue.

Within each box was written the subject's ostensible occupation and his relationship with any of the other suspects.

"Here's what we've got so far," Harker reported. "Rathbone tells Sullivan that he and the guys from the Palace are organizing a new business, the Fort Knox Commodity Trading Fund. They've rented a small office on Federal Highway. Sullivan goes to work there tomorrow as a secretary, the Fund paying her salary.

"Suarez says Coe is pushing shares of the Fund in his boiler room, and Clark says Sparco is doing the same thing in his brokerage. Clark also confirms that Bartlett is in on it. The only one whose connection remains iffy is Frank Little, but I'm betting he's a partner, too.

"And that's about all I've got so far, sir. It's possible, of course, that the Fund is an out-and-out swindle, it really doesn't exist, and they're selling shares in soap bubbles."

"But you don't believe that?" Crockett asked.

"No, sir. If the whole thing is just one big goldbrick, why go to the bother of renting an office and hiring a secretary?"

"Just as a front?"

"Maybe," Harker said, "but I think there's more to it than that. They're having letterheads and business cards printed up, like this is a company that's going to be in business for a while."

"Registered?"

"Not with the SEC, the Chicago Board of Trade, the Chicago Mercantile Exchange, or the State of Florida. They may have offshore registration, but I've been unable to find any evidence of it. I'm hoping Sullivan will be able to tell us more about the nature of the Fund after she's been working in their office awhile."

Crockett thrust his hands in his pockets, hunched his shoulders, stared down at the chart. "Of course," he said, "we could pick up the entire mob right now, on charges of security fraud, mail fraud, and conspiracy. And maybe throw the RICO book at them for good measure."

Harker stared at him. "You don't really want to do that, do you, sir?"

"No," Crockett said, "because the moment we put the cuffs on Rathbone, he'll clam up about the source of that self-destructing check. Have you learned anything more about it?"

"According to Sullivan, Rathbone said that scam's on hold."

"Do you believe that?"

"No—but no more of those queer checks have been reported."

"Ullman is still working on the bank officer?"

"Yes, sir. He's become very buddy-buddy with Mike Mulligan. So I'm expecting a break there."

"Soon, I hope," Crockett said. "The Washington brass keep pushing me. All I can do is keep pushing you. And all you can do is keep pushing Ullman."

"I intend to," Tony said.

"Good. Anything else?"

"Yes, sir. Have you come to any decision about bugging Rathbone's town house?"

"No," Crockett said, "not yet. I'll let you know." And he tramped out of Harker's office.

Tony sat down behind his desk, bent over the chart. He felt aswirl in swindles, and not all of them by the crooks: The good guys, in the course of their investigations, were pulling their share of cons, too. Harker was troubled by it, couldn't convince himself of the need to "fight fire with fire." His distress went deeper than that.

He presumed that if you were forced to live in a slum, eventually the ugliness of your surroundings would seep into your nature. Maybe without even being aware of it, you'd begin to think ugly thoughts, say ugly things, act in ugly ways.

Similarly, he now found himself in an environment where everyone lied, schemed, cheated. He had done it himself in the Navigator Bar in Boca. He wondered if, over time, this atmosphere of connivance might corrupt him to such an extent that deceit became normal and he would palter as naturally as he breathed.

He stared down at his chart, at the name of Rita Sullivan. She was a good cop, his most valuable operative, and he appreciated the job she was doing. But he wondered if he had become so tainted by this world of deception that he was now capable of conning himself.

26

Henry Ullman took it easy with Mike Mulligan, playing him slowly and not asking too many personal questions. The bank officer seemed to enjoy meeting Ullman for drinks every evening after work. Once he invited the investigator to his home for dinner. His condo looked as if it had been decorated by a department store, and was so spotlessly clean that it was difficult to believe anyone lived there.

Ullman told him the same cover story he had given James Bartlett: His name was Samuel Henry, and he was a mortgage loan officer at First Farmers' Savings & Loan in Madison, Wisconsin. He had come to south Florida to see if he and his wife could relocate. Mulligan accepted this fiction without question, especially since the two men spent a lot of time talking shop, and Ullman was obviously knowledgeable about banking procedures.

They were in the back booth of the Navigator on Friday evening when Mulligan said, "Sam, how about dinner at my place tomorrow night?"

"You've already fed me once," Ullman protested. "Now it's my turn."

"No, no," Mulligan said, smiling. "Maybe some other time, but tomorrow is going to be a special occasion. I'll send out for Italian food, and after dinner a couple of guests are going to drop by."

"Oh? Friends of yours?"

"Sort of," Mulligan said. "I think you'll like them."

On Saturday night, Ullman arrived at Mulligan's apartment bearing two cold bottles of Chianti, having learned that practically everyone in south Florida preferred their red wine well chilled. The food had already been delivered and was being kept warm in the oven. Mulligan had ordered antipasto, veal piccata, spaghetti all'olio, and arugula salad.

They each had two martinis before sitting down to eat. They finished a bottle and a half of Ullman's Chianti during dinner. Then Mulligan served big snifters of brandy. By that time the little man was feeling no pain, blinking rapidly behind his horn-rimmed glasses and occasionally giggling. He tried to tell a joke about an Englishman, a Frenchman, and an American, but forgot the punch line. Ullman wondered if his host would still be on his feet when his guests arrived.

They showed up around ten-thirty: two tall, thin women who appeared to be in their late thirties. They were introduced to Ullman as Pearl and Opal Longnecker, sisters, who worked at a Crescent Bank branch in Deerfield Beach.

Both women were rather gaunt, with lank hair and horsey features. They were drably dressed except for their shoes: patent leather pumps; kelly green for Opal, fire-engine red for Pearl. They sat primly on the couch and politely refused the offer of a drink. They spoke little, but answered questions in a heavy southern accent.

Ullman made them for a couple of rednecks and hoped, for the sake of Crescent Bank's public relations, their jobs—maybe data entry work— were in a back room where their speech patterns and appearance were unimportant. He couldn't understand what staid, respectable Mike Mulligan had in common with these unattractive and uncommunicative women.

After about ten minutes of desultory conversation, Opal rose and announced, "I gotta use the little girls' room."

"I'll come with you," Pearl said, standing.

Ullman noted they went directly to the bathroom without asking directions.

"What do you think of them, Sam?" Mulligan asked.

Ullman took a sip of his brandy. "They seem very nice," he said. "But quiet."

The host had a fit of giggling. "You'll see," he said, spluttering, "you'll see. You're the guest, so you take the bedroom. I'll make do on the couch."

"What?" the investigator said, bewildered. "What are you talking about, Mike?"

"You'll see," the little man repeated, and sloshed more brandy into his glass.

The Longnecker sisters came out of the bathroom about fifteen minutes later. They were laughing, holding hands, practically skipping.

"Whee!" Opal cried.

"It's party time!" Pearl shouted, eyes glistening. "Time for all good men to come to the aid of the party. Let's go, big man." And she held out her hand to Henry Ullman.

He turned to look at Mulligan. The bank officer had taken off his glasses and pulled Opal onto his lap. His hand was thrust beneath her skirt. He saw Ullman staring at him.

"Go ahead," he urged. "Pearl will do you good."

Henry followed her into the darkened bedroom, but then she turned on all the lights.

"I like to see what I'm doing," she said.

"Shall I close the door?"

"What the hell for? Wait'll you hear Mike huffing and puffing. It's a scream!"

She undressed so swiftly that he was still taking off his socks when she was naked, lying on the bed and kicking bony legs in the air.

"C'mon, hurry up," she demanded. "I been waiting all week for this, and I'm hot to trot. Oooh, look at the big man. What a sweet cuke!"

He had never had a woman like her before and wasn't certain he'd live to have another. She was demented, insatiable, and wrung him out. She was still at it twenty minutes later, long after he had collapsed, drained. Suddenly she stopped, jumped out of bed.

"Little girls' room," she said, panting. "Don't go away."

Ullman lay in a stupor, thinking this was above and beyond the call of duty, and wishing he might find the strength to rise, dress, and stumble out of that madhouse. But then naked Opal came bounding into the lighted bedroom.

"Turnabout's fair play!" she yelled, and he saw in her eyes what he expected to see.

It was another half-hour before he could get away from her, stagger to his feet, go reeling into the bathroom. He soaked a washcloth in hot water and swabbed off his face and body.

Then he started looking for it.

He checked all the boxes, jars, and bottles in the medicine cabinet, but it wasn't there. It wasn't behind the frosted glass doors of the bathtub. Then he did what he should have done in the first place: lift the porcelain lid of the toilet tank.

There it was: a watertight mason jar containing at least a dozen little glassine envelopes filled with a white powder. He took out the jar, unscrewed the lid, removed one of the envelopes. Then he tightened the lid, replaced the jar in the water-filled tank.

Ullman opened the door cautiously. There was talk and laughter coming from the living room. He heard the voices of the two women and, as promised, the huffing and puffing of Mike Mulligan. He slipped into the bedroom, put the glassine envelope deep in the breast pocket of his jacket.

Then he went back to the living room. Mulligan, his body fish-belly white, mouth smeared, eyes bleary, was sprawled on the couch, and both women were working on him. They all looked up when Ullman entered.

"Party time!" he bawled.

27

A new discount drugstore had opened on Federal Highway and had quickly become a mecca for every hustler in Broward County. All because the owner was using peel-off price labels on his merchandise and wasn't yet aware of how he was being taken.

David Rathbone stopped by to stroll through the crowded aisles. He selected Halston cologne for himself and Chanel dusting powder for Rita. He casually switched the price labels with those from a cheap after-shave and an even cheaper face powder, and brought his purchases to the desk where a harried clerk was trying to cope. She rang up the sale without question, and Rathbone carried his bargains out to the Bentley, reflecting on the credo of con men everywhere: "Do unto others before others do unto you."

He drove to the office of the Fort Knox Commodity Trading Fund, north of Atlantic Boulevard. He parked and carefully removed the incorrect price label from the box of Chanel dusting powder. Then he entered the office. Rita was listening to a transistor radio, sandaled feet on her desk. He leaned to kiss her cheek.

"Hi, boss," she said. "What's going on?"

"A present for you," he said, handing her the powder. "Just for the fun of it."

"Thanks a mil," she said, sniffing at the box. "Hey, this stuff is expensive."

"Only the best for you," he said, touching her cheek. "We travel first class."

"Oh? Are we going to travel?"

"Maybe," he said. "Someday. Any excitement around here?"

"Oh sure," she said. "A real hectic morning. The stationery store delivered the letterheads and business cards."

"Let me take a look."

She showed him the five boxes of business cards bearing the name, address, and phone number of the Fund, plus the names of the Palace gang in elegant script.

"No titles," Rita pointed out. "Are you president, or what?"

"We're all equal partners," he said. "No titles. I like these letterheads and envelopes. Very impressive. Listen, I have a little work to do here, and then I've got to go visit a client."

"Yeah? Man or woman?"

"A widow lady named Birdie Winslow. Every now and then she gets antsy about her investments, and I have to hold her hand."

"Make sure that's all you hold. Honey, I'm bored. This is a real nothing job."

"Hang around until I'm finished, then turn on the answering machine, lock up, and go get some sun. It's a super day."

He went into the inner office and closed the door. Rita took a single business card from each of the five boxes and slipped them into the top desk drawer. Then she fished an emery board from her shoulder bag and went to work on her nails.

David came out of the inner office in less than twenty minutes.

"That was quick," she said.

"I've had my fun, and now I'm done. Maybe I'll take those business cards along with me. If we see the gang for drinks tonight, I'll hand them out. They'll get a kick out of them."

"You guys are like kids with a new toy. Are we eating at home tonight?"

He thought a moment. "Why don't we have dinner at the Palace? Then we can have drinks later in the Lounge."

"The Palace? I've never eaten there. How's the food?"

He flipped a palm back and forth. "So-so. They have a double veal chop that's edible. But I don't eat there very often. It's the kind of restaurant that never throws out unused butter, half-eaten rolls, or unfinished steaks. They recycle everything."

"Isn't that illegal?"

He laughed. "Come on," he said, "you know better than that. So they make beef bourguignonne out of leftover steak. Who's to know?"

"I'm not sure I want to eat there," she said.

"Don't tell me you're a straight arrow," he said. "If you found a wallet on the street with a hundred bucks in it and the owner's phone number, would you return it to him?"

"Probably not. I'd keep the money and drop the wallet in a mailbox."

"So would I. So would anyone with an ounce of sense. If the owner is dumb enough to lose his wallet, he's got to pay for his stupidity. Would you steal a towel from a hotel?"

"I might."

"Not me. It's not a class act."

"What's boosting a hotel towel got to do with eating other people's garbage at the Palace?"

"I'm just proving to you that everyone cuts corners. I wouldn't swipe a hotel towel, but I'd clip a mooch for every cent he's got. I enjoy outwitting suckers, but I'd never bash one over the head in a dark alley. I have my standards."

"I guess you do at that."

"Just remember the Golden Rule: He who has the gold, rules. See you later, honey."

She watched him drive away, then went into the inner office. She had to admit they hadn't stinted on the furnishings: new steel desks and file cabinets, leather-covered chairs and Simbari prints on the freshly painted walls.

There was nothing in the unlocked desk except a few scratch pads and pencils. She wondered what "work" David had been doing in there. Then she saw three pieces of crumpled paper in the shiny brass wastebasket. She scooped them out, went back to her own desk, and examined them. They seemed to be three lists of words, five on each list:

1. Machines, melons, mousetraps, mittens, mangoes.

2. Chairs, computers, cherries, corkscrews, catalogs.

3. Hammers, hubcaps, honeydews, heels, hats.

Three of the items had little checkmarks next to them: melons, chairs, and hammers.

She phoned Tony Harker.

"Where are you?" he asked.

"In the office. David was here for a while but he's gone now. I'm taking off in a few minutes. I'm going to hit the beach and tan my buns."

"That I'd like to see," Tony said. "Anything going on?"

"*Nada*. Except they delivered the business cards and letterheads. I lifted one card from each box and figured I'd mail them to you."

"Good idea. Is there one for Frank Little?"

"Yep."

"Bingo. That ties him up with the Fort Knox Commodity Trading Fund—whatever that is. Now we know they're all in on it."

"Something else," Rita said, and told Harker about the crumpled pieces of paper she had found in the wastebasket. She read the three lists to him.

"Mean anything to you?" she asked.

"Not a thing. Just a collection of nouns."

"Three words have little checkmarks next to them: melons, chairs, and hammers."

"It still means nothing to me," Harker said.

"Maybe I'll mail the lists to you along with the business cards. You might be able to make sense out of them if you see them."

"No," Tony said quickly, "don't do that. Rathbone might come back looking for them. Make copies of them as exactly as possible. Mail me the copies. Then crumple up the original lists and toss them back in his waste-basket."

"You don't miss a trick, do you?"

"I miss *you*," he said in a low voice. Then: "Did Rathbone say where he was going?"

"To visit a client. A widow named Birdie Winslow. That's the first time he's mentioned the name of one of his mooches."

"I'm making a note of it. Is her first name spelled with a *y* or *ie*?"

"Beats me. He just said Birdie Winslow."

"Okay. I'll try to get some skinny on her. Anything else?"

"Nope."

"Then go toast your tush."

"Hey, I like that," she said. "I really do think you're beginning to lighten up. My therapy is working."

"Thank you, nurse," he said. "What would I do without you?"

She smiled and hung up. But a moment later she had forgotten about Tony; she was thinking about David, wondering if he really was going to see a client or if he had another bimbo on the side and was planning a matinee. As he had said, everyone cuts corners, and she couldn't believe fidelity was one of his virtues.

She was right; David didn't visit Birdie Winslow. But an assignation with another woman was not on his agenda. Instead, he met with Termite Tommy in the parking lot of the Grand Palace.

The two men sat in the Bentley and cut up the proceeds from the dissolving check scam.

"Gross was 27K plus," Rathbone said. "The pusher drew two thousand as I told you. That leaves 25K plus in the kitty."

"Manna," Tommy said. "How do you want to split?"

David turned sideways to stare at him. "Thirds," he said, "You, me, and the printer."

"You crazy?" Tommy cried. "I thought we were going to stiff the Kraut."

Rathbone put a soft hand on the other man's arm. "Don't you trust me, Tommy?" he asked.

"Remember that old sign in saloons. 'In God We Trust. All others pay cash.'"

"There'll be more cash than you can count if you go along with me on this. First of all, the Treasury check went through without a hitch. But Tommy, how many times can we pull that dodge? We'd have to find a different pusher for every operation, and you know as well as I do that the more people you let in on the action, that's how much your risk increases. There's a better way of using that queer paper. And giving the printer a third will tickle his greed."

"Yeah? What's on your mind?"

"Persuade the German to use the paper for making fake twenties and fifties."

"He'll never go for it," Tommy said. "That's what put him behind bars the last time."

"No, it wasn't," David said. "What put him behind bars was that the feds caught him selling and grabbed the queer. But if he prints on self-destruct paper, where's the evidence?"

"The feds won't have any evidence, but the customer won't have any money either. They'll have paid for a bag of confetti. It'll shred away before they have a chance to push it. Then they'll come looking for us."

"Just listen a minute, will you? The German prints up the fake bills on that freaky paper. But we don't try to sell the bills for the reason you just said. Instead, you and I open bank accounts with phony ID and make cash deposits. It's credited to our accounts. Then who cares if the cash dissolves three days later? The bank takes the loss. And we withdraw clean money whenever we want."

Termite Tommy looked at him. "Nice try, David, but how much cash can we deposit before the banks get suspicious?"

"They're not going to ask questions if we keep each deposit under ten grand. And what if they do? We can always say we sold our car for cash. We each open maybe a dozen accounts so all the queer doesn't go to one bank."

"I don't like it."

"Tommy, my scam will have two big advantages. First of all, it cuts out the need to use pushers. There's a saving right there. Second of all, we'll be getting face value for the queer. How much was the German making before he was nabbed? Twenty percent? Thirty?"

"About that."

"There you are! We do it my way and we make twenty on a twenty and fifty on a fifty."

Tommy was silent. He had turned his head away and was staring out the window.

"Now what's bothering you?" David asked.

"It means I'd have to become a pusher," the other man said in a low voice. "I'm not sure I've got the balls for it. Ten years ago I'd have jumped at the chance. But that time I did in stir did something to me, David. I never want to go back in there again. Never!"

"All right, Tommy," Rathbone said, "I can understand that. Look, you brought me this deal; it's only right that I pay my way. I'll do all the pushing. I'll open accounts in a dozen banks. You get the cash to me as quickly as you can. I'll stick it in the banks as fast as I can, while the money is still fresh. I'll take all the risk."

"You'll really do that, David?"

"Of course I will. Because that's how positive I am that this thing is going to work."

"I'm not sure I can talk the German into printing bills again."

"Why don't you let me meet him? I'll convince him that this is the way to go."

"And we split three ways? On the face value?"

"Absolutely."

"Yeah," Tommy said, "maybe that's the way to handle it. I'll go back to Lakeland and set it up. Then I'll give you a call, and you drive over. Now what about the payoff on the fake Treasury check?"

"I'll bring it to you and the German when I come to Lakeland."

Termite Tommy nodded and got out of the Bentley. "I'll be in touch," he said. "Goodbye, David."

Rathbone lifted a hand in farewell. Then, watching the other man walk back to his battered pickup, he said softly, "Goodbye, Tommy."

28

A black man from the Drug Enforcement Administration had a desk in the bullpen next to Roger Fortescue's. His name was Hiram Johnson, and he was working a case involving a ring peddling a new laboratory drug called "Rapture" to schoolkids in Dade and Broward counties. The two investigators—the only blacks in the room—discovered they were both graduates of Howard University, and whenever they had the chance, they had lunch together, or a few beers, and talked shop.

They were scoffing fried fish in Long John Silver's on Federal Highway when Fortescue brought up the subject of Haiti.

"A lot of drugs coming in from there?" he asked.

"Indubitably," Johnson said, which was the way he talked. "But you must realize, my dear confrere, that very limited quantities of controlled substances *originate* in Haiti. Like Panama, Haiti is a transshipping point.

Because it's closer to the U.S., y'see. Heavy shipments of la dope come in on freighters or flights from Colombia, or Bolivia, or wherever, and are packaged in Haiti for delivery in bulk to Miami or New York."

"Is the stuff flown here or brought in by boat?"

"Both. And smuggled through in hollowed-out lumber, under false bottoms in furniture, in cans of flea powder—a thousand different ways. A few years ago we intercepted a shipment of toothpaste, each tube filled with heroin."

"Toothpaste?" Roger said. "Unreal."

"The villains are extremely clever," the DEA man went on. "Every time we uncover one subterfuge, the rascals come up with another. Just last year the Spanish police intercepted a million dollars' worth of cocaine concealed in a shipment of coconuts. A neat little plug had been drilled out of the shell of each nut, the meat and milk removed, the coconut filled with coke, and the plug replaced. A lot of arduous labor involved there, but justified by the profits, I do assure you, bro."

"Coconuts," Fortescue repeated. "That's cool."

After he left Johnson, Roger drove to a locksmith's shop on Dixie Highway. It was owned by Louis Falace, an ex-con. After spending almost thirty of his seventy-four years in the clink on several burglary raps, Falace had decided to go straight and had opened Be Safe, Be Sure, a successful store where he sold locks, bolts, chains, peepholes, window guards, alarms, and other security devices designed to thwart the kind of Breaking & Entering artist he had once been.

Fortescue, who had helped send Falace away on his last trip to the pokey, stopped by occasionally to see how the old man was doing. There was no enmity between crook and cop; they were both professionals.

"Lou," Roger said, "I need your advice. There's this place I want to get into, but it's surrounded by a high, chain-link fence. The gate faces a street and is usually lighted, so I don't want to go in that way. I figure I've got to cut a hole in that fence or take a ladder along and go over it. Which do you think is best?"

The old man smiled. He had new dentures, and they glistened like wet stones. "No cutta hole," he said. "No climba over."

"No?" Fortescue said. "Then how do I get in?"

Falace went into a back room and returned in a moment carrying a folding entrenching tool with a khaki cloth over the blade: standard U.S. Army issue.

"Go *under*," Falace said. "Dig just deep enough to wiggle beneath the fence. When you come out, fill in the hole, make it nice and neat. Everyone says, 'How did he get in?'"

"Lou, you're a genius," Roger said. "I'll return your little shovel."

"Don't bother," Falace said. "I don't go digging anymore."

Fortescue's next stop was at a sporting goods store. He bought a baseball. It cost $7.99 plus tax. He carried his purchase (in a little plastic bag with handles) out to the car and before he examined it, he entered "$7.99 (baseball) and 48 cents (tax)" on the page of his notebook where he recorded his out-of-pocket expenses.

The ball was in a small box marked "Official Major League Baseball." It came from a company in Missouri, but in fine print it stated: "Contents assembled in Haiti." Fortescue smiled.

Then he inspected the ball itself. It had a white leather cover stitched in red, and it felt as hard as a rock. On the side of the baseball was printed: "Cushioned cork center." Roger had no idea what the rest of the ball contained and didn't want to cut the cover open to find out.

He drove home with his baseball and folding shovel. Estelle was out—probably shopping—and the kids were at school, so Papa went to bed and had a fine nap.

That night, just before twelve o'clock, he assembled all his gear.

"You better not wait up," he said to Estelle.

"I wasn't going to," she said. "What's that you're carrying?"

"A baseball."

"Oh? A night game?"

"Something like that," he said.

He went back to his hidey-hole in the deserted fast-food joint and took up his position at the window facing the FL Sports Equipment warehouse. The gate was open, floodlights were on, an unmarked van was being loaded with cartons. Frank Little, as usual, stood to one side keeping a tally.

The van didn't leave until almost one-thirty A.M. Then Little closed the gate and locked it. He went into the blockhouse, and a moment later the floodlights went off. But there was a light in the rear of the office. Fortescue waited patiently. Finally the light was extinguished. Frank Little came out, locked up, and drove away in his snazzy Cadillac convertible. The investigator waited in the darkness another half-hour. Then, when it seemed likely that Little wouldn't return, he went outside and got to work.

He picked a spot at the rear of the warehouse where he couldn't be seen from Copans Road. He unfolded his little shovel, locked the blade into place, and started digging. The Florida soil at that spot was sandy and loose, and the hole went swiftly. The only trouble was that displaced dirt kept sliding back into the excavation, and Roger had to shovel it farther away.

It took him about thirty minutes to scoop out a trench deep enough so he could lie down and roll under the chain-link fence. But first he went back to the restaurant to get the baseball, bull's-eye lantern, and set of lockpicks. Then he squeezed under the fence, rose, dusted himself off, and started exploring.

What concerned him most was that there might be an alarm system: electronic or infrared. The last thing in the world he wanted was to be poking around and suddenly have the floodlights blaze and a siren go "WHOOP-WHOOP-WHOOP!" He was well aware that he was engaged in an illicit enterprise and whatever he found could not be used as evidence. Still, as every cop learns early in his career, there are many ways to skin a cat.

He made a cautious circuit of the warehouse, using his lantern sparingly, and finally decided his best means of entry was through one of the small, fogged windows in the rear. Locked, of course. It would have been easy to take off his dungaree jacket, wrap it around his fist, and punch out a pane of glass to get at the rusted window lock. But he didn't want to leave such an obvious sign of a break-in. So, mumbling angrily at his own lack of foresight, he went back to his trench, rolled under the fence, fetched the little crowbar from his hideaway, rolled under the fence again, and went to work on the locked window.

It took almost ten minutes of prying before the lock snapped and the window slid up with a loud squeal. He waited awhile, and when he heard no shouts of "Stop, thief!" or the sound of approaching sirens, he climbed through the window and looked around the warehouse, using his lantern with his fingers spread across the lens to dim the glare.

It was a cavernous place, smelling of damp. But all the cartons and crates were stacked on pallets close to the front entrance, which made his job easier. Even better, one of the top cartons was unsealed, and when Roger lifted the flaps he saw at least fifty white baseballs piled in there.

He slipped one of the balls into his jacket pocket, replaced it with the baseball he had bought that afternoon, then began his withdrawal. Out the window. Lower the sash carefully. Check to make certain he had all his gear. Wiggle out under the fence. He filled in the trench and tamped it down, leaving it "nice and neat," just as Lou Falace had instructed.

He was home within an hour, the house silent, family sleeping peacefully. He sat down at the kitchen table and examined the stolen baseball. It looked just like the one he had left in its place: white leather cover, red stitching, printing on the side: "Official Major League Baseball. Cushioned cork center."

He found a sharp paring knife and very, very carefully slit open a few of those red stitches. He began squeezing the hardball with both hands, gripping it with all his strength. After a while white powder began to spurt out of the cut and pile up on the tabletop.

He put the ball aside. He licked a forefinger and touched it cautiously to the white powder. He tasted it, made a bitter face.

"Bingo," he said.

29

Simon Clark considered writing a letter home to his wife, merely to tell her he was alive, well, and living in Fort Lauderdale. But then he thought better of it; she'd have absolutely no interest in his health or whereabouts. Their childless marriage had deteriorated to the point that while they occupied the same domicile, they communicated mostly by notes stuck on the refrigerator door with little magnets in the shape of frogs and bunnies.

This sad state of affairs had existed for several years now, exacerbated by the long hours he had to work and her recent employment at a Michigan Avenue boutique. That resulted in her making many new friends, most of whom seemed to be epicene young men who wore their hair in ponytails.

So rather than write a letter, Simon mailed his wife a garishly colored postcard showing three young women in thong bikinis bending over a ship's rail, their tanned buns flashing in the south Florida sunlight. He wrote: "Having a fine time; glad you're not here," and didn't much care if she found it amusing, offensive, or what.

He had a gin and bitters at his hotel bar and decided to drive over to Mortimer Sparco's discount brokerage and check on the status of his investment in the Fort Knox Commodity Trading Fund. It wasn't listed anywhere in *The Wall Street Journal*, and Clark didn't expect it ever would be.

As he was about to enter the brokerage, a woman was exiting and he held the door open for her. She was a very small woman, hardly five feet tall, he reckoned, and seemed to be in her middle thirties. She swept by him without a glance or a "Thank you," and he had the distinct impression that she had been weeping.

Old men in Bermuda shorts were still watching the tape on the TV screen in the waiting room, and there was one geezer, presumably a client, sleeping peacefully in one of the wicker armchairs. His hearing aid had slipped out and was dangling from a black wire.

"Could I see Mr. Sparco, please," Clark said to the receptionist. "My name is Simon Clark."

"Oh, I know who you are, Mr. Clark," she said warmly. "But I'm afraid Mr. Sparco is in a meeting. He won't be free for at least an hour."

"All right," Simon said. "Maybe I'll try to catch him this afternoon."

He went outside, wondering if he should drive to headquarters and work on his weekly report to Anthony Harker. Then, realizing he really had nothing to report, he decided to goof off for a few hours, perhaps have some lunch, and return to the brokerage later.

He left his rented Cutlass where it was parked and crossed Commercial to the Grand Palace. He walked through the empty dining room to the Lounge at the rear. There was a table of four blue-haired women, all laughing loudly and all drinking mai tais, each of which had a plastic orchid floating on top. There was a single woman seated at the bar, the small woman Clark had seen leaving Sparco's brokerage. He stood at the bar, not too close to her, and ordered a gin and bitters.

As he sipped his drink, he examined the woman in the mirror behind the bar. If she had been weeping when he first saw her, she certainly wasn't now. In fact, she was puffing on a cigarette, working on a boiler-maker, and chatting animatedly with the bartender. Simon thought her attractive: a gamine with a helmet of short blond hair.

He waited until the bartender was busy making fresh mai tais. Then he stepped closer to the woman.

"I beg your pardon," he said, smiling, "but I believe I saw you at Sparco's brokerage, and I wondered if you're a client."

She looked at him, expressionless. "No," she said, "I'm not a client. I'm Nancy Sparco, the schnorrer's wife."

"Oh," Simon said, startled. "Sorry to bother you."

"You're not bothering me. Bring your drink over and talk to me. I hate to booze alone. People will think I'm a lush, which I'm not."

He took the barstool next to her.

"You've met my husband?" she said.

He nodded.

"A prick," she said. "A cheap, no-good, conniving prick. But that's neither here nor there. What's your name?"

"Simon Clark."

"Where you from, Simon?"

"Chicago."

"Nice town. Greatest shopping in the world. Married?"

"Yes," he said, "but I'm not working at it. Neither is my wife."

"I know exactly what you mean. My marriage isn't the greatest either."

"May I buy you a drink?" he asked.

"Why not. Where are you staying, Simon?"

"At a hotel on the Galt Ocean Mile."

"Good," she said. "As long as it's not the YMCA."

Two hours and two drinks later they were in his hotel room. He thought her the wittiest woman he had ever met: vulgar, raunchy, with a limitless supply of one-liners, some of which went by too fast to catch.

When she undressed and took off her cork wedges, she was positively *tiny.*

"My God," he said, "this is like going to bed with a Girl Scout."

"A Brownie," she corrected. "You'll notice my collar and cuffs don't match. But the lungs aren't bad—right? The best silicone money can buy. I'll never drown."

She showed him how they could manage, with her sitting atop him. He was amenable, but she wouldn't stop talking, and he was laughing so much he was afraid he couldn't perform. Finally he told her to shut up, for five minutes at least.

"May I groan?" she asked, but then was reasonably quiet while she rode him like a demented jockey.

When they finished, she took his wrist and lifted his arm into the air. "The winner and new world champion!" she proclaimed. "When's the rematch?"

"In about twenty minutes," he said. "Shall I call down for drinks?"

"Please," she said. "A whiskey IV. Mommy needs plasma."

Later in the afternoon, when they were just lazing around and sipping sour mash bourbon, she said, "Don't go back to Chicago, Simon. Not just yet."

"It depends," he said.

"You got any money?" she asked suddenly.

He wondered if she was a pro, and she caught his expression.

"Not for fun and games, dummy," she said. "I'm no hooker. I mean real money."

"I'm not rich, but I get by."

She sighed. "I've got this great idea for a new business. It would be profitable from Day One. So I go to my dear hubby for start-up cash, and the asshole stiffs me. He's loaded, but it's all for him, none for me."

"Maybe he wants to keep you dependent on him."

"Yeah, that's probably it. He knows if I ever had my own income, it'd be goodbye Mort."

"What's this new business you want to start?"

"An escort service," she said. "Covering the Miami-Lauderdale area. Listen, next to drugs, tourists are Florida's biggest cash crop. Men and women come down here on vacation and want a good time. But they don't know anyone. They don't know where to go, what to see. I'd provide escorts—young, good-looking guys and dolls—they could hire for an hour, an evening, a day, a week, to show them around, best restaurants and so forth. Keep them from getting lonely. What do you think?"

"Sex?" he asked.

She shrugged. "It wouldn't be in the contract, but if the escorts want to make a private deal, it would be up to them. As long as my agency gets its fee. I pay the escorts a percentage and pocket the rest. The escorts can keep the tips, if any."

"You know," he said, "it just might go."

"Can't miss," she said. "I could even arrange boat charters and things like that. And I'd screen the escorts carefully. All clean, tanned kids. South Florida is full of beach bums, male and female. I'd recruit a choice staff who have table manners, know how to dress and talk and dance and show the tourists a good time."

He poured them more bourbon. "What do you figure your start-up costs would be?"

"Twenty-five thousand at least. Possibly more. Because I want this to be a class operation. And listen, there are a lot of ways to make an extra buck. Like getting kickbacks from restaurants and nightclubs for steering clients there. Ditto for jewelry stores, hotels, and expensive boutiques. It could be a gold mine. You got twenty-five grand to spare?"

"I wish I did," he said. "As a matter of fact, I did have it a week ago. But then I met your husband."

"Mooch!" she jeered. "You can kiss those bucks goodbye. What'd he put you in—penny stocks?"

"For starters. But those made money."

"The old come-on. Did you see any of the money he said you made?"

"Well . . . no. It was reinvested, plus more."

"Uh-huh, that sounds like Mort. What are you in now?"

"Something called the Fort Knox Commodity Trading Fund."

"Yeah," she said, "I heard him talking on the phone about that. I don't know what it is, but all his buddies are in on it so it's got to be a scam. I call them Captain Crook and his Merry Crew."

"Your husband is Captain Crook?"

"Nah, he's just one of the crew. The Captain is a guy named David Rathbone, a handsome devil who hasn't got a straight bone in his body."

Clark did some heavy thinking. "Maybe I can get my money back from your husband," he said.

"Fat chance! Once he's got his paws on your green, it's his, to have and to hold till he croaks."

"If I *could* get it back," he persisted, "maybe we could talk some more about your escort service."

"Hey," she said, "that would be great."

"Tell me something," he said. "If I could come up with the money you need, would you leave your husband?"

"Is the Pope Catholic?" she cried. "I'd be gone so fast all he'd see would be palm trees waving in my wind."

"And move in with me?" Clark asked, staring at her.

She didn't blink. "I learned a long time ago, you don't get something for nothing in the world. You bankroll my business, and I'll do whatever turns you on."

"Okay," he said, "then we've got a deal. Give me your home phone number so I can reach you if anything breaks. You can always call me here at the hotel. Leave a message if I'm out."

She nodded, rose, and began dressing. "How soon do you think it'll be?"

"It may take weeks," he said. "Even a month. Try to be patient."

"I'm good at that," she said. "Meanwhile we can be getting to know each other better."

"It couldn't be much better than this afternoon."

She left, and he showered and dressed. Then he went downstairs to drive to headquarters. Now he had something to put in his report.

Something, but not everything.

30

They started for Lakeland early in the morning, David driving the Bentley.

"We should be there by noon," he said, "if the traffic isn't too heavy. My meeting will take an hour or so. Then you and I'll have lunch and do some sightseeing before we head back. We should be home around eight o'clock."

"Whatever you say, boss," Rita said, yawning. "I think I'll grab a little shut-eye. You didn't let me get much sleep last night. Where did you learn those tricks?"

"Mommy taught me," he said, laughing.

"You've never mentioned your parents, David. You did have parents, didn't you? I mean you weren't just found in a cabbage patch?"

"Oh, I had parents," he said, keeping his eyes on the road. "Plus two brothers and a sister. All of them so straight they were practically rigid. I was the Ebony Sheep, in trouble since the age of seven when I was caught playing doctor and nurse with the little girl next door. I knew even then I'd cut loose from that family as soon as I could."

"You ever hear from them?"

"Hell, no! And that's just the way I want it."

"Don't you have an urge now and then to write or phone them? After all, they *are* your family."

"Go to sleep," he said, and she did.

It was a hot, hazy day with not much breeze stirring. They drove northward on U.S. Highway 27, through part of the Everglades, around Lake Okeechobee. The scenery kept changing: dense woods, arid patches of scrub pine, condo developments, lakes and canals, swamps, golf courses, somnolent little towns, and roadside diners that advertised alligator steaks. Everyone they saw was moving slowly in the heat. Some of the women carried parasols, and in every patch of shade, no matter how small, a hound lay snoozing.

They stopped once to gas up and gulp a cold Coke. Then they pushed on and were in Lakeland a little after noon. It looked like any other whitewashed Florida city with elderly tourists rocking on the verandas of ancient hotels. But there were a lot of out-of-state cars, and the souvenir shops were doing a brisk business in carved coconut masks, shell picture frames, and necklaces of shark teeth.

"What do the people who live here do besides clip the tourists?" Rita asked. "I mean, how do they make a living?"

"Probably take in each other's laundry," Rathbone said. "I hope I remember the directions. Yep, here's the street, and there's the church. Now I make a right, go five blocks and hang a left. We dead-end at a park."

"You're going to have a meeting in a *park*?"

"That's the way the printer wanted it," David said. "I wasn't about to argue. Ah, here we are."

He pulled into a turnaround and stopped the car. Ahead lay a broad spread of flat lawn, nicely manicured, and trimmed palm trees surrounding a stretch of clear water, more pond than lake. There were meandering walkways, benches, clumps of scarlet hibiscus. Lovers were strolling, a family was picnicking on the grass, two small boys were trying to get a kite aloft on a windless day. It was a painted scene, artfully composed, gleaming with sunlight.

"Nice place for a do-or-die meeting," David said. "I'll wander around, and my guys will see me or I'll see them. You take the car, drive downtown, do some shopping, have a drink. Just remember to be back here in an hour. Don't forget me."

"I won't forget you," Rita said. "Maybe I'll look for a place where we can have a decent lunch."

"Good idea," he said. He took a manila envelope from the glove compartment, and she recognized it as the same one that had contained the Crescent Bank money. He kissed her cheek and got out of the car.

"Don't talk to any sailors," he warned.

"In the middle of Florida?" she said, laughing. "That would be some trick."

She drove away without looking back. It took her less than twenty minutes to find a reasonably modern hotel. At least it was air-conditioned and had a public phone in the lobby. She called Anthony Harker in Lauderdale, collect.

"What the hell are you doing in Lakeland?" he asked. "No ocean there."

"He's got a meeting in a public park, if you can believe that."

"Oh? With whom?"

"Beats me. But he talks of 'guys,' so it must be more than one. He took the envelope of cash I got from the Crescent Bank in Boca. And he let something slip. I asked him how come he was having a meeting in a park, and he said that's the way the printer wanted it."

"The *printer*?" Tony said, voice excited. "You sure he said printer?"

"That's what he said."

"Beautiful. The first good lead we've had on that phony check. No way you can get a look at the printer?"

"Nope. Not without risking my cover."

"Then play it cozy. I'll take it from here. How many first-class counterfeiters can there be in Lakeland? I'll find him. Nice work, Rita. When am I going to see you?"

"I'll try to finagle something. An afternoon or evening."

"Try," he urged. "I went to the beach over the weekend."

"You did? Great! Did you get a tan?"

"No," he said, "I got a red. But at least I didn't break out or peel."

"Good for you," she said. "Now go for the bronze."

She hung up and wandered about the hotel. She found a little restaurant and bar tucked into one corner. It was decorated in Key West style, with overhead fans and planked tables scrubbed white. Not a soul in the place except for the bartender, who looked to be one year younger than God and was reading a romance paperback titled *Brazen Virgin*.

Rita ordered a frozen daiquiri and it turned out to be excellent, not too tart, not too sweet.

"Kitchen open?" she asked him, looking around at the empty room.

"I can open it," he offered.

"You're the chef?"

"And bartender. And waiter."

"I'd like to bring a friend back for lunch in about an hour," she said. "Could I see a menu, please."

"I'm also the menu," he said. "Today I can fix you some eggs, any style; a hamburger I wouldn't recommend for a nice lady like you; or homemade lentil soup."

"How about a salad?"

He thought a moment. "Would you settle for canned shrimp? I got all the greens; they're fresh. And I make my own dressing."

"You've got a deal," she said. "How about some white wine to go with it?"

He rummaged in a cupboard and dragged out a dusty bottle of Pouilly-Fuissé. "Here's some pooly-foos," he said. "Will that do?"

"Just fine. Put it on ice to chill. Okay?"

"I think I got a corkscrew," he muttered. "Somewhere."

She had a second daiquiri, then drove back to pick up David. When she reached the turnaround, she saw him out on the lawn with the two boys, trying to launch their kite. He was running like a maniac, but the kite just kept bumping along the ground behind him. Then he saw the Bentley, waved, handed the string to one of the kids.

He came over to the car, grinning. He really was a beautiful man, she decided: blond hair tousled, flashing smile, everything about him alert and active, taut body bursting with energy. The golden boy at play.

"I couldn't get it up," he said.

"That's the first time you've had that problem. How did the meeting go?"

He made the A-OK sign. "Couldn't have been better. We're going to be *rich* rich."

"Good," she said. "That's better than *poor* poor. Let's go eat."

On the drive back to the hotel, she told him about the ancient bartender-chef-waiter-menu, and the lunch they were going to have.

He laughed. "I love that pooly-foos," he said. "But who cares what he calls it as long as it's cold. I could drink the whole bottle myself."

"My God, you're wired," she said. "That meeting was a real upper."

"It went great," he said. "One little drawback, but I know how to get around that."

They were the only diners in the restaurant, and the old man fussed about them anxiously. He poured their wine with a trembling hand and beamed at their approval. He brought the salad in a big wooden bowl,

enough for four, and let them help themselves. The shrimp were unde-
niably canned, but there were a lot of them, and everything else was fresh
and crisp.

"You picked a winner," Rathbone said to Rita. "I wonder why this
place isn't mobbed."

"No chrome, no plastic, no chili dogs or french fries. By the way, he
also makes the world's best frozen daiquiri."

"For dessert," David said.

They sat sprawled for almost an hour after they had finished lunch and
the table had been cleared.

It was getting close to three o'clock, and the bartender had disappeared
into the kitchen. There were occasional muted sounds from the lobby and
outdoors, but quiet engulfed the room, and they spoke in hushed voices,
not wanting to shatter the spell.

"About our being rich," David said, "I meant it. I have two deals in
the works that are shaping up as winners, plus my investment service. I
figure to give it another year and cash in."

"And then?"

"Off we go, into the wild blue yonder."

"Both of us?"

He lifted her hand, kissed her fingertips. "Yes," he said. "Both of us."

"You won't have to hustle anymore?"

"Not if the payoff is as big as I figure. I don't mean we'll be able to
light our cigarettes with hundred-dollar bills, but we'll be able to live very
comfortably indeed. We won't have to count pennies."

"You'll really take me with you?"

He kissed the palm of her hand. "You remember the morning after our
first night together?"

"When you told me to move in?"

"Right. I said it was love at first sight. You thought I was conning you,
and maybe I was. Then. But I'm not conning you now. I love you, Rita.
More than that, I *need* you. You're the most important thing in my life."

"That's heavy," she said.

"It's the truth. It's why I'm getting into these new deals. To make
enough for *both* of us to have the good life. You like all the perks that
money can buy. So do I. Neither of us wants to live like a peasant."

She looked down at their linked hands. "You're right," she said in a
low voice. "I've never had as much as you've given me. Have I ever said,
'Thank you'? I'll say it now: Thank you."

"You don't have to thank me. I don't want your gratitude; I want your
love. And besides, you've paid me back just by being there when I need
you. Did I tell you I'm addicted to you? Well, I am. But what about you?

I've never really asked if you'd be willing to spend the rest of your life with me. It would mean leaving the country and probably never coming back. Could you do that?"

She gave him a twisted smile. "I don't know. When you talked before about cashing in and taking off, I thought that's all it was—talk. But now you're serious, aren't you?"

He nodded.

"I don't have to give you an answer right now, do I, David?"

"No, of course not. Maybe my deals will go sour. And then I'll have to change my plans. Or postpone them. But you'll think about it?"

"Yes," she said, "I will."

"Good. Now let's go home."

"Are we going to the Palace tonight?"

"I'd rather not," he said. "Let's spend it together. Just the two of us."

"I'd like that," she said.

31

Anthony Harker's office was jammed. He had brought in folding chairs so his crew had a place to sit, but it was shoulder-to-shoulder and everyone was smoking up a storm. The air conditioning wasn't coping. But Harker wasn't having an allergic reaction.

"Okay," he said, "here's what we've got. Roger, we'll start with you. That stuff in Frank Little's baseball tested out as high-grade cocaine."

"Thought it might," Fortescue said.

"You figure he's importing and selling?"

"I'd guess not. I think he's just a trafficker. His customers make their own buys. The stuff comes to Little's warehouse in baseballs from Haiti, and the dealers pick it up there. It's like a distribution center. He charges a fee for providing a service. But he's not pushing the stuff himself."

"That reads," Harker said, nodding. "I've persuaded Mr. Crockett to hold off raiding the warehouse until we learn more about Little's operation. If we get called for stalling the raid, we can always say we were trying to track the source and the guys making the pickups—which is the truth."

"That would take an army of narcs," Fortescue said.

"Maybe not," Tony said. "We're trying to get more bodies assigned to us. They'll tail those vans and trucks you spotted to their eventual destinations. It looks to be a big, well-organized distribution system, and we'll hold off busting the warehouse until we know the identity of Little's customers."

"That coke I found in Mike Mulligan's toilet," Henry Ullman said, "you figure it came from Frank Little's baseballs?"

"The lab says no," Harker said. "It was high-grade cocaine all right but had a different chemical signature—whatever that is—from the stuff Fortescue found. Henry, you think Mike Mulligan is snorting?"

"I don't think so. I've become close pals with the guy and he shows no signs of it. He loves the sauce, but I think he just uses the coke to get women. Some of them are young and attractive, too. He pays off with the dust, and it's party time every Saturday night."

"Where's he getting it? Does he buy it?"

"I doubt it. Not in that quantity. If he was paying for it, he'd have been dead broke a long time ago. According to your snitch, David Rathbone said that James Bartlett claimed Mulligan was on the pad. How's this for a scenario: Bartlett is laundering drug money through the Crescent Bank, and Mike Mulligan is his contact. Mulligan is a bank officer; he could fiddle the deal. And Bartlett pays him off with coke."

"That's possible," Tony said. "Likely, in fact. You know, we started out tracking a gang of con men and swindlers, and now it's beginning to look like they're up to their ass in dope. Suarez, Clark, have you heard anything about Coe or Sparco pushing any kind of drugs?"

"Not me," Manny Suarez said. "Coe smokes a joint now and then, but all he's pushing right now is that crazy commodity fund."

"The same with Sparco," Simon Clark said. "He's selling shares in the Fund like there's no tomorrow. I checked all my contacts in Chicago, and no one in the commodity pits ever heard of the Fort Knox Fund and there's no record of any trades under that name."

Harker sighed. "All right," he said, "just keep on doing what you're doing, but try to dig a little deeper. That Fund may be an out-and-out fraud or it may be a front for something bigger. I think it is, but can't pin it down. That's all for now."

They rose and began folding chairs so they could get out of the office.

"Wait a minute," Tony said. "I want the four of you to take a look at something and tell me if it means anything to you."

He opened his desk drawer, took out copies of the lists Rita Sullivan had fished from David Rathbone's wastebasket. He handed them to Ullman.

Henry read them, shook his head. "They don't make any sense to me," he said, and handed them to Suarez.

Manny read them over twice. *"Nada,"* he said. "Just words." He passed them along to Clark.

Simon scanned them quickly, shook his head, gave them to Fortescue.

Roger read them, shrugged, returned them to Harker. "Means nothing," he said. "Just—" He stopped suddenly. "Wait a minute. Let me have another look." He took the lists back from Tony and studied them again. "Uh-huh," he said, grinning. "Five words beginning with C, five with H, five with M. C, H, M. Put them all together and they don't spell Mother. But they could be code words for cocaine, heroin, and marijuana."

Harker stared at him, then took a deep breath. "Thank you very much," he said.

After they left, Tony called Lester Crockett's secretary. "Five minutes," he said. "That's all I need."

"Hang on a moment," she said. "I'll check with him."

He waited, took his inhaler out of his shirt pocket, tossed it into the bottom desk drawer.

She came back on. "All right, Mr. Harker," she said. "Five minutes. Right now."

"On my way," he said.

He stood in front of Crockett's desk and told him about the lists of words from Rathbone's wastebasket. He handed over the copies.

"I couldn't make any sense out of them, sir," he said.

Crockett read the lists slowly. Then again. "Nor can I," he said.

"I showed them to my men. Roger Fortescue caught it. The lists start with C, H, and M. Standing for cocaine, heroin, marijuana."

Crockett looked at him and nodded. "Possible," he said.

"Probable, sir," Tony said. "And if so, Rathbone, his pals, and that Fund are involved in drug dealing. Those lists are potential code words. The nouns with checkmarks are the ones Rathbone selected. I guess they need code words for messages, documents, and telephone conversations concerning their deals."

Crockett nodded again.

"It's all supposition," Harker said. "Smoke and mirrors. But I think there's a good chance the Fort Knox Fund is trading commodities all right: coke, shit, and grass. Now can I put central-office taps on Rathbone's phones and bugs in his town house?"

"All right," Crockett said, "you win. Draw up a detailed plan of how all this is to be accomplished and the evidence justifying it. We'll have to get a court order."

"Will do," Tony said.

"And you're still determined not to tell Sullivan about the bugs?"

"She has no need to know," Harker said stubbornly.

Crockett didn't say anything. Tony turned to leave, then stopped.

"I was supposed to be covering white-collar crime," he said. "As I told my men a half-hour ago, it now looks like the sharks we're tracking are into drug dealing. And Rathbone is dabbling in counterfeiting. It's unusual for criminal leopards to change their spots. How do you account for it, sir?"

The chief clasped his fingers across his vest, stared up at the ceiling almost dreamily. "The something-for-nothing syndrome," he said. "Con men depend on human greed for their livelihood. If it wasn't for greed, swindlers would have no victims. What do they call them—mooches? Most people have get-rich-quick dreams. How else can you explain the popularity of lotteries? The sharks exploit that dream and profit from it. But their defeat is inevitable. Because they themselves are not immune to the dream. Your swindlers and sharpers see the enormous profits being made in the drug trade, and they can't resist trying to get a piece of the action. They are just as unthinkingly greedy and vulnerable as their mooches. In fact, they are mooches, too."

Tony Harker laughed. "Maybe we all are mooches."

Lester Crockett brought his gaze down from the ceiling and stared at him. "Maybe we are," he said. "Greedy in irrational ways. Not only for money, but for fame, pleasure, power." He paused. "Perhaps even for love," he said. "Your five minutes are up."

32

A few of the yaks in Sid Coe's boiler room worked till midnight, culling their lists for West Coast suckers.

But Manny Suarez and most of the others quit work around six or seven o'clock. Ten hours in that noisy sweatbox were enough; they had to unwind, have a cold beer, replenish their store of nervous energy for the next day's wheeling and dealing.

"Suarez," one of the yaks called as Manny was heading for his Ford Escort, "do you have a few minutes?"

"Yeah, sure. You wanna go have a coupla brews?"

"Not at the moment," the man said, coming up close and lowering his voice. "I have a private matter I'd like to discuss with you. Let's sit in my new Porsche. I just took delivery."

It was a midnight-blue 928S4 model, and Manny could believe the talk that the owner was the highest-paid yak at Coe's, averaging a reported two grand a week in commissions. His name was Warren Fowler. He was an older man who dressed like an investment banker and never removed his jacket no matter how steamy it got in the boiler room. Suarez thought he talked "fancy."

"Nice car," Manny said, stroking the leather upholstery. "I even like the smell."

"It's advertised as capable of doing one-sixty," Fowler said, "but I haven't let it out yet. Would you like one just like it?"

"Oh sure," Suarez said, "but I don't rob banks. Not my shtick, man."

"You won't have to. Tell me something: Do you enjoy working for Coe?"

"It's hokay. The moaney's good."

"Good? Compared to what Coe is netting, it can't even qualify as peanuts. Ten-percent commission—that's obscene!"

"Yeah, sure, but he's taking all the risk. The feds move in, and he's liable for fraud, and he goes to the slam. You and me, we can cop a plea and maybe get off with probation or a slap on the wrist. But Sid would do hard time."

Fowler shrugged. "I doubt if he'd get more than a year or so. Just the cost of doing business. And when he came out, I'm sure he'd still have all his profits in overseas accounts."

Suarez turned sideways to stare at him. "What's on your mind? You want us to go on strike for more dough?"

"Don't be absurd. But about six months ago a gentleman came to me with a proposition that sounded too good to resist. I've tried it, and it's turned out to be just as good as it sounded. This man wanted me to talk to a selected few of the other high-producing yaks to see if they'd be interested in doubling their income. I've spoken to four so far, and they've all joined up. Now I'd like to lay it out for you. I should tell you immediately that I get a bonus for every yak I bring into the scheme. But my bonus is nothing compared to the money you'll be making."

"So now you've given me the buildup. Let's hear the rest of the script."

"It's simplicity itself. Here's how it works: This man has established a small office in West Palm Beach. It's really just a mail drop. Now suppose I close a deal for five thousand. My regular commission would be five hundred. But if Coe isn't hanging over my shoulder, I tell the mooch to mail his check to that office in West Palm Beach. When the money arrives, I get seventy-five percent or a sweet $3,750. How do you like that? The man running the mail drop takes twenty-five percent for renting the office, cashing the checks, and the risk."

"It's a rip-off."

"Of course it is. But there's poetic justice there. Coe is sweating his peons and paying a ridiculously small commission for our hard work. Now the clipper is getting clipped. Nothing wrong with that, is there? But of course you can't do it with all your deals or Coe's income would fall off drastically, and he'd smell a rat. I usually limit myself to one big sale a week, and I've advised the other four yaks to do the same. The important thing is not to get too greedy. Coe will never notice if you're skimming one deal a week. Just make it a biggie."

"And you've been pulling this for six months?"

"That's correct. And our esteemed employer doesn't have a glimmer of suspicion that he's being royally rooked."

"If he ever finds out, he'll have your kneecaps blown away."

"How can he possibly find out? The man who devised this scheme is very insistent that we keep our take modest. Even at that, I estimate the five of us are costing Coe close to a hundred grand a month. Serves him right."

"This guy who's running the chisel," Suarez said, "what's his name?"

"You have no need to know that," Fowler said. "Just take my word for it that he pays off promptly. He's content with his cut."

"He should be," Manny said. "With five yaks nicking for him, he's probably clearing twenty-five big ones a month."

"He's entitled. After all, old boy, it was his idea. Well, what's your decision? Coming in with us? You'd be a fool not to. And if I thought you were a fool I would never have solicited you."

"Lemme think about it tonight," Suarez said. "Hokay? I'll tell you tomorrow."

"Excellent," Fowler said. "If you decide to join us, you get the address of the West Palm Beach office and can begin doubling your income."

Manny drove home in a thoughtful mood. Since working at Instant Investments, Inc., he had been turning in his weekly take to Anthony Harker—but not all of it. He had been skimming two or three yards a week and sending money orders home to his wife in Miami. He figured the government would never miss the money, and if the boiler room was raided, Suarez was confident that Coe kept no records of commissions he had paid his yaks.

But this chiseler in West Palm Beach was an unknown. If he got busted, the feds might find records detailing all his transactions, and then, conceivably, Manuel Suarez would be in the *sopa*. He decided that as a matter of self-preservation, he'd better play this one straight.

Later that evening he got out of his hostess' bed and stumbled into the living room. He called Harker's night number and when Tony came on, Suarez told him all about the proposition from Warren Fowler.

Harker laughed. "Beautiful," he said. "The screwer gets screwed. And

I'll bet it's one of his Grand Palace buddies who's doing the screwing. Probably David Rathbone. Swindling friends is his style."

"What do you want I should do?" Suarez asked.

"Go for it. And try to find out for sure who's running the scam."

"Hokay," Manny said.

33

Lester Crockett tried to get additional personnel to do the job on Frank Little's warehouse, but Washington reminded him that he was already over budget; he would have to make do with the men he had. So he did the next best thing: He cut a deal with the local office of the Drug Enforcement Administration.

"I don't like it any more than you do," he told Harker. "But we'll have to live with it."

The deal took a long afternoon of often rancorous argument to arrange, but eventually an agreement was hammered out that had as many compromises as the Treaty of Ghent.

The DEA would take over surveillance of FL Sports Equipment, Inc., and responsibility for tracing the Haitian source of the coke-filled baseballs and trailing the vans and trucks that picked them up at the warehouse. In return, the DEA agreed not to bust the operation or collar Frank Little without Crockett's prior notification and approval. Hiram Johnson, one of Crockett's men and Roger Fortescue's buddy, was assigned to liaise with the DEA's investigative team.

So it happened that on a blustery night in late November, Fortescue conducted Johnson to his hideaway in the deserted fast-food joint adjacent to Little's warehouse. The hurricane season had ended, but the weather had turned mean and brutal. A northwest wind was driving gusts of cold rain, and both men were drenched before they could duck into the restaurant, Roger leading the way with his lantern.

"Loverly," Johnson said, peering around. "Perfect for weddings and bar mitzvahs."

Fortescue showed him the office where boards covering the window could be moved apart to provide a clear view of the goings-on at FL Sports Equipment.

"All the comforts of home," Roger pointed out. "I even dragged in this swell crate so your guys will have a place to sit while they peep."

"Primitive," Johnson said. "Definitely primitive. But as they say in real estate circles, the only three things that count are location, location, and location."

Within a week, the DEA, working through a dummy corporation, had leased the empty building and were ostensibly converting it into a new restaurant. A sign went up—FINNY FUN—and underneath a promise that read "Coming Soon: Fresh Fish."

The exterior renovation went slowly; the outside of the building showed little change. But inside, in the small office, DEA specialists built a fully equipped command post with telephones, two-way radios, video cameras, bunks for two men, a hot plate, and enough canned provisions to feed a regiment. The toilet was put back into working order, power was restored, and the kitchen faucets flowed.

The cameras were the first equipment installed, and were put into use immediately with hypersensitive film to record nighttime activities. The arrival and departure of vans and trucks taking delivery of Little's baseballs were radioed to teams of agents parked along Copans Road, and the shadowing began.

Having played his role, Roger Fortescue ambled into Anthony Harker's office.

"I guess I'm out of a job," he said.

"Not quite," Tony said. "How would you like to go to Lakeland?"

34

The rain ended during the early morning hours. The air smelled of fresh-cut grass, salt sea.

Theodore mopped up puddles on the terrace and turned the cushions. Rita and David had breakfast out there: grapefruit juice, toasted raisin bread with guava shells and cream cheese, coffee laced with cinnamon.

"I forgot to tell you," Rita said. "I came home early, and the phone in your office was ringing. Why don't you put your office phone on the regular line so someone can take messages when you're out?"

"I don't want to mix my private life with business," he said, smiling at her. "If it's important, they'll call back. Probably one of my clients."

"That Birdie Winslow you mentioned?"

"Oh, did I mention her? Yes, it probably was. She demands a lot of attention. Really more trouble than she's worth. I may have to drop her."

"How old is she?"

"Older than you, believe me. And heavier. Much, much heavier."

"Pretty?"

He fluttered a hand back and forth. "So-so. Passable, but not my type."

"Who is your type?"

"You. How many times do I have to tell you?"

"I never get tired of hearing it," she said, squeezing his arm. "What're your plans for today?"

"I have to see my travel agent. I've got to go to England for a few days. Tomorrow if I can get a flight."

"Me, too?"

"Nope. Not this time."

"That's what you said last time."

"You'll get your chance," he assured her. "Maybe sooner than you think. We'll have to visit Irving Donald Gevalt and get you fixed up with ID and a passport."

"Why can't I use my real name?"

"I don't think that would be wise," he said.

He spent the morning in his office, reviewing the accounts of his clients and drawing up a schedule of investments each would make in the Fort Knox Commodity Trading Fund. Birdie Winslow called shortly before noon.

"I phoned you all day yesterday," she complained. "I suppose you were gallivanting around."

"I wish I had been," Rathbone said. "But I had to attend a seminar in Boca on zero-coupon bonds. Very dull stuff."

"Can we have lunch today?"

"Oh, I'm so sorry," he said. "I have a luncheon appointment with a Palm Beach banker. He's probably on his way here right now, so I can't cancel."

"Then how about dinner?"

"I'm sorry," he repeated. "I'm flying to Germany tonight. Just for a few days. Maybe we can get together when I get back."

"David, you're not avoiding me, are you?"

"Of course not. It's just that I've been so busy. Making money is hard work, you know."

"Uh-huh. Well, I have something *very* important to talk to you about. I could come over to your office."

"Oh, it's in such a mess right now," he said, "I'd hate to have you see it. Tell you what: I have to stop at my travel agent after lunch to pick up my ticket. Suppose I come by your apartment for a short time at about three o'clock."

"Divine!" she said. "I'll have your vodka gimlet all ready for you."

"Wonderful," he said.

He had lunch with Jimmy Bartlett at an outdoor café on the Waterway. They sat at an umbrella table and watched the big boats coming south for the winter.

"I had a visit from Termite Tommy," Rathbone said. "He claims the German doesn't want to engrave new plates for the bills. Says his hands aren't steady enough. Which is probably true; the old guy was half in the bag when I met him in Lakeland."

"So the deal is off?"

"Not yet. The printer wants to buy one of those new color laser copiers, an office machine. He says it does beautiful work. Sharper than the original. If he can use his self-destruct paper to pick up copies of twenties and fifties, we're in business."

"Worth a try," Bartlett said. "Even if it's a half-ass reproduction. We're going to salt it in with the drug cash anyhow. And from what you say, it'll disintegrate before anyone has a chance to spot it as queer."

"Right. But I told Tommy to bring me a sample before I go ahead on this."

"He still thinks you're going to deposit the funny money in bank accounts?"

"That's what he thinks. Which brings me to our big problem. To get this thing rolling, I had to promise Termite Tommy a third and the printer a third. But that would leave only a third for you and me to split. Not enough, considering the risk we're running."

"I agree. And the idea was ours."

"Yours. The German is the producer and worth a third. But Tommy is just a go-between, a messenger. He's not contributing anything. So the problem is how to cut him out of the loop."

"Finished your lunch?" Bartlett said. "Then let's move to the bar and have a real drink."

They sat close together at the thatched bar and ordered margaritas.

"What kind of a guy is this Tommy?" Bartlett asked.

"A boozer," Rathbone said. "A natural-born loser. I thought he was out on parole or probation, and it would be easy to set up a frame and send him back to the clink for a while. But now I find out he served his full time. So, as they say, he's paid his debt to society and he's home free."

"He could still be framed," Jimmy observed. "It doesn't have to be anything heavy; just get him sent back for a year or two. Our operation isn't going to last any longer than that."

"I know," David said, "but there's another factor. The guy's psychopathic about going back behind bars. I'm afraid that if he's even arrested for speeding, he'll rat to save his ass. Then I'm down the tube."

Bartlett looked at him with a crooked smile. "And if you go, I go—is that what you're saying?"

"Something like that," Rathbone admitted.

From where they sat they could watch an enormous yacht moving slowly toward the Atlantic Boulevard bridge. There was a small helicopter lashed to the top deck, and on the afterdeck two older men in white flannels and blue blazers were horsing around with three tanned young women in bikinis. They all had drinks, and their laughter carried across the Waterway.

"From the way you describe it," Bartlett said, "there's only one solution."

The bridge rose, the shining yacht disappeared down the Intracoastal. The two men turned to stare at each other.

"Let me ask around," Jimmy said.

"How much would it cost?" Rathbone asked in a low voice.

"Not much," Bartlett said.

They finished their drinks in silence, rose, lifted hands to each other, and separated. Rathbone returned to his car and lighted a Winston. He was startled to see that his fingers were trembling slightly. He smoked slowly, and by the time the cigarette was finished, his jits had disappeared. He drove two blocks to his travel agent.

He could have saved money by flying directly to San José from Miami. But he elected to go first to San Juan, then to Panama City, and finally to Costa Rica. He reasoned that if, for some reason, he was dogged, it would be easy to spot a tail making the same plane changes he did. He had learned to trust his instincts, and right now they were telling him to play it cozy.

"Need a hotel room in San José?" the agent asked.

"No," Rathbone said, "I'm staying with friends."

He glanced at his gold Rolex, saw it was time to be heading for Birdie Winslow's apartment. He considered bringing her a gift, then decided not to; it would be smart to chill that relationship.

She met him at the door wearing lounging pajamas in psychedelic colors that made him blink. She threw her meaty arms about him in a close embrace that stifled him.

"You bad boy!" she cried. "Never home when I phone. Never come to see me."

"I've really been busy, Birdie," he said. "And then this trip to Spain came up unexpectedly."

"I thought you said you're going to Germany."

"Spain *and* Germany. And I haven't even started packing yet. So I'm afraid I can't stay very long. You said you had something important to talk about."

"Something *very* important," she said. "But first you sit yourself down, and I'll serve you a vodka gimlet just the way you like it."

This one had two ice cubes, but he postponed tasting it, fearing the worst.

"Now then," he said, "what's this all about?"

"Come over here and sit near me," she said, patting the couch cushion. "You're so far away."

Obediently he heaved himself out of the armchair where he had hopefully sought refuge and sat next to her. She put a heavy hand on his knee.

"David, you told me you live in this cramped one-bedroom apartment, and today you mentioned how messy your office is. I really don't like this apartment all that much, and my lease will be up in a few months. So my wonderful idea is this: Why don't the two of us take an apartment together? A really big place with enough room for your office and a nice living room and terrace where we could do a lot of entertaining. I think it would be fun, don't you?"

He lifted his drink slowly and swallowed half, not tasting it.

"Birdie," he said, "that's a heavy decision to make. You know, we're the best of friends now, but living together is something entirely different. I've known couples who have tried it, and within a week or so they're at each other's throat."

"I just know that could never happen with us because we get along so well together. David, you're not involved with anyone else right now, are you?"

"Oh no," he said. "No, nothing like that."

"Well, there you are! You're by your lonesome and so am I—which is really silly when you think about it. I mean paying two rents and keeping two kitchens and all. If we lived together, we could share the rent and have this fabulous big apartment we could decorate just the way we want it. What do you think?"

He finished his drink. "Birdie, first of all I want to thank you for suggesting it. It's quite a compliment to me. But I'm not sure we could make a go of it. Sometimes I work till midnight and even later. I have clients visiting and business meetings in my office. I even—"

"Oh, I'd respect your privacy," she interrupted. "You don't have to worry about that. And we could have all your friends over for cocktail parties and dinners. I thought we might get a place right on the beach, with a terrace. And sometimes I'd make a nice, home-cooked meal when we didn't feel like going out. I'd even keep your office neat and all tidied up so you wouldn't be ashamed of it."

"You make it sound very attractive," he said, trying to smile. "But as I said, it's a big decision, and I think we should both consider it very carefully and talk more about it before we make up our minds."

"Oh, I've already made up my mind," she said gaily. "I think it would be *divine!*"

"Well, I promise you I'll give it very serious thought."

"And you'll let me know?"

"Of course."

"When?"

"Suppose we do this: When I get back from Europe, we'll get together and discuss it in more detail. Meanwhile, I promise you, I'll be thinking about it very, very carefully. Neither of us wants to rush into something we might regret later."

She swooped suddenly to kiss his lips. "I'd never regret it," she said breathlessly. "Never!"

He drove home recklessly, speeding, jumping lights, cutting off other cars. And steadily cursing as he frantically devised scenarios to finesse his way out of this outrageous complication.

He went directly to his office and revised his plan so that Birdie Winslow's total wealth would be invested in the Fort Knox Commodity Trading Fund. Then he sat back and tried to figure out how this new development would affect his schedule.

When Rita came home from work, he was seated on the terrace working on a big iced gimlet and staring out over the ocean.

"Where's *my* drink?" she demanded.

He looked at her a moment without replying. Then: "Remember this morning you asked when you were going on a trip with me, and I said it might be sooner than you think."

"Sure, I remember," Rita said. "So?"

"I was right. When I get back, we'll go to Gevalt and get you new ID and a passport."

"Whatever you say, boss," she said. "Now can I have a kiss and a drink, in that order?"

"Whatever you say, boss," he said, and felt better.

35

The rip-off of Sidney Coe's boiler room went pretty much the way Warren Fowler described it. Manny Suarez closed a deal with a mooch in Little Rock, Arkansas, for $2,000 in the Fort Knox Fund stock. He told the sucker to mail his check to the West Palm Beach office. Then he informed Fowler of the sale.

"When do I get my moaney?" he asked. "And who pays me?"

"You'll get paid as soon as the check clears," Fowler assured him. "Then I'll give you your seventy-five percent."

"The check will be made out to Instant Investments, Inc. So how does your friend cash it?"

Fowler shrugged. "That's his problem. Maybe he peddles the checks to another goniff at a ten-percent discount. That would still leave him fifteen percent clear. But I suspect he may have opened an account in an out-of-state bank in the name of Instant Investments. In any event, you'll get your money from me."

"Just don't go out-of-state," Manny said, and both men laughed.

Suarez took Saturday off and drove up to West Palm Beach. He had never been there before and it took him a half-hour to locate the office. It was in a grungy neighborhood, on the second floor over a gun shop. There was a card thumbtacked to the locked door. All it said was "Instant Investments. Please slide mail under door."

Manny went downstairs to the gun shop and waited patiently while a clerk sold a semiautomatic rifle to a pimply-faced youth with a banner, *Death before dishonor*, tattooed on his right bicep.

When the kid left, carrying his rifle in a canvas case, Manny approached the clerk. He was an oldish guy, heavy through the chest and shoulders. He was wearing a stained T-shirt that had printing on the front: GUNS DON'T KILL PEOPLE. PEOPLE KILL PEOPLE.

"The owner around?" Suarez asked.

The beefy guy looked at him. "Who wants to know?" he demanded.

Sighing, Suarez took out his shield and ID from the Miami Police Department. The clerk inspected them carefully.

"You're outside your jurisdiction, ain'tcha?" he said.

"Cut the crap," Manny said. "Where can I find the owner?"

"I'm the owner," the guy said, "and I got all my permits and licenses, and you can look at my books anytime you want."

"I'm not interested in your guns," Manny said. "Who owns the build-ing?"

"I do."

"You rent the upstairs office?"

"That's right."

"Who rents it?"

"Some outfit that does mail order."

"What kind of mail order?"

"I don't know and I don't care."

"What's the name of the guy running it?"

"Who the hell knows? I don't."

"You must have some name. The name on the lease for the office."

"There ain't no lease. It's rented month to month."

"Who signs the rent checks?"

"There ain't no rent checks. I get paid in cash."

Manny stared at him. "You keep jerking me around," he said, "and you're in deep shit. I'll visit the locals and see what we can do about closing you down. Like is the fire exit clearly marked, is the toilet clean, do the sprinklers work, how do you handle your garbage, and so forth. Is that what you want?"

"The guy's name is Smith."

"Don't tell me it's good old John Smith."

"Robert Smith. I got his home address writ down on a piece of paper somewhere."

"Find it," Suarez commanded.

It took him another half-hour to locate the address, or rather where it should have been. It was a weedy vacant lot next to a small factory that made novelties such as whoopee cushions, dribble glasses, and plastic dog turds. Manny drove back to the gun shop.

"You again?" the owner said.

"Me again," Manny said. "This Robert Smith, does he come to his office every day?"

"Nah. Two, three times a week."

"To pick up his mail?"

"I guess."

"What does he drive?"

"A black BMW."

Manny whistled. "The mail order business must be good," he said. "Tell you what: I'm going to phone you every day next week. I want you to get the license number of that BMW. I'll keep calling until you get it. Hokay? I know you want to cooperate with your law enforcement officers."

"Oh yeah," the guy said. "Sure I do."

"Uh-huh," Suarez said. "Well, here's your chance."

"This Robert Smith, what's he wanted for?"

"He's been cheating on his girlfriend. She claims he's been sleeping with his wife."

He called the gun shop on Monday. Robert Smith hadn't shown up. But he was there on Tuesday morning, and the owner gave Manny the number on the BMW's license plate. Suarez phoned Tony Harker.

"The guy who has that office in West Palm Beach," he said. "The one who's ripping off Sid Coe. He calls himself Robert Smith and he drives a black BMW. Here's the license number."

"Got it," Harker said. "I'll check it out with Tallahassee. Call me back tonight."

Manny phoned him at his motel, a little before midnight.

"Well?" he said. "Is it David Rathbone?"

"No," Harker said, sounding disappointed. "It's Mortimer Sparco."

36

They were slouched in armchairs in Harker's living room, bare feet up on the shabby cocktail table. They were nursing beers. It was cool enough to turn off the air conditioner and open the windows. They heard the scream of a siren speeding by on A1A.

"That's the 911 truck," Rita said. "You know what they call this stretch of road? Cardiac Canyon."

"I'm liable to have one," Tony said, "if I don't get a few days off to unwind."

"So?" she said. "Take them."

"Can't," he said. "Too much happening. Things are really heating up. Right after you called I put a man on Rathbone at the Miami Airport, and we got a look at his ticket. He thought he was being cute, going to Costa Rica by way of Puerto Rico and Panama. So I had to arrange for a different agent to pick him up in San Juan, and another at Panama City. So he wouldn't spot the tail. A lot of phone calls, a lot of work to coordinate all that in a short time."

"And he's in Costa Rica now?"

"The last I heard. He got off the plane in San José, where a fourth agent took up the trail. This is costing Uncle Samuel a mint."

"He can afford it. What do you suppose David is up to?"

"You want me to guess? I'd guess he's preparing to make a run for it sometime soon. He probably has fake ID from that Gevalt guy, and he's been building up his offshore bank accounts. Maybe he's bought a house or hacienda, whatever they call it, in Costa Rica, and he's planning his retirement. Taking all his loot with him, of course. Has he said anything to you about leaving the country?"

Rita took a swallow of her beer. "Not a word," she said.

"Well, I'll bet he's working on it. If he follows the pattern, he'll stick around long enough to make one final killing, then take off. We'll have to move in on him before that. The agent tailing him right now in San José will try to find out what name he's using. Then we'll be able to check other property and bank accounts in the Bahamas and Cayman Islands. If we can nail him under RICO, we'll take everything but the fillings in his teeth."

"Have you discovered what the Fort Knox Fund is?"

"Working on it. I think it's got something to do with drugs, but I haven't pinned it down yet."

She slumped farther down in her chair. "Drugs? David wouldn't have anything to do with drugs. He's strictly small-time."

"Don't kid yourself. If there's easy money to be made without too much risk, he'll be dealing and pushing like all the other punks. And drugs are only half of it. There's a good chance he's also working some kind of counterfeiting scam. I should know more about that next week. Rita, you've got to get rid of the notion that your Prince Charming is just a naughty boy clipping widows and divorcées for a few bucks. This man is a vicious criminal, and he's dangerous. Do me a favor, will you?"

She looked up at him. "What?"

"Get out. Now. I won't pull you because it'll look like you weren't doing your job. But if you request reassignment, Crockett will find another slot for you; I know he will. And no one will blame you."

"No," she said. "I signed on for this particular job, and I want to be in on the kill. You have no complaints about the way I've handled it, do you?"

"No," he said in a low voice. "No complaints."

"Then let's have another beer and go to bed. And no more bullshit about taking me off the case. Okay?"

"Okay," he said. "If that's the way you want it."

Her tanned body was a smooth rope and entwined about him, her long hair making a secret tent for them both. The heat of her flesh made him wonder if he could be scorched by her intensity.

He heard himself making sounds he didn't recognize and couldn't stop.

And then she was crying out, grasping him. It was only later, when he reached to caress her face, that he felt the wet and wondered if it might be tears.

"Better than a few days off," he murmured. "To unwind."

"That afternoon I met you," she said. "In your office. I thought you were nerdy."

"Did you? I suppose I was."

"Was," she said. "Not now."

"The nerd turns," he said. "No more inhaler, no more allergies, no more nervous stomach. Marry me."

She laughed.

He propped himself on an elbow, peered down at her in the gloom. "I'm serious," he said. "Marry me."

She reached up to touch his cheek. "Tony," she said softly.

"That's really why I want you off the job," he said. "I want you out of his bed. I want you to resign. I want you to marry me."

"Oh darling," she said, "you want, you want, you want. It's very nice to hear, but I want, too. To be independent. Do it my way. I like my job, and I'm good at it; I know I am."

"Listen," he said, "I composed this speech. Can I recite it to you?"

"Sure. Go ahead."

"You're the only woman I've ever met who can lighten me up. When I'm with you, I grin. If it's not on my face, it's inside. When you're away from me, I work nights and weekends and I don't know what I'm killing myself for. But when I'm with you, my life makes sense. It has meaning. I'm not only jealous of the time you spend with Rathbone, I'm jealous of the time you spend alone, doing your nails or sleeping or whatever. I want us to be together every minute. Obsessive? I guess. What it all boils down to is that I love you and want to spend the rest of my life with you. End of speech."

She sat up in bed, hugged her knees. "Thank you," she said huskily. "You really know how to puff up a girl's ego. But you're talking about a big decision, Tony."

"I didn't expect you to yell, 'Yes, yes, yes!' But will you think about it? Consider it carefully and seriously?"

"Of course," she said. "This is my first proposal. Plenty of propositions, but only this one proposal. So I don't really, honey, know how to handle it. You're right; I better think long and hard about it."

"Do that," he said, leaning forward to kiss her knee. "Please. Don't just reject me out of hand. I've got some money—not a lot but some—and I make a good living; you know that. Also, if I can put Rathbone behind bars, that'll help my career. I just want you to know that I can support you, but if you want to keep on working, that's okay, too. But preferably not as a cop."

"Wow," she said, "you've really tossed me a fastball. I don't know what to do. Yes, I do."

She was so loving he wanted to shout his rapture. Her warm mouth drifted, tongue flicked, prying fingers tugged him along to ecstasy.

"Rita," he said, gasping, "I can't take this."

"Yes, you can," she said, and wouldn't stop.

She pleasured him as if she had a debt to pay, and only his gratification would wipe it out. Her ministrations became increasingly rapid; she seemed driven by a wildness that calmed only when he was drained of sense and vigor.

Then she slid out of bed, went into the bathroom, and didn't emerge for at least ten minutes. By that time Harker was standing shakily and gulping a fresh brew. She took the can from his hand and finished it.

"I've been thinking," she said, speaking rapidly. "Not about you and me but about business. Earlier tonight when we were talking about the case, and I said I wanted to be in on the kill, I meant I want to be around when the whole thing is wrapped up. But I don't want to be there when you take Rathbone. After all, I've led the lamb to the slaughter, haven't I? So I'd appreciate it if you could give me plenty of advance notice of when you intend to bust everyone and I'll make myself scarce. You can understand that, can't you?"

"Oh sure," he said.

37

Harker told Roger Fortescue about the self-destruct paper and how Rathbone pushed a counterfeit Treasury check made of the stuff through a Boca bank.

"Rathbone went to Lakeland and met with a man he referred to as the printer," Tony said. "That's the only lead I've got. It's all yours."

"Sheet," Fortescue said. "I better get some more skinny before I go up there or I'll just be spinning my wheels."

So he spent almost two days at his desk in the bullpen, making phone calls and requesting assistance from strangers. It took that long because invariably they stalled until they could check his bona fides. Then sometimes they'd call back, but usually he had to make a second or third call. But he never lost his temper, figuring to catch more flies with honey than with vinegar. And he was properly apologetic for the extra work he was causing and grateful when his inquiries yielded results.

He started with the Secret Service and was shunted from office to office until he was connected with a cranky agent who finally agreed to ask his computer if there was any record of a counterfeiter working out of Lakeland, Florida.

The computer spit out the name of Herman Weisrotte, German-born but a naturalized citizen. He had just completed a stay in stir for wholesaling twenties and fifties. Quality stuff, too. The computer even provided a physical description and his last known address in Lakeland.

So far, so good.

Then, because he had the smarts of a street cop, Fortescue called the warden's office in the prison where Weisrotte had done time and asked a very nice lady for the name of the forger's cellmate. It turned out that during the last year in jail Herman had shared living quarters with a convicted swindler named Thomas J. Keeffringer, recently released, who had committed his depredations over a five-state area, but mostly in south Florida.

This time Roger phoned a friend, Sam Washburn, an old bull who had spent most of his working life in the Detective Division of the Fort Lauderdale Police Dept. Then he had retired to spend his remaining years making birds and animals from shells his wife picked up on the beach. Sam had given Fortescue a shell owl which Estelle had promptly given to her mother who gave it to her minister who, at last report, was desperately seeking someone who would accept it.

The moment Fortescue mentioned Thomas J. Keeffringer, Washburn started laughing. "Termite Tommy!" he said, and told the investigator about the con man's scam using bottled bugs and sawdust to convince mooches to sign on for costly termite control.

"Is he a heavy?" Roger asked.

"Nah, he's a pussycat. Likes the sauce. A dynamite salesman. I heard he's out. What's he been up to?"

"I'm not sure. Maybe counterfeiting."

"That's a switch. Boosting mouthwash is more his style."

So now Fortescue had two names and an address in Lakeland. He went home to pack.

"How long will you be gone?" Estelle wanted to know.

"It depends," he said.

"Thank you very much," she said. "I may not be here when you get back. The bag boy at Publix has eyes for me."

"Lots of luck," Roger said.

He arrived at Lakeland late in the evening and checked into a motel with a neon sign that advertised TV—HAPPY HOUR—POOL PARTY ON SAT. Fortescue's room smelled of wild cherry deodorant and had a framed lithograph of the Battle of Shiloh on the wall over the bed. He wasted a few hours watching television.

In the morning he checked in with the locals as a matter of professional courtesy. He talked to an overweight detective who was working on an anchovy pizza and drinking Jolt for breakfast.

"Yeah, we brace the Kraut every now and then," he said, his mouth full. "He looks to be straight. He's got this little store where he prints up letterheads, business cards, and stuff like that."

"He wouldn't be printing the queer again, would he?"

The dick wiped his smeared lips with a paper napkin. "That I doubt very much. First of all, the guy's an alkie. Talk to him later than four in the afternoon, he just don't make sense. Second of all, he never seems to go nowhere. So how can he be pushing?"

"No funny money showing up in town?"

"Now and then. Nothing big. And most of the queer is spent by snow-birds who don't know what they got. Some of it is miserable stuff."

"Ever hear of Thomas J. Keeffringer, known as Termite Tommy?"

"Nope. That's a new one on me. Why all the interest in Weisrotte and this Termite Tommy?"

"Beats the hell out of me," Fortescue said. "They just sent me up here to see if these guys are behaving themselves."

"They could have done that with a phone call."

"Sure they could," Roger agreed, rising. "Well, I'll nose around and see if anything smells. If I find anything, you'll be the first to know."

"Uh-huh," the detective said, starting on his second slice of pizza. "When pigs fly."

Fortescue looked up the address of Weisrotte's Print Shop in the tele-phone directory and located it without too much trouble. He parked two blocks away and walked back. It was a dilapidated place with a dusty plate-glass window cracked across one corner. The interior was more of the same: a long, littered room crammed with cartons of stationery; presses of all sizes, some of them rusty and obviously unused; yellowed, flyspecked samples of business cards, letterheads, and envelopes pinned to a corkboard above a scarred sales counter.

The only piece of equipment that looked modern and new was a big white-enameled machine on casters. It had plastic shelves protruding from both ends, and in front was a push-button control panel that looked as complex as the dash on a 747.

An old man was working a small treadle press in the rear of the shop. When he saw Fortescue standing there, he came shuffling forward, wiping his palms on his ink-stained apron. He looked to be pushing seventy, with the suety face of a heavy drinker, bulbous nose a web of burst capillaries.

"Mr. Weisrotte?" Roger asked.

"Yah," the printer said, peering at him through inflamed eyes.

"You print business cards?"

"Yah."

"How much?"

"Thirty dollars a thousand."

"Wow," Roger said, "that's stiff."

"Iss quality work," Weisrotte said. "Any color ink. Iss thermographed. Raised printing. Six lines of type. Take it or leave it."

"I'll ask my boss," Roger said, and turned to leave. Then he paused and pointed at the gleaming white machine. "What the hell is that thing?" he asked.

Weisrotte came alive. "Iss color laser copier," he said proudly. "The latest. Iss beautiful, no?"

"Yeah, that's some piece of machinery. What'll they think of next."

As he exited from the shop a bozo was climbing out of a dented pickup truck parked at the curb. He was tall, skinny, and dressed like an undertaker. He headed for Weisrotte's door.

It's not enough to be a smart cop; you also need luck. Fortescue decided to try his.

"Hey, Tommy!" he cried. "How you doing, man?"

The guy stopped, turned slowly, stared at the agent. "Do I know you?" he asked in a toneless voice.

"Sure you do," Roger said cheerily. "Leroy Washington. I just got out a couple of weeks ago."

Keeffringer shook his head. "I don't make you," he said.

"I know," Fortescue said, laughing. "All us smokes look alike. I was in Cellblock C."

"Yeah? Where did you work?"

"They had me all over the place, but mostly in the kitchen."

"That was lousy food," Tommy said, relaxing.

"I know, but we did the best we could with what they gave us. You live in Lakeland?"

"For a while."

"Yeah," Roger said, "me, too. I just stopped by to visit an old girlfriend. Then I'm going down to Lauderdale. More action."

"Lauderdale?" Termite Tommy said. "I'm heading there later this afternoon. Need a lift?"

Fortescue jerked a thumb at the battered pickup. "Not in that clunker," he said, grinning. "Thanks anyway, but the girlfriend is fattening me up so I think I'll stick around a few days. Hey, it's been good talking to you, man. Maybe I'll bump into you again on the Lauderdale Strip."

"Maybe you will," Tommy said. "Nice seeing you again, Leroy."

Fortescue ambled slowly down the street in case Keeffringer was watching. But the moment he turned the corner, he walked quickly to his parked Volvo. He reckoned this was too great to pass up; he'd probably do better with Termite Tommy in Fort Lauderdale than tailing the Kraut around Lakeland.

He packed swiftly and checked out of the motel. He drove back to Weisrotte's shop and was gratified to see the mangled pickup still in front. Fortescue found a place to park about a half-block away where he could watch the action. Keeffringer had said he was heading for Lauderdale later that afternoon, so Roger left his car and found a fast-food joint not too far away. He bought a meatball submarine, a bag of fries, and a quart container of iced Coke. He returned to his stakeout and settled down.

It was almost three o'clock before Termite Tommy came out. And in all that time, Fortescue hadn't seen a single customer enter the shop. Which probably meant the German wasn't buying his schnapps with the income from printing business cards.

He gave the pickup a head start, then took off after it. He didn't stick too close, figuring Keeffringer would probably cut over to take Highway 27 south, and even if he lost him at a light he could always pick him up later; that decrepit truck would be breathing hard to do fifty mph.

But he never did lose Termite Tommy, even as traffic heavied south of Avon Park and Sebring, and even when they drove through a couple of heavy rainsqualls that darkened the sky and cut visibility. They hit Fort Lauderdale a little after nine o'clock, and Fortescue decided that if Tommy had driven all this way for a shackup with some bimbo, he himself would have a hard time explaining to Tony Harker why he had deserted his assignment in Lakeland.

Keeffringer seemed to know exactly where he was going. He cut over to Federal Highway, turned onto Commercial, and pulled into the parking lot of the Grand Palace Restaurant.

"Welcome home," Roger said softly, feeling better.

He parked a block away and sauntered back. He returned in time to see Termite Tommy come out of the side entrance to the Palace Lounge. With him was a blond guy wearing a white suit. When they passed under the restaurant's outdoor lights, Fortescue thought the newcomer might be David Rathbone. But he couldn't be sure, having seen only that photograph Harker had.

Roger watched as the two men climbed into a parked car, a big, black job that, from where he stood in the shadows, he guessed was either a

Rolls or a Bentley. They were together less than five minutes, then got out of the car. They shook hands. Rathbone, if that's who it was, went back into the Palace Lounge. Termite Tommy returned to his truck and pulled away. Fortescue could have taken up the tail again but didn't.

"The hell with it," he said aloud.

He drove home, and when he walked in carrying his suitcase, Estelle looked up from her sewing and said, "Have a nice vacation?"

But she rustled up a great meal of cold chicken, spaghetti with olive oil and garlic, and a watercress and arugula salad. She also warmed up a wedge of apple pie and topped it with a slice of cheddar, just the way she knew he liked it.

She watched him wolf all this down and asked, "Didn't you have any lunch today?"

"Oh I did, I did," he said. "Instant ptomaine."

He opened his second bottle of Heineken before he called Harker at his motel. He gave Tony a brief account of meeting Weisrotte and how he tailed Termite Tommy back to Lauderdale.

"He met a man in the parking lot of the Grand Palace," he reported. "I think it was probably David Rathbone, but I can't swear to it. A good-looking blond guy wearing a white suit. They sat together in a car that was either a Rolls or a Bentley."

"Rathbone drives a black Bentley," Tony said. "It was probably him and his car. Find out anything about that self-destruct paper?"

"Sheet," Fortescue said, "I barely had time to turn around. But while I was in the German's printshop, I spotted something interesting. He's got a brand-new color laser copying machine."

"Oh-oh," Harker said.

38

"When's this guy going to show up?" Rathbone demanded.

"Hey, take it easy," Jimmy Bartlett said. "You've been awfully antsy lately."

"You're right," David said. "I'm getting impatient. And when you get impatient, you make mistakes. I'll try to slow down. But did we have to meet in a crummy place like this?"

Bartlett shrugged. "He picked it, and at the last minute. Look, the guy is playing a double game. If his agency finds out he's turned sour, he'll draw ten, at least. And if the Colombians even suspect he might be a plant—which he isn't—he's dead meat. So can you blame the guy for being paranoid? He's just meeting us as a personal favor to me. He'll show up—after he's made sure the place isn't staked out."

They were sitting in the bedroom of a motel far west on Atlantic Boulevard. The room smelled of roach spray, and the wheezing air conditioner in the window was no help at all. Bartlett had brought along a bottle of Chivas and a stack of plastic cups. They got a tub of ice cubes from the machine in the lobby, and were working on strong Scotch and waters.

"Before he shows," Jimmy said, "let's talk a little business. That queer twenty you got from Termite Tommy is a gem. *Was* a gem. I went to dig it out just before you picked me up, but it wasn't there. Just a pile of confetti."

"I told you," Rathbone said.

"David, this is the greatest invention since sliced bread. The possibilities are staggering. We'll start with a deal I've got coming up in a week or so: a big deposit at the Crescent Bank in Boca."

"Mike Mulligan covering for you?"

"Oh sure; he's true blue. The deposit will run at least a hundred grand. Probably more. I suggest we begin by salting it with thirty thousand of the queer and taking out thirty Gs of genuine bills."

"Whatever you say, Jimmy."

"If it goes okay, we'll increase our take from future deposits. Can you get thirty grand of those color prints from Tommy?"

"In twenties?"

"Better make them fifties and hundreds, half and half. Twenties will be too big a bundle."

"All right. I'll let him know."

"And if Tommy is out of the picture, you'll be able to deal directly with the printer?"

"Absolutely. He—"

But then there was a single knock on the door, and both men stood up. Bartlett put the door on the chain, opened it cautiously, peered out. He saw who it was, closed the door, slipped off the chain, then opened the door wide.

"Hiya, Paul," he said. "Glad you could make it."

The man who entered was tall, broad-shouldered, with a confident grin. His madras sports jacket and linen slacks didn't come off plain pipe racks. He moved smoothly and, before saying a word, walked into the bathroom and out again, opened the closet door and looked in, even went down on one knee to peek under the bed.

He rose, dusting his hands. "No offense," he said to Bartlett, "but I'm alive and mean to stay that way. Who's this?"

"David. He's in the game. Paul, meet David. David, meet Paul."

They nodded. No one shook hands.

"Warm in here," Paul said. "Why don't we all take off our jackets."

"Paul," Bartlett said gently, "we're not wired; take my word for it."

"Sorry," the newcomer said, still grinning. "Force of habit. Hey, Chivas Regal! That's nice."

"Help yourself," David said. He sat on the bed, let the other two men take the spindly armchairs.

"So?" Paul said, taking a gulp of his drink. "What do you want to know?"

"An overall view of the world market," Jimmy Bartlett said. "What's going to happen in the next year. Your opinion, of course. We know you don't have a crystal ball. We just want your informed guess on the future fluctuation of the product price. Cocaine especially."

"Okay," Paul said, "but all this is just between us. Right now there's a product surplus. That should evaporate within three months. Demand will hold steady; supply will contract."

"How do you figure that?" David asked. "Government raids? Interception of shipments?"

Paul laughed. "Forget it," he advised. "Washington claims they stop ten percent at the borders. The truth is, if they're grabbing two percent they're lucky. No, the reason for the coming shortfall is more basic than that. The U.S. is saturated, all markets covered, no possibility of any great expansion. So the cartels are turning to the European Community. What's the market over there right now? Modest for heroin and marijuana, underdeveloped for cocaine. There are a few wealthy snorters, no one is free-basing, and they don't even know about crack. Plus you've got to realize that by 1992, the borders between countries in Western Europe will be a sieve; it'll be no problem at all to move the product. So the cartels' merchandising and sales managers have planned an all-out campaign to flood the whole continent with coke. It's already started in a small way, but eventually the European demand should be as strong or stronger than the American. That has got to mean reduced shipments to the U.S. and higher prices. You asked for an educated guess; that's mine."

"How high do you think it'll go?" David said.

Paul pondered a moment. "Assuming general inflation remains at its present level, I can see a wholesale price increase in the U.S. to 30K a kilo within a year. That may eliminate one social problem because the price has got to be about 10K before it's economically feasible to produce five- and ten-dollar vials of crack. But at the same time the price is rising in the U.S., it'll be reduced dramatically in the European Community. The

Colombian marketing experts know there's a two- or three-year wait before a strong consumer demand develops. Cocaine addiction takes that long. Heroin and crack work much faster, of course. But the cartels have the money to invest and the patience to wait for the market to build. And cutting the wholesale price is the quickest way to open up Western Europe, but it'll mean a higher price per kilo in this country. Yes, I think it'll go to thirty grand within a year, and I wouldn't be surprised to see it hit fifty thousand in two or three years as more production goes overseas."

"Paul," Bartlett said, "who knows about this decision to target the European Community for coke? Do the domestic dealers know about it? The retailers?"

"I doubt that," the drug agent said, pouring himself another drink. "They're only interested in today's profits. They know from nothing about long-term planning and international marketing strategies. But the Colombian cartel executives realize they've got to develop worldwide demand if their growth is to maintain its current rate of increase. And after Western Europe, of course, there is always Russia, Japan, China. These men may not be Harvard MBAs, but they recognize the reality of the global economy and their need to expand their international trade. And price manipulation is one way of achieving that."

"Thank you, Paul," Jimmy Bartlett said. "You've given us exactly what we wanted. Can we contact you for an update in a month or so?"

"Whenever you like," Paul said, finishing his drink and rising. "I don't care how you use the information, as long as I'm not named as the source. By the way, this was a freebie, Jimmy. I owed you one for tipping me about that rat from Panama. Now we're even. If you want updates, it'll cost."

"Understood," Bartlett said. "Thanks again."

"Nice meeting you, David," Paul said.

"Nice meeting you, Paul," David said.

After he departed, the door locked and chained, Rathbone and Bartlett mixed a final drink.

"You believe him?" David asked.

"I trust his judgment and inside knowledge of the industry. He deals with some very important men. If he says the kilo price of coke is going to rise in the U.S., then it will. He'd have no reason to con us."

"I'll take your word for it. So we can plan purchases and sales by the Fort Knox Fund on that premise, that prices are going up because of a coming scarcity?"

"I think so. Let's start out on a small scale, wait a month or so, and then see if Paul's predictions are on the money."

"Okay," Rathbone said, "I'll contact Frank Little and set up a meet with his biggest client. We'll try to sell for eighteen to twenty thousand a kilo. How does that sound?"

"About right. Ask for more than twenty, but fight anything lower."

"What quantity?" Rathbone asked.

"How much is in the Fund's kitty right now?"

"About a quarter-mil."

"Then let's try to peddle fifteen kilos. We'll have enough cash from Sid and Mort's mooches before we make the buy."

"Suits me," David said. "How much should we offer on the buy?"

"Say 12K per kilo. We may have to pay more and sell for less. But let's aim for a net of 100 Gs. Now to get back to Termite Tommy...I talked to two professionals, the Corcoran brothers, well qualified to handle our problem. Their price is ten thousand. But they're going to be up in Macon on assignment for a few weeks. I could get the job done cheaper, but I'd feel better if we waited for these men to return from Georgia. They're really the best in the business."

"Ten grand?" Rathbone said. "I thought it would be less."

"Oh hell," Bartlett said, "you can buy a kill for fifty bucks if you want to trust a hophead. Do you? I don't."

"I don't either. You're right; this is not something we want to chisel. All right, we'll wait until the Corcorans are available. Meanwhile I'll get that thirty thousand in queer from Tommy. Now let's get out of this shithouse."

They rose, finished their drinks, looked around to make certain they were leaving nothing behind.

"Hey," Jimmy Bartlett said, "did I tell you my younger son won a catamaran race off Key West?"

"No kidding?" David Rathbone said. "That's great!"

39

Simon Clark was aware of one of the basic tenets of con men, corporate raiders, and investment bankers: Never gamble with your own money. Although he was not ultra-rich, his net worth was sufficient to bankroll Nancy Sparco's new business if he chose to. He did not so choose.

The sting money he had invested with Mortimer Sparco's discount brokerage, if it could be recovered, would be more than enough to get Nancy started. Thus, in effect, the U.S. Government (actually the taxpayers) would finance her escort service in south Florida.

The puzzle was how to reclaim the money before the boom was lowered on Sparco and all his assets seized. Clark thought he might be able to finagle it if he could be present when the bust went down. Sharks like Sparco invariably kept a heavy stack of currency on hand for bribes and getaway insurance. It wouldn't be the first time a law enforcement officer had glommed onto a criminal's money during the confusion of an arrest.

But Clark decided that robbing the robber was just too risky; there had to be a better way of regaining the cash that had presumably purchased shares in the Fort Knox Commodity Trading Fund.

He put that problem aside temporarily and concentrated on his own future and the path it might take. While stealing Sparco's poke during the arrest had its dangers, there would be much less peril in lifting a list of the broker's clients. With that in hand, Clark would have a strong base for starting his own discount brokerage, pushing the same penny stocks that had made Sparco a wealthy man.

But running a brokerage, even semi-legitimately, required many registrations, licenses, and permits. And the SEC was always looking over your shoulder. Clark preferred a simpler swindle, with the risk-benefit ratio more in his favor. He decided his best bet might be to follow David Rathbone's example and become an investment adviser or whatever you wanted to call it.

With a limited number of wealthy clients with deficient money smarts, Clark reckoned he could do very well indeed. His background as a U.S. ADA would inspire confidence, he had an impressive physical presence, and his courtroom experience had taught him that when sincerity is demanded, style is everything.

So when he wasn't on the phone to Denver and Chicago, learning more details of Sparco's price manipulation and market domination of certain worthless securities, Clark went looking for permanent housing and an office location. He figured that by using leverage he could hang out his shingle for about a hundred thousand tops. He could do it for less, of course, but recognized the value of front in a business based on clients' faith in his probity.

The only opportunities he had to relax and enjoy south Florida came when Nancy Sparco visited his hotel room, two or three afternoons a week. Then they drank too much, talked too much, loved too much and, as she said, "told the whole world to go screw."

She showed up one afternoon when rainsqualls from the southwest had driven all the tourists off the beach and flooded the streets. Clark saw at once, despite a heavy layer of pancake makeup, that she was sporting a black eye. He embraced her, then held her by the shoulders and stared at the mouse.

"Who hung that on you?" he asked.

"Who?" Nancy said bitterly. "It wasn't the Tooth Fairy. My shithead hubby."

"Does he do that often?"

"No," she admitted. "Maybe a couple of times since we've been married."

"Was he drunk?"

"Nah. Just pissed off when I told him he couldn't screw his way out of a wet paper bag. I guess I shouldn't have said it, but I can't stand the guy anymore. I pray for the day when I can give him the one-finger salute and walk out. Pour me a drink, will you, hon. I've got to take off my shoes; they're soaked through."

He mixed bourbon highballs, and they slumped in armchairs and watched rain stream down the picture windows.

"I never belted a woman in my life," Clark said.

"I know you haven't, sweetie, because you've got class. But I don't have it so bad. A friend of mine, Cynthia Coe—her husband, Sid, runs a boiler room—is a real battered wife. Sid has a rotten temper and he's a mean drunk. When he's crossed, he takes it out on Cynthia. Really slams her around. Once he actually broke her arm."

"Why does she put up with it?"

"Why? M-o-n-e-y. After he beats the shit out of her, he starts crying, apologizes, swears he'll never do it again, and gives her cash, a rock, a gold watch, a string of pearls. Then a month later he's at it again. She says that when she's got enough money and jewelry put aside, she's going to give him the broom. But I doubt it."

"Maybe she enjoys it, too."

"Maybe she does," Nancy said. "A lot of nuts in this world, kiddo. I'm glad you and I are normal." She pulled off her dress and the two of them fell on the bed.

Afterward, Nancy asked, "Listen, you haven't forgotten about my new business, have you?"

"Of course not. I'm working on a couple of angles. You'll get your funding."

"When?"

"A month or so."

"Promise?"

"Yep. Nancy, I'm thinking about moving down here."

She sat up on the bed. "Hey, that's great! I love it! But what about your wife?"

He shrugged. "She'll be happy to see the last of me."

"Divorce?"

"Or separation. Whichever is cheaper. I'll leave it to my lawyer to cut a deal, but it's going to cost me no matter what."

"You plan to get a job down here?"

He didn't answer her question. "Tell me something, Nancy: Does your husband keep a list of his clients at home?"

She stared at him. "Oh-ho," she said, "you do have a plan, don't you? Thinking of joining the game?"

"I might," he said. "I'm tired of being a spectator."

"Well, I never saw Mort's client list. He probably keeps it in the office."

"Probably."

"But he does have a personal list of people he calls Super Suckers. Lots of loot and not much sense. That guy I told you about, Sid Coe, has his own list, and so does David Rathbone, another shark we know. They all have a Super Sucker list. Sometimes they get together and trade names like kids trade baseball cards."

"That's interesting," Clark said. "You think you might be able to get me a copy of your husband's list? It's worth a grand to me."

"In addition to the money for my escort service?"

"Of course. Two different deals."

She thought a moment. Then: "Five thousand," she said. "Those names are valuable. Money in the bank."

"How many names?"

"At least twenty. Maybe more. Widows, divorcées, senile old farts, and some younger swingers whose brains are scrambled. But all rich."

"Twenty-five hundred?" he asked.

"You got a deal," she said, and reached for him.

40

"Look," Frank Little said to the man from New York, "I'll introduce this guy to you by his first name only. That's the way he wants it. Okay?"

"Sure," Lou Siena said. "I like a man who's careful. But who *is* he?"

"His full name is David Rathbone, and he runs an asset management company down here. But that's just a front. He spends most of his time in Colombia and Bolivia, advising the cartel bosses on how to launder their money, what legit investments to make, and how to move their cash around to take advantage of currency fluctuations. He's one smart apple, buddy-buddy with the cartel big shots. The only reason he agreed to this meet was that about a year ago I tipped him to a rat in Panama who could have caused a lot of trouble. David passed the guy's name along to the Colombians, and they handled it. So David owes me one."

"Uh-huh," Siena said, glancing at his watch. "I just hope he's on time. I got to get down to Miami by five o'clock."

"He'll be here," Little assured him. "Have another belt and relax."

They were in the back room of the blockhouse office of FL Sports Equipment, Inc., on Copans Road. And next door, in the deserted fast-food restaurant, the DEA agents in their command post had filmed the arrival of Lou Siena in his silver Lincoln Town Car. And they made a written record of the license number on his New York plates.

Little's office was strictly utilitarian, with a steel desk, steel chairs, and filing cabinet. There was a small safe disguised as a cocktail table, and on it were arranged a bottle of Chivas Regal, a tub of ice cubes, a stack of paper cups, and a six-pack of small club sodas.

"I still don't see the need for a signed contract," Siena said, pouring more Scotch into his cup.

"Lou," Frank said, "how long have we been dealing? Five, six years?"

"Something like that."

"And never a hassle. Which means we trust each other—right? I'm asking you to trust me on this. I want to expand my business. All I've been doing is transshipping. You make your own buys. It's delivered here, and you pick up. I've just been a go-between, a middleman, and you know I'll never make it big on my cut. So now I want to simplify the whole operation and become a distributor to wholesalers like you. I'll make the initial buy, get it put into the baseballs in Haiti just like before, bring it in, and you'll buy directly from me. That'll save you time and trouble, won't it?"

"I guess."

"Sure it will. And you can't blame me for wanting a bigger cut, can you? Now about the signed contracts. . . . You know the cartels are strictly COD. But where am I going to get the cash to make a fifteen-kilo buy? I've lined up a broker who'll make me a loan with very low vigorish, but first he wants to see some proof that I'm good for the money. And what better evidence could he want than a signed contract stating you're willing to pay X number of dollars for those fifteen kilos in three months. Lou, you're a big man. Your name means more to the broker than mine. That's the reason for the signed contract. We'll use a code word for the coke, of course."

"You said X number of dollars for the fifteen kilos. What's X? How much you asking per kilo for delivery in three months?"

"That's why I asked David to come over and give us the lowdown on where the market is heading. I don't want to cheat you, and I don't want to cheat myself. I just heard a car pull up outside. That must be him. Excuse me a minute."

And next door, the DEA agent operating the TV camera reported to his partner: "A black Bentley just pulled up. One guy getting out. Caucasian male, five-ten or-eleven, one-eighty, blond, good-looking, wearing a vested black suit, white shirt, maroon tie. Take a look at the Bentley through your binocs and let's phone in the license number, along with the plates on the silver Lincoln. Headquarters can get started on the IDs."

"Lou, this is David," Frank Little was saying. "David, meet Lou. Mix yourself a drink and sit down."

"I'll have one," Rathbone said, "but only one. I've got to make this short. A heavy exporter is flying in from Mexico City, and I promised to meet his plane. What do you want to know?"

"Your overall view of the market," Little said. "Coke especially. Where's it going—up or down? What'll the kilo price be three months from now? Six months? A year?"

"Right now there's a product surplus," David said. "That will disappear within three months. Demand will remain steady or increase; supply will contract. In the U.S., the price per kilo will go up, up, up."

"How do you figure that?" Siena said.

Then, demonstrating almost total recall, Rathbone repeated the words of the renegade narc. But while Paul had merely reported, David used his words in a hard sell, leaning forward, staring steadily at Lou Siena, an easy enough trick if you concentrated your gaze on the space between a man's eyes.

He was a dynamite yak, very earnest, very sincere, very convincing. He spoke authoritatively of the global economy, the internationalization of trade, the significance of 1992, the decision of the drug cartels to concentrate their main marketing efforts in the European Community. He explained how they planned to reduce the kilo price to lure consumers in Western Europe, which would, inevitably, lead to higher prices in the U.S.

Lou Siena listened closely, fascinated. This was the first time he had heard such detailed financial information about his industry from a man who was obviously knowledgeable about the big picture and yet had enough street smarts to recognize how the relaxation of border regulations between European countries would facilitate drug trafficking.

"There's no doubt about it," David concluded firmly. "You'll see the wholesale price of high-quality cocaine hit 30K per kilo within three to six months, and I wouldn't be a bit surprised to see it go to 50K within a year. Any questions?"

"Yeah," Siena said. "How do I know you're giving me the straight poop?"

David stiffened, narrowed his eyes, looked coldly at the New Yorker. "What possible reason would I have to scam you? I'm meeting you today for the first time. I don't know what kind of deal you and Frank are cooking up, and I don't want to know. You asked for my opinion, and I gave it to you as honestly as I know how. And I resent the implication that I'm involved in some kind of a con game."

"Okay, okay," the other man said hastily. "I guess you're leveling."

Rathbone nodded, finishing his drink, and stood up. "I don't care how you use what I told you, but just don't quote me as the source. I wouldn't care to have it get back to my close friends in Bogotá that I'm leaking inside information."

"Don't worry about it, David," Frank Little said. "You can depend on Lou and me. Thanks for your help."

"Now we're even," Rathbone said. "I wish you luck. See you around." Then he was gone.

"What did you think of him?" Little asked Siena.

"I guess he's straight. Like he said, what possible angle could he have?"

"Right. So let's figure coke will be up to 30K within three to six months. How about taking those fifteen kilos at 25 per?"

Then they started haggling.

An hour later Rathbone phoned Little from the office of the Fort Knox Fund. Rita was perched on his desk, filing her nails, bare legs crossed. As he talked, David stroked her knee.

"How did you make out?" he asked.

"Nineteen-five," Frank said.

"Not bad."

"I did my best, but he wouldn't come up. It's about five Gs more per kilo than he's been paying."

"So he bought my spiel?"

"Definitely. Very impressed. Said he'd like to meet with you again."

"Fat chance. Did he do the contract?"

"Signed, sealed, and delivered. Fifteen thousand chairs at nineteen-five per thousand. And the guy won't welsh, David. He's very hot on personal honor."

"Honor?" Rathbone said, laughing and leaning forward to kiss Rita's knee. "What's that? You did a good job, Frank. See you at the Palace tonight to celebrate?"

"I'll be there."

Rathbone hung up and grinned at Rita.

"Good news?" she asked.

"The best. We're going to be rich."

"I thought we were."

"You know what they say: You can never be too thin or too rich."

"I'll take care of thin," she said. "Rich is your department."

"I'm getting there," he said. "Now let's pick up a bottle of something cold and dry, and then go home and get some sun."

"Beautiful," she said. "I like this life."

41

Mr. Crockett had become increasingly tetchy of late, and Tony Harker could only conclude the man was under increasing pressure from Washington to show some results. And because the chief was feeling the heat, his lieutenants were, too, and in turn were leaning on their subordinates.

Harker sat on one of those uncomfortable folding chairs in front of Crockett's desk and flipped through a sheaf of messages, telexes, and photographs.

"Here's what we've got so far, sir," he reported. "David Rathbone, using the name Dennis Reynolds—same initials you'll note; so he doesn't have to throw away his monogrammed shirts, I guess—has purchased a home about twenty miles west of Limón in Costa Rica. Our man down there says it's a big ranch-type place with about ten acres of orchards and a vegetable garden. Plus a swimming pool. Right now there's an old couple living there, taking care of things."

"Mortgage?" Crockett asked.

"No, sir, he paid cash. Reportedly about a hundred thousand American. And under the name of Reynolds, he has a balance of about twenty thousand in a San José bank. We're still looking for Dennis Reynolds bank accounts in the Bahamas and Caymans."

"He's getting ready to run?"

"Not quite yet, sir. I questioned Sullivan, and she says Rathbone has mentioned nothing about leaving the country. I figure he's waiting to make a big kill with his counterfeiting scam and the Fort Knox Commodity Trading Fund before he skedaddles."

"Tony, what *is* that Fund?"

"Drug trading," Harker said promptly. "Got to be. What a ballsy idea—to organize a commodity fund that trades only in controlled substances. And then to sell shares to the public to finance the business! If that's not chutzpah, I don't know what is. Anyway, the DEA traced those two cars parked outside Frank Little's office. The Bentley belonged to David Rathbone, as I figured, and he fits the agents' description of the driver. The other car, a Lincoln, is registered in New York to a nephew of Lou Siena. He owns Siena Moving and Storage and is currently under investigation by the Manhattan DA for allegedly running one of the biggest cocaine operations in the city."

"Interesting," Crockett said, drumming his fingers on his desktop. "You believe that links Rathbone and Little with the drug trade?"

"Definitely. The DEA is getting a court order to tap Little's office and home phones."

The chief frowned. "They're certainly moving swiftly on this, aren't they? I trust they'll remember their agreement to consult with us before making any arrests."

"I think we better keep up with them," Harker said. "Rathbone was seen meeting with a suspected drug dealer. That's additional evidence to justify tapping his home phones, wouldn't you say?"

Crockett nodded.

"And the office of the Fort Knox Fund?"

"All right," Crockett said. "Let's go for broke."

"And can we tape conversations in Rathbone's home?"

The other man stared at him. "You never give up, do you? How do you propose to do it?"

"At first I thought it would have to be a black-bag job. Our man would break in when no one's home and place mikes and transmitters. But that's too risky. Rathbone lives in a development where there are a lot of people around. If our agent was spotted, the whole operation would go down the drain. I talked to some phone people, and here's what they came up with: It'll be easy to tap incoming and outgoing calls at the central office. But to pick up other conversation inside the apartment, Rathbone's phones will have to be fitted with a special bug. It's a small, sensitive mike that picks up talk within about twenty feet and transmits it over the phone lines. It doesn't interfere with the normal functioning of the phone. In other words, Rathbone's line will be continually open to carry conversation taking place inside the apartment as well as incoming and outgoing calls."

"And how do you suggest we place these bugs?"

Harker grinned. "I'm going to scam the scammer. The phone people can feed interference into Rathbone's lines. All his calls will be jammed with static and crackling. He'll call the phone company to complain, and they'll send a man—*our* man—out to inspect his phones. That's when they'll be equipped with the bugs. Rathbone's static will clear up, and he'll be none the wiser."

Crockett made an expression of disgust. "I don't like all this," he said. "Whatever happened to privacy in this country? I find the whole concept of bugging and taping repugnant."

"Yes, sir," Tony said, "I agree. But can we go ahead with it?"

Crockett sighed. "Yes, go ahead. I'll have our attorney file for a court order with a friendly judge. And you're not going to tell Sullivan what we're doing?"

"No, sir, I'm not."

"Tony," his boss said in an almost avuncular tone, "I hope you know what you're doing."

"I hope so, too," Harker said, gathered up his papers, and left.

Simon Clark and Manny Suarez were waiting in his office. Tony dropped into his swivel chair and began drumming his fingers on the desktop, just as Crockett had done.

"Fortescue is back in Lakeland," he told the two men, "keeping tabs on the printer. And Ullman is up in Boca playing games with Mike Mulligan. But I didn't want to wait for your weekly reports. Things are beginning to move, and I'm trying to stay on top of them. Clark, what's happening at Sparco's brokerage?"

"The guy's into penny stock fraud up to his eyeballs," the agent said. "At the very least, I've got enough for the SEC to bring civil charges. And with a little more digging, I think we can rack him up on criminal charges, too. This shark and his Denver pals are breaking every securities law on the books and getting rich doing it."

"Yeah?" Suarez said, interested. "How they do that?"

"They've got a dozen gimmicks, but basically what they do is organize a shell company or find some rinky-dink outfit that doesn't have a prayer of success. One of the broker-dealers underwrites a stock offering at maybe a couple of bucks a share. They each buy a block of stock for themselves. Then they get busy high-pressuring suckers, usually by phone, touting the stock at inflated prices. Since it's not listed anywhere, they charge whatever the traffic will bear. When the price is inflated high enough, the promoters sell out to their customers. But if the suckers try to sell, there are no buyers. The most Sparco and his merry band of thieves will do is roll over the suckers' money into another fraudulent investment. And the suckers, hoping to recoup, send in *more* money. The whole dirty deal is a cash cow."

"We'll hold the penny stock swindle as an ace in the hole," Harker said. "What I really want to do is tie Sparco to the Fort Knox Fund. That outfit was organized to deal drugs. Sparco's brokerage is selling Fort Knox stock, so we've got him on umpteen conspiracy charges."

"Plus mail fraud and wire fraud," Clark added.

"Right. What I think will happen when we collar all these crooks is that one of them will cut a deal. Take my word for it, these are not standup guys."

"Which one do you think will rat?"

Harker thought a moment. "My guess would be James Bartlett. He's already done time for bank fraud, and an ex-con will sell his mother to keep from going back into stir. Manny, what's going on at Sid Coe's boiler room?"

Suarez shrugged. "We're still pushing shares in the Fort Knox Fund, but now Coe has added postage stamps. We tell the mooches they can make a killing on commemoratives."

Clark laughed. "No way," he said. "Most commemoratives of the last thirty years are selling for less than face value. The only way to break even is to stick them on letters."

"All I know," Suarez said, "is that I pitch stamps, and the moaney keeps rolling in."

"One thing I've been thinking about," Harker said, "is that when we eventually get these villains in court, we'll score a lot of points with the jury if we can enter as evidence a thick file of complaints from mooches who have been taken by Coe and Sparco. Manny, can you get me a copy of Coe's sucker list? Then I'll contact all of them with a form letter asking for details of their dealings. That should touch off a flood of weeping and wailing."

"No chance," Suarez said. "Coe treats the sucker lists like moaney in the bank. He says he pays a guy in Chicago big bucks for those names. He gives you the list when you get to work. When you leave, you turn it in. And he's right there to make sure you do. I guess he don' wanna yak to swipe a list and start freelancing."

"Could you call me from work and give me names and addresses on the phone?"

Manny shook his head. "Coe walks that boiler room like a tiger. Always leaning over our shoulder, listening to our spiel. If he ever heard me giving out his sucker list over the phone, he'd try to kill me. I mean it. The man is mean."

Harker pondered a moment. Then: "Do you ever go out to lunch?"

"Sometimes. Or to grab a beer."

"How about this . . . You go out for lunch or a beer and take the sucker list with you. I'm parked nearby with a photographer. We photograph every page on the list. It shouldn't take too long. Then you go back to work and turn in the list as usual when you leave."

"I guess," Suarez said slowly. "Maybe it'll work if he don' notice the list is gone while I'm out. Hokay, I'll take the chance."

"Good," Harker said. "I'll line up a photographer and let you know when this little con is scheduled. Are you still clipping Coe for Mort Sparco?"

"Oh sure," Manny said. "At least a coupla big sales a week."

Simon Clark straightened up in his chair. "What's that all about?" he asked. "Sparco is clipping Sid Coe?"

Harker laughed and told him the details of how the discount broker had turned several of Coe's yaks and was taking the boiler room operator for a hundred grand a month.

"That's what friends are for," Tony said.

Clark's smile was chilly. "An interesting story," he said.

42

Rita Angela Sullivan switched on the answering machine and left the office early, bored out of her skull with that stupid job. David insisted on opening the mail himself, and the few times the phone rang it was usually a wrong number or someone trying to sell a timeshare in a Port St. Lucie condo.

So she locked up, headed for home, and her spirits rose. Christmas was only a week away, but you'd never know it from the weather: a dulcet afternoon with burning sun and frisky breeze. The holiday decorations along Atlantic Boulevard seemed out of place, and the white foam sprayed in the corners of shop windows looked more like yogurt than snow.

She had already mailed her cards and sent her mother a nice blouse from Burdines. She had bought a bottle of Courvoisier for Tony Harker. It came in a plush-lined gift box with two crystal brandy snifters. For David, she had shopped long and hard, and had finally settled on a slim black ostrich wallet with gold corners. It cost almost $500, but she didn't begrudge that. After all, it was his money, and she was certain it was a gift he'd love: elegant, expensive, and showy.

She went directly to the kitchen when she arrived home. Blanche and Theodore were there, preparing an enormous bouillabaisse that Rita would reheat for dinner. They were also working on a chilled jug of California Chablis, and Rita had a small glass. It tasted so tangy that she filled a thermos to take up to the terrace.

"Still having trouble with the phones?" she asked.

"Is worse," Blanche said. "So much noise!"

"I told Mr. Rathbone," Theodore said. "He called the phone company, and they're sending a man out to check the lines."

Rita carried her thermos upstairs and undressed slowly. Then she collected beach towel, sunglasses, oil, radio, and went out onto the terrace. The westering sun was unseasonably florid, and heat bounced off the tiles. If it hadn't been for that lovely breeze, she would have been lying in a sauna.

She oiled herself, wishing David were there to do her back, and then rolled naked onto the towel-covered chaise. She lay prone, lifting her long, thick hair away from the nape of her neck.

Whenever she tried to concentrate on the decisions facing her, that passionate sun made her muzzy and melted her resolve. She found her thoughts drifting, just sliding away, until her mind was a fog, and all she could do was groan with content and let the sun have her. But this time, determined not to become muddled, she sat up again, feet on the hot tiles. She turned off the radio and leaned forward, forearms on thighs, and reviewed her options as rationally as she could.

She had no doubt that Tony Harker was speaking the truth when he said he loved her and wanted to marry her. That dear, sweet man could cleverly deceive the black hats he was hounding, but she was convinced that his dealings with her were frank, honest, open.

No question about it: The guy would be a great husband. He'd work at it and do his damnedest to make a marriage succeed. He could be stuffy at times, but he wanted to change and was changing. Rita took some credit for that, but mostly it was Tony's own efforts that were making him less uptight. More *human*.

But despite the thaw, he still represented Duty, with a capital D. He was a straight arrow and would never be anything else. If a conflict ever arose between his personal pleasure and the demands of his job, Rita knew which path he'd take.

If Tony was good malt brew, David was champagne. It made Rita smile just to reflect on what a rogue he was. She knew all his faults, but she knew his virtues, too. He was generous, eternally optimistic, attentive to her needs, and loving. He was also the most beautiful man she had ever known, and that counted for something.

She admitted he was a swindler, but did not agree with Harker's harsh condemnation of Rathbone as a sleazy crook, a shark, and possibly a drug dealer and counterfeiter. Those were heavy crimes and, Rita decided, totally out of character for David.

It was also out of character for him to propose; she knew marriage played no part in his plans. The guy lived by his wits and had the typical con man's aversion to commitments. After his divorce, he was free, unencumbered by legal responsibilities, and he intended to stay that way.

Both men were good in bed, but in different ways. Tony was all male. He was always *there,* solid and satisfying, if predictable. With David, she didn't know what to expect. Kinkiness was the norm with him and sometimes, during their lovemaking, he feverishly sought role reversal as if he needed desperately to surrender and be used. Punished?

Rita lay back upon the chaise. She had sense enough to admit that neither man was totally or even mainly fascinated by her mental prowess or scintillating personality. She propped herself on her elbows, looked down at her tight, tawny body, at the sleek, black triangle, and wondered how long she could depend on *that.*

43

Termite Tommy climbed into the Bentley and put a battered briefcase on the floor.

"Thirty grand in fifties," he said. "Queerest of the queer. Want to count it?"

"Of course not," Rathbone said. "I trust you."

"Going to stick it in banks?"

"I've already opened four different accounts," David said. "I've got to keep each deposit under ten thousand. By the way, I had to make initial deposits of my own money to cover the minimum on checking accounts. My expenses come off the top. Okay?"

"Sure. David, I think you better get this stuff in the banks as soon as possible. That nutsy German can't swear to how stable this batch of paper is."

"How long do I have?"

"Better figure two days tops."

"All right, I'll deposit it first thing tomorrow morning."

Termite Tommy lighted a cigarette. "How soon do you plan to cash in?"

Rathbone shrugged and opened the windows. "A week or two."

"That long?"

"Tommy, I can't put money in one day and draw it out the next. Even a brainless banker would wonder what the hell was going on."

"The problem is I need cash in a hurry. Legit cash. There's a payment due on that color laser copier, and the German and I have the shorts."

"How much do you need?"

"Ten grand."

"By when?"

"Yesterday. We've been stalling the guy who sold us the machine, but now he's threatening to repossess."

"Ten thousand?" Rathbone repeated. "I'd advance it out of my own pocket if I had it, but right now I'm in a squeeze. Look, let me see if I can hit a couple of friends. If I can raise the ten, I'll give you a shout and you come down and pick it up."

"I'd appreciate it," Tommy said. "I hate to put you in a bind, but I don't want to lose that copier."

"Neither do I," David said. "Leave it to me; I'll raise the loot somehow."

"Soon," the other man said, climbing out of the car. "The sooner the better."

Rathbone watched him get into his pickup truck and drive away. Then he opened the briefcase and inspected the money. Tommy and Herman Weisrotte had done a good job weathering the bills, and none of the serial numbers were in sequence.

He drove to the home of James Bartlett on Bayview. Jimmy opened the door wearing a lime-green golf shirt, lavender slacks, pink socks, white Reeboks.

"You're a veritable rainbow," David said and held up the briefcase.

"Got it?" Bartlett said. "Good. Let's go out to the pool. I have a pitcher of fresh lemonade and a bottle of port. Ever try port in lemonade?"

"Never have."

"Refreshing, and it's practically impossible to get stoned."

They sat at an umbrella table, the briefcase on the tiles. Bartlett mixed them drinks in tall green glasses.

Rathbone took a sip. "Nice," he said. "A little sweetish for me, but I like it."

Jimmy kicked the scarred briefcase gently. "All there?" he asked.

"I didn't count it, but I don't think they're playing games. The bills look good to me, but Tommy says the Kraut isn't sure how long the paper will last. He gives it two days."

"No problem," Bartlett said. "My deposit at the Crescent in Boca is scheduled for tomorrow morning. After it's in the bank, I don't care what happens to it."

They sat comfortably, sipping their drinks, watching sunlight dance over the surface of the pool. They could hear the drone of a nearby mower, and once a V of pelicans wheeled overhead.

"By the way," Bartlett said, "the Corcoran brothers are back in town. They're ready."

"Price still ten thousand?"

Jimmy nodded. "They'll make it look good. Guy gets drunk, ends up in a canal. But we've got to figure a way to get him down here from Lakeland and finger him for the Corcorans."

Rathbone stared at him. "I've got a way," he said. "Tommy needs a fast 10K. Says there's a payment due on the copying machine. You'll have the legit cash by tomorrow?"

"Noon at the latest. The courier from Miami is coming tonight. Almost two hundred thousand. I sign for it. He leaves. I take out thirty grand in legit bills and replace them with this 30K of queer. Tomorrow morning I drive up to Boca and deliver the package to Mike Mulligan. He gives me a signed deposit slip. That's it."

"All right," David said. "I'll call Tommy and tell him I've raised the ten thousand he needs. He comes down to Lauderdale, meets me at the Palace, and I hand over the ten grand. That's when the Corcorans pick him up and do their job. Their fee will be in Tommy's pocket. How does it play?"

"Like *Hamlet*," Bartlett said. "I'm glad you're on my side. But what happens when Tommy doesn't return to Lakeland? The German will wonder what happened to him and worry about losing the machine."

"I'll drive up there and snow him," David said. "I'll tell him Tommy got drunk, messed up, and is in the clink. He'll buy it. I'll give him ten grand for the machine and promise more to come. And I'll get him started on a new batch of the queer. Okay?"

"Sounds good to me. Order fifty thousand in fifties and hundreds. I have a feeling this deal is going to work out just fine."

"Can't miss."

"Then why do you look so down?"

"I guess it's because I've got to finger Tommy for the Corcorans."

"It has to be done."

"Sure," Rathbone said. "When are we going to Miami to make a buy for the Fund?"

"I'm working on it. The dealer I want to use is in Peru right now, but he's due back in a week or so."

"How much do you think we'll have to pay?"

"I'm hoping to get it for 13K per kilo. That would give the Fund a profit of ninety-seven thousand, five hundred on our first deal."

"Beautiful," David said. "Will your guy take a check?"

"I don't see why not; we're not asking immediate delivery. We have enough in the Fund's account to cover it, don't we?"

"More than enough. Will he sign a contract?"

"I think he will. We don't have the muscle to enforce it, but he doesn't know that. But contract or not, he'll make delivery. He's an honorable man."

"We're all honorable men," Rathbone said, and they both laughed and poured more lemonade.

44

Henry Ullman was sticking close to Mike Mulligan in Boca. Four evenings a week he met the banker for drinks at the Navigator Bar & Grill. And on Saturday nights, Ullman took a bottle or two to Mulligan's pad, and they hoisted a few while waiting for the guests to arrive.

Ullman figured the mousy banker had about a dozen women on the string. Some showed up alone, there were a few duos, and one trio: all reasonably clean and attractive, not too old, and marvelously complaisant after dipping into the toilet tank in Mulligan's bathroom.

Henry wondered if, in the line of duty, he should be banging women zonked out of their gourds on high-quality coke. It was an ethical dilemma, and it bothered him for at least thirty seconds.

He didn't have drinks at the Navigator with Mulligan on Friday evenings because on Fridays the Crescent was open till seven P.M. to cash paychecks and take deposits. Mike worked late, and Ullman spent the evening writing out his weekly report for Tony Harker. It was usually a brief, uneventful account, although Henry included the names of Mulligan's female guests and their addresses if he could discover them.

Then, one Saturday night, just two days before Christmas, he showed up at Mulligan's apartment with two bottles of Korbel brut, and the weekly orgies came to a screeching halt.

When the banker opened the door, he looked like death warmed over. His poplin suit had obviously been slept in, there were food stains on his vest and gray stubble on his chin. Even worse, the man was crying; fat tears were dripping down his cheeks onto his wrinkled lapels.

"Mike," Ullman said, closing the door quickly behind him, "what in God's name is wrong?"

Mulligan shook his head, said nothing, but collapsed onto the couch. He leaned forward, face in his hands, shuddering with sobs. Ullman took his champagne into the kitchen. The place was a mess: unwashed dishes, encrusted pans, a broken glass. The agent found a bottle of bourbon in the freezer. He poured a healthy jolt into a clean tumbler and brought it to the banker.

"Come on, Mike," he said gently, "take a sip and tell me what's wrong."

Mulligan took the drink with trembling hands and gulped it down. Then coughed and coughed. Ullman waited for the paroxysm to subside, then asked again, "What's wrong?"

The other man wouldn't look at him; he just stared dully at the carpet. "I'm thirty thousand short at the bank," he said in a low voice.

"And that's what knocked you for a loop? It's just a bookkeeping error, Mike; you'll find it."

Mulligan shook his head. "It was a cash deposit. I signed for it without counting it. Then, last night, I discovered it was thirty thousand short."

"I don't understand," Ullman said, but beginning to. "How much was the total deposit?"

"Almost two hundred thousand."

Ullman whistled, then put an arm across the man's thin shoulders. "Tell me all about it," he said softly. "I may be able to help."

"I was just doing a favor for a close friend. I swear that's all it was."

"So you accepted cash deposits over ten thousand and didn't report them?"

"So much paperwork," Mulligan said. "Besides, we only held the funds for a short time and then they would go out in drafts."

"But Crescent profited while the money was in the bank—right? Short-term paper? Overnight loans?"

"Yes."

"Who authorized the drafts? The depositor—your close friend?"

"No. The president of the corporate account authorized the drafts."

"Who was that?"

"Mitchell Korne. It was just a name to me. I never met the man."

"Who were the drafts paid to?"

"Another bank."

"Where?"

"Panama."

"How long has this been going on, Mike?"

"Two years. At least."

"You knew it was drug money?"

Mulligan stared at him with the wide-eyed, innocent look of a guilty man. "I suspected but I had no proof. It could have been the cash proceeds from a real estate sale."

"Oh sure," Ullman said. "Or a yacht. Let's get back to your shortage. When was the deposit made?"

"Yesterday morning."

"In the lobby of the bank? Over the counter?"

"No. Back door."

"So the tellers didn't know about it?"

"No."

"Someone else in the bank must have known. Vice president? President?"

"They knew, but they let me handle it."

"I can imagine. All right, the two hundred grand was deposited at the back door of the bank yesterday morning and you signed for it without counting it."

"It would have taken a long time. It was Friday and I was busy. Besides, previous deposits had always been accurate to the dollar."

"How was the deposit made? I mean how was the cash delivered? In a shopping bag?"

"A suitcase. A cheap vinyl suitcase."

"What did you do with it—put it in the vault?"

"No. I brought it home."

"You did *what*?"

"I couldn't leave it in the bank. The examiners are coming in first thing Tuesday morning, the day after Christmas."

"Good enough reason. Where is the suitcase now?"

"In the bedroom, under the bed."

"No wonder you've got the jits. Mike, why don't you just tell your friend he was thirty thousand short and he'll have to come up with it."

"He won't believe me. He'll say all his previous deposits were accurate. He'll say I signed for the total amount. He'll say I have to make up the loss."

"So? You have thirty thousand in liquid assets, don't you? And if you don't, the bank does. If Crescent's top brass is in on this, they won't squeal too loud."

"Don't you think I've thought of that? But what if we keep getting shortchanged on the deposits?"

"There's an easy answer to that: Tell your friend to get lost."

Mulligan lowered his head. "I can't do that."

"Why not?" Ullman said. "Because he's got you by the short hair? Because for two years he's been paying you off with that white stuff you keep in your toilet tank?"

The banker's head snapped up. His mouth opened; he stared at Ullman, horrified. "You're from the police, aren't you?" he said.

"Sure I am," the agent said cheerfully. "But that doesn't mean I don't like you. I really want to help you."

"You just want to put me in jail."

"Nah. You're more valuable out. Look, if you cooperate maybe we can cut a deal. You'll get a fine and probation. Your career as a banker will be over, but you won't be behind bars with all those swell people. That's worth something, isn't it?"

"When you say cooperate, I suppose you want me to name my friend, the man who made the deposits."

"James Bartlett?" Ullman said casually. "No, you won't have to name him."

Mulligan gasped. "How did you know?"

"You just told me. What do you say, Mike? Will you play along?"

"I don't have much choice, do I?"

"Not much. Now you go take a quick shower, shave, and put on fresh clothes. Then I'm going to drive you down to Fort Lauderdale to meet a couple of men you can deal with."

"It'll be late," Mulligan objected. "They'll probably be asleep."

"I'll wake them up," Ullman promised.

"Am I under arrest?"

"Let's just call it protective custody. Now go get cleaned up."

"May I have another drink?"

"No. You'll want a clear head when you start talking to save your skin."

Mulligan went stumbling into the bathroom. Ullman went into the bedroom and dragged the vinyl suitcase from under the bed. He snapped it open and took out all those lovely bundles of twenties, fifties, and hundreds bound with manila wrappers. He stacked them neatly on the bed, then peered into the emptied suitcase. What he saw made him happy: a layer of confetti that felt oily to the touch.

He left the fluff there, repacked the currency, and closed the suitcase. Mike Mulligan, showered and shaved, came into the bedroom to dress. Ullman took the suitcase into the living room. Then he went into the bathroom and lifted the jar of glassine envelopes from the toilet tank. He took that into the kitchen and found a shopping bag under the sink. He put the cocaine in the bag and added his two bottles of champagne. He went back into the living room, poured himself a shot of bourbon, and sipped slowly.

They were ready to leave a half-hour later. Mulligan carried the shopping bag, and Ullman lugged the suitcase of cash. The banker carefully locked his front door, and then they waited for the elevator. The door slid open. Pearl and Opal Longnecker got out and stared with astonishment at the two men.

Ullman smiled at the sisters. "The party's over, ladies," he said.

45

They spent a quiet New Year's, recovering from the noisy party at the Palace Lounge the previous night. It was a gray, sodden day; there was no sunning on the terrace. They read newspapers and magazines, watched a little television, lunched on cold cuts and potato salad. Both were subdued, conversing mostly in monosyllables, until finally David said, "The hell with resolutions; let's have a Bloody Mary."

"Let's," Rita said, and they did.

After that they perked up and began discussing all the outrageous things that had happened at the New Year's Eve party. Frank Little had dragged Trudy Bartlett under the table, and Nancy Sparco had to be restrained by her husband from completing a striptease atop the table.

"Great party," David said. "I'm going to miss those people."

"Miss them? Are you going somewhere?"

"Eventually," he said, smiling. "And so are you." He glanced at his watch. "But right now I have a business meeting. Shouldn't be gone for more than an hour or so."

"You'll be home for dinner? Blanche made a veal casserole for us."

"I'll be back in plenty of time," he assured her.

"If you're going to be late," she said, "give me a call. The phones are working fine now."

"What was wrong—did the repairman say?"

"A short at the junction box, or so he claimed. Whatever it was, he fixed it and checked all the phones."

"Good. Lend me your car keys, will you? The Bentley's low on gas and nothing will be open today."

He drove Rita's white Corsica. It was only five o'clock, but the waning day was gloomy, and he had to switch on the wipers to keep the windshield clear of mist. He had deliberately picked this particular day and this particular time, figuring the gang would be home recovering from the party. And when he walked into the Palace Lounge through the side entrance, he was happy to see only Ernie, behind the bar and washing glasses used the night before. David swung onto a barstool.

"Happy New Year, Mr. Rathbone," Ernie said. "I'm surprised you're still alive. I didn't think you'd wake up for a week."

"Happy New Year, Ernie, and I feel fine. Mix me the usual, please. That was a dynamite party."

"I should do that much business every night," the bartender said.

He went back to his chores. Rathbone reached into his inside jacket pocket to make sure the envelope was there. Then he lighted a cigarette and sipped his vodka gimlet. Now that the time had come, he found he was calm, acting normally, hands steady.

He had just started his second gimlet when two men came in through the side entrance. Rathbone inspected them in the bar mirror. They matched Bartlett's description of the Corcoran brothers: short and burly with reddish hair cut in Florida flattops. Both were wearing cotton plaid sports jackets over black T-shirts. They took a corner table, and one of them came over to the bar.

"Beer," he said curtly.

"They almost cleaned me out last night," Ernie apologized. "All I got left is Miller's."

The man nodded. "Two bottles," he said.

He paid, then carried the bottles and glasses back to the table. The brothers sat stolidly, drinking their beers, not conversing. Rathbone finished his drink.

"More of the same," he called.

When Ernie started mixing his drink, David slid off the barstool and went into the men's room. He checked both stalls. Empty. He glanced at himself briefly in the mirror over the sink, then waited, not looking in the mirror again. In a few minutes one of the Corcoran brothers entered. He stared at Rathbone.

"From Jimmy Bartlett?" David asked.

The man nodded.

"The guy should be here any minute. He'll come through the side door. He's tall, skinny, and may be wearing a black suit. He'll join me at the bar, and we'll have a drink together. I'll slip him a white envelope. He'll probably take off first, but if he doesn't, I'll take off and leave him alone. He drives an old pickup truck. It'll be parked outside in the lot."

"Our fee's in the envelope?" Corcoran asked. His voice was unexpectedly high-pitched, fluty.

"That's right."

Corcoran nodded again, stepped to a urinal and unzipped his fly. David left hurriedly, went back to the bar, took a gulp of his new drink.

It was almost fifteen minutes before Termite Tommy showed up. He saw Rathbone at the bar and came over to stand next to him.

"Hey, Tommy!" David said heartily. "Happy New Year!"

"Same to you. And many of them."

"What're you drinking?"

"Jim Beam straight. Water on the side."

"If you had the kind of night I had, you better have a double."

"Yeah," Tommy said, "it was kinda wet."

David ordered the bourbon and another gimlet for himself. "Sorry you had to make the trip today," he said.

"That's all right. You got the dough?"

"Uh-huh."

"Good. We make the payment on the machine, everything's copasetic."

Rathbone took the envelope from his jacket pocket and handed it over, making no effort to hide the transfer. In the mirror, he saw the Corcoran brothers finish their beers, rise, and leave.

"Ten K," he said to Tommy. "Legit hundreds."

"I appreciate it, David. Everything go all right at the banks?"

"No problems. I'll start withdrawing next week and give you a call when you can pick up the balance due. Listen, I've got to split. My lady is expecting me home for dinner."

"That's okay; I'm leaving, too. Got a long drive ahead of me."

Rathbone stood, took his new black ostrich wallet from his hip pocket as if he was about to pay the tab.

"Thanks again," Termite Tommy said.

"Keep in touch," David said lightly.

Tommy took a swallow of water, then left. David put his wallet back in his pocket and sat down again.

"Another, Ernie," he called.

The bartender shook his head. "You're a bear for punishment, Mr. Rathbone," he said.

When he brought the drink, he leaned across the bar. "Did you see those two guys?" he asked in a low voice.

"What guys?"

"At the corner table. They had a beer, then went out."

"I just glanced at them. Why?"

"A couple of hard cases," Ernie said.

"You're sure?"

"Sure I'm sure. Wasn't I a cop for too many years? You wouldn't want to be caught in a dark alley with those yobs, believe me."

People entered, stayed for a drink or two, departed. Others took their place. The Lounge was quiet, jukebox stilled, conversation muted. David knew none of the customers, which was just as well; he didn't want to talk to anyone. He had another drink. Another. Another.

He floated in a timeless void, the room blurred, Ernie wavered back and forth. He could not concentrate, which was a blessing, but stared vacantly at the stranger in the mirror and watched the glass come up, tilt, pour out its contents. The throat constricted, the stranger grimaced and gasped.

" 'Nother," he said in a loud voice.

Ernie looked at him but said nothing. He was mixing the gimlet, taking his time, when he saw David fall forward onto the bar. He just folded his arms and his head went down. He sat there hunched over, not moving.

The bartender sighed, put aside the drink. He dug out his little red address book and looked up Rathbone's home phone number. He called from the phone behind the bar.

"The Rathbone residence."

"Rita?"

"Yes. Who's this?"

"Ernie. At the Palace Lounge."

"Oh. Hiya, Ernie. Happy New Year."

"Same to you. Listen, Mr. Rathbone is here, and he's a little under the weather. I hate to eighty-six him, but he's in no condition to drive. He'll kill himself or someone else."

Silence a moment, then: "I'll call a cab. I should be there in twenty minutes, half-hour at the most. Don't give him any more to drink and try to keep him from leaving."

"Okay."

"And thanks for calling, Ernie."

When she hurried in, raincoat slick with mist, David was still sprawled over the bar. Rita stood alongside and looked down at him.

"How many did he have?" she asked Ernie.

"Too many. And fast. Seemed like he just couldn't stop. It's not like him."

"No," Rita said, "it's not. What's the bill?"

"Don't worry about it. I'll catch him another night."

"Thanks, Ernie. The valet brought the car around to the side entrance. Will you help me get him out?"

Ernie came from behind the bar. Rita shook David's shoulder, first gently, then roughly until he roused.

"Wha?" he said groggily, raising his head.

"Come on, Sleeping Beauty," she said, "we're going home."

She and Ernie got him to his feet and supported him, one on each side.

"All right, all right," he said thickly. "I can navigate."

But they didn't let go of him until he was outside, leaning against the Corsica, his face pressed against the cool, wet roof.

"Let me get some fresh air," he said.

"Thanks again, Ernie," Rita said. "I can take it from here."

The bartender went back inside. Rita opened the car door. But suddenly David lurched away, staggered several steps, and vomited all over a waist-high sago palm. He remained bent over for five minutes, and Rita waited patiently, listening to him retch.

Finally he straightened up, wiped his mouth with his handkerchief, and then threw it away. He came back to the car slowly, taking deep breaths.

"Sorry about that," he said huskily.

"It happens," Rita said. "Get in the car and I'll drive us home. Have a cup of black coffee, you'll feel better."

"I don't think so," he said.

When they arrived at the town house, he went directly upstairs to take off his spattered clothing. Rita sat on his bed and listened to the shower running. He was in there such a long time she was beginning to worry. But then he came out in a white terry robe, drying his hair with a towel.

"I'd like a cognac," he said. "Just an ounce, no more, to settle my stomach."

"You're sure?" she said.

"I'm sure."

"All right, I'll bring it up here for you."

"No, I'll come downstairs."

In the kitchen, he measured out an ounce of Courvoisier carefully. He took a cautious sip, then closed his eyes and sighed.

"You okay?" she asked anxiously.

"I will be. Let me mix you something. A brandy stinger?"

"Just right," she said.

They took their drinks into the living room and sat on the couch.

"I don't suppose you feel like eating that veal casserole."

"Jesus, no!" he said. "I never want to eat again. But you go ahead."

"I can wait. Maybe you'll feel like it later."

He stared at her, then picked up her hand, kissed her knuckles. "Know why I love you?" he asked.

"Why?"

"Because not once, at the Palace, on the ride back, or since we've been home, have you hollered at me or asked why I made such a fool of myself."

"I figured if you wanted to tell me, you would. I don't pry; you know that."

"It was that business meeting I had."

"It didn't go well?"

"It went fine."

"I don't understand."

"Forget it. I'm going to. Oh God, what would I do without you? You're my salvation."

"Don't make a federal case out of it, baby. You got drunk and I brought you home. No big deal."

"You were there when I needed you; that's what counts. Rita, I swear to you I'll never do that again."

"Even Ernie said it wasn't like you."

"Did you pay my bar tab?"

"He said he'd catch you another night."

"He's a good man. He called you?"

"Yep."

"And Florence Nightingale came running. Thank God. Listen, hon, I've been thinking; maybe we should take off sooner than I planned. Say in about six months."

"Whatever you say; you're the boss."

"On that drive home tonight, I got the feeling that things were closing in. Waiting around for just one more big deal is a sucker's game. Let's take the money and run."

"Where to?"

He grinned. "A secret. But believe me, you'll love it. Plenty of hot sun."

"A beach?"

"Not too far away. But a big pool."

"A private pool?"

"Of course."

"That's for me," she said.

"Will you have a lot of preparations to make?"

"Nope. Just pack my bikinis. I'll write my mother and tell her I'll be traveling awhile and not to worry."

He kissed her hand again. "You think of everything. You're not only beautiful, you're brainy." He raised his glass. "Happy New Year, darling."

46

She called Tony Harker a little before noon and told him that Rathbone had driven up to Lakeland and wouldn't be back until late that night. Tony locked up his office and ran. He was at his motel with a cold six-pack of Bud by the time Rita arrived. Ten minutes later they were in bed, blinds drawn, air conditioner set at its coldest.

She had never been more impassioned, but now he had the confidence of experience and her ardor didn't daunt him. They coupled like young animals eager to test their strength, and if there was no surrender by either, there was triumph for both.

When finally they separated, they lay looking at each other wildly. It had been a curious union, so glowing that it frightened both for what it might promise. It exceeded the physical, gave a glimpse of a different relationship that, if nurtured, might remake their lives.

"What happened?" he asked wonderingly, but Rita could only shake her head, as confused and fearful as he.

The real world intruded, and they laughed and pretended it had merely been a dynamite roll in the hay and sexual pleasure was all that mattered.

But having experienced that epiphany, they desired to know it again, despite their dread, if only to prove such rapture did exist. So after a time they made love again, slowly and deliberately, and waited for that unequaled ecstasy to reappear. But it did not, leaving them satiated but conscious of a loss.

"Have you been taking lessons?" Rita asked him.

"Yes," he answered. "From you. My God, your tan is deeper than ever." His forefinger stroked the fold between her thigh and groin. "You're not worried about skin cancer?"

"Ahh," she said, "life's too short. And I drink too much, smoke too much, and pig out on fatty foods. It's stupid to give up all the pleasures of life just to squeeze out a few extra years. That's for cowards."

"Dying young doesn't scare you?"

"Sure it does. But what scares me more is living a dull, boring life." She sat up. "Let's talk business for a while," she said. "Have your guys come up with anything on David and the Palace gang?"

"Lots of things. I really think we're going to rack up the whole crew. Rita, why did Rathbone go to Lakeland?"

"He didn't say, and I didn't want to push."

"Has he mentioned anything about taking off permanently? Leaving the country?"

"Not really. A couple of times he's complained about how hard he works and how he'd like to retire. But it all sounds like bullshit to me. He's making a nice buck; he'd be a fool to cash in. And David's no fool."

"Don't be so sure of that. He's making a lot of mistakes."

"Like what?"

"Oh, this and that," Harker said vaguely. "Has he ever mentioned the names Herman Weisrotte or Thomas Keeffringer?"

"Nope. Never heard of them."

"How about Mitchell Korne?"

She shook her head. "No again. Who are all these guys?"

"Their names came up in our investigation. I'd like to tie them to Rathbone."

She drained her beer, got out of bed, began to dress.

"Hey," he said, "where you going?"

"You're itching to get back to the office," she said. "I can tell."

"Well, yeah, I've got a lot to do. Things are beginning to move."

"You're really after his balls, aren't you, Tony?"

"Rathbone? You betcha! I want him stuck out of sight for ten years at least. Maybe more."

"What'd he ever do to you?" she said in a low voice.

He stared at her. "What the hell kind of a question is that? I'm in the crook-exterminating business. Rathbone is a crook. So I'm going to exterminate him. Logical enough for you?"

"All right, all right," she said hastily. "Don't get steamed. It's just that you seem to have a personal feud with the guy, even if you've never met him."

"I know what he's done. Is doing."

"But it's more than just a cop doing his job. It's like a crusade. You're never going to let up until you nail him."

"You've got it. But screw Rathbone. What about us?"

She stood in front of the dresser mirror, combing her long black hair. "What about us?"

"You promised to think over what I said. Marriage. Have you?"

She whirled suddenly, hair flying. "Yes, I've thought about it. I think about it all the time. Don't lean on me, Tony, please don't. I told you it's a heavy decision, and it is. Right now I don't know what I want to do."

He came over to her and held her in his arms.

"Don't be angry with me, darling," he said. "I don't want to pressure you, but you mean so much to me that I get anxious. I don't even want to think about losing you."

She reached up to stroke his cheek. "I'm not angry with you, baby. It's just that I'm trying to figure things out, and it's going to take time."

"How much time?"

She pulled away. "Six months. Tops. How does that sound?"

He blinked once. "All right," he said. "Six months."

47

Roger Fortescue went home for Christmas Day and New Year's Eve. The rest of his time was spent in Lakeland, keeping a loose stakeout on Herman Weisrotte's printing shop and occasionally tailing Thomas J. Keeffringer just for the fun of it.

He hadn't uncovered a great deal. The German slept in a little room behind his shop, and Termite Tommy kipped in a motel even more squalid than Fortescue's. The two men spent a lot of time together, and the fact that Weisrotte rarely had a half-dozen customers a day convinced Roger that these two villains were engaged in some nefarious scheme that enabled them to get plotched almost every night at the Mermaid's Tail, a gin mill only a block away from the printshop.

It was, Fortescue decided, just about the dullest duty he had ever pulled, and only his nightly phone calls to Estelle enabled him to keep his sanity. But then, a few days into the new year, things started popping, and what had been a boring grind became a fascinating mystery.

It began when the agent realized he hadn't seen Termite Tommy around for three or four days. He didn't come to the printshop, and when Roger checked his motel, the surly owner said he hadn't been there since New Year's Day, and if he didn't show up soon with his weekly rent, the owner was going to chuck his sleazy belongings into the gutter.

Fortescue, sitting in his Volvo and keeping an eye on Weisrotte's shop, wondered if Tommy had split with the German and decided to try his larcenous talents elsewhere. But it didn't make sense that he'd take off without emptying his motel room. It could be, of course, that he was shacked up with a ladylove somewhere and would soon reappear.

While Roger was trying to puzzle out what had happened, he saw a black Bentley pull to a stop, and he straightened up in his seat. A handsome blond guy got out of the car, glanced around, and then sauntered into the German's shop. The agent made him for David Rathbone, but jotted down the license of the Bentley to double-check later.

Rathbone was in there almost two hours. Then he and Weisrotte came out and headed for the Mermaid's Tail, Rathbone talking a mile a minute.

The agent figured it was safe enough for him to move in. Rathbone had never seen him before, and if Weisrotte recognized him—so what? He was just a guy who had dropped by once to price business cards. So Fortescue entered the saloon, ordered a beer at the bar, and looked around casually. His targets were in a back booth, Rathbone still talking nonstop and the German downing shots of straight gin like there was no tomorrow.

This went on for almost an hour while Roger nursed a second beer. Then the two men got up, and Rathbone paid the tab. They started for the door, and as they passed, Fortescue noted the diamond ring on Rathbone's left pinkie. At least a three-carat rock, he estimated, and wondered how many mooches had contributed their life savings to the purchase of that sparkler.

Rathbone got the printer back to the shop and went in with him for a few minutes. Then he came out, lighted a cigarette, and got into the Bentley. By that time Fortescue was in his Volvo, and he tailed Rathbone until it became obvious the man was heading south, probably returning to Fort Lauderdale. Then the agent turned back and drove to his motel, trying to figure out the significance of what he had just witnessed.

He came up with zilch and decided maybe he'd give Tony Harker a call, report what had happened, and let him chew on it awhile. But before he did that, he made his nightly call home. He jived with his sons awhile, got their promises that they were doing their homework and weren't planning to rob a bank, and then Estelle came on.

"Guess who called you this morning," she said.

"Elizabeth Taylor?"

"Even better. Sam Washburn."

"Yeah? What'd he want?"

"Didn't say. But he claims it's important and said to call him."

"Probably got another owl made of shells he wants to unload on me."

"Don't you take it! Don't you dare!"

"Trust me," he said.

He hung up, found Washburn's number in his notebook, and called the old retired cop.

"Roger Fortescue," he said. "How you doing?"

"Hey, old buddy!" Sam said. "Your wife said you were out of town."

"I am. I'm calling from Lakeland."

"What the hell are you doing there—picking oranges?"

"Something like that. What's up, Sam?"

"You remember the last time we talked you asked me about Thomas J. Keeffringer, aka Termite Tommy?"

"Sure. What about him?"

"Well, he showed up down here."

"No kidding. What's he up to now?"

"Not a whole hell of a lot," Washburn said. "At the moment he's occupying an icebox in the morgue."

Silence. Then: "Sheet," Roger said, "how did you find that out?"

"There was a short article in the *Sun-Sentinel* this morning. I called to ask if you had seen it, but then Estelle told me you were out of town, so I figured you hadn't. Anyway, according to the story a kid was testing his new scuba gear in a canal out near Coral Springs. He spotted an old pickup truck on the bottom. Nothing unusual about that. You know how many people ditch their clunkers in the canals and then claim the insurance, saying it was stolen."

"I know, Sam," Fortescue said patiently, "I know."

"But when this kid got close to the pickup, he saw there was a guy sitting behind the wheel. So he got out of the water, called the cops, and they drug the truck out. The guy behind the wheel was Termite Tommy himself."

"Cause of death?"

"They're not sure yet. I phoned Jack Liddite at Homicide, but he doesn't think it'll be their baby. He said the ME's report isn't complete yet, but it looks like Tommy got smashed, didn't make a curve, and just drove into the canal. They found an empty liter of juice in the cab of the truck. That's all I got. But you sounded like you were working the guy so I wanted to make sure you knew about it."

"Thanks, Sam," Fortescue said. "I really appreciate it."

"Glad to help, old buddy. By the way, I got a shell penguin for you. It's a beaut."

"That's great," Roger said faintly. "Love to have it."

Then he called Tony Harker. He told him about Keeffringer's disappearance, the meeting between David Rathbone and Herman Weisrotte, and the discovery of Termite Tommy's body in the Coral Springs canal.

Harker didn't hesitate. "Get back as soon as possible," he said. "The printer's not going anywhere; he'll be there when we want him. You schmooze with your buddies down here and see what you can pick up on the homicide."

"They're not even sure it *was* a homicide."

"I think it was," Harker said. "Don't you?"

"Yes," Fortescue said.

48

They rehearsed their roles on the drive down to Miami. Both men were quick studies, and it didn't take long to cobble up a scenario and decide how it was to be played.

"Korne is not a megadealer," Jimmy Bartlett said, "but big enough. Most of his stuff goes to New Jersey and New England. He isn't in New York, but the last time I spoke to him, he was talking about expanding into Montreal and Toronto. He's an ambitious lad."

"Lad?" David Rathbone said. "Just how old is he?"

"Mitch? I don't think he's thirty yet. He's come a long way in a short time."

"Do you call him 'Mitch' to his face?"

"I do, but I suggest you address him as Mr. Korne. He likes it when older men use Mister."

"How did he get so far so fast? Is he a hard case?"

"Not personally. But he hires very dependable muscle and pays them well. I think the secret of his success is his business sense. He's a Harvard MBA, you know, and treats drugs like any other consumer product. That's what he calls dopers—consumers. He talks about his product line, distribution network, the need to maximize profitability, and so forth. Bribery of officials he calls Public Relations. His only regret is that he can't advertise. But he's considering putting a brand name on all his products as a guarantee of quality."

"I'll snow him with Wall Street lingo," David said. "The smarter they are, the harder they fall."

"By the way," Bartlett said, "how did you make out with the German in Lakeland?"

"In like Flynn. I could have sold him the Brooklyn Bridge. He bought the story of Termite Tommy being in the slammer. He promised to get started on our 50K of queer fifties."

"And he agreed to accept twenty percent of the face value?"

"He did after I got half a jug of Beefeater in him. That guy must have a liver as big as the Ritz."

"Who cares," Bartlett said, "as long as he does the job."

The offices of Mitchell Korne Enterprises, Inc., were located in one of the raw, pastel-colored towers jazzing up downtown Miami. The firm was registered as an importer of South and Central American furniture, lamps, and decorative accessories. This business showed an annual profit apparently sufficient to justify a lavish suite of offices that doubled as a showroom for the company's legitimate imports.

Cocaine, marijuana, heroin, hashish, and other illicit substances were imported and marketed by another division with its own financial structure, personnel, and distribution. Both divisions, overt and covert, were controlled by the CEO, Mitchell Korne, although it was rumored that Mitchell Korne Enterprises, Inc., was actually a sub rosa limited partnership with several investors who financed the operation in return for an enormous quarterly cash distribution.

Korne's private office had none of the carved wood and Aztec-patterned upholstery of the reception room. It was severely modern: glass, chrome, leather, and built-in bookcases of polished teak. There were Japanese prints framed on the walls, and behind Korne's high swivel chair was a plate-glass picture window with a startling view of the Miami skyline and a small patch of blue water sparkling in the January sunshine.

After the introductions, they sat around a cocktail table: a single sheet of stainless steel supported on black iron sawhorses. There were no ashtrays in the room, no family photographs, mementos, or anything else that might yield a clue to the occupant's background and character. The office was as impersonal as an operating theater, and as sterile.

Korne was a tall, scholarly-looking young man with a hairline mustache and glasses framed in gold wire. Rathbone made him for a cold fish but was impressed by the dealer's three-piece suit of dove-gray flannel.

"How was Peru, Mitch?" Jimmy Bartlett asked.

"Impressive. I saw one huge valley that was almost totally coca shrubs. Very reassuring. Supply won't be a problem for the foreseeable future."

"Which means, Mr. Korne," Rathbone said, "that distribution and marketing will be the keys to your bottom-line profitability."

Korne looked at him with interest. "Yes, I think that's a reasonable assumption."

"David," Bartlett said, "why don't you make your presentation now. Mitch is a busy man."

"Of course," Rathbone said. "I'll keep it as brief and on-target as possible. Mr. Korne, I'm from Indianapolis, and a number of associates and I have formed an ad hoc organization that is exploring a variety of ways in which undeclared income might be invested."

Korne nodded. "I understand," he said.

"The associates I speak of are from Indiana, Illinois, and Iowa plus Ohio and western Pennsylvania. We have come up with a concept we feel has high upside potential and limited downside risk. In our home states are an enormous number of small colleges and universities. I can't quote the exact figure, but I assure you it's in the high hundreds. We feel the educational institutions in this area represent an exciting untapped market for your products. We propose to establish a network of distributors that would initially consist of one sales representative in each college and university. If initial results validate our optimistic computer analysis, we would eventually attempt to place a retail salesperson in every fraternity, sorority, and dormitory in every college throughout the target area."

Mitchell Korne straightened up in his suede director's chair, then leaned forward intently. "A very interesting game-plan. What specific product did you have in mind? Crack?"

Rathbone shook his head. "I don't think so. You must remember that these college students are relatively wealthy. Crack is consciously or unconsciously linked with poverty. But cocaine is considered daring, glamorous. Look at all the movie stars and rock singers who have admitted frequent use."

Korne nodded again. "Yes, I think your decision to avoid crack is wise. It is certainly not a recreational product. Tell me, Mr. Rathbone, have you done any market research?"

"No, sir, we have not," David said. "Which is the reason I am here today. We—my associates and I—have decided to conduct a test in a limited number of demographically selected markets. We feel it will take three months to have trained sales personnel on station. We would like to purchase fifteen kilos of high-quality cocaine to be delivered in three months. As proof of our dependability and serious intent, I have been authorized to pay the agreed-upon price immediately."

"I see," Korne said, sitting back. "And what price did you have in mind?"

"Ten K per kilo."

The dealer smiled coldly. "I'm afraid not. It is far below the present market price, and the weight involved would not justify such a heavy discount."

"I realize," Rathbone said, "that the sale of fifteen kilos hardly represents a significant transaction to a man in your position, Mr. Korne. But I want to emphasize that this initial purchase is merely for a market test. If our computer predictions prove viable, I have every expectation of requiring a vastly increased and regular delivery of the product in the future. What I am suggesting, Mr. Korne, is that if you are willing to take a chance on us in the formative period of our operation, you will find us a grateful and loyal customer in the years to come."

"Another consideration, Mitch," Bartlett said softly, "is that you will have the use of a hundred and fifty thousand dollars for the three months prior to delivery. Surely the profits from investing those funds, even for a period of ninety days, will help offset the difference between what David is prepared to pay and the going rate."

Korne stared at Rathbone a long time while the other two men remained silent. Finally Korne said, "I like your idea of direct distribution to the colleges. Of course, a great deal will depend on the personality of your local salespersons, but I'm sure you are aware of the need for cheerful service and customer satisfaction. Very well, I'm willing to take a flier. If you'll accept delivery in Miami in three months, you may have fifteen kilos at 10K per kilo."

"Thank you, Mr. Korne," Rathbone said.

"Call me Mitch," the other man said.

On the drive back to Lauderdale, still astounded by their good fortune, they calculated the take on the fifteen kilos. Sold for $19,500 per kilo to Lou Siena. Purchased at $10,000 per kilo from Mitchell Korne. Profit: $142,500.

"Amazing!" Bartlett said. "He didn't haggle a bit. I thought sure we'd have to up the ante to 12K per kilo."

"And he signed the contract for chairs and accepted the Fort Knox Fund check," Rathbone marveled. "Jimmy, we've got to get another, bigger deal in the works immediately. Different buyer, different seller, but let's stick to the same plot. It worked once, it'll work again."

"Fine with me," Bartlett said. "Let's have a meet with Sparco, Little, and Coe. We'll tell them the good news and figure ways to build up the Fund's working capital. It's a marvelous con, David."

"Only it isn't a con," Rathbone said. "Not really. The scenarios might have been a swindle, and maybe we're clipping the marks who bought shares in the Fund, but essentially the deal is legitimate. We're buying low and selling high. That's the religion of Wall Street, isn't it?"

49

The tape clicked off, and Tony Harker switched it to fast rewind. Then he went into the cramped kitchenette and made himself a sandwich. The tape had rewound by the time he returned to the living room, and he settled down to listen again, reflecting that in the distant future his son might ask, "What did you do, Daddy, when your world was falling apart?" And he might reply, "I ate a bologna on rye with mustard."

He heard Rita Sullivan and David Rathbone, apparently on New Year's Day, discuss a party they had attended the previous night. He heard Ernie call Rita to come to the Palace and take care of Rathbone, who was "under the weather." He heard the subsequent conversation inside the town house during which Rathbone made it obvious that he was planning to leave the country in six months, and Rita practically promised to go along.

It was possible, of course, that she had been playing her assigned role, trying to lure Rathbone into revealing his destination. But that was hard to believe; a few days later Rita, seated in the chair now occupied by Harker, had assured him that Rathbone had spoken of leaving only in general terms. She had been vague about that, but definite in promising Tony to answer his marriage proposal in six months. That would be after Rathbone had skedaddled. And Rita with him?

There were other things she should have told him but hadn't: the description of Rathbone's intended hideaway, a place in the sun, not too far from the beach, with a big private pool. That matched Rathbone's ranch in Costa Rica. And she mentioned nothing of his business meeting on New Year's Day, probably at the Palace, that "went fine" but resulted in Rathbone drinking himself into insensibility.

All those lapses were worrisome enough, but it was the content and tone of her conversations with Rathbone, obviously in a bedroom, that shattered Tony Harker. He could not believe that she was such an accomplished actress that she could fake the passion in the things she said and, presumably, did.

The intimacy and fervor of the pillow talk between David and her was at once arousing and depressing. He listened to it, feeling like a sick voyeur but unable to turn off the machine, knowing that even if he did, the hurt would not end.

When, finally, the tape ran out, he still heard the moans of delight. And he sat alone in a shoddy motel room, trying to puzzle out reasons for her possible duplicity. It was easy to say Rathbone was handsome, wealthy, loving, and she had succumbed to his charms. But Tony had to believe there was more to it than that. Rita was a hardheaded cop who could spot a phony a mile away. Yet here she was apparently embracing phoniness and willing to risk her future with an insubstantial man whose entire life was based on sham.

What were Harker's options in response to what he had heard? He could confront Sullivan with the tapes. Her defense, he reckoned, was that she was doing her assigned job. She had delivered information on the Fort Knox Fund, hadn't she? And on Rathbone passing the forged Treasury check. And on the activities of Irving Donald Gevalt.

She could claim that she had done what she was ordered to do. But how she accomplished her assignment was her business, not Harker's. And how could he answer that? He could not, but the worm still gnawed.

He might take the actual tapes to Lester Crockett rather than submitting an expurgated précis, and let the boss decide where the truth lay. But that, Harker decided, would be surrender of his responsibility. Sullivan was *his* agent, and if he was willing to profit from her work, he should be willing to accept the blame if she turned sour.

He was convinced that the entire case was progressing well and nearing its denouement. Pulling Rita out might well rob the investigation of vital intelligence. He needed her as much as he needed Clark, Fortescue, Suarez, and Ullman.

And there was always the possibility—slim though it might be—that she *was* acting a role with Rathbone. And that she would deliver David's head to Tony Harker as soon as she had the evidence.

He hoped with all his heart that might be true. But he was tied in knots, felt the familiar pressure, and began searching frantically for his inhaler.

50

He put it off as long as he could, answering her importunate phone calls with "Birdie, I can't talk right now; I have people in my office." Or, "Birdie, I have to go up to Palm Beach on business; call you when I get back." Or even, "Birdie, I have a miserable case of the flu, and I don't want to risk giving it to you."

But finally her calls took a nasty tone, and he decided to get it over with. The last thing he wanted at this stage of the game was a scorned woman blowing the whistle on him.

He bought a gold-plated compact for her and had it engraved with a cursive monogram, B.W. He paid for the gift with a stolen credit card, one of many that Ernie sold to trusted customers for fifty bucks a pop. The name on David's card was Finley K. Burden, and they hadn't yet redlined his account.

Mrs. Winslow met him at the door of her apartment with a glacial smile and a greeting that was barely civil. She waved him to an armchair. No snuggling on the couch and no offer of a vodka gimlet just the way he liked it—for which he was grateful.

"Birdie," he said, "that's an absolutely smashing suit you're wearing. Donna Karan, isn't it?"

"No."

"Well, I think it's divine. Birdie, I want to apologize sincerely for not having gotten back to you sooner. I just can't begin to tell you how sorry I am. But I've never been so busy in my life. The goods news is that your investments are doing wonderfully; so far your net worth has increased almost forty percent, and I think it'll do even better this year. I realize that's no excuse for my neglecting you, but I want you to know that I have been working very hard to increase the value of your account."

"Thank you," she said faintly.

He stood, went over to the couch, sat down close to her. He took the gift-wrapped package from his jacket pocket and presented it to her with his dazzling smile.

"For you," he said. "A peace offering."

She held the gift but made no effort to open it. "You know, David, I'm very angry with you. You never came to see me over the holidays, and I didn't even get a Christmas card from you, and you've been almost rude to me on the phone."

He looked at her, shocked and outraged. "You didn't get my card? That's terrible! My secretary said she mailed it a week before Christmas."

"Maybe you need a new secretary."

"Maybe I do," he mourned. "It was a special card I picked out just for you. I'm so sorry, Birdie, but I assure you I didn't forget you."

"I'll take the thought for the deed," she said primly. "But I must tell you honestly that I was so furious at the way you were treating me, I came very close to taking my account away and demanding all my money back."

He was instantly solemn. "First of all, you have every right to do that. The money is yours, and anytime you want to end our business relationship, the assets will be returned to you without delay."

"I'm happy to hear that."

"But before you do it, all I ask is that you consider your financial future carefully. What would you do with your investments? Who would handle them for you? There is an enormous amount of paperwork and very specialized expertise required. Birdie, I don't wish to brag, but I doubt very much if you'll find another asset manager able to provide the kind of return I've been earning for you. Do think it over carefully before you make a decision you may later regret."

"I thought we had more than a business relationship, David, but I guess I was wrong."

"No," he said firmly, "you are not wrong. Of course it is more than a business relationship; we both know that."

She looked at him challengingly. "Well then, what about our taking an apartment together? You never have given me a definite answer."

He rose and paced slowly back and forth in front of the couch. He had contrived a scenario he thought would fly.

"Birdie, I've considered it long and hard. I still feel the risks are tremendous. We know how we feel about each other, and I'd hate to do anything that might jeopardize that feeling. You honestly believe we could make a success of living together. I'm more cautious and conservative than you, just as I am in handling your money. But I've come up with a solution I think is reasonable, and I hope you'll agree."

"What is it, David?"

"Right now I'm heavily involved in a dozen business negotiations for you and my other clients. The pressures are enormous, requiring every bit of my energy and time. At the moment, I couldn't possibly think of moving. But I think I'm beginning to see light at the end of the tunnel. I estimate that in six months I'll have things organized and running smoothly. Then you know what I'd like to do?"

"What, David?"

"I'd like to take a vacation. I haven't had a real one in years—just business trips. I'd like to take at least two weeks off, maybe a month, and travel through Europe, Russia, maybe even Japan and China. A long, leisurely vacation that'll enable me to unwind and recharge my batteries. I'd like you to come with me—at my expense, of course. Not only will we have a wonderful time, seeing all the sights, visiting Paris, London, Rome, Moscow, Tokyo, but we'll be living together for at least two weeks. It'll be like a trial run. If we find we enjoy each other's company twenty-four hours a day, then that will certainly be proof that we can make a success of living together when we come back home. What do you say? Will you be willing to make the trip with me in six months?"

She tossed the wrapped gift aside, heaved off the couch, rushed to him, enfolded him in a suffocating embrace.

"*Divine!*" she cried. "Of course I'll go with you, David. We'll have the time of our lives, you'll see, and really get to know each other better."

"And you're willing to wait six months?"

"Of course, you silly boy, because I'm positive, just *positive*, that we'll come home closer than ever and eager to get our own place—together. Oh, I'm so excited! I'm going out tomorrow and start shopping: dresses and shoes and maybe new luggage. There's so much, I've got to make a list of all the things I'll need."

"You do that," he said with a tender smile, "but meanwhile look at your gift."

She ripped away the fancy wrapping, opened the box, removed the engraved compact, and stared at it with widened eyes.

"Oh David, it's beautiful! Just what I wanted."

"I thought it would be," he said.

51

It had been a frustrating morning for Manny Suarez. He and the other yaks were hawking the Fort Knox Commodity Trading Fund, commemorative postage stamps, and pork bellies, but it was one of those days when the mooches just weren't biting. Sid Coe was in a vile mood, stalking up and down the boiler room and screaming, "Close the deal or there's no meal! Get the buck in or get the fuck out!"

Finally, a little after noon, he went stomping downstairs, muttering and cursing. The yaks figured they were safe for a while because it was common knowledge that Coe was humping the comely receptionist in his private office during his lunch hour. Manny Suarez folded up the sucker list, stuck it in his hip pocket, and ducked out.

Just as he had promised, Tony Harker was parked a block away in a white Chevy van. Harker sat behind the wheel. In the back, a bearded young black waited with a classy Leica camera and a battery-powered floodlight. Suarez slid in next to Harker and handed the sucker list to the photographer. He put the list on the floor, turned on his light, adjusted the lens and started snapping.

"How's it going, Manny?" Tony asked.

Suarez flipped his hand back and forth. "*Comme çi, comme ça.* Moaney is tight today. The boss is goin' nuts."

"Stick with it," Harker said. "I don't think it'll be much longer. Ullman brought in a canary who's singing his heart out. We're going to nail the whole bunch, including your boss."

"I wanna be there when you take him," Manny said. "Hokay?"

"Sure, I was planning on it. I guess you'll be glad to get back to Miami."

"Oh, I don' know," Suarez said, thinking of the Cuban lady and the cash he was skimming from his commissions. "It's good duty. Maybe you can use me again?"

"Could be," Harker said. "After this case is closed, there'll be something else. It never ends."

"Have gun, will travel," Manny said.

The photographer tapped Tony's shoulder. "Finished," he said. "I took two of each page, different exposures. We're covered."

"Good," Harker said. "Here's your list, Manny. I hope there's no hassle."

Suarez shrugged. "He don' even know I'm gone."

But he did. When Manny walked into Instant Investments, Inc., Sid Coe was waiting for him, his face twisted with fury, and the agent knew he was in trouble.

Coe jerked a thumb toward his office. "In there, bandido," he said, his voice gritty.

Suarez followed him inside, and Coe slammed the door.

"Where you been?" he demanded.

"Having a beer," Manny said. "Hokay?"

"Where's your sucker list?"

"Right here," Manny said, taking it from his hip pocket.

"What the fuck you taking it out of the office for?"

"So no one swipes it. I got this list marked with all my best mooches. Why should I let another yak make deals with my pigeons?"

"Yeah? Let me see it."

Suarez handed over the pages. Coe scanned them swiftly.

"You're lying, you little shit," he said. "All you got marked are Hispanic names. You stole my list that I paid good money for. You sneaked it out of the office against what I told you and had it copied. You're figuring on going into business for yourself."

"Not so," Manny said, spreading his hands. "Ask up and down the street. Where could I have it copied in twenty minutes?"

Coe stared at him angrily. "No one messes with Sid Coe. You're fired. Get your ass the hell out of here."

"Sure," Suarez said, "as soon as you pay me commissions for three days' work. You owe me."

"I owe you shit," Coe said. He opened his desk drawer, took out the heavy .45 automatic, and placed it on the desktop. He turned it with his forefinger until the muzzle was pointing at Manny.

"Look what I got," Coe said. "Now get out."

Suarez lifted the tail of his white guayabera shirt to reveal the short-barreled .38 Special holstered on his hip. "Look what I got," he said. "You wanna see who's the fastest draw in the East?"

Coe looked up at his face, his eyes. Then he took out his wallet, extracted two hundred in fifties and threw them on the desk.

"You fuckin' spic," he said. "You're all alike."

"Yeah, I know," Manny said, picking up the bills. "We wanna get paid for the work we do. Un-American—right? See you soon, Mr. Coe."

"Not if I can help it."

"You can't," the agent said, smiling. "Too late."

He left Coe trying to figure that and went out onto Oakland Park Boulevard. He found a phone kiosk and called Tony Harker. But he wasn't back in his office yet, so Manny drove to a place that served Tex-Mex and had a big bowl of peppery chili and two icy bottles of Dos Equis. Then he called Harker again.

"I got canned," he reported.

Tony took it in his usual laid-back style. "Too bad," he said. "Any heat?"

"Some. He's a mouthy guy. But nothin' I couldn't handle."

"Good. Well, come on in; I've got another job for you."

"Yeah? What is it?"

"Roger Fortescue could use some help. He's investigating a homicide."

"No kid?" Suarez said. "Sounds inarresting."

52

A real estate agent found Simon Clark a nice two-bedroom condo on the Waterway down near Las Olas. It was completely furnished and had a terrace facing east. He signed a year's lease and moved in. He figured that eventually he'd have to go back to Chicago and pack up clothes, law books, and personal belongings, and have them shipped down. But that could wait; he had bought enough Florida duds to dress like a native, and the condo was equipped with linens and kitchen stuff, so he was all set there.

He inspected possible office space on Commercial, but he really didn't want to be located there, so he kept looking. The agent, Ellen St. Martin, was helping him, and the last time they spoke, she reported she had a lead on a small but elegant office up near Boca Raton. That would be a long daily commute, especially during the tourist season, but Simon didn't plan on a nine-to-five job, and it was important to have a flash front.

Nancy Sparco had delivered a copy of her husband's Super Sucker list, and it looked good to Clark: twenty-four names, addresses, and telephone numbers with notations on net worth, personal peccadilloes, and the kind of scams they bought: oil wells, grain futures, computer leasing, real estate, even fish farms and Arabian mares.

His Chicago checking account was getting low, and it hurt him to run up unpaid balances on his credit card accounts, considering the usurious interest those bastards charged, so Clark figured it was time to hit Mort Sparco. He thought about buying a gun—God knows it was easy enough in Florida—but decided against it. With the ammunition he had, a gun just wasn't necessary.

He arrived at the discount brokerage a little after one P.M., but had to cool his heels in that ratty reception room for almost a half-hour because "Mr. Sparco is busy with a client right now." Clark doubted that, but waited patiently until the summons, "Mr. Sparco will see you now," like the guy was a brain surgeon or something.

The broker was Mr. Congeniality, greeting Clark warmly, shaking his hand, getting him seated in a low club chair alongside his desk.

"Well now," he said briskly, "I suppose you want a progress report on your investment in the Fort Knox Fund. I can sum it up in one word: *dynamite!* Let's see, you put in a total of about sixty thousand, didn't you?"

"About that."

"What would you say if I told you the value of your stock now is close to seventy-five? Is that a barn-burner or isn't it?"

"Mr. Sparco," Clark said, "I'd like to cash in. I've decided to move back to Chicago. But first, of course, I have to pay off my father's home-equity loan. So if you'll sell my stock as soon as possible, I'd appreciate it."

He had to admire the broker. Sparco didn't seem shocked or startled, and his affable smile didn't fade. Instead, he leaned back in his swivel chair, took a cigar from his desk drawer, bit off the tip and spat it into his wastebasket. Then he lighted the cigar with a wooden kitchen match scratched on the underside of his desk. He blew a plume of smoke at the ceiling.

"Now why would you want to do that, Mr. Clark?" he asked pleasantly. "The fact that you're moving back to Chicago needn't make any difference; you can keep your account open here. We have a number of active clients who go north eight months out of the year. They phone collect whenever they want to trade or ask a question."

"I don't think so. I'd like to sell my Fort Knox Fund and close out my account. How soon can I get the money?"

"But why should you want to unload such a money-making investment? You're already showing a twenty-five-percent profit, and that stock has nowhere to go but up."

"I want to sell," Clark repeated stubbornly. "I want my money. Immediately."

Sparco showed the first signs of discomposure, tapping his cigar frequently on the ashtray rim, blinking rapidly. He licked his lips a few times, leaned toward Clark, tried a smile that didn't work.

"That might present some difficulties," he said. "As I'm sure you've noticed, the Fort Knox Fund is not listed on any of the exchanges. That means we'll have to negotiate a private trade for you. It may take some time."

"You mean I can't get my money?"

"Oh no," Sparco said. "No, no, no. Your investment is perfectly safe. It's just not as liquid as you might have thought."

"How long will it take to sell it?"

"Well, that's hard to say. We'll certainly make a best-faith effort to unload it, but I can't guarantee you'll get top market price."

"That's all right," Clark said. "I'll forget about the profit. I'll be satisfied if I just get my sixty thousand back."

"Mr. Clark," Sparco said earnestly, "one of the first things I learned about this business is that a broker should always try to fit the investment to the client. It's not always a matter of dollars and cents; it's frequently an emotional thing. The client should be *comfortable* with his investments. If he's not, then I'm not doing my job."

Clark listened closely to this spiel, wanting to remember the phraseology since it might prove valuable in his new career as a shark.

"Now it's obvious to me," the broker continued, "that you are not comfortable with the Fort Knox Fund, regardless of how well it's doing. All right, I accept that. Around here, the client calls the shots. Now what I suggest is this: Instead of closing out your account, you roll over your funds, including your profit, into another investment. I can suggest a number of equities as good or better than Fort Knox. I see no reason why you can't double your money in six months or less."

Simon Clark was silent, staring steadily at the other man. The silence went on so long that the broker began to fidget, relighting his cigar with fingers that trembled slightly.

Clark sighed, leaned back in the armchair, crossed his legs. "Mr. Sparco," he said quietly, "I want sixty thousand dollars from you. Cash, not a check. And I want it now."

"That's ridiculous!" the broker burst out.

"Do you know Sidney Coe?" Clark asked suddenly.

"What?"

"Do you know a man named Sidney Coe?"

"No, I've never heard the name."

"He runs a business on Oakland Park Boulevard."

Sparco shook his head. "Don't know him."

"He has a really rotten temper," Clark said. "Alleged to be a wife-beater. A dangerous, violent man."

"What's that got to do with me?"

"Well, since I've been in Florida I've had the time to poke around a little. I've talked to some interesting people and found out some interesting things."

"So?"

"So one of the interesting things I discovered is that office you rent up in West Palm Beach."

The cigar dropped from Mortimer Sparco's mouth onto the desktop. He made no effort to retrieve it but sat rigidly, gripping his chair arms.

"I also discovered," Clark went on, "that you've succeeded in turning several of Sid Coe's yaks. Although from what I understand about the man, it probably didn't take much persuasion. My informant tells me you've been clipping Sid Coe for about a hundred grand a month."

"What the hell's going on here?" Sparco cried.

"It's called blackmail," Clark said tonelessly. "I'm sure you've heard of it. Either I get my sixty thousand immediately or I leave your office, go directly to Coe's boiler room, and show him the evidence of how you've been jobbing him."

"What evidence? You've got no evidence!"

"A signed statement from your landlord in West Palm Beach who copied the license number on your black BMW. A Polaroid photo of the sign on the door of your office up there. It says Instant Investments, the name of Coe's business. And I can finger the yaks who've been working this scam with you. I figure all that'll be enough to convince Sid Coe. Ten minutes after I leave him, he'll come busting in here with steam coming out his ears. What do you think he'll do to you, Mr. Sparco? I hear he carries a gun."

Sparco gnawed furiously at his thumbnail. "Suppose I pay," he said. "Just suppose I give you back your sixty grand. How do I know you won't hit me again?"

"Easy," Clark said. "You pay me. Then you close down that West Palm Beach office. Tell the yaks the picnic is over. Drop the steal and figure a new way to cheat your friends. I'll be up in Chicago and won't know a thing about it."

"I haven't got 60K in the office."

"Sure you have. All you chiselers keep bribe and getaway cash available."

"I've got maybe thirty grand. No more than that. I'll have to go to the bank."

"That's okay," Simon Clark said cheerfully, rising. "I'll go with you."

53

David Rathbone had a long, tiring day. He drove to Lakeland in the morning, picked up the fifty thousand in queer from Herman Weisrotte, then turned around and drove back to Fort Lauderdale. On the trip home he stopped for a club sandwich and a bottle of Rolling Rock.

He delivered the cash to Jimmy Bartlett, then dropped in at the Palace Lounge to pay his tab for New Year's Day.

He had one vodka gimlet at the Palace, then started home. On impulse, he pulled off Atlantic Boulevard on the east side of the Intracoastal and parked in the concrete area under the bridge. There were a few other cars there, a few night fishermen dipping their lines in the glimmering channel.

Rathbone lighted a cigarette and tried to unwind. He knew Rita was waiting for him, but at that moment he wanted to be alone, watch the boats moving up and down the Waterway, and think about where he had been, where he was, where he was going.

It had been in his early teens that he had suddenly realized, almost with the force of a religious experience, how stupid most people were. They were just dumb, dumb, dumb, and nothing in his life since that revelation had changed his conviction that the great majority of Americans had air between their ears.

Why, there were people who believed wearing a copper bracelet would prevent arthritis, people who believed they could beat a three-card-monte dealer, people who believed in astrology, flying saucers, and the power of crystals. There were even people who believed professional wrestling was on the up-and-up. How could you respect the intelligence of the populace when a con woman could travel the country collecting contributions by claiming to be the penniless widow of the Unknown Soldier?

Rathbone came to regard this mass stupidity as a great natural resource. Just like oil in the ground, gold nuggets in a stream, or a stand of virgin forest, it was there to be exploited. The ignorance and greed of most people were simply inexhaustible, and a man would be a fool not to harvest that bounty. It was no sin to profit from the mooches' need to believe what they *wanted* to believe, ignoring reason and common sense.

Now he was in south Florida, a paradise for con men and swindlers.

Frank Little had once said that Ponce de León was looking for the Fountain of Youth but had found the Golden Mooch. The phrase had caught on with the Palace gang; they referred to Florida as The Land of the Golden Mooch. And best of all, hundreds of marks arrived every day, to live in a sunlit, semitropical climate, play shuffleboard, and listen to the siren song of the sharks—the human variety.

There just seemed to be no limit to the credulity of Florida mooches. They eagerly gulped the most rancid bait, and the saying amongst Florida sharpers was, "If the deal is so lousy that even a doctor won't bite, take it to a dentist." Deluding Floridians, Rathbone decided, was shooting fish in a barrel, and he questioned if he was doing the smart thing to leave the state in six months.

But he recalled the advice of an old slicker he had met when he first arrived in south Florida. This guy had been on the con for fifty years and had accumulated a nice pile for his old age, mostly by wholesaling counterfeit brand-name perfumes he concocted in his bathtub. But he had retired and now, just to keep himself busy, he was running a magic shop in Miami, selling tricks and illusions.

"Remember, kid," he had rumbled to David, "Easy Street goes two ways. You're young now, and you think it'll last forever. It never does. The swindles don't die—the old ones work as well as ever—but eventually you'll get tired of the game. Too much stress, too much pressure, never knowing when a mark might turn nasty and cut you up. Do what I did: Save up a stake, and then take the money and run. The game is really for young guys with balls and energy. But after a while you get to the point where you want to live a straight life, quit looking over your shoulder, and start smelling the roses."

There was probably some truth in that, Rathbone acknowledged, but he couldn't buy it all because it meant the way he was living now would eventually prove to be unsatisfying.

In six months he might cash in, but he knew that moving to Costa Rica wouldn't be the end of his plots. He'd be a bamboozler till the day he died simply because that's the way he was.

And the opportunities never seemed to end.

Like the fifty thousand in funny money he had just delivered to Jimmy Bartlett, to be salted into a deposit at a Palm Beach bank.

"The German gets twenty percent of the face value?" Bartlett had asked.

"That's right," Rathbone said. "I had to lean on him—he wanted thirty—but he finally agreed after I told him there'll be bigger jobs coming."

"Good," Bartlett said. "You're an A-Number-One yak."

Actually, Rathbone had conned the printer into accepting fifteen percent of the face value of the queer. David planned to skim that extra five percent for himself.

But Jimmy Bartlett, friend and partner, didn't have to know that.

54

Mike Mulligan would have confessed to being Jack the Ripper if they had asked him. They read him his rights, but he said he didn't want an attorney present during his questioning. Lester Crockett gently suggested it might be a wise thing to do, but Mulligan insisted: No lawyer.

So they had him sign a statement that he understood his rights but didn't wish any legal assistance. Just to make sure, they videotaped the reading of the rights and the banker's disclaimer.

Then he started talking.

Crockett did the questioning, with Anthony Harker and Henry Ullman as witnesses. The entire session was videotaped, and later Mulligan read the typed transcript and signed it. All this took place over the Christmas weekend.

Mulligan confessed that as an officer of the Crescent Bank of Boca Raton, he had accepted deposits of cash in excess of $10,000 from James Bartlett for the account of Mitchell Korne Enterprises, Inc., of Miami. In return, he had been supplied with cocaine by Mr. Bartlett. Mulligan had never used the drug himself—he was insistent on that—but had given it away to "friends."

He described how the deposited funds were eventually moved out of the Mitchell Korne account to a bank in Panama. He named the other officers of the Crescent Bank who were aware of these deals. But he bravely accepted complete responsibility for the money-laundering scheme and stated his intention to take his punishment "like a man."

"I think, Mr. Mulligan," Crockett said gravely, "that your punishment may prove to be milder than you anticipate. It all depends on your cooperation."

"You mean I won't have to go to jail?"

"Possibly not. What we want you to do is return to your job at the bank and carry on as before. Do not—I repeat, *do not*—inform your co-conspirators at the bank of your arrest. What we require is that you inform us promptly when James Bartlett calls to arrange for another deposit. Is that clear?"

"Yes."

"You will agree to accept that deposit, and then tell us the date and time. Meanwhile, Mr. Ullman will move into your apartment temporarily. He will also accompany you to and from work. In other words, Mr. Mulligan, you will be under constant surveillance. Understood?"

The banker nodded.

"Good," Crockett said with a bleak smile. "We appreciate your assistance."

Ullman and Mulligan left the office, with the agent's arm about the banker's thin shoulders.

Crockett waited until the door was closed, then shook his head softly. "No fool like an old fool," he said. "But at least he seems determined to make amends."

"Yes, sir," Harker said, "but we may have a king-size problem. When we nail Bartlett making the deposit, we'll have to scoop up all the other perps at the same time. Otherwise they'll hear of Bartlett's arrest, and the roaches will disappear into the woodwork. I think we better start working on the logistics of the crackdown right away. We'll have to make sure every suspect is covered, plus have enough men to confiscate the records of Rathbone, Coe, and Sparco. We'll also want to arrange for a coordinated DEA raid on Frank Little's warehouse, and pick up Herman Weisrotte and Irving Donald Gevalt. Then there's the problem of Mitchell Korne in Miami."

"I'll inform the Miami DEA office about that gentleman," Crockett said. "I presume they'll want to initiate their own investigation. Yes, I think you'd be wise to begin planning the roundup immediately. Then when we get the word on the Bartlett deposit, we'll be able to move quickly." He paused, stared at the other man, then asked curiously, "What role do you have in mind for Rita Sullivan?"

"I don't know," Tony said. "I'll have to think about it."

Simon Clark came into Harker's office and dumped a thick file on his desk.

"That's it," he said. "Everything I've been able to dig up on Mortimer Sparco's penny stock swindles. I can't do more without subpoenas."

"Got enough for an indictment?"

"More than enough. But it's all raw stuff. It really needs a staff to organize it and follow the leads."

Harker thought a moment. "I've got plenty on my plate without this," he said. "Besides, as I told you, this penny stock scam is a sideshow. I want to nail Sparco for dealing drugs. He'll do heavy time on that."

"Good," Clark said. "He's a slimy character."

"What I think I'll do," Harker went on, "is ship this file up to my old buddies in the SEC. They've got the manpower and contacts to handle it."

"That makes sense," Clark said. "Can I go back to Chicago now?"

Tony looked at him in surprise. "In the middle of winter?" he said. "That *doesn't* make sense. Don't you like Florida?"

The agent shrugged. "It has its points, I guess, but I prefer the big city."

"Well, I have another job for you before you cut loose. There's an old guy named Irving Donald Gevalt involved in all this. He claims to be a rare book dealer, but he's really a paperman. He's supplied David Rathbone with phony ID, and I suspect the others in the gang use him, too. See what you can find out about his past history and present activities."

"You want me to try making a buy?"

"It wouldn't do any harm. And if Gevalt gets spooked and tells Rathbone, it might make him sweat a little. I'd like that."

"All right," Clark said, "I'll see what I can do. When are you going to bust everyone?"

"Soon," Harker said. "I'm working on the details right now. I'll probably want you to lead the team that takes Sparco."

Clark did a good job of covering his shock. "Whatever you want," he said casually. "Meanwhile I'll get to work on Gevalt."

"He's supposed to have a wife one-third his age," Harker said, smiling. "I hear she wears the world's smallest bikini."

"I couldn't care less," Simon Clark said. "I'm a happily married man."

They sat around a littered table in the Burger King and worked on double cheeseburgers, french fries, coleslaw, and big containers of cola, using up a stack of paper napkins.

"Jack Liddite is handling the file," Roger Fortescue said, "and he's not happy about our nosing around."

"You're a smoke and I'm a spic," Manny Suarez said. "Why should he be happy?"

Harker grinned at both of them. "Screw Jack Liddite," he said. "Whoever he is."

"A homicide dick," Fortescue said. "And he wanted to know what our interest was in Termite Tommy. I mumbled something about his being involved in pushing queer, but I don't think he believed me."

"Homicide?" Tony said. "So it *was* murder?"

"Well, Tommy had enough alcohol in him to put the Foreign Legion to sleep, and when he went into the canal, he smacked his head a good one on the dash. But what actually killed him was that someone stuck a sharpened ice pick into his right ear. It took the medical examiner awhile to find it, but that's what did the job."

Suarez started on his second cheeseburger. "It would be nice," he said, "if he was out cold from the booze before he got stuck."

"Yeah," Roger said, "that would be nice. So where do we go from here?"

Harker slopped ketchup on his french fries. "You said Tommy left Lakeland on New Year's Day?"

"That was the last his motel owner saw him."

"Could he have been murdered that night?"

"Possible," Fortescue said. "It falls within the ME's four- or five-day time frame. He couldn't be more exact than that. After all, the guy had been marinating in canal water awhile."

"Let's figure he drove down here from Lakeland and got it that night," Tony said slowly. "The last time he came down he went to the Palace Lounge on Commercial."

"Right," Fortescue said. "Met David Rathbone."

"Well, on the evening of New Year's Day, Rathbone got smashed in the Palace Lounge. So drunk that the bartender had to call Rathbone's woman to come collect him."

The agents didn't ask how he knew that. They munched their burgers in silence.

"It's theen stuff," Manny said finally.

"Sure, it's thin," Harker agreed. "But what else have we got?"

"Okay," Fortescue said, "so let's figure that before Termite Tommy ends up in the canal, he goes to the Palace Lounge and meets with David Rathbone. Then he leaves, and Rathbone stays and gets plastered. If that holds, then someone at the Palace might remember Tommy being there on New Year's Day. Maybe the parking valet. Maybe the bartender."

"The bartender's name is Ernie," Harker said.

"Ernesto," Manny Suarez said. "I like it. Roger, let's you and me go talk to Ernesto."

"Let's run a trace on him first," Fortescue said. "I like to know who we're dealing with."

"This is fun," Suarez said. "Better than selling pork bellies."

Tony said, "Just be sure to ask Ernie if David Rathbone met with Termite Tommy on New Year's Day."

Roger stared at him. "Regardless of how Ernie answers that, he's going to call Rathbone and warn him the moment we leave."

"I know," Harker said happily.

55

It had chilled off to 59°F overnight, but the morning of Friday, January 26, was sharp and clear, and the radio weatherman predicted the afternoon would be sunny and in the low 70s.

They decided it would be too nippy on the terrace, so they came down to the dining room in their robes. Theodore served a down-home breakfast of fried eggs, plump pork sausages, grits, and hush puppies.

"No office for you today," David said. "I think we'll pay a visit to Irving Donald Gevalt and get you fixed up with a passport."

"In my own name?" Rita asked.

He thought a moment. Then: "No, I don't think so. We'll use the ID of Gloria Ramirez you used at the Boca bank. You'll have to provide a photo, but that's no problem."

She glanced around to make certain Theodore was out of the room. "David, will Blanche and Theodore be going with us?"

He shook his head. "Unfortunately, no. Too many complications. Right now they've got fake green cards Gevalt provided. If I can work a deal, they may be able to join us later."

"What are you going to tell your clients when we leave?"

He grinned at her. "Nothing. They'll find out eventually. But by then we'll be long gone."

"Poor Birdie Winslow," Rita said. "She'll be devastated."

Rathbone laughed. "Did I tell you she wanted me to move in with her? Scout's honor. She had visions of the two of us sharing a big condo on the beach."

"What did you tell her?"

"I told her I already had a roomie."

They went upstairs to dress and, a little before noon, drove out to the Gevalt Rare Book Center. The old man seemed delighted to see them. He called into the back room, and a few moments later his wife, still wearing her fringed black bikini, came out with two wine spritzers for Rita and David.

"None for you?" Rathbone asked.

The gaffer shook his head sadly. "Even such a mild drink my stomach cannot stand. A glass of warm milk before I go to bed: That's my speed. This is a social visit, David?"

"Not entirely. You provided a package of paper for Rita in the name of Gloria Ramirez."

"I remember. Any problems?"

"None whatsoever. But now we need a passport in the same name. Something that looks used."

"Of course. Visa stamps and so forth. You have a photo?"

"We'll bring you one."

"Not necessary."

The young blonde went into the back room and came out carrying an old Nikon with an attached flashgun.

"The camera is ancient," Gevalt said with his gap-toothed grin, "but it does good work. Like me. David, could I speak to you a moment in private?"

His wife began to take close-ups of Rita while the two men moved away to a corner of the littered shop.

"Yesterday a man came in," Gevalt started. "He is wearing Florida clothes, but he talks like the Midwest. Hard and fast. A big-city man. He asks if I have a first edition McGuffey. I ask him what edition does he want? Is he looking for a reader, speller, or primer? He begins to hem and haw, and it is obvious to me he knows nothing about rare books. Finally he says he has heard I can provide identification papers. He needs a birth certificate and Social Security card and is willing to pay any price."

"You ever see this guy before?" Rathbone asked.

"No. Never."

"It's possible one of your clients talked, and this man overheard and really did need paper."

Gevalt shook his head. "If any of my clients talk, they wouldn't be my clients. I am very choosy, David; you know that. No, this man was law; I am convinced of it. Something about him: a clumsy arrogance."

"What did you say to him?"

"I became very angry. Told him I was a legitimate businessman making a living selling rare books, and I would never do anything illegal, and he should leave my shop immediately. He left, but it still bothers me. It is the first time anything like that has happened. David, do you feel I am in danger?"

"Of course not," Rathbone said. "Even if the guy was a cop—and you're not sure he was—it was just a fishing expedition. You handled it exactly right. If the law had anything on you, you'd be out of business already. You have nothing to worry about, believe me."

The old man looked at him, and his rheumy eyes filled. "Worry?" he said. "That's all I do—worry. About that stupid man with his first edition McGuffey. About one of my motels which is losing money because the manager is dishonest. *Dishonest*, David! And also I fear my wife has a lover. Oh yes, I have seen him lurking around. A muscular young man and he has—oh God, David, I hate to mention it but he has a tattoo on his right bicep. And you tell me not to worry!"

Rathbone put a hand lightly on Gevalt's shoulder. "It will all work out," he said soothingly. "The important thing is to think positively. I always do. Who can remember last year's problems? Everything will turn out all right, you'll see."

The old man took out a disgraceful handkerchief and blew his nose. "You're right, David," he said, snuffling. "I must think positively."

On the drive back home, Rita asked, "What were you and Gevalt talking about while I was having my picture taken?"

Rathbone laughed. "The poor old man thinks his wife has a boyfriend. A hulk with a tattoo."

"Can't say I blame her. What would you do if you found out I had a boyfriend?"

"Couldn't happen," David said. "If I can't trust you, who can I trust?"

56

The previous day's tapes were delivered to Anthony Harker's motel every morning at about seven A.M. He listened to the first run-through while he was shaving. He found he was listening to but not hearing the personal portions, much as one might look at something without seeing it. He closed his mind to the intimate murmurs and cries; they had, he kept assuring himself, nothing to do with him. He was interested only in names, dates, hard facts.

On Saturday morning, January 27, he heard Rita and David discussing a visit to Gevalt. Then Rathbone joked about not informing his clients before he decamped, and Birdie Winslow was mentioned. That rang a bell with Harker; Rita had given him that name weeks ago, but he had never followed up on it.

He made himself a cup of instant coffee and chewed on a stale bagel. Then he went to the office, planning to put in a full day. Work was the only relief he could find from brooding on what was tearing him apart: those murmurs and cries that had nothing to do with him.

He found a note on his desk from the night duty officer. It was a message from Henry Ullman in Boca: Please call him ASAP. Harker popped an antihistamine capsule, and phoned.

"It's on," Ullman reported. "Bartlett called Mulligan last night. He's going to make a deposit at the bank on Friday, February second, at noon. Got that?"

"Got it," Tony said. "Next Friday morning at noon. Hank, you handle the collar. I'll get some warm bods to you early on Friday to help out. Two men be enough?"

"Plenty," Ullman said. "I don't expect Bartlett to turn mean. What about the other bank officers involved?"

"We'll scoop them up later. I'm hoping Bartlett will make a deal with us. Then we'll have corroborative evidence for Mulligan's confession. How's the little man acting?"

"Believe it or not, I think he's excited. It's probably the most dramatic thing that's ever happened to him."

"Except for those Saturday night parties."

"Yeah," Ullman said, laughing. "The Great Toilet Tank Capers. He'll never forget those."

Harker now had a date and a time, D day and H hour, and could begin firming up the destruction of the Palace gang. But before he got to work on schedules and personnel deployment, there was something he wanted to do first: He looked up Birdie Winslow in various telephone directories and finally found her in Pompano Beach. He was startled to discover she lived less than a half-mile from him.

Before he called, he pondered on his best approach. If he told Winslow the truth about her "financial planner," she'd probably scream bloody murder, demand all her funds back from Rathbone, and tip off the shark that the law was closing in. Harker decided to play it cool.

"Birdie Winslow?" he asked.

"Yes. Who is this?"

"My name is Anthony Harker. I hate to bother you, but I've been considering employing a money manager, and David Rathbone is one of the possibilities on my list. Mr. Rathbone has provided me with a list of his clients so I can check his track record. I was hoping you'd be kind enough to spare me a few moments. I'm in your neighborhood, and I promise not to keep you long."

"Well," she said, "I planned to go shopping today, but I guess I can spare a little time. How soon can you be here?"

"Twenty minutes," Harker said. "Thank you very much—uh—is it Miss or Mrs. Winslow?"

"Mrs.," Birdie said. "And your name is Harder?"

"Harker. Anthony Harker. I'm on my way, Mrs. Winslow, and thank you."

She turned out to be a buxom matron, a bit blowsy in Harker's opinion.

She was wearing a black gabardine suit, and both jacket and skirt were too snug. Like many overweight women, she had legs which were exceptionally shapely, the ankles slender. But the scarlet patent leather pumps didn't help.

She was pleasant enough, got him seated in an armchair, and offered him a drink which he declined. She sat on the couch, but even at that distance he could smell her perfume, a musky scent he thought much too heavy for this woman and this climate.

Her apartment was as overstuffed as she, with too much of everything in lurid colors and clashing styles. Near the door, he noted, was a stack of matched luggage, so new that the manufacturer's tags were still tied to the handles.

"Mrs. Winslow," he started, "I appreciate your seeing me on such short notice, and I'll try to make this as brief as possible. As I told you on the phone, I'm planning to hire someone to handle my investments, and naturally I want to learn as much as I can about the person I select. If I ask questions you'd rather not answer, please tell me and I'll understand. Believe me, I have no wish to pry into your financial affairs. I'd just like to know whether or not you can recommend David Rathbone as an asset manager."

"Oh, ask anything you like," she said blithely.

"Could you tell me how you happened to meet him and become his client?"

She thought a moment. "Why, I believe it was Ellen St. Martin who introduced us. Ellen is the real estate agent who found this apartment for me, and she suggested David was the perfect man to take care of my finances. After my husband died, I just couldn't handle all the investments he had made. And then I had the insurance money, of course. Ralph left me very well fixed, I'll say that for him. Then I met David and was quite impressed with him."

"You investigated his record?"

"Oh yes. I spoke to several of his clients, and they all were very enthusiastic about what he had done for them. Why, he had increased their investment income forty or fifty percent a year."

"And has he done as well for you?"

"He certainly has! I think my net worth has increased at least that much since I've been with him, and that's been less than six months."

"Remarkable," Harker said. "Do you receive monthly statements from Mr. Rathbone?"

"I surely do."

"And monthly statements from the brokers he deals with? Confirmation slips on your trades?"

"Oh no," she said gaily, "none of that. David said it's just unnecessary paper. After all, everything's included on his monthly statements."

"Uh-huh," Tony said. "When you started with Mr. Rathbone, I suppose he had you sign some documents. A full power of attorney perhaps, or a management contract."

"I know I signed some papers, but David said they weren't important, and I could get my money back from him whenever I liked."

"You didn't ask if Mr. Rathbone is registered with the Securities and Exchange Commission or the Florida Department of Securities?"

"No, but I'm sure that if he's supposed to be registered, then he is. You could ask him."

"Of course, I'll do that. Did he ever mention if there was an insurance policy in effect to protect your account from fraud or theft?"

"No, the subject never came up. But as long as David will return my money whenever I ask, there's no need for an insurance policy, is there?"

"No," Harker said, realizing this woman was hopelessly naive, "no need. Mrs. Winslow, would it be too much if I asked to see your most recent statement from Mr. Rathbone? I'd like to get some idea of the type of investments he prefers."

"I don't see why not," Birdie said, rising. "You'll see that David is making me lots of money."

The statement she brought him was, he noted, a computer printout. But that didn't mean a thing. It was a perfect example of GIGO: Garbage In, Garbage Out. The statement listed several Certificates of Deposit at Texas and California banks Harker had never heard of. All were allegedly paying over thirty percent. But the bulk of Mrs. Winslow's wealth appeared to be invested in the Fort Knox Commodity Trading Fund.

"This Fort Knox Fund," Tony said. "What is that?"

"Oh, that's something David heard about through close friends on Wall Street. He got me in on the ground floor, and it's just made oodles of money."

"But what exactly *is* it?"

"I'm not sure, but I think they buy and sell things. You know, like wheat and corn."

Harker nodded and stood up. "Thank you very much, Mrs. Winslow. You've been a big help, and I appreciate it."

"I hope I've convinced you that David is really the best in the business. Everyone says so."

"Well, he's certainly high on my list," Harker said. "I expect to be having a long talk with him very soon." He started to leave, then paused at the stack of new luggage. "Planning a trip, Mrs. Winslow?" he asked, smiling.

Unexpectedly she giggled like a schoolgirl. "Well, if you promise not to tell anyone, I'm taking a long vacation in about six months—with David!"

Harker kept the smile frozen on his face. "That sounds like fun," he said. "Seems to me that you and Mr. Rathbone have more than a business relationship."

"He's a *divine* man," she said breathlessly. "Just *divine!*"

Tony nodded and got out of there, not knowing whether to laugh, curse, or weep.

The moment the door closed behind him, Birdie Winslow picked up the phone and called David Rathbone.

57

On Monday, January 29, Suarez and Fortescue had lunch at the Tex-Mex place Manny had discovered. They ate cheese enchiladas, rice, refried beans, tortillas, guacamole salad, tacos, nachos, plenty of hot sauce, and two beers each. As they devoured this stupendous feast, they had their notebooks open on the table and exchanged skinny on Ernie the bartender.

"Full name Ernest K. Hohlman," Suarez reported. "Claims to be forty-four. Divorced. Got a young daughter. They live in a condo up at Lighthouse Point. Ernie was on the force in Manhattan. He came down here about five years ago and went to work at the Palace Lounge. When I called the NYPD, they said he resigned, but I finally got hold of a landsman who was willing to *hablilla* for a while. He says Ernie was allowed to resign quote for personal reasons unquote after he was caught shaking down crack dealers."

"Pension?" Fortescue asked.

"*Nada*. But he owns his condo, drives a white Toyota Cressida, and has almost fifty Gs of CDs in the bank. Neat for an ex-cop and bartender."

"You have a gift for understatement," Roger said. "Well, I talked to all my snitches and my snitches' snitches, and I've got a pretty good idea where Ernie's gelt is coming from. The guy is a world-class hustler. I mean he's into *everything*: books bets and peddles pot, coke, stolen credit cards, and merchandise that 'fell off the truck.' Also, he pimps for a young call girl, a real looker. His daughter."

"That's not nice," Manny said.

"No, it's not," Fortescue agreed. "I think that maybe after we finish this heartburn banquet we should go visit Ernie and point out the evil of his ways."

"How we gonna handle it? You wanna try the good cop-bad cop routine?"

"Nah," Roger said. "He was a cop once himself; he'd recognize the plot. Let's both just be nasty."

"Hokay," Suarez said. "I can do nasty."

They drove over to the Grand Palace in Manny's Ford Escort. It was then almost three o'clock, and there was only one parking valet on duty. He was a young black who looked like he could slam-dunk without jumping.

"Let me talk to him alone for a few minutes," Fortescue said, and Suarez nodded.

They waited until the Escort was parked, and the valet came trotting back. Roger drew him aside.

"A moment of your time, bro," the agent said, and showed his ID.

The youth raised his palms outward. "I'm guilty," he said. "Whatever it was, I did it."

Fortescue smiled, took a morgue Polaroid of Termite Tommy out of his jacket pocket, held it up.

"You do this?" he asked.

"Jesus!" the valet said. "He looks dead."

"If he isn't," Roger said, "he must be cold as hell in that icebox. Ever see him before?"

The boy studied the grisly photo with fearful fascination. "What happened to him?" he asked.

"He died," the officer said patiently and repeated, "Ever see him before?"

"Yeah, he was around a few times. Drove an old beat-up truck. We called him El Cheapo because he always parked his heap himself."

"That's the guy. Did you work on New Year's Day?"

"Nope. There was only one valet on duty that day. Al Seymour. I was home and I can prove it."

"That's good," Fortescue said. "Now I won't have to goose you with a cattle prod."

The youth was horrified. "You don't really do that, do you?"

"All the time," Roger said, motioning to Suarez. "This job has a lot of fringe benefits."

They entered the Palace Lounge through the side door. There were three men drinking beer at one table, and a middle-aged couple working on whiskey sours at another. The only other person in the room was the man behind the bar. He was reading a supermarket tabloid. He put it aside when Roger and Manny swung onto barstools.

"Yessir, gents," he said, "what's your pleasure?"

"Mine's pussy," Suarez said, and turned to his partner. "What's yours?"

"A boneless pork loin with yams," Fortescue said, and displayed his ID.

"The sheriff's office?" the bartender said. "I know some of the guys there. They stop by occasionally. What division you in?"

"Community relations," Roger said. "This is my partner, Manuel Suarez. Your name is Ernest Hohlman?"

"That's right. Everyone calls me Ernie."

"Uh-huh. Did you work here on New Year's Day, Ernie?"

The bartender stalled a beat. "Sure I did," he said finally. "Got paid triple-time because of the holiday."

The agent placed the morgue photo of Termite Tommy on the bar. "Know this guy?"

Ernie glanced at it. "Nope. Never saw him before in my life."

"That was queek," Suarez said. "Wasn't that queek, Roger?"

"Quick?" Fortescue said. "Sheet, it was fuckin' instantaneous. Take another look, Ernie. A nice long look."

The bartender stared. "Dead?" he asked.

"Couldn't be deader," Manny said cheerfully. "Ever see him when he was alive and kicking?"

"No, I don't make him. Listen, this is a busy bar. Maybe he stopped by once for a drink. You can't expect me to remember every customer."

"Did he stop by on New Year's Day?" Suarez said.

"I don't recall him being here."

"That's odd," Fortescue said. "The parking valet on duty that day, Al Seymour, says this guy was here."

"Maybe he was, maybe he wasn't. I can't swear to it either way. You men want a drink? On the house?"

"No, thanks," Fortescue said. "We never drink on duty, do we, Manny?"

"Never," Suarez said. "Against regulations."

"David Rathbone a customer of yours?" Roger asked suddenly. "One of your regulars?"

"Mr. Rathbone?" Ernie said cautiously. "Yeah, he stops by occasionally. Hey, what's this all about? If you could tell me, I'll be happy to help you any way I can. I used to be a cop myself. In New York."

"Yeah, we heard about that," Suarez said. "I wouldn't want to be a cop in New York with all those crack dealers running around with Uzis. How come you left the NYPD, Ernie?"

"I just got tired of the cold weather up there."

"Cold?" Manny said. "I thought maybe it was because it was too hot. So David Rathbone was in here on New Year's Day?"

"He could have been. I really don't remember. Hey, those guys are signaling for another round of beers. I gotta go wait on the customers."

"Go ahead," Fortescue said, "but don't try to make a run for it. The place is surrounded."

"Very funny," Ernie said.

By the time he returned behind the bar, the two officers had decided to lean a little harder.

"We're going to level with you, Ernie," Fortescue said. "After all, you used to be a cop so we know you'll cooperate."

"Sure I will," Ernie said.

"So we'll tell you some of what we've got. The clunk in the photograph was a two-bit con man who went by the moniker of Termite Tommy. We know he was here on New Year's Day. That night someone stuck an ice pick in his right ear. We're talking homicide, Ernie. We also know David Rathbone was here on New Year's Day. Now all we want to know is whether or not Rathbone and Termite Tommy met, maybe had a drink together, maybe talked awhile."

"I don't remember," Ernie said.

"Oh Ernesto," Suarez said sadly. "You are not cooperating, and you promised."

"Listen, I can't tell you something I don't remember, can I?"

"Try," Fortescue urged. "Surely you recall how Rathbone got drunk that evening and you had to call his woman to come get him. You remember that, don't you?"

Ernie wiped the top of the bar with a rag, making slow circles, not looking at them. "Well, maybe he had a few too many," he said in a low voice. "Yeah, now I remember; he got smashed."

"But you don't remember his meeting with Termite Tommy?"

They waited, but Ernie was silent.

"Why you protecting this guy Rathbone?" Suarez demanded. "He's your brother or something? You talk or you don't talk, he's going to take a fall. But you don't talk, you fall right along with him."

"Me?" Ernie said indignantly. "Take a fall? What the hell for? I haven't done anything illegal."

Manny sighed. "Tell him, Roger," he said. "Tell him the good news."

"Well, first of all, Ernie, is the problem of your making book. That's not a capital crime, I admit, but you gotta agree it's illegal. And then we got the grass and coke you been peddling. Not pushing it exactly, but it's available here just for your friends—and from what we hear, you haven't got an enemy in the world. Then we have the stuff that 'fell off the truck' and the stolen credit cards. That adds up to quite a total, wouldn't you say, Manny?"

"Oh yeah," Suarez said. "Years and years."

"Now we haven't dotted all the i's and crossed all the t's on these things," Fortescue said to the bartender. "You've been a cop; you know the drill. We get a squeal or pick up a tidbit from a snitch, and then we go to work, turning over rocks to see what's underneath. That means pounding the pavement and ringing a lot of doorbells. You could save us all that time and trouble."

Suarez tugged at his sleeve. "The *puta*, Roger," he said.

Fortescue snapped his fingers. "Right, Manny," he said. "Thanks for reminding me. That hooker you're running," he said to Ernie with a bright smile. "Your daughter. We'll have to pick her up and take her in for questioning, of course."

"The gossip sheets will love it," Manny said. " 'Ex-Cop's Daughter Accused of Soliciting.' On local TV, too."

Ernie had listened to all this like a spectator at a tennis match, his head turning back and forth as each agent spoke. But when his daughter was mentioned, he froze and stared directly at Roger.

"Listen," he said hoarsely, "maybe we can make a deal."

"I don't see why not," Fortescue said.

58

Simon Clark imagined that having decided to flip from the side of the law to the side of the lawless, he might suffer guilt or shame. But he discovered that converting from a U.S. assistant district attorney to a south Florida shark was no more painful than switching jobs, going from one corporation to another.

All it entailed was redirecting his energies and talents. His skills at organizing, managing, setting goals and achieving them—all that was still important. Even more crucial was his courtroom experience, the ability to convince and manipulate witnesses, judges, and juries. He called this "human relations," and he knew how vital they would be in his new business.

Best of all, of course, was that he would now be self-employed, and no longer have to play the degrading game of office politics. To be one's own boss—that was exhilarating but scary. If the profits of success were to be all his, so would be the losses of failure. Still, he was convinced the risk-benefit ratio was in his favor.

On Tuesday evening, January 30, he sat at a florid imitation of a Louis Quinze desk in his new condo and worked on his accounts: cash on hand, debts, expected income. He figured he could squeak by for six months without cutting a deal. But he was confident that long before his funds were exhausted, he would be flush with Other People's Money, and on his way to becoming wealthy.

He had already made progress. He had learned, for example, that his real estate agent, Ellen St. Martin, would be willing to introduce him to potential mooches in return for a finder's fee. And he found that one of the best places to meet and cozen pigeons was at public seminars on investing hosted by legitimate stock brokerages. And, of course, to get him started, he had that copy of Mortimer Sparco's Super Sucker list.

He was reviewing the list when his phone rang, and he knew that if it wasn't a wrong number, it was either Nancy Sparco or Ellen St. Martin. It was Nancy.

"Hi, big man," she said breezily. "Feel like having company?"

"At this time of night?" he said. "How come?"

"Because my jerko husband is out playing poker with his crummy pals and won't be home till midnight."

"All right," Clark said, "come on down."

"Don't I always?" she said. "Be there in a half-hour."

He had discovered her favorite drink was Pimm's Cup No. 1 with seltzer and a lemon slice, and he had stocked the makings. He had a drink ready for her when she arrived, and was working on his second gin and bitters.

"I'm glad you called," he told her. "I've got something for you."

"An erection?" she said. "Just what I wanted."

"Even better than that," he said, and took two envelopes from the desk drawer. He handed the thin one to her. "Twenty-five hundred for the Super Sucker list." He thrust the plump one into her hands. "And twenty-five thousand for your new business."

She opened the flaps frantically, and when she saw the green, she just squealed.

"Oh you sweetheart!" she cried. "I love you, love you, love you!"

He watched, amused, as she counted the money with nimble fingers. Then she looked up, still amazed.

"You got your stake back from Morty?"

"Uh-huh."

"How did you manage that?"

"Oh, I just persuaded him. He listened to reason."

"Bullshit," she said. "You must have held a gun to his head. But I don't care how you did it; it's a whole new life for me."

"Listen," he said, "don't stick all that money in your bank account. If a cash deposit is ten grand or over, the bank's got to report it to Uncle Sam."

"I know that, dummy. Don't worry, I'll spread it around. Then it's ta-ta, Morty."

"You're moving out on him?"

"You bet your sweet ass. By this time tomorrow, my hubby will be frying his own calamari. I always hated that stuff."

"Where are you going when you leave?" Simon asked.

She shrugged. "Probably check into a motel temporarily until I can find a decent place."

He drained his drink and mixed himself another. "How about moving in with me? Temporarily. I've got an extra bedroom."

She looked at him shrewdly. "Expect me to pay half the maintenance, utilities, and food bills?"

He was offended. "Of course not," he said huffily.

She patted his cheek. "Simmer down, sport," she said. "I'm willing to pay my own way. But if you want to take it out in trade, that's okay, too. Tell me something: What are you going to be doing while I'm setting up my new business?"

"Setting up *my* new business. I told you I'm going to join the game."

"I thought you were just blowing smoke."

"No, I meant it. I'm going to become an investment adviser."

She looked at him doubtfully. "Don't you need a license for that?"

"Nope. Anyone can call himself a financial planner or a money manager. You don't need a license to steal. All you need is a plentiful supply of mooches. When you get your escort service organized, maybe you'll be able to steer some marks my way."

"Of course I will, honey. After all you've done for me . . . Hey, let's celebrate our new careers with a bang."

She tugged him by the hand into the master bedroom, a flossy place. She stripped down swiftly. She was wearing white nylon panties with a red heart embroidered on the crotch.

"See?" she said. "I've got a heart on, too."

She flipped down the top sheet, then suddenly stopped.

"Wait a minute!" she yelled.

She ran into the living room, came back with the two envelopes of money. She dumped them around to make a green, crinkly layer, then threw herself naked on top.

"I've always wanted to do this," she said throatily, and rolled around, burrowing into the money, eyes closed, mouth open, almost panting with pleasure.

Then she opened arms and legs to him, and that's how they screwed, on a bed of cash.

59

At noon on Tuesday, David Rathbone drove over to Bartlett's home on Bayview Drive in response to Jimmy's phone call. The two men sat in the Bentley in the driveway, and Rathbone lighted a cigarette.

"You're smoking too much," Bartlett observed.

"And drinking too much," Rathbone added. "So what else is new? Why the hurry-up call?"

"I'm making a deposit at the Crescent in Boca at noon on Friday. Mitchell Korne says it will be more than a million."

"Wow," Rathbone said. "And you can quote me on that."

"I think we can safely take out two hundred grand," Bartlett said, "and replace it with our funny money. Providing the German can print that much by Thursday night."

"Printing isn't the problem," Rathbone said. "It's getting the stuff at the last minute, while the bills are still in one piece. Print it up too soon and we'll have a sackful of shit. How about this: I'll drive up to Lakeland first thing tomorrow morning and tell Weisrotte we want the queer by late Thursday afternoon. Then on Thursday, I'll drive back to Lakeland again to pick it up."

"That's a lot of driving."

"For two hundred thousand I'd drive to LA and back."

"All right then," Bartlett said, "let's do it your way. You get the stuff to me by late Thursday, and we're in business. I haven't read anything more about Termite Tommy, have you?"

"Not since that first story. It just fell out of the news. I guess the cops figure he got drunk and drove into the canal. They have more important things to worry about than the accidental death of a lush."

"Of course," Bartlett said.

Rathbone drove back to the town house and went directly to his office. He jotted some numbers on a pad. Two hundred thousand dollars. Deduct the German's fifteen percent and Bartlett's forty. That left Rathbone with ninety thousand clear. He grinned at that. Not bad for two trips to Lakeland.

He was working on his personal ledger when the office phone rang, and for a moment he was tempted to just ignore it until the caller gave up. But then he figured it might be Bartlett wanting to add more details on the deal. He picked it up.

"David Rathbone Investment Management."

"David!" Birdie Winslow said, and her laugh was a trill. "How nice to catch you in. I've been calling and calling."

"I've been awfully busy, Birdie," he said. "How have you been?"

"In seventh heaven," she said, "dreaming about our trip. I can't begin to tell you all the wonderful things I've bought. Luggage and dresses and hats and shoes and just everything."

"Why not," he said. "You deserve it."

"But that's not why I called. I just wanted you to know that I think I've won you a new client."

"Oh?" he said, suddenly cautious. "How did you do that?"

"Well, you know that man you gave my name to, that Anthony Harker, he stopped by last Saturday and asked a lot of questions about you and if I was satisfied with your services, and of course I said I was, and I think by the time he left he was convinced that you were the right investment adviser for him. He said he was going to have a talk with you. Have you heard from him yet?"

"Anthony Harker? No, not yet."

"Well, I'm sure you will. I showed him my last statement, and he was just amazed at how much money you were making for me. I told him you were the best in the business, and everyone said so. Aren't you proud of me?"

"I certainly am," he said. "Thank you for the recommendation."

He finally got her off the phone and sat awhile, staring at his big green safe. Then he dragged out his telephone directories and looked up the name. No Anthony Harker in Lauderdale, Boca Raton, or Pompano Beach. He sat back and lighted another cigarette with hands that were not quite steady. He recalled what Irving Donald Gevalt had told him, and wondered if Anthony Harker was interested in McGuffey first editions.

He left for Lakeland early Wednesday morning, January 31. Rita was still asleep, so he scribbled a note saying he'd return in time to take her to dinner and maybe stop by the Palace for a few drinks with the gang.

It was a cool, crisp morning, but he knew it would warm up later. He didn't wear a suit, just linen slacks and an aqua polo shirt with a bolo tie, the clasp set with a thirty-carat emerald-cut blue topaz.

He drove with the windows down; the new world smelled sweet and clean. But he was in no mood to enjoy it; all he could think about was what Gevalt and Birdie had told him. Live like a jackal, he told himself, and you develop an animal instinct for danger. And right now he had the feeling he was being stalked, but by whom and for what reason he could not fathom.

So intent was he on trying to puzzle it out that he was not aware of how fast he was driving until he was pulled over by a state trooper on Highway 27.

"Know what you were doing?" the officer asked, writing in his pad.

"To tell you the truth I don't," Rathbone said with a nervous laugh. "My wife's having our first baby in a hospital in Lakeland, and I'm in a hurry to get there."

"Nice try but no cigar," the trooper said, handing him the ticket. "I clocked you at eighty, at least. Take it easy and maybe you'll live to see your first kid."

"I'll do that," Rathbone said, and then, after the officer went back to his car, "Up yours!"

He was in Lakeland by noon and was happy to find Weisrotte reasonably sober. He told the printer he wanted two hundred thousand in fake 100s by late Thursday.

"Zo," the German said. "And when my share do I receive?"

"Early next week," Rathbone promised. "You can count on it. You're the most important man in this operation, Herman, and we want to keep you happy."

"Goot," Weisrotte said, and insisted Rathbone have a glass of schnapps with him before leaving. It was caustic stuff, and David wondered if the printer used it to clean his presses.

On the drive home he tried to convince himself that he was foolish to worry; the guy at Gevalt's could have been a rube hoping to buy forged ID at an old-book store, and Birdie's Anthony Harker could have been a legit investor looking for an adviser. But none of that really made sense, and Rathbone felt someone closing in on him, a faceless hunter who came sniffing at the spoor, hungry for the kill.

He was pulled over again for speeding; same stretch of highway, same trooper.

"How's the wife?" the officer asked, writing out the ticket. "Have the kid yet?"

"Not yet," Rathbone said with a sick smile. "False alarm."

"Uh-huh," the trooper said, handing him the ticket. "Have a nice day."

He was in a vile mood by the time he got home, but after a vodka gimlet and a hot shower, he felt better, reasoning that he had been in squeezes before and had always wriggled out. The important thing was to keep his nerve.

The sight of Rita helped lift him out of his funk. She wore a tight miniskirt of honey-colored linen and an oversized nubby sweater with a deep V-neck that displayed her coppery tan and advertised the fact that she was bra-less. Her gypsy hair swung free, and when they sauntered into an elegant French restaurant on the Waterway, she made every other woman in the place look like Barbie.

They did the whole bit: escargots; a Caesar salad for two; rare tournedos with tiny mushroom caps and miniature carrots; Grand Marnier soufflé; and chilled Moët.

"This is living," Rita said. Then: "Why are you staring at me like that?"

"Ever hear of a man called Anthony Harker?" he asked.

She fumbled in her purse for a cigarette and signaled the hovering waiter for a light. "Nope," she said. "The name rings no bells with me."

The bill arrived, and Rathbone offered his stolen credit card. It went through without a hitch, and he gave munificent cash tips to the waiter and maître d'.

They drove to the Palace and found everyone partying up a storm at the big table: Trudy and Jimmy Bartlett, Cynthia and Sid Coe, Frank Little, Ellen St. Martin, and, by himself, Mort Sparco.

"Where's Nancy?" Rathbone asked him.

"The bitch walked out on me," Sparco said glumly. "This afternoon while I was at work. Took most of her clothes, jewelry, and a bottle of extra-virgin olive oil I've been saving."

"Don't worry about it," Rita consoled him. "She'll be back."

"Damned right," Mort said. "Where's she going to go? She'll be lost without me."

Rathbone went to the bar for drinks, but Ernie wasn't on duty; Sylvester, a waiter from the dining room, was filling in as bartender.

"Where's Ernie?" David asked.

"Called in sick, Mr. Rathbone. Hasn't worked for the past two days. He wants you to phone him. Here's his number. He said to be sure and tell you to call him from outside, not from here."

"Okay," Rathbone said, stuffing the scrap of paper into his pocket. "Now let me have a couple of brandy stingers."

"What's a stinger?" Sylvester asked.

Rathbone went behind the bar and mixed the drinks himself.

It was the kind of night he needed. He caught the bubbly mood of the others, and his premonitions disappeared in the noise, jokes, laughter, chivying, and just plain good fellowship of these splendid people. When he and Rita departed a little after midnight, they waited, hand-in-hand, for the valet to bring the Bentley around, and they sang "What'll I Do?"

Theodore and Blanche had left a light on downstairs. They had also left the air conditioning turned so low that the town house felt like a meat locker. David switched off the air and opened the French doors.

"I'm going upstairs and change," Rita said.

"Go ahead," Rathbone said. "I'll pour us a nightcap, and then I have to make a phone call."

He brought two small snifters of cognac from the kitchen and placed them on the glass-topped cocktail table. Then he settled down in one corner of the big couch and used the white phone on the end table. He took the scrap of paper from his pocket and punched out the number.

"Ernie?" he said. "This is David Rathbone."

"Hiya, Mr. Rathbone. Where you calling from?"

"From my home. Why?"

"I just didn't want you to call from the Palace. The phone there may be tapped. My own phone probably is. I'm not home now. I'm staying with a friend."

"Ernie, what's all this about? Why should the Palace phones be tapped? Or yours?"

"Listen, Mr. Rathbone, two cops from the sheriff's office came to see me at the Lounge on Monday. I thought at first they were a couple of clowns wanting to put the arm on me for a contribution—if you know what I mean. But it was more than that. They showed me a picture of a dead guy they said went by the name of Termite Tommy. The picture had been taken in the morgue. This Termite Tommy had been wasted. Someone stuck an ice pick in his ear."

Rathbone leaned forward and picked up one of the brandy snifters. He took a deep swallow, then held the glass tightly.

"They wanted to know if this guy had been in the Lounge on New Year's Day. I told them I didn't remember. But they said they knew he had been there; one of the parking valets had seen him. Then they asked if you had been there at the same time, Mr. Rathbone."

David finished the cognac, put the empty glass on the table, picked up the other one.

"I tried to cover for you, Mr. Rathbone, really I did. But they knew all about your passing out and how I had to call Rita to come get you. Now how in hell did they know that?"

"I have no idea," Rathbone said hoarsely.

"Well, they knew, all right. They kept asking if you had talked to that Termite Tommy, if the two of you had a drink together. Mr. Rathbone, you've always treated me decent so I got to level with you. Those jokers knew all about my little sidelines, so I'm talking a deal with them. Or rather my lawyer is. I'm sorry, Mr. Rathbone, but my ass is on the line. If they want to throw the book at me, I'm liable to end up doing heavy time. I've got to cooperate with them. You can understand that, can't you, Mr. Rathbone?"

David gulped down half of the second brandy. It caught in his throat and for a moment he was afraid he might spew it up. He swallowed frantically again and again. Finally it went down, burning his stomach. Then:

"What did you tell them, Ernie?"

"Just that you were there at the same time as Termite Tommy. That the two of you had a drink together and talked awhile. That's all, Mr. Rathbone, I swear it. Oh, I also told them about those two bums who were having a beer at the other table while you and Termite Tommy were talking. Remember those guys? The cops want me to go through the mug books and see if I can make them. Maybe they're the skels who used the ice pick."

"Maybe," Rathbone said.

"Anyway, I wanted you to know what's going on. Ordinarily, I wouldn't gab about any of my customers—you know that—but my balls are in the wringer and I've got to make the best deal I can. You can appreciate that, can't you, Mr. Rathbone?"

"Sure, Ernie. It's okay. No great harm done."

"I'm glad to hear that. I just didn't want you to think I was a rat. I wish you the best of luck, Mr. Rathbone."

"Thanks, Ernie," David said. "The same to you."

He hung up and finished the second cognac. He took the empty glasses back to the kitchen and started to pour new drinks. He stopped suddenly, remembering. At least Ernie hadn't mentioned his passing a white envelope to Termite Tommy or how he, Rathbone, had gone into the men's room and had been joined there by one of the thugs.

Perhaps Ernie hadn't seen either incident. Or had witnessed them but just didn't recall. Or did recall them and hadn't told the cops. Or had told the cops and wasn't admitting how much he had blabbed.

But it really didn't matter, Rathbone concluded. The important fact was that he had been seen in the company of a homicide victim shortly before the murder. Sooner or later, he knew, the cops would come looking for him.

First Gevalt, then Birdie, and now this. . . . For one brief instant he thought it might be smart to run at once, that night. But he immediately recognized it as stupid panic. Even if the cops came around in the morning, he could stall them for a day or two. He could tell them he had met

Termite Tommy quite by accident in the Palace Lounge on New Year's Day. They had been casual acquaintances. They had a drink together, wished each other Happy New Year, Tommy left, and that was that.

The cops might not buy the story, but it would take time and a lot more digging before they discovered Rathbone was holding out on them. And by the time they tied him to the Corcoran brothers—if they ever did—he'd be long gone.

His need to stall the fuzz, even for a short while, was obvious: He couldn't run until Bartlett's deposit on Friday was a done deal. Jimmy would take his forty percent, and David would pocket a cool $120,000. Screw Herman Weisrotte! If that drunken Kraut wanted to sue in Costa Rica for his fifteen-percent cut, lots of luck! But there was no way Rathbone was going to run before he made that marvelous score.

He carried the fresh drinks into the living room, feeling up again. Rita was coming down the stairs barefoot, wearing the yellow terry robe he had given her the first morning she awoke in his bed.

"You okay, honey?" she asked, looking at him closely. "You look like something the cat dragged in."

"I was a little shook," he admitted, "but I'm better now. That phone call—an old friend of mine up north just died."

"Ah, too bad. What did he die from?"

"Cancer," David said. "Sit down and drink your drink. There's a lot I want to talk to you about."

She curled up alongside him on the couch, and he put an arm about her shoulders.

"How soon can you be ready to leave?" he asked her. "I mean leave the country for good."

"I told you," she said. "Give me twenty minutes."

He laughed and hugged her. "You're a wonder, you are," he said. "It won't be until after this Friday. It all depends on when I can book a flight for us. But let's figure early next week—okay? Now listen carefully: I'm driving up to Lakeland tomorrow and may not be back until late in the evening. I'll leave you two grand in cash, and I want you to go out to Gevalt and pick up your passport. Got that?"

She nodded.

"Now on Friday afternoon, you and I are going shopping. I have charge accounts at Burdines, Jordan Marsh, Lord and Taylor, Macy's, Saks, and Neiman-Marcus. Make out a list of everything you want. We're going to charge up a storm at all those stores."

She turned her head to look at him. "And we'll be gone before the bills come in—right?"

"Right! So forget about the cost. Just buy everything you want."

"But what'll I need—fur coats or bikinis? Where are we going?"

"Costa Rica," he said. "A climate a lot like Florida's. Even better. I have a ranch down there you're going to love. It's out in the country, but not too far from the beach or the city. Plenty to do, plenty to see. And you already *habla* Spanish."

"Oh God," she said, "it sounds great. I'll bet they have wonderful plantains."

"And fantastic melons," he said. "The place is a paradise."

He picked up her drink and led her upstairs to the bedroom. She took off her robe, sat on the edge of the bed, watched him undress.

He knelt on the floor at her feet. He pressed her bare knees together and leaned his chin on them, his eyes turned upward to her face.

"I've got to tell you something, Rita. I've been a grifter all my life, and loving you is maybe the first straight thing I've ever done. It's a super feeling."

She clasped his face, lifted his head gently.

"Come to mommy," she said.

60

On Thursday morning, February 1, Anthony Harker listened to the previous day's tapes in his motel room. Then he packed all the reels in a battered briefcase and lugged it to the office. He finally decided Crockett had to know. He wasn't going to dump the problem in his lap, just present the evidence and tell Crockett what he planned to do. He owed the chief that much.

Crockett was already behind his desk, as trim as ever in his vested suit with a neatly knotted polka-dotted bow tie. He listened closely as Harker ran through the checklist on his clipboard.

"Roger Fortescue will drive up to Lakeland tomorrow morning in time to be there by noon. He'll arrest Herman Weisrotte. Two Secret Service men will provide backup.

"Henry Ullman will collar Bartlett at the Crescent Bank in Boca at noon. He'll be assisted by FBI special agents.

"Manuel Suarez will take Sidney Coe. Manny will lead a squad from the Fort Lauderdale police. In addition to Coe, all the yaks will be booked.

"I figured Simon Clark would bust Mortimer Sparco's brokerage, but

Clark asked if he could pick up Irving Donald Gevalt instead. That's okay with me, so I arranged for an SEC team to hit the brokerage. They know what to look for.

"The DEA will coordinate their raid on Frank Little's warehouse. At the same time they arrest Little, they'll grab all his customers they've been able to identify.

"I'll lead a team from the Broward County Sheriff's Office against David Rathbone's town house. The warrants authorize his arrest and seizing whatever records we can find in his private office.

"Ernest Hohlman, the bartender at the Palace Lounge, picked out two ex-cons from the mug books who might be involved in the murder of Termite Tommy. They're Brian and Thomas Corcoran, brothers, with rap sheets as long as your arm. Heavy stuff like armed robbery and felonious assault. There's a warrant out for both of them right now.

"I should warn you, sir, that some if not all of the assisting agencies are sure to rush to the newspapers and TV cameras as soon as the operation goes down."

"That's all right," Crockett said. "There'll be enough glory to go around, and we don't want any for this organization. We may need the cooperation of those people in the future, so let them get their headlines. Have you been able to keep a lid on all this?"

"I think so," Harker said. "There have been no leaks that I know of."

Lester Crockett leaned over his desk, clasped his hands, looked directly at the other man.

"Tony," he said, "you haven't mentioned Rita Sullivan. What part have you planned for her?"

Harker hoisted his briefcase onto Crockett's desk. "Sir," he said, "I've been providing you with abstracts of the tapes from David Rathbone's home. Now I think you better listen to the complete tapes. I know what must be done, but you should be aware of my reasons."

Crockett nodded. "If you feel it's that important, I'll do it now. Is there a machine available?"

"Yes, sir. In the bullpen. I'll have it brought in here."

He wasn't summoned back to Crockett's office until late in the afternoon. The reels were stacked on the chief's desk. He motioned Harker to a chair and stared at him.

"You should have told me sooner, Tony," he said quietly.

"I wasn't sure. Not absolutely sure. She could have been playing her role."

Crockett shook his head. "I was afraid of something like this. And so were you."

"No! I didn't expect anything like that to happen."

"I think you did," Crockett said, "but perhaps you wouldn't admit it to yourself. If you were sure of her, you would have told her about the taps on Rathbone's phones and the bugs inside the house."

Harker was silent.

"I'm sorry, Tony," Crockett said. "People do turn sour, you know. And sometimes the best. Will you handle it?"

"Yes, sir. Before noon tomorrow. What's the most we can offer her?"

"Immediate resignation for reasons of health. Nothing on her record, but never another job in law enforcement. Oh God, what a fool!"

"Rita?" Tony said. "Or me?"

Crockett looked at him sadly. "Both of you," he said. "But perhaps 'fool' isn't the right word. 'Victim' is more accurate."

"Mooches," Harker said bitterly.

61

Friday morning, February 2. It was a squally day, no sign of the sun, ripped clouds scudding before a northeast wind. There were spatters of rain, an occasional zipper of lightning, thunder rumbling in the distance like an artillery barrage.

It must have poured during the night; streets on the way to the office were flooded, and a royal palm was down across Federal Highway. Tony Harker splashed through puddles to a coffee shop, but his stomach was churning and he ordered a glass of milk and dry rye toast.

He wondered why he felt no exultation. He was bringing a complex investigation to a successful end, but he had no sense of satisfaction. In fact, this final day was almost anticlimactic. He saw it as cleaning up after a wild party: a mess of cold cigarette butts, empty bottles, stale food, and broken glass. Nothing left to do but throw out the garbage.

His first call was to the sheriff's office, requesting that two plainclothesmen be sent in an unmarked car to stake out David Rathbone's town house. They were to collar Rathbone at noon if Harker hadn't shown up.

He spoke to Manuel Suarez and Simon Clark, and gave them final orders. He called Henry Ullman in Boca to make certain there was no last-minute hitch in their plans. There was no way to reach Roger Fortescue; Harker assumed he was on the road en route to Lakeland. He called his contact at the DEA and was assured everything was on schedule.

Finally, at 9:10 A.M., he called the office of the Fort Knox Commodity Trading Fund. He was connected to an answering machine, and hung up.

He called every ten minutes after that with the same result. He had resolved that if he couldn't contact Rita at the office by eleven o'clock, he'd
call her at the town house and run the risk of Rathbone's answering the
phone.

But at 10:20, she answered the office phone. "The Fort Knox Fund,"
she said perkily. "Good morning."

"Harker here," he said. "You alone?"

"Yes."

"I've got to see you right away. It's important."

Silence for a beat or two. "Will it take long?" she asked finally. "We're
supposed to go shopping this afternoon."

"No, not long. An hour at the most."

"All right. Where?"

"My motel," he said. "I'm leaving now."

He hadn't devised any scenario or even decided in what order to say
the things that had to be said. So he'd have to wing it, and he wasn't
much good at improvising.

She came into his motel apartment wearing a clear plastic slicker over
a peach-colored jumpsuit. Her wind-tossed hair was glistening with mist,
and she was laughing because the flowered umbrella she carried had
turned inside out. She tossed it into a corner and stripped off her raincoat.

"Let's move to south Florida," she said, "where the sun shines every
day. Got a cold beer for me?"

"No," Harker said, and she whipped her head around to look at him.
"Sit down," he told her. "I'll make this as brief as possible."

She sat, crossed her legs, took out a pack of Winstons. She slowly went
through the ceremony of shaking out a cigarette, lighting it, inhaling.

"What's up?" she asked quietly.

He was standing behind an armchair, gripping the top. But he found
his knees were beginning to tremble, so he paced a few steps back and
forth.

"I promised to tell you before we moved on Rathbone. I'm telling you
now. We're taking him today."

"Oh?" she said, inspecting the burning tip of her cigarette. "When?"

"Noon."

"Thanks for giving me so much advance notice," she said, making no
effort to hide the sarcasm. "Who's going to arrest him?"

"I am. With men from the sheriff's office. The town house is staked
out right now. Did Rathbone ever tell you where he might go if he left
the country?"

"No, he never said."

Harker laughed, a harsh sound that sounded phony even to him. "Not a word about his ranch in Costa Rica? Close to the beach and city? The two of you leaving early next week? But first let's go shopping and charge up a storm."

She reacted as if he had struck her across the face. Her head flung back, tanned skin went sallow; she stared at him with widened eyes, trying to comprehend.

"Bugs!" she finally spat out. "The place was bugged!"

"And the phones tapped," Harker said.

"And you never told me?" she cried. "You prick!"

He sat down heavily in the armchair, suddenly saddened because despite what she had done, her first reaction was to accuse him.

"It's all a can of worms, isn't it?" he said. "I've learned that logic doesn't always work with human beings."

"What makes you think you're a human being?"

"Oh, I'm human," he said. "I'm just as fucked-up as everyone else."

But she wouldn't let it go at that. "No," she said, shaking her head, "you're vindictive, malicious. You're getting your jollies out of busting David, aren't you? Big deal! That guy's just a con artist who's ripped off a few rich people, and you've gone after him like he's a serial killer. He'll never spend a day behind bars, and you know it. He'll get himself a sharp lawyer. He'll make full restitution—and he's got the money to do it. He'll promise to straighten up and fly right, and he'll get off with a wrist tap. You'll see."

"I told you a dozen times," Harker said, "and you wouldn't listen. Rathbone's been doing more than stealing pencils from blind men. In addition to a dozen financial felonies, we've got him on drug dealing. What did you think the Fort Knox Fund was trading? Their commodities were cocaine, heroin, and marijuana. And we've got him on counterfeiting and bank fraud. Why do you think he made all those trips to Lakeland? It was to pick up packages of the queer printed by an ex-con up there. And we also want him on suspicion of being an accessory to murder. When he got drunk in the Palace Lounge on New Year's Day, he had just fingered a guy who was later found dead in a canal. Someone had stuck an ice pick in his ear. So much for your poor, misunderstood con artist who's going to make restitution and dance away whistling a merry tune. In a pig's ass he will!"

She had listened to this diatribe with lowered head. Now she looked up, and he was shocked at how old she appeared.

"Are you telling me the truth, Harker?" she asked.

"It's the truth," he said. "That bastard is going to do hard time."

"He's beautiful," Rita said in a low voice. "You know what they'll do to him in prison?"

"I know," Harker said.

She pulled herself from the chair and began to walk about the room hugging her elbows. She was silent a long time, and he glanced at his watch to make certain time wasn't running out.

"David's got a lot of puppy in him," she said finally, speaking in a monotone as if thinking aloud. "He likes to be petted and played with. And sometimes spanked and told what a bad boy he is. Prison will kill him."

Harker said nothing. She stopped pacing and stood before him, looking down, hands on her hips.

"Can we cut a deal, Harker?" she asked him.

His expression didn't change. "What kind of a deal?"

"You said you wanted to marry me. Did you mean that?"

He nodded. "I meant it."

"I'll marry you," she said, staring at him, "and do my damnedest to be a good wife. In the bedroom and in the kitchen. I won't cheat on you, and I won't leave unless you kick me out. For that you let me make a call right now. David's smart enough to get away. He'll duck the stakeout, go out a back window or through the pool area. Just let me phone him. If he doesn't make it, I'll still keep my part of the deal."

Harker felt like weeping. "You must really love him," he said.

"Love?" she said, almost angrily. "What's that? Poets and songwriters know all about it, but I don't. Sure, I have affection for him, but that's a small part of it. Mostly it's guilt for having conned him. It's knowing I helped put him away, and realizing I'm going to live with it till the day I die."

"You've helped put villains away before. Did it bother you?"

"No," she said, "but this is different. He said he was going straight with me, and it turned out to be a scam. What does that make me?"

Harker didn't answer.

"Well," she said, "time's getting short. Do you want to marry me? Have we got a deal?"

"No," he said.

She looked at him with a gargoyled grin, all twisted and ugly. Her hands clenched, knuckles white. She was trying to hang on, but it didn't work. She broke and collapsed into the armchair, black wings of hair covering her face, shoulders rocking back and forth. What moved him most was that she wept silently, no sobs, no wails, just soundless grief.

He relented then and went looking for something to drink. The only hard stuff he had was a bottle of Popov. He poured it over ice and brought one of the drinks to her. He took her hand and pressed her fingers around the glass. The feel of her velvety skin still had the power to stir him.

He sat down in his chair again, took a gulp of his drink, watched her. Her body finally stopped shaking. She straightened, jerked her head back to get hair away from her face, drained half the glass of vodka.

"Why did you do it?" he asked her. "You don't have to answer, but I'd really like to know. Was it the loving?"

"Part of it," she admitted, taking a deep breath. "And part was the way he treated me, like I was the most valuable thing he had ever owned. And part was the lush life. David really knows how to live."

"What kind of bullshit is that?" Harker demanded. "You talk like it's a special talent. Everyone knows how to live. All you need is money."

She smiled wanly. "That's what David always said. His favorite expression. Well, he had the money."

"Sure he did. But look how he made it, and look where it got him."

"So you've got me on tape," she said. "Am I going to be charged?"

"No," Harker said. "There'll be no charges. You'll be allowed to resign for reasons of health. Nothing on your record. But no more jobs in law enforcement. Crockett okayed it."

"So he knows, too?"

Harker nodded.

"Anyone else?"

"No, just Crockett and me."

She sipped her drink and stared at him. "Why didn't you tell me about the bugs and the taps? Was it because from the first you were afraid I'd turn?"

"That's what Crockett thinks," he said, not looking at her. "But I don't think that's the whole reason. I think part of it was jealousy. Listening to you and Rathbone in bed together was like pounding on a wound."

"You were right," she said. "You *are* fucked-up. What's going to happen to me now? What'll I do?"

Harker shrugged. "I'm not worried about you," he said. "You'll find another David Rathbone. Or another me," he added.

She finished her drink, and with it her breezy courage returned. "And what about you, kiddo?" she said. "No more fun and games with me on motel sheets. That was the best loving you'll ever have."

"I know."

"You'll get your allergies back," she jeered. "And your nervous stomach and your sun poisoning."

"I'll survive," he said, not certain he would. He glanced at his watch. "After twelve. They've taken Rathbone by now."

They fixed her umbrella, and he locked up and accompanied her down to their cars. They faced, not knowing whether to shake hands, kiss, or knee each other in the groin.

"Will I see you again?" she asked.

He looked upward, hoping for an omen: the muddy clouds parting and a shaft of pure sunlight striking through to bathe them in gold. He saw only zigzags of lightning splitting the sky, heard only the growl of far-off thunder.

"Will I?" Rita persisted.

"Maybe," Tony said.